D1015693

JINN

WITHDRAWAL

WITHDRAWAL

JINN

MATTHEW B. J. DELANEY

ST. MARTIN'S PRESS ≋ NEW YORK

JINN. Copyright © 2003 by Matthew B. J. Delaney. All rights reserved. Printed in the United States of America. No part of this book may be used or reproduced in any manner whatsoever without written permission except in the case of brief quotations embodied in critical articles or reviews. For information, address St. Martin's Press, 175 Fifth Avenue, New York, N.Y. 10010.

www.stmartins.com

Book design by Jonathan Bennett

ISBN 0-312-27670-2

10   9   8   7   6   5   4   3   2

F
DEL
TC#L20020368978

Lord God, our war is over.
We are nothing but dead men
—and the Kingdom has come to an end.

—COUNT OF TRIPOLI, FOLLOWING THE BATTLE OF HATTIN, A.D. 1187

———

I didn't tell half of what I saw,
because no one would have believed me.

—MARCO POLO, FROM HIS DEATHBED

$24.95

JINN

The eight landing craft formed a jagged line of gray ship's metal across the tumbling Pacific Ocean. The small boats rose and dived through the rough waters, the ocean's shimmering green phosphorescence pounding against the ship's straight metal sides before misting over the helmeted heads of F Company. Private Eric Davis stood corralled between Marines, their helmets dripping salt water, their fatigues dark and wet. He hunched his shoulders as the landing craft caught the crest of another wave, diving through it in a nauseating roll, more water spraying onto the men.

Two months earlier he had been home in Boston. Then there was the draft. A month of training in Mississippi, his station in the Pacific, and the rest was a blur of sleepless nights aboard rolling ships, lying on canvas bunks, one on top of the other, listening to the occasional air raid warnings as Japanese Zeros buzzed above, circling like hungry vultures over their prey.

The landing craft hit another sickening drop, forcing Eric to spread his legs wider to hold his balance as more water sheeted down on him. They had been circling the island for ten minutes, the warm sun baking their helmets, drying the salt tightly against their skin. Over the metal sides of the landing craft, the men turned their heads, watching the Navy's shells slam into the thick vegetation across the beach.

Turning suddenly, the LCM slanted toward the shore. A Marine Air Group torpedo bomber roared overhead, its single prop cutting the air as it blasted by, making one last pass at the beachhead.

Men around him began to vomit. Some leaned their heads over the sides of the landing craft, others covered their mouths with the little paper bags they had been given before boarding. Davis watched the man next to him, bent at the waist, the egg-colored vomit spilling out around his fingers as he made a vain attempt to cover his mouth.

That morning the soldiers had been woken at 3 A.M. The mess boys of the USS *Pennsylvania* were wearing pressed white jackets and serving up plates of eggs and bacon, while jazz thrummed through the intercom speakers. Eric felt sick when he saw the food. When the military allowed a good meal, it usually meant the men had it coming heavy from the Japs that day. His shipmate Alabama used to say that a decent one was close to a last one, like granting the condemned prisoner his final dinner before the gallows.

The day after a landing, the colored regiments clearing away the dead from the beaches always found a good amount of half-digested eggs mixed in the sand, punched out by bullet wounds to some soldier's gut. They used to serve onions mixed in with the meal, but medical corpsmen found that the smell in the Red Cross tents was too overwhelming. The onion scent literally permeated out through the wounds, mixing with the odors of blood and defecation. Standing well out to sea, the USS *Galla*, a transport craft from New Guinea, had nine bagged bodies ready to begin the journey home to be buried. Someone had neglected to store them far enough aft, so, in their quarters, the crew could smell them decay.

Most of the Marines were silent as they ate their breakfast, sitting around the metal mess tables under the bare lightbulbs of the ship, listening to the droning of the engines and the slapping of the ocean against the metal sides. Night after night, Davis lay in his cot, his arms stretched behind his head, with the thought of death on an unknown beach growing stronger in his nose. Davis, who had been on the *Galla* before transferring to the USS *Pennsylvania,* could smell it again, seeming to waft up from the eggs.

He thought of home, his mind wandering back to Jessica. Hanging near the head of his cot were the three letters he had from her, stored in a tight roll in one of his bandoliers. He found her handwriting comforting, not so much for what it read, but in its femininity, the shapes of the words themselves. The way each letter seemed to flow together in her familiar style.

Before, before the war, before the smell of the dead, he used not to notice when they might be apart. Now, however, it was her face that came to him in the darkness behind his closed lids. Maybe he just liked the idea of a pretty girl caring for him, but, for whatever reason, Davis found himself thinking of her. Especially the way her hair smelled. He used to press her hair against his face, burying himself deep in its sheen. That sweet smell. *God, how I loved that.*

An explosion slammed his ears, his helmet vibrating against his skull. The damp chin strap, dangling loosely, swung back and forth, hitting him like a wet noodle across the face. The helmet fell down across his eyes, momentarily obscuring his vision. He pushed it back in time to see a section of the beach ahead of them disappear in a red burst of sand and broken branches. The shells from the *Missouri* landed in the thick palms lining the edge of the beach, sending splintered wood sections into the air for a moment, before they splashed back into the rolling tide.

Eric turned his head, leaning to the side to look out across the ocean. Behind them, safely out to sea, the *Missouri* and the *Nebraska* launched their last rounds of protective fire. Dotted against the horizon, the battleships' guns seemed harmless against the vastness of the sea surrounding them, their puffs of gunpowder smoke appearing as benign as milky clouds from burst mushrooms.

The metaphor was lost by the whistle of the automobile-sized shells as they passed overhead, screaming angrily, before slamming into the beach ahead of them.

Their craft continued forward, steadily moving toward the whirl of burning jungle and frothing sand. The LCM ducked again, water spraying against its sides and shooting up into the air in white fountains. Behind him, the ship's diesel engines groaned onward, a pulsating metallic sound, the tone rising and falling with the rolling of the ocean. Sometimes up, sometimes down, but always the monotonous droning. The driver stood above, his face tight and gleaming with seawater beneath his helmet, protected by a metal wall that reached past his waist.

Eric felt a tug on his sleeve.

"Cigarette?" Jimmy Scotti was holding out a thin white stick, while another unlit one dangled precariously from his top lip. His voice was contorted, his mouth tight as he tried to talk while keeping his lips pinched around the cigarette in his mouth.

"No, thanks." Eric shook his head.

Scotti shrugged and put the cigarette carefully into his front pocket, shielding it from the water.

"This is a mess, huh?" Scotti said suddenly, his voice sounding tense.

"What's that?" Eric asked.

"This," Scotti answered simply. "This whole fucking thing. Out here on the waves, landing on some Jap-infested island."

Eric nodded, thinking for a moment. "You know, I've never seen a Japanese person before."

"What?"

"I've never seen anyone Japanese before."

"You're shitting me."

"No." Eric shook his head. "I swear, there was one guy down the street who I thought was Japanese, but turned out he was from China."

Scotti snorted in surprise, then, lifting his head, shouted to someone in the front of the boat, "Hey, Leonard!"

"Yeah?" came the muffled reply from one of the helmeted heads.

"Davis here never seen a Jap before."

A few of the helmets turned toward the back of the craft with mild interest.

"Yeah? Fucking-A," Leonard's reply came, muffled over the sound of the crashing sea and the roar of the engine. "Well, he's about to see a whole fucking bunch of 'em at once."

Scotti nodded at this reply. "Never seen a Jap before . . . fucking Japs," he whispered in amazement to himself, shaking his head. The cigarette was still dangling from his mouth, and Scotti tightened his lips, bringing a silver lighter up toward the white paper.

Eric watched Scotti trying to light the cigarette, the flame dancing around the end of the smoke, his hand too unsteady to hold the lighter in place. "I can't get this damn thing lit." His voice sounded angry. "It's too damn wet out here."

Disgusted, he took the cigarette out of his mouth and tossed it overboard, the white stick sucked up instantly by a rolling wave. Eric looked forward, seeing the shore approach steadily. They were close enough that he could distinguish each of the individual trees lining the sand, the gracefully arching palms rising like sentinels guarding the entrance into the jungle beyond.

There was a soft thud from the beach ahead. It was followed by a whistling noise, as if someone had left a teapot on to boil for too long. Around him, men were beginning to cringe, pulling their heads toward their shoulders like turtles. Davis lowered his head as well, gripping his rifle more tightly.

The whistling increased, until reaching a full shriek. There was a pause, then the water next to them exploded into a froth of white as a Japanese 75mm shell smacked close by the craft. The men ducked into the puky mess in the bottom of the landing barge, ceasing to watch the approaching coastline.

"Three minutes!" shouted the driver, perched in the metal-plated wheelhouse above them.

"Get ready," the captain shouted out above the noise of the sea. He was an older man of about thirty-five, with a wide face covered by stubble and acne scars. Shells began exploding in the water around them, violent bursts of white foaming the water, which kept their heads down below the sides of the landing craft.

"Tighten up those helmets," the captain shouted. "Keep the waterproofing on your weapons."

Eric pulled the loose strap tightly underneath his chin, till the helmet pressed against his head. Around him men were doing the same.

"When we hit that beach, keep moving, never stop." The captain was holding the edge of the landing craft, steadying himself against the rolling sea.

There were murmurs and nods among the men. The captain straightened his helmet. "If you feel sick, go ahead and vomit now, get it out of the way." The captain looked around at the men. "Any man that tells you he's not afraid is crazy. Put it aside."

Another explosion tore into the water ahead of them, spraying light steam across the men. Eric crinkled his nose—it smelled like someone had loosened his bowels already. The smell wafted backward from somewhere in the front of the ship.

"Hell, I ain't scared," Scotti was mumbling to himself, rocking back and forth. "Goddammit, I'm gonna be all right." He kept repeating it, until the words flowed together into a chant. He ran his hands over his face, stopping for a moment to rub his glistening eyes, then his fingers frantically began to dig at his chin strap. "This fucking thing's too tight. I can't breathe in this."

"Sixty yards!" the driver shouted from behind, holding up one finger above his head.

Numbly, Eric made the sign of the cross over himself. Beside him, a guy who'd just been transferred into the unit was unwrapping a piece of gum. He put the stick in his mouth and went to work chewing nervously, crumpling up the paper and placing it back in his pocket.

Suddenly Eric had an intense urge to urinate. He crossed his legs over, trying to push the sensation away. The sky had begun to cloud over, and rain was falling in thin drizzles, striking against the ocean in gray slanted lines.

The beach ahead was covered in gray-black sand, stretching back about seventy yards before meeting an impossibly thick jungle. Above the line of the jungle, wisps of fog curled around a steep range of mountains, while the surf crashed in low waves against the shore. A thin stream of smoke rose into the air from the great jungle-surrounded volcano, Mt. Bagana. Out at sea, the *Missouri* and the *Nebraska* had ceased their protective fire and the landing craft advanced in eerie silence. The talking among the men had halted, each man staring forward in nervous expectation as the rain dotted hundreds of tiny circles on the surface of the gray ocean around them.

Through the thin mist, Eric saw a sudden flash of red on the island. Then a second, and a third. There was an instant of silence, the final moment of quiet, before Japanese bullets tore at the sides of the landing craft. *Pa-ching, pling, pling.* Then there was another noise, different from the hard crack of metal against metal. It was softer, like a broomstick smacking a plump feather pillow. Just as it sounded, one of the soldiers jerked backward with a short cry, collapsing to the floor of the landing craft.

"Here it comes," the captain shouted. "Stand ready."

The bullets began snapping around them, popping against the metal hull of their LCM with incredible speed. The jungle was flaring with hundreds of pricks of red muzzle flashes, appearing almost as lightning almost as lightning bugs in a dark wood. Eric ducked beneath the sides as much as he could, listening to the random cracking. He was suddenly glad to be in the rear of the craft, ten full rows of men ahead of him forming a protective wall of bodies.

There was a heavy thundering, and a searing heat swept across his face. The landing craft next to theirs had been struck by a Japanese 75mm. Flames erupted from the back, and Eric could hear the cries of the men burning in the intense heat. Thick smoke swirled in small cyclones as the wreck continued to motor forward, running blindly toward the gray-black shore.

"Jesus Christ," Scotti cried to himself.

A sudden jolt against the bottom of their landing craft caused the LCM to shudder, the engine whining in protest.

"Reef!" the driver called from behind.

"Fuck, we're supposed to be going in on the goddamn high tide."

The jolt struck again, and the small ship yawed dangerously to the right, threatening to spill over into the sea. They were still about ten yards from the beach. If they went over, they'd have to swim. One of the men nearest Davis let go of the minesweeper he was carrying, dropping into a huddled ball at the base of the craft as he clutched his gut. Someone near him was praying softly, almost chanting. "Hail Mary. Hail Mary."

Next to him, the new guy spit out his gum, while from behind, Eric heard Scotti muttering something. He gripped his carbine tightly, reminding himself to keep it up over his head if he had to go through water. The beach approached suddenly, and the LCM ground to a momentary halt as it struck hard ground. The engines groaned and pushed toward the shore.

All around him, the hissing of bullets rent the air, moving with inescapable speed. He could hear them approach and blow past him, drilling loudly against metal or sometimes impacting with a muffled thump against flesh.

The craft jarred to a second stop, striking against the sandy bottom and throwing the men forward. A roar of fearful anger rose from a few of the soldiers as they prepared themselves for combat in the moments before the flaps fell. Davis closed his eyes for a moment, sucking in his breath, trying not to wet himself.

There was the sudden sound of metal chains being released and sliding forward. The heavy flap fell, splashing into the water and opening up the LCM.

It had begun. Someone was shouting, "Go! Go! Go!" and there was a frantic push forward.

Immediately men began falling, ripped open raw and bloody with numbing quickness. Eric felt the rush, the wild mindless race off the craft and onto the shore. Ahead of them stretched the pitted grayish sand, deeply scorched with rings of black ash by the Navy's heavy bombardment. X-shaped metal joints stuck up jaggedly from the beachhead, the tide washing around them as it rolled up to the jungle. Beyond the joints, multicolored tracer bullets were arching out of the trees, reaching toward the American landing craft, racing to meet the oncoming soldiers.

All along the beach, American landers were running aground, men pouring out in low, crouching runs. Davis shuffled his feet back and forth, still in the back, pressed tightly against the other soldiers. There was a sharp scream, and suddenly the air was filled with feathers. Soft floating down filled the air. It was surreal, dreamlike; the cries of the men, the pounding of the guns, all amidst the gently falling feathers.

A bullet had torn into one of the men, ripping open the standard-issue Kapok life jackets each of the soldiers wore. Davis surged forward through the clumps of feather-like material, a few of them sticking in wet clumps to his face and body.

As he reached the edge of the ramp, his foot caught on someone lying sprawled on the bottom of the landing craft, and he fell forward onto his chest. He pushed off the ground and stepped off the ramp, his boots sinking into the thick wet sand. The ocean water was cool and heavy, soaking into his clothes, weighing down his legs. He slogged forward, his body charged with the electricity of expectation, waiting for the blazing, crushing impact of metal against his body. What would it be like? Where would it hit? His face? His legs, chest?

His boots dug deeply into the wetness, sucking him in like quicksand. He remembered the familiar nightmares of something chasing you from behind as you feel your feet growing heavier, your movements slower, and a coldness pressing in at your back.

Men continued to collapse without warning, their bodies falling and forming dark clumps against the sand. A wave crashed in from behind. Knocked off-balance, Eric staggered forward a few paces, trying to pull his heavy boots underneath him to catch his body. He failed, falling facefirst into the wet sand. As he lay, the water swirled past him, its salty warmth bloody, dyed into a red ocean.

He froze for a moment, burying his face in the muck, listening to screams and the fire of weapons around him. Something heavy fell against this legs, and turning back he saw Rafuse's distorted face peering at him, his hand gripping Eric's leg tightly, a low gasp seeping out of his mouth.

Eric's eyes strayed down Rafuse's body, stopping around his stomach. Where his belly should have been was nothing but a mass of blood and protruding red. Something long and squirming had broken through Rafuse's midsection, and was lying on the sand, rolled like a snake, a quivering mess of blood and guts.

Rafuse's hand moving toward Eric's face, small bits of intestine clinging to the end of his finger. Horrified, Eric slid backward across the sand like a crab, moving out from underneath the heavy weight of Rafuse's body. He backed against something soft, and looking down he saw the leg of a fallen soldier.

Next moment he was up and running, moving as quickly as he could away from those red snakes squirming out of his friend. Ahead was a fallen tree, knocked down by the shell fire and swaying up and down with the rhythm of his feet on the damp sand.

Half-surprising himself, he reached the protective wood and threw himself down into the sand. He pressed his body tightly against the trunk, staring at the bits of rock and bark underneath. Behind him, fallen men were crawling across the beach or lying on their backs, screaming out names known only to them.

The heavy firing from the jungle continued, the red tracer bullets weaving a cross-stitch pattern over the sandy shores, breathing invisible death. In trickling numbers men began joining him behind the fallen tree. They flopped onto the sand, faces filled with the surprise of still existing, that their guts hadn't yet turned into snakes trying to break out through the skin.

Even in its slow death, the giant old tree provided shelter one last time. It protected them from the angry bullets that struck against the rotting wood, trying to burrow their way through and reach the men.

Soldiers around him were unfastening their shovels from their packs, digging shallow foxholes in the sand. Eric looked back across the beach. The smooth sand was dotted with the lumpy forms of the men who hadn't made it to the tree, their bodies rocking back and forth in the water. An LCM was rolling in on the waves, its engines vibrating in the rough water. The craft hit the beach and the flaps fell. Medics with a red cross painted on their helmets poured out, carrying packs filled with supplies.

A Japanese shell landed on the beach, just beyond the barbed wire. It fizzled in the sand for a moment, before exploding, sending hot bits of shrapnel into the bodies of the men. One of the medics went down, his hand pawing at his own pulpy face.

Eric chanced a quick look over the rounded mass of the tree. Set back in the dark shade of the jungle he could see two pillboxes, solidly constructed of coconut logs and dirt, and connected by trenches and a series of rifle pits. He ducked back down and pulled a grenade from his belt. Pulling the pin, he waited a moment and tossed the ball of metal toward one of the pillboxes. Other Marines around him were doing the same, their arms throwing the grenades in quick succession.

There was a series of quick explosions, like the bursting of small paper bags filled with air, and some of the return gunfire diminished. "Let's get over!" someone shouted. Nobody moved. Looking to his side, Eric saw that the voice was coming from a man he didn't recognize, with the stripes of a captain on his helmet.

Around him, men were stripping off their equipment, trying to lighten their packs. Davis pulled off his Navy life belt, two inflatable tubes that strapped around his chest.

"Keep it tight! Keep it tight!" a new captain shouted, not making sense, the veins in his neck bulging.

Men were pressed flat on their stomachs all around Eric, hiding their bodies in depressions in the mud, lifting their heads to fire occasionally into the jungle, their rifles recoiling with each shot. Spent cartridges littered the ground, glowing brass mixed in the black mud.

The heavy fire continued, spraying into the sand and mud around them. Rain continued to fall in slanting drizzles, soaking quickly into the earth and men. Beads of water dripped from the brim of Eric's helmet.

Men were beginning to stream over the log, running bent over into the jungle, moving toward the log-and-earth pillboxes. Resting his rifle on the fallen tree, Eric fired at the Japanese positions. His gun ejected the spent cartridge and he fumbled in his bandolier for another clip. Jamming it back into the gun, he pumped out bullets blindly, his Garand making a *pop, pop, pop* sound like an amusement park air rifle.

His clip spent, he stood up and tried to vault over the top of the trunk. Catching his foot on the ridged bark, he sprawled forward into the mud. As he scrambled quickly along the ground, a searing heat suddenly branded Davis's arm, and he fell flat. His shoulder was bleeding through a tear in his fatigues, the sight of his own blood startling him. Something inside urged him to move. No longer thinking, he rushed forward, barely conscious of the other men around him, also moving along the ground in the same hunched-over position.

He saw a dirty soldier running quickly through the jungle, heading toward the Japanese bunker. Eric raised his rifle and pulled the trigger, firing at the only Japanese person he'd ever seen. The man jerked, his body spinning around as the bullet impacted, sending him to the jungle floor.

More Japanese soldiers were streaming out of the log structures. Their cries of attack carried through the jungle as they charged to meet the oncoming Americans. A man with a sparse beard and dark eyes appeared suddenly in Davis's face. Davis swung the barrel of his rifle forward, pulling the trigger. The man disappeared from view, falling backward into the mud, and Davis advanced without further thought.

Men had begun to fight with their hands, close enough so the blood from the dying beat across the faces of the living. American soldiers had reached the pillboxes, swarming across in scattered groups like ants.

"Burn 'em out!" someone screamed, as one of the soldiers, his back weighted down with a long, silver-colored fuel canister, stood outside the entrance of one of the boxes. A stream of flames shot out of the soldier's weapon, exploding through the opening and filling the structure with fire.

"Light it!" an American near him urged.

A shirtless Japanese soldier, his chest patched with dirt, broke from one of the trenches, confusedly running toward the American forces. A Marine struck him heavily across the face with the butt end of his rifle, and the man collapsed to the ground stunned, blood streaming from his nose.

The Marine was silent as he struck the fallen soldier again, cracking his skull under the blows from the end of the heavy rifle. Afterward, he stood up, arching his back as if stretching and wiping his forehead with the back of his forearm.

The heavy fighting had ended, but the dense jungle cloaked the few remaining

Japanese soldiers around them. Marines were moving warily, sending arching flames into trenches, dropping grenades into camouflaged foxholes. Eric collapsed with fatigue into the sand. Adrenaline shot through his body, pitting into his stomach like a drug. He bent over and vomited eggs onto the sand. Wiping his mouth with his free hand, he spit, then leaned on his rifle for support.

One of the guys had a forgotten Japanese flag and took it out, smiling. "Hey," he shouted. "A Rising Sun!"

Davis turned his eyes toward the noise and saw it was Scotti. He was waving the flag over his head and standing on one of the pillboxes. He pointed to one of the men. "I'm a fucking Jap!" He laughed.

From somewhere in the jungle a rifle cracked. Scotti dropped the flag and clutched his throat, pawing at his neck, his face turning red as if he were choking. His hands dropped to his side, and Eric saw a half-dollar-sized bullet hole where the man's Adam's apple had been. Scotti collapsed to the ground.

Gradually the gunfire slowed to sporadic shots, individual recoils sounding from the jungle before finally dying out altogether. Davis lay back on the ground, closing his eyes. He heard the waves rolling along the sand and the crackling of the burning Japanese pillboxes. Occasionally a man would groan with pain. He looked up as a flock of parakeets flew across the jungle border, cutting back and forth in perfect formation.

Turning his eyes away from the sky, he gazed around at the wasted dead. Japanese and American soldiers covered the jungle floor, some sprawled over one another in strange embraces, blood from their wounds intermingling. A heavy rain had begun to fall, striking the wide green leaves of the canopy above. The entire jungle seemed to shimmer with wet color.

On the ground, lying close to him, was something like a man. The soldier was burned so badly that Eric couldn't tell if he were American or Japanese. His eyes were gaping holes, his black lips skinned back, his teeth showing white against the burned skin. Drops of water, falling from the trees sizzled as they hit the man's face, little bursts of steam rising from the superheated charred flesh.

Two hours later, Eric sat in the sand, his back propped against a log, while one of the medics placed a white bandage across the wound in his arm. He looked out over the beach, watching the Pacific waters rolling up the sand in gentle waves. The coast was lined with the drab green steel of equipment. Large squat landing barges had delivered the first of the light tanks and half-tracks, which roamed the edge of the jungle burning diesel fuel. The M3A1 tanks, the Honeys, armed with 37mm guns, coughed up diesel smoke and grumbled as their tracks clawed through the fine sand.

A rough tent had been strung between two palms, and most of the wounded and dying had been carried underneath the dark green fabric. The air inside was stifling. Davis preferred baking in the sun on the beach to being inside with those men, all half-crazed with pain.

Most of the dead had been cleared from the beach. They lay in long lines just inside the perimeter of the jungle, pulled out of the way of the heavy equipment. Later they'd be searched for personal letters, which would get mailed. Then their bodies would be bagged up and taken out on the next ship.

The first bivouac was being established about a quarter mile from the shore. The trees, nothing more than burned stumps after the naval bombardment, were cleared, the ground flattened, and office tents erected. Men, stripped to the waist, their tags glinting in the sun, labored to clear out the heavy brush.

"Rough go of it?" the medic attending Davis's arm asked.

"Yeah, pretty rough," Davis replied.

"Hell, we're getting it rough all up and down here," the medic observed thoughtfully.

The MO finished patching Davis's wound and stood up, arching his back and stretching.

"You'll be all right. Get yourself a Purple Heart, take home, show your girl."

"Thanks," Davis said, pulling himself to his feet.

The MO nodded and wandered off toward the medical tent. A wounded man was screaming inside, thrashing around on the sand while two MOs held him down as a third jabbed a long needle into his arm.

Davis turned away, walking back across the sand, his arm feeling heroically numb. Three of the guys he knew from the *Pennsylvania* were lounging around in the shade of a coconut tree. They were smoking cigarettes and watching the half-tracks drive across the beach.

Davis joined them, leaning up against the rough bark of the coconut tree and sliding to the ground.

"What, you kidding me? Hundred to one, I'd rather be over in Europe than the Pacific right now," a twenty-four-year-old named Jersey Walker was saying to the other men. "Shit, you got better climate, no bugs, better food."

"And the Nazis aren't crazy like the Japs. You ever heard of a Jap surrendering?" said Kelly Keaveney from New York. Keaveney had an endless amount of energy, which he seemed to pull from throughout the day. His movements were quick, his laugh explosive, punctuated by even quicker body movements. Even his hair seemed energized. Bright red, sticking in curly tufts from his head.

"And don't forget all them Frenchwomen," replied Jersey. "We see a woman what, once a month? And that's if we hit port."

"Y'all got that right," another man, J.J. Mulry, nicknamed Alabama after his home state, said. Alabama was thin, with tight, almost gaunt cheeks and hollowed eyes. He reminded Davis of the images of starving Confederate soldiers he had seen in his Civil War history class. Alabama had an easygoing air to him, almost lazy in his movement, everything seeming to be slowed down.

"I don't even know what the hell we're fighting about. I say the Japs can have these damn islands. I'm not using 'em, I could care less. Take the whole damn Pacific. I'm from New York, shit if I care," Keaveney said.

Amen," Alabama replied. "And this heat? Shit, only thing heat like this is good for is sipping cold liquor drinks out on a front porch. First thing—"

Keaveney leaned over, interrupting Alabama with a quick hit on the shoulder before gesturing out across the beach. Davis shook his head, clearing away the sleep. Their staff sergeant, Alexander Seals, was wading through the thick sand toward them.

"Aw shit, here we go," Alabama murmured, picking up his rifle and pretending he was inspecting it.

"Look at this, huh?" Seals joked as he approached. "You must have the cleanest armaments in the entire U.S. armed forces."

He stopped and looked down at Mulry. "I swear, every time I come walking by, you pick up that damn thing and pretend like you're cleaning it."

"I am cleaning it," Alabama said mildly.

"Uh-huh."

"Hey, sir," Keaveney said. "We were all just talking. We decided we'd rather go fight the Germans than the Japs. Like a town meeting, we voted on it."

"Oh yeah?"

"Yeah."

"What do you think this is? A fucking travel agency?" Seals asked. "Next time we do one of these wars, I'll see if I can get you stationed someplace nice."

"I never been to Europe before," Keaveney said.

"So? I never been to Atlantic City," Seals answered. "Maybe next time we'll declare war on New Jersey just so as I get to go."

Alabama chuckled.

"All right, jackasses, listen up," Seals said to the group. "Twelve days ago. B Company landed on the island farther north. They've got a bivouac about six miles above our position. A unit of forty men from B moved southwest into the jungle, but as of a week ago, nobody's heard a peep from them."

"So?" Keaveney said.

"So, we're the closest position, and the general wants us to send in a small recon unit to see if we can locate them."

"Oh c'mon now," drawled Alabama. "They got Japs runnin' round all over here like swarms o' ants. We go in there, we ain't got much chance o' coming back out."

"I'll file your complaint," Seals answered. "Along with Keaveney's request to move to Europe, in the don't give a rat's ass drawer."

"They don't know what happened to 'em?" Davis asked.

Seals shook his head, pulling a scrap of paper from his front pocket. "Last message we got came about one week ago. Was a strange voice. Nobody recognized it."

"What did it say?"

Seals read the scrap of paper. "It said, '*Ultio ultionis possidere.*'"

"What the hell does that mean?" Alabama asked.

Seals looked at him for a moment, then squinted out across the ocean.

"It's Latin," he said finally. "It means, revenge shall be mine."

They left the beach that afternoon, and, by nightfall, the sixteen-man unit had pushed almost three miles into the island. It had been the hardest three miles Eric Davis had ever walked. Everything in the jungle seemed to hate him. It was either biting, scratching, or oozing around him. Mud waist deep that left two-inch leeches quivering and pulsating on their bodies, wasps the size of half-dollars, giant snakes that moved delicately across tree branches over their heads—everything was alive and angry. They'd passed through mangrove swamps and scrub thickets, and the constant vine-draped giant forests that towered skyward above them. By the time the sun was beginning to set they still hadn't seen another living person.

Seals halted them in a small clearing for the night. The soldiers collapsed to the ground. Eric sat on his pack as darkness descended, seeping through the leaves of the jungle. Around him, exhausted men were clearing spaces to sleep and setting up their rickety tents. Davis was sharing a tent with Alabama, Keaveney, and Jersey Walker. Jersey's real name was Joe Walker, but he'd been a boxer before the war, and his fighting name had been Jersey Joe Walker, just like the up-and-coming Jersey Joe Walcott. He looked like a boxer, with a thick neck and a head so close to his shoulders that it seemed to be melting into the rest of his body. He was known for being mean back in the States, picking fights in bars over other guys' girls, causing trouble. Word was that he joined the Marines to avoid going to prison.

Alabama was inside the tent already, his boots off, flexing his bare toes in the night air. "That wasn't no joy walk today," Alabama said, picking at his feet with his bare hand. "I felt like I was walking through a greenhouse full a wet leaves."

Keaveney was digging the rain trench around the tent. He'd gone down about six inches before he gave up, throwing the shovel away in exhaustion.

"No kidding," Davis said, pulling himself off his pack and standing up. "You pull duty tonight?"

"Naw," Alabama answered, lying back into the tent. "You?"

"Yeah. Two-hour shift: 2 to 4 A.M.," Davis answered, referring to the night watch.

Keaveney and three other men were setting up the perimeter to the camp. Davis watched them digging the foxholes and positioning the two machine guns. They had a dog with them. A Doberman mix named Pete, who tracked down hidden Japanese soldiers. The dog was casually burying its nose in the ground, rooting around in the wet leaves before snorting, turning, and collapsing on the ground in a tight ball.

The greenery had begun to turn black as the light faded, their giant leaves becoming dark silhouettes against the graying sky. During the day, the light misty rain had been almost unceasing, penetrating the thick overgrowth of trees above them, gradually soaking through their clothes, until every part of his body seemed wet and he almost couldn't remember a time when he'd been dry.

With the coming of night, the air began to cool off, and the rain slowed, gradually diminishing to sporadic bursts of drizzle. In the far distance was the heavy rumbling noise of mortar fires. Eric had heard there was some action on one of the ridges about

six miles away from them. He closed his eyes and listened. The rumbling was soothing, like listening to the approach of distant thunder.

Someone in the camp cleared his throat, a wet hacking sound followed by a spit
into the green leaves around them. Another soldier was using the rope in his pack to
make a clothesline, extending the twine between two trees.

Conversation was subdued, the men tired.

Alabama was already asleep in the tent, his bare feet sticking out the front. Keaveney wiped off his hands and, laying his Garand rifle on the ground, scooted inside
next to him.

"You coming in?" Keaveney called out to Davis.

"Yeah," Davis replied, stripping off most of his equipment and crouching in front
of the flaps. Inside, the men were crammed tightly together, lying almost one on top
of the other. The tent's fabric was moist and smelled of mildew, making the air stuffy
and close.

"Jesus Christ, it stinks in here," Davis said, squeezing in and lying on his back next
to Keaveney.

"It's like wet socks and farts," Keaveney replied, laughing slightly.

"It's the fruit bars in the Ks," Jersey answered. "Gives me gas."

Davis kept his eyes open, resting his head on his hand, and began looking out at the
night sky through the triangular opening of the tent. Around him in the flat grove he
saw red embers glowing, the fire ends of lit cigarettes from some of the men out smoking. They seemed to hover in the air, gliding from point to point as their invisible
owners moved. He lay back on the ground, surprisingly comfortable.

"Hey, Seals?" a voice whispered in the darkness from somewhere outside the tent.

"Yeah?"

"I gotta go use the bathroom."

"Who is that?"

"It's Anderson, sir."

"All right, but take someone with you."

"Yes, sir." Anderson's voice picked up a little as he spoke to the group. "Who wants
to go?"

"I will." Another whisper to Eric's left.

The whispers of voices echoed around Eric, their owners indistinguishable in the
darkness.

Eric heard a rustling, as someone opened up the inside of his pack.

"Aww, shit, anyone have any toilet paper I could borrow? Mine's soaking wet from
the rain," Anderson said to the group.

Eric smiled and heard chuckles around him, the embers of cigarette ends bobbing
up and down.

"Use some leaves," someone offered. "I saw some big wet ones over there, it'd be
like a huge wet nap."

"Yeah, funny. How about I shit on your head."

There were more chuckles.

"All right, I got a dry roll here. You drop this on the ground and get this wet, Anderson, and I'll use your shirt to wipe my ass next time."

Eric heard the sound of leaves being walked on as Anderson picked up the toilet paper.

"Hey?"

"Yeah?"

"You set to go?"

"Yeah."

The two men headed away from the clearing, pushing deeper into the jungle. Eric lay on his back, looking once more up at the stars overhead. He remembered the night he was shipped out for basic. There was his girlfriend Jessica, the heavy blind groping under the bleachers of the empty, dark football field. The taste of the Coca-Cola she'd been drinking, the feel of the hard grass on his bare skin, then afterward lying on his back and looking up at the summer night sky. He tried finding the same stars when he reached the Philippines, but they were no longer there. Lying now and looking out through the tent flap, he tried again. The sky was different than it was back home, the formations and clusters changed.

Everything was foreign in the South Pacific, even the stars. Somewhere, where he couldn't see, he knew the moon to be full, its reflective light illuminating the sky, creating a dark, yet not entirely black, palette for the stars.

Above him stretched the branches of large palms, gently swaying and swishing in the breeze, their shapes silhouetted against the night sky. From deep in the jungle he heard a monkey hooting loudly. There was a pause and an answering hoot called out, the two animals communicating with each other in the darkness. Eric continued to stare up through the trees, listening to the wind rustle through the wet branches. Around him insects were playing, until they sounded like a thousand bows drawn long over violin strings.

He shut his eyes. In a minute he was asleep.

Somewhere in the darkness of the jungle something cracked, the noise of wood splintering. Davis opened his eyes. He was staring up at a dark shape waving slightly just above his face. A giant bat swooping down from the trees.

Disoriented, it took him a moment to realize it was only the fabric of the tent, moving slightly in the wind. Tired, he closed his eyes again, listening to the heavy breathing of Alabama, Jersey, and Keaveney in the tent with him. He tried remembering what had woken him up in the first place. He vaguely remembered hearing the noise of something moving through the underbrush outside.

His eyes jerked open again. He heard a noise. A heavy breathing sound, almost like the grunting of a pig, coming from somewhere outside the tent. There was a series of hurried whispering, and a low laugh from the jungle.

"Hey." He shook Keaveney.

"Wha'?" Keaveney said, rolling over.

"Wake up," Davis said, shaking him harder. "I hear something."

"What?"

They both lay in the tent, listening. Outside a slight wind was blowing through the jungle canopy, rustling the leaves. The night insects were humming together in non-stop rhythm.

"I don't hear anything. Just the trees, you prob—"

"No, there it is," Davis hissed.

The whispering noises had begun again, then a chuckling. It sounded like there were two people outside the tent, maybe three, about twenty yards away in the jungle. Davis leaned forward, peeking out through the tent flaps. In the middle of the camp, something rose. There was a low growling noise as the shape hunched its back. Pete, the soldier's dog, was standing, ears raised, lips curled back as it stared out toward the dark jungle.

The strange laughing continued, quietly. Davis tried concentrating on the words, but the whispers were so indistinct he couldn't catch anything.

"Jesus," Keaveney said, now wide-awake. "You think it's the Japs?"

Davis shook his head. "Doesn't sound like Japanese."

"Yeah, but who the hell else would be out here?"

"Maybe it's some of our guys?"

"Should we check it out?"

"Are you crazy? I'm not leaving the tent," Davis said.

"Who's on duty now?" Keaveney asked.

"Sadlon and Hartmere."

The whispering was rising, until it sounded like whoever was out there was arguing. The voices combined into a frantic hissing noise, the words indistinct. Then there was more chuckling, followed by a screeching noise.

"Jesus that's spooky," Keaveney whispered, trying to keep his voice light, but he was right. The noise was unnerving.

Davis sat up, opening the flap of the tent, his eyes trying to pierce the jungle. He saw only the dark shapes of the leaves blowing slightly in the wind. In the clearing were the tents of the other men. They were quiet. Nobody else seemed to be awake.

He strained his eyes toward the edge of the clearing, trying to see the perimeter guards. In the night's darkness, however, his line of vision ended well before the machine gun emplacements. Again, he heard the hushed voices.

"Hello?" he called out into the jungle.

Immediately the whispering stopped. There was the sound of leaves being disturbed, like something heavy moving off through the underbrush. Someone was out there. He listened to the fading noise, then the whispering began again, this time farther away. Whatever it was seemed to be walking away.

Davis turned back into the tent. "It's moving away."

"That's good," Keaveney said confidently. "I'm going back to sleep."

"Whoa . . . wait a minute. Don't you think we should check it out?"

"Do you want to check it out? Because I'm not going out there. No way in hell am I that curious. That's why we have people on watch."

Keaveney was lying on his side. "I'm just pretending I didn't hear a thing."

"You serious?"

"Listen, if it was Japs, I'm not going out there and fucking with that."

"What if it wasn't Japs? I don't think they were speaking Japanese."

"Well, I'm not fucking with that either, I don't want to be running around in the jungle at night. Bad enough during the day, when you can see what's going on."

Davis checked his watch. A little before 1 A.M. He still had another hour before he was supposed to post up for guard duty. A sudden wave of fatigue flooded over him. *I'll just sleep for a little while,* he thought, *just until I get woken up at two.*

Davis lay back in the tent. He quickly fell asleep.

His eyes jerked open again. The whispering was back, just outside the thin fabric of the tent. It was closer this time—whatever it was had moved back toward them. Now the noise was coming from inside the camp. Davis was immediately wide-awake and listening. The sounds were a strange mixture of whispering and high-pitched laughing, like a strange group conversing with each other.

He felt the back of his neck grow cold. They were miles into the jungle. *Who would be out there?* Davis turned his head, looking through the triangular opening of the tent. It was a clear night. The moon was low in the trees, breaking through the foliage and casting a pale light across the clearing of the camp. With his eyes, he tried to pick out familiar objects from the darkness. Another tent, the stump of a tree, anything he could recognize.

Something ran across his field of vision. He had just a quick glance, a fleeting impression of something pale, moving on two legs, but crouched over, low to the ground. It had been the size of a man, but its body was strangely curved or disfigured. Davis shivered involuntarily.

What time was it? He peered at his watch, trying to read the numbers in the darkness. Fuck.

It was just after 2:30 A.M.

Sadlon and Hartmere were supposed to have woken him half an hour earlier for the start of his shift. He clenched his teeth, thinking. His turn was up for the watch. If he didn't go, Seals would be pissed tomorrow. On the other hand, he didn't want to leave the comfortable warmth of the tent and go out there by himself. Next to him. Keaveney and Alabama were both sleeping soundly.

Davis slowly slid forward in the tent, reaching for his boots. He shook them out, knocking free any insects that might have crawled inside. Sitting in the opening of the tent, he began tying the laces and surveying the camp.

Everything was quiet, except for the constant hum of the insects in the kunai grass. The whispering voices had stopped. The five tents were arranged randomly around the clearing, their fabric sides billowing in and out from the wind. Another breeze blew in, smelling of the ocean three miles away. Davis turned his face toward it, breathing in the slight salty smell.

His boots strapped on, he picked up his Garand rifle and walked slowly across the camp toward the machine gun post. He could see where the strips of barbed wire had been strung out, forming a weak perimeter fence. Just before that were two dark openings in the ground, rectangular blocks, each the size of a man, cut into the dirt. They were foxholes, but in the moonlight they looked more like open graves.

Both of them were empty.

A dark form lay next to one of the coffin-shaped holes. Davis nudged the shape with his foot. It was soft, yielding against the toe of his boot. In the darkness, it was just a bulbous outline. Davis leaned over. Taking out his lighter, he flicked the flame, holding the light toward the ground.

He felt the back of his throat twitch as he fought down an attack of nausea. Lying crooked on the ground was the dog, Pete, his neck snapped jaggedly backward, his tongue hanging limply from his mouth.

"Jesus," Davis whispered, leaning over Pete, the shadows thrown from his lighter flickering off the matted fur.

Suddenly conscious of the darkness of the jungle around him, Davis snapped shut the lighter, pale colors flooding his eyes as his vision moved to adjust. The light machine gun was propped up on a swivel stand just outside the foxhole. In the darkness, it had a strange crooked appearance, like the silhouette of a sitting man.

Beyond the machine gun, the jungle faded into black, where tree branches seemed to turn into rushing enemy soldiers, fallen logs into crouching Japs. Insects were thrumming loudly in waves of sound. Water fell in bulbous droplets from the leafy canopy above, smacking occasionally against Davis's helmet. There was a rustling noise, like something pushing through the thick branches.

Davis had heard that when the Japanese attacked at night, they called with bugles and shouted war cries to distract the Americans. Another quick snapping of a branch in the distance jolted Davis with a sudden rushing intensity. Something was out in the jungle. He slowly lifted his carbine, crouching lower to the ground. His knee brushed against something warm on the ground, and he pulled back in disgust as he realized he was crouching almost on top of the dead dog.

There was another noise, something strange. He cocked his ear, listening closely, trying to make it out.

It was the sound of laughter.

Slowly, Davis eased himself forward until he was positioned just behind the machine gun post. A silver-colored metal box lay in the mud near him. He opened the top, pulling out a heavy flare gun. Cracking the barrel of the gun, he loaded in a flare.

Ahead of him, the noise of laughter died down, replaced by a furtive whispering, like two people arguing. Davis listened carefully, trying to pick up individual words. The language the voices spoke was strange, flowing quickly together, almost like a chant. Holding the silver flare gun in the air, he rested his finger against the trigger. There were more sounds coming from the jungle in front of him. The crackling of something walking through the heavy underbrush, then more hissing whispers, followed by a calling sound, like the hooting of an owl.

Keeping the flare gun raised, Davis pulled the trigger.

The red light arced up into the air, rushing from the barrel with a popping noise. Almost instantly, the jungle around the campsite was lit with a reddish glow, the shadows bouncing back and forth as the flare slowly tumbled back to earth. The dark shadows faded away from between the trees, opening up the jungle with light, allowing Davis to see ahead of him.

Something was out there.

A man was standing in the jungle, almost twenty yards deep, visible through the thick foliage. He was pinioned to the tree, his arms stretched outward, his legs bound together. His head was resting at his feet, separated from the body. Davis could see that the mouth was open and stuffed with mud, bits of leaves and wet twigs protruding from between two blue lips. On the man's shoulders, where his head should have rested, was instead the head of a monkey. A chimpanzee. The chimp's eyes were glazed over and dead, its head fastened somehow to the body of the murdered soldier.

Davis recognized the man. It was James Sadlon, one of the two Marines who had been on guard that night.

"Jesus Christ!" Davis said aloud in surprise.

The flare was falling into the trees, the light quickly beginning to fade, as the shadows started to creep back between the trees. Then the flare was extinguished, and the jungle was plunged back into darkness.

Around him, Davis heard the wild, frantic rustling of tent fabric as men clambered out. There was a gunshot, the orange muzzle flare flashing for an instant, followed by a shrill scream from the jungle ahead. Davis raised his own weapon in confusion, squeezing the trigger and feeling the sharp jar of the recoil against his shoulder.

Something dark whistled through the night air, striking him heavily against his exposed forehead, just underneath the brim of his helmet. Grunting in pain, he fell backward onto the muddy jungle floor as around him the clearing was alive with the sounds of gunfire and heavy bootfalls.

Eric lay in his bed, his eyes open, looking out through the open flap at the dawn sky. Curls of fog surrounded everything, tucked close to the jungle floor, breaking around plants and men. Around him, he could hear the camp slowly coming to life. Men were standing up, arching their backs and stretching, rubbing out the tension of a night of sleeping on the ground. He heard someone cough deeply, spitting out something wet.

Eric rolled over on his side and pulled his canteen from out of his pack. Unscrewing the lid, he put it to his lips, trying not to choke on the metallic-flavored warm water that entered his mouth. There were beads of condensation on the metal canister. He wiped the water droplets off onto his hands, trying to rub off some of the mud that had collected there.

He rolled over onto his side, his brain seeming to flow sluggishly and painfully against the side of the skull. A black lump had formed on his forehead from where he had been struck the previous night. He ran his fingers over the sensitive skin. Keaveney leaned over on his elbows, looking at the mark with a low whistle.

"You got whacked pretty good there, huh?"

Davis said, "Hurts like hell."

Keaveney glanced appreciatively at the mark before sliding out of the tent. Davis rubbed the sleep from his eyes. Next to him, Alabama was awake, lying on his sleeping back and eating the fruit bar from the K-Ration pouch. He seemed tense, chewing each bite unusually quickly. He was thinking about something. Finally, he turned to Davis.

"So you think what you saw last night was Japs?"

"I guess so."

Alabama was silent for a moment, thinking.

"I don't know," he said finally, shaking his head. "Seems strange is all. How in the hell did they get two of our guys, armed guards, without them even firing a shot?"

"Quiet, I guess."

"No man is that quiet."

"What?" Eric responded slowly. "You think it was something else?"

"Now I didn't say that," Alabama said. "I don't know what that was last night. I didn't see it for myself, so I can't really say. All I know is that I been feeling something bad coming on. There's something in this jungle that ain't right. Something evil is in here with us, I can feel it. Ain't gonna be long 'fore we find it either."

He rolled back over onto his back, staring up at the flaps of the tent. "Ain't gonna be long at all."

Seals, the unit sergeant, was already up and walking around the camp. Davis could hear him shouting.

"You get your ass outta that goddamn tent, Keaveney, before I break it down on top of you."

Keaveney muttered something indistinct.

"What the hell you say?" Seals responded.

Drying his hands on his pants, Eric Davis sat upright, stretching his arms over his head. Everything around him was a grayish white, surrounded by the covering of fog.

"Let's get going, eat up something this morning." Seals was striding up and down the line, kicking men who still slept. Soldiers were reluctant to open their eyes, to leave dreams of warm beds and their girlfriends, to wake up to a reality of mud and killing.

"Everybody up. You've got two minutes before you get my foot in your ass. Let's go."

Eric hurriedly gathered his gear. Everything seemed damp: his pack, his clothes, even his rifle seemed cold and wet. They formed a ragged line of thirteen men outside the tents, facing Seals. Most of the men looked tired and worried, large dark circles gathering under their eyes like runny mascara.

Alabama had his helmet in his hands, scratching the top of his head. Keaveney was jawing a stick of gum, the white flashing in and out between his teeth. A light rain had begun falling, dripping through the thick leaves like water through a strainer, covering the men in cool wetness.

Eric wiped the rain away from his eyes, waiting for Seals to begin.

"As you know, we had an encounter with the enemy last night. Two men are missing. Any of you that came out here thinking they were gonna make friends with the Japanese. That this was just gonna be some kind of camp-out. Franks and beans, fireside stories, nobody getting killed." Seals paused for a moment, staring at them. "Well, you best get that idea out a your head right now."

Seals exhaled a big breath. Trickles of sweat had gathered above his lip; he rubbed the back of his head with his hand.

"Let's go find out what happened last night. Groups of two, stay together, look for bodies, watch for traps, don't want no daytime surprises."

They began moving forward, gripping their rifles tightly, their heads turning nervously as they pressed deeper into the jungle. The thin rain was lightly poking cold down the back of his neck. A light mist covered the ground, and from that whiteness. Leaves seemed to close around him, their dark shapes looming suddenly out of the fog, threatening to swallow him up inside their covering. He pushed aside branches with the barrel of his gun, moving his head, his eyes burning with nervous intensity.

Alabama was beside him, breathing heavily, and Keaveney was on the other side of him. Turning his head, Davis saw the rest of his company was doing the same, cautiously pressing forward, brushing aside the leafy branches that scratched at their face. The fog was thick enough that if a man lay down, he could hide in it. For a moment Davis had a vision of himself finding a nice dry spot in the fog and just hiding out.

Then he saw Sadlon's body.

The soldier was still pinioned roughly to the giant trunk of a towan tree, his back arched and folded. Deep gouges were across his face and chest, and Davis could see white flecks of bone showing through the flesh. A slash mark was cut across Sadlon's belly, a flowering red mass of intestines poking out from under the skin. Flies had already begun to gather on the body, trickling across the bloodier sections in little jittery masses.

The head of the chimpanzee was beginning to sag under its own weight, the eyes staring vacantly at the ground. Alabama saw him a moment later, making a hissing sound and turning his head away with a soft, "Gah-damn."

"We got him," Eric shouted out. "He's over here."

Davis's first impression was that Sadlon had been gored by something, the marks looking as if they came from a jungle cat.

"This ain't right," Alabama said, looking down at the body.

The other men were converging on them. Davis could hear them coming through the fog. Slowly, they melted out of the milky whiteness, standing in front of the dead body with looks of shock on their faces.

"Oh Jesus," Jersey said as he reached the scene and looked down at the mess of a human. Eric could see the base of his throat twitching as he fought down the urge to vomit. Other Marines joined, forming a ring around the body. Eric heard the sound of someone unable to control the nausea, his ration meal being regurgitated onto the jungle floor.

"Good Lord," Seals said, looking at the mutilated body.

"Cut him down from there," he said after a moment. "And get that fucking head off him. Jesus."

Davis and Alabama stepped forward, taking knives and slitting the thick cords that pinioned the man's arms around the tree. His body sagged forward, collapsing in a wet heap on the ground. They looked at each other.

"I'm not touching that," Alabama said after a moment, staring at the chimpanzee head.

Seals turned away, staring blankly into the trees for a moment before he squatted, bending over the body and pulling Sadlon's letters from his pocket. Slipping them into the front of his jacket, he took his helmet off for a moment, wiping his brow. Then, slipping out his own knife, he cut the sutures holding the chimp's head to the man's body. The chimpanzee head rolled free after a moment, coming to rest in a bit of leaves.

"I won't leave a man like that," Seals said. He stood up, picking up the chimp's head and hurling it into the jungle.

"Who the hell you think did this?" Alabama asked quietly.

"Who do you think?" Seals said. "Japs are a bunch a goddamn animals."

Alabama nodded, but Davis noticed that he didn't seem convinced.

The men all stared at their boots for a moment, before Seals said, "Someone say a prayer for him."

The men looked at each other, then turned toward Jersey. He'd gone to a Catholic high school.

"Like what?" Jersey asked.

"Anything goddammit, just say something for him," Seals answered sharply.

"Man's dead," Alabama said. "He ain't gonna be too picky."

Jersey nodded, mumbling out a quick prayer. The men all crossed themselves. Sadlon's eyes were staring up toward the sky, vacant and glassy, like dead fish eyes. Seals reached out and closed them.

Placing his helmet back on his head he stood up straight. "Let's get him buried. Don't want the Japs coming back through here looking for souvenirs."

He strode off a few steps away from the body before stopping and turning around to face the men. "War brings dead bodies," he said. "That's the whole point of it. You make more dead than your enemy, and you stand a pretty good shot at winning the war. You'll see a lot more of them before this thing is through. Get used to it now. Nothing here you haven't seen before."

"I haven't ever seen anything like this before," Keaveney said, staring down at the gored body lying folded over on the ground.

"What'd you say?" Seals said sharply.

"Nothing."

"Well good. All right." Seals clapped his hands and turned away. "Let's get to work and bury him before it gets too hot out here."

It took three soldiers about half an hour to dig a hole deep enough in the wet jungle floor. Eric and the rest searched around for the second missing Marine. They found nothing. As if he'd been swallowed up by the jungle itself.

An hour later they had left Sadlon's body behind, the green jungle carpet disturbed by a rectangular section of freshly laid dirt, his rifle and helmet serving as a marker. Stretching into a jagged line, they followed a small path of mud leading deeper through jungle. Fourteen Marines pressed forward, cigarettes dangling from mouths, weapons raised in one hand, the other extended out to the side, balancing as they slogged through the rot.

The jungle was stifling, making their skin feel as if layers of oily rags had been placed over their bodies. Leeches oozed up from the mud, squiggling on bootlaces and pant legs. Giant bees, the size of half-dollars, landed on their uncovered skin, attracted by the saltiness of their sweat. The bees were gentle, unless provoked, lapping at the sweat for a few minutes before flying off again. Eric felt a shiver through his body as they landed on his uncovered face, crawling around, sometimes moving toward his eyes or his mouth. Entering his ears. Scorpions scuttled away from them as they passed, moving low to the ground, their tails bent backward.

They paused to rest, and thankfully Eric stopped and took a draught of warm water from his canteen.

Cries of "I'm out!" traveled up and down the line as men tilted back their empty metal containers.

Eric felt something on his leg. Looking down, his pants seemed to have come alive, the fabric twitching and moving. He was covered in ants.

"Aww, shit!" he cried, unbuttoning his pants as quickly as he could. He kicked off his boots, heavy with mud, and his dirty socks, until he stood in just his underwear. His clothes, a quivering pile of moving ants, lay in front of him.

"What'cha got there? Ants?" Alabama asked.

He picked up one of Eric's socks, inspecting it closely for a moment, then dropping it back to the ground before the ants had a chance to run up his hand. "Don't want to get bit by those sons a bitches. That'll sting worse than a bit a Louisiana hot sauce."

"Yeah, thanks."

"You musta stepped in a nest."

Eric looked around on the ground and saw a small mound of loose dirt piled up to the side of the path. The dirt had been compressed in the middle, a large boot print stamped firmly on the top. He'd stepped on a nest, all right.

Eric carefully beat his clothes with a stick he tore loose from the ground, the ants scurried around in mindless panic, eventually leaving the clothes and heading back in a trail toward their nest.

He put his clothes back on slowly, still expecting the fiery hot bite of ants to sink into his skin.

Ten minutes later, they pressed forward again, moving unsteadily along the path. They were entering a coconut grove—the brown ring-barked trees became more spaced out, and walking became easier. The brown balls of coconut littered the ground. Soldiers were picking them up and cracking the hard shells against trees, drinking the watery white milk inside as they walked.

Suddenly Seals raised an arm, halting the men for a moment, before waving them to the ground. Eric dropped the coconut he was working on, pressing himself against the ground and gripping his carbine. He watched with sadness the coconut next to him, lying where he'd dropped it, the white milk slowly oozing out of a narrow crack in the shell.

Nothing around him seemed to be moving, except for a sloth working its way slowly across a branch above. Seals crouched, indicating that they wait as he slowly pressed forward, moving through the trees. Eric rested his head on the ground, breathing in the smell of the mud and listening to the rustling of the great palm leaves above them. The temperature was hot as usual, but in the shade of the coconut grove it wasn't at all unbearable.

He looked up again and saw Seals staring off into the distance, looking up a ridge ahead of them. Eric saw nothing. Seals paused for a moment before jogging back to the first man on the ground and whispering something into his ear, pointing up toward the ridge. He saw that private turn around and whisper into the ear of the man behind him, gradually the secret working its way down the line. By the time it got to him, Eric half expected the words to be so messed up, forgotten, and rearranged by multiple mouths, that it would end up something like, "The Yankees Win the Series in '46."

It wasn't.

"There's a Jap bunker . . . out there, among them trees on the ridge, .30 caliber." Alabama hissed into Eric's ear. "Seals wants three men up front."

Eric nodded and passed the message back. Men's hands started going up along the line, volunteers. Eric raised his hand along with the others, half-afraid to be chosen.

He was.

Nodding when Seals pointed to him from the front, he rose and, in a crouch, moved slowly forward. As he passed, the Marines on the ground nodded to him, wishing him luck.

At the front, Seals was squatting on the ground, holding a stick and playing with it in the dirt. The three men assembled around him. Alabama, Davis, and a Texan named Martinez.

"Looks like we got an emplacement up there," he pointed with the stick to a point on the ridge above them. Eric looked up and saw a coconut-log-and-dirt structure set back into the hill. It seemed quiet.

"Probably something smaller than 75mm," Seals said, running the stick over the ground. "Could be anything."

"Thirty caliber?" Martinez asked.

"Probably," Seals answered. "Thirty caliber, yeah. Same as on the beach, except we got more cover here."

Seals broke the stick in half. "Davis, you and Alabama take left. Martinez and I'll take right. Keep down until you have the shot. Those .30 calibers can lay down a good rain from up on the ridge, and we sure as hell don't want to get wet."

Seals used one of the stick halves and pointed to a small outcrop of rocks just slightly up the hill, to the left of the bunker. "Sit tight by those rocks. And get those packs off."

Alabama and Davis nodded, pulling off their packs and laying the unnecessary weight on the ground. Martinez and Seals moved off through the jungle, pushing their way through the thick leaves. They were standing on the edge of a clearing. Ahead, through the waving kunai grass, was a slightly sloping ridge. At the top was the bunker.

Alabama tapped Davis on the shoulder, and together they moved cautiously forward, skirting the edge of the clearing. The air was filled with the raucous calls of parakeets and the screeches of monkeys, the noise covering over the slight, *whisk, whisk,* of their footsteps through the wet undergrowth. After pushing a few yards through the jungle, Davis felt as if he'd stepped into a cool shower. His hair was soaked through, and his clothes clung to his body in wet, sticky clumps.

Alabama was using the barrel of his rifle to push aside the wet leaves. They would occasionally slip, springing back toward Davis's face with alarming speed, sometimes catching him across the eye.

"Hey, watch that," Davis whispered.

"Sorry."

They moved about thirty yards forward before coming to an outcropping of rocks in front of the clearing. Sliding down, Davis pressed himself against the warm, dry stone surface, feeling its heat radiate through his body. They were close enough to the bunker that Davis could see the individual chinks in the logs, the ax marks cut into the wood. The structure was made of mud and thick coconut trunks, almost blending in with the surrounding environment. They could have walked within ten yards of the spot and not noticed that it was there. It was peaceful, reminding Davis of his own family's cabin in New Hampshire.

The similarity ended with the .30 caliber machine gun barrel that protruded from a narrow slit in between the logs.

"Looks pretty quiet," Alabama whispered.

"Yeah."

"I mean I don't see nothing. The place looks abandoned, like they just up and left."

"Maybe."

Eric was panting hard, his palms pushing hard against his rifle. He realized with surprise that his index finger was slowly depressing the rifle's trigger. Forcing himself to slow his breathing, he relaxed slightly, his finger pulling up from the trigger.

The Japanese bunker was silent. A slight breeze blew through the clearing, gently blowing the small tufts of grass that grew out from the chinks in the logs.

"Don't look like anyone's home," Alabama repeated.

"You wanna go up and knock?"

"Shit no."

"So what do we do?"

"Why don't we fire a few rounds inside there, see if we can't shake something out?"

Looking across the rock, they could see Seals and Martinez making their way quietly up the slope across the clearing, on the other side of the bunker. They were almost crouching as they walked, their bodies low to the ground. Seals parted the thick leaves, looking toward Davis and Alabama on the other side.

Alabama caught the sergeant's eye, then pointed to the bunker and shook his head in a motion indicating that the fortification appeared to be empty. Seals nodded, slowly moving forward by himself. Martinez stayed behind him, crouching underneath the thick cover of greenery.

"He's got balls, huh?" Alabama said admiringly as he watched Seals crawl toward the bunker.

"I don't know about that," Davis replied. "He just might be a fucking idiot."

Seals advanced, the kunai grass of the clearing coming up just past his knees as he walked. He was crouched low, his rifle held at waist level. The grass parted with each step and lay in a crushed trail behind him, like he was walking through a beach of deep sand.

He disappeared behind the wall of the bunker.

"Where'd he go?" Alabama asked.

Davis opened his mouth to reply, when the sound of an explosion changed his mind. A spout of dirt and loose grass was launched into the air from behind the bunker. There was the short sporadic crackle of rifle fire.

Alabama was on his feet, running forward, one hand holding his helmet in place. Surprised, Davis hung back for a moment, clinging to the cover provided by the rock. When Alabama suddenly stopped, Davis went into action, standing up from behind the rock and starting forward.

"It's all right," a man's voice cried.

Seals stepped out from behind the bunker.

"Place is empty," he said.

Alabama exhaled, rolling his head. "Jesus. You scared the shit outta me."

Davis ran up, joining them. "What's going on?"

"There's nobody inside," Seals repeated.

"Seriously?" .

"Nothing, it's empty."

Davis looked around the rest of the clearing. They were standing on a slight ridge overlooking the rest of the jungle. Behind the bunker was what appeared to be a small Japanese bivouac. A few tents were scattered in the deep kunai grass, their fabric sagging in the middle, some of them lying in collapsed heaps on the ground. Empty cartons of rations and cigarette butts lay in piles in the clearing, along with metal canisters of ammunition, their contents half-strewn around. The grass was littered with empty canteens and discarded packs, clips of ammo and a thousand other items of assorted military junk; but there were no soldiers.

"Where is everyone?" Davis asked, looking around.

Seals shrugged. "Don't know."

"Maybe they all gave up," Alabama said, kicking a bandolier with his foot. "Took the first ferry back to Tokyo."

Around them, the entire clearing was covered in the brassy glint of spent ammunition shells. They littered the ground by the thousands, their cylindrical forms lying in the grass.

Davis bent and picked one up, fingering it thoughtfully. "They were shooting at something up here."

Alabama nodded. "Spent enough ammunition to shoot up all o' Chicago. I didn't even think our guys were up here this far."

"They're not," Seals confirmed. "Least they shouldn't be."

"Then who the hell were they shooting at?" Davis asked.

Alabama shrugged. "Don't know."

He looked around the clearing—the shells were everywhere. "Looks like they were getting attacked from all around them. They got cartridges all over here."

"Lookit here." Alabama was bending, examining the side of one of the fallen tents. The pale green fabric was covered by dried, blackish spots.

"It's blood," Davis said.

"Looks like," Alabama answered. He stood up, looking around the clearing.

Davis was moving toward the far end of the clearing. The grass was pressed flat against the ground, ridged boot prints covering the soft earth The air was humid, and he swished his hand in front of his face, urging away the tiny insects hovering around his eyes. The hill sloped downward before meeting the edge of the jungle on the far side. Something near the line of the trees was fluttering in the wind. Davis cocked his head, staring at the object. It was a piece of cloth, hanging from something large suspended off the ground.

There were more of these objects, spread along on a straight line across the edge of the clearing. Suddenly Davis recognized what they were.

"Oh my God," he whispered to himself, then turned back toward the other men. "Jesus Christ, you guys gotta come look at this. Hustle up!"

Alabama and Seals jogged toward him, their canteens jangling against their hips as they ran.

"What is it?" Alabama asked breathlessly, staring at Davis as he approached.

Davis said nothing, only nodded toward the edge of the clearing.

Alabama turned his head slowly, looking out across Davis's line of sight.

Along the line of the jungle was a series of straight wooden poles, standing upright from the dark soil. Suspended from each was a Japanese soldier. Someone had pierced the soldiers through their stomachs, then raised the poles until the men hung limply from the top, ten feet above the ground, where they sagged like drooping flowers. Most of their clothes were tattered, bits of exposed flesh visible through the tears, the loose fabric swishing in the wind.

Insects had begun to collect around the bodies, giant winged creatures, which buzzed and zipped back and forth in the air. The poles were spaced evenly, about six feet apart. They appeared to be buried deeply in the ground, showing no signs of leaning one way or the other, even with the weight of the impaled men.

Davis felt strangely calm as he viewed the scene, almost dumbfounded with amazement at the spectacle.

"What the hell happened here?" Alabama asked softly, turning toward Seals.

"I don't know," Seals replied.

"Did our guys do this?"

Seals shook his head. "Don't know."

"Well . . ." Alabama said slowly. "What do we do about it?"

Seals reached down and plucked a few strands of grass, playing them back and forth between his fingers. After a moment he said, "Nothing. We don't mention it to the other guys. We don't do anything."

He turned away from the sight of the men hanging from the poles. "Let's get back up top."

The three men walked quietly back up the ridge, toward the bunker. As the shock began to wear off, Davis's stomach felt unsteady, rocking back and forth in a pit of nausea. They reached the top and heard a jangling noise coming from the jungle. Davis looked up to see Martinez jogging through the clearing, two large metal canisters suspended from his back, the fuel containers for the flamethrower clanging together as he moved.

"Christ," Alabama said. "I don't know how you stand to walk around with them things on your back. It's like carrying a full-size barbecue."

Martinez shrugged amiably, smiling and lighting a cigarette.

"Yeah, that's smart," Alabama said. "You got twenty pounds of gasoline strapped to your back. Go ahead, light up a cigarette. Fucking idiot."

"Hey," Seals's voice sounded suddenly. "Got something."

Seals was standing in the entrance of the bunker, staring at the dirt floor. The three other men joined him, following his eyes down. Set in the middle of the floor was a small, wooden trapdoor. Seals leaned down, pulling up the door, which came free in his hand. Beneath it was a rectangular hole dug into the ground. The sides of the hole were constructed of tightly packed dirt, the walls leading into complete darkness.

"They got tunnels," Seals said. "Martinez?"

"Yes?"

"Burn them out."

"Yes, sir."

Martinez stepped forward, raising the flamethrower. Standing in the doorway of the bunker, he adjusted the fuel gauge on the canisters and pointed the long weapon toward the hole in the ground. There was a rushing noise, and a jet of flame shot from the end of the metal gun in Martinez's hand.

He arced the flames down the hole, where they exploded through the opening, torching the ground around. Standing off to the side, Davis could feel the heat radiating outward and heard a popping noise as the flames singed the ground.

Martinez released the trigger and stepped back. The inside of the bunker was smoking slightly, the logs tinged with black. Around the hole, more black soot covered the ground.

"All right," Seals said. "Let's get down there."

"What?" Alabama asked.

"You heard."

"Sergeant, they're dead. Why go down there?"

"I didn't know this was a democracy, Alabama. Since when do I have to tell you why?"

Alabama shook his head. "Yes, sir."

Seals moved forward, squatting over the opening, a rectangle about two feet wide and three feet long. A thin trail of smoking steam wafted lazily from underground, like a candle that had just been blown out. Bracing himself against the dirt, he swung his legs over and slowly lowered himself.

He dropped out of view.

"He's crazy," Alabama murmured.

"Yeah, he is," Davis said, moving toward the hole.

Sliding the strap of his rifle around his shoulder, Davis placed his hands on the earth and swung his feet out. Below him, he could see only a square of darkness. The flames had made the soil warm, almost hot to the touch, and it felt like lying in the sand during a blazing summer day. As he lowered himself into the hole, the heat radiated around him. The effect was almost relaxing, like stepping into a sauna.

"You see anything?" Alabama asked.

Davis dropped, falling a few feet before his boots impacted against the solid ground below.

"It's a tunnel. 'Bout five feet high," Davis replied.

Seals was ahead of him, holding a flashlight and shining the beam forward. The light seemed to die against the walls of the tunnel, soaked up by the dark soil. Overhead, a rectangular shaft of sunlight streamed through the opening, projecting a pale rectangle onto the dirt floor.

Seals was moving forward quickly, heedless of the unknown blackness ahead of him. One hand swung the flashlight from side to side, while the other gripped his rifle. Davis followed him, his finger nervously pressing against the trigger of his weapon. The walls were narrow, and Davis's shoulder brushed the sides, breaking off small clumps of dirt.

Ahead of them, where the tunnel seemed to expand into a small room, there appeared a strange, flickering, red light, which cast long shadows on the walls of the tunnel.

The shadows seemed to be moving, as if someone were stepping in front of a fire. Behind Davis, Alabama was struggling through the hole; then Martinez followed.

"Whadya see?' he asked in a low whisper.

"Don't know," Davis replied, turning his head slightly back. "Some kinda light. Weird-looking."

The tunnel stretched about ten yards forward, before widening out into the dugout room. Seals went forward, stepping into the room and disappearing, moving toward whatever was causing the reddish flicker.

Davis followed more slowly, resisting the urge to call out for the unseen sergeant.

The tunnel ended, and Davis stepped into the room beyond. The area was dug out from the soil, with a series of coconut-log posts and beams holding up the roof. The area was about twenty feet by fifteen feet, with a bed made of dried kunai grass and logs against the corner, next to a small reed mat and a table. On the table was a tea set and a few personal effects brought from Japan. A tiny bookcase was against the wall, with four carefully stacked books, the writing all in Japanese. Draped from between two of the log posts was a large white sheet scrawled with Japanese characters and a large rising sun.

The room was cozy, comfortable even, almost like a boyhood fort. Except it wasn't. Everything was on fire.

The bed of grass was burning, the flames curling up the dried stalks. Thin trails of flames streamed up the draped white fabric and danced along the bookshelf. Orange burned along the posts, igniting the books. They were standing in a room of fire, ignited when Martinez used the flamethrower.

A thick layer of smoke was beginning to build. The fire sucked in drafts of air from the opening outside, the breeze bursting down the tunnel, ruffling Davis's clothes and causing the flaming fabric hanging from the ceiling to sway. The shadows cast on the far wall appeared to shift and move in unison with the white cloth.

Suspended from the back wall of the room was a human body, the body of a Japanese soldier. He was wearing only a pair of dirty pants, rolled up almost to the knee, with no shoes or socks, and was hanging from one of the burning posts, his arms outstretched to either side, his bare feet together. Someone had hammered nails into his hands and feet, crucifying him to the wood. His dirty skin hung loosely from his body so that Davis felt it might slide off to the floor, leaving just a bare skeleton on the wall.

His body had been slashed by something sharp. Long gouge marks streaked down his chest, opening up part of his gut and allowing his intestines to hang freely out. They were as dried and shriveled as strings of black seaweed.

"Jesus," Davis said. "What happened to him?"

"It's like he's been cut up and left to dry like a dead pig," Alabama said. "Who in the hell did that? You think our guys did that? Cut him up like that?"

"We don't have any men within ten miles," Seals answered, staring at the body.

"What about that recon unit that's gone missing," Alabama said. "The one we're looking for. Maybe they came through here and did this."

"What about those guys up on the poles?" Davis answered.

"Shut up, Davis," Seals said angrily.

"What guys on the poles?" Martinez asked.

"Nothing," Davis responded.

"Something been bothering me about this whole thing," Martinez said. "If they killed everyone, how come there're no bodies?"

"Maybe they took 'em with them," Alabama answered.

"Through the jungle? I can't hardly walk through the jungle with just my pack. How the hell can you haul an entire platoon of dead soldiers away?"

"Yeah. No American soldier'd do something like this anyway." Alabama gestured at the mutilated body.

"Or anything else we've seen," Davis said, thinking of the ten men hanging from the wooden poles.

"Strange things can happen to a man in war," Seals said slowly. "A man doesn't know what he's capable of, till he gets out here, where killing is just a part of getting by."

"You saying our guys did this?" Davis asked.

Seals shrugged. "I've seen men so caught up in killing, they'd slit their own mother's throat, just to see her bleed. It's like a drug, killing a man. Makes you forget who you are, how you were raised. Once you reach that point, you don't care 'bout nothing else except killing. Besides, Alabama's right, we still don't know where that recon unit is. Maybe they did come through here."

Alabama shook his head, and spit. The room was filling up with smoke, the flames climbing the timbers and across the bookshelf. The body hadn't caught on fire and remained nailed to the wall, the man's head sagging toward his chest.

"We gotta go," Seals said.

"We're just gonna leave him up there?" Alabama asked.

"Not our responsibility."

"Maybe. Still, it just don't seem right. Leaving a man nailed to a wall like he was a picture."

Davis's eyes had begun to water from the smoke, and his mouth tasted sour. He wanted to get out of there. Suddenly there was a cracking sound. Davis first thought one of the support timbers had snapped until Martinez grunted and leaned forward, his arms pressed against his stomach.

"You all right?" Alabama asked, watching with surprise as the man dropped to his knees. Davis looked down at Martinez's fingers, and was surprised to see that blood was flowing freely between then.

"What the . . . ?" he began to say, before there was another popping noise and he felt an instant burning in his shoulder, as if someone had held a lit match to his skin.

"Ahhh! Fuck!" he shouted, as it slowly dawned on him what the popping noise was. Someone was shooting at them.

He dropped to his knee, raising his rifle. The room was almost entirely filled with thick, black smoke, but Davis could faintly see that, just past the room, the tunnel continued. Through the smoke, he could see a shirtless man ducking behind a mound of earth. He was reloading his rifle, looking down at the magazine as he did so. Davis raised his rifle, firing a few rounds toward the soldier with a *tchh. Tchh. Tchh*. Alabama was still standing flat-footed, watching Davis, his eyes wide.

"Someone's shooting at us," Davis said. "Get Martinez out of here."

Alabama shook his head, then bent, grabbed Martinez by the shoulder, and began pulling him along the dirt floor of the tunnel. Davis squinted against the acrid smoke and fired again blindly. There was an answering shot, and Davis heard a fragment of sharp metal explode past his head. He couldn't see ahead, the smoke and fire blocking out the rest of the room. Alabama had dragged Martinez to the opening and was trying to push him up. The soldier was still conscious, swearing loudly, one hand held over his opened gut. He was bareheaded, his hair slicked down to his scalp in greasy streaks of sweat. "I need a hand here, Davis. I can't get him out."

Davis moved past them, climbing out of the opening. He sucked in the air outside with relief, like cooling ointment going into his scorched lungs. Bending back toward the hole, he grasped Martinez around the chest, and, with Alabama and Seals pushing from the rear, they pulled the wounded man up.

Davis carried him out of the tunnel. Weak from the lack of oxygen, he staggered slightly under the dead weight before laying him in the thick kunai grass just outside the bunker.

Alabama and Seals followed them, both breathing heavily. Alabama's body was slumped over at the waist, and Davis thought he might be shot, too, until he opened his mouth and vomited the contents of his stomach all over the ground. Drawn by the sound of the shots, Davis could see the rest of the men breaking out of the jungle, running through the kunai grass toward them. Martinez groaned loudly, pressing his hand against his stomach as if he were trying to hold his insides in.

There was a noise from the tunnel, a quick scraping sound, like the scattering of loose dirt or small rocks. Alabama walked cautiously back to the hole in the ground, looking into it. He jumped back in surprise.

"What is it?" Davis asked.

"It's a Jap," Alabama said. "Prolly the one that shot up Martinez."

"You kill him?"

Alabama leaned forward again, looking into the hole.

"He ain't got no gun," he said slowly. "What do I do?"

"What do you mean he doesn't have a gun?"

"He ain't armed. And it looks like he's wounded his own self."

Leaving Martinez for a moment, Davis stepped back toward the tunnel and looked down. Almost eight feet below him, lying in a heap at the base of the tunnel, was a Japanese soldier. His head was propped against the dirt wall. A dark red splotch of blood on the floor showed just over his left shoulder. He recognized the man, the one who had shot at them.

He was lean, each of his ribs showing clearly underneath his skin. He looked up at them with glazed eyes, mumbling something in Japanese. The tunnel was filling with thick black smoke, which billowed out from the opening as if it were a chimney. The wounded soldier was trying to cover his mouth with a strip of fabric torn from his shirt, but his body still shivered with racking coughs.

"What should we do?" Alabama asked.

Davis shrugged. "Leave him there, I guess."

"We leave him, he's gonna die down there," Alabama said slowly.

It was true. The wounded soldier wasn't strong enough to pull himself out of the tunnel. He'd either burn to death, bleed to death, or die from smoke inhalation. The choices weren't promising.

"Martinez is gonna die, too," Davis said. "This is the guy that did that."

"Yeah, I guess you're right."

Davis turned and walked back toward Martinez. He had opened his mouth, sucking in air. Streaks of blood covered his teeth. From behind him there was a grunting noise. Davis turned around to see Alabama pulling the Japanese soldier from out of the hole.

"Jesus, man, what the hell you doing?" Davis asked, running back. "That's crazy. You lost your mind?"

"We can't just leave him there. That ain't right. He's gonna die anyway, might as well let him die in peace with a full stomach."

"Oh now you want to feed him, too? We lugged those rations all through the jungle, and now you want to just give them up."

The Japanese soldier was lying in a curled heap on the ground. He grabbed Alabama's foot, holding it, and looking up at him. The soldier nodded, saying something quickly in Japanese which could only be interpreted as a thank-you.

The rest of the men from the unit joined them a moment later, clustering around Martinez and the Japanese soldier. "Where'd he come from?" Kelly Keaveney asked.

"He's down in that tunnel," replied Alabama.

The soldier began saying something in Japanese. His eyes were wide as he spoke, his fingers clutching at Alabama's pant leg.

"What the hell's he saying?" Jersey said.

Alabama shrugged. "Hey, Reder," he shouted to one of the other men. Martin Reder had grown up in San Francisco and spoke a tolerable amount of Japanese. He was the only man in the unit that knew any at all.

Reder was a young, smart kid, with close-cropped hair and a wide, pleasant face. He was standing, looking down at Martinez, but when he heard his name, he jogged quickly over to Alabama.

"Yeah, what's up?"

"You understand him?"

Reder listened closely to the mumbled Japanese. The wounded soldier seemed to be very agitated, his eyes wide and staring, jumping back and forth between the Americans.

Reder listened for a moment, then he shrugged slightly. "Sort of."

"Well? What the hell's he saying?" Alabama asked. "You know I can't understand a word a this damn language. Just like listening to chickens fighting."

Reder spoke quickly to the wounded soldier. Hearing the Japanese phrases, the soldier turned toward Reder and began speaking more clearly. His wound was hurting him, and every few moments he paused to suck in a breath and wince. His face was growing more pale every moment, as if the blood were literally draining from his body through the tiny bullet hole.

"He's dying," Davis whispered.

"What's he say?" Alabama asked, nodding toward the Japanese soldier.

Reder shook his head, his eyebrows knitted together.

"Not sure," he said. "Something about ghosts coming out of the jungle. Or spirits. The word doesn't translate exactly."

"Ghosts?" Alabama repeated skeptically.

"Sort of," Reder replied. "More like spirits. Evil spirits. Like of the dead."

"That's bullshit," Alabama answered. "Ask him again."

Reder looked at the soldier, saying something in Japanese. The soldier shook his head, and mumbled back a few words.

Reder nodded and looked up, lifting his helmet off his head before spitting into the ground. "Yeah, he says it wasn't ghosts. Something solid, like a man, only not a man. They came from the jungle."

The bunker was in flames, long curls of angry orange that rose above the jungle canopy. Keaveney had leveled the portable torch at the log walls, bursting jets of fire into the wood. A thick cloud of smoke poured up into the sky, making Davis a little nervous. Now every Jap for three miles around could see exactly where they were. In the trees, terrified monkeys and parrots were screeching, watching the blaze burn wildly. They had cut two rolls of bamboo, wrapping them together to make two poles. Between the poles was wrapped tent fabric, strung around the bamboo and forming a rickety stretcher. They rolled Martinez over onto his side, a stream of blood leaking out of his stomach as they turned him, then slid the stretcher underneath.

The Japanese soldier lay on the ground, his hand pressed against the wound in his chest.

"What about him?" Alabama asked, nodding to the Japanese soldier.

"Leave him," Jersey answered. "I guess. Can't really take him with us. We don't have enough men to carry another stretcher."

"That don't really seem right," Alabama said. "Just leaving him here."

"Well we can't do anything."

"We could try and carry him."

"Carry him where?" Jersey replied.

The two men were beginning to argue, their voices rising.

"Shit, I dunno," Alabama answered.

Lying on the ground underneath them, the Japanese soldier watched the two Americans, seeming vaguely to follow the conversation. "Jesus Christ, man," Jersey said, shaking his head. "Listen to yourself. You want us to carry him through the jungle. He's the enemy. We're not supposed to help."

"Can't just leave him."

"Don't be such a dumb-headed ignorant hick."

"What?" Alabama said sharply. "What the fuck you just say?"

"Nothing," Jersey said, shaking his head in disgust.

Alabama moved quickly forward, bringing his fist up to strike. Jersey ducked out of the way, punching Alabama sharply in the jaw with a quick left jab. Alabama's neck snapped backward, his helmet falling to the ground. He came back at Jersey quickly, swinging one wild fist. The rest of the soldiers moved toward the men to restrain them. Seals stood to the side, passively watching the argument.

"Aren't you gonna do something," Davis shouted toward him.

"They want to fight," Seals replied. "Let them. Anger is good."

Jersey had knocked off Reder with a quick back elbow, and Reder pulled away, blood pouring down his face. Seals watched the confusion for a moment more, a half smile on his face. Without a word, he pulled out his pistol, walked to the wounded Japanese soldier, and put the weapon to the man's head.

"You goddamn sonof—" Alabama was yelling, his fist pulling back.

The gunshot cracked loudly in the open clearing and something dark splattered across the front of Alabama's shirt. He dropped his fist, the anger melting from his face, as he looked down with confusion at the dark spots. In unison, the heads of the men turned from Alabama toward Seals. Seals was standing upright, slowly lowering his pistol to his side, a reddish streak across his face. On the ground at his feet was the dead Japanese soldier, a black opening the size of a half-dollar just above his temple.

"Problem solved," Seals said. "You want to fight, that's how you do it. You kill. No thought, no guilt."

Seals inhaled deeply, seeming to be very relaxed, less tired. Davis felt suddenly cold, Seals seemed . . . better somehow. His face healthier, his eyes more alive.

"Take a man's life," Seals said. "Makes your own that much stronger."

Seals turned, wiped the barrel of his gun against his pants, and walked away.

They continued through the jungle in silence, moving away from the clearing, still shocked from the killing. Eric looked back up the ridge once, just in time to see the weakened logs of the bunker collapsing on themselves, the structure tumbling inward, destroying everything inside. Between them, Alabama and Jersey carried the stretcher with Martinez. He was lying on his back, groaning and cursing occasionally in Spanish.

"This isn't right," Reder said, holding a piece of torn cloth against his nose. "We should call this off, get home."

Davis nodded. "Yeah."

"I saw those men back there, those men on the poles."

Davis turned to him.

"When the rest of the guys were making a stretcher for Martinez, Seals wandered off over the ridge. I followed him, and I saw those Japanese, those men, hung up on the poles."

Davis nodded. "I saw them, too; so did Alabama."

"What does it mean?"

"Don't know. Something is going on. Something bad."

"Seals, he didn't seem to mind. You want to know what he did?"

"What?"

"I was watching him. He walked down to those poles and was staring up at the men with this weird look on his face, kind of like he was eyeing something good to eat. Then he ran his hand along one of the poles, and I saw it come away wet with blood, and he just looked at it."

"Then what happened?"

"Then I saw him climb one of the poles. He took his knife and cut out something from one of the man's faces. I couldn't see it too well, but I know he put something into his pocket."

"Bullshit."

"No." Reder shook his head. "I saw it. He cut something off the man's damn face and put it into his front pocket."

Davis was silent a moment, and Reder continued, "I don't care about the missing men, I just want to get home. I don't want to be here."

Davis nodded in agreement. He didn't want to be there either.

Dysentery had begun to hit the men in force. Eric felt his guts twisting apart inside him, and every hour they had to stop so men could rush into the jungles around them. Everything around them was choked with life. Life killing life. Plants had poisons, insects stung, animals bit, everything was untrusting and vengeful. At first he'd been tempted to pick the beautiful red and orange flowers that sometimes dangled in large clumps across the trail. Now the thought didn't cross his mind. There could be a scorpion inside, or the motion might trigger a horde of wasps, or even worse, if the flower was poisonous, its toxins would slowly seep in through your skin until an hour later your nerves began shutting down.

They rested during the early afternoon, the hottest part of the day, reclining against tree roots, their packs spread out in front of them. Jersey and Alabama gratefully lowered the stretcher to the ground, rubbing their sore wrists and fingers. Eric rested against his back, looking up into the tangle of plants overhead. He followed the brownish grayish trunks up from the ground, as they shot upward all around him, like rockets reaching into the sky before exploding outward into the green leaves high above the jungle floor.

There was a rustling noise above him, the shaking of branches. Looking up, he saw a small Siamang ape sitting high on a branch over him, its feet clasped tightly together around the bark, one of its long arms reaching into the leaves above. The Siamang, with its small black face encircled by white fur, was staring down at him, shifting its weight back and forth, rocking its head. Eric rummaged into his pack and pulled out a section of candy bar he hadn't finished yet. Tearing off a small chunk, he threw the section away from him, where it landed on the jungle floor just underneath the Siamang's tree.

"Let's get moving," Seals said after a while.

Eric turned away from the Siamang, watching as men around him slowly and painfully pulled themselves to their feet and hoisted their packs back onto their shoulders, picking up their rifles and helmets.

Eric shoulders were raw, and he winced with pain as he felt the weight of the pack's straps dig back into the chafed wounds. Once they'd walked for a while, a numbness set in, but it was painful after they'd stopped. The men started off again through the jungle. As they walked away, Eric glanced backward. The Siamang was quickly climbing down its tree, keeping one eye warily on the receding men, moving toward where Eric had thrown the candy bar. It grasped the smooth piece of chocolate in its delicate fingers and, placing it carefully in its mouth, disappeared again into the trees.

Eric turned back toward the group.

They crossed a brown, sluggish river, before the trail continued, disappearing again into the jungle. Stretching forward, beckoning them farther inland. One of the men ahead of Eric was holding a colorful, small-beaked parrot. The bird's feathers were splotched with deep reds and blues, and it clung tightly to the Marine's two outstretched fingers. He let his hand fall to his side for a moment as they walked, and the parrot still clung to the fingers, hanging upside down and swinging beside the Marine like a brightly colored pendulum.

Shouldering his rifle and reaching out with his free hand, the man plucked a small brown ball hanging from a tree limb over the trail. When he crushed the ball in his hand, the brown skin split open, and a pulpy orange fruit burst out. He held the parrot out in front of him as he walked, holding the fruit up to the bird's small red beak. The parrot cocked its head slightly, looking at the man for a moment, before it dug into the fruit with its beak, pulling off a small chunk of pulpy orange. The soldier's hand returned to swinging along at his side, and the bird, suspended upside down, happily swallowed the fruit.

Eric noticed that men were turning to their left up ahead, staring somewhere off the trail into the jungle. Eric turned, too, as he passed, peering into a small clearing between the trees. Seated on one of the giant curving roots was a large stone carving of something vaguely human-shaped, but with elongated arms and legs and the head of a bull. Its right arm was held up, one finger extended, wagging a warning at the men.

Another creature stood off to the right, leering at them through a break in the trees with its stony grin. The second statue was closer to the path, and Eric was startled to find himself looking up at least six inches into the thing's eyes. The sculpture was much larger than he had originally thought, carved from what appeared to be one large stone. The carving was evidently old since the surface of the stone was covered in a thin green plant growth. A seedling struggled out, its small leaves breaking through a tuft of soil caught in the crook of the creature's arm.

Other men were glancing quickly at the statue as they passed, staring for a moment into the creature's unmoving eyes of stone.

The rest of the day passed slowly before night began once again to seep into the jungle. The hoots and calls of nocturnal animals started, sounding the alarm of oncoming darkness. Taken almost by surprise at the sudden loss of light, the men hurriedly pitched a camp off the trail, cutting back the overgrowth to form a clearing.

The soldiers around Eric were all carefully easing their packs from their shoulders, arching their bodies backward, their hands pressed against the smalls of their backs. Davis sunk to the ground, feeling the blood rushing in his legs and the swollen arches of his feet. Unlacing his boots, he slipped them off, staring at the splotches of blood staining the socks in various places. He slowly peeled his socks off. The blood was from a combination of blisters and leeches, burrowing into his skin. He pulled off the squiggling black leech bodies, hurling them into the jungle around him. He cleaned the areas with a quick pour from his canteen, the brownish iodized water stinging as it flowed across his foot.

Across from him, Seals was taking off his pack. Davis's eyes fell over the man's front, and remembering Reder's words, he looked at Seals's front pocket. The pocket bulged like there was something inside. It was indistinct, clothed in fabric, but appeared to be round, about the size of a marble.

Davis looked up quickly and saw that Seals was staring at him. Surprised, Davis maintained the gaze for a moment. Seals reached up and gently patted his front pocket and smiled. Davis turned quickly away.

"My fingers are about to fall off," Alabama groaned, as he and Jersey lowered the stretcher. "I can't feel nothing."

"No kidding," Jersey affirmed.

The dusk moves quickly to darkness in the jungle, seemingly passing over the sunset, as if the sun were rushing to seek its business in a more hospitable part of the world. They set up their tents quickly. Lying on his back, Eric looked up again at the night sky through the open flaps. Slowly, as his eyes adjusted to the darkness, he saw a patch of soft green luminescence glowing in the trees above him. As he watched, another patch somehow materialized, then another, until above him was a canopy of glowing green. Even spots on the ground, were glowing softly, painting the rain-forest floor an eerie green.

The other men noticed it, too.

"What is all that?" Alabama whispered.

Eric thought for a moment of stories he'd heard as a kid of enchanted forests, filled with goblins and trolls. The hovering green lights, glowing in the darkness, seemed cast by spells. He felt along the ground for the long shape of his rifle, anticipating the green-covered stone statues they'd passed along the trail slowly coming to life deep in the jungle behind them, their stony limbs creaking, as they mechanically pressed forward, breaking through the trees toward the men, the evil grins captured on their faces.

"It's fungi," Jersey's voice answered from somewhere close by. "Luminescent fungi. It's in the rotting leaves of the trees."

Eric was strangely disappointed in the realness of the answer. Fungi. Not what he was expecting. Nothing ever really seemed to be as mysterious or as wonderful as what you first thought it to be. He leaned back again, looking into the sky and thinking of what was inside Seals's pocket.

Eric woke suddenly to something tearing at his insides. The air was chilly and still black with night as he rushed behind the concealing trunk of a palm to relieve himself. The moment he squatted, he felt almost as if his entire insides were pouring out in one relieving explosion. Exhausted, he returned to his sleeping spot and curled up again, trying to ignore the wetness of the dew that was slowly seeping in through his clothes. There had been rain during the night. He could feel the ground through the tent fabric, moist and soft, and he felt himself sinking down into it, like trying to sleep on a wet sponge.

Then he heard the scream.

The noise came from somewhere out in the jungle. A low moaning, followed by another sharp cry. "What the hell's that?" Alabama hissed. Davis couldn't see him, but could hear Alabama breathing heavily, lying on the ground nearby.

Eric was wide-awake, listening. Around him, the other men were moving slightly, sitting up uncomfortably on the soft ground. There was a loud *click*, as someone pulled back the bolt of his carbine.

"Jesus, man, what is that?" Alabama repeated, as the scream sounded again.

"Could be Japs," Keaveney's voice sounded in the dark. "They always scream before they attack."

"Don't sound like Japs," Alabama replied. "Sounds like someone out there getting tortured."

"Yeah," Davis responded, as the cry came again.

"It sounds like Hartmere, don't it?" Alabama murmured, mentioning the Marine missing from their unit the previous night.

Davis shook his head. "I can't tell. Could be anyone. Just sounds like screaming."

There was a crashing noise, like something running through the jungle toward them.

"Get ready!" Seals's voice shouted in the darkness.

"Oh God," Alabama whispered, scrambling to his feet.

There was a slight moon above, and the pale light filtered through the thick jungle canopy, refracting off the wet leaves and softly illuminating the jungle. The screaming continued, moving closer to them, traveling quickly through the thick jungle. Davis rose to his knees, butting the rifle against his shoulder as he stared through the thick vegetation. In the shadowy moonlight, the trees formed vague outlines, which blended together as they rose upward. The rain continued to fall thinly from the leaves, pattering lightly against the men.

Something burst out of the jungle. Davis caught a flash of white before something struck him in the shoulder. He fell backward, his finger squeezing the trigger, launching off a round. Already primed with nervous energy, the rest of the men began to shoot, rifling bullets into the jungle. The shooting lasted for almost thirty seconds before Seals's voice called, "Cease fire, cease fire!"

Davis was stunned, lying flat on the ground, something heavy resting against his arm. He shook his head and sat up.

"Everyone all right?" Seals called out. "Davis, you shot?"

Davis grunted, patting himself down. "No. Something hit me."

"What?"

He felt around on the ground with his hand, trying to find the object that had flown from the jungle. His fingers bumped something warm that seemed to be covered in soft, long fur. He picked the object up, holding it in front of his eyes, peering at it in the darkness.

The moonlight reflected off the white object. Davis blinked with surprise. He was looking at Private Hartmere, the missing Marine from the previous night. The man was staring at Davis with glazed, rolled-back eyes. Davis was confused for a moment until he realized what was in his hands.

He was holding Hartmere's head.

Davis shivered in disgust, dropping the head onto the ground and sliding away from it.

"What is it?" Keaveney asked.

"It's his head," Davis replied. "Something cut off his head."

They sent out a group to search the jungle, but the men came back with nothing. They buried the head in the thick mud under the roots of a banana tree. Then they slept.

The tropical dawn turned night into day. Davis glanced inside Seals's tent, which stood by itself at the edge of the encampment, surprised to see that the tent was empty. He glanced around, seeing only the wide, leafy vegetation of the jungle, but no Seals. The nighttime insects were still out, their long hums sounding around him. The air was pleasantly cool and damp, a refreshing change from the intense heat of midday.

Davis relieved himself again behind a tree and, walking back, took a second look around the camp, still seeing no sign of Seals. Lying just inside the flaps of Seals's tent, Davis saw the man's fatigue vest and again became curious about what Reder had said he'd seen put into the pocket. Davis moved quietly toward the vest, feeling a strange nervous feeling flood his stomach. The fabric was rough and damp, and Davis's finger slid along the front stopping at the first pocket. He undid the button and peered inside. Empty.

He was disappointed for a moment, before remembering that there were two pockets on the left side of the vest. He bent over again and undid the second button. He slipped his hand inside and felt something warm and gelatinous. He peered down into the flap. Inside was a round white ball that glistened with wetness. He turned the ball over and recoiled in disgust.

It was a human eye.

"Some believe the eye is the window into the soul."

Davis heard the voice behind him. He stood up, turning slowly around. Seals stood in the clearing, staring at him. His shirt was off, his skin glistening with sweat. Streaks of mud cut across his upper torso, just above a long swath of blood. One arm was resting at his side, while he held the other behind his back, as if he were obscuring something from Davis's view.

"If you take a man's eyes, you take his soul," Seals said slowly, giving Davis a cold look.

Davis nodded dumbly, dropping the vest back into the tent.

"I'm sorry. I didn't mean to go through your stuff," he said feebly.

Seals shrugged. "Doesn't matter. You saw what you saw."

"Whose blood is that?" Davis asked, looking at the red streaks across Seals's chest.

Seals laughed. "Well . . . it's not mine, that's for sure."

From behind his back, he pulled out a long knife, the edge shining with blood. He looked at the knife for a moment, before passing it back and forth across his pants, cleaning the blade until it shone. He took a step toward Davis.

"You really should watch yourself, where you choose to stick your nose. A war can be a dangerous time, lot of accidents can happen."

Davis took a step backward, his hand slowly moving down for his own sidearm. Suddenly there was the sound of a tent flap being pulled open. Both Davis and Seals turned simultaneously and saw Alabama slowly pulling himself out of the tent. He looked at them curiously, and said, "Morning."

Seals nodded. "Morning."

Then Alabama pulled himself all the way out and walked toward the jungle to relieve himself. Davis turned his back on Seals and walked to his own tent, sliding back inside next to Jersey. He heard the fall of footsteps as Seals walked past the tent. The steps stopped just outside, only a foot away through the thin fabric from Davis's head. Next to him, Jersey was snoring soundly, his breaths long and smooth.

Then a voice. "The angel of darkness is visiting with us."

Davis closed his eyes, and the footsteps moved away as Davis could hear the rest of the men beginning to wake up around him.

Twenty minutes later, they began quietly to move out, packing up their gear and racing against the inevitable onrushing heat of the day. The murky mist had returned, oozing through the jungle, obscuring everything. Eric caught only glimpses of the Marines around him. A helmet, an arm, a shoulder blade cutting through the white mist, only pieces of the men around him. The leather of his boots had stiffened during the night, and he felt them beginning to rub again into his already swollen feet.

The path dipped sharply, the Marines leaning backward as they walked down the slope. The jungle around them was quiet, only an occasional hooting sounded or the drip of water against leaves. They passed a pair of roosting birds seated together on a tree limb, their bodies intertwined into one indistinguishable body.

The ground leveled out, and the jungle began to clear. Ahead of them was an open area of long grass, gently undulating in the wind, the tips swaying. The grass was almost up the chests of the men, stopping just below Eric's sternum. Ahead of them, the thin stalks reached upward, gliding up a sloping hill. In the steel gray of dawn, nothing moved or sounded except for the whispering voices of the men.

Seals held up a hand, waving the men forward. "Single file line. Slowly and quietly."

The helmeted men watched him, nodding, and began to move into the grass. As each man stepped forward, he was almost instantly swallowed up by the long waving green, disappearing from view as the blades closed behind him like the ocean's waters. Eric stepped slowly, feeling the rushing of the grass around him, brushing his arms and legs, his rifle held out in front. A little rain had begun again, the cold rain of early morning, before the drops are warmed by the sun.

Just ahead, Eric saw the guy with the brightly colored parrot. He was holding the small bird in front of him, whistling lightly to it. The bird had cocked its head, watching the soldier's lips move, and imitating him, making a soft, chirping noise. The soldier smiled and, shouldering his rifle, reached into his pocket, the parrot nudging him impatiently. He pulled out a handful of seeds and held the seeds in the flat of his hand while the parrot pecked away.

Something cracked in the distance, and Eric heard a faint angry buzzing noise, before the head of the Marine virtually exploded, spraying Eric's face with brain tissue and bone fragments.

"Get down! Get down!" someone shouted, as more cracks sounded, bullets whistling through the grass.

Eric hit the ground hard, almost knocking the wind out of him. In front of him lay the Marine's twisted body. The parrot was standing next to the fallen soldier, confused and suddenly alone, its brightly colored head cocked at an angle, staring at the man's body. Small flecks of blood stained the parrot's orange breast. It chirped quietly, and Eric realized that it was still a baby.

The crack of rifle recoils were surrounding him now, breaking the silence of the field. Heavy fire from ahead. Davis could hear them getting it hot from above. Someone shouting "Yang-ees! Yang-ees!" in broken English. He did a quick look, lifting his head. A bright tracer bullet whistled by his ear. Down he went again.

"We got heavy fire coming from up on that ridge," Seals shouted, his finger pointing ahead.

Alabama was crouched near Davis, hunching his shoulders up around his neck. "Ahh, Jesus, we got a whole nest o' Japs up there."

Eric nodded, then on his hands and knees he moved blindly forward, moving in the direction of the gunfire, carefully avoiding a swarming nest of ants as he crawled. They were all moving now, crawling through the thick grass. Grass was everywhere. All around. Blinding, like moving through water. Still they moved, Davis becoming disoriented, trying to follow the direction of the gunfire.

The ground slowly began to rise, and he crawled up a slight ridge. Carefully he raised his head again, holding his helmet in place with his hand. He had moved off to the left of the Japanese position. The ridge overlooked the rest of the sloping hills, and he could see men moving through the grass beneath him, American helmets appearing for an instant to fire off rounds before diving back into the grass.

He watched the fighting for a moment from his spot on the ridge. Alabama lay below him, giving it heavy now with M1 rounds, his eyes wide and bulging, his mouth popping like a fish as he gasped for air.

Between the Marines and the Japanese position was a wide expanse of deep, empty grass. No-man's-land. Or was it? Looking closer, Davis saw that something was already there. It was moving quickly, headed down from one of the ridges toward the Americans. Whatever it was, it was keeping low to the ground, concealed by the long green stalks, moving faster, the tips of grass wavering and shaking, something pressing them down. Davis caught glimpses of gray skin.

Rifle fire close by sent him back to the ground, and his view of the ridges disappeared as he went below the grass line and crawled back toward the rest of the men. Then from out of the grass, he stumbled on Reder. Reder, shot in the chest, lying flat on his back, rolling slightly back and forward.

Spent cartridges littered the ground around him, falling into the crushed grass. Blood everywhere—on Reder's front, on the grass, on the ground. Davis slid across on his hands and knees through the grass until he was crouching right in front of Reder.

"Stay here, stay with me."

Supporting Reder's head in one hand, with the other he gently peeled back the shirt to look at the bullet hole.

Reder was sucking air. "Can't move it. Can't breathe either." His tongue was red with the blood invading his mouth. "I need a fucking medic up here." He sobbed, holding Eric's arm tightly.

Eric glanced at the wounds; Reder had actually taken two bullets, shoulder and lower rib cage.

"OK," Eric said, nodding and smiling, "I'll go get you some help, hang in there."

He began to move off. "Wait . . ."

Eric turned back to the wounded man. "What?"

"Promise me you'll come back," Reder said weakly. "I don't want to die out here."

Eric nodded. "I promise."

Davis moved off through the high greenery, keeping low to the ground. *Head up, find our guys, head down, keep moving.* Then he heard something. Something moving quickly toward him. *Shit.* Davis stopped short, pulling his rifle from his shoulder, hunching in the grass. *Stay small. Stay small. Don't let anything see you.* The thing was moving fast, coming toward Davis, big tufts of grass being displaced. Japs making a rush? That was trouble, Davis too far from his unit to reach them.

He crouched in the grass, rifle up, ready. Stalks crackling and snapping, something coming hard. Silence.

Then came a scream.

Reder. Turning his head, Eric saw the man thrashing around. Something had hold of him. Something was dragging him back into the grass. Reder screamed again, eyes popping, trying to brake himself with his unwounded arm. Then he was pulled quickly out of sight, deeper into the cover of grass. Jesus. Something had snatched him out of the grass.

Stunned, Eric crouched, frozen. There was a snarl and then a cracking noise. Then nothing, only the empty space of crushed grass where Reder had been and a wide swath of blood along the blades of grass from where he'd been dragged.

He began firing blindly into the grass, bullets streaming through the tall strands, clipping apart the stalks. He heard the snarling noise again, followed by a low grunting, which gradually diminished as the thing moved away through the grass. Whatever it was, it was gone. So was Reder.

Davis lifted his head and saw three Japanese soldiers, moving quickly, running across the slope. The war was still going on. Raising his rifle, he fired a quick four-shot burst, watching as one of the soldiers turned swiftly and disappeared. He ducked again and moved forward, coming out of the grass suddenly onto Alabama. He was crouched on the ground, reloading his rifle, and spun up at Davis, turning at him with his bayonet.

"Jay-sus," Alabama said. "Don't sneak up on me like that. Scared me half to death."

"You seen Seals?"

"Naw, he's around here somewhere. This grass is thicker than a fog."

"Where's Martinez?" Davis asked.

Alabama gestured with his head vaguely. "Left him back a ways. He's out cold on that stretcher. He'll be all right. Jersey and I put him down."

Davis thought of the thing in the grass. Wondered if Martinez really would be all right, lying out there somewhere. Out there with whatever was hunting down their wounded.

"Reder bought it."

Alabama turned. "Yeah?"

"Something fucking came outta the grass and grabbed him. Dragged him back."

"What? A Jap?"

No, something else.

"I don't think so, this was too strong for that. Grabbed him right up."

Alabama lifted his head and fired a few quick rounds. Return fire from the unseen Japanese position flared up on the far ridge. Behind them, a Marine named Baynes had his head above the level of the grass, his rifle raised, shooting quickly as he stepped back on his heels.

"Get your head down, man!" Alabama said.

"Baynes!" Eric hissed back.

"What?"

"Stop shooting like that, you'll get your head taken off."

Baynes turned and looked at them blankly. He reloaded and lifted his head again.

That's when the bullet caught him in the cheek, piercing his mouth and shattering his teeth. He collapsed on the ground instantly.

Davis cringed and looked away.

Ten minutes passed, and Jap fire was getting slower. They were wearing them down. The Japs were moving off the ridges and back into the valley, where they'd lay somewhere in the jungle and the whole thing would start again until there weren't enough men to fight. The sun was hot, baking the grass and the men, but storm clouds sat fat and black on the horizon. Davis prayed for rain. Cooling rain. He sat on the ground, pulling strands of grass apart with his fingers and waiting for the whistle to blow the all clear. Ten yards away, Baynes lay dead. Davis could see part of his skull opened up from where the bullet had entered. Flies were already collecting around the blood.

Alabama had moved off to find Seals, then up the ridge to clear the Jap position, leaving Davis back with Baynes. Not that Baynes would know any different, the man was dead the second he hit dirt. Davis pulled another bit of grass up, putting it into his mouth, rolling the green around on his tongue. It tasted bitter. Explosions in the distance somewhere. Shouting. A rumble of thunder down in the valley. Rain was falling somewhere. Rain was always falling, somewhere.

Then he heard it.

A growl. Or more of a low bellow, like the sound a bull makes. Coming from somewhere off to Davis's right. Somewhere hidden in grass. Davis's rifle lay on the ground at his side. Keeping his eyes fixed into the darkness of the stalks, he slowly moved for it. Something was out there. Whatever had taken Reder's body was still out there, watching him. Hands to his rifle, he lifted it, the stock creaking slightly as he moved it.

The growl sounded again, five yards closer. Then the crunch of footsteps in the grass. Something coming toward him, stalking him, the sound coming from somewhere near Baynes's body. Slowly Davis began backing up, away from the body and whatever wanted it. Grass fell back into place as he moved, slowly obscuring his view of Baynes. Then came the bellow again and the sound of something heavy being dragged through the underbrush. Of something dragging Baynes away.

Another hour passed, and still Davis waited. Occasionally the bellow would sound from somewhere near him. Something out on the perimeter, watching him. Rain began to fall, slanted and steel-colored. The day turned dark, thick black clouds covering the sky. A strong wind moved through the field, blowing through the grass, the stalks appearing a grayish white as the storm approached. Eric wiped the water from his face, trying to clear his eyes. Gripping the wet wood of his rifle, he began moving up toward the ridges.

Ahead of him explosions were sounding. He stood up slightly, gazing out over the waving grass. The wind had ripped a palm leaf from a tree at the edge of the jungle, and Eric watched the large green leaf carry across the field, blowing over where the rest of the Marines were standing. They had reached the Jap position, dropping grenades into the holes the Japanese had dug. More explosions sent up tufts of dirt into the air, where it was picked up by the wind and carried off.

Alabama was firing off rapid rounds into one of the bunkers; Keaveney was behind him with a mounted .30-caliber machine gun. Eric could hear a whistling sound in his helmet as the air whipped past his ears. A crack of lightning broke the sky, blazing down above the stormy jungle off to the west. The air felt like an electric sea around him.

Ahead, he heard a whistle blow, sounding the all clear. Marines were standing up around him, appearing suddenly from their positions hidden in the tall grass, wading forward toward the captured ridge. Another crack of lightning broke the dark sky, followed by a long, drawn-out rumbling growl of thunder.

Squinting against the rain, he looked out over the grass. Something was in there, moving. He could see it, an occasional glimpse of its gray skin as it scurried through the tall waving green. It was loping quickly forward, running up behind one of the soldiers. Eric recognized Alabama. Eric shouted a warning, but his voice wouldn't carry in the strong wind and beating rain.

Hearing his name being carried vaguely through the wind, Alabama stopped and looked up toward the ridge where Eric was standing. Eric waved his hands over his head. Alabama smiled, a cigarette dangling from between his teeth, and waved back, holding his rifle up in the air.

Then his expression changed. His body jerked sharply. Something was pulling at him from the grass, attacking him. A moment later he was gone. Disappeared, pulled down into the long grass.

Davis broke into a run, wet stalks of grass whipping against his body. He tumbled, foot catching on something, then was up again, pushing his helmet back from his eyes and moving swiftly forward. Alabama was lying in the grass, a patch of red on his shoulder. Still alive. Bellowing sounds and footsteps retreating off into the grass.

Davis dropped in front of him, his fingers stabbing out for Alabama's neck, reaching to feel his pulse.

"Holy Mother," Alabama groaned. "What in the hell was that?"

He rolled over on his side, reaching up toward his bloodied shoulder as he winced in pain.

"You all right?" Davis asked.

"Yeah," Alabama answered. "I'm all right. What the fuck just hit me?"

Davis looked through the stalks of grass.

Nothing was there.

"You'll be fine," Seals said, peeling apart the torn shirt fabric over Alabama's arm and inspecting the injury. The rest of the Marines stood watching. They were standing on the ridge of the sloping hill, the grass rising to just past their waists. From the top of the hill, they could see across the rest of the valley, the wide expanse of the jungle stretching out until meeting the jungle. The gray sky continued to drizzle rain onto dull green grass and the standing Marines.

"Some bad news. We've got more Japs," Seals said, nodding toward the jungle at the base of the hill. "Took off in a cave down there."

"How many?" Davis asked.

"Two," Seals replied, squatting and unloading some of his gear. "Maybe more."

"Can't we just forget about them?" Alabama asked, looking toward the jungle. "Just keep moving?"

Seals shook his head. "Nope. We gotta get them out now. Can't have them coming up behind our flanks. Davis, Alabama, Keaveney, and Jersey, let's check it out. Rest of you sit tight up here."

The five men made their way down the hill and into the humid jungle. Ahead of them was a rocky outcropping, rising from the thick vegetation on the ground. The rocks rose almost fifty feet, covered in thick vines with moss, small plants, and lichen clinging to the moist surface. Rainwater trickled down the cliff, forming small streams on the bare sections of rock. At the outcropping's base was a black hole in the rock, an opening about the size of a man leading back into a cave. Drips of water fell in quick succession across the opening, forming a puddle underneath.

Seals was waving to the five men up on the ridge, telling them to come down. The wind had picked up even more, tearing at Eric's clothes, the dangling chin strap on his helmet blowing up against his face.

"They're in there. In that cave." Seals had to raise his voice above the wind.

The men nodded, hunching their shoulders against the rain, and together they moved down the slope toward the grotto. As they stepped inside the doorway, the sound of the wind and rain immediately died down. Instead there was a low moan, trapped air echoing on the narrow rock walls. Reaching into his pocket, Davis pulled out his Zippo lighter, holding it above his head. The flame flickered, casting distorted shadows along the slick walls around them.

The cave itself was narrow, wide enough to allow only one man at a time. The soldiers squeezed forward, packs scraping against rock, the sound echoing ahead of them. All around them it was black, the flames from the few small lighters the soldiers had lit barely piercing the dark.

As they moved forward, the sound of the rain and the wind outside died away completely. A slow, creeping silence descended on them, until there was nothing to listen to except the scraping of boots along the rock. Water from the ceiling dripped on them. Eric held the lighter up over his head to see the source of the drips. Above them, illuminated by the small flame, he saw writing high up along the walls. Strange curving writing Davis had never seen before.

Alabama whistled. "Look at all that writing. Who the hell do you think did all that?"

"I can't even see an end, it's like it just goes on forever," Jersey replied.

There were drawings, too, simple figures of men painted crudely on the walls. The pictures seemed to be all similar. He could feel there was some kind of pattern, then he realized the drawings were arranged chronologically, spanning backward through time. Nearer the bottom, at the level with their heads, were diesel-powered ships, then above that were sailing craft of all kinds, some with masts and riggings, others with single sails.

Why only ships, Davis wondered. Then it struck him. These ships must all have visited the island at some time in history. Whatever made these drawings had been on this island for hundreds of years, maybe more. The ships were the only contact whoever had done this had with the outside world.

In the far corner he saw a crudely drawn vessel with long sets of oars and a wide single sail. There were small scratch marks around the ship. Looking closer, Eric saw that the marks were actually drawings of men. They were falling over the side, their arms outstretched, mouths open in horror. A shipwreck from thousands of years ago. Whatever had made these drawings had been there to witness it.

"Uh-oh," Jersey whispered, pointing up toward the wall. "Look at this."

Turning his head, Eric saw something drawn in the corner that was eerily familiar. There was an image of another ship painted on the wall, one with a sharp bow and stacked smoke column. Something had been drawn on the ship's side. The number 302. Their number.

It was their transport ship. They were up on the wall with the rest of the doomed vessels.

"What is going on?" Alabama whispered.

"I don't know. I don't like this though," Eric answered, his pack scraping against the wall as he moved forward.

Something had been following them since they'd landed on the island.

The pictures faded back into darkness as Eric and the rest of the Marines moved deeper into the caves. He turned his head back for one last glimpse, the drawings fading into black. He just hoped they'd get out of there to see the transport ship again.

The floor of the cave was smooth, Eric had little trouble keeping his balance. Occasionally a gust of wind from outside would pass through the dark tunnels, causing the flames of the lighters to waver and issuing a deep moaning sound as it passed through the rocky chamber. Eric couldn't tell if it was still raining outside, and, without looking at his watch, he had no idea how much time had passed.

The feeling was like being deep beneath the ocean, cut off from everything on the surface, floating, lost in a world of murky darkness. He almost expected to look up and see the iridescent glow of strange fish, their eyes phosphorescent in the incredible, lonely darkness. The walls were slightly damp, the floor beneath them covered with a fine black dust. Bending, he rubbed the dust between his fingers. His hands came away black.

"It's volcanic," Jersey said, looking at Eric's fingers. "This whole mountain is actually a volcano. Mt. Bagana, the central mountain on the island. There were some books on it in the galley."

"It's extinct, right?"

"Well, technically, but no volcano is really extinct. They could—"

Jersey cut off in midsentence as Seals suddenly held his hand up. The cavern snaked forward, and ahead of them they heard a scraping noise, as if someone had lost his footing and slipped onto the slick rock.

Seals held his finger to his lips, and the men began quickly moving forward. Eric Davis held his rifle firmly, stopping the clip from jostling as he moved. The sound ahead of them stopped, and there was a sudden flare-up of light in the tunnel ahead. As they jogged, Davis noticed the sides of the cave slowly beginning to change. He noticed the solid rock gradually becoming brick, the jagged ceiling beginning to form a smooth arch. There was a light ahead. A single torch.

Then he heard a bellow. Deep, somewhere farther in the cave. Whatever had been in the grass was there. With them in the darkness.

"Fellas," Davis said, "I think we should get out of here."

The light ahead of them died suddenly, but in the distance they heard a cracking noise followed by a long scream.

They could hear a pattering of feet, see a figure running toward them. Down the long tunnel, Davis could see it was a Jap. He was running blindly, a stream of blood pouring down the side of his face. As his legs moved, he turned backward, looking with terror at something behind him, farther into the tunnel.

"Do not move!" Seals shouted toward the man, shouldering his rifle.

The man turned his head toward the noise, waving his hands and saying something in quick Japanese. He was shaking his head.

"Don't fucking move!" Seals warned, placing his finger over the trigger.

"No, no, America," the Japanese man said in broken English, still running toward the Marines. Davis wondered where the other soldier was. They had followed two men into the cave, and now only one was running toward them.

"No, help, help," the Japanese soldier said. "You help."

The Japanese soldier had a pistol and he raised it, firing shots wildly as he ran toward them, the muzzle flashing in quick succession. Davis ducked his head, burying his face into the rock as chips of stone flew up toward him. Blindly, he pulled the trigger of his carbine until with a *ping* the clip was ejected. The rounds struck the man flat in the chest, knocking him backward onto the stone.

There was a grunt, and Alabama rolled over on his back, clutching his arm with his opposite hand. He stood up a moment later, cuts on his forearm.

"You all right?" Davis asked.

Alabama nodded, pressing tightly against his arm. "Yeah, it's not a bullet, it's a chunk of rock from that damn wall."

As the men stood there, they heard a long moan, like the sound of the wind traveling through the tunnels. Davis cocked his head, listening.

"Wind?" he asked slowly.

"That ain't no wind," Alabama replied. "That's something else."

The moan came again. Then a snorting bellow. The rest of the tunnel was quiet, each man listening carefully, their guns played out toward the rear of the tunnel, where the light faded and pitched the rock into total blackness.

"Let's pull back." Seals was in a crouch, slowly backing up, looking carefully down the tunnel.

They kept moving, back and back. Hearing heavy breathing behind them, something following. Ahead was a jagged oval of light, and, moving toward it, they stepped out of the cave. The jungle was cool, the rain falling dripping on them from the leaves above.

"How's the arm?" Seals asked, leaning toward Alabama.

"It's all right," Alabama replied. "Winged me mostly. Unless it gets me home, then in that case I got hurt real bad."

"Didn't that Jap look like he was running from something, something farther back in the tunnel?" Jersey said quietly.

"Yeah it did," Davis agreed. "He kept looking back over his shoulder."

"Wonder what would make a man run like that," Jersey said. "Right into the hands of his enemy."

"Where's Martinez?" Seals asked suddenly.

Seals, Davis, Alabama, and Keaveney had rejoined the rest of the group on the side of the hill.

"We left him at the bottom of the hill," Jersey answered. "Couldn't carry him up with our rifles."

Seals nodded. "All right, let's get down and pick him up."

One of the grenades had lit the grass, and behind the sergeant small orange flames released waves of hazy heat into the air. A Marine was pulling the dead Japs toward the flames, dragging them along the ground before throwing them into the fire one by one.

The sergeant turned back toward the brush fire. "Baynes, see if you can put that fire out. Don't need every Jap on the island knowing where we are."

"Baynes is dead," Davis said simply.

"Oh." Seals raised his eyebrows. "All right, Keaveney then."

The rest of the men headed down the steep slope.

At the bottom of the ridge, they broke through the grass and saw Martinez's stretcher lying on the ground.

It was empty.

Streaks of blood stained the fabric, which had been torn in a jagged strip down the middle. The torn portion lay in a bundle next to the makeshift bamboo poles. "Where'd he go?" Alabama asked, jogging the rest of the way and standing over the broken stretcher.

The rest of the Marines joined him. "He was right here," Alabama said defensively, pointing to the stretcher. "Right here when we left him."

"Where'd he go?" Seals asked. "That man was shot up. He can't just walk out of here."

"I know it," Alabama said. "He can't move around. It's like something came and took him."

They split up into two groups, prowling the grass for Martinez. Alabama cut through the stalks with a machete, moving away from the stretcher, cutting a swath up the hill. Davis moved back into the jungle, stepping into the oppressive heat, while the rest of the men moved in the clearing, parallel to the ridge. In the distance at the top of the ridge, Keaveney was still working to put out the brush fire. The wind was blowing over the hill, pressing the grass forward in waves. The field was empty.

Martinez was gone.

The men left the stretcher behind, sitting in the long grass of the clearing and pushed onward through the jungle. The air was warm and humid, filled with the smells of the jungle, while the sky above them was gray with a solid mass of clouds. They were walking in a single file line, rifles slung up over their shoulders. Most of the men had taken off their shirts, tying them around their heads, the long tails hanging down their backs underneath their helmets. Alabama was one man ahead of Davis, a strip of dirty cloth bound tightly around the laceration on his arm.

They were winding their way below the ridge of a hill, moving back toward the jungle. Rain was falling in spatters, cleaning the mud and bits of grass from their skin. Davis was still thinking of the bellowing noise he had heard in the cave, that deep snorting. Something had carried off Martinez, something had killed all those Japanese soldiers and chased that Jap out of the tunnels. Something was on the island with them.

There was a sudden commotion in the line ahead of him. Men were jumping back away from the edge of the jungle, and Davis could hear shouting. Jersey was pointing at something with one hand, while he slowly brought his rifle up with the other. Alabama began running forward, jogging to catch up with the other men, and Davis followed him, his helmet jangling on his head as he bounced across the uneven ground.

After a moment, they broke through the thickest section of undergrowth and found themselves standing in a clearing. The roots of a giant tree extended upward almost six feet, rising to meet in thick ridges running along the massive trunk. High overhead, the leafy canopy extended outward, blocking the sun and making the ground slightly cooler underneath.

Davis slowly looked up, following the line of the tree. Wedged between two branches, its tail curled over by encroaching vines, was a crashed Japanese Zero fighter plane. Davis could see the red circle, the mark of the Japanese sun, painted on the gray metal skin of the plane, partly obscured by branches. The window was fragmented into spiderwebs of cracks, while a line of bullet marks punched through the frame swept backward along the plane's body toward the tail.

"Our guys must o' shot it down," Alabama said. "Crashed here."

The pilot hung from the trees, his parachute fully extended and caught above him, wrapped around branches. He was dead, his body sagging, still held fast by the parachutes harness. His feet, still in their boots, dangled just above the highest towas root. Seals turned toward Davis and Jersey, then indicated the dead pilot. "Search him for intelligence."

Davis and Jersey nodded, climbing up the side of the root and making their way toward the dead pilot. Below them, the rest of the men laid their packs down, opening up the silver foil packets of rations. Alabama lay back against the root, his eyes closed, his helmet drawn over his face.

The dead pilot was swaying back and forth like a giant pendulum hung from the tree and Davis had to put his hand against the man's leg to steady him. Carefully, he and Jersey began sticking their hands into the pilot's pockets, fishing out his wallet, loose bits of paper, and three empty rounds of ammunition. Davis could feel the cold flesh through the thin fabric of the pockets, soft and yielding, like cold meat. The pilot had nothing of interest on him.

"Everybody up," Seals said, suddenly. "Get over by the plane. We've got to take some pictures for *Life* magazine."

Davis stared at him for a moment. Seals seemed to be acting completely normal. He had felt sure that Seals had murdered Reder, but now he thought he might have been mistaken.

"You serious?" Davis asked. "Hell, we're gonna be in *Life*?"

"General says we need to promote the war back home, so . . ." Seals had a large camera, which he was positioning on the top of a root, the lens turned toward the plane. "We're taking pictures for *Life* magazine."

Interested, the men gathered in front of the downed plane. Davis and Jersey left the pilot hanging, moving over to join the rest of the group. The tail of the plane was suspended in the air, while the nose and wings were impacted deep into the earth. Three parrots were sitting on the glass canopy, grooming each other's wings with their large orange beaks.

The soldiers crowded together beneath the plane, jostling each other for a better position. Most had their shirts off, still wrapped around their heads forming military green turbans. Davis stood on the end, between Alabama and Jersey, his rifle propped against his shoulder. Seals was bent over the camera, fixing the auto-set mechanism. He sighted through the lens once, adjusting the shot of the men, then quickly ran over to join them, standing at the end of the group, nearest the crushed nose of the plane.

There was a whirring noise, then the shudder clicked once, capturing the moment.

The men relaxed as Seals went to retrieve the camera. Alabama sighed, turned to Davis, and said slowly, "Something's wrong about this island." He breathed in the hot, fetid air. "I can feel it."

He slung his rifle over his shoulder and turned back toward the lines of trees. "Something's wrong."

TWO DAYS LATER

Awake. Pain. Head throbbing almost unbearably. *Where am I?* His entire body rising and falling, he closed his eyes again. Something exploded near him, spraying his body with small bits of what felt like dirt or pebbles. Davis struggled to open his eyes again.

He was lying on a stretcher, covered in his own blood. Two guys he didn't know were carrying him. Running under heavy fire. Davis could hear the breathing of the man just above him, see the sweat trickling down the sides of his cheeks.

A second explosion sounded, the displacement of fiery air blasting Davis's exposed side. They were moving quickly through the jungle, the two Marines who carried him running unsteadily over the damaged ground. He heard the snap of machine gun fire, the heavy thump, thump, thump, of a .30 caliber as red tracer bullets whirled over his head like the colored lights of an amusement park ride. He looked down at himself, amazed at the blood that seemed to be pouring from his body, the white bandages wrapped around his side that were stained a sickly red color. He groaned once.

"Hang in there, buddy," the voice above him sounded. "Almost out."

What's happening? How did I get here? He raised his head slightly, looking through the line of trees to a strip of white just beyond the jungle. They were running toward the beach, and, looking around him, Davis could see other Marines running, their backs slumped, their heads down, all running through the jungle and back toward the beach.

None of them were men he recognized. His hand reached across his body, passing over the three dime-sized blood spots, patched over by rolls of bandages, just below the line of his ribs. Shot. But how? His mind was thick, sluggish, as he tried to recall what had happened.

Memories started to come clear. Flashes of them, forming a chain of events. The past two days. Everyone dead. Something had come for them out of the jungle. Something had been waiting for them. He reached for his pants pocket, the wide heavy pocket sewn into the sides of his military pants. It was still there. The small wooden box he had found. The box that meant everything.

They were all dead—Jersey, Alabama, Seals, Keaveney, everyone. Or he hoped they were, for their own sakes. Some things are worse than death.

In the distance, across the wide beach, he could see the transport ship *Galla* waiting out on the emerald-colored ocean. Behind him, the Japanese positions continued to lay down heavy fire, attacking the retreating Marines, trying to prevent them from escaping the island. If the Japanese knew what was hidden in the jungle, if they had any idea, they would be fleeing, too. Some of the Japs had known, but they were all dead. Among the living on both sides, only Davis knew.

Some things are more evil than war.

Awake. Where? A room. An infirmary room. Lying on a cot. Eyes closed again. He smelled the hard scent of metal, and stale cloth, with a lingering sweet smell of burning oil. Listening, he heard only a constant squeaking sound, like a hammock rocking back and forth between two tree limbs, while, with his body, he felt a softness against his back. And beyond that there seemed to be a deep rumbling vibration.

Cautiously he opened his eyes. A small room of green metal walls. He must be back on the transport ship he had seen from the beach, the *Galla*. Around him, Davis saw a series of cloth bunks, stacked on top of each other. They all appeared empty, and one of them was rattling slightly, moving to the gentle rocking of the ship and causing the squeaking noise he'd heard.

On the wall was a Vargas Girl calendar, with the girl of the month dressed appropriately in a revealing Navy blue. Underneath the calendar was a long counter. Davis saw rolls of gauze pads and tongue depressors and a stethoscope stacked neatly in the corner.

He raised himself, feeling his brain flowing painfully against the side of his skull like a jellied egg. It felt like the worst hangover he'd ever had. Grimacing, he noticed something sticky around his throat and, reaching up, felt a layer of gauze pads wrapped tightly around his larynx. His head had also been wrapped, and his scalp was painful to the touch. There were more bandages around his abdomen.

Looking around the room again, he saw something in one of the bunks. Another man was lying in a similar bunk across from him, his face turned to the wall, apparently asleep. Davis was unable to make out the guy's face in the darkness.

The handle to the door began to turn slowly. Eric heard voices and laughter as the door opened a crack. He saw an orderly in white pants and shirt standing in the doorway looking back down the hall and talking to someone. Davis lay back in bed, his head resting on the pillow again, feeling exhausted.

The orderly was young, and smelled sterile. He smiled amiably at Davis as he stepped into the room, wearing a name tag that read, "Lyerman."

"Feeling better?" Lyerman asked.

Davis opened his mouth to answer, but instead of his voice, only a strange wheeze escaped from his lips. The orderly noticed the sound and nodded.

"Your vocal cords were crushed out in the jungle," he said. "You won't be able to speak for a while."

The orderly was humming to himself, packing bandages into a jar on the counter by the set of sinks.

"They found you out in the jungle," Lyerman said. "Must have been pretty heavy. Haven't brought anyone else out. Just you and that guy over there."

The orderly indicated the figure lying in the bunk. Curious now, Davis turned toward his infirmary mate. The man's head was still facing the wall, features hidden. The orderly finished at the counter, walked over to the man in the cot. A light came on as Lyerman examined the man. Davis, seeing the man's face for the first time, wanted to scream.

It was he.

The man from the jungle. The one who had come for them. With the yellow eyes. Davis opened his mouth to cry out, but no sound came. Nothing. Not even a whisper. His crushed vocal cords. The orderly was turning to him, pressing him gently back into bed.

"You need to rest or you'll burst," the orderly said strangely. "Like a watermelon filled with blood."

Lyerman was smiling. Eric struggled, trying to rise, opening his mouth, no sound coming. The *Galla* orderly took out a needle and inserted it in a glass bottle. Eric shook his head no, trying again to sit up, but his body was too weak, and Lyerman easily kept him down.

Holding Eric firmly, he pressed the needle into Eric's arm. Eric looked past the orderly toward the sleeping man. They were bringing him off the island. They were bringing him with them.

"There you go," Lyerman whispered, as Eric began to relax. "Just sleep for a little bit, you'll feel a lot better."

Eric lay back on the bed as the drug began to take effect.

The orderly picked up Eric's wrist, looking at his watch as he checked Eric's pulse for a moment. "You'll be fine. I'll let you rest."

Putting Eric's wrist back on the bed, the orderly slowly withdrew from the room. When he reached the doorway, he turned back toward the bed. Eric held his hand out toward him, trying to call him back, but the orderly looked at him for a moment, smiled, and turned out the lights. Leaving him alone.

Lyerman opened the door, and, outside, Eric heard laughter and talking. Then he was gone.

There was silence in the room for a moment, then the creak of a bed.

Turning his head slowly, Eric saw the other man faintly in the darkness. Drugs were moving through Eric's veins. Everything was slowing. He was growing sleepy. Things were beginning to fog over. The man from the jungle had turned toward him, was staring at him. It didn't matter anymore. No place to go. His time had come.

Then a ringing sound. From where? Deep in the ship. The sound insistent. An alarm, and then the banging of doors and the pounding of feet along metal corridors. The noise was familiar to him. It was an air raid siren.

They were being attacked.

The ship suddenly shuddered, and Davis heard a faint explosion from somewhere above. There was the heavy firing of antiaircraft rounds, and he could imagine the men running around up on deck as Japanese Zeros buzzed overhead. Another explosion sounded, as the alarm continued its monotonous ringing, and the medic room gradually began to lean. *The ship must have been hit,* Davis thought to himself peacefully.

Across the room, the man was still lying in bed, seemingly oblivious to the commotion. Struggling, Davis was finally able to rise from the cot. He swung his feet to the floor and slowly stood. Rolls of gauze began sliding down the counter on the far wall as the room slowly turned over onto its side, the floor sloping. Drawers opened up along the wall, the metal instruments inside spilling out with a clatter onto the floor. An entire row of bunks broke free from the wall, the mattresses and frames sliding across the floor.

Davis was thrown to the other side of the room, landing hard against the thick metal door. Struggling, he pulled himself up, using the door handle as support. Leaning against the wall, he pressed his face against the small portal opening of glass in the center of the door. Through the thick window, he could see out into the corridor beyond. Outside was commotion. Water was pouring into the hallway, traveling down a companionway to the right in a flooding wave. Men were running up and down the corridor, splashing through the foot of water on the floor, trying to keep their balance as the ship continued to list to one side. Davis could hear them faintly crying back and forth to each other, the sound muffled through the thick metal of the door. Overhead, an alarm was flashing red, casting strobes across the walls and the panic-stricken men.

Somewhere deep in the ship there was a bursting noise and a scream of metal, the sides of the ship beginning to collapse as salt water poured in. The *Galla* was beginning to give way, the crushing ocean blasted into its holds. In the hallway, the water-line was rising. Davis saw bits and pieces of the ship floating down the corridor, loose sheets of waterlogged paper, a seat cushion, someone's shoe. Davis tried the handle of the door, but it only jiggled, the door refusing to open. He tried again, putting his weight into it, but there was no response. The door was locked from the outside. He was trapped inside the medical room.

A strange feeling of hopelessness began to sink into him, like the drug, seeping through his veins. The water was almost up to the bottom of the portal window, and Davis watched it continue to climb inexorably upward, covering the glass in tiny increments, blocking out the light bit by bit. As the water rose, Davis found with some interest that he was looking through the glass portal, peering through the water, like staring through the lens of a swimming mask. The ocean had completely filled the narrow hallway, but Davis could still see the flashing red alarm glowing strangely underneath the water. Someone was swimming toward him, kicking rapidly and pushing aside the debris that floated in the water. Davis saw that it was a nurse, holding her breath, coming toward the window.

She banged against the window with her fist, eyes large bulges, veins bursting in her head. Davis watched her in horrid fascination, watched her drown in front of his eyes, finally floating off, bubbles of air escaping from between her lips. He could feel the ship sinking, groans of metal sounding all around him. The red alarm light went out with a pop, and the corridor outside was thrown into blackness. Davis turned away from the window, looking into the murky darkness of the medical room.

He could feel a pair of eyes on him, sense that the man was staring at him. Something was beginning to glow in the darkness, a yellowish swirling red. He could feel the room growing colder. And slowly he saw a pair of eyes emerge from the darkness. A pair of glowing eyes. And he was trapped with them, sinking to the bottom of the sea.

"You got the shot?"

"*Oui.*"

"It good?"

"*Oui.*"

"All right, roll camera and pan left . . . slowly, that's right, slowly . . . OK." French director Pierre Devereaux was standing, feet braced against the rolling ocean, on the slick fantail surface of the American research vessel *Sea Lion*. He and his crew of five had been on board for two weeks, filming a documentary on deep-water recovery systems for the French television station *La Découverte*.

"Did you get the submersible in the shot?" Pierre asked, looking toward the cameraman.

"You did not say."

"Yes! Yes, of course I wanted it, that's what this shot is." Pierre raised his hands over his head, before a roll of the ocean caused them to shoot back to the sides of the ship for support. "That's what the shot is, the ocean, then pan to the submersible. You don't have the shot if you don't have the submersible. That's what the shot is about."

"OK, *ça va*." The cameraman sighed. "I'll redo it." His American New York Yankees hat turned backward, he pressed his eye against the camera again, retaking the shot. "But you did not say you wanted it."

Ignoring the comment, Pierre looked out through the open sub hangar, squinting across the gleaming azure surface of the Pacific Ocean. They had passed by Bougainville Island, one of the battle islands during the WWII Pacific campaign, two days earlier. The hangar of the *Sea Lion* protruded from the stern of the research vessel, and almost level with the ocean itself. As the ship rolled through a high crest, warm seawater sloshed through the roll-up doors and glided partway up onto the floor of the hangar, turning the cement green and slick.

Pierre let the water roll around the base of his boots before watching it slowly retreat across the hangar floor and into the ocean. At first he found the idea of water actually entering the ship unnerving, but after two weeks on board, he'd gotten used to it, even enjoying the sensation of being dry, while standing almost in the ocean itself. Behind him, the two American sub pilots, Randy Rutherford and Nat Rink, were bent over the submersible, loosening the composite-plastic joints of the sub's two joystick-controlled mechanical arms. The French filmmaker's camera, fixed to a tripod placed in the corner of the sub hangar, was sweeping over the lazily turning sea again, gradually moving across until ending with a frame centered on the bright yellow, pod-shaped underwater submersible and the two pilots.

The submersible itself, nicknamed the *SeaHorse*, had been designed and built at a cost of $22 million by IFREMER, the French Institute of Research and Exploration of the Sea, and was one of only a dozen submersibles in the world capable of diving past twenty thousand feet. The expedition was being funded by the Joseph Lyerman Institute, whose head, the wealthy American magnate Joseph Lyerman, had strenuously objected to the presence of Pierre and his crew. IFREMER had insisted on the filming, however, as a condition for the use of their *SeaHorse* in the operation. The later IMAX production would bankroll their own independent operations for the next few years, leaving them free of the demanding control of Lyerman's institute.

Inside, the *SeaHorse* was capable of squeezing three people into its eight-foot-long, four-inch-thick titanium sphere. The pilots, both Americans, moved away from the mechanical arms, slowly wiping away a thin layer of seaweed that had collected across one of the four-inch portals on the left side of the craft. Both Americans were wearing one-piece temperature-controlled dark blue piloting suits. Pierre had insisted on them as being more photogenic.

Behind them, trawling slowly beneath the warm Pacific waters, was the MR-1, a torpedo-shaped device used to map the ocean floor beneath the *Sea Lion*. The MR-1 transmitted sonar signals to the ocean bottom, then recorded the signals as they bounced back. They had been pulling the MR-1 for the past week, towing the device in a back-and-forth pattern designed to cover every inch of an eleven-mile-by-ten-mile search grid.

The entire operation was very cutting-edge, which Pierre liked. Giving the picture thus far the feel of an updated Jacques Cousteau film. Cousteau without all that washed-out late-1970s film color. Pierre had hoped to make a nautical adventure film, man entering the last great unexplored region of the planet, that sort of thing. Unfortunately for him and for IFREMER, they had encountered a slight hitch; they hadn't found anything yet. They hadn't even had the chance to drop the *SeaHorse* down past a thousand feet, and Pierre was really hoping to get some underwater footage from below ten thousand feet. Mixed in with that ambient music, something dark, *Titanic*-esque, and that could really have been an effective scene. For the scene, though, you needed the *SeaHorse* to be in operation and for the *SeaHorse* to be in operation, you needed to find something. And they had nothing.

Part of the problem, Pierre was beginning to understand, was the objective of the expedition. Pierre had assumed it was just to search the ocean's floor for wreckage, any wreckage, of sunken WWII American war vessels. Slowly, though, he'd begun to realize that they appeared to be searching for something specific. One specific ship. The Pacific covered an area of 69.4 million square miles, Pierre had looked it up. That was a pretty big haystack in which to find a single needle.

"Get the two pilots working, underwater explorers, very American, very American," Pierre was almost shouting in accented English, to his cameraman. "Very good. Good shot. Like John Wayne of the ocean, *oui*? The suits look beautiful, you two, beautiful."

Lately Pierre had decided to reconsider the focus of the film, less adventure and more human interest. Focus on the man behind the expedition, Lyerman himself, like that IMAX team had done with the Mt. Everest picture a while back. Develop the characters first, and the adventure will follow. Of course the Everest project had Liam Neeson doing narrative work, which always helps. And they had that Everest disaster to follow, eight hikers tragically lost . . . the drama! Talk about drama, Pierre had nothing but stock footage of seagulls and the two Americans in their Disney suits. *Merde!*

Pierre was hoping to get Gerard Depardieu to do both a French and an English narration, but if nothing happened, the narration wasn't going to help. The IMAX was meant for the big screen; Pierre was practically making a book on tape. That's why he needed to refocus, take a look at the men behind the expedition. Lyerman, for instance. Who was this American? What was he looking for? But the problem with Lyerman was that nobody seemed to want to talk about him. He runs everything, but nobody knows anything. Pierre was pretty sure almost everyone on board, except for the pilots, who were possibly ex–U.S. Navy, was in his employ, but still nobody would talk. And then there was that Panamanian fellow on board, always lurking around, watching everything. That man gave Pierre the creeps.

Around the *SeaHorse*, the pilots finished cleaning off the portal and stepped around to the other side of the submersible.

"Remind me again why these French people are here," Nat, one of the American pilots, whispered to his partner.

"We needed *SeaHorse*," Randy replied.

"We should get our own."

"They don't just have these for lease at Rent-A-Center. They're pretty hard to come by, you know," Randy responded, turning his head slightly away from the camera.

"Yeah, but couldn't we just sell T-shirts or something, hold a phon-a-thon? Buy one ourselves?" Nat gestured toward the camera. "I feel like Kate Moss at the Paris fashion show."

"When you finish," Pierre shouted to them, "turn toward the camera and give the thumbs-up, OK? All Americans love the thumbs-up, right?"

Nat rolled his eyes, smiling. "Jesus . . . the French."

The two pilots stepped out from behind the submersible, looking toward the camera. Pierre was watching them, standing behind the bent-over cameraman and smiling, his own two thumbs raised in the universal thumbs-up pose. He nodded to them enthusiastically, raising his arms even higher.

"These fucking Americans . . ." Pierre whispered to his cameraman. "They are all such cowboys."

"This is ridiculous," Nat said softly to Randy, holding his thumbs up.

"Yes it is." Randy held his up, cocking his head to the side and smiling.

"Beautiful, love it, you two are beautiful." Pierre turned to the camera. "That's the shot there."

As the crew finished packing up their equipment, a man joined them on the end of the fantail. He stared absentmindedly for a moment out across the ocean's surface, watching the waves rise and fall in rhythmic motion. He kept his hands in his pockets, but as he stood, his cuffs pushing up to reveal a small Panamanian flag tattooed on his wrist, his feet slowly became wet from the ocean water that splashed over the fantail.

Fourteen members of the *Sea Lion* crew and the French contingent of six were seated around the long table in the ship's mess, their conversation broken by the pleasant *click* of metal silverware.

"So when we dive tomorrow," Pierre was saying to the entire assembly, waving his fork in the air over the table, "I want to capture the spirit of American adventure, you know? Capture the essence of what it means to be American."

The meal was broiled marlin, caught early in the day by one of the crew. Each crew member had their own bungee-corded fishing line over the side of the *Sea Lion* during the day. They placed bets on whose line would bring up the biggest catch, the winner getting the honor of providing dinner for that night.

Pierre took a forkful of his marlin. "Too bad there's no hamburgers here, eh? Very American, yes? Hamburgers? McDonald's, Have It Your Way, *oui?*"

"Actually, I think that's Burger King," Nat replied, chewing the tough fish.

Nat had opened his mouth to say more, when the door opened suddenly.

"I think we've got something." Seung Yi, head of the ship's aquatic research lab, suddenly burst into the mess, holding a piece of paper in his hand.

Dropping his fork to the plate, Captain Philip Smith stood up slowly, his eyebrows knitted in expectation. "What?"

"We may have found it," Yi answered, a flickering smile passing over his lips.

The captain swallowed slowly before peeling his napkin off his lap, bunching it into a ball and tossing it on the table. He gestured toward the doorway. "Let me see."

Nat and Randy followed the captain down the narrow corridor of the *Sea Lion*, walking toward the sonar control room. Pierre and the French cameraman scurried after them, walking quickly to catch up, the cameraman, a cigarette dangling from between his lips, inserting a new tape.

The control room was small and packed tightly with equipment, screens lighting the room in a strange purplish glow. The light from the corridor flooded into the room, as Yi opened the outside door and stepped in, followed by the captain, Nat, and Randy. Nat blinked quickly, trying to adjust his vision to the purple-tinted darkness.

The navigational and detection equipment room of the *Sea Lion*, otherwise known as the "tech room," was the nucleus of the ship. Along with the conventional radar and sonar equipment, Yi controlled a LORAN C navigational system, three satellite links for telephone and fax, VHF, HF, and single sideband radio. Weather reports also came directly to the tech room, updated every fifteen minutes, while the GPS tracker kept the ship's location exactly detailed.

Yi sat behind a main computer terminal, just underneath a large video sonar screen that reminded Nat of a conventional radar array. Behind them, the two Frenchmen pushed their way inside, making the room uncomfortably crowded.

"Your cigarette," Yi said to the cameraman. "You can't smoke in here."

Yi made a motion to his lips, then shook his head, miming his words.

Pierre nodded, and the cameraman shrugged, pressed the cigarette out lightly underneath his shoe, and placed the unused portion behind his right ear. He hoisted the camera to his shoulders and began recording.

In front of him, on the circular sonar screen, Nat saw an array of glowing blue dots on a black background. The dots radiated outward like the spokes of a bicycle, their uniformity broken occasionally by glowing clumps. A single line wound its way around the circular screen, like the hand of a clock, reminding Nat of a conventional radar reading.

"OK, I think we might have found something below us, resting on the floor." Yi pointed to a separate screen, a tightly spun web of lines appearing on a computer-generated grid of the seafloor. "Now these data are all from the MR–1 we've been towing behind us. As it picks up the sonar signals bouncing off the seabed, it can generate an accurate picture of exactly what's down there."

Nat felt a slight nudge against his back as the cameraman moved forward slightly, trying to get a better glimpse of the screen.

"What we get when we superimpose the sonar data on the computer-generated picture of the ocean floor is something like this." Yi typed rapidly on the keyboard in front of him. The computer monitor went blank for a moment. The screen flickered, then the ocean floor reappeared, a box-shaped object sticking out unusually from the relatively smooth ocean bottom.

"What is that?" the captain asked, pointing toward the strange object.

"Good question," Yi responded, swiveling the chair around, leaning back, and looking up at them. "Exactly, what is that? Well, it's some kind of object about a hundred feet long and twenty-four feet high."

The captain leaned forward, looking closely at the screen. He pulled his baseball hat back slightly, exposing an outcropping of white hair, and thoughtfully scratched his forehead. "How do you even know that's a ship? Or that it's not a carrier? Wasn't the *Hornet* sunk around here?"

Yi said, "From this, we don't really. A typical WWII carrier is going to be about eight hundred feet long, which this object here isn't even close to, right? So this could just be some kind of rocky outcropping or a ledge or what have you." The scientist swiveled his chair back to the keyboard. "The shape is almost too symmetrical, however, to be naturally occurring." Yi punched again at the keyboard until the screen went black again. "I investigated the area with EOSCAN, which uses a sonar signal that can penetrate the mud of the ocean floor, but will bounce back from anything like a ship's metal hull." Yi paused for a moment and turned toward the camera. "Can I use product names on film?"

Pierre nodded. "Just go, it's OK for now. We edit later."

Yi smiled and turned back toward the screen. "So turns out, there's a lot more to this thing beneath the mud. It must have hit the ocean floor pretty hard and jammed itself down."

Yi drove his fist into his open palm, indicating the motion of the ship's bow pressing itself into the mud as the sinking ship impacted the seafloor.

"What'd you get?" Randy asked.

Yi clicked the mouse once, and a new image began to form on the monitor. "There's about another two hundred or so feet beneath the mud and sediment."

The captain whistled softly as the new image took shape on the screen, a computer-generated cross section of the ocean floor, constructed from the multiple sonar echoes and *pings* bouncing off solid masses thousands of feet below them.

Nat saw that across the black background was a relatively straight green line, representing the ocean floor. Cutting across the line was the box-shaped object below them, running down past the line, ending at a mark buried thirty feet into the mud. The end was narrower, shaped like a ship's bow.

Yi had noticed the same thing and pointed to the screen. "Here, if you see, it looks like the bow of a ship, right? And if we rotate the image"—Yi typed something into the keyboard—"we can get a better idea of what's below."

On-screen the image slowly began to move around a center axis. On the screen in front of him, Nat saw the contoured outlines of the sunken ship rotate, the tapered bow leading on a gentle slope upward. Where the body of the ship reached the line of the mud, there was a sharp break, as if the ship had snapped as it made contact with the ocean floor.

"If you'll notice," Yi began slowly, speaking like a professor to his class, "there doesn't appear to be any carrier deck in this image; it just looks like the body of the ship itself. This could be because what we're looking at is not the *Hornet*, or it's very possible that the ship broke into several different sections as it sank. Similar, for instance, to what happened to the *Titanic* as it sank."

"It's not the *Hornet*," a voice said suddenly. The man with the Panamanian flag tattooed on his wrist, their financial backer, was standing in the doorway, staring at the monitor screen. "This is something else. Something much more important."

Yi pointed to the obvious break on-screen. "Right here is where the body of the ship seemed to snap, so it's very possible that there are other pieces elsewhere on the ocean floor."

"Have you found them yet?" the captain began, looking toward Yi.

Yi shook his head. "Not yet. They could be miles away from this central site. If the MR-1 keeps trolling, we should have this entire area mapped in a few days."

The captain nodded and stood up straight, turning toward Nat and Randy. "How'd you two like to have something to look at during the *SeaHorse* warm-up tomorrow?"

"Hell yeah," Randy said, smiling and rubbing his hands.

"You?"

"Sure, yeah," Nat agreed. "I'm in."

"Good." The captain smiled slightly, his lips barely visible through his heavy beard. He rested a hand on Yi's shoulder. "How far down is this?"

"It's about 10,280 feet down," Yi replied slowly. "It's deep. Real deep."

The next morning, Nat woke with the familiar feel of nervous anticipation he experienced before every deep-water dive. In the bunk next to him, Randy was still snoring quietly, his face, rubberized by sleep, pressed deep into the pillow. Nat glanced through the portal over his bed, looking out over the gently moving Pacific Ocean, the sunlight, tinted blue from the waters, streaming in through the circular glass.

"Hey"—he shook Randy once—"wake up."

The intercom over his bed sounded, the captain's voice coming across in a burst of static. "OK, rise and shine, little ones, we've got the dive scheduled right at noon."

Randy turned over, putting his back to Nat and the intercom, his face toward the wall.

Nat ignored the move, sitting in his boxers on the edge of his own bed, still groggy, his hair crushed and angled all over his head. He yawned, and felt the bed behind him, fighting the temptation slowly to ease himself back under the covers.

There was a knock on the door.

"Yeah?" Nat shouted out, looking toward the doorway through his slightly closed eyelids.

The door slowly pushed inward, followed by one of the French camera assistants, camera mounted on his shoulder, cigarette dangling from his mouth.

"Oh no." Nat shook his head, waving his hand. "Now is not a good time."

The assistant cameraman smiled, continuing to roll the tape.

"I'm tired, I look like shit, come back in ten minutes." Nat moved his head, trying to get eye contact. "You understand English?" He held up ten fingers, and talked in the loud, unaccented voice of someone speaking to a person hard of hearing, "Ten minutes. *¿Comprende?*"

The assistant kept rolling tape, panning over from the sleeping Randy to the upright Nat.

"You're one a those sons o' bitches that don't even speak proper English, right? Get your boss, Pierre, he speaks English, get him."

At the mention of Pierre, the assistant cameraman turned suddenly toward Nat.

"Yeah, Pierre, go find Pierre. *Findez-vous* Pierre." Nat waved his hand toward the door.

The assistant cameraman nodded, turning toward the doorway for a moment, then looking back at Nat.

"Pierre," Nat reassured.

The assistant cameraman smiled in faint understanding, then moved through the doorway, shutting the door behind him.

"Jesus Christ." Nat smiled in frustration, lying back in bed, letting his legs dangle over the edge. "It's like *Candid Camera* around here."

"Who was that?" came Randy's voice, muffled and slow from the pillow.

"One of the French camera guys."

There was a pause.

"Kinda early for that, huh?"

"Yeah, no shit."

Nat looked out the window once more, toward the ocean.

He shook Randy again. "C'mon, let's go dive."

After a quick breakfast, the two pilots stood in their dark blue uniforms on the deck of the *Sea Lion*, squinting against the bright South Pacific sunshine. All around them was the general nervous buzz of increasing preparedness, the crew shouting and talking with one another as they ran diagnostic computer tests and checked the cranes before the dive. The French IMAX unit was near the port side of the ship, the two female IMAX divers struggling into slick black wet suits, while Pierre directed the cameraman's shooting, and a sickly-looking man held up the boom mike.

The bright yellow *SeaHorse* sat quietly nearby, the eight-foot-long pod-shaped unit having been lifted from the sub deck by the *Sea Lion*'s giant crane earlier that morning. The bulbous black glass window bulged from the front of the craft, between the two, thin robotic arms the pilots had replaced the previous evening. Attached to the submersible aft side was the Urchin, a smaller, remote-controlled camera-operating device. While underwater, the Urchin would be deployed from the *SeaHorse* on its 250-foot umbilical cord, to enter areas of the sunken ship that were too small or too dangerous for the larger, manned, submersible. When they reached the bottom, Randy would operate the Urchin while Nat maintained control of the submersible itself.

From the sonar room stepped Yi, shielding his eyes against the outdoor brightness, walking quickly toward Randy and Nat.

"How are you two feeling?" he asked amiably as he stepped toward them.

"All right, you know," Nat began slowly, then shrugged. "Nervous."

"Yeah, same," Randy added.

Yi said, "OK, the ship below is resting on a slight incline, nothing too bad. But just as a warning, it's about five hundred feet away from a deeper crevice, so you want to stay away from that."

He turned toward Randy. "Now, you're going to deploy the Urchin when you arrive at the site, correct?"

Randy nodded. "Yeah, that's right."

"OK. Good. Now there are three minicams on-board the *SeaHorse*. One inside the cabin with you, and the two mounted just outside your port window. Now, as you know, you'll be in contact with us while you're below, but you're so deep . . . if something goes wrong down there . . ." Yi shrugged, letting his voice trail off.

"We're fucked," Nat finished the sentence.

"Maybe." Yi smiled. "But nothing should go wrong; we ran the tests this morning again. Everything checked out all right. We can use the responder on the ship's bridge to track your sonar *pings*, so we'll be keeping an eye on you, OK?"

"Yeah."

Yi paused for a moment, then smiled. "And third seat is going to be occupied by the IMAX cameraman. And I don't think there's any discussion on that."

"Jesus." Randy exhaled, turning out to the ocean for a moment. "Yeah, all right. Just make sure he keeps quiet."

"We told him already, and they agreed. And he's leaving his cigarettes up here. I guess he went down with the team that explored the *Bismarck*, so he's got some experience."

"OK." Randy's voice was noncommittal.

There was a brief moment of silence.

"Listen, there are some important people backing this expedition, this search, whatever. If what they are looking for is down there . . ."Yi raised his eyebrows, looking directly at Randy this time. "Understand?"

There was another moment of silence before Yi clapped his hands.

"All right." Yi stepped back. "Well, I'll let you get ready now. Good luck down there."

He extended his hand, and both Randy and Nat shook it. Then, smiling, Yi turned and walked back across the gently rolling deck to the sonar room. There was a brief crackle of static sounding from a loudspeaker placed on the GPS tower, toward the bow of the ship. The prerecorded female voice sounded politely, yet flatly, over the entire deck before reverberating out to sea. "All submersible personnel, please report to their dive stations. Dive will begin in ten minutes. Again, would all submersible personnel, please report to their dive stations. The dive will begin in ten minutes. Thank you."

Nat turned away from the set of speakers. "Here we go." And he followed Randy toward the submersible, waiting for them on the deck. To their left, the French IMAX cameraman was shaking hands with the rest of his crew, their expressions set with the formality of a funeral. The two divers stood ready, cameras in hand. They were going to film the first hundred meters of the submersible's descent into the Pacific.

The Panamanian was standing by the railing, staring out to sea with a thoughtful expression on his face.

"We'll see about getting you your money's worth, eh?" Nat called out to the man.

The man turned and regarded both the pilots. "It's down there. I can feel it."

Nat looked at Randy for a moment, then shrugged.

Two men in yellow hard hats stood on either side of the removable ladder as Nat climbed up the side of the *SeaHorse* and lowered himself through the top hatch. Inside, he felt cramped almost immediately. In front of him, the instrument array of the cockpit glowed a faint green. The six-inch-thick Plexiglas cockpit portal was about five feet in diameter, and as Nat sat on the small padded chair just to its right, he looked out and saw the two female divers climbing down the ladders into the warm waters of the Pacific.

Randy followed him, grunting as he squeezed into the tight chamber, sitting in front of the remote guidance system for the Urchin. "I think I'm gaining weight," he complained as he adjusted his suit.

After Randy came the IMAX cameraman, first lowering his camera into the submersible, then easing himself inside, feetfirst, sitting down hard on the passenger seat, wedged just in front of the propulsion motor in the back of the craft. Sitting in silence, Nat felt a trickle of sweat run down the base of his neck. The submersible was baking under the Pacific sun, slowly turning into a giant titanium oven. His stomach felt empty and was beginning to hurt. Standard dive procedure disallowed any food within twelve hours of the dive itself.

"Your assistant was up early this morning," Nat called back over his shoulder to the IMAX cameraman.

"Yes. His English not so good. But he is very hard worker."

Above them, there was a clanging of metal as the workmen closed the hatch, sealing it from the outside. That was the last fresh air for the next ten hours. In front of the heliport, the skeletal crane, rising from the deck of the *Sea Lion*, began to rotate slowly toward them, trailing a half dozen stabilizing steel ropes.

There was a jarring sense of movement as workmen began rolling the sub along the deck in its specially made cart, moving the yellow pod toward the crane. A *Sea Lion* diver climbed up the ladder alongside the pod, waiting on the top for the crane to lower the eight-inch-thick hawser, the giant rope used to hoist the *SeaHorse*. Through the portals, Nat saw the workmen in the hard hats pulling away the ladders, sliding it across the deck on its two sets of wheels.

As the crane lowered the hawser and the support ropes, more workmen fastened them to the *SeaHorse*, then, giving the thumbs-up sign, they gradually pulled away.

"Here we go," Nat whispered, slipping a piece of gum into his mouth.

There was a short jerking sensation, and the *SeaHorse* lurched into the air. The lifts were always dangerous. Sometimes an unexpected heavy gust of wind could toss the small submersible around like a mobile.

The A-frame crane began to swing out toward the ocean, and Nat felt the familiar sudden lightness in his stomach, like a free fall from a roller coaster. Then, with the grinding of metal, the crane stopped. The *SeaHorse* glided back and forth like a pendulum, suspended fifty feet over the rolling Pacific, before the sound of chains being cranked began, and, with an elevatorlike bump, the submersible was slowly lowered.

As it hit the water, the pod began to roll gently with the waves. The choppy waves ran across the front of the Plexiglas window, dividing Nat's view into part air and part sea. Along the top half of the portal, the light blue sky was broken by occasional tufts of clouds, while below, the cross section of waves slapped lightly against the window, and, underneath, Nat saw the pale aqua constancy of the ocean. A diver from the *Sea Lion* swam into view, a cloak of bubbles rising from his mask and surrounding his body. He moved toward the pod, unlatching the various support ropes until the pod floated freely on the surface.

Lifting his neck and looking down, Nat could see the two French scuba photographers, filming the operation. The radio crackled, and Yi's voice came through the small speaker mounted on the starboard side of the craft. "OK, you guys are set to dive. Good luck."

Randy pressed the intercom, said, "Thanks," and turned to Nat. "Well, should we get this going?"

"Yeah."

The cameraman smiled and nodded. "A-OK."

"A-OK." Nat shook his head. "All right. Let's do this. *Voyage to the Bottom of the Sea.*"

Nat pressed forward on the thrust joystick, and the submersible slowly began sinking beneath the water, the waves sliding along the Plexiglas portal until the ship was submerged completely beneath the sea. Looking up, he saw the turning water's surface, then the sky, warped and distorted through the lens of the undulating waves.

They began passing the two female French divers at around fifty feet. Their long hair was suspended in the water around them as they hovered in the ocean, kicking gently with their long tan legs as they filmed the descent of the *SeaHorse.*

"Why can't the American ships ever get crews like that?" Nat murmured. "We should get individual booths for a show like this."

Randy tapped Nat lightly on the knee, pressing one finger across his lips, then nodding back toward the camera.

"Oh, yeah, I forgot we're being filmed back there, I gotta watch what I say." Nat smiled, looking back out the portal to catch the final glimpse of the French divers. He watched them slowly swim upward, their legs propelling them toward the surface.

With a sigh, he turned back to the flat blue water in front of the submersible, watching as the colors gradually darkened to a sheer black as the sub dropped farther and farther from the surface. Finally, the only lights came from the dim green displays in front of them, as their dive deprived them of almost all senses except for the slighting whirring of the air-recirculation fan and the plastic-tasting air in their mouths.

They continued to fall, one meter per second, toward the ocean bottom, encapsulated in an eight-foot-wide pod, thousands of feet under the indifferent water.

"Hey," the voice sounded softly. "HEY."

A crab was pressing softly against Nat's leg, looking up at him with its two blank coal eyes.

He pushed it away in disgust, but another crab reappeared, walking on its stilt legs toward his body. "Jesus." He shuddered as he felt something grab his arm.

He shook his head slowly, opening his eyes.

"Wake up." Randy was shaking his arm lightly. "We're almost there."

"Whoa." Nat rubbed his face, yawning. "Strange dream. I'm getting those ten-thousand-foot dreams again."

His legs were burning from the cramped seat, the muscles almost numb. He pushed backward, stretching as much as he could in the limited space. Most of underwater diving was pure boredom. The overall trip, both up and down, would take about ten hours, much of it just sitting, staring out at the uniformly black water surrounding the Plexiglas cockpit sphere. The sensation was like taking an all-night plane flight in coach. The pod was dark, the greenish instrument panels allowing Nat to see just a dim outline of Randy.

Behind them, the French cameraman was using a small penlight to read a Zola novel, the pages of the book folded backward on each other. Nat closed his eyes again, listening to the soft churning of the water around them. There was a slight tapping on the window near his ear. The noise stopped, then started again, the same gentle tap, almost like someone was outside tapping on the glass.

Curious, Nat lifted his lids, turning toward the portal. Something clicked against the window again. The outside was so black, he saw only his own reflection, distorted in the glass.

"You hear that?"

"What?"

"That, like, tapping sound or something coming from outside?"

Randy tilted his head, listening for a moment. "Naw"—he shrugged—"I don't hear anything."

Nat closed his eyes again, waiting a moment in silence. Suddenly there was another tap on the window. He jerked up. "All right, there is definitely something out there. You can't hear that?"

"Nothing."

Behind them, the cameraman continued reading.

"I'm turning the outside lamps on for a second, hang on." Nat leaned forward, turning up the starboard side series of lamps mounted toward the rear of the submersible. There was a brief humming sound, then, with a flicker, the massive underwater lamps shot on, bathing the surrounding waters with light.

Caught in the light, a sea creature was staring at Nat through the portal by his head. Its face was pressed almost against the glass, its mouth slightly open, showing off rows of dagger-sharp teeth as it looked in with two dead eyes. It was a kind of fish Nat had never seen before, and the thing was hovering just outside, its fins moving in slow circles as it descended along with the *SeaHorse*. The body was large, eight feet long, its bulbous face filling almost the entire portal. Nat shivered involuntarily, feeling suddenly nervous that the thing outside was watching them.

"That's an ugly guy," Randy murmured, leaning over Nat to get a closer look. "Never seen anything like that before."

"Naw." Nat shook his head.

Behind them, the Frenchman was shouldering his camera, pulling back to get a good shot of the creature. Seemingly annoyed to be caught suddenly in the bright lights of the pod, the fish turned slightly away from the Plexiglas, hovering again, before turning full away and powering itself off into the darkness with its thick tail. Nat relaxed, watching the dark form gliding off into the murkiness eight thousand feet down. He leaned forward, turning off the outside lamps, watching the light melt away, fading everything in the water around them to black.

He turned forward, watching the bubbles stream by the front of the pod. In the blackness through the window, he suddenly saw a light blinking, hovering in the water about twenty yards away from their pod. Nat rubbed his eyes for a moment, then looked out again. Now there were two lights. They seemed to be moving together, then a third joined them, like a group of underwater fireflies.

"You see that?"

"Yeah," Randy said. "Most deepwater fish have some kind of iridescence to them. Small packets around their eyes or fins that glow in the dark, then when they get attacked, they can jettison the packets, distracting their attacker while they make an escape."

Nat watched the small glowing lights increase outside, gradually growing in number, dancing in the black waters. It was almost peaceful, like watching fireflies flit through a nighttime field. One swam directly across the Plexiglas in front of them, its foot-long snakelike body undulating through the water, its sharp teeth bared. Nat drew back in revulsion. Suddenly, from somewhere outside the small sub, came a low, undulating moan, followed by a higher-pitched screeching noise, like the sound made by humpback whales.

"What the hell was that?" Nat whispered nervously, gripping the side of the *Sea-Horse* and squinting through the Plexiglas portal.

"No idea . . ." Randy moved toward the instrument panel. "I'm gonna use the sonar, see if there's anything out there."

"You sure that's a good idea?" Nat replied cautiously. "We don't want to piss anything off, know what I mean?"

"It should be all right," Randy said quietly, activating the sonar display. "I'll send out a few *pings*, see what comes back."

The sonar of the *SeaHorse* made three quick droplet sounds, sending off the short signals.

"Uh-oh," Randy murmured, squinting at the computer display.

"What? I don't like hearing 'uh-oh,' what 'uh-oh'?"

"There's something out there, about a hundred yards away. Something big." Randy checked the display again, rubbing the glass with his finger and shaking his head. "Real big."

"Aw, man." Nat turned away from Randy, looking out the Plexiglas window, into the blackness of the water ahead of them. Involuntarily, he touched the portal, rubbing his fingernail against the glass.

Ahead of them, the droplets of glowing light had begun to separate, quickly moving apart from each other, as if the fish were all swimming away from something.

"Look at that." Randy pointed to the rapidly spreading points of light. "It's like they're all running away."

They heard the high, wailing noise from outside again, the sound reverberating through the titanium hull of the *SeaHorse*, echoing all around them. The other deepwater fish had spread way out, their lights racing away quickly in separate directions.

"It's like there's something out there that's chasing them away," Randy whispered, watching the accelerating movement of lights.

The pod began to rock slightly, disturbed by an unexpected pulse of water, as if something outside were beating the water, throwing out rippling waves.

Behind them, in the third seat, the Frenchman was looking around, his face bearing an expression of vague unease. At this depth, the air inside the pod was very cold, but

Nat saw a trickle of sweat breaking from the cameraman's temple, moving quickly toward his neck, before the cameraman swiped at it with one finger, his hand still holding the reading penlight.

The penlight!

From a distance, the small pointed light looked almost exactly like the beads of light on the fish outside the pod; and something out there was hunting them.

"Quick, put out the light!" Nat grabbed for the light, feeling the submersible rock again as another wave struck its titanium shell. He pulled the penlight from the cameraman's startled hands, quickly shutting it off.

He turned back toward the cockpit window. From out of the darkness of the water came an even blacker silhouette of something large, pushing itself forward with giant sweeps of its tail, its entire body, almost sixteen feet long, waving as it glided through the water, heading toward the pod.

The deepwater creature continued to move forward. Nat sucked in his breath, sitting unmoving, surrounded by the pressing ocean.

Another wailing call struck against the metal frame of the pod. Randy looked up from the instrument panel, his eyes wandering over the inside. The call was answered by another, from something back beyond the pod, the cry sounding lonely.

"Jesus, what is that?" Nat whispered. "A whale?"

"Maybe . . . but most don't dive this deep."

Ahead of them, the creature hovered for a moment, about twenty yards away from the pod, before slowly turning and, with a sweep of its tail, moving away, receding into the water's darkness.

Nat exhaled deeply, smiling as he pushed the air from his lungs. "Whoa . . . that was a rush, huh?"

Behind them the Frenchman shifted uncomfortably in his seat, his camera lying forgotten on the floor between his feet. He jabbered something quickly in French.

"That's right, man, scared shitless." Nat smiled, leaning back and patting the man's knee.

Randy leaned forward and checked the sonar readings. "Looks like we're only about two hundred feet from the wreck. It should be coming into view pretty soon."

As Randy used his hands to tell the cameraman they were descending on the wreck, Nat leaned forward in the cockpit, looking through the curved Plexiglas toward the ocean bottom.

"OK, let's raise the lights." Randy pressed a red circular button on the left side of the console. Instantly the two halogen lamps on either side of the submersible shot to life, bathing the water in light and turning the ocean from black to a ghostlike whiteness. Below them, rising from the sandy ocean bottom, were the skeletal remains of a ship. They leered up at them, lying across the bottom like a giant forgotten toy, the ship's once strong gray metal lines encrusted with outcroppings of coral, crawling with crabs and deepwater tube plants.

Nat whistled softly, saying nothing. He slowed the descent of the pod, the lights casting strong shadows over the sunken ship, exposing the vacant and abandoned decks where men had once stood and died. As they passed over the giant artifact, the Frenchman had his camera pressed against the side portal, capturing the view. They appeared to have descended just to the front of the stern, the rest of the craft visible ahead of them, before the bow plunged into the sand, buried upon impact. The metal was crusted and discolored, and in some places, had become twisted together, but through the mess of almost sixty-five years, Nat could still see the ship almost as it was the day of its final battle.

The pod's propulsion units had kicked in, and Nat moved the joystick forward, propelling the *SeaHorse* in a slow glide across the ship's deck. His analytical mind slowly began to click into gear.

"Look at that jumble of metal down there." Randy was pointing toward a large structure rising from the decks. "That looks like it might be the pilothouse."

Nat nodded. "I think we've got a couple of 20mm antiaircraft guns just beneath that." He indicated the two heavy guns, their black-holed barrels pointing upward, failed sentinels of the doomed ship.

They continued gliding over the ship, moving toward its buried bow.

"Well." Randy sighed. "This isn't a carrier, that's for sure."

Nat nodded. "Yeah, I saw that. Looks like some kind of transport ship. There's no lift elevators, no landing area."

Nat watched a long-tailed ratfish swim quickly along the bottom sand, frightened away by the lights, kicking up plumes of watery dust as it moved.

"What do you want to do?" he asked.

"Well," Randy began slowly, with a slight shrug, "might as well bring a piece up. We can always just take it back to Boston."

The pieces were destined for the new Boston Naval Museum, scheduled to be opening up in the fall. The museum was a showcase for naval warfare, and many of the exhibits had actually been salvaged from the ocean's bottom. "Yeah, all right," Nat concurred. "You want me to send up the transponder signal?"

"Go ahead."

Stretching to his side, Nat initiated the sonar transponder signal, an exact sonic code that traveled up to the *Sea Lion* above them. They could hear the machine sending the signal, a tapping sound somewhat like Morse code. The cameraman leaned forward, tapping Randy lightly on the shoulder. "For the tape," he said in English, then nodded at the wreck. "Explain, a little bit, OK?"

"Oh yeah, sure." Randy smiled, twisting his body toward the camera. "How's my hair?"

The Frenchman pulled the camera to his shoulder, adjusting the eyepiece. A small light over the lens began blinking red, and he waved his hand.

"OK, now basically," Randy began, speaking to the camera, "we've come upon the wreck of what we believe to be some kind of World War II seagoing craft. We're now going to attempt an underwater extraction of one section."

Randy paused for a moment to glance out the pod window. "OK, uh, the noise you might be able to hear now, that sort of *click, click* sound, is the *SeaHorse*'s transponder." He placed the palm of his hand on the small machine set on the side of the pod by Nat's head. "Now this sends up a signal to our host ship on the ocean surface, telling the ship to send down the buoyancy lift bags. These devices are used in most all heavy underwater salvage operations, the *Titanic* for example, and are basically large bags filled with diesel fuel. In this case, I think each bag is filled with . . . what?" He turned to Nat. "Four thousand gallons of fuel, creating something lighter than water."

"Yeah, something like that," Nat returned, carefully steering the *SeaHorse* over the wreck site.

Randy nodded, pausing for a moment, out of things to say, shrugged and stared into the camera. The cameraman nodded, shutting off the recorder and smiling. "OK, very good."

Randy relaxed slightly, stretching back into his seat. "All right, since we have about an hour to kill before the flotation bags get down here, you want to explore a little?"

"Yeah, sure. Let's send out the Urchin?"

"Yeah, we'll see what's going on down here," Randy said, moving forward to press the release button for the Urchin, the small remote-controlled underwater unit. There was a mechanical unlocking sound from outside the rear of the submersible as the Urchin detached from the *SeaHorse*. Randy was bent over the controls. In front of him was a small joystick, just underneath a black-and-white television screen showing the image relayed from the Urchin's onboard camera.

As Randy pressed the joystick forward, Nat watched the tiny Urchin whisk by the pod's side windows, its tether dragging behind it, as the unmanned sphere glided toward the site of the wreck. The three men watched the video screen as the wreckage from the site gradually came into focus. The Urchin was approaching a section of twisted metal, a giant gaping hole ripped open in the port side of the ship. Old antiaircraft guns, their bodies disengaged from the protective shells, lay scattered across the sandy floor, covered almost entirely by particles of rust. Vacant windows, the glass long since shattered, stared outward. The Urchin maneuvered easily, entering through the torn-away hole, moving into the interior of the ship.

Inside the wreck, the video screen showed a long, narrow corridor, stretching back toward the stern, just in front of the Urchin. Nat looked out the portal window, seeing the Urchin's umbilical cord stretching forward, disappearing into the torn section of the wrecked ship. Beyond that, the Urchin was barely visible, its position indicated by the faint glow from its onboard lights illuminating the gray of the inner ship.

"You wanna see what's down that hall?" Randy pointed to the grainy black-and-white image of the hallway on the monitor in front of them.

"Yeah, go ahead."

Randy pressed forward on the joystick, and slowly the Urchin began moving down the corridor, not walked upon in almost sixty-five years.

"This is amazing; look at how intact it is," Nat murmured, watching the screen.

Behind them, the Frenchman nodded his agreement, leaning forward and craning his neck to look at the screen. Randy replied, "That's what they saw in the *Titanic*; the damage was almost random. Some sections of steel piping were destroyed, while in other parts of the ship they found crystal chandeliers completely intact."

"Strange."

The Urchin was continuing down the corridor, its spherical body completely hidden from view, the unmanned craft seemingly swallowed up by the wreck.

Still watching the screen, they saw the corridor come into focus as the Urchin moved through it slowly. The walls were tilted slightly to the right, the entire wreck itself almost on its side on the ocean bottom. The grayish paint still clung to the walls of the corridors, and the words CAUTION: LOW CEILINGS were still visible in faint red lettering across one side.

The corridor receded straight ahead into darkness. As the Urchin moved forward, its lights penetrated ahead. Something was down there, swimming directly toward the camera.

"Whoa, mama," Nat said, staring into the video screen. "Look at the size of that thing."

A giant eel was moving down the corridor. Disturbed by the sudden presence of the Urchin's light, its body pulsated as it swam toward then moved past the Urchin. There was a glimpse of its long, open mouth and dead eyes before it swam past the camera, its body undulating behind it like a Slinky.

"Wonder what else is down there," Randy murmured as he pressed the controls forward.

An open doorway, a sudden rectangular blackness, came into view, the heavy metal door flung open, leaning back into the ship. The Urchin moved toward it, turning its light into the room beyond.

Inside, a collection of giant pots and pans had gathered in one corner of the room, lying together where they had fallen during an impact sixty-five years earlier. Small tube plants and coral had grown around the pots, gently breaking down the metal over time. Silver-colored metal doors and cabinets circled the room, some of them yawning open. The cabinets led up to a black stove, the grill covers still in place, a skillet sitting on top, as if ready to cook one last meal.

Three giant canisters stood on end in one corner of the room. The Urchin moved forward, camera scanning over the surface. On one of the rounded sides was the word FLOUR, another read, SUGAR. The writing on the other canisters was unreadable, wiped away by the passing of time.

Everything in the room seemed overlarge, a kitchen designed to feed hundreds of men.

"Must be the galley," Randy said, backing the Urchin into the hallway again. "Too bad we don't have a map of the ship, we could find our way around a little better."

Nat coughed lightly, then leaned forward, lowering his voice to a whisper. "Hey, do you think there's any chance we'll come across any . . . you know . . . remains down here?"

Randy smiled, shaking his head. "No way. I don't think so, anyway; they've never found human remains on any of the wrecks. These things have just been down here for too long. Why do you think that eel was so big? Good food source."

"Jesus." Nat sat back, running his fingers through his hair. "That thing we saw was eating the bodies?"

Randy chuckled. "Naw, I'm just kidding. This thing went down in '43, way too long for there to be anything down here except eels, coral, and barnacles."

The Urchin was moving forward again, passing farther down the hallway. A second vacant doorway gaped open on the left. The Urchin glided forward, before shifting to the left, its camera and strong lights burning away the darkness of the abandoned room.

Inside were two thickly padded chairs, the padding torn apart by a family of crabs, but reclined slightly and facing toward a large, still-intact mirror mounted on the wall. The light from the Urchin glinted off the mirror, rippling eerily about the room in waves. For a moment, Nat glimpsed the Urchin's reflection in the mirror, a spheroid hovering in the middle of the room, the umbilical cord trailing out the door.

"Looks like we got a barbershop in here," Randy said, gradually panning the Urchin's camera across the room. An old pair of scissors lay rusted and forgotten on the ground underneath the mirror, along with shards of glass and a boxlike object Nat recognized as a shaving cream dispenser, everything covered in the familiar undersea growth.

"Get in close." Nat pointed to a few small rectangular objects lying on the floor. "Can you see what those are?"

"Yeah, sure," Randy replied, pushing the joystick forward. Gradually the objects grew larger on the screen, until they filled out the entire frame.

"What is that?" Randy whispered softly, almost to himself.

Nat squinted. "I can't really make it out. Can you focus it more?"

"Hang on." Randy twisted the auto-focus on the camera lens. The image responded, first growing fuzzier, then becoming clear.

"Huh," Randy grunted. "Would you believe that?"

They were photographs. Three of them. Still intact, set inside what must have been waterproof frames.

The glass had been crusted over partially by barnacles, but through the film, Nat saw the faces of the lost crew. The first was an image of about thirty smiling men in Navy uniforms, standing together in front of the giant guns of a battleship.

The next was a photograph of three men sitting behind a table playing checkers. They were looking up from the board, smiling at the camera. Underneath in black marker someone had written, "Halsey, Murdoch, and Danny-Boy."

Beside that was a third, a photograph taken more than sixty years earlier in the same room the Urchin was in. Two smiling men were sitting in barber's chairs, their faces a lather of shaving cream, their heads poking up from large smocks tucked in around their necks, then folded over their legs. The chairs had been swiveled out away from the mirror, facing them toward the camera. Behind the men, where Nat had just seen spider crabs walking and a floating jellyfish, were a stack of magazines and three wicker waiting chairs, lost long ago, melted into the ocean.

Nat felt a strange pain of sadness.

"Hey, let's get out of this room," he whispered.

"Yeah, let's go." Randy pulled the Urchin backward, the photographs fading into the forgotten anonymity of shipwrecks and ocean bottoms.

Behind them, the Frenchman sighed. "Very sad." Leaning back into his chair, he became lost for a moment in his own thoughts.

The Urchin was gliding slowly out of the barbershop, the forgotten padded chairs fading off to the side of the camera's view. Out in the corridor again, the Urchin pressed forward, moving slowly between the narrow walls.

"Let's check out one more room," Randy whispered, carefully easing the Urchin down to avoid a section of caved-in roof.

Ahead was a third doorway. A painted sign, lying on the floor of the corridor, read RECREATION ROOM, then underneath that, NO ALCOHOL. The Urchin glided forward, moving toward the doorway. The remote craft turned into the opening and met a solid wall of metal.

"Huh, this room must be closed off, door is still shut," Randy muttered, moving the Urchin up. On the monitor, Nat saw a quick glinting flash of something on the door.

"You see that?"

"What?"

"Something shiny, like silvery or something on the door." Nat pointed to the screen. "Just up top there."

The Urchin slowly panned upward, exposing the door covered in reddish rust-colored barnacles, until reaching a small, round section set back in the door and unusually clear of underwater growth. The section reflected some of the light from the Urchin's lamps, refracting it toward the lens of the camera.

"Looks like a window," Randy said.

"Guess so; glass looks pretty thick, too. Can you get the camera to look through it?" Nat asked.

Randy nodded. "Yeah, probably. Let me just get it closer."

Randy carefully maneuvered the remote submersible toward the round window until the camera lens was pressed up against glass. Adjusting the focus, he saw a new image gradually come into view.

"Oh, man," Randy whispered, looking at the screen.

Behind them, the Frenchman hissed in air, leaning backward and crossing himself once.

With the solid steel door shut and locked, the room inside had formed a watertight seal against the imploding ocean. Even as the ship had sunk and lain on the ocean bottom, the seal hadn't been broken, leaving a completely dry, perfectly preserved room. It looked like some kind of lounge area. Books and magazines were scattered over the floor. Cutouts of Vargas Girls had been tacked overhead, along with various black-and-white photos of long-forgotten beauties of the day, the tape still clinging to the walls, holding them in place. A Ping-Pong table was turned on its side. Nat recognized the room from one of the pictures in the barbershop.

A giant wood-covered radio stood quietly in the corner, the knob still turned to ON. And there was something else.

There were men inside.

Four of them, their bodies so well preserved they looked almost like mannequins striking poses around the room. They were all fully clothed in pale, light blue Navy uniforms, while one of the men was wearing a white cap, tufts of his dried blond hair poking out from underneath. He was lying back on a sofa, his skin dried and leathery, almost mummified, his eyes like old apricots. One arm lay languidly to his side, falling off the sofa, the tips of his fingers just grazing the red-carpeted floor, while the other was stretched back over his head. Underneath him, a second man lay across the floor, his shoes stacked neatly by his side, exposing his bright white socks. His head was propped against the base of the sofa, his thin lips pulled back exposing two rows of teeth, left looking unusually long by the dried, receded gums.

The other two were also on the floor, heads propped up against the far side of the sofa, their bodies dried out and vacant, but their clothes still fitting snugly around their bodies.

The light from the Urchin passed through the thick glass of the portal window and glinted on their still-shiny buttons.

As the ship sank, the four men must have made their way into the recreation room, sealing the door behind them. Through the glass portal, they must have seen the corridor outside fill up with water, watched as their fellow sailors drowned, perhaps banging on the portal as their lungs filled with the ocean. Judging from the size of the room, the four men inside probably asphyxiated in a few hours. That time would have been spent in utter blackness, with the knowledge that there was no way out, no hope of survival, feeling the ship sink around them, then, judging from the state of the room, the crashing sensation as the big wreck hit bottom. Nothing after that but silence.

And here they all were, stuck forever in a capsule from the Second World War.

The Urchin pulled away from the window, the image of the men and the recreation room slowly vanishing.

"Let's get the Urchin out of there," Randy said slowly, pulling the joystick back. "The flotation bags should be here any minute anyway."

Nat remained silent, only nodding slightly.

The Urchin navigated its way safely back through the corridor, then Randy paused, leaning forward on the controls.

"What?" Nat asked.

Randy shook his head, staring at the monitor. On screen the Urchin had fixed on a single round object, an old life preserver half-buried under metal piping. Faintly visible black lettering wound its way around a cushioned side—USS GALLA.

"It can't be . . ." Randy whispered.

"What? What is it?"

"The *Galla*. We found it."

"I didn't even know we were looking for it."

Ignoring him, Randy backed the Urchin out of the hallway, the small craft reappearing suddenly through the cockpit window of the *SeaHorse*. Instead of bringing the Urchin back to the *SeaHorse* dock, Randy pushed forward on the control, causing small jets of water to propel the Urchin toward the bow.

"I should have checked, I should have known better," Randy muttered, as the Urchin approached the bow, skimming along the metal sides of the sunken ship. There, printed in black letters visible beneath layers of sea growth was more lettering. USS GALLA was printed again, even fainter, on the metal. Randy stared at the screen for a moment, Nat still not understanding the significance of the ship's name. Randy looked at Nat for a moment, then turned to Pierre in the back.

"No cameras."

"Excuse me?" Pierre asked, surprised.

"No filming. No cameras. From this point on. You understand. Nothing," Randy said sharply.

"But we had an agreement."

"Fuck the agreement. If you turn that camera on, so help me . . ."

Randy turned back to the monitor, still tense, guiding the Urchin back to reconnect with the rear of the *SeaHorse*.

Above them, the transponder signals from the sinking flotation bags had been increasing in number. Looking up through the pod portal, Nat could see several pinpoints of light, the guide lights of the bags, a thousand feet above them. There was a bump as the Urchin docked with the *SeaHorse*, the remaining umbilical cord slowly being pulled in.

Over them the guide lights continued to grow bigger, the bags slowly coming into view, being pulled down by piles of old anchor weights. Randy maneuvered the *Sea-Horse* away from the wreck, to avoid being crushed underneath the descending bags. As the bags hit the ocean bottom, creating a solid cloud of sand and debris from their impact, the rec room and the mummified sailors were forgotten for a moment.

"OK, hit bottom," Randy said, moving his hands toward the joystick.

The inside of the *SeaHorse* was quiet, some unknown tension taking hold of everyone. Randy was still tense, his back stiff as he worked the controls. The *SeaHorse* glided forward, using its robotic arms to gather the tether ropes of the four giant flotation bags, which hovered in the water like hot-air balloons. The piece of wreckage Randy and Nat had selected to be brought to the surface was lying in a tangled twist of metal about thirty yards north of the main wreck site. It appeared to be a section blown apart from the starboard side of the wreck, probably from a torpedo impact.

Randy reached for the radio. "Little fish to big fish. Over."

There was a long pause, then a burst of static. "Go ahead. Over."

"We've found the needle. Over."

Another pause, then the voice Nat thought he recognized as Yi saying, "Repeat, please."

"We've found the needle. Bringing up a section now. Over."

A new voice came on now, one with the slight accent of a native Spanish speaker. "You have found it? Over."

"That is correct. Over," Randy replied.

"You will observe radio silence from now on. No pictures or photography of any kind, do you understand? Over."

"Understand, yes. Over."

"Very good, best of luck. Over and out."

Randy switched off the radio, turning his attention back to the controls. Through the glass, the giant salvage piece loomed up from the mud.

The *Titanic* crews brought up a part of the *Titanic* weighing about fifteen tons. Nat estimated this section to be similar in size. Randy had finished cutting off the weights tethered to the bags, making each one almost neutrally buoyant, allowing the *SeaHorse* to nudge them closer to the wreckage fragment.

Slowly the *SeaHorse* did its job, attaching each of the four bags securely to the smaller wreckage.

"What's going on?" Nat finally said. "What's with the secrecy?"

"Don't know." Randy shrugged. "Just doing what I'm told to do."

"By who? How come I've never heard of any of this before now. That makes me nervous; I don't like these unexpected problems."

Randy turned to him. "The only real problem right now is that the Pacific is a pretty warm ocean. This may not rise any higher when the balloons hit the less dense warmer water. Otherwise, we're fine."

Nat watched carefully through the cockpit window, while from behind them, the Frenchman sat still, the camera sitting silent in his lap. The fragment they were going to raise was about twenty yards long and thirty yards wide, but was so covered in growth that its function on the working ship was difficult to tell.

"Hmm . . . strange," the cameraman murmured.

"What?" Nat twisted his body back.

"Look, that part is clear. Nothing growing there." He was pointing out toward a far section of the fragment.

Randy shook his head, half-listening while keeping his eyes fixed on the instrument panel. "That's impossible, everything is gonna be covered by rust by now."

Nat glanced up, squinting through the darkness. "No . . ." he began slowly. "He's right. Look."

The wreckage fragment was covered with hundreds of the typical gray-green stalactite-shaped growths, hanging from all the surfaces of the ship, covering the entire wreck with a crusted blanket. Out on the tip of the fragment, the growth had stopped suddenly, in a giant arc around one portion, leaving the area completely clean, as if the section had fallen into the ocean only very recently.

"That's amazing," Randy began, looking up for the first time. "The central characteristic of all wreck sites is that they're covered in particles of rust." He turned back toward the cameraman, explaining himself. "Those are just basically giant colonies of microbes that eat the metal off the ships. As they grow, they cover the entire ship. That's what leads to the eventual disintegration of most underwater sites. I've never seen any wreck that didn't have that."

The *SeaHorse* had finished attaching the tether ropes of the inflatable bags to the wreckage fragment. The transponders worked on a timer. In thirty minutes, the weights would be automatically cut from the balloons, allowing them to rise to the surface and bring the fragment with them. This gave the *SeaHorse* enough time to glide away from the entire operation, in case something went wrong and the wreckage fragment broke free, crashing ten tons of steel back to the ocean floor.

Randy checked his watch. "We've got time. I'm going to have to go look at that."

The *SeaHorse* began to glide forward, moving slowly over the fragment, heading toward its far end. Above them, the giant dark shadows of the flotation balloons hovered silently, moving slightly in the currents.

"Looks just like brand-new," Randy said in amazement, looking down on the cleared section as they passed over. "You can still see the rivets holding the plates together."

The metal stretched forward, forming a slight overhang over the ocean bottom. Underneath the overhang was a door. As the submersible moved closer to the door, Nat saw a round glass portal, still intact, looking into whatever room was beyond.

Randy noticed the door and the glass portal, too, already maneuvering the *SeaHorse* forward.

"Door Number 1 was pretty horrible; let's see what's behind Door Number 2?" Nat said in his best, deep, game-show-host voice.

"We're not going to look inside, we're going to block off the glass," Randy said.

"Block off the glass?"

"Cover it."

"What the . . . how? What are you talking about, cover the glass, where is this cloak-and-dagger shit coming from?"

The *SeaHorse* was still moving slowly toward the glass portal set in the door on the side of the ship. Like the rest of the area, the glass seemed unusually free of rust growth. The door was only a few feet above the rippling sand, giving the appearance that they were visiting someone's underwater house.

Randy stopped, turned to Nat. "We cover the windows because I've been told to cover the windows."

"OK . . . slowly here, don't bump the wreck, we don't want to start an avalanche," Nat said cautiously. "Who told you?"

"Don't ask."

Nat paused, thinking. "So what's inside?"

"Don't know."

"Aren't you curious?"

Randy paused. "No. No I'm not."

"Listen," Nat said, leaning forward. "What if there's something on this ship? Something dangerous, or something valuable. Don't you think we should at least know what it is . . . to cover ourselves down the line? Just between us, nobody else has to know we even looked."

Randy stopped, hands hovering over the controls, thinking for a moment.

"We've got time, we can take a look, see what's inside. If it's nothing, all right fine. If it's something . . . well, we can deal with that later. I don't want to find out later on that we towed a prototype for the first atom bomb into Boston Harbor."

Slowly, Randy nodded. "All right. We'll look. But only for a minute, then we cover it up."

"That's it."

Randy eased the *SeaHorse* forward until the bubble window of the cockpit pressed against the round portal of the wreck. The portal itself was about a foot in diameter, and Randy turned the *SeaHorse's* powerful lamps toward the door, playing around with the angle until they could see inside.

Everyone in the submersible left his seat, straining forward, eyes pressed against the Plexiglas of the *SeaHorse*, looking directly into the room beyond the portal.

"*Mon Dieu . . .*" the Frenchman whispered softly, then repeated in English, "My God."

Inside was another perfectly preserved room. Cloth cots were pressed against one wall of the room, their linens rumpled, as if they'd been slept in. Along the wall nearest the portal was a counter, covered with gauze pads, surgical scissors, antiseptic lotion, and Ace bandages. Underneath that, were cabinet doors, some of which had been thrown open, revealing layers of crisply folded white sheets. A clean metal bedpan glinted in the light from the submersible, lying on the floor, thrown sometime from one of the cabinets.

"Looks like a hospital area, or some kind of first aid room," Nat said, his forehead almost pressing against the window of the *SeaHorse* as he struggled to get a better view.

The walls had been painted a faint sea blue color. Against the far wall was a series of straight-backed chairs for visitors and a calendar pinned to a corkboard. The calendar was open to a Vargas painting of a woman dressed in Navy blues, her impossibly long legs crossed, her head tilted back in a laugh. Underneath, the month and year read, "June 1943."

Nat whistled softly. "Nineteen forty-three." He shook his head. "Long time ago."

The calendar was surrounded by newspaper clippings and cartoons, pressed into the corkboard, all of which were too far for Nat to read. Underneath the board, something was lying in a crumpled heap on the floor. The object was about six feet long, covered by brown blankets and twisted strangely along the wall's base. Nat had to turn his head slightly to the side before he realized what it was.

A man.

The blankets came up to the man's waist, revealing a light blue hospital-issue cotton shirt. His head was twisted toward the wall, hiding his face, but his hair was a brownish blond, sticking up in tufts like dried wheat grass from his head.

"We got another body in here," Nat said.

"Where?"

"Underneath that corkboard there." He pointed through the portal.

There was a dark smudge of writing across the back of his shirt. It was the man's name.

Eric Davis.

"Must have been fighting on Bougainville. This looks like a ship's hospital; he was probably wounded and getting a ride home when the *Galla* sank. Poor bastard."

Nat scanned the room some more, moving his eyes away from the crumpled body. On the floor in front of one of the cots, something was shimmering in the light from the *SeaHorse*. It looked almost like water, but that would be impossible after all that time.

Looking closely, he realized it was a small handheld mirror, lying faceup on the floor of the infirmary. A black mound was just next to the mirror. It took Nat a moment to recognize the mound as a shoe, covering a human foot. A man was seated in one of the chairs, his skin almost alive, his eyes seeming to sparkle in the lights, his face fixed so that he appeared to be staring directly at Nat.

"Whoa . . ." Nat murmured, then as he watched, the man buried in this underwater tomb for the past sixty-five years did the impossible.

He smiled.

"Jay-sus Christ," Nat said, jumping back from the window, startling Randy and the cameraman. "Did you see that?"

"What, what?" Randy sounded suddenly nervous, holding Nat's arm firmly.

Nat was looking away, keeping his head turned toward the portal. "There's a guy alive in there."

"What?" Randy almost laughed, then his smile grew uncomfortable. "Where?"

"See the corkboard." Nat continued to look away, reciting the vision from memory. "Look at the row of chairs next to it, there's a guy sitting in one."

There was a moment of quiet as Randy leaned forward, looking through the portal into the room. Finally, he said in a quiet voice, "I don't see anything."

"What? He's not smiling?"

"I mean there's nobody sitting there, I don't see anyone else in the room except for our friend Davis on the floor there."

"What the hell . . ." Nat murmured. Confused, he turned back toward the front, looking through the portal again. The chair was empty. He sat back, running his hand through his hair. "Weird," he whispered. "I could have sworn there was somebody sitting there, looking right at me, then he smiled."

Randy glanced toward the cameraman, who shrugged. "I saw nothing."

"Probably just mind tricks, things get weird when you've been this deep for so long," Randy said reassuringly.

"Yeah." Nat's voice was reluctant, and he leaned forward to look back through the portal.

The man was seated in the chair again. And this time, as Nat watched, the man raised one hand, wagging a single finger toward him.

Nat turned away from the portal, grabbing Randy's shirt. "Look!" He pulled the copilot forward, pressing him against the glass. "Whoa, easy there." Randy smiled cautiously, looking through the portal. He sighed, then began to pull back. "I still don't see anything."

Nat leaned in. The chair was empty. "That can't be." He shook his head. "I, I swear. Someone's in there . . . alive. He's trapped. We need to get him out."

Randy gently pried Nat's fingers off his shirt, holding his wrist. The motion seemed one of gentle consolation, until Nat realized Randy was checking his pulse. He jerked his hand away tersely. "I feel fine."

Randy looked at him. "Listen, this wreck has been here for a very long time. Nobody would still be alive."

"Yeah?" Nat said suddenly, pointing into the room through the portal. "Then look at that."

The cameraman sucked in his breath.

"What the—?" Randy whispered.

The crumpled body of the man named Davis had vanished from its spot on the floor underneath the corkboard. Only the brown blanket remained, pressed flat against the ground, as if the body underneath had just evaporated.

"Whoa . . ." Randy shook his head. "What's going on here?"

A light on the submersible's console began blinking rapidly, a small alarm sounding. Everyone looked down. "Warning," a prerecorded female voice began, sounding from speakers set near the back of the submersible. "Launch begins in five minutes."

"The balloons lift for the surface in five minutes," Randy said, staring at the console.

"Can you override it?"

"No." Randy shook his head. "The signal comes from up top, it's automatic. Nothing we can do. This whole piece is going up."

"Well, what about the guy in there?"

"Just a minute." Randy held his hand up. "We don't know for sure anyone's even in there. Nobody could have survived for that long."

"But look, we all just saw it with our own eyes. Did that body just get up from under that blanket and walk away?"

Simultaneously, the three men in the pod leaned forward, staring in through the portal, half-afraid to see what new changes there would be.

There were none. The blanket remained on the floor, nobody in sight, nothing moving.

"There . . ." Randy began slowly. "There's nothing—"

Something inside the room banged against the portal, inches from their faces. They jumped back in surprise.

"Holy shit," Nat cried, grabbing his chest, trying to slow the painful jumping of his heart.

The thing pressed against the portal glass was a human face. Its skin was so dried and discolored, Nat couldn't tell if it were a man or a woman, but its hair was the same sandy dried yellow as the body that had been lying under the blanket. The thing's jaw had dropped open, exposing a cracked inner mouth, and as they watched, the thing began banging its head against the window.

It was as if it wanted to get outside, but there was no life in its face at all. The eyes were dried and vacant, the skin taut against the bone. And across the cheeks and nose ran three parallel scratch marks, so deep they showed the bone fragments underneath. The head kept pounding at the glass, loosening its jaw until the chin hung limply, sagging under its own weight, the skin of the cheeks beginning to rip. The cameraman was whimpering softly, crawling to the very back of the submersible, as far away from the Plexiglas cockpit window as he could.

"Christ, get us outta here," Nat shouted, pulling at Randy's arm.

"Wait a minute." Randy held a finger up, his mouth open in awe, but his voice sounding strangely analytical. "I still have to cover the window."

"Cover the window? Are you crazy?"

The head pounded again against the portal glass, before sliding out of view, leaving just an empty round blackness of glass. Quieting down, the three men in the submersible leaned forward again, looking tentatively back through the empty portal. Another face suddenly pressed itself against the glass, causing the three men to jump back again in surprise. This one was different, more alive, the skin shining in the lights, its hair jet-black and curly. The head looked like a man's, but something was so wrong with it. Something evil. Nat pulled away from it.

The face was smiling, almost grinning, its sharp teeth protruding from its mouth. What drew Nat's attention the most were its eyes, glowing a murky yellow and green, the colors flowing together in swirls like slowly mixing paint. The thing reached up with one arm, tapped on the portal glass once with a yellowing fingernail, then pointed to something on the door. Nat looked down. It was pointing to the door latch. It wanted someone to open the door, to free it from its prison.

Instinctively, Nat shook his head, pulling away from the window.

The effect was instantaneous. Watching Nat's reaction, the thing's grin fell, suddenly being replaced with a snarl as the humanlike lips curled up, baring sharpened teeth. The head rolled back, the mouth opened, and it screamed. The noise must have been piercing, but the thick walls of glass muffled it to a rolling shriek that filled the inside of the submersible.

The Frenchman grabbed Randy's shoulder, shaking him. "Let us go, let us go. *Mon Dieu, ce qui est celui? Nous devons sortir d'ici tout de suite! Ce n'est pas humain, cela est un démon!*"

It screamed again, pounding on the glass with its clawed hand.

"Yeah, man, let's get the fuck out of here," Nat yelled, sitting back hard in his seat.

"Launch will begin in one minute," the recorded voice said suddenly over the submersible speakers, warning of the impending flotation of the four giant bags.

"The window covering."

"Fuck the window, let's go," Nat said.

Randy sat back and was reaching toward the controls when the entire pod shook violently. A toolbox sitting on a ledge overhead was knocked clear, falling and smashing against Nat's leg.

"Jesus," Nat said, gritting his teeth against the pain. "Take it easy."

"I didn't touch anything," Randy answered, holding his hands in the air. "That came from something outside."

There was a crushing sound from outside, and the submersible shook violently again, a hydraulic tube coming loose, spraying fluid all over the interior.

Nat turned, looking out the pod's side window. Something dark and large was moving outside, gliding through the waters.

"There's something out there," he cried, turning toward Randy. "Get us outta here."

The impact came again, knocking the submersible on its side, equipment spilling out onto the three men. Something hard hit Nat in the head, radiating a pain through his skull. The world was turning around him, until he was falling out of his seat, his shoulder smashing against the ceiling of the submersible. He could vaguely hear the whirring of the *SeaHorse*'s engines, but another impact rolled the sub downward, where, through the Plexiglas windows, Nat saw the ocean bottom coming up quickly to meet them.

A hose broke free of its encasement, filling the pod with hot steam. Nat was knocked off his seat, sprawling backward toward the rear of the pod, his chin landing hard against the Frenchman's knee. The pod was turning over again, rolling like the inside of a washing machine, causing a constant rattle of loose equipment against the titanium sides.

Randy was struggling to pull himself back behind the console, grasping the side of his chair and slowly easing himself forward. Something impacted again outside the pod, knocking them downward. Through the pod window, Nat caught a glimpse of something swimming quickly by, the size of a large shark, except thicker, and a lighter gray color.

Randy tried again to reach the controls, but the pod was already spinning out of control. Nat saw the ocean bottom come up quickly, the *SeaHorse* smashing into it amidst a flurry of sand and crushed rock.

"Liftoff sequence complete," he faintly heard the recorded voice say over the screaming of the three men trapped in the pod.

There was a metallic grinding sound, as the transponders signaled for the flotation bags automatically to cut away the scrap metal holding them down.

The pod rolled on the ocean bottom for a moment, before suddenly coming to rest, lying on its back, the front cockpit facing up toward the surface. Nat touched his head, his fingers coming away dripping with blood from a gash somewhere in his scalp. He was lying on top of the crumpled Frenchman. Gently easing himself off, he heard the Frenchman groan, moving onto his side and rubbing his rib cage. Whatever had attacked them outside had vanished, leaving them with only the hissing of the broken pipes inside the pod.

Nat sat up, his brains rolling around in his head like a loose egg, seeming to smash painfully against his skull as he moved. He grunted, closing his eyes again and gently massaging the back of his neck.

"Oh no," Randy cried, looking up through the cockpit window and shaking his head.

Their pod had slid down a small embankment, and above them was the wreckage fragment the diesel flotation balloons were bringing to the surface. The balloons had cut away their scrap metal anchors, and the heavy weights had fallen to the ocean bottom, all of them sliding down the embankment in a roar of foaming sand and water, heading toward the damaged pod.

Randy was making a strange gurgling sound in his throat, his eyes wide, holding one arm up as if to ward off the ten tons of loose anchor chains and ballast weight crashing toward the pod. The Frenchman, who had stopped groaning, was unconscious in the back, his face pressed tightly against the metal side of the submersible.

Nat closed his eyes as the scrap metal hit the *SeaHorse*. Inside the pod, there was a rumbling and scraping so loud that Nat covered his ears. It was like being in the middle of an avalanche, and the entire pod was shaking violently. A rusted-out anchor hit the cockpit window, causing a spiderweb of cracks to radiate out. Nat expected a burst of ocean, the salty coldness flooding the pod, but somehow the Plexiglas held.

Then the avalanche was over. Something struck Nat hard in the head, and a wave of blackness spread over him.

He opened his eyes. Something seemed wrong, slightly off. It took a moment for Nat to realize what was different—the pod was too quiet. The reassuring hum of the batteries was gone, there was no power.

Randy realized it at the same time, struggling forward.

"We lost power," he said after a moment, then leaned back against the pod wall.

"Can't we just float back to the surface?" Nat asked quietly.

"We could, but all that scrap metal is pressing on us outside. It's too heavy; we can't lift off."

Randy sat back down on the tilted floor, then leaned back, pressing his fingers against the Frenchman's neck.

"He's out, alive, but knocked out."

Nat nodded. With no power, they couldn't send a distress signal to the surface. Not that it mattered anyway. There were only a handful of submersibles able to dive so deep, and they were spread out all over the world. It would take at least a week to get one down there. They wouldn't be alive that long.

Nat nodded and looked up through the cockpit window overheard, a giant skylight up into the ocean. The only lights came from lamps attached to the four balloons. They had begun to lift slowly off the ocean floor, rising toward the surface, carrying the piece of wreckage with them.

He could see the hospital room's door, the strange time-encapsulated room with the living man inside. As the balloons lifted off, the door moved upward, the lights from the balloon lamps highlighting it against the dark Pacific waters.

A face was pressed against the portal glass. The same face they had seen earlier, its yellowish eyes peering at them inside their wrecked submersible. It smiled for a moment, then disappeared, as the room inside the wreck slowly moved upward.

Nat watched the entire structure rising away from him like a slow-moving jellyfish. Soon the lights from the balloons grew as small as pinheads, suspended in the blackness of the ocean, before disappearing entirely.

Then there was nothing but the darkness of the bottom of the ocean and the rasping of his lungs pulling oxygen from the already failing air supply. He wondered, faintly, if years from now, new explorers would discover their submersible and marvel at the three mummified remains inside.

As the quiet returned to the ocean bottom, the small iridescent fish began to return, their pale blue lights blinking overhead and shifting overhead like the fireflies Nat remembered.

On the ocean's surface, the warning alarms were beginning to sound on the *Sea Lion* as the metal object rose from the bottom. The Panamanian was leaning over the side of the *Sea Lion*, smelling the salt air and watching the rippling waves, his face eager with anticipation. They were making preparations to cover the salvaged piece when it rose; Lyerman didn't want anyone getting a look at his prize possession.

"Won't be long now," the captain said. "I'm worried, though. Our boys should have come up by now."

The man shrugged, thinking that it was no matter. What was important was that the cargo arrived safely. A voice cried out toward the bow of the ship, and the man turned his head. There was a great crashing of waves, and four giant flotation balloons surged up to the surface amidst a great plume of white foaming water.

"Looks like we got it." The captain smiled. "Lucky day."

The man watched the captain walked up toward the bow.

The Panamanian smiled. "Lucky day indeed."

Detective Will Jefferson lay on his sofa, watching *Late Nite*, an open bag of chips sitting on his chest. Overhead the ceiling fan spun lazily in tight circles while his aquarium gurgled, the water glowing a dark blue as fish swam among the coral and plants. Feeling around underneath him for the remote, he pulled it out from between the cushions and changed the channel. A West Coast Red Sox game came on for an instant, then an infomercial, then back to *Late Nite*. It was Friday. The phone rang.

"Yo, my man, Jefferson? You awake?"

"Yeah, I'm awake, my girlfriend just left."

"Shut the fuck up, what are you doing? Watching late-night TV and eating potato chips again?"

Jefferson glanced at the bag of chips at his feet. "Something like that. What's up?"

"We've got a double murder down here at the Lyerman Building. Real chop up job."

"Oh yeah, who?"

"Couple of kids." Brogan paused. "Looks like it's game time. You ready?"

"Right now?"

"Yeah, I'm downtown, just look for the sirens."

Jefferson shrugged, crumbs of potato chips falling off his shirt and onto the floor. "I don't know, man, I'm pretty busy right now."

"Right. I'll see you down here in twenty minutes."

Jefferson sighed. "All right . . ."

"Cheer up, could be worse."

"Yeah, how?"

"That new girl. The tech. She's here."

"Who, that model?"

"One and the same."

"What's her name again?"

"McKenna Watson."

"That's right," Jefferson said. "What's she wearing?"

"Come down and find out," Brogan said. "Don't take 93, its all backed up."

"Why?"

"Some construction they're doing, opening up a new tunnel out in the harbor, just started today," Brogan said. "Oh, and Jefferson. You afraid of heights?"

"Am I afraid of heights? What the hell you talking about?"

"Well, you'll see," Brogan replied. "Just get down here."

Jefferson could see the police sirens from a block away, the silently running lights of the squad cars throwing a blue glaze against the rain on his windshield. An ambulance was parked at the corner of the building, two drivers leaning against the van's sides and joking with each other. Officers were everywhere, directing traffic around the building, talking to the crowd, standing inside the lobby. One of them nodded to Jefferson as he approached, pointing him toward the roof.

"The roof?"

"Yeah, this one's a bitch on a rainy night like tonight. Feel sorry for you guys, I'll be home in bed before your team even gets started."

"How do I get up there?"

The officer pointed in through the revolving glass doors. "Go in through the lobby and ask the guy behind the desk. He'll show you up."

Jefferson nodded and pushed through the door.

Cold night air seeped around him as he stepped out of the elevator and onto the roof. For the last few weeks, Jefferson had been in Florida helping his old neighbor set up in a retirement community down there. Stepping onto the roof, he realized he was glad to be back. He had missed the work.

A thin rain was falling, slanted and cold, from the clouded sky. Jefferson remembered reading in the *Globe* that the roof of the Lyerman Building had taken three months to finish. A path of wood chips meandered out from the elevator, running between rows of poplar trees and benches made from rosewood. A black, waist high security gate, partially concealed by the leaves of the trees, ran the length of the roof. In the middle of the roof was a rectangular, glass-encased greenhouse. The windows were open, and, inside, Jefferson could see orange and red roses, their just-flowering buds waving in the slight wind from the air circulation fans.

Beyond the greenhouse was a fountain, three horses wrapped around each other, their mouths spitting streams of water that met together over a small, gurgling pool. Jefferson caught a glimpse of large orange goldfish lazily swimming circles in the water. Near the fountain was a small solarium of brick and glass. Inside was an ornate writing desk that looked Thai, a big-screen television, and a sofa. Not a bad setup.

Jefferson was beginning to feel the excitement of a new case.

Brogan was standing just outside the study, one foot resting on the surround of a bubbling hot tub. He was wearing white surgical gloves and holding a wineglass, inspecting the rim for a moment before smelling the liquid inside. Green lights in the tub lit the water, highlighting the rising steam.

Four technicians were walking a grid pattern across the roof. Brogan looked up as Jefferson approached. They'd first met each other in the Army. Jefferson had joined because he didn't know what to do with his life. Brogan had joined because he had known exactly what he didn't want to do. End up in prison like his two brothers.

Brogan was a big man. Construction worker build or maybe an older heavyweight boxer. His hair was cut close and jet-black, his arms long, apelike in appearance with large hands. His nose had been broken years before, giving his face a crooked appearance. He whistled when he breathed through it. His wife used to call it his teakettle nose. That was before she died.

Still holding the wineglass, Brogan looked up, and said, "Smells expensive."

"Doubt it's Pabst Blue Ribbon," Jefferson replied. He slipped on a pair of surgical gloves and bent toward the wine bottle still sitting on the ledge of the hot tub.

"Château Carruades de Lafite-Rothschild," Jefferson pronounced slowly, reading the label. "I think I had some of this at the last Sox game at Fenway."

Brogan carefully placed the glass on the ledge of the hot tub and stood up, arching his back.

"What do we got?" Jefferson asked.

"Two vics," Brogan replied. "Called in tonight at 12:16 A.M., approximate time of death 10:45 P.M."

Jefferson turned toward the edge of the roof. The police photographer was leaning over two figures lying on the path. The strobe flashed white for a moment as he snapped pictures.

Jefferson pointed toward them. "Who?"

"Jill Euan, twenty-one, college student at Tufts, originally from Dallas, Texas."

"And?"

"And . . ." Brogan said slowly. "Kenneth Lyerman. Son of Joseph Lyerman."

"*The* Joseph Lyerman?"

"One and the same."

"Jesus . . ." Jefferson said.

Joseph Lyerman had achieved status of mogul along with the likes of Rupert Murdoch and Warren Buffett some forty years before, when Ted Turner was still growing lawn grass and practicing taxidermy in his college dorm room. Just as the Rockefeller name was associated with Standard Oil and Carnegie's with U.S. Steel, the Lyerman name was associated with a list of major corporations ranging from media holdings to technology companies. There was even a brief foray into automaking with Lyerman's U.S. Auto Corporation's production of three automobile lines in the mid-seventies. Cornelius Vanderbilt once said, "I have been insane on the subject of moneymaking all my life." Joseph Lyerman made Vanderbilt look conservative on the topic.

Jefferson remembered reading an article on the man and thinking that at his present salary, he'd have to work for, oh, only a thousand years before he caught up with Lyerman. The man was now in his mid-eighties, yet was as involved with his companies as he had been in his fifties. Jefferson's grandfather was in his midseventies and sat around and fished all day when he wasn't listening to the Red Sox on the radio.

"Notify?" Jefferson asked.

"Joseph Lyerman found the bodies, placed the call. Lyerman knows. We've got someone on the phone now with Dallas PD. It's an hour earlier out in Texas, and we thought it best to notify them as soon as possible."

A whirring noise sounded as one of the techs ran a handheld vacuum over the bench nearest the two bodies. He emptied the contents into a plastic bag and placed it on the evidence cart. Jefferson watched the tech and thought of that new girl, McKenna Watson. The Beauty of Boston. He'd never seen her personally, but that was the word anyway. And word travels fast in the force when a beautiful woman is concerned.

Brogan looked at the bubbling water in the hot tub.

"Can we get someone to turn this off, already? Please?" Brogan shouted in an exasperated voice across the roof. "Christ Almighty . . ."

"How's Lyerman?" Jefferson asked.

Brogan shrugged. "Don't know. Haven't talked to him yet."

"We keeping this land bound?" Jefferson asked. "Land bound" meant staying off the police radio, a policy used when celebrities or famous figures were involved in investigations, to prevent the media from monitoring the scanners.

"Yeah," Brogan replied. He turned his collar up against the rain. "This weather isn't helping any. We're gonna have nothing to work with after this shit lets up. Captain's on my ass, too. Almost shit a brick when he found out who the kid's old man was."

"I bet," Jefferson said.

Brogan pulled a silver thermos from the pocket of his raincoat. Unscrewing the lid, he poured the steaming liquid into a silver cup.

He offered the cup to Jefferson. "Coffee?"

"No, thanks."

"Baby had another 3 A.M. wake-up last night," Brogan said, sipping the coffee. "She wouldn't stop crying."

Jefferson smiled, hunching his shoulder against the light rain.

The jets of water in the hot tub suddenly stopped, and the surface of the water went smooth.

"Finally," Brogan murmured. Then, turning toward the tech, he said, "Let's get this drained and tested."

Brogan took another sip of coffee, then asked, "You want to see the show?"

Jefferson nodded. "Sure."

The two men walked across the field toward the benches. There was a ring of yellow police tape sectioning off the area. Jefferson and Brogan slipped plastic bags over their shoes to prevent tracking something in and contaminating the site.

Lying on the ground were two figures, one male, one female. The man was wearing swimming trunks, the girl a white robe, which had come undone. Underneath was a black tight-fitting two-piece swimsuit. She was lying faceup on the path, an arm sprawled over one of the benches, her legs lying limply together. The guy was facedown, his head pressed into the woods chips on the path.

When she was alive, Jefferson could tell the girl had been beautiful. A model even. Her hair was long and chestnut-colored, clumped together in parts, glued by dried blood. Her body was trim and fit, her legs tan and stretching out.

Her throat had a U-shaped dark line across the front. Jefferson used to feel strange appreciating the sexual qualities of the dead. Things change. Look at the tits on her, must be fake. Great legs. Beautiful face. Now he was so used to the dead that most times it was like looking at a photograph. And anything you'd say about a photograph, guys he worked with would say about the dead. Hell of a thing to get used to. Thank you, Boston. Could be worse, at least this wasn't D.C. or New York, where they scooped them up off the sidewalk every other day.

"Lucky guy, huh?" Brogan said, taking another sip of coffee.

"Yeah." Jefferson nodded. "Nice-looking girl."

Brogan loosened his tie as he talked, unbuttoning the top button. "So you want me to fill you in on what's been going on?"

Jefferson nodded. Would be nice.

Brogan nodded, took out a Palm Pilot, and scrolled through the screens.

"I remember when detectives used pencil and paper."

"Get with the times, brother. OK, let's see . . . all right, here we go. Call comes in at 12:16 from Mr. Lyerman. Doesn't come in directly, though, goes straight to the top, doesn't come 911."

"Wasn't 911?"

"No, called up the captain. Lyerman knows him personally."

"OK."

"Now this is weird the part," Brogan said. "There was another call to 911, earlier in the night, but from this same address. That call came in at 10:15."

"Ten-fifteen? Before the homicide ring?" Jefferson asked.

"Exactly." Brogan scrolled down on his pocket organizer. "The homicide call was actually the second ring out of this address."

"What was the first about? The one at ten-fifteen?"

"Possible B&E."

"Breaking and Entering?"

"Yeah. And here's the weird thing. About four minutes after that call is placed, we get another ring from one of the security guards on duty here. This guy says the B&E call was a false alarm."

"To 911?"

"Yeah."

"So we called it off?"

"Sure. He had the proper authorization code, knew the alarm procedure. Says he was the one that phoned it in originally."

"We get the name?"

"Yeah, we've got it somewhere," Brogan said.

Jefferson said, "Then Lyerman calls in the homicide almost two hours later?"

"That's right," Brogan affirmed. "Strange, huh?"

"That *is* strange."

"That ain't the half of it," Brogan said. "Check out what we found over here."

Brogan walked to the edge of the roof, stopping just before the black railing. The top of the rail was flecked with reddish spots. Next to the red marks were small traces of dirt. Jefferson lowered his face to the railing, looking closely at the marks and the black granules.

"What is that? Blood?" Jefferson asked.

"We took a scraping," Brogan said. "But gut instinct tells me no. I think it's something else."

Brogan pulled a white paper and foil package of chewing tobacco from his front pocket. Taking out a large plug, he placed the greasy leaves in his mouth, moving them toward his cheek, where they stuck out of the corner in a little leafy bundle.

"What about this other stuff," Jefferson said. "Looks like dirt."

"Yeah, I don't know," Brogan said, then, standing up, shouted back to one of the technicians. "Let's get a vacuum over here, all right?"

Something was lying on the ground, just underneath the railing. It was small and dark, covered in cloth. Jefferson bent, picking it up with his surgical gloves.

It was a doll.

The doll's head was large, flopping from side to side on its flimsy cloth neck. The face was made of porcelain, with large eyes and a frowning mouth, beneath which was a long black beard. It was dressed in red-and-white robes, with images of green dragons stenciled finely in gold thread across the fabric.

Thin strings ran from the doll's hands, feet, and head, attaching to a wooden crosspiece. Holding on to the crosspiece, Brogan lifted the doll off the ground, where it dangled in the air.

"What the hell is it?" Brogan asked.

"Looks like a marionette puppet."

Brogan nodded, bringing the doll over to the railing, until its small feet just touched the top of the metal. As he moved the strings back and forth, the doll began to dance in a strange, jerky fashion. Its body twitched to and fro, the frowning head bobbing up and down.

"Creepy little guy, isn't he?" Jefferson said as he watched the doll jerking back and forth.

"Yeah, no shit. Like Howdy Doody meets the *Exorcist*." Brogan stopped the strings, carefully carrying the doll over to the evidence cart. He placed the figure inside a large plastic bag, then, sealing the bag shut, laid it on the cart.

"We'll check with Lyerman, see if he knows anything about that," Brogan said, still looking at the doll, now lying quietly inside the plastic bag.

Brogan stood up. "Hey, you know McKenna is here?"

"No shit, really?" Jefferson asked, looking around the roof. "Now?"

Brogan nodded toward the two bodies. "I shit you not, brother."

"Didn't think she'd still be here with the rain."

"Yeah, well, she is. She's a cool lady. Classy broad."

"Classy broad? What are you, Frank Sinatra?"

Cool lady. Classy broad. Coming from Brogan, those were high compliments. Jefferson followed his gaze back across the roof toward the bodies. A woman was bending over the male vic, probing his scalp with latex-gloved hands. Her back was toward him, her brown hair pulled into a ponytail. Slowly she moved down the length of his back, pulling down his swimsuit and exposing his buttocks to insert the rectal temperature probe.

"Ahh, the smells of romance and rectal probes are in the air," Brogan said, throwing his arm around Jefferson. "Well, shall we meet our lovely new tech? God, I would love to have her take my rectal temperature sometime."

"Get the fuck outta here."

"I think she's got her eye on you though, brother."

"Right."

"I'm serious."

"OK."

While Jefferson had been down in Florida, Brogan had already worked two cases with McKenna. Most people had better odds surviving a single case with the man than they did in getting off the *Titanic* alive. Two cases, was like the *Hindenberg*.

"Hey, McKenna, get your hand out of that man's pants," Brogan said, as they approached.

Her back was to them and she stood up slowly turning toward the sound of Brogan's voice. She was tall, five-foot-eight or -nine, with hair so smooth you wanted to reach out and run your hands down it. She was facing them, and then McKenna Watson smiled. Really smiled. Not just rehearsing the act, but really smiling. Genuine. And somehow in that moment she seemed familiar to Jefferson. All at once. Without being able to remember how or where. Like recognizing the details, the curve of the lips, the color of the eyes, but somehow not being quite able to put the whole of them together.

She brushed back a loose piece of hair with her wrist and smiled again.

"McKenna," Brogan said. "You know my partner, Detective Jefferson?"

McKenna turned to Jefferson, and she looked confused, for just a moment. Something in her eye, a glimmer of what? Recognition? Pleasure?

"Detective Jefferson, pleasure to meet you," McKenna said. "I'd shake, but . . ."

She nodded to her latex-gloved hands.

"No problem," Jefferson returned. "How's everything coming?"

"All right." She shrugged. "I just checked the temp probe, the core body temperature has fallen off a lot, so the time of death was probably about two hours ago"—McKenna checked her watch—"a little before eleven tonight."

She bent over the body of the dead man and held up his limp wrist, flicking his fingers lightly.

"No rigor yet," she continued.

From her bag she pulled out two plastic hand wraps, carefully sealing up the man's hands, tying the bags off around the wrist. "There's nothing evident under either of the two victims' fingernails, but we'll check that out when we get to the lab."

McKenna stood up and peeled off her latex gloves, carefully placing them in the evidence cart. "There has obviously been some mutilation to the upper torso, extending downward toward the midsection. If you notice here, these three parallel gashes extend directly across the midline of the body. They are repeated here, on both arms and the right shoulder, resulting most probably from the victim's raising his right arm in a defensive posture.

"The pattern of the marks indicate that the attacker was right-handed, and unusually tall. There was no evidence of skin or blood underneath the victim's fingernails, and the extensive bleeding of all the marks indicates the gashes were not postmortem."

"You mean this guy was alive when this happened to him?" Brogan asked.

"Unfortunately for him," McKenna replied.

"May I?" Jefferson bent in front of the body.

"Sure, go ahead."

Using a small penlight, with his gloved hand, Jefferson carefully felt along the man's scalp, gently rocking the head back and forth and feeling his neck. *Someone worked this guy over pretty good.* Looked like he'd been mauled by a pack of wild bears. And it didn't look any better up close.

Holding the light in his mouth, he gently probed at the wounds with both hands.

"This guy got turned into a flank steak, huh?" Brogan said, spitting a bit of tobacco into a plastic cup he was holding.

Jefferson's finger pressed into a gash on the man's stomach. He felt something hard and sharp. Inserting a scone finger, he carefully pulled the object from the wound and held it in front of the penlight.

"Look at this." He held the object up for Brogan and McKenna.

The object was about two inches long and curved, with almost razor-sharp edges. It was brown in color and looked like some kind of hook.

"What the hell is that?" Brogan asked.

"I don't know. Can you hand me one of the bags?" Jefferson nodded toward the evidence cart. Brogan handed him a bag, and he slipped the sharp, hooked object inside and sealed it for further examination at the lab. He looked around for McKenna. She was standing a few feet off talking into a cell. She looked back at him, one hand cupped over the receiver end of the phone.

"The coroner's people want to know if they can remove the two victims," she said.

Jefferson stood and peeled off his latex gloves. "Yeah, I'm done here. You?"

"I'm all set," Brogan answered.

McKenna nodded and spoke into the phone, nodding some more, before clicking the cell phone shut and slipping it into her pocket.

"So, what do you think?" she said.

Jefferson looked at the bodies. The uncovered skin of the man was glazed with beads of rainwater. The woman's robe was wet, plastered tightly to her body. The rain had prevented the blood from drying, and drips of pinkish water flowed down the victims' bodies and onto the ground. Jefferson thought the whole thing looked like someone had doused them both in runny pink watercolor paint. The contrast of colors was almost interesting. Monet on the rooftop. From a detached perspective anyway.

"We're on the roof of one of the major buildings in Boston. Unless we're dealing with Superman. I'm sure someone saw the guy who did these two come up here," Jefferson said.

"Yeah, someone or something."

"What do you mean?"

"I mean that if nobody saw the perp, there are cameras everywhere up here. Shouldn't be a problem pulling the tapes."

Jefferson stood dumbly for a moment. "Tapes?"

"Surprise," Brogan said. "Happy birthday."

McKenna looked at him. "You didn't know?"

"What?"

Brogan laughed, spitting again into his cup. "We're on *Candid Camera* up here, guy."

Brogan moved slightly to his right, and behind him, sitting on the corner of the roof, Jefferson saw a blinking red light. A video camera. Twenty yards away was another one. The place had more tape than a 7-Eleven convenience store. Sometimes you just get lucky.

"Jesus . . ." Jefferson said slowly. "There are surveillance cameras up here?"

Brogan nodded. "You got it, buddy. Two of them."

"Two cameras?"

Brogan smiled. "What say we go take a look at the tapes."

According to McKenna, who had verified it with the security desk, the tapes for the cameras were kept in the basement of the building. Jefferson and Brogan took the glass elevator down, watching the numbers descend as the elevator ran along the outside of the building, whirring softly as the lights from the city streamed across the black glass.

Brogan was quiet, turning to watch the view.

"Hey, you all right?"

"Yeah." Brogan exhaled. "It just gets me sometimes."

"What's that?"

"Look at where we just came from. Here's that kid up there. God bless his soul, but he's got the hot tubs, the fucking fancy wine, while guys like you and me are working hard every night, cleaning up the mess, and just getting by." Brogan turned toward Jefferson.

The doors of the elevator opened with a *ping*, and they stepped into the empty lobby.

"All right, where the hell's the basement?" Brogan asked, a little worked up, looking around at the marble floor.

In the corner, a waterfall gurgled, and from hidden speakers somewhere in the room, Jefferson could hear the sound of rainfall and the occasional squawk of tropical birds.

Their shoes tapped on the polished floor as they walked across it.

"Nice place," Jefferson murmured.

"Yeah, this ain't bad. I like this jungle theme. It's like my mother-in-law's place with all these plants." Brogan pressed one of the green leaves between his fingers. "Hey, these plants are real."

"Here we go," Jefferson said, standing near the fountain.

Behind the waterfall was an unmarked elevator door.

He pushed the button and waited for the car to arrive. Brogan spit once into the fountain next to them, the tobacco juice disappearing into the foam. Jefferson stared back out at the lobby, distorted and shimmering as he looked through the sheet of water.

The security office was at the end of a long, cracked-concrete corridor dotted by an occasional shiny black oil stain. Along the walls and ceiling ran gray pipes of various sizes, intermingled with plastic-covered wires. The scene was lit by industrial-looking fluorescent fixtures that depended from the ceiling. At the end of the corridor was a metal door with the words, SECURITY PERSONNEL ONLY in block letters across the top.

Brogan knocked. A moment later they heard a muffled, "Come in."

The Lyerman Security Office was small and dark. Rows of black-and-white television screens lined the wall, their glare providing the main light for the room. Underneath the wall of televisions was a long, slightly bowed desk, topped with a computer, a stack of *Entertainment* magazines, an open box of donuts, and a few photographs in frames.

John Dombey was the guard on duty. His blue uniform was tight around his body, smooth and shiny over his rounded stomach. White powdered sugar dusted the front of his shirt, and Jefferson saw the man's clip-on tie lying in a heap on the desk. The picture of American efficiency. The man was greasy, and Jefferson wished the room were larger. He didn't like being so close to the guy.

"I had a feeling you might be coming to see me," Dombey said, reclining in his chair, his lips spreading apart in a smile. Like oil spreading over a pan.

"You've been keeping an eye on things up there?" Brogan asked.

"Of course. You guys are giving me something to do down here."

Jefferson looked up at the television screens. Two of them showed views from the roof. He saw the coroner's assistant using a stretcher to carry out Lyerman's body, his big form inside the zippered bag. The body was heavy, and the two men were having trouble lifting it over the bench. In the other screen he saw McKenna, carefully dusting off a corner of the bench, looking for prints. Again, that feeling of familiarity. Weird.

Brogan snapped his finger suddenly. "You with me, buddy?"

"Yeah, sorry."

"Good-looking gal," Dombey said, staring at the screen. He had the face of a snowman. Round and soft, with small black eyes. "Real nice."

Brogan smiled, sliding the pocket organizer from his pocket. He flipped open the screen, looking at the small keypad.

"When did you start work tonight?" Brogan asked.

"I got here a little before 8 P.M.," Dombey replied.

"And what happened?"

He shrugged. "The usual, Don Becker was here already, he works the noon-to-eight shift, so I took his place. We talked for a little bit, he left around eight-twenty, maybe eight-thirty."

The guard reached into his pocket and pulled out a white plastic stick about three inches long. He placed the stick in his mouth and pulled in deeply.

"Nicotine inhaler." He shrugged holding the stick out. "I'm trying to quit."

Dombey was staring at Brogan now. The smile still greased across his face, but was slipping slightly. Confused. The oil in the pan drying up. Brogan looked at him for a moment, before he pointed to his own face. "Nose got broken five, six years ago when I got kicked in the head. It makes my face look a little crooked. It takes some people a little bit of time to figure out what's wrong exactly, so I like to let 'em know right up front."

Dombey nodded. "Oh, right. What happened?"

Brogan shrugged. "Just got kicked. Found the guy later. Broke his leg."

"Oh . . ." Dombey said, and nodded again, the smiled fading again. Not a story most people know how to respond to. Brogan had actually broken both the guy's legs. And his nose, for good measure. But that part didn't make it into the story usually. Didn't have to. Brogan was scary enough even without all the details.

Jefferson nodded to Dombey. "So after you relieved Mr. Becker, what happened next?"

Dombey took another silent pull on the inhaler. "Well, I started my shift. Nothing unusual really, it's pretty quiet this time of night, you know."

Dombey dragged again on the inhaler. Maybe the guy had a Freudian oral fixation. Maybe he competed with his father for his mother's love, and it pissed him off. Or maybe he was just lying.

"Did you see anything unusual on the roof?" Brogan asked.

Dombey shrugged slightly. Frowning as if he were thinking, he repeated, "The roof?"

Jefferson glanced at Brogan out of the corner of his eye. "Yes, the roof, Mr. Dombey, did you see anything unusual?"

Another drag.

"No. Not really."

Brogan tapped the screen showing the view of the roof. The body of the girl was lying in full view, sprawled out across the bench. "You don't call this unusual? I don't know, Jefferson, you call that unusual?"

Jefferson nodded.

"Because I'd say that's pretty strange," Brogan continued. "Two bodies showing up all of a sudden like that, that's not like an everyday occurrence."

"Christ," Dombey whispered to himself, looking at the inhaler. He dropped the plastic stick onto the desk and pulled a real cigarette from his front pocket. He held it in his mouth for a moment, fishing for a lighter.

"All right, listen, you can't tell Lyerman about this, OK?"

"Why not?" Jefferson said.

"I could lose my job is why. I'm not supposed to be watching what goes on up there."

The greasy smile was gone. The guy's oil was all dried up, leaving him nervous and shaking while he tried to light the cigarette.

"So you *were* watching the roof?" Brogan repeated.

Dombey lit the cigarette and took a pull. "Aww, hell. Yeah, I was watching."

He leaned closer to the two officers, his voice lowering like he was going to confide a secret. "Listen, I used to make nine bucks an hour in this shit-ass job. I sit here in this dark little room eating donuts and smoking cigarettes eight hours a day, then I go home, go to sleep, wake up, and do it all over. I figure I got a right to watch sometimes, you know?"

Jefferson couldn't tell what he was getting at. Then he remembered the girl on the roof, the hot tub, the wine. The sex. And Dombey was always down here, eating his donuts, and watching the show like it was *Monday Night Football*. Jesus. At least he was being honest.

Brogan caught on suddenly, his face almost breaking into an amused smile. "So you were watching the two of them go at it?"

"Yeah, man, I mean, you know, what the hell else have I got to do here, sit around on my fucking brains all night and look at the conference room cameras. Christ. I'd go fucking crazy." Dombey pointed to the television screen. "This is like a pay-per-view movie every night."

Brogan nodded. Jefferson nodded. The man had a point.

"Did Lyerman ever find out?" Jefferson asked.

"Yeah, well that's the thing." Dombey took another pull of his smoke. "Once about a year ago, he and this girl weren't getting heavy in the usual spot, which is right on that bench there."

Dombey pointed to the padded bench in the middle of the screen and lowered his voice. Jefferson had flashbacks to high school locker room conversations.

"She was this beautiful blonde," Dombey said. "Knockout. And she's all playful with him. Can't wait. So, instead of taking him to the bench, she drops his fucking pants right near the railing on the side of the roof and starts working him like a Popsicle."

"You saw all that?" Brogan said, leaning forward and lowering his voice.

"No! That's the thing, they're out of the camera's field of view. I can only see them if they're in the visual field of the two cameras, either on the bench or in the hot tub. Anywhere else, and I miss the show."

"What'd you do?"

"Well, I could just see a little bit, but the main part was off-screen, so . . ." Dombey put the cigarette in his mouth to free up both his hands. The smoke trailed up around his head. Leaning forward, he touched the screen with the shot of the bench with his finger. The screen flashed once, then Dombey moved a small joystick on the desk in front of him. "So . . . I just used the manual controls to position for a better view."

The camera angle panned to the right as Dombey moved the joystick until the railing and side of the roof were in full view. "Bingo, I'm back to late-night television."

The image on the screen now covered the railing on the edge of the roof. In the distance, Jefferson could see the lights of the Hancock Building.

"So I kept moving the camera," Dombey began again, "so I could follow the action. Except, let me tell you something, this girl is wild. She's on the railing, she's on the sofa, they're behind the trees, it's like trying to keep up with a sexual rubber ball. But I'm doing my best. Until they move back to the Jacuzzi area, and, as I moved the camera with them, I notice Lyerman is staring right back at me. He's watching the camera move. He's figuring out what I'm doing, and I know I'm fucked."

Dombey took another pull from his cigarette, the end glowing a deep red for a moment. "Employee loyalty is real important around here, they take things seriously, they catch you fucking around on the job . . ." Dombey's voice faded. He shrugged.

"So what happened?"

"Well, I watch Dombey tell the girl to wait on the bench, then he disappears. Five minutes later the door opens, and he's standing there in some kind of fruity robe reaming me out. He's pissed as hell. 'What the fuck? I oughta kill you!' Just in my face about it. I try and get him to calm down, and he shoves me against the console here."

Dombey took another pull on the cigarette.

"He worked me over pretty good. I couldn't even fight back—he's the fucking boss's son—I'd have lost my damn job. I just tried to protect myself. He got me bad though. I spent a week in the hospital." Dombey pointed to a metal file cabinet about four feet tall in the left corner of the room by the door. "You see that right there? That cabinet there?"

Brogan turned to look. "Yeah."

"You want to know why that's new?" Dombey smashed out the cigarette in a tray. Standing up, he stood in front of Jefferson and Brogan, holding a lighter from his pocket in front of his right eye. He held the flickering flame in front of his face. Nothing happened. The shark's eyes didn't move. The pupil didn't dilate.

"Guess why my eye doesn't respond to light or movement?" Dombey said. "The cabinet is new because he bashed my head in with the old one. Crushed the optic nerve in my eye. Nerves don't regenerate, I lost sight in one eye forever."

"Jesus," Brogan murmured.

"Yeah, I'm sorry that the girl is dead. But I couldn't give two shits about that rich prick. His father found out about the 'incident,' as they called it. He heard his son had assaulted one of his employees, almost put him into a coma. Immediately the old man is at the hospital, in my room past midnight because he arranged with the hospital to see me during nonvisiting hours, asking if I'm gonna press charges.

"Except with people like this, they don't ask, they tell you what's gonna happen. If I take my old job back and shut up, he says, I get my wage doubled." Dombey shrugged. "I'm still working here. You guess what happened."

There was silence in the room, the only sound the flicking of the lighter as Dombey lit a new cigarette. He stared off vacantly through the thin trail of smoke rising above his head.

Almost a full minute passed before Dombey spoke again. "After that, old man Lyerman insists on having a bodyguard up on the roof at all times, whenever his kid's up there with a girl. He was there to step in and protect any of those girls from getting killed, just in case the Lyerman kid lost his temper again.

"But you know what? That kid never even apologized for what he did to me. I lost my vision, and he can't even apologize for that? Fuck him. I'm glad he's dead. I really am."

The guard stopped talking, pulling angrily on his cigarette. Brogan glanced at Jefferson for a moment and cleared his throat.

"So were you here the whole night?" Jefferson asked.

Dombey looked up sharply from his meditation.

"Yeah, I was here. I didn't kill him if that's what your getting at, but I was down here when it happened."

"Then why didn't you call us?"

"Well, I notified Mr. Lyerman first, and he went up to go see what was going on. You know, I seen him up on the roof, checking things out. He called down and told me not to call the police unless I was instructed. Yeah, I was here when everything happened." Dombey looked at the floor for an instant, inspecting his shoes. "It doesn't matter any. Couldn't see anything anyway."

"Why is that?" Brogan asked.

"Well, all the cameras in this building? They all use cellular transmission to relay the picture down here. That means there's no wires involved with any of them, they can just transmit the signals directly down here. So, security can just pick the camera up and move it wherever they want. After they installed the system, though, they found out the problem with using cellular frequencies is that sometimes it causes distortion interference. Fucks things up."

"What do you mean?"

"Well . . . here I'll show you." Dombey looked around the room for a moment. "Do either of you guys have a cell phone on you?"

"Yeah, sure," Jefferson said, reaching into his pocket and pulling out his. Taking it from him, Dombey flipped open the lid but kept the phone turned off. Leaning into the computer console, he pressed a few buttons, and one of the images on the screen immediately changed.

"Recognize that?" Dombey pointed to the new image on screen.

Leaning forward, Jefferson saw three men in a small room. The room was lined with television screens, and one of the men had his face turned toward the camera. It was Dombey. An instant later Jefferson realized he was looking at an image of himself and Brogan. The picture on the screen was of the security room they were standing in. Turning around, he saw a small camera mounted high on the wall, one red light blinking as it looked down on them.

Brogan grunted with surprise. "That's us, huh?"

"Exactly. You can wave to the camera if you want." Dombey held the cell phone open. "OK, so now everything is working well. Picture is clear, you can tell everyone in the room. But watch this."

Dombey turned on the cell phone, the dials illuminating green. Immediately wavering lines cut through the image on the television screen. The picture was distorted so wildly, Jefferson couldn't recognize anything anymore. The image was totally destroyed.

"What's going on? Where'd our picture go?" Brogan asked.

"Exactly. They installed the cameras to run on a cellular frequency because it was more convenient. They didn't realize that anyone using a cell phone would mess with the transmission of images from the security camera."

Dombey turned off the phone. Immediately, the screen returned to normal.

"Unfortunately for you two, Lyerman decided to make a cell phone call right before he was knocked off. I've got the tapes right here for you to look at, but I'm afraid there's nothing much to see. You just get a little make-out footage of him and the girl, before he clicks on the phone and everything goes distorted. That lasts for about an hour before the battery wears out and the phone turns off. And then, that's when I saw the bodies."

Dombey held the phone back out to Jefferson.

"Looks like the two of you are in for a little more trouble than you thought."

Jefferson and Brogan took the elevator up to the thirty-fifth floor, Lyerman's private offices.

"We found a photograph on the boy's body," Brogan said as they rode upward.

"What of?"

"Just him, looks like he's skiing," Brogan answered. "We're going to give it back to the old man after we run it for fingerprints."

"Was he the only son?"

"Yeah, think so," Brogan replied. "I don't know who the mother is."

There was a *ping*, the elevator stopped, and the doors slid open.

Almost in unison with the opening of the elevator doors, a blocklike man sitting behind a desk just beyond the elevator rose from his seat. A big Samoan guy. Two gold hoop earrings in either ear. In front of the man was a small radio, which he turned down as they entered the room.

Beyond the elevator door was a small reception room. Two pastel paintings of sailboats hung from the walls, flanked on either side by brightly glowing halogen lamps, which painted arcs of yellow light on the wall behind them.

"Can I help you gentlemen?" the guard asked from behind the large walnut desk.

He was wearing black pants and a deep purple shirt and tie, which clung tightly to his chest and massive arms. Looked like a nightclub bouncer. He leaned forward, resting his hands on the desk in front him.

"We're here to see Mr. Lyerman," Brogan said, moving his eyes around the room.

"He may be busy now, please wait one moment while I notify him," the guard replied. "May I ask your names?"

Very polite. Just like he was paid to be. Wonder how he'd act if he wasn't being paid. The guard spoke softly into a telephone on the desk. He listened for a moment, nodded slightly, looked up at the two detectives, then whispered again. Brogan was staring intently at the guard, his neck bulled out around his collar, doing the big dog stare down. The Samoan ignored him. Which is a very tough thing to do.

Jefferson noticed a security camera perched high on the wall, its lens trained on them. He wondered if Dombey was in the basement watching them.

"You can go right ahead, gentlemen," the guard said, replacing the phone in its cradle. "Mr. Lyerman is ready to see you now."

A buzzer sounded, and a glass door behind the guard's desk swung slowly open. They passed through the doorway into a long, carpeted hallway. Some kind of desert motif. Photographs of the American Southwest hung from the wall. Sweeping sand, rock-covered mountains, and cactus plants. The air was hot, dry.

As they approached, the pictures slowly began to change, shifting to images of dark redwood forests. The lights dimmed and a mist began to stretch across the floor, clinging just above the carpet and moving slowly in pale billows around their feet. An owl hooted, followed by another answering hoot, and, above him, Jefferson heard the swishing of wind through trees. Turning his face, Jefferson actually felt a breeze. The room had completely transformed.

"I read about this in *Time* magazine at my sister's house," Brogan said, as they walked through the simulated forest. "It's something new that one of Lyerman's companies, VisionWare, is working on."

At the end of the hallway was a pair of double doors. A thin sheet of water streamed from the ceiling, falling in front of the doors before disappearing into a space in the floor. As they approached, the water suddenly stopped, allowing them to pass. Ahead of them were double doors. Brogan rapped on the dark wood with his · knuckles.

The doors buzzed open.

Lyerman's office was huge and black. Black marble floors. Black sofas and chairs. An enormous black desk with a shining marble top was centered in the room. The entire wall behind was glass, looking out over the city. Two large palm plants sat in dark pots on either side of the window.

Along the walls were shelves filled with art, all depicting people moving. Greek vase of athletes running. Mayan statue of a handball player. Roman bronze of a discus thrower. *Guy must be some kind of athlete,* Jefferson thought.

Lyerman himself was seated behind the desk watching them.

"Hello, Detectives, thank you for coming up to see me," Lyerman said. "Did you find your way here all right?"

And then Lyerman moved out from behind the desk. Only he wasn't walking, he was gliding. Seated in an electric wheelchair, his right index finger sliding over a small plastic panel attached to the side of the chair. Jefferson stared for a moment longer than he should have.

"I can see you're surprised," Lyerman said. "Didn't expect to find a cripple?"

"No, no, it's not that," Jefferson said. "Well, I just thought that, with all the art, you'd be . . . you know . . ."

"A runner?"

"Something like that, yeah."

"Not in sixty-five years, I'm afraid. My neck, my head, and my right index finger, that's all I'm left with."

They stood around for a moment more. no one speaking. Then Jefferson was surprised to notice there was someone else in the room. A little guy, about five-six, very thin. He looked Central American, and he was wearing a white cotton suit, which stood out sharply against the black of the room. Maybe Jefferson was surprised because he hadn't noticed the man from the start.

Then Brogan nodded. "Like that hallway."

"I'm glad you enjoyed it, it's something we're very proud of. Fully interactive spaces."

"What is that?"

"We've become accustomed to our surroundings being completely static. When you stand in a room, you expect a picture on the wall to be the same when you leave the room as when you entered. What if, however, that picture could change to reflect your mood? Calm images for a calm mood. Happy images for a happy mood. And so on. The decor of the room actually reflecting how an individual feels at any given moment. You think something is one way, but then it changes to be something completely different."

"Sounds deceptive."

Lyerman shrugged. "People don't want to face reality. That's why we have television."

"And that's what VisionWare is working on?"

"Among other things."

Lyerman turned, and the chair whined its way toward the desk. The thin man stepped forward a foot until he was standing behind his boss. Up close, his skin was very tight against his bones and so smooth that it shone under the lights. As he moved, the cuff of his right sleeve rode up slightly, revealing a small blue-and-white flag tattooed on his wrist. Panamanian, Jefferson decided, definitely. Lyerman still hadn't acknowledged the man, nor had the Panamanian looked at either of the two detectives. Instead, he kept his gaze straight forward, fixed on a point somewhere at the end of Lyerman's desk.

Lyerman turned the chair around behind the desk, faced the two detectives, and waited. He already knew that his son was dead. He'd found the bodies himself. Jefferson had gotten used to the fact that most parents can't stop talking when they find out. Telling homicide detectives about how their son was just accepted to college or was the star catcher on his high-school baseball team, or any number of stories that would let them forget the fact that their son was sitting in a bag somewhere on his way to the medical examiner's office.

But not Lyerman. This guy was ready to wait it out.

"First off, Mr. Lyerman," Jefferson said, "let me just express my sympathies for you on your loss."

"Thank you. I appreciate the sentiment."

"We just have to ask you a few routine questions here. About what time did you originally find the . . . your son?"

"Sometime close to midnight."

"And what did you do?"

"I called the police."

"When was that?"

"I couldn't say really."

"About."

"I really couldn't say. I lost track of time."

"OK, that's all right, we'll have it on record."

The Panamanian hadn't moved once during the conversation, concentration fixed on the far corner of the desk. *He must be Lyerman's helper,* Jefferson thought. He looked more closely, noticing a small scar over the right temple, a line of white that didn't reflect the lights. The man's eyes suddenly flicked up like a lizard's, catching and holding Jefferson's for a moment, then they were back again, staring at the desk. Jefferson decided that the guy gave him the creeps.

"Mr. Lyerman," Brogan was saying, "does your son have a personal bodyguard?"

Lyerman nodded. "Yes. He does."

"Why is that? Were you afraid for his safety?"

"Only in the general sense," Lyerman said. "I'm a very wealthy man, Detective Jefferson. Money can cause problems for those who have it. I hired a bodyguard for my son to prevent these problems from occurring."

"Was he on duty tonight?"

"No, he wasn't."

"Why not?"

"My son sent him home, apparently. I don't really know why."

"Do you have his number?" Jefferson asked. "We'd like to contact him."

"My man up front will give it to you," Lyerman said.

"Mr. Lyerman, we found a doll on the roof," Brogan said. "Does that mean anything to you?"

"A doll?"

Lyerman suddenly looked very tired and old.

Jefferson glanced sideways toward Brogan, then said to Lyerman, "You OK?"

"Yes, I'm sorry. What were you saying?"

"The doll we found. Mean anything to you?"

"No, it doesn't."

"Don't you want to see it first, before you decide?"

"Yes, you're right. Perhaps I should see it."

Jefferson took doll out of the plastic evidence bag and, leaning across the desk, held it up in front of Lyerman. Lyerman looked at it for a moment, staring at its blank face, and shook his head. "No, I'm sorry."

"No problem," Jefferson replied, putting the doll back in its evidence bag.

"Now"—Brogan was peering at the floor, his eyebrows knitted in thought—"I'm very curious about something. I've been thinking about it, and I can't figure it out."

"What's that?"

"Well, the first call to 911. The one logged in at ten-fifteen from this location."

"What about it?"

"That was a Breaking and Entering call," Brogan said. "Who called that in?"

"I'm not sure," Lyerman replied.

"Huh. Then four minutes later, a second call was placed to 911, canceling the alarm."

"Again, I'm not sure," Lyerman replied. "It's very possible."

"Do you know who placed that second call?"

"No, I don't," Lyerman replied.

Brogan reached into his pocket and pulled out a slip of paper. "Call was logged as coming from a Harold Thompson. Name sound familiar to you?"

"Not really, no," Lyerman answered. "My office manager might be able to help you there. I have a lot of employees."

Brogan nodded, then said, "So after the first call is placed, you go up to the roof and find the two victims. That correct?"

"As I said, I wasn't aware the first call was even placed. But if you're asking if I went up to the roof shortly after 10:15, the answer is no."

"No? But you did go up to the roof? And when was that?"

"I did go up to the roof. But it was after the security guard called up here, some-time shortly before midnight," Lyerman replied.

"You in the habit of going outside while it's raining? You can do that all right in that thing?" Brogan pointed to Lyerman's wheelchair.

"It wasn't raining then."

"Uh-huh. And how long after you first found the bodies did you notify the police."

"Roughly?"

Brogan cleared his throat sharply, looking up from taking notes. "Yes, Mr. Lyerman, roughly."

"About twenty minutes."

Brogan's eyes opened, pretending to be surprised. "Twenty minutes? Why so long?"

"I wanted to be alone with my son."

"OK. And who did you call?"

"The police, as I said."

"Nine-one-one?

"No. A friend of mine in the department."

"Why not just 911?"

Lyerman closed his eyes and put his head back, as if he were thinking out a difficult problem. "I'm not sure I understand the reasoning behind these questions."

"You don't have to understand the reasoning," Brogan replied. "I don't care either way if you understand."

"Well, I don't waste my time answering questions that are asked for no reason."

Brogan and Lyerman stared at each other across the desk, their mutual hostility evident.

Lyerman smiled, then said, "Detective Brogan, would you please come around the desk. I want to tell you something privately. Detective Jefferson, would you mind standing by the door for a moment?"

Brogan glanced back at Jefferson, who was moving to the door, then walked around the desk to stand next to it. Lyerman moved his index finger, a gesture Brogan almost missed, indicating that Brogan should come even closer. When Brogan was close enough to satisfy Lyerman, Lyerman stared at him and spoke so low that at first it was difficult for Brogan to catch what was said.

As Brogan finally understood Lyerman's words, his fist went white knuckle. Slowly he stood up, backing away from Lyerman, his eyes angry. Killer eyes. Eyes that came out right before Brogan took a brick to someone's head. Jefferson, stepping away from the door, heard a faint hissing sound from the wall. He turned and saw Plexiglas panels sliding down over the works of art on the wall. Noticing Jefferson's glance, Lyerman broke the stare with an amused smile, looking up toward the Plexiglas panels.

"That, up there on the wall"—Lyerman raised his head, indicating the artwork— "it's valued at just a shade over eight million dollars. The wall has sensors to detect rises in body temperature. A rise in body temperature may indicate an increase in anger, and therefore a higher probability someone may have a violent outburst that could endanger the pieces."

Lyerman continued to look at the wall; the Plexiglas barriers were locked into place.

"I guess one of us is angry," he said with a faint smile.

Jefferson looked at his watch. "Well, I don't want to take up too much of your time. Soo . . ."

He glanced at Brogan. Brogan shrugged.

". . . I guess we'll get going," Jefferson finished.

Lyerman nodded. "Thank you for coming to see me."

Jefferson and Brogan turned to leave. As they reached the doors, they heard Lyerman's voice from behind them. "Detectives?"

"Yes," said Jefferson.

"That picture of my son you found."

"Yes?"

"I won't need it."

"No?"

"When you're in this chair," Lyerman said, "you learn to remember things in your mind. I've got all the pictures I need right there."

Jefferson nodded silently, then Brogan pushed open the office doors, and they stepped out. As they walked down the hallway, Jefferson heard the faint hiss of the Plexiglas barriers over the artwork sliding back into the wall.

"What the hell was that about?" Jefferson asked, as they stepped outside.

"What?"

"Whatever just happened in there. What did Lyerman say to you?"

Brogan shook his head. "You don't want to know."

That was as far as the conversation was going to go. Jefferson nodded as they passed out of the long redwood forest hallway. They pushed open the double glass doors and stepped into the lobby on the other side. The Samoan guard in the purple shirt was waiting for them. He nodded as they stepped toward him.

"Mr. Lyerman called and said you had a request concerning one of our employees. I've written the guard's personal information on this card. He is still an employee with Mr. Lyerman, so he's under certain obligations, but there would be no problem if you wanted to go speak with him."

The guard stiffly handed Jefferson the card. Jefferson took it with two hands. Still holding the card, Jefferson nodded his thanks, and the two officers left the lobby and stepped into the elevator.

In the elevator, Jefferson glanced at the card for the Lyerman kid's private body-guard.

Harold Thompson, 200 Harbor Street, Apt 3.

It was the name of the man who had made the original 911 call.

When they got outside, the rain had stopped. The black night sky had turned a dull gray under the flashing lights of the patrol cars. An ambulance was parked just outside the double glass doors of the Lyerman Building. The back of the ambulance was open, and two men in white EMT outfits were loading a stretcher covered in a white sheet into the back. Brogan and Jefferson paused for a moment to watch. A pale female hand slipped out from underneath the sheet as the two men lifted the stretcher. Jefferson caught a glimpse of neatly painted red fingernails.

Overheard, Jefferson heard a humming noise and saw a helicopter for Fox TV gliding by, lit sharply against the buildings.

Brogan sighed. "Jesus, poor girl. What the hell is she doing mixing with a guy like Lyerman?"

"Money?" Jefferson responded, turning back toward their car.

"Yeah, I guess. Don't much seem worth it now though."

"Never does." Jefferson opened the car door. "After the fact, anyway."

Harold Thompson lived in the market district, close to the waterfront. Even late at night, crowds of people filled the sidewalks around them, spilling out into the street in an endless flow around their car. In the backseat lay the doll they had found on the roof. It was sealed in a plastic evidence bag, its porcelain eyes staring upward, the frown still fixed on its face.

Brogan was looking quietly out the window.

"How did Lyerman know about the photograph of his son?" Brogan asked suddenly.

"What?"

"That photograph of Lyerman's son skiing. We found it in the son's robe."

"So?"

"So how did Lyerman know it was there?" Brogan asked quickly. "I only told you about it when we were in the elevator."

"Maybe he knew his son carried it with him."

Brogan shook his head and pulled something from his pocket.

"Jesus, man," Jefferson said, looking at the photograph. "That's supposed to be evidence. You can't just take that with you."

Brogan waved his hand dismissively. "Look at the development date on the back of the picture. It's only last week. I don't even think Lyerman knew the picture existed until tonight."

"You think he had his lackey search the bodies on the roof before calling us?"

Brogan shook his head. "No. I think he was listening to our conversation on the elevator. They've got cameras everywhere in that building, they must be able to listen, too."

"Probably."

"What if there are tapes for that?" Brogan said. "Even if we can't get the visual tapes of the murder. What if we can listen to the audiotapes, if there were recording devices on the roof."

"We'll ask Thompson," Jefferson said. "Maybe he knows."

After passing Harold Thompson's address and finding a parking space, Jefferson turned the wheel slowly, maneuvering the car toward the sidewalk. The crowd around them was unyielding, and their sluggish movements threatened to hit the pedestrians. Brogan rolled down his window and stuck his head out, waving one hand wildly.

He pulled his head back inside.

"Fucking zoo," he snorted. "Use the lights."

Jefferson nodded and flipped on the lights, blaring a short burst of the siren. Heads around them turned toward their car, attracted by the sudden flashing blue. Slowly, people began moving aside. Turning off the siren, the two officers stepped out into the warm city night. The summer air was fragrant with the smells of cooking. Brogan adjusted his tie and sniffed delicately.

As they walked back toward the building they had passed, the street vendors began to pack up and leave. Stretching along the sidewalk were small plain doorways set into rounded stone alcoves. Jefferson paused before a metal door painted brown.

He glanced at the address card in his hand. "This looks like it."

"It locked?" asked Brogan.

Jefferson reached out and cautiously tried the handle. The door clicked softly and swung inward.

"Nope."

Reaching beneath his coat, Brogan slid his Beretta up and quietly pulled back the slide. With a metallic *clink*, he chambered the first round, before sliding the gun back underneath his coat. Jefferson looked at him and raised his eyebrows slightly.

Brogan shrugged. "As far as we know, this could be the guy that did it. Better safe than sorry . . . you know?"

Jefferson nodded, and the two men slowly opened the door. Inside was a small vestibule. The floor was covered with peeling plastic tiles, and the room smelled of urine. Along the wall was a short row of metal mailboxes. Jefferson glanced at them quickly; most of the names had peeled off or were written in pen directly onto the boxes themselves, previous owners' names crossed out as new tenants moved in.

THOMPSON was printed neatly in block letters on an old piece of masking tape across the box for Apartment 3. Jefferson nudged Brogan and tapped the metal with his finger.

"This place is a shit hole," said Brogan, looking at his newly polished shoes, then up at pool of slushy liquid at the base of the doorway. "Shouldn't have worn the dress shoes."

"Guess the bodyguard business isn't paying as well as it used to."

Opposite the entrance was a second dented door, over which was a glass window embedded with chicken wire. There was crack in the glass, like someone had once taken a baseball bat to the window. Through the opening a stairway led up and out of sight. Brogan tried the door, but the knob refused to turn.

"Should we see if he'll buzz us up?" Jefferson asked, looking back toward the rusted intercom on the wall by the door.

"Naw, let's not give him a chance to run," Brogan responded. Taking out a small set of metal tools, Brogan bent over the lock, working to crack it open. After easing a thin rod between the doorframe and the lock, there was a clicking noise, and he pushed the door backward.

Standing back up, Brogan put the kit back into his pocket. "Spent two years working burglary, might as well put that to use."

The two officers slowly climbed the stairs and passed down a long hallway. The doors of the hall were closed. Jefferson heard the muffled noise of a television playing behind one, a couple arguing behind another. They stopped in front of Number 3.

Jefferson rapped lightly on the door.

"Just a minute," came a female voice from deep behind the door.

There was a pause, then the door slid tentatively open an inch. A woman's face appeared at the crack of the doorway, peering out at the two men.

"How's it going?" Brogan said pleasantly. "Is Harold Thompson around? We're old friends of his, and we were in the neighborhood and thought we'd drop in."

"He doesn't live here," the woman said, before making a quick move to shut the door.

Brogan shoved his foot in the doorway, and asked, "Well, do you mind if we come in and look around, Mrs. . . . ?"

Brogan reached into his coat and pulled out his badge.

"Old friends, huh?" The woman stared hard at the gold medallion, before looking at Jefferson, and saying, "You a cop, too?"

Jefferson nodded, trying to smile pleasantly.

"All right, come on in. And it's Ms., not Mrs. My name is Latia."

The door shut for an instant, and they heard the sound of a chain being slid back. A moment later the door reopened, and the woman's back was already to the two men as she walked into her apartment.

"I don't know what you two guys are looking for. I told you, I don't know any Harolds," she said over her shoulder.

The two men fell in behind her as she walked. The apartment was small, but surprisingly clean. A bookcase was just inside the doorway, standing next to a large gilt mirror. To the left, a hallway stretched back, ending in a closed white wooden door. To the right, a doorway opened up into a small living room. Jefferson saw a black leather sofa underneath two windows. Long ivy plants hung from the window frames, and through their green leaves, Jefferson could see the lights of the building next door. The woman turned suddenly, facing them.

"Yeah . . . all right look, let's cut the bullshit, OK?" the woman said, still standing in front of the kitchen. "What the hell you want to speak to Harold about?"

"So you know him?" Brogan asked.

"Yeah, I ain't gonna lie. I know him, but what he's done is all in the past. He served his time already, now he's got himself a job. He's a law-abiding citizen and all. He don't deserve to be getting hassled all the time by you people coming round here."

Putting the statue on the table, Jefferson raised his hands. "Hey, I think we're getting off on the wrong foot here. We're not here for Harold. We just need to ask him a few questions."

Brogan nodded. "That's right."

"Hmm," Latia replied, still standing defensively, one leg cocked forward. "You're not gonna hurt him?"

The two detectives shook their heads.

"This one looks like he's got the crazy bug in him." She pointed at Brogan. "Keep that under control, you hear?"

Looking around, Jefferson noticed a pair of men's pants draped across the back of a faded easy chair in the living room.

"So . . ." said Jefferson casually. "Does Harold live here with you?"

Latia's hands dropped to her side, her defensive posture melting away as she stepped back into the kitchen.

"Yeah, he's here from time to time. You know, he mostly lives here, but sometimes he's out by himself. You know how it is."

She stood by the kitchen sink, pouring a glass of Kool-Aid from a pitcher out of the refrigerator. She held the red liquid up to the light for a moment before taking a sip.

"Is he here now?" Jefferson asked.

She shook her head. "No. He works late tonight."

"Where does he work?" Brogan asked.

"Downtown, security at the Lyerman Building."

"He like working there?"

"Yeah." Latia shrugged. "He says it's all right. Used to work for ComGas till he got laid off about five months ago. He . . ."

Her voice trailed off.

From out in the hallway Jefferson and Brogan heard the sound of footsteps and whistling. Latia looked quickly up from her drink; she seemed genuinely surprised.

The door to the apartment swung open, and a voice said, "Hey, baby, I'm home. I bought some things for dinner."

"Expecting company?" said Brogan softly.

"I got some fish for us, I'll cook tonight if . . ." Harold Thompson's voice trailed off as he entered the living room and saw the two strange men waiting for him.

The room went quiet. The man who entered was big, and his six-foot-six frame filled the small doorway like he was the door itself. His expression didn't seem mean, kind of sleepy if anything, his eyelids partially closed. He was the type of guy that rarely got into fights. Given his size, most people never bothered to start trouble with him.

In his arms he held two large paper bags. Jefferson saw a box of spaghetti poking out the top of one of them. "You Harold Thompson?" asked Brogan.

"Yeah," replied the big man tentatively. "Who are you guys?" Then, looking over at the woman, he added, "You all right, baby?"

"I'm all right," she replied.

"I'm Detective Jefferson, this is Lieutenant Brogan. We'd just like to ask you a few questions."

"Yeah, sure," replied Harold. "What about?"

Harold squeezed past them in the narrow hallway and stepped into the kitchen. Laying the bags on the counter, he began removing the groceries inside and placing them neatly next to the refrigerator.

"Go ahead, I'm listening," Harold said as he pulled out a glass bottle of spaghetti sauce and opened the refrigerator door.

"You are a bodyguard for Kenneth Lyerman, correct?" Brogan asked.

"That's right."

"Why was that? Was Kenneth receiving threats?"

Harold paused for a moment, holding three tomatoes in the palm of one of his huge hands. He shook his head. "Not that I know of, but he's a rich kid, they always got enemies somewhere."

"Well, it's a funny thing there, Harold," Brogan began.

"Yeah, what's that?"

"We heard you were sticking around Kenneth so as he didn't knock around any of his lady friends. But that's just something we heard, nothing to that, right?"

Harold stopped unloading the groceries and looked at the two officers. He leaned over and whispered something in Latia's ear, kissing her on the cheek after he finished speaking. She nodded and left the room with her Kool-Aid, walking back down the hall and disappearing behind the closed door. Jefferson heard the muffled voices of a television being turned on.

The groceries all on the counter, Harold began folding up the brown paper bags. "What is this about?"

"Kenneth Lyerman was found after midnight on the roof of the Lyerman Building. Murdered. Him and this young woman," Brogan responded.

Harold exhaled sharply and shook his head. "Damn."

"He was all cut up. Pretty bad, looks vicious," Brogan said, trying to gauge the man's reaction.

Harold gripped the kitchen counter for a moment before looking up. "You two want to go sit in the living room and talk?"

"Yeah, sure," Jefferson said.

The three men made their way into the small living room. Harold pulled up a chair in front of the leather sofa and gestured for the two detectives to sit. Jefferson sat on the sofa, sinking comfortably into the soft leather. Brogan sat next to him.

Harold sat in the chair opposite, hanging his head slightly. "I always knew that boy was in for trouble sometime, but getting himself killed? Man, I had no idea it'd end like that."

"What do you mean he was 'in for trouble sometime'?" Jefferson asked, pulling his notebook out.

"Well, just things I'd heard. Like he'd got cleaned out by the Super Bowl, had to square with some dude, that he knocked up some girl and she had to get an abortion. Things like that."

Jefferson pulled the plastic-covered doll from his coat pocket and showed it to Harold. "You ever seen anything like this before?"

Harold took the doll, the plastic crinkling in his hand. "No. Looks Chinese though."

"What makes you say that?"

"Chinese lettering on the back of the robe. Means good life and luck. I've got the same symbols tattooed on my arm."

Brogan nodded.

"You mentioned something about him having a gambling debt," Brogan said. "To who?"

"Aww, man, let me see." Harold closed his eyes and dropped his head, trying to remember the name. "Chinese guy, uhh . . . something Lee, I think."

"They all got names like something Lee. Can you remember better'n that?" Brogan asked impatiently.

Harold snapped his fingers and looked up. "Richard Lee. That's the dude's name. He's up in Chinatown. Got a restaurant called the Green Tea."

"What about tonight? Did you work tonight?" Jefferson asked.

"Sure."

"What time did you start?"

"Around six, just after dinner."

"And what happened?"

"Not much. Kenneth went out around eight-thirty to this club downtown, called Apollo. I was with him there for about an hour, before he met this girl he used to know. Real nice girl, Jill, I think. Anyway, he wanted to leave after that, so I drove him back to the Lyerman Building."

"Then what happened?"

"He and the girl went up to the roof. I waited on the floor below, making sure nobody went up."

"Did anyone try and get up there?"

Harold shook his head. "No, but . . ."

"But what?"

"About thirty minutes later Ken comes running down, saying he saw someone up there. I went up, checked out the whole roof, but didn't find anything. Ken was convinced though, so I called the police."

"He said he saw someone up there?" Brogan said. "Must have been hard for someone to get up to the roof and you not see them."

"Impossible for anyone to get past me, I was standing right at the doorway."

"And you didn't go the bathroom or leave at any point?"

"Nope."

"They have alarms up on the roof?" Brogan asked.

"Sure."

"What kind?"

Harold smiled slowly. "I can't really tell anyone how the alarm system works. It's part of my contract."

"Motion sensors?"

"I can't really say."

Brogan sighed, exasperated. "C'mon, we're here on a murder investigation. You telling me you can't say?"

"I don't know," Harold said dully, his eyes glazing over.

"What about the aud—" Brogan began, but Jefferson cut him off quickly.

"Of course you don't know," Jefferson said soothingly. "You don't want to tell anyone anything you shouldn't and then lose your job. Mr. Lyerman is very strict about things. He doesn't want anyone to know about how tight security is."

"Damn right." Harold livened up. "Never seen it so tight in my whole life."

"We were talking to Lyerman about the system's audiotapes," Jefferson fished. "How it's difficult to keep track of all the tapes."

"They're not that difficult," Harold said. "He keeps them all in order chronologically, then just reuses the tapes every four days."

There were audiotapes of the roof; Jefferson kept still.

Instead, he changed the subject. "So Lyerman told you to call off the alarm?"

"That's correct," Harold agreed. "Told me to call the dispatcher and tell them to cancel the alarm. He was in a big rush, too."

Brogan chuckled. "Probably couldn't wait to get back up to that woman on the roof."

Harold looked at him for a moment, his face confused.

"No," Harold said after a moment. "It wasn't Kenneth that told me to cancel the alarm. It was Mr. Lyerman, Kenneth's father, who told me. I don't even know how he knew. The man must have eyes in the back of his head."

The streets were empty by the time they stepped out of Harold's apartment, the only sound the rattle of cars on the highway overhead. Jefferson sat on the curb while Brogan walked to get their car. *At 8 P.M., Dombey starts working the night shift in the security room. At 10 P.M., Kenneth, the girl, and Harold arrive at the building. Around 10:15 P.M., Harold places a call to 911. Four minutes later, Lyerman calls off the alarm. Why?*

And if there were security cameras all over the building, how did anyone get up to the roof to commit the murder?

Brogan pulled up alongside the curb, head out the open window. "You ready, brother?"

Jefferson joined him in the car.

"You want to check out this Richard Lee tonight? See what he's got to say about Kenneth's gambling debt?"

Jefferson checked his watch. It was 2:30 A.M.

"You think it's too late?" he asked.

"Yeah, I'm sure Chinese Triad gang members go to bed around nine. He's probably all tucked in to sleep now, we better not disturb him."

"All right, we'll check him out now. You know where he's at?"

"Yeah, I know where he'll be," Brogan said, pressing the gas, the car lurching beneath them like the beginning of a roller coaster.

Just past midnight, Ron Saint sat in his apartment eating the last of a cold pizza he'd removed from the refrigerator. The dough was moist and flimsy, but he kept chewing, driven by hunger. Through the open window, a soft breeze carried in the sounds of someone's car radio playing in the street outside. As he pushed the last piece of crust into his mouth, he heard the slight banging of a bed against the wall of the next room. Saint knew the sex habits of each of his neighbors. He couldn't avoid it—whenever the room was quiet he could hear them.

His television was on, turned to a rerun of *Jeopardy*. Keeping his eyes on the screen, he took a sip from his soda. The groaning next door was becoming louder. Saint was having trouble hearing the answers to the questions on the show.

He found out that he was much better at *Jeopardy* since he had gotten out of Blade Prison, got more of the answers now. He'd done some reading in there, had a little bit more knowledge about things like Lakes of the World and Shakespearean Quotes. He'd also put on thirty pounds of muscle while in jail and learned to fight, knocking his way up to lightheavy champion of the Massachusetts prison system. Not much to do when you're doing time except read, lift weights, and box.

"Hey!" He pounded against the wall.

The phone rang.

"What's up, Saint, how you doing, man?"

Saint paused before answering. "I'm all right, Five, what's up?"

"Man, we got a job we're doing. A lawyer's place in Beacon Hill."

"A job? When?"

"Right now, tonight. In an hour."

Next door the groaning was rising to a furious pace. The banging against the wall was growing louder. Saint could hear springs creaking.

"Yeah, so? What's that got to do with me?" Saint answered.

"We want you in on this. We need a big guy like you."

"What's the job?"

"Nothing big, don't worry, nobody gets hurt. We figure we pull about five grand each. It's a document someone wants. A manuscript. All we gotta do is take it."

"You know I'm out of all that. I'm working now," Saint said, playing with a loose piece of pizza crust.

"Doing what?"

"Maintenance."

"Yeah, bullshit, I talked to Thompson. He said you're cleaning toilets at Wakefield Elementary. What you making there? Seven bucks an hour?"

"Seven twenty-five." Saint leaned forward and changed the television channel. A baseball game came on. The Sox were playing out on the West Coast.

"Yeah, well, why you home tonight, it's a Friday?"

"I'm sick."

"Yeah, right, you home on a Friday because your boss got you working at 5 A.M. six days a week. And if you don't show, he calls the parole office, tells them you violated or some shit. Besides, even if you didn't have to work tomorrow morning, you think you'd be out with a girl? Shit, what kinda girl is gonna want a muscle-bound ex-con making seven bucks . . . oh, excuse me, seven twenty-five an hour."

Saint paused, looking around his apartment. The paint was flaking off one of the window frames. He'd meant to fix that, but just hadn't had the time.

"So you in?" Five's voice repeated.

The phone hissed static for a moment. Saint listened to the groaning next door slowly dying down into a relieved moan. He pressed the telephone against his lips.

"Yeah. I'm in."

They picked him up twenty minutes later. The black '86 Buick Century rolled up outside his apartment before coming to a stop with the motor running. Five was driving, and a man named Q was sitting in the passenger seat. Saint sat down in back, squeezing in next to a large stuffed bear, still wrapped in clear plastic.

"Hey, move that over," Five said, turning his head back. "That's for my baby girl's birthday."

Saint pushed the bear to the other side of the car, where it sat in the corner, staring at him with its big, round, plastic eyes.

"Where we going?"

"Beacon Hill," Five answered, turning the wheel and pulling out into the almost empty street.

Q laughed at something. He was sitting in front of Saint and drinking gin out of a plastic Gatorade bottle. He was wearing a black-and-white warm-up suit, the plastic swishing as he moved his arms.

Saint crinkled his nose. "You wearing cologne, Q?"

Q laughed again. "Yeah, man, I'm swinging by an old girl's place later."

On the dash, the green luminous numbers of the clock read just after one o'clock. Q was shaking his head and keeping time to a song he was singing by beating his hand against the top of his knee.

Five kept driving, looking straight forward.

"Damn," Q mumbled to himself, his eyes glazed. He leaned in closer to Five, his voice lowered some, but Saint could still hear. "Man, how much we figure to get tonight?"

Five turned his head away from Q, his face disgusted. "Damn, Q, your breath stinks. How much you have to drink?"

Q shrugged and leaned back in his seat. "Whatever."

Five leaned forward and turned on the radio, pushing the buttons and flipping through the stations. An old song came on, reminding Saint dimly of high school.

"What the hell you putting this bullshit song on for?" Q slurred, reaching for the radio and turning the dial.

Saint shook his head and looked out the window. They were passing through Chinatown. Neon signs lit the windows of shops, the Chinese characters glowing and flashing in red and orange. They stopped at a red, and Saint glanced in through the window of a late-night take-out restaurant. He saw a single waiter in a white outfit slowly mopping the restaurant's tile floor. Another man in a black, hooded sweatshirt was pounding on the restaurant's glass window, trying to get the waiter's attention.

The light changed to green, and the car moved off, the restaurant passing out of view.

"How we getting in here?" Saint asked.

"I know a man," Five replied.

"Who?"

"A man," Five answered simply. "He used to be a guard, at Blade."

"A guard? What the hell you trust him for?"

"Naw, he's cool. He ain't like that. He got fired at Blade, so now he's looking out for his own self. I met him when I was doing time there for that misunderstanding."

The misunderstanding had been that Five had shot someone outside a club in Boston.

"Why'd he get fired?" Saint asked.

"I dunno, something about him snooping around Blade where he wasn't supposed to be," Five answered. "But he says he'll pay us each five thousand if we can get this manuscript tonight. This lawyer, Timothy Sinatra, he got it now, he's some kinda art collector. We get it and sell it to Older. Plus whatever else we rip off Sinatra, that's just cream on the cereal, know what I mean?"

Saint thought for a moment. If Five was telling them they'd each get five grand, then that probably meant the real figure was twenty grand or so. Five had a way of skimming off the top.

Q leaned forward, reaching underneath the seat. He pulled out something made of black metal that gleamed in the passing streetlights. Holding it in front of his face, he caressed the metal with his hand. It was a Beretta 9mm handgun.

Saint looked out the window, pretending not to notice.

"Hey, put that down, man," Five said, pushing Q's arm below the car window. "You don't want someone seeing us drive by with that shit."

Q lowered the gun onto his lap. He pulled the slide back with a sharp metallic *click*, chambering the first round. He murmured something to himself and raised the gun again, sighting along the barrel at a woman walking down the street carrying a white plastic bag of groceries in each hand. Q pursed his lips, making the sound of a gunshot with his throat, his hand pulling up in a mock recoil as he aimed at the woman.

"What the fuck did I just say, Q? Put the damn gun down."

"Damn. All right." Q shrugged and put the gun back into his lap.

Five shook his head, staring forward out the windshield. "Jesus."

They passed out of Chinatown, heading for Beacon Hill. Near the Boston Common, the car stopped at another light. Five men were huddled together in the cold, their breath rising in thin plumes above their heads as they talked.

Q took another drink from the Gatorade bottle of gin.

"See, this here is some inventive shit, man." Q pointed to the Gatorade bottle. "I put my drinks in this plastic bottle so it never breaks. And when I'm done, I just screw the cap back on"—Q demonstrated by screwing the white cap back on—"to prevent spillage and shit. It's like revolutionized the way I drink my alcohol."

Five nodded and smiled. "Yeah."

Q started playing with the gun again, pretend firing it.

Out the window, Saint saw they'd driven into Beacon Hill. The streets were lined with cobblestone sidewalks, while gas lamps flickered inside their glass cages. Around them, older brick buildings rose, heavy bronze knockers on the doors. Expensive cars were parked quietly along the street—Saint caught glimpses of a few blue Volvos and a black Mercedes.

Slowing the car, Five braked and looked out the windshield at the buildings around them.

"All right, it's around here somewhere," he said, driving more slowly.

The streets were narrow and one-way, the sidewalks empty and quiet. They passed a small park of vacant benches and bare-limbed trees.

Five pulled up, parked the car, and turned off the ignition. "We're here."

"Yeah." Q smiled and gripped the weapon tightly in his hand.

"Which one?" Saint asked.

"There." Five pointed to a nice four-story brick building, on the corner of the one-way street. Saint saw a narrow cobblestone driveway extending back behind the brick house. On the third floor, Saint saw that one of the windows was lit. Something was flickering inside, the soft glow of a television, and as he watched, someone passed by the window, visible just for an instant. Something else in the room was glowing a soft red, but from the street Saint couldn't see what it was.

Five nodded, seeing the movement inside. "OK, good, they're still up."

Five pulled a .22 from underneath the seat and slipped it into his pocket. "All right, we set?"

Saint nodded, and Five opened the car door, the overhead light turning on and cold air streaming inside. Saint stepped out, joining Q on the sidewalk. Together, the three men walked toward the building. Saint glanced up again at the lit window. Nothing was moving, only the flickering of the television set.

Q pushed his hands deep into the pockets of his jumpsuit, walking with his shoulders pulled up, the plastic swishing around his legs.

"What the hell you wear those pants for, Q?" Five asked, looking at the wind pants as they walked. "You can fucking hear those things a block away. You see any gyms around? You think we're gonna be working out tonight?"

Q shook his head, smiling. "Man, like I said, I'm seeing my girl after this. And this outfit makes me look good."

Five shook his head. "What the fuck's wrong with you, Q? You have an attention deficit disorder? Are you aware of what we're doing out here? We're about to rob these motherfuckers, and you're thinking about looking good for your girl. Fuck, man, I don't understand how someone intelligent enough to come up with putting his drinks in a plastic bottle can be so stupid sometimes."

Q scoffed, and murmured, "Hey, all I know is that I look good. I'm doing this robbing in style."

The three men walked toward the driveway, pausing for a moment, looking around. The streets around them were empty.

Moving forward, they walked up the driveway, passing behind the brick building until they were out of view of the street. A black Land Rover was parked in the driveway, and Q paused a moment to admire the leather interior. Behind Sinatra's building was a tiny space of grass and a chain-link fence that blocked off an alley. Lining the strip of grass was a brick wall, and pressed up against the wall was a small garden. A short set of five stairs led down from a green metal door near the brick wall. The windows on either side of the door were both illuminated, the lights inside turned on.

"OK, we'll get in through here. They put a spare key under the fourth brick over from the stairs," Five whispered.

He pulled three black shapes from out of his pockets. "Here, take these."

They were ski masks.

They all took the black masks. Saint and Five put theirs on. Q stood there, felt the fabric with his fingers, then turned the mask inside out.

"What the hell are you doing?" Five asked.

"I can't wear this shit. This shit's 30 percent wool. It'll make my face break out," Q said, reading the label on the inside of the mask.

"What?"

"I told you, I can't wear a wool mask. I need something softer or it'll chafe my skin."

Five shook his head. "I can't believe I'm hearing this."

"Sorry, man, I can't rob these people unless I'm comfortable," Q repeated. "Maybe if you put a little more money into our equipment, this wouldn't happen. There's a convenience store down the street. I'll run over and see if they got something that's all cotton."

Five pushed his hand into his pocket, rummaging around. He pulled out something white and shimmering and shoved it toward Q.

"What the fuck's this?" Q said, holding the white silken thing.

"Panty hose."

"Panty hose?" Q shook his head. "Where the fuck you get 'em?"

"They're my girlfriend's. She left them at my place, and I was bringing them back to her."

"Man, I ain't gonna wear your girlfriend's nasty drawers on my head," Q whined, holding the white panty hose. "Who the fuck you think I am?"

"You're acting like a fucking bitch. Shut up and let's do this," Five said, clenching his .22 tightly.

Q paused for a moment before he shrugged. "All right, man, cool. I'll put this shit on, but you just remember who's got the bigger gun."

Q took the white panty hose and pulled them over his face, mashing his features beyond recognition. One of the stockings legs dangled limply around his chest.

"Ooh, these are smooth. Your girlfriend must have nice legs, man," Q whispered.

Ignoring him, Five was bent over the bricks, lifting them to search for the key. He walked toward the door holding the silver-colored key in his hand. He slipped the key into the lock and turned it. The door opened smoothly. Light flooded out from the hallway. The other two men joined him, stepping in through the back of Sinatra's building.

They were standing in the lawyer's small laundry room. A washing machine and dryer stood in the corner. On the floor by the door were piles of old newspapers and boxes of empty soda cans waiting to be taken out to the curb for recycling. Ahead of them, a long hallway stretched, ending at the front door of the building. A twisting circular staircase descended from the floor above, meeting on the right with the hallway.

From somewhere above Saint heard the subdued voices of a television set playing softly in one of the rooms.

"Saint, you take the front door and keep your eyes open," Five whispered, pointing to him. "The two of us'll go upstairs."

Q was holding tightly to the Beretta, keeping it pointed up. He began to move forward, his wind pants swishing together as he walked. The sound seemed to travel up the hallway.

"Shit, Q, you gotta take those pants off, they're gonna hear us coming," Five said.

"I'm not taking my pants off! You crazy?"

"Damn, man, you don't have to be embarrassed about your skinny-ass chicken legs, I already seen them before."

"Shit, you think I'm embarrassed? Fuck it." He pulled his pants to his ankles until he was standing in just his boxers. "I'll rob these people butt-fucking naked if I have to."

His boxers were silk, covered in red hearts, with the words "I Love You Baby" across the back.

There was a pause as Saint and Five stood staring at him. Five started trembling, holding his hand over his mouth, the corners of his lips rising in a smile. Q stood in front of them, the white panty hose over his head, his pants around his ankles, wearing the ridiculous boxers.

"Q, man, what the fuck?" Saint whispered through a smile.

"Man, I didn't know I'd be showing you guys these. Like I said, I'm going to my girlfriend's after this. She gave me these boxers for my birthday, so she likes it when I wear them." Q slipped his pants over his shoes and piled them on the floor. "Yeah, so fuck y'all, laugh all you want. We'll see what's up when she's giving me what I need." Q pointed to himself.

"Jesus, man, we don't even need these guns now. You show yourself upstairs wearing all that, they'll give us the manuscript just to get you outta here," Five whispered.

"Yeah, OK, are you done here? Can we get this show going? I thought we were robbing someone, because I know I didn't come all the way over here just to hang out by some dude's washing machine."

Five nodded. "OK, let's go then."

Q left his pants in a pile on the floor, and the three men walked quietly through the hall of the lawyer's house. Five and Q turned to the right, heading slowly up the stairs, their guns held in front, Q in his boxers, wearing the white stockings over his head. Saint stationed himself by the front door, glancing out the window. The street was empty, the flames from the gas lamps flickering silently in their glass encasements. Near the lawyer's door was a dining room with the lights dark, and farther on Saint glimpsed a large kitchen. Heavy-looking pots were hanging from hooks on the ceiling.

From upstairs someone screamed, then he heard Q's voice, the words indistinct but the tone angry and loud. Glass shattered from above.

"Don't do anything stupid, Q," Saint whispered to himself.

Saint checked his watch. They'd only been in the house for seven minutes. The downstairs was quiet, and Saint glanced around the room. A long Oriental carpet reached down the hallway, running under a chandelier, whose multitude of glass arms hung loosely like the tentacles of an octopus. The dining room was dark, the pale glow from streetlamps casting elongated shadows across the floor.

There was a table just inside the dining room, something sitting on top of it. A roll of yellowed papers tied with a piece of string. Saint moved to the papers, slowly unrolling them and spreading them out on the table. This was it. What they'd been looking for. Damn, that was easy. Easiest five grand Saint ever made! Saint rolled the papers up again, slipping them inside his jacket pocket.

He turned to call upstairs to Five and Q, when his eye caught something in the room.

A sharp pain jolted Saint's heart, electrifying his stomach. Someone was in one of the dining room chairs. Sitting still in the dark. Staring right at him. He cried involuntarily from surprise.

The figure in the chair sat frozen.

Saint looked again. "Hello?"

He moved slowly forward. In the dim light from the window, Saint saw that the figure was a woman. She was young, attractive, with short brown hair and wearing a long gray robe that flowed down around her bare feet.

Saint held his hands up, whispering, "Miss?"

She continued to stare forward, her eyes wide, her mouth stretched back in terror. Saint stepped slowly, his hands held up, suddenly feeling guilty.

"I don't want you to be scared, but listen," Saint whispered, glancing cautiously up the stairs. "These guys I'm here with now? These motherfuckers are crazy, so you need to hide before they get down, OK?"

Upstairs he heard another crashing noise, something heavy thudding against the floor.

He moved slowly toward the woman. As he stepped, his foot landed in something dark, pooled on the dining room's polished hardwood floor. She must have spilled something in her fright. In the darkness the liquid looked like thick coffee.

The woman remained motionless, her face terrified. Saint reached out and, with his gloved hand, lightly touched her shoulder. Her head rolled back unnaturally, dangling limply as she stared vacantly up at the ceiling. There was a dark red gaping line across her neck. Her throat had been slit.

"Jesus. Fuck!" Saint hissed in disgust, stepping back from the dead woman. Her head sank to her chest for a moment, carrying her entire body off the chair, where it thudded to the floor.

He backed up through the puddle of dark liquid on the floor, revolted, as her blood stained his white sneakers.

Moving quickly away from the dining room, Saint stepped back out into the hall. His face suddenly felt hot, and he was gasping for breath. He pulled the ski mask up, sucking in the cleaner air, his throat twitching as he fought down a wave of nausea.

What the fuck is happening? Who killed that woman? It couldn't have been Q or Five, I was with them the whole time. Then it occurred to him. *Someone else is in the house with us. A killer.*

Saint turned toward the front door, ready to leave, when he noticed that the door was unlocked.

As he stood there, something pattered softly against his shoulder, a bit of wetness splattering the bare skin of his neck. Raising his hand, his finger came away red. The liquid pattered down again, striking against his ear.

He looked up, toward the source of the drips, turning on the light to see what it was. Above him, there was writing, scrawled across the ceiling,

Fear Him who has the power to cast into hell

The lettering was wide, painted with something red and wet, which dripped, staining the carpet below in blotches. There was a knock on the door to the outside. He quickly turned off the light. Something was standing outside on the stairway, rapping softly. Saint backed away from the door as he heard a grating sound, like long fingernails being drawn across the metal doorframe. Afraid, he turned and ran up the wide staircase toward the second floor. The stairs were covered with thick carpeting, and his feet dug in deeply and silently as he moved. The upstairs was quiet. The living room was to his right, a muted television flickering silently. Two white couches had been placed to the sides of the television, a glass-covered coffee table between them. On the back wall was a mirror, the glass broken and lying in pieces on the floor.

Three china dolls stood on the mantel over a large stone fireplace. One of the dolls had been knocked over, its china head cracked against the hard stone.

In the corner of the room a phone lay off the hook, the busy signal sounding softly. As Saint stood listening, the sound ended abruptly, as if the line had suddenly been cut.

The circular stairway continued to wind upward, toward the third floor. Saint moved cautiously up, his feet sinking into the thick carpet. The floor above had a long hallway, and three rooms, their white doors closed firmly. Saint listened closely, but heard only a faint dripping sound coming from behind one of the closed doors.

He slowly opened the first door; it yielded easily, emitting a faint whisper as it glided over the carpet. Inside was a bedroom. A large, plush bed was pushed against the corner wall, the sheets drawn back and disarranged. The closet doors were open, clothes piled onto the floor. Saint picked up the handle of a phone by the door and put the receiver to his ear. The line was still dead.

The next room was also empty. African masks and the stuffed heads of wild game were mounted on the walls. A gazelle head looked out vacantly, suspended over a large, heavy, polished oak desk. A plush dark leather chair was pulled out from the desk, and on the decorated carpet next to the chair the head of a large caribou had been knocked to the ground, its glassy eyes staring upward.

A large gun cabinet stood in the corner, a series of rifles lined up inside. Saint tried the handle, but the cabinet was locked. Stepping away from the cabinet, he saw the body for the first time.

He was lying on his stomach, his body obscured from the doorway by the large desk. Where the head should have been, there was the stuffed head of a hyena, the lips drawn back in mocking laughter.

There was a door in the back of the room, partially open, a pair of legs showing through it. Saint looked inside and saw Q's boxers, circles of blood glistening on the shimmering fabric. He saw enough to know that Q was dead, mutilated.

Saint shuddered and slowly began backing out of the room. From somewhere below him, lost in the house, he heard a door slam, then the hurried pattering of feet across the floor.

"All right, Saint, be calm," he whispered to himself.

At the end of the hallway was the third door, still closed. Saint advanced cautiously, putting his ear to the wood. Listening, he could hear a soft dripping noise coming from within. The door handle felt cold, his hand clammy against the metal.

Something creaked on the stairway behind him. Turning, he saw a shadow suddenly striking against the wall. Something was on the stairs, silhouetted against the wall of the hallway by the lights of the second floor. The shadow was elongated, almost taking a human form. Except something seemed wrong, almost unnatural. Saint's heart pounded painfully as he stared at the shadow, trying to decide what troubled him. It was as if the figure were stretched out, pulled and lengthened until becoming distorted, almost beyond recognition. The arms were long and ended sharply, the body tall and thin with a strange head that in shadow seemed to have more of a snout than a face, as if some kind of deformed scarecrow were standing on the stairwell.

As he watched, the shadow twitched suddenly, jerking up the stairs silently. Its long arms hung immobile down the sides of its body, its body moved side to side as it crept upward.

Saint turned back to the door with the dripping sound. Turning the knob, he pulled the door open into the hallway. Inside was a white bathtub, suspended off the ground by four porcelain feet. Five was huddled strangely in the tub, and as Saint burst through the door. Five jumped up until he was standing.

"Five, man, Jesus, what the fuck is going on?" Saint cried.

Five remained silent, his body swaying back and forth as he stood, his feet seeming to dangle limply beneath him.

"Five, you all right?"

Five stared at Saint with glazed eyes. A rope had been tied around his neck. Saint's eyes followed the rope up to where it wrapped over a rod on the ceiling and started down again, tying off on the inside knob of the door. Saint touched the rope, uncomprehending, but feeling it taut, as if it were holding a heavy weight.

In the tub, Five was silent, his body continuing to sway. Saint heard the dripping noise again. He watched a droplet of blood collect in a small bulb on the tip of Five's finger, trembling for a moment, before falling into the bathtub.

Five was dead.

The standing was an illusion. He was being suspended by the rope tied around his neck, his entire body pulled upward like a giant marionette puppet. Saint shut the door, and Five's body collapsed back into the tub. Whoever had done this had made it a game. Five's body had been tied to the door. When the door opened, the rope pulled his body up out of the tub. As Saint closed the door, the illusion of life was lost, and Five lay in a crumpled, distorted heap in the tub again.

"Oh God," Saint whispered, fearful tears coming to his eyes.

He turned around the bathroom, looking for an escape. Outside, through the closed door, he heard the stair creak again.

Jefferson and Brogan pulled off 93, heading into Chinatown. Just before 3 A.M., and the hookers were out doing their business, clustered around streetlamps and teetering back and forth on impossibly high shoes. Brogan waved to a few familiar faces as they slowly cruised down one of the side streets. A big black Lincoln Navigator sat parked, engine running, in a small lot, two guys sitting inside, talking on their cell phones and keeping an eye on the girls.

"Look at these two upwardly mobile African-Americans in baseball caps and hockey jerseys," Brogan said, nodding to the pimps in the Navigator as they passed by. "Climbing the urban corporate ladder, amen, brother. God Bless America."

They were driving into Chinatown to meet with Richard Lee, the gangster that Lyerman's bodyguard had mentioned, at the Green Tea, a small tea shop squeezed between an apartment building and a convenience store.

The sign out front of the Green Tea had plain lettering, in both English and Chinese. The doorway was set beneath the sidewalk, with a small concrete stairway leading down.

The two detectives parked the car and walked down to the teahouse. A bell rang somewhere as they opened the glass door. Inside was warm and well lit. A large aquarium, set behind bamboo leaves, bubbled quietly just in front of the doorway. Jefferson saw three enormous goldfish swimming calmly in the tank, their large bug eyes regarding him vacantly.

The aquarium blocked the view into the teahouse. Jefferson had to step farther into the room in order to see the place. The Green Tea was small and sparsely furnished. A few tables with chairs lined the wall, and in the center of the room was a large gray stone. The stone's top had been leveled and smoothed off, creating another table. Three chairs were spaced around the stone, and Jefferson saw a man and two women bent over drinking tea, a black teapot resting in the center of the created table.

They were young, well dressed, and looked like students on their way to a nightclub. Each of them turned to look toward the doorway for a moment as the two men entered, but quickly resumed their conversation.

On the walls hung silken canvases painted softly with black Chinese lettering and images of mist-obscured mountains. A few plants sat in pots along the floor, spaced evenly with colored vases that stood on pedestals. The rest of the tearoom was empty.

"Nice place," Brogan said. He rose on his toes, his arms behind his back, looking around at the nearly empty room. "What is this, help yourself? I don't see anyone who works here."

Soft violin music was playing in the background, just audible over the hushed tones of conversation of the three students. Jefferson heard a door open somewhere in the back, and an attractive blond hostess in a red silk gown appeared from a small alcove at the end of the tearoom. Her hair was long and straight, framing her blue eyes and long eyelashes. She smiled at the two men as she moved toward the front.

"Whoa . . ." Brogan whispered. "I gotta start coming to these teahouses more often."

The blonde paused in front of them. She bit her lower lip and glanced at Jefferson. "Just two of you?"

"Excuse me?" Jefferson asked.

"For tea?" she said. "Just the two of you?"

"Oh no." Jefferson smiled and turned toward Brogan. "We're not here for tea. We're here to speak to Richard Lee."

Her eyebrows darted down for an instant, a tiny wrinkle appearing between them, before she relaxed her face and smiled again. "I don't know if he's here. Can I tell him your names?"

"Sure," Jefferson responded, smiling back. "I'm Detective Jefferson, and this is my partner, Lieutenant Brogan."

Brogan smiled politely.

"One moment," the blonde whispered, and turned away, her hair whisking behind her.

As she walked toward the end of the tearoom, Brogan exhaled.

"Jesus Christ, I can't stop smiling around her."

"I know," Jefferson said. "I couldn't help it. The pope would smile around her."

They watched as the blonde moved smoothly between the tables of the tearoom, disappearing again behind a swinging door. At the sound of Jefferson's voice, the student nearest the door turned around slowly. He had his back to them, but as he turned toward the doorway, Jefferson saw his face.

Jefferson was surprised at how much older he looked from the front. From the side, Jefferson saw a black earpiece in the man's ear, a thin black wire running from the piece and disappearing into the front of his shirt. Jefferson was getting that feeling, that electric tingling just before something went down.

Minutes passed, Jefferson kept his eyes fixed on the man with the earpiece so he was surprised when he heard a voice, "Richard will see you now."

Jefferson looked up to see the hostess smirking at him. The blonde kept her eyes on Jefferson, but nodded toward the man with the knife. "Mr. Lee is an important businessman. Security is tight in his restaurant, especially when two strangers wearing guns arrive in the middle of the night."

"We're police officers," Jefferson said.

"You *say* you are police officers," the hostess corrected. "We had to verify that for ourselves."

She began walking toward the back. Jefferson and Brogan followed close behind. The swinging door in the back of the Green Tea led to a narrow hallway. Shelves stocked with food lined the walls, and open bags of sugar were pushed up against the wall. The narrow walkway was dark and smelled of stale food and vinegar. A security camera mounted on the wall seemed almost out of place. There was nothing there worth guarding.

At the end of the hallway was a red metal door, a peephole in the center. The blonde knocked twice on the door, and Jefferson saw the peephole darken from the other side as someone stuck his eye to the door to see who was knocking. There was a pause, Jefferson heard a chain sliding back, and the door slowly opened.

A heavyset Chinese man with a thin trace of a beard greeted them at the door. He was wearing an orange Nike workout shirt, stretched tight across his chest, matching orange Syracuse hat, and white shorts. A gold stud glittered from his ear as he moved his head.

"Hey, Veronica," the man said, licking his lower lip and staring at the blonde. "How you been?"

"I've been all right, Greg." Veronica smiled, then pointed to Jefferson and Brogan. "These gentleman are here to see Richard."

The man's face hardened for a moment, and he moved slightly in front of the open doorway as he eyed the two officers. "Richard say that was all right?"

"Yeah," Veronica said. "I just talked to him."

Greg shrugged and stepped aside, allowing Veronica, Brogan, and Jefferson to pass. They were making a lot of new friends.

The single room beyond the door was well lit by standing halogen lamps. The floor was carpeted in gray, and a white leather sofa was pushed against the wall. Three kids in their early twenties were lounging on the carpet in front of a Sony wide-screen television playing video games. They were laughing and barely looked up as Brogan and Jefferson entered the room. A stereo on a table in the corner was blaring American rap music. Another stereo sat wrapped in plastic on the floor, next to two more television sets in unopened cardboard boxes.

"Are these Richard's kids?" Jefferson asked, bending close to Veronica's ear to speak over the music.

She smiled. "Not exactly."

A door to the side opened up and a thin twenty-two-year-old Chinese kid in silk boxers stuck his head out. His hair was shaved, and a thick gold chain dangled around his bare chest. Behind him, Jefferson glimpsed a bed, the sheets bunched up together.

A redhead in a bathrobe was sitting on the edge of the bed smoking a cigarette and playing with her bare feet on the carpet.

"Hey, Veronica, what's up girl?" the kid shouted loudly, smiling and raising his hand.

"These are the two men that wanted to see you," Veronica responded, pointing to Jefferson and Brogan.

"Oh yeah . . . sure, what's up? Hang on a sec."

The kid pulled his head back into the bedroom and slammed the door shut again.

"*That's* Richard Lee?" Brogan asked, his eyes wide with surprise.

"In person." Veronica smiled. "Kinda young, huh?"

"Yeah, I guess so. He's about the same age as the kid that cuts my lawn."

The three kids on the floor didn't seem much older, each in their early twenties. They were all wearing Nike sneakers and baggy jeans. They each had enough gold on them to feed a small family.

"Aww . . . shit!" one of the kids swore as his game ended, slamming the controller on the floor as the other two laughed. As the kid threw down the controller, his shirt lifted up for a moment, and Jefferson caught a glimpse of a black Beretta tucked into the waistband of his jeans.

The bedroom door opened, and Richard Lee stepped out. Jefferson glanced through the doorway and glimpsed the redhead lying back down on the bed, watching TV.

"So, what's up, guys?" Richard was wearing loose-fitting jeans, and a blue silk shirt which hung open exposing a thin muscular chest. He padded toward them in his bare feet.

"You have someplace we can talk in private maybe?" Jefferson said.

"Yeah, sure," Richard said.

He gestured toward the man in orange guarding the door. Speaking quickly in Chinese, he pointed toward Brogan and Jefferson. The guard nodded and, leaning against the wall, turned back toward the book he was reading.

Richard nodded toward the guard reading the book and spoke softly to Jefferson and Brogan. "He in college." Richard smiled and spoke louder for the man in orange to hear. "He become big lawyer someday, defend Golden Tigers, huh?"

Richard clapped his hands and turned to Veronica. "Why don't you go out front, I'll speak with these two now, OK?"

Veronica nodded. "Yeah, sure Richard."

As she turned to leave, Richard watched her walk away. The guard in orange opened the door to the hallway for her, and she disappeared, her silk dress rustling.

"Very beautiful girl, huh?" Richard said, his head still turned toward her. "Very pretty."

Richard turned back toward the two officers and clapped his hands. "But you two didn't come to the Green Tea for beautiful girl. Come on, we talk."

Richard opened the bedroom door again and gestured forward with his hand. Inside was small and tastefully designed. The enormous bed with gray silk sheets and comforter stood in the middle of the room. Along one side of the bed was a large wall of granite. Shelves had been leveled off in the rock, and unlit candles sat in the small alcoves. Small evergreen bonsai trees stood next to the candles, and a thin fountain of water streamed down the rock, disappearing somewhere beneath.

The tall redhead lay back in the bed. A pewter ashtray in the shape of a rounded dragon lay on the bed next to her, the base filled with used cigarette butts. Her bathrobe had fallen partly open, and one of her toned bare legs was stretched out across the bed. Her head was propped up with a pillow, her red hair cascading around her as she watched a taped episode of *Friends* on TV. Her eyes were glazed, barely moving. On the floor next to the bed was a small mirror, streaks of white powder still clinging to the glass.

The redhead barely looked up as Richard and the two officers passed through the bedroom, walking down a hallway decorated with Chinese calligraphy. Richard opened another door, and inside was a small office. Across one of the walls was a dark-ened one-way mirror looking out into the tearoom. The three students were still seated outside, their mouths moving silently as they continued to talk. From there, Richard must have watched the action in the tearoom taking place.

"What made you decide we were police officers?" Jefferson asked.

Richard took a seat behind a desk in the room and leaned back in the chair. A sil-ver Glock lay on the desk in front of him.

He smiled. "I called the police . . . obviously." He smiled again. *Of course. Gang leaders must call the police department all the time.* "I simply asked them if they knew a Detective Jefferson and a Lieutenant Brogan. The lady who answered the phone was very polite."

Richard leaned back in his chair.

"So . . . I'm here, you're here," he said, putting his hands behind his head. "You found me."

"First of all, you mind putting that away." Brogan indicated the Glock on the desk. "Guns make me nervous."

"They're supposed to make you nervous," Richard said, but the gun disappeared into a desk drawer. "That's the point of them."

Jefferson stepped forward. "We'd like to ask you about your relationship with Ken-neth Lyerman. Was he a friend of yours?"

"No, no, no." Richard shook his head. "He was a business associate."

"A business associate," Jefferson said. "You mean he gambled through you?"

"Gambled?" Richard looked confused. "No, he didn't gamble through me. We worked together, as partners."

Brogan laughed aloud. "Yeah, right."

Richard shrugged. "I know you came here thinking I was a gangster, right? A mur-derer. An animal. I am not Triad, not Chinese gangs. I simply provide a service that is forbidden by our laws. Nobody is hurt, yet I'm labeled a criminal."

"So what was your exact relationship with Kenneth Lyerman."

"He provided capital for restaurants, I provided the labor."

"The labor?" Jefferson asked.

"Sure," Richard said. "These are Chinese restaurants, and I provide them with Chinese workers."

Jefferson nodded, beginning to catch on. Richard was bringing immigrants into the country from China to work in these restaurants.

"Are they illegals?" Jefferson asked.

Richard sighed, folding his hands in his lap. "Have you ever been to China, Detective Jefferson?"

Jefferson paused, taken aback by the question. "No."

"I give people an opportunity in this country. People who have nothing in China."

"And Kenneth Lyerman helped you with that?"

"No. Not exactly," Richard answered thoughtfully. "He helped me for the money, not for the Chinese. Then, of course, he is not Chinese. What does he care?"

Richard seemed to be telling the truth, and he hadn't hinted at all that he knew Lyerman had been murdered. He'd be cold as ice if he could sit behind that desk and talk about Lyerman if he had whacked him earlier that night by himself.

"Lyerman is dead," Jefferson said. "Murdered. Tonight. Did you know that?"

Richard nodded. "I did."

Jefferson glanced over at Brogan. "Yeah, how?"

"Why else would two homicide detectives be asking questions about him in the past tense?"

"Did you do it?"

Richard smiled. "No. I don't like violence. I view it only as a means to protect one's interest. As a defense, not as an attack. I had no reason to wish ill toward Lyerman. He was not a nice man, but he was my business partner."

Jefferson nodded, then reached into his pocket and pulled out the small doll they had found on the roof.

"Does this look familiar to you at all?" Jefferson asked, handing Richard the plastic-encased figure.

Richard smiled, taking the doll with both hands and staring at its porcelain face.

"Sure," he said. "I know what this is. It is a Chinese puppet from the old puppet theaters. They were used to ward off demons."

"Demons?" Brogan asked.

"That's why their faces are so distorted, to frighten away the demons and evil spirits," Richard answered.

"Hang on a sec." Richard leaned forward, pressing an intercom button on his desk. "Let me get someone up here who knows more about this than I."

He spoke rapidly in Chinese for a moment. "He'll be with you in just a moment. He's a very old man, still familiar with the customs of China. More so than I."

Jefferson and Brogan heard footsteps coming up the long hallway behind them. Turning, they saw an elderly man, wearing a tight-fitting sweater and thin cotton pants with sandals. His face was so lined he reminded Jefferson of the doll itself.

The man stepped into the room, looking at Jefferson and Brogan through thick spectacles.

"Uncle Zhang," Richard said, rising from his chair, nodding to the man and saying something in Chinese.

The man named Zhang nodded back, followed by more words of Chinese.

Richard showed Zhang the doll, and the old man looked at it for a moment, before placing the doll back on the desk. He spoke with Richard for a full minute.

"What'd he say?" Brogan asked.

"He said that he knows this doll. It is Chinese Demon doll, and he gave it to Kenneth Lyerman."

"He gave it to him?" Brogan said incredulously. "Why?"

"He says that Lyerman had the mark of the demon on his forehead. That he had been marked, and he needed the protection the doll might give."

Zhang followed the conversation for a moment before speaking again.

"He asks where you found this doll," Richard said.

"Tell him we found it on the roof of a building, near where Lyerman was found dead."

Richard spoke, then the old man replied.

"He asks who you are, and I tell him that you are investigators, here to find out who killed Lyerman. He tells me that this answer is very easy. Of course it is evident who killed Lyerman."

The old man spoke some more, and Richard listened, holding up one finger to have the man slow down.

"He asks if the body had marks on it," Richard said.

"Yes, it did," Jefferson said, forming a claw with his fingers and running his hand across his chest. "Parallel cut marks, like he'd been slashed."

"He is familiar with such marks," Richard said. "Many years ago, they found a man dead in the bamboo fields near his village in China. This man had the same marks on him. Father Zhang asks about the man's heart? Was it eaten by worms?"

"Eaten by worms?" Brogan asked.

"He says that the ancient belief is that if a man's heart is eaten by worms, his body cannot find peace in the afterlife. His soul has been destroyed."

"We haven't done the autopsy yet," Jefferson answered. "I don't know what his heart looks like."

Zhang spoke quickly again, nodding toward Jefferson and Brogan.

Richard shook his head, then looked up at the two officers. He smiled once.

"What did he say?" Jefferson asked.

"He says you should drop this investigation. That this case is no good, for either of you."

Richard put his arm around the old man's shoulders, gently leading him out of the room and down the long hallway. He returned a moment later, and sat behind the desk.

"I am sorry," he said. "Uncle Zhang is very old. Maybe a little confused. His ways are the old ways, from old China. A place that maybe no longer exists. You know? He speaks of dolls and worm-eaten hearts. Not much help to your investigation, I guess."

Brogan shrugged. "You never know."

"Now, Richard," Jefferson began slowly, "where were you this evening?"

Richard smiled. "You have to ask, right?"

"We have to ask," Jefferson agreed.

Richard sighed, leaning back in his chair. "I'm taking a summer school class at Northeastern. I was at class tonight, until almost ten o'clock."

"What kind of class?" Brogan asked.

"Nothing really," Richard said quickly. "Not important."

"Richard, we'll find out anyway," Brogan said.

Richard turned away, arms folded over his chest, staring sullenly up at the ceiling.

"What's the class, Richard?" Brogan asked firmly.

Richard looked toward the officers. He lowered his eyes. "It's a class in French cooking."

Brogan turned a moment toward Jefferson, a smile waiting to break across his face. He turned back to Richard. "You're shitting me."

Richard shook his head. "No, I'm not. They've got these international cooking classes there at night. I'm trying to be a chef maybe sometime, maybe get a real restaurant, not just a teahouse." Richard gestured toward the gun in the drawer. "Can't live by that all your life."

"Well, you stay a good citizen, and your restaurant is gonna boom. You ever see a skinny cop? Just the precinct alone could keep your place in business," Brogan said.

Richard smiled. "Hey, I thought you guys just ate donuts."

Through the one-way glass, Jefferson saw the group of three students rising to leave. Empty cups of tea and crumpled napkins remained behind on the table. Veronica immediately glided over to clean up, her blond hair falling around her ears as she bent to pick up the empty cups.

Brogan clapped his hands suddenly. "Well, I think we've taken enough of your time."

"Thanks for stopping by. Kenneth wasn't a friend of mine. He wasn't a good person, but I'm sorry to hear he was killed. Nobody deserves that."

"You're right," Jefferson said slowly. "Don't think about it, it's out of your hands. We'll let you get back to that redheaded female friend of yours back there."

The two men turned away from Richard, heading back down the hall. Before they passed out of sight, Jefferson glanced back for an instant. He caught a glimpse of Richard, leaning back in his chair, his shirt hanging open, staring into space, deep in thought. The silver Glock lay on the desk in front of him again.

Jefferson turned the corner, and Richard disappeared from view.

Reginald Tate checked his watch for the third time in the past ten minutes. He shook his head once and a soft, "Damn," drawled from his lips. Around him the park was quiet and dark. The pond glimmered in the moonlight, the swan boats shut down and chained together near the shore by the dock. The trees around him rustled slightly, showing the pale undersides of their leaves as a breeze passed by. He rolled down the sleeves of his flannel shirt and hunched his shoulders against the slight chill.

He checked his watch again. This shit was getting old. He stood up from the bench, rubbing the numbness from the backs of his legs and twisting his head slightly, cracking the tension out of his neck.

Except for the two hours it had rained, he had been dealing from the same bench since eight o'clock. He'd been moving CoCo, cooked cocaine, for most of the night, but business, brisk before and after the rain, had trailed off around two, and he'd just been sitting there for the past half hour. It hadn't been a good night. Usual crackhead bullshit, trying to pay with a couple dirty one-dollar bills and trade the rest for some old piece of shit jacket or something they'd boosted from somewhere. If they'd been around, they knew it was cash only, but you'd get the ones new to the game or still trying to pull shit.

There was loud laughing from across the street. The door to the bar on the street corner banged open, and two women stumbled out together, arms intertwined, holding each other up. Except for the difference in their hair, they could almost pass for twins, both wearing tight-fighting black pants and tank tops.

Reggie turned back toward the park, looking across the grass toward his partner. Jay was fifty yards away, sprawled out on a poncho playing a video game by the light of one of the park lamps.

"What the hell you doin', Jay?" Reggie whispered to himself. "Shit, you supposed to be pretending to be homeless. This ain't a fucking arcade."

Jay never has any future thinking, thought Reggie. *He's always living for the moment.* Alonzo, the BeeKeeper, the man who supplied Reggie and took a 40 percent cut of his take, had a barbershop down the way. He used to bring the young kids from the streets into his back room, sit them down, and start the talk. The talk was a twenty-minute speech on being Black and poor. The BeeKeeper was thirty-six, and he used to love to tell the kids that he'd started out on the benches, started out in the projects, just like them. Now he had a degree in computers, owned a shop, and had three cars.

"When you get on that bus, you get there," Alonzo used to say, then point to the two closed drawers of a cabinet in the back room of the barbershop. Behind Door Number 1 was a new pair of sneakers. Behind Door Number 2 were ten bottles of cooked cocaine, CoCo.

Door Number 1 was just a pair of shoes.

Door Number 2 was a business opportunity.

If you took Door Number 1, you walked out of the shop and never saw Alonzo again. If you took Door Number 2, you worked for the BeeKeeper. The ten bottles was a loan. You took that out to the street, sold it, collected the money, and bought more CoCo from Alonzo. Then you stepped on that, took it back to the street, and sold it again. Reggie remembered being in the BeeKeeper's room and making the choice. Now he was up to four hundred bottles.

He'd served time for doing what he did. Two years in Blade State Penitentiary. And that time out there was no motherfucking joke. The lines of men just waiting to get at your ass. The hard rock everywhere, the warden, even the pit. Man, he still remembered that pit. Behind down there, by yourself in the dark, serving solitary.

Reggie shook his head, stood up again from the bench to straighten Jay out, when he spotted someone moving in the trees across the pond. He was walking unsteadily, looking around, then staring across the pond at Reggie. Another customer unsure how to act. Reggie checked his watch again, waiting for him to make up his mind. A moment later, either the guy figured everything was safe, or the craving for a fix got too strong, and he began walking cautiously toward Reggie.

Even from across the pond, Reggie could tell the dude was a mess, wearing an old tight pair of jeans, dirty high-top sneakers, and a mesh baseball cap. Probably not an undercover, they usually came looking too sharp, with lots of gold and slick clothes; and in some kind of color, Black or Hispanic. Not white trash nasty like this guy.

Reggie knew most of the police who worked this block anyway. They didn't have the energy to bring in an undercover he wouldn't recognize from another precinct. He wasn't moving that kind of weight yet. It was almost insulting that the cops didn't think he was big enough.

The guy in the mesh hat had reached the wide stone bridge across the narrowest part of the pond and was slowly making his way across, gripping one of the sides for support. Reggie mentally tried to speed him up, moving each of his awkward steps more quickly. It was getting late, he wanted to get the hell out of here.

As the guy pushed forward, Reggie checked his finances in his head. He'd moved about forty-five bottles of CoCo that night, at ten a bottle. Alonzo would call him tomorrow morning. "How much pollen you make last night?" Seven hundred dollars, making Alonzo more—almost 280 dollars. Not bad for a night, that's more than Reggie used to make in a week back when he worked at Phillip's Pizza Place. He still had a quarter ki stashed in the fake bottom of his refrigerator. He could step on that, mixing it with flour or powdered laxative and get about nine hundred bottles of low-grade coke. That way you made yourself a safe reputation, customers know you don't cut in any surprises, like DeCon or powdered detergent.

He was selling the pure shit tonight, trying to make new customers come back tomorrow. Once his CoCo ran out, he'd have to see about getting more from Alonzo. He was starting to become the BeeKeeper's biggest Bee. Alonzo had forty Bees like Reggie, going out onto the street and collecting the pollen for the BeeKeeper.

Or maybe get out of this shit altogether. Waiting around on this damn bench half his life.

He felt his beeper begin to vibrate silently against the small of his back. He pulled it out and checked the number. It was Laura, his girl for the past month. He shrugged and snapped the beeper back behind his coat. He'd call her in a minute.

The crazy-looking white trash motherfucker was suddenly standing in front of him, jittery as hell. Reggie crinkled his nose involuntary as the stench of piss hit his nostrils. Reggie looked up at the guy's hat—it read SOMERVILLE CONSTRUCTION across the top, with a poorly drawn picture of a bulldozer underneath.

"Hey, man, how you doing?" The guy in the mesh hat seemed nervous, mindlessly scratching the back of his neck with dirty fingernails and staring around the park. He had a light scruff of a beard slowly coming, growing in patches around his chin and neck.

"What's up?" Reggie asked blandly, looking as if he were bored.

"Nothing much, man, you know, just getting by."

There was a brief pause. The man's head bobbed up and down like a parakeet's, his hand still scratching the back of his neck. Reggie almost checked his watch again. *Fuck it. I don't need this shit for ten dollars.* He thought about rolling over and seeing Laura right away. She would have put her kid to bed. She worked afternoons for a cleaning service, but he still needed to get there soon before she went to sleep.

"Hey, I thought maybe you could help me out? I got twenty dollars here." He held out a crumpled-up twenty-dollar bill.

"What you want for twenty bucks?"

The mesh hat man shrugged. "I dunno, maybe something, like a couple bottles?"

Reggie shook his head, playing with the guy. "Naw, I don't sell drugs."

The mesh hat man looked confused for a moment, the bill hanging in the air, clenched between his greasy fingers.

"Lemme see your money." Reggie reached up and took the bill from the man's hand. He inspected it closely, wondering for a moment where this guy even got twenty dollars. The front was clean, but somebody had drawn a little heart on the back with the initials, "V.R. + M.D." scrawled in the middle.

Reggie handed the bill back. "I don't want that, that shit's got writing on it."

"But that's all I got," the man whined.

Alonzo had shown him what a marked bill look like. They were all more subtle than a big heart drawn on the bill, but maybe Boston PD was trying something else. Reggie paused for a moment, holding the bill, debating with himself. *Fuck it. This guy's rat nasty. He isn't undercover.*

Reggie paused, staring at the bill. "All right, I guess, but you better not be fucking with me." Reggie took the twenty and put it on the bench next to him.

From his pocket he pulled out a small cylinder about the size of a pen. A laser pointer. He pointed it at Jay, still reclining under the tree playing video games, and a red point of light appeared on Jay's jeans. Reggie's little brother had brought home a laser pointer from school one time for a science project. Reggie had become obsessed with it, and went out the next day to an electronics store in town and picked up his own. He loved using it; he always felt like Wesley Snipes, holding the laser sight of a sniper rifle trained on some unsuspecting victim. He would never admit that though, he'd feel foolish telling anyone. People would start treating him like a kid.

Reggie moved the light around, attracting Jay's attention.

Jay looked up, and Reggie touched his head twice, the signal for two bottles. Jay nodded and stood up slowly; like a drunk rising from an alcoholic stupor. Staggering forward, he stepped toward the dock hanging out over the pond. During the day, hundreds of people, parents and kids, happy couples, waited around on the dock for the swan boats to pick them up. At night, Reggie hid the small glass vials of CoCo taped in a bag underneath the wooden boards of the dock.

Jay bent over, reaching underneath the dock for a moment, before staggering back to his resting spot. He paused for only an instant, just enough time to dump the two bottles into a trash bin by the water's edge.

Reggie looked at his feet. Seeing an old crushed McDonald's cup, he picked it up and held it out to the mesh hat man.

"Throw this away for me, all right?"

"What?"

"Throw this away, there's a trash can right over there." Reggie nodded toward the waiting garbage bin.

The man's eyes glazed over, uncomprehending. He stood there, his body slowly swaying back and forth, trying to figure out what was going on.

Reggie hung his head. "C'mon, man, just take the damn cup and throw it away . . . in THAT trash can right over THERE." Reggie bugged his eyes out and stared at the trash can, nodding over and over again to encourage the man.

The junkie man's eyes suddenly snapped into focus, and he smiled, turning away from Reggie without taking the cup and walking quickly toward the trash can. Reggie shook his head, before throwing the cup on the ground. Wiping his hands slowly across his pants, he watched the man, his head bobbing up and down again, approach the trash can. *Stupid-ass motherfucker. No IQ test to be a junkie, that's for damn sure.*

Reggie looked up for the two women who had come out of the bar. They were gone, the street was empty. Across from him, the junkie was rooting around in the garbage. He found the two bottles of CoCo and, pocketing them, made his way off through the park. That was good. Reggie hated when they couldn't wait and started piping in the park. That's when the PD started taking notice and cracking down on operations. Besides, this was a park for kids; there shouldn't be junkies all around, dropping their dirty shit everywhere for children to pick up. Alonzo kept bottles of low-grade CoCo back at the shop, the shit was mostly baking powder, but it got you high all right. Every two weeks, he'd give two out for free along with a trash bag. He'd send them out to the playground to clean up, and if you came back with a full trash bag, you got two more bottles.

Reggie placed his hands on the bench, about to push himself off, when he saw a police cruiser drive slowly. *Shit, I don't need something like this now.* He looked at the ground, trying somehow to blend in with the bench. The police car continued to roll by, driving slowly along the deserted street. Reggie watched as the car was almost past, when suddenly the lights flashed on with a burst of siren.

"Fuck," Reggie hissed, looking down at the ground and watching the car through his raised eyebrows. Turning his head slightly, he saw his partner, Jay, staring bug-eyed at the flashing sirens. He slowly rose to his feet, pocketing the GameBoy, and turned, ambling off quickly through the park, his hands pressed deep into his pockets as he moved away from the police car.

Reggie didn't move. He'd probably just get checked for bottles and kicked out of the park.

Across the grass, the doors of the police car remained closed, the lights flashing silently. Then there was the sharp screech of tires and the car angled back out into the street, the sirens sounding again as the car gunned away from Reggie toward some more pressing emergency somewhere in the city. Reggie relaxed as the big car sped away, disappearing around the corner of the park. He looked around again.

Jay was gone somewhere, probably running for his bicycle parked behind the subway station. Reggie smoothed down the creases along the front of his pants, feeling the roll of money tucked into his pocket, and was slowly standing up from the bench when a bit of movement caught his eye. Someone was walking toward him from the pond side of the park. *Another score? Is it even worth sticking around?*

Reggie looked more closely at the figure, feeling something tug on his stomach, "Fuck . . ."

The man was Boston Police Department. Must be from the cop car that he'd seen before, circled around and parked where Reggie couldn't see him, then gotten out and walked.

"Fuck, fuck . . ."

They didn't like walking unless they were really going to bust someone. And Reggie was still on parole. *Shit! What to do? Run? Maybe* . . . But the cop probably had a partner somewhere out there, and he'd hate to run into the long end of some night-stick. And besides, Reggie didn't like running, too stressful. He'd rather just deal with it, then make it home and worry if someone got an ID on him. Almost impossible anyway, wearing the boots and jacket, damn beeper shoved in his belt. The officer was still coming toward him, and Reggie was thinking that it might be a mistake, until a flashlight suddenly flipped on, aimed directly at him from across the park, and a voice called out, "Stay right there! Don't move."

Reggie waved, easing himself back down onto the bench. While he waited for the cop to get to him, Reggie surveyed his surroundings. Green grass, cut by large gravel paths, extended forward, boxed in by the concrete sidewalks that circled the park. At the far edge, was the small granite-block housing for the Boston Common subway station. The lights inside had been turned off, leaving only the hazy blue lamp over the emergency telephone connected to the side of the building. To his left, the park continued until it reached the Park Street Church and, adjacent to it, the black iron-posted fence surrounding the old Granary Burying Ground. Reggie could dimly see the stone grave markers. Over the wavering trees, in the distance, rose the skyscrapers of downtown Boston, their lights blinking in the night.

Then the cop was standing right over him, shining the light up and down his body.

"How you doing tonight?" he asked.

The officer looked old, the workings of a three-day shadow on his face, and as he got closer, Reggie wrinkled his nose in surprise at the smell. Was he drunk? He stank like alcohol, bad. It made Reggie uncomfortable. The man's face looked life-battered. Sagging flesh, puffy eyes, skin dark and leathered from spending too much time outside.

"All right," Reggie answered, still squinting in the light.

Reggie held his breath and looked down at his shoes.

"You know why I stopped you?" the cop asked.

"No."

"Little late to be out, isn't it?"

"Naw, I was just out getting some air, you know."

The cop was staring at him strangely now, his pupils dilating lazily back and forth, the black circles expanding and contracting like ripples in a pond. There was a moment of silence, the cop not saying anything, just staring.

"So, uh," Reggie said after a moment. "Can I go?"

The cop still ignored him, the black ripples swimming inside his iris. Reggie looked at him more closely. Something seemed off. The uniform looked too thin, the material flimsy and bunching up in places. Even the cop's shield looked wrong, dulled somehow, like it was made of plastic.

"Who was your friend?" the cop finally said, Reggie assuming he was talking about Jay.

"Who?"

"That man who was sitting down there, playing a video game."

"Don't know him."

"I think you do. Did he see me coming?"

"I told you, I don't know him."

"Do you have any vehicle parked in this vicinity?"

"Huh?"

"A vehicle," the cop said. "Near here?"

"No. I can walk here from home."

The officer nodded, turning his head to scan around the empty park.

"Do you have a license?" the cop asked.

"Yeah . . . sure," Reggie said slowly, reaching down and taking his wallet from his pocket. He began to slide out the license from inside, when the cop interrupted him, taking the entire wallet from his hand and looking at it for a moment before sliding it into his own front pocket, where it bulged out from beneath the blue fabric.

"Whoa . . . yo, hold up, man, you can't be taking my whole wallet. That ain't—"

"You were selling drugs here."

Reggie's voice took on a vaguely hurt tone. "What? Naw, you don't even know me."

"Stand up."

"What?"

"Stand up."

Reggie nodded, not wanting to talk back to this cowboy, and slowly got up from the park bench.

"Turn around, spread your legs, and place both your hands on the top of the bench. Head down."

Complying, Reggie slowly turned around and leaned forward toward the high back of the bench. He felt hands patting down around his waist, moving across his pockets, then down his legs. The hands touched his wrist, and Reggie jerked at the cold skin. It felt like someone had draped cold seaweed over his body.

"And you're wrong, Reggie," the voice came from behind him. "I know everything about you."

The patting continued, the hands moving around his feet, looking underneath the tongues of his shoes, checking the elastic of his socks. Gradually, the search moved up toward his waist again, then along his back. The constant motion moved around toward his front, feeling along his rib cage.

"Let me ask you something," the cop said. "Were you ever scared out there?"

"Out where?"

"On Blade. In the pit," the cop replied. "Were you ever scared?"

Reggie thought back to Blade Prison. To inside the pit. To the something that had been down there, that had hunted them. How did he know about that? Nobody knew about that, except the cons who had served down there and the warden. And how did this cop know who Reggie was? Reggie was good with faces, he would have recognized this cop. The guy looked like a bum anyway. If he wasn't wearing the uniform, he'd look like one of Reggie's typical customers.

"Were you scared?" the question came again, the cop's voice taking on a tone of subdued excitement.

"Yes," Reggie whispered.

His head still hanging down, Reggie glanced at the two hands moving up his body. The nails were long, dirty, and jagged, the fingers streaked with blood.

Surprised, Reggie raised his head, craning his neck to look behind him. Something grabbed him, forcing him to look at the ground. From behind him, he heard a gurgling noise.

"You have anything in your shoes, boxers, or pockets?" a calm voice said.

"No, sir," Reggie responded, rapidly growing more uncomfortable.

Behind his head, Reggie heard a strange noise.

"What the . . ." Reggie spun around, looking behind him.

The cop was staring at him, his puffy eyes suddenly bloodshot. He looked ready to explode. His face was darkening, the loose skin around his cheeks twitching like the flanks of a horse. Reggie took a step to the side, getting clear of the bench behind him, watching as the cop's eyes slowly rolled upward for a moment, showing only their whites.

"Yo, shit . . ." Reggie whispered, staring openmouthed. Like the roll of a compass, the cop's eyes slid back into place. He turned his head sluggishly, focusing on Reggie.

This time, Reggie ran.

He moved quickly, breaking across the rolling slope of the park, cutting through the trees toward the street. Ahead of him, the streetlamps were glowing brightly, lighting up the sidewalk. The bars and shops were all closed for the night, their windows dark. The grass was wet with dew and Reggie could feel dampness seeping in through his shoes, staining the bottoms of his jeans. He turned, looking back as he moved. The cop had begun walking purposefully toward him, his arms moving back and forth mechanically at his sides, his head set straight forward, the yellow eyes following Reggie as he ran.

Reaching the street, Reggie saw a car moving toward him—a green Toyota. He ran out into the street, waving his hands over his head, trying to flag the car down.

The Toyota accelerated, and Reggie had to jump back to avoid being hit. He caught a glimpse of a thin-faced woman bent over the steering wheel, gripping it tightly as she passed quickly by. As he moved out of the way, Reggie landed hard against the side of a parked Jeep, his tailbone smashing painfully against the metal surface.

He darted between parked cars and moved quickly along the empty sidewalk until the big front gates of the Granary Burying Ground loomed in front of him. The thick metal bars of the entrance were locked, but Reggie pulled himself up and over, his jacket catching on the sharp, pointed top and throwing him down shoulder first where he hit the ground hard on the other side. He crab-crawled forward over the grass, night filtering across the graveyard around him. Darkness filled up every little crevice and chink of rock in the small, scattered tombstones, reaching out slowly across the grass to envelop the solid granite mausoleums.

When Reggie had first started working the park benches next door, he'd hidden something in the graveyard. He hoped it was still there. And it was. A silver .38 Special. Underneath a small square of turf behind the gravestone of Eleazar Johnson, 1783–1836. Breathing heavily, he kept low to the ground, slowly raising his eyes above the level of the stone.

The cemetery was empty.

Gravestones tilted at jagged angles, their stone cool in the moonlight, while above him, the sparse clouds slid silently across the night sky like billowing sails of ships.

Then from the corner of his eye, he caught a flash of movement. A glimpse of something running between the graves, then nothing.

Reggie began walking slowly backward, gun raised in front of him. He caught it again. The same fleeting motion off to the side. A quick blur of a black shadow moving, almost mirroring his own movements. Reggie stopped and stared, finding some confidence in the .38 Special. He tilted his head, trying to peer through the grayish darkness of the graveyard. The stones, tilted at uneven angles, glowed in the moonlight, while the spaces between them were filled with darkness, of unreflecting dirt and grass. Even looking closely, it was difficult to tell if anything was out there.

"Hey, I got a gun now," Reggie said aloud. "You still want some of this?"

The graveyard was silent.

Reggie jumped back, almost dropping the .38. A figure was standing across the cemetery, watching him. Reggie leaned forward, staring hard into the darkness. The figure was not wearing a cop's uniform.

"Hey? What's up?" he called out, but the figure remained silent.

Reggie looked back, staring through the metal fence at the street. No sign of the cop. He turned to the figure and noticed it was closer to him now. A moment of panic hit Reggie; he wished he hadn't strayed so far from the street. He looked back at the figure. Again, it was closer to him.

Something was odd, the shadow of the figure was so crooked, bent at strange angles with long, almost sharp-looking arms, and legs which curved inward at the knee. Reggie took a step backward. The figure took a step forward.

"Yo, I don't know who you are, but you better step back!"

The figure continued to advance, following Reggie in short, jerky movements. Without a sound, the figure picked up speed, breaking into a sort of rhythmic jog toward him. Reggie braced his arms and pulled the trigger, the .38 cracking to life, exploding against the palm of his hand. The figure jerked for a moment, but kept advancing. Reggie fired again, missing completely, a gravestone exploding in a puff of stone dust as the bullet struck.

As the figure passed from underneath a pair of trees, the moon shone directly down, breaking apart the shadows that had obscured Reggie's vision. Reggie could see what was coming toward him. He screamed.

Reggie heard a short, low roar and felt a sharp pain rip across the back of his shoulder. Falling forward, his foot caught against the edge of a tombstone and he landed facefirst in the grass. An immense weight pressed against his back momentarily, and he felt hot breath against the back of his neck. He closed his eyes.

Reaching back, he pulled the trigger of the .38 blindly, hearing the bullets strike something like flesh. While he was still on the ground, the weight suddenly lifted from Reggie's back. He jumped up and continued moving, the gravestones flashing past him as he moved swiftly forward, eyes searching for some sort of safety. He was in a section of low stone buildings, individual crypts. Moving into the center of the rows of buildings, he ducked, pushing his shoulders against the solid stone of one, squeezing between two carvings of angels blowing trumpets.

Behind him there was a growl, and he heard footsteps moving through the grass to his right. Scooting along the ground, keeping his head down, Reggie slid along the wall of the mausoleum. In front of him the graveyard stretched into the distance, broken by tombstones rising from the ground like jagged molars. He reached the front of the small stone building, where two heavy metal doors met in the center.

He heard the footsteps again, between the gravestones. It was searching for him.

The metal doors were secured by a chain and a rusted lock. He pulled on the lock; nothing happened. Placing the .38 on the ground, he pulled again, harder, with both hands. The chain rattled slightly under the pressure, but the lock remained closed. Noticing a shovel ten feet away, he got it and returned to the lock and chain. As he inserted the digging end of the shovel between the lock and the doors, the chain clinked painfully loud against the metal doors.

Reggie froze, holding his breath. The footsteps had stopped, as if someone were standing in the graveyard, listening. Slowly, Reggie reached for the revolver. The footsteps started again, the gentle thumps on the other side of the building, moving slowly toward Reggie.

Something was coming.

Reggie put the revolver in his pocket and worked with the shovel to break the lock. He lifted the chain away from the metal door and pressed harder. The footsteps were beginning to fall faster, and the lock continued to remain shut.

The figure had reached the other side of the crypt, and Reggie could hear its breathing, coming in short, rasping tugs. Reggie could feel tears brought by fear beginning to form at the corners of his eyes. Fearful pain flowing through his body, he fought the urge to surrender, to lie down in the grass. Instead he pulled down again in one sharp jerk, and, without warning, the lock snapped open.

He stared in amazement for a moment, before shaking his head and tossing the shovel into the grass. The footsteps were almost to the edge of the crypt. In another moment, their owner would turn the corner, and Reggie was in plain view. Easing open the doors, he slipped into the building through a two-foot-wide opening. Finding a bar intended to keep people out, he lowered it into its holder. *With luck,* he thought, *that will keep it from getting in.*

Inside, the small building was black, with only a thin sliver of light filtering underneath the small crack of the two doors. He stood quietly, his hands reaching blindly in front of him. He began moving forward slowly until he ran into something hard and box-shaped. Running his hands across its front, he realized it was a single large coffin, set up on a stone platform in the middle of the room.

Reggie breathed deeply, trying to slow his heart rate and quiet the ringing in his ears. The crypt was dusty, bits of cobweb striking against his face, choking him and clinging to his hair as he moved blindly behind the coffin. Dust, undisturbed for decades, fell in an almost constant stream onto him. His eyes were burning, and he could taste grit in his mouth.

Something moved outside. Reggie held his breath and listened. He could hear the footsteps of something in the graveyard as it approached the crypt. The steps seemed to stop for a moment, then walk swiftly away from the door, turn, and head off in a different direction, as if confused. Pressing his ear against the door, Reggie could hear a snuffling sound, only a few inches from his head. Looking at the bottom of the doors at his feet, he saw the sliver of light between the door and the ground broken by moving shadows. Something was standing outside the door.

The shadows breaking up the light moved, disappearing entirely. Reggie heard a soft scratching sound outside on the granite walls of the building. Then there was silence. Reggie breathed sharply outward, feeling the nervous energy flow out of him. He realized he had been holding his breath. He backed slowly away from the door. Behind him, his outstretched hand suddenly came in contact with the coffin he had previously run into.

The air inside was cool and smelled of dirt. Dirt. Reggie suddenly realized the floors were only made of dirt. If that thing wanted to, it might be able to dig its way underneath the doors and up inside the crypt.

There was a pause, then something heavy struck the doors. The metal groaned under the impact and warped instantly inward, but the bar held. A moment passed, and another impact followed; this time the doors shuddered, their hinges threatening to break. Another impact, and loose bits of dust fell from the ceiling, showering Reggie with dry soil. The air became thick and dirty, and Reggie held his hand to his mouth, trying to filter clean air through his fingers.

Outside something was smashing against the door, trying to break its way in.

"Oh Jesus Christ," Reggie said to himself. "Jesus, God help me."

He pulled the trigger of the .38, the bullets sparking against the inside of the metal doors.

The pounding continued outside. The top corner of one door suddenly folded inward with a screech of twisted metal, and moonlight streamed through, creating a square patch of light on the dirt floor of the crypt. The pale light was suddenly blocked by a silhouette, as the figure stuck its head through the opening to look in. Reggie whispered to himself as a pair of eyes fixed on him. The figure's mouth twisted into a smile of triumph.

Reggie had one bullet left. He placed the gun against his temple, feeling its cold metal against his skin for a moment.

He pulled the trigger.

Detective Jefferson blinked sleepily as the sunlight streamed in through the cracks in the blinds. Sitting up, he raised the blinds entirely, allowing the sun to fill the room. Outside, the buildings of the city rose around him. A soft breeze dragged through the half-open window, and he could hear laughter and the occasional aluminum *ping* of a bat against a baseball as kids played ball in the park across the street. He grabbed the remote off the bedside table and clicked on the small TV across the room.

A pleasant-looking blonde appeared on the screen, the afternoon news anchor for Channel 10. Jefferson padded across the carpet and into the kitchen in his boxers and bare feet. Grabbing some milk and cereal, he sat down at the kitchen table and absent-mindedly watched the first part of the news.

". . . will meet one week from today to discuss these measures. And in other news today, the body of a man and woman were found atop the Lyerman Building."

There was a brief clip taken from the news helicopters. Jefferson saw the top of the Lyerman Building, lit up by the forensic spotlights. He saw Brogan bending over one of the bodies. The scene must have been shot just before Jefferson had arrived.

"The bodies were discovered sometime late last night. No word yet on cause of death," the anchorwoman continued. The screen flashed to another shot of two men loading one of the bodies into the back of the ambulance. Jefferson saw himself in the background talking with Brogan.

"In other news, an unidentified body was discovered this morning in the Granary Burying Ground, right across from the Boston Common. We do know the victim was an African-American male between the ages of twenty and twenty-five, but nothing further is available at this time."

Jefferson looked up sharply from his cereal, staring at the television screen. "This begins our three-part series on violent crime and gun control in the city, called *Shootings in the Street*."

Jefferson clicked off the television and checked his watch. The phone rang.

"You watching the news, buddy?"

It was Brogan.

"Yeah, we got another body?"

"Looks like it. He was found him this morning, same as the two we found on the Lyerman. Word is the Feds have been asking questions."

"They think it's a serial?"

"Sounds like it."

"You been down there yet?"

"No, I got in just now. I'm gonna head over in a bit. You want me to wait for you?"

"Thanks, yeah, I'll be down in thirty minutes."

"Take your time, the guy'll still be dead."

Twenty minutes later, Jefferson pulled up in front of the Eighth Precinct. The building itself was cut entirely from white granite, and a constant flow of people filed up and down its front steps. He went in.

The station was filled with bleary-eyed releases from a night in lockup. Three prostitutes in short skirts and ripped nylons filed past Jefferson, unlit cigarettes in their hands. They pushed open the outside door and, standing on the steps blinking against the sun, smoked together and stared with glassy eyes out onto the street.

Jefferson passed the front desk and went through a set of swinging doors to his desk. His foot caught on the peeling tile of the floor, causing him to stutter-step forward to catch his balance. The chief had been complaining to City Hall for years to get a budget increase, but so far it hadn't happened. Brogan was seated behind his desk, hunched over with a phone pressed against his ear. He didn't look up as Jefferson walked by and collapsed into the padded leather chair by his own desk, directly in front of Brogan. Jefferson suddenly felt exhausted and glanced slowly around the homicide office. Two windows, perched high on the wall, let in sunlight filtered through dusty glass. A map of Boston was tacked up against one wall, next to a poster drawing of a giant foot crashing down on a crack pipe with the words "Boston Police and You, Stamping Out Crime" written in black across the bottom.

Brogan said something sharply into the phone, then hung up, tilting his chair backwards. "Jesus, fuck . . ."

"What's up?"

"Just got off the phone with Lyerman. Asked him about the audiotapes on the roof that we're pretty sure he has . . ."

"Yeah?"

"Says he can't confirm or deny their existence, but said that if there were such tapes, we'd need a court order to listen to them as they might contain private corporate information. You'd think we weren't trying to find out who murdered his child. Anyway . . ." Brogan said, cracking his knuckles thoughtfully. "How's it going with you?"

"All right."

"You ready to go fight crime?"

Jefferson shrugged. "Yeah, sure."

"OK, hang on a minute, let me just call home and check in with Amelia, see if she wants me to bring home dinner tonight," Brogan answered, reaching for the phone again.

Amelia was the woman who took care of Brogan's kids on a near-full-time basis. Six months before, Brogan's wife had been coming home late on a Friday night from her job as a nurse at Mass General. Her two-door light blue Dodge Neon had been hit head-on by a group of MIT students in a Ford Expedition who'd been going the wrong way up the I-95 off-ramp. The Neon, with Michele Brogan inside, had been crushed between the Expedition and the heavy cement blocks that lined the ramp. Traffic backed up for miles before they could clear away the two automobiles. The kids had all returned to classes the following week, finished their requirements, and graduated. His wife, on the other hand, lay in a coma for three days before a blood clot in her brain finally killed her.

Brogan had been left with a mortgage, two young daughters, and a scattering of pictures of his wife. Jefferson remembered attending her funeral, watching Brogan stare with soft wet eyes as they lowered his wife's casket into the ground, holding his four-year-old daughter's hand, while the baby sat in a white plastic rocker on the grass.

Since that day, Brogan hadn't mentioned his wife once. He still kept her picture at the station, but it was no longer on his desk. Jefferson had caught a glimpse of it once, hidden in Brogan's desk drawer. The man had been looking at it when he thought he was alone in the office.

"No rush, they couldn't get the forensics guys over there yet anyway." Brogan glanced up from the phone as he dialed.

"Why not?"

"Shooting at a liquor store in Dorchester, they were working that first."

"It'd help if we had more crews."

"No shit, brother."

The ride to the Granary Burying Ground was a short one.

Even from a block away Jefferson could see the line of black-and-whites parked outside. There were three squad cars and an ambulance, the lights shining dully in the morning sun. A crowd of people had gathered along the sidewalk, shielding their eyes against the bright sun and watching the proceedings. Jefferson saw a large white van parked on the corner with WCVB CHANNEL 5 BOSTON printed along the side. Brogan pulled to the curb and shut off the ignition. The two men exited the car and began walking.

"You know, my wife and I used to come here when we were dating and walk around." Brogan stepped through the open black iron gate of the cemetery. "It always used to be the only quiet place in the city."

A group of men in suits were gathered in one corner of the cemetery.

"They found the body a little way into the cemetery. Over this way." Brogan pointed ahead as he walked. "It looks like the guy tried to hide out in one of those burial buildings. What are they called again?"

"Mausoleums."

"Yeah, that. Anyway, they found him in one of those. Like I said, he was probably trying to get away from something. Not too much luck I guess," Brogan added as he indicated the mausoleum ahead of them.

Even from a distance Jefferson could see the gaping black hole in the center of the building, where the doors had been torn apart.

A female voice suddenly called to them. "Jefferson and Brogan, imagine seeing you two here again."

McKenna was standing by one of the grave markers. She was wearing a pair of latex gloves, hair pulled back into a ponytail. Jefferson had that familiar feeling again. Like he'd known her before. Or maybe that was just wishful thinking. She was across the graveyard from them, shielding her face from the sun.

She was the most beautiful woman Jefferson had ever seen in person, and he mentioned it to Brogan.

"Agree with you there, buddy," Brogan said. "Even counting all the strip clubs you, me, and Vincent hit back in our Army days. Better even than the classy ones where you can't touch the girls."

Brogan, always the romantic.

"You know, McKenna." Brogan called out, as the two officers walked through the grass toward her, "if I had to be knocked off right now, God forbid, I'd want you to check my body all over for clues. I mean that."

McKenna chuckled. "You two came just in time, the party's about to get started. I was worried you weren't going to make it."

"What've you got so far?" Jefferson asked.

"Well, we've got a dead, young male victim by the name of Reginald Tate, age twenty-two. One of the beat cops who took the call recognized him immediately."

Brogan looked up at McKenna. "Reggie bought it? Nice kid. Drugs, but other than that, he wasn't bad. I met him in court last year."

McKenna nodded. "We found him this morning, and have been trying to track down his parents and notify them before the media finds out. Checked his beeper, last number was from a Laura Ginsberg of South Boston. We haven't checked her out yet, but I'm sure she's just a girlfriend or sister."

"You think this was drug-related?" Jefferson asked.

McKenna looked at him for a moment, a strange expression on her face. She paused before answering, "No . . . this was something else." She looked like she was going to keep going, but said instead, "Well, you'll see."

"You find money on him?"

"Yeah, a roll. Little over seven hundred," McKenna answered.

Brogan whistled through his teeth. "Whew, seven hundred, Reggie was moving up. Not bad for a night's work."

"So how'd he die?" Jefferson asked.

McKenna sighed slowly, turning toward the mausoleum. "That's the strange thing; it looks like he committed suicide."

"Suicide?" Brogan was startled. "You kidding me?"

"He was shot once through the head, point of entry from the right temple. We found the weapon, a .38 Special, beneath his feet."

"A .38 to the temple? That must have made a fucking mess," Brogan replied.

"We don't know if it was a suicide or not, ballistics will confirm what type of gun he was killed with, but I suspect the markings from the bullet will match the .38 we found beneath his feet, and it'll have his fingerprints all over it. Of course, what happened to him afterwards was *definitely not* self-inflicted. You'll see . . ."

Jefferson was confused. *Why work the whole night, make seven hundred bucks, then go into a graveyard and blow your head off?* Brogan was apparently thinking the same thing.

"Why would he commit suicide? Was he alone?" Brogan asked.

McKenna shook her head. "No, he definitely wasn't alone. Looks like he was being chased."

McKenna pointed toward an older couple standing together being interviewed by Gregg Stanley, one of the homicide detectives. The man looked tired and had one of his arms around his expensive-looking wife. Her eyes were blurry, the makeup beneath them smudged, as if she'd been crying.

"Those two over there say they saw a young black man fitting Reggie's description rush out of the park calling for help."

Brogan looked over at the couple. "They do anything?"

McKenna smirked. "Young black man running out of a park late at night dressed like that? Yeah, they turned and walked the other way . . ."

"So what do you think happened?"

"We're still trying to figure that." McKenna stepped over one of the gravestones and walked slowly toward a small cleared path between the grass. "We've got some footprints."

Jefferson bent over the ground. The late-night rain, which had ended before they had left the Lyerman Building, had turned the dirt path slightly to mud, and he saw several sets of footprints planted clearly in the thick, yielding substance. They all seemed to be made from the same shoe, except for one.

"Look at this." He motioned to Brogan and McKenna.

"Yeah, we saw that, too," McKenna said. "Someone must have been walking a pet through here. Just once I'd like to get an uncontaminated site."

Jefferson stared at the print, trying to picture what type of pet it could have been.

Pressed down in the mud, superimposed over one of the footprints, Jefferson saw clearly an impression of three thick toes, each with a long nail.

He shivered involuntarily; it was like nothing he'd ever seen.

"So, you want to see what's left of Reginald Tate?" McKenna was standing just off the path, looking toward the cordoned-off mausoleum.

"Yeah, sure," Jefferson replied, and the three officers walked along the path toward the crime scene.

A small group of police in uniform milled outside the building. Yellow tape, stretched across the area, strung from a dead gray tree at one end and tied around a tombstone at the other, fluttered in a slight breeze. As he approached, Jefferson heard two of the cops joking about something. One of them was laughing and slapped the other one on the shoulder. Noticing Brogan and Jefferson, they immediately grew silent. One of the men nodded as they walked by.

"Now, as I said, we figure Mr. Tate was initially attacked back over on the path." McKenna pointed back toward where the footprints in the mud lay. "After the altercation, our victim made his way here, entered through these doors, and hid inside."

Jefferson began inspecting the outside of the mausoleum. The heavy granite stone was chipped in places, with loose bits having fallen into the grass as if someone had hammered at the structure with something heavy. The two carved angels that flanked the doors gazed toward heaven with impassive eyes. One of the angel's wings had a large crack in it that ran vertically downward in a jagged line.

"Looks like my house after my daughter's birthday party." Brogan said, inspecting the destroyed exterior of the building.

The doors themselves were constructed of a heavy black metal. Looking at their profile, Jefferson could see they were several inches thick. At the top corner of the frame, the black metal bent jaggedly inward, allowing light to stream through the opening and fill the burial space inside. One of the heavy metal hinges to the door had been torn loose and hung freely from the frame, allowing the door to be pushed inward after whoever opened it had removed the security bar across the doors. Large vertical scratch marks ran in deep grooves down the black metal, and Jefferson could see several dents and pit marks. Jefferson squatted in front of the structure to look more closely at the markings.

"Something hit this door hard. Look at these marks here. It's like someone went to work on it with a sledgehammer." He picked up a few pieces of loose granite from the side of the mausoleum and held them.

"Yeah, well wait till you see inside," McKenna said, shielding her eyes from the sun as she looked back across the broad graveyard toward the news crews standing around on the sidewalk outside. She noticed a silver Camry pull up to the curb near the news vans, two officers waving the car forward. A middle-aged Asian man stepped out of the car wearing jeans and a golf shirt. From across the cemetery, Jefferson recognized him.

"That can't be Dr. Wu?" Brogan asked. "Can it?"

"Looks like him," Jefferson said. Dr. Wu was the Chief Medical Examiner for the county. He was a lab rat, doing the autopsies for most major homicides cases in the city but leaving fieldwork to his subordinates.

"Dr. Wu," Brogan called out to the man as he approached, carefully picking his way up the cemetery path. "Surprised to see you here."

Wu nodded, shaking hands all around. "Purely observational. Believe me. I haven't been on scene in over ten years, not since I was a tech just out of med school. Chief asked me to come down on this one, said he just wanted to make sure everything ran smoothly. First time I've ever heard that before. Frankly, I think it's a waste of time. I have faith in all my people. They wouldn't be my people otherwise."

"Well, Doc, we were just about to step inside. Care to join us?"

"I'm just observing, I'll be in the background," Wu said, nodding.

Somewhere in the distance a bird began to sing, its tune sounding hollow in Jefferson's ears. Brogan pushed open the doors, and they all stepped inside.

It was dark, the air thick. The building was cramped, the ceilings only about eight feet high. The previous night was probably the first time the place had been open in a hundred years.

Brogan waved his hand in front of his face. "Man, smells worse than three-week-old Chinese food in here," Brogan said, then looked sideways at Dr. Wu. "Sorry, Doc, didn't mean anything by the Chinese crack."

Dr. Wu shrugged, waving a hand dismissively. Even the doctor looked like he was having a tough time breathing.

Jefferson paused a moment, letting his eyes adjust to the darkness. Toward the center of the room was a large rectangular coffin. The lid was covered in a thin film of dust, but Jefferson could see that a resting man had been chiseled into the coffin's lid. The figure seemed peacefully asleep, his arms crossed on his chest, his eyes closed. Jefferson was moving closer, to look at the man's face, when he saw something dangling from above, a few feet to the side of the coffin.

He instantly felt a wave of nausea overtake him.

From the ceiling hung a human body. Reggie Tate. Spikes had been driven into his hands, pinning them against the granite roof of the building. His feet hung limply, suspended over the ground. One foot was bare, the other clad in a loosely tied sneaker. Below the body a pool of blood had collected, combining with the dirt and caking into black splotches on the earthen floor and dark circles on the sleeping face of the figure carved on the coffin lid. The man's entire insides hung limply out of his body, his chest and gut ripped open. The air inside was oppressive with the smell of blood.

Jefferson thought of meat lockers and butcher shops. Except this time, it was a man that had gotten cut up.

What was left of his shirt hung open, dangling loosely around his midsection. Part of Reggie's chest was exposed, and Jefferson could see a stylized B with a dagger through the middle burned into the soft skin of his chest; the symbol for Blade Prison. He must have served time there.

"Jesus Christ," Jefferson whispered softly.

"Yeah, no shit," answered Brogan.

From behind them there was a noise, and a young-looking officer quickly entered the small enclosure.

"Detectives, the press is still outside," the young officer declared. "They want to know . . . oh my God! Oh, man, what is that?" The young officer staggered back, looking up at the body and holding his hand over his mouth. He tripped over the doorway and fell backward onto the grass outside. Jefferson heard the sounds of vomiting as he turned back to inspect the corpse.

"Hey, don't let any of the reporters see that," Brogan shouted outside.

Jefferson rubbed his stomach, his face a twisted into a grimace. "I'm feeling pretty upset here, too."

Brogan glanced at the hanging corpse, bits of dirt and dust collecting on its protruding intestines. He cleared his throat and turned away. "I think I'll hold off on that."

"We think that Reggie did commit suicide, technically, but then someone else came in, obviously, and did this." McKenna turned toward the walls of the burial crypt. "We're having a hell of a time with the walls, too. Trying to figure out what all that means could take weeks."

"Why? What's up with the walls?" Jefferson asked.

"Take a look at them. They're covered in some kind of crazy writing. I've never seen anything like it."

Jefferson stepped forward and looked carefully at the walls of the mausoleum. He saw that McKenna was right. They were covered with strange writing, all drawn in thick black ink. He bent toward the wall, his disgust overcome by his curiosity.

"What is this? Blood?"

"I wish," McKenna said. "We had one of the bioforensic guys look at it. It's partially digested human excrement. It's Reggie's shit. Whoever did this tore out entire sections of Reggie's intestines and used them like a pen, squeezing out the excrement inside to write along the wall."

Brogan's eyes bulged for a moment, and he swallowed hard. "My Lord."

In disbelief, Jefferson turned back to the wall and inspected the black streaks more closely. He saw bits of rice clinging to the wall, Reggie's last meal, mixed in with the blood and pressed against the granite. What used to be inside Reginald Tate was now painted black streaks covering the walls of the small tomb.

"I think I'm gonna be sick," Jefferson declared. He bent over, closing his eyes, waiting until the feeling passed. He felt Brogan's hand on his shoulder.

"You all right, buddy?"

"Yeah."—Jefferson wiped his hand across his dry mouth—"I'm all right, I just need a minute."

Jefferson breathed deeply through his mouth, feeling the wave in his stomach die down. In all his years of working homicide he'd seen some amazingly revolting shit— bodies lying in water for three weeks, men shot in the brain, the bullet exiting through the eye, severed limbs from auto accident. But in all that time, he'd only puked once before, six years earlier when some crack mother nuked her baby in a microwave. What he saw in the mausoleum was up there with that. Jefferson cleared his throat and looked up.

Around him, in Reggie's excrement, Jefferson saw a roughly drawn village, with images of skulls strewn along the ground and drawings of groups of men.

"We already got photographs of this whole place, so we can check up on it later, but still I've never seen anything like this before in my life." McKenna peeled off the latex exam gloves she was still wearing.

Jefferson continued to stare at the pictures. He imagined the killer last night. In this same room. Hunched over, using Reggie's insides as a paintbrush. The drawings extended around the entire walls, and Jefferson had to turn around completely to view all of them.

In one corner of the room was a passage written in English:

And shaking his mane dripping with blood.
Made a garland for himself with his enemy's entrails

"You get pictures of this one, too?" Jefferson asked.

"Yeah, we got it all. We still have to sweep this place for fingerprints and hair samples and the usual though. We tried bagging the victim's hands . . . but we couldn't, for obvious reasons."

Jefferson nodded and suddenly felt exhausted from the long hours of the case. The tomb seemed small and stiflingly hot, the smell of the dead seeping inside Jefferson. He knew his clothes would probably smell for a week.

He stepped through the doors into the sunlight. Brogan soon joined him.

The two men stared across the graveyard, watching the other officers search the grass for evidence.

"Have you ever seen anything like this?" Brogan asked.

"No," Jefferson said, staring back at the broken crypt. "No, I haven't."

By the time they had finished up at the graveyard, it was already midafternoon. Most of the crowd had thinned, grown tired of waiting around for something to happen. Behind them, still in the mausoleum, a crew was trying to bring down the body of Reggie Tate from where it hung inside the small crypt, while Wu watched, still in his role as observer. Nobody had been able to get the spikes out, so they had to call in a pipe cutter from one of the construction crews working on the new tunnel a few blocks away.

Brogan was moving quickly down the path, walking toward the car, occasionally pausing to glance at the name on a gravestone. Jefferson hung back, walking slowly side by side with McKenna.

McKenna had picked a twig off the ground and was playing with it between her fingers. "How you holding up?"

"I'm all right," Jefferson responded. "It just seems like you should get used to this sorta thing, you know?"

McKenna nodded and squinted across the graveyard, looking against the mid-afternoon sun.

"I think if you can start getting used to something like this"—she nodded toward the mausoleum—"maybe you've been in this too long."

She looked at Jefferson for an instant, before turning back toward the sun, squinting hard. "You know, my father was a cop. I remember Christmas morning, he left for shift, and was gone until that night. There were three suicides that day. That was his Christmas, taking dead bodies off nooses hanging from the rafters."

She shrugged and looked at her hands, snapping the twig and throwing the piece to the ground. "But yeah, I guess you do have to get used to it after a while. Either that, or it starts tearing you apart."

Jefferson vaguely remembered hearing something once about McKenna's family and her past. Something bad. He couldn't remember what. He wasn't sure what to say, so he kept quiet. A quick breeze blew up, pulling at his clothes and catching McKenna's hair, lifting it away from her face.

Jefferson's arm was tingling, wanting to drape itself over McKenna's shoulder. She turned away from the sun, looking at the ground, her forehead creased slightly, eyelids half-closed dreamily. Looking past her, across the cemetery, he saw a gray community van pulled up along the sidewalk, two college-age kids bending down to look at something lying beyond his line of vision in an alley. Curious, Jefferson watched them for a moment, one of the kids bending over whatever was on the ground.

"What are you looking at?" McKenna asked.

"Who are they?" Jefferson asked, distracted by the two kids and the community van.

"City volunteers, probably. They do these outreach programs for the homeless and things like that," McKenna said. "Why, you interested in doing some good deeds?"

"Not exactly. I'm just wondering what they're looking at," Jefferson said, taking a few steps forward. "I'm gonna go check it out."

"I'll go with you," McKenna said.

They began walking across the graveyard, ducking underneath the yellow police tape and moving around one of the television trucks. The van was parked half on the curb, the words CITY VOLUNTEERS painted in red lettering across the side. Jefferson remembered the group now, mainly college kids that did community service work in urban areas. As he approached, the kid kneeling suddenly jerked up, pulling his hand away quickly as if he'd touched something bad. He looked around quickly, saying something to the other kid, then noticed Jefferson. His eyes fixed on the shield hanging from Jefferson's coat pocket.

"Hey, hey, you're with the police? Yeah?"

"That's right."

"This guy, we found him, he's cold. I don't think he's breathing," the kid said, sounding a little scared, but excited at the same time. "I think he's like dead or something. He's all blue, it's fucked up."

Jefferson stopped and turned back toward the cemetery. "Dr. Wu, little help over here?"

Dr. Wu walked quickly down the cemetery path, as Jefferson waved his hand. "We got someone down here. Might need medical attention."

Jefferson quickened his pace, jogging the last few yards until he was at the front of the alley. Between two old brick buildings was a space about five feet wide that ran down almost forty yards before ending abruptly in two Dumpsters. A few feet from the alley's entrance lay the body of a man, just out of sight of anyone passing along the sidewalk. Even without bending to check, Jefferson knew the man was dead.

Wu joined him a moment later. "What's up?"

"We just found him like this," the kid who had been doing the talking said quickly. "We're out in this area checking up on people living in the street, and this guy was always around here. I thought he was just like passed out from boozing, so we're usually supposed to move on, but I took a look at his face and thought there was . . . Jesus, I go to the music school, this isn't my thing at all, man. . . ."

Wu bent down, his fingers pressing against the side of the man's throat. As their skin touched, the man's eyes opened for an instant, his mouth forming an O, sucking in air. Startled, Dr. Wu moved back quickly, but the man was quicker, reaching out with one hand and grabbing the doctor's wrist. The man's mouth moved for an instant more, the lips looking to form words, his dirty fingernails digging deeper into Wu's wrist. His eyes focused for an instant, turning on the doctor. Then, as quickly as it had come, the focus was gone, the man's face relaxed, and he fell back onto the street, his hand releasing its grip.

Immediately, Wu was pulling up, looking down at his arm.

"Jesus, you all right?" Jefferson asked.

"I believe so, just startled me."

"Holy shit, man, that was fucking crazy, he went like nuts, man," the kid said.

McKenna looked down at Wu, seeing a small puncture wound just below his right wrist, a pinprick of blood visible on his skin.

"You're bleeding," McKenna said. "You should get that looked at."

"It did penetrate the skin," Wu murmured, staring down at his own wrist. "This is why I stick to lab work."

"You better watch for like AIDS, man, that'll kill you," the kid was saying, bobbing up and down on his toes, still excited.

Still holding his wrist, Wu looked up. "I'm going to take a walk over and see if the ambulance crew have anything for this."

"Go ahead," McKenna said. "I can handle this here."

Wu turned and walked purposefully away, heading for the ambulance still parked on the corner. McKenna bent down over the man, her fingers moving to the side of his throat, this time cautiously. She held her hand still for a moment, her eyes on Jefferson, then shook her head slowly. Nothing. The man was curled almost into the fetal position, his skin a light bluish color, his lips slightly darker, like he'd been eating blueberries. His eyes were wide, as if he had seen something horrible, his face contorted, the tongue sagging out of his mouth like an engorged slug. The man looked dirty; with his long black fingernails and greasy hair, he had the hardened look of someone who had lived on the street for years.

McKenna had slipped on a pair of latex gloves and was slowly turning the man's head back and forth. "I don't see any marks on him. No blood. Looks like this could just be natural causes."

"Probably," the kid said importantly. "We've seen him before. He's been living in this area for years. I've heard they just go sometimes. Heart attacks or whatever. Just like that. I don't know about that second coming he just had, return to the living thing going on."

The kid was beginning to annoy Jefferson, but he had a point. Sometimes people just died. And Jefferson wasn't sure what was worse, getting strung up like Reggie Tate or dying in complete anonymity like this guy. Forgotten by society. They'd be lucky if they ever got a name on him. Looking more closely, Jefferson did notice there was something odd about him. He squatted in front of the dead man, pushing against shoulder and turning his body slightly so that the body rolled over on its back. That was a little strange. He looked like he was wearing a police uniform. Not a uniform, though, more like some kind of cheap Halloween outfit. The kind they sold at convenience stores around Halloween.

McKenna noticed it, too, because she said, "What's he wearing? Is he dressed like a cop?"

"Looks like," Jefferson said.

The kid stepped forward. "We get all kinds of strange clothes down at the clothes drop. People just give them away. Maybe it was someone's old Halloween outfit. Don't suppose he was too picky what he was wearing, being on the street and all."

Jefferson shrugged. Possibly. It still seemed strange. The bottoms of the pants were dirty with mud, like the kind of mud that was in the graveyard. Just a coincidence, maybe. If the kid was right, and the guy lived in this area, he'd probably been in that graveyard before. It was shaded nicely during the summer, you could get out of the sun more easily there.

"Yo, Jefferson." Brogan's shout came from behind him, pulling Jefferson out of his reverie.

He stood, shielding his eyes against the sun and looked back toward where their car was parked on the street. Brogan was waving his arm, then holding his hands apart past shoulder width like he was showing off the size of an imaginary fish he'd just caught. Something big had just come up. Something Brogan didn't want to shout across the park and past the ears of the listening television people. Jefferson held up a single finger, looked down at the body, then back to McKenna.

She stood. "Don't worry, I can handle this."

"Yeah?"

She nodded, opening her mouth to speak, then changing her mind. Whatever she might have said was silenced by the presence of the two kids and the dead man.

"Yeah . . ." Jefferson said again.

McKenna handed him a slip of paper. "My number. Call me later."

"Yeah."

Jefferson pocketed the number, then turned and jogged back across the street. Brogan was leaning half into their car parked on the corner, holding up the radio. "They found another body; we gotta get going, buddy! Play time is over."

Brogan started speaking as he pulled the car away from the curb. "I just got a call from Vincent. He's OIC at the crime scene for now."

Detective Vincent worked homicide with Brogan and Jefferson. They went back a long way, to when they'd first met while serving in Bosnia. "Yeah?"

"They got a bunch a bodies at some place over in Beacon Hill."

"You think there's a connection with our guy?"

Brogan nodded. "Vincent thinks there might be. If there is, you can bet we'll be lead detective team."

The car pulled off down the street. Jefferson took a last glance over his shoulder, back toward the graveyard. Three white television vans were still parked out front, and Jefferson saw an attractive young female reporter staring into the camera and speaking, the white granite mausoleum directly behind her. Jefferson could almost imagine what she was saying. "Police today found yet another victim in a series of grisly murders that have been holding the city of Boston hostage since last night. Blah, blah, blah . . ."

He turned back to the front.

"Well, looks like no shortage of work for homicide, huh?" Brogan said.

"Yeah, that's the truth."

"Too bad we don't get paid by the hour," Brogan said. "We'd be making a killing."

"Amen."

Brogan was on the radio again, just finishing up. He turned to Jefferson, and said, "We got an ID on that Beacon Hill address. It's Timothy Sinatra's place."

"Wait, Timothy Sinatra, the lawyer?"

"Yeah, that's him."

"Didn't he get Ferrara off on those murder charges a few years back?"

"Yeah, he worked a miracle, too, and got that rapist fucker Paul Driscoll out walking the streets because of a search and seizure violation."

"Yeah, I remember that," Jefferson said. Paul Driscoll had raped five women at Boston University over a period of eight months and taken pictures of each of his victims. Police found the pictures while they were investigating Driscoll, but his lawyer, Timothy Sinatra, was able to talk the judge into ruling the evidence inadmissible. Without the pictures, the DA's case fell apart, and Driscoll walked.

"So Sinatra got whacked, huh?"

"Guess so," Brogan answered. "Vincent thinks it's our guy, but, knowing Sinatra, it could be any number of people he managed to piss off during twenty years of getting criminals back out on the street. Looks like we got two guys breaking into the place and a whole bunch of dead bodies. Real weird shit from what I hear."

Ahead was a series of black-and-whites parked alongside the curb. The narrow street leading to the Sinatra house had been partially blocked off, and a uniformed officer stood in front, waving traffic away. The shades had been pulled down over the bottom-story windows of the town house, giving it a vacant look. A small crowd was gathered across the street, including more news media.

Brogan turned on his flashing lights as he pulled up toward the uniformed officer directing traffic. The officer nodded and waved their car through. Brogan parked behind a police cruiser. As they opened the door, Jefferson immediately heard voices shouting at them from across the street.

"Detectives, is this the work of Boston's latest serial killer?"

"Have there been any developments in the Lyerman case, and do you feel that this murder is linked to the others?"

The usual media frenzy was developing. Several reporters were standing behind the wooden police barriers on the other side of the street. They were leaning forward, excited, holding out recorders and shouting questions to Jefferson and Brogan as the two officers passed by.

"They're out like a horde of mosquitoes today," Brogan whispered to Jefferson, as they moved away from the reporters and proceeded to the Sinatra house. Another uniformed street cop nodded and opened the door for them.

"I wouldn't wear anything you want to keep nice in there," the officer said as they passed by. "It's pretty bad."

Jefferson figured his suit was dry-clean material anyway after being inside the mausoleum. Working a crime scene was like being in a room filled with heavy smokers. The scent of a rotting body just got into your clothes, your hair, even your skin, lingering for hours in your nostrils. The department had actually started allowing homicide detectives to write off dry-cleaning bills as business expenses.

A double layer of plastic had been placed just beyond the entrance door to seal up the house, preventing any insects from leaving. "I think I'm helping to put my dry cleaner's kid through college just on my suits alone," Brogan murmured, as they pushed through the sealing plastic. It was almost like passing through an underwater air lock, moving from the outside, into some unknown region.

Jefferson saw a few black flies, buzzing excitedly against the clear plastic, unceasingly trying to reach the outdoors again, unaware they'd been trapped inside the town house for the rest of their short lives. After death, the human body becomes a nesting and feeding area for hundreds of different types of insects. Airborne insects arrive first, attracted by the almost undetectable smell and warmth of a new body. Later, after the initial decay, as the smell of rot rises to a pungent level, different types of insects arrive.

The first of these to stake a claim are blowflies, tiny creatures that lay their eggs on the body, especially around the holes created by wounds or in any natural orifices.

Jefferson hated insects, almost to the point of a phobia. As they passed through the plastic, he sucked in his breath and readied himself. The smell hit them first, hammering their nostrils, noxious and overwhelming. Unusually strong even for a crime scene.

"Wow, that's ripe." Brogan scrunched up his face, turning his head slightly away from the smell.

Jefferson only nodded, clearing his throat once and looking at the pattern on his tie to distract himself. They stood in the foyer, just inside the entranceway. Ahead of them was a wide curving staircase, reaching upward underneath a crystal chandelier.

To their right was an open dining room. The smallish room was crowded with detectives and very dark, only a thin amount of light filtering in through the edges of the closed blinds. The officers all seemed to be circling slowly around something in the middle of the room. Jefferson couldn't yet see what it was. One of the men, wearing a dark blue suit, was leaning over inspecting the floor, white latex gloves on both hands. His tie was tucked into his pants, and the sleeves of his white shirt had been rolled up to his elbows, his coat somewhere else. Turning his head, he smiled, as Jefferson and Brogan entered the room and stood up to greet them. It was Vincent.

Vincent was a thin Italian, with constant black facial hair, even after he shaved. His skin was dark, almost Mediterranean in color, which meant that, as he was fond of saying, he didn't have to "wear all that SPF shit out at the beach like you Irish kids do." Brogan and Jefferson had known him for years; they had all served in Bosnia together.

You would have thought he was the nicest guy in the world, unless you had seen him at Zvornik, in Bosnia. But then again, they had all gone a little crazy there, not just Vincent. Now he was well liked by everyone he worked with, and in his midthirties was a detective in the Boston PD.

"Hey, guys, thanks for coming." Vincent stood up and walked toward them. Behind him, Jefferson caught a glimpse of something white, before the image was blocked out by the backs of other detectives. "I'm glad you're here."

Vincent peeled off the gloves and threw them in the waste disposal unit by the doorway. He shook each of their hands. "From what we're seeing, this looks like it's going to tie in with your guy. If that's confirmed, the chief wants you two to lead the investigation. Technically I'm OIC at this scene, but it's your case; I'm just here for the legwork."

"Fair enough," Jefferson responded.

"What'cha got?" Brogan asked.

"Well"—Vincent hesitated for a moment—"take a look."

He stepped back, and, for the first time, Jefferson had a glimpse into the room. A woman in a white bathrobe lay back on a chair pulled away from the long dining room table. Her robe was wrapped loosely around her tan legs, pouring loosely to the floor. Her arms hung limply at her sides, one hand dangling just above the carpeted floor.

Jefferson moved his gaze up. Over her shoulders, where Jefferson imagined her face to have once been, someone had cut off her head and replaced it with the stuffed head of a yellow-and-black-marked cheetah. The cheetah's lips were pulled back in a snarl, and the head itself, which was too big for the woman's body, spanned out almost the width of her shoulders. It was fastened tightly with cords that had been threaded through the skin on the woman's neck. Her head was in the corner, eyes open, staring at the room.

"Holy Mary and Joseph," Brogan murmured, involuntarily backing away from the horribly disfigured body. "What could do that?"

Vincent shook his head. "We don't know." He pointed to the darkened windows. "We had to keep all the blinds closed to keep the press from peeking in the window. If they got a picture of this, the city would be in a panic. This is worse than Zvornik, huh?"

"Hoowah," Brogan replied, still staring at the woman, his eyes wide, his mouth hanging open.

"Hoowah," Jefferson answered softly.

Jefferson had grown uncomfortable at the mention of Zvornik. A while back, they had all agreed not to mention the town's name again; it was as if that night didn't exist for any of them.

"We've got four more bodies upstairs. It's all equally weird shit. All with their heads cut off, replaced with the stuffed heads of animals." He pointed to the woman. "This was Patricia Sinatra, wife of Timothy Sinatra. He's upstairs, too, the head of a jaguar sewn to his shoulders. And there's another man, Gary Older, who was the family cook here during the week."

Stepping into the foyer, Vincent pointed up toward the ceiling. "Look at that."

Above them was written:

Fear Him who has the power to cast into hell

"What's all that mean?" Jefferson asked.

"Don't know." Vincent shook his head, then pointed up the stairway. "Then there are two other guys up on the third floor. We don't know how they fit into this. They're both small-time thugs, and I can't figure what the hell they were doing here. I recognize one of them, went by the nickname Q. I personally sent him away to Blade Prison for two years. We're checking that maybe Sinatra was representing them in court. We do know that the cook was also an ex–Blade man."

"What, a con?" Brogan asked.

"No, this guy was an ex-guard. He worked at Blade for twelve years before getting canned a month back. Heard he didn't take it so well."

A uniformed officer came by the group with a clipboard. He handed it to Vincent, who quickly signed it and passed it back. The officer disappeared around the corner into the next room.

"Where did the animal head come from?" Brogan asked, still staring in disbelief at the body in the chair.

Vincent shrugged. "Off the wall of Sinatra's game room up on the third floor."

Jefferson was beginning to feel sick from the lack of air. The entire town house had been sealed up to study the insects that had inhabited the body, but that meant there was no air circulation. Jefferson could almost feel himself breathing the air, thick with the smell of death and sluggish inside his lungs. A black blowfly landed on Jefferson's neck, crawling quickly toward his ear. He brushed it away in disgust. The place was swarming with insects, buzzing around in circles underneath the overhead light and rattling against windowpanes.

"Another weird thing about this," Vincent began.

"What's that?" Brogan waved his hand across his face, flushing out the few tiny gnats that had collected just under his nostrils.

"There must be thousands of insects in here, right?"

"Yeah, they're everywhere," Brogan replied. "That's what you'd expect at a blood-bath like this."

"That's true," Vincent concurred. "But the thing is, there isn't a single insect on any of the bodies. Not one. The victims have been here for most of the day, there should at least be some infestation. There's nothing. The insects won't touch the bodies. It's like they were attracted into the place by the smell, but once they got here, they won't even go near the victims."

For the first time, Jefferson noticed that was true. Looking around the room, he saw uniformed officers swiping the backs of their necks, scratching their arms, trying to swipe the flies. The only thing that seemed clear was the disfigured woman in the chair. Jefferson didn't believe that insects had much intelligence, but it was as if what had happened to the woman was too unnatural for even the insects to touch her.

Vincent walked toward the doorway, motioning them to follow. "Here, let me show you something else." A heavyset officer was kneeling by the doorway, dusting the wooden frame with carbon powder for fingerprints. He was sweating heavily in the stifling air, and grunted as he stood up to move out of Vincent's way.

Vincent turned back to Brogan and Jefferson. "We've been pulling some good prints so far, takes time, but we're trying to speed it up." He began slowly moving up the great staircase, talking back over his shoulder. Brogan and Jefferson followed him. "When we started dusting upstairs, we found something unusual."

They moved up to the second floor. Jefferson caught a quick glimpse of a living room, books lying flat on the floor and a cream-colored sofa overturned. Upstairs was another long hallway, with doorways on all sides. Vincent strode down the hallway and entered the second door on the left. Jefferson and Brogan followed. It was a wild-game trophy room. The stuffed heads of animals—zebra, grizzly, deer—hung from the ceiling, circling around the room over a thick-looking walnut desk. A gun cabinet was pushed up against one wall, long rifles locked securely inside. Just beyond the cabinet was a dead body, the grinning head of a hyena on his shoulders.

"Who's this?" Jefferson asked.

"Older," Vincent replied, "the ex–Blade prison guard. His head is in the corner behind you. And in the room through that door over there is where we found Q, the ex-con. For some reason I can't explain, he was wearing boxer shorts."

"So Older was working for Sinatra?"

Vincent nodded. "Sinatra apparently knew a lot of the cons and guards at Blade, since he represented a good number of them in court. He had Older on staff here, just as a cook. Older would steer him to new clients from time to time."

Jefferson leaned over the body. "May I?"

"Knock yourself out," Vincent replied.

Jefferson slapped on a pair of latex gloves, tucked his tie into his shirt, and crouched over the body of the man. He averted his eyes from the headless top, the large stitch marks of thick cord connecting the head of the hyena to the man's shoulders. Instead, he patted the body down with the palms of his hands. There was a rectangular lump in the man's back pocket, and Jefferson slipped his fingers inside, carefully pulling out a leather wallet. He opened the wallet up with his gloved hands, first checking the billfold, eyeing a short stack of green bills and white gas receipts. Moving outside in, he began checking each of the card holders, pulling out credit cards, movie store cards, supermarket cards, a driver's license identifying the man as Gary Older, and a few pictures. He glanced for a moment at one of the pictures, a plain-looking woman standing in front of the St. Louis arch holding a small baby in her arms.

Carefully he slipped the picture back into its pocket and began inspecting the wallet's other flap. Inside was stuffed a small slip of folded paper. Taking it out, he slowly unfolded it. Scrawled across the front was a series of seven digits; a phone number. He flipped the paper over, on the back were three letters—"R J D."

Jefferson copied down the letters and phone number into his notebook, then carefully slipped the paper back into Older's wallet.

"Everything going all right?" Vincent's voice startled Jefferson.

"Yeah, yeah," Jefferson said, standing up. "Everything's fine."

He surveyed the rest of the room.

Opposite the body, someone had placed a ceramic garden gnome, the small grinning figure standing on the carpet just beside one of the walls. The gnome was similar to anything found on lawns, but the thing gave Jefferson the creeps. Jefferson wondered what it was doing there.

The ceramic figure was only about two feet high, but it was unnerving, the way the thing looked at the officers with its dull eyes, standing on the carpet about ten feet away from the slowly decomposing body. One of its arms was hanging by its side, the other extended up and away from its body. The little hand of the extended arm was wrapped around something pale and long. Jefferson stepped farther into the room to get a better view and felt his head spin.

Grasped tightly in its little hand was a severed human finger.

Brogan cleared his throat, holding his hand over his mouth as he swallowed hard. He turned away from the room, staring with half-closed eyes out toward the hallway.

"When we dusted this room, we picked up a lot of skin oils along that wall." Vincent pointed to the large blank space on the wall, just next to the garden gnome. "So we flooded the room with laser light to see what was going on."

Jefferson nodded understanding. Forensic scientists often used laser light to detect the presence of fingerprints. The light caused the chemicals in any fingerprints to fluoresce.

Vincent shut the door behind them. With the lights turned off, the room was pitch-black. Jefferson involuntarily tensed as the door closed and the light vanished, leaving them in complete darkness with a dead body and the garden gnome. He wasn't sure which was worse, the body or the gnome. The skin along his leg was prickling.

"Jesus, let's get some light in here," Brogan murmured, his voice tense.

"Yeah, no shit," Jefferson responded.

A shifting of metal sounded from in the room, then Vincent's voice, "OK, just a minute, I had to get this thing set up."

There was a brief *click*, and instantly the room was filled with a soft, iridescent bluish glow. The light reminded Jefferson of a candle, leaving smudges of wavering darkness in the far corners of the room. The effect was actually very peaceful, like swimming in the bottom of a luminous blue ocean.

In the light, the chemicals in human oil began to fluoresce, revealing the invisible fingerprint marks and handprints in the room. Jefferson saw smudges of prints, random and haphazard marks made about the room. Only in one area did the random marks come together.

Across the wall, just over the distorted ceramic figure, written in glowing fluorescent human oil, was crudely drawn,

Four came from the Galla
No bribe mollified them,
Nor did they satisfy a woman's body,
But hated children
And tore them from their parents' laps

Jefferson was silent for a moment, standing in the darkened room, staring at the wall. Brogan leaned toward him, his breath hissing against his ear. "Who is doing this?"

"I don't know."

Next to the writing was the garden gnome. Something had painted over its face in fluorescent oil, outlining and distorting its smile, turning the lips up into an evil grin and slanting the eyebrows down in anger. The effect was strange, giving the gnome a hateful appearance, like a little demon.

Jefferson began to wish the bluish laser light would go out, allowing everything to return to normal.

"Seen enough?" Vincent asked.

"Yeah, I think so," Jefferson responded.

Vincent nodded and turned on the overhead light. Jefferson blinked involuntarily, squinting against the glare. He turned to the wall; the writing had vanished. The decapitated body still lay chest down on the carpet, a thick, dried pool of red staining the carpet.

"Well . . ." Brogan said. "Given what we've seen, here and at the Burying Ground and at Lyerman's, there's no doubt it's the same guy."

"So you two taking the case over?" Vincent asked.

"Looks like."

Vincent held his palms up. "No complaints here."

Vincent opened the door into the hallway again, letting some air flow back into the room. Jefferson breathed deeply, filling his lungs with the relatively clean air from the rest of the house, feeling as if he'd just surfaced from a long underwater dive. There was a knock on the open door. A uniformed police offer stood in the doorway holding out a portable phone.

"I've got a call here for either Detective Jefferson or Lieutenant Brogan," the officer said, cupping one hand over the phone's receiver.

Brogan glanced at Jefferson for a moment. "I'll take it."

Jefferson nodded and turned back toward Vincent. Brogan took the portable phone and, placing one finger in his ear, went out in the hallway to talk.

"So that's about it," Vincent began, scratching the back of his neck. "Like I said, we've got some good prints, and I'll have run those back at the lab, see if anything comes up."

"We're about at the same place right now. Nothing big turned up. I hate waiting like this, but that's what we might have to do." Jefferson glanced at the ceramic figure of the gnome. "This is definitely a bad one."

Vincent grunted in agreement. "Got that right. If you want to check it out, looks like Older had a private office here."

"Where's that?"

"Down the stairs, all the way at the back of the house on the left."

Jefferson nodded thanks and stepped back into the hallway, leaving the gnome and the dead man behind. He made his way past uniformed officers and white-suited evidence teams. Brogan was standing in the hallway, talking animatedly to someone on the phone. He didn't look up as Jefferson passed by, but Jefferson heard him say, "Not ready yet . . ." to whoever was on the other end of the line.

Down the stairs, Jefferson moved down the posh hallway leading to the rear of the building. Decorated with ornately framed portraiture paintings and a watercolor landscape, the hall reminded him of the West Wing of the Museum of Fine Arts, and he briefly entertained the idea that the hallway alone must have cost more than his entire apartment. At the end was an open doorway, leading into what Vincent had said was Older's private office.

The office was small and crammed with books. Hundreds of book bindings, their colors muted by age and dust, faced outward from three ceiling-high shelves lining the walls. Jefferson scanned the titles, catching glimpses of *Crime and Punishment* and *The*

Count of Monte Cristo. Two large windows flanked either side of the room, breaking up the continuity of the bookshelves, and allowing hazy light in through their yellowish panes. Green branches were pressed against one of the windows, stretching out from a large elm standing just outside, the light filtering through the leafy screen entering the room with an almost greenish hue, illuminating the dust motes that spiraled through the air upon Jefferson's entrance.

Jefferson took out his cell phone, dialing the number McKenna had given him. Her service answered, so he left a message, telling her about the writing they'd found on the ceiling. *Four came from the Galla . . .*

In the center of the room was a walnut desk, topped with an old-fashioned ink blotter, a manual typewriter, and two sets of pictures in frames. In each of the photographs, Jefferson recognized the image of plain woman from the picture Older carried in his wallet. Jefferson wondered if the woman knew her husband was lying dead upstairs.

He made a cursory inspection of the desk drawers, seeing nothing but pencils, papers and a stack of *National Geographic* magazines in each of them. A phone sat on the corner of the desk, and Jefferson lifted it, listening to the dial tone for a moment. Reaching into his pocket, he pulled out his notebook and turned to the page where he had copied the phone number and the three letters.

He dialed the number. There was a pause on the line, then a *click*, and Jefferson found himself listening to the ring of a phone somewhere. He looked out the far window, to a view across the street. Two kids were playing Frisbee, tossing the red disc back and forth, while a German shepherd frolickled underneath the floating plastic, snapping its teeth playfully, its barks sounding muted from across the street.

The ringing abruptly ended—someone had picked up.

He turned away from the Frisbee players, pressing the phone hard to his ear and listening.

There was heavy breathing, as if someone had used a lot of effort to answer the phone. For a moment Jefferson thought the person on the other end of the line might be in danger of having a heart attack, a phone-induced homicide, then a voice, "Hello?"

"Hello?" Jefferson said quickly. "I'm sorry, who's this?"

There was a pause, and Jefferson could hear the wheezing breath continue.

Then the voice came again, thin, scratchy, reminding Jefferson of the noise produced by electronic voice boxes used by heavy smokers.

"Who is this?" asked the voice.

"I'm sorry, I might have wrong number, who am I speaking with?" Jefferson asked.

The breathing continued for a moment, then there was a long chuckle at the end of the line. Jefferson listened with amazement to the noise, when the voice finally said, "Detective Jefferson . . . I'm not sure how you came by this number, but I would suggest never calling here again. You have no idea what you're getting yourself into."

Jefferson felt cold, like insects crawling over your face or fingernails across a blackboard.

There was a sharp *click* on the line.

"Hello?" Jefferson said quickly. "Hello? Who's this? Hello?"

He pulled the phone away from his ear, looking at it for a moment with a concerned stare, expecting it to say something more. He tapped the receiver repeatedly, but heard only a dial tone. Placing the phone back in the cradle for a moment, he quickly picked it up again, redialing the numbers.

There was a *click*, then he heard the grating noise of a busy signal. Whoever was at the other end of the line had taken the phone off the hook. Disconcerted, Jefferson slowly replaced the receiver in its cradle. He made a mental note to run a reverse check on the number once he was back at the station. He had recognized the voice, but like an old song to which you can't quite remember the words, the name of the person on the other line was beyond recall.

Sunk in thought, he wandered across the office to stare at a large painting hung from the wall: DeRanier's *Demon's Gate*. Devils with jagged teeth and sharp eyes had descended to Earth, tearing apart the bodies of men. He turned his attention to the picture frame, a massive, gilded affair of swirls and carved scrolls. Older seemed to have a thing for demons. Everybody's got to have their interests.

In each of the four corners of the frame was the carved head of a cherub or an angel, cheeks puffed out as they appeared to be blowing a strong wind onto the painting itself. And there it was. A shiny, smooth spot on the lower right-hand corner of the frame. He tilted his head, staring at the spot. The area was small, about an inch long, and oval in shape. Curious, he leaned forward, lifted his hand, and pressed his thumb against the spot. It fit perfectly.

He pressed his thumb against the spot again, and felt his fingers wrap naturally around the rest of the frame. His index finger pressed against a small latch on the underside of the frame. He depressed the latch, there was a clicking noise, and the frame swung out, away from the wall, opening like a book on a set of hinges affixed to its left side.

With the frame pulled back, Jefferson could see a square of metal set into the wall. It was a safe, a safe hidden by the painting. He leaned forward and saw three black dials set into the metal. Each dial was notched with letters, spanning from A to Z. A lever extended from the right side of the safe. Jefferson gripped the lever, pressing against it, but the metal refused to turn. The safe was locked.

Jefferson pulled out his notebook and glanced at the three letters written beneath the phone number.

He set the lettered dials accordingly, turning the first to R, the second to J, and the third to D. Trying the lever again, he found that it turned easily in his hand. There was a *click*, and Jefferson swung the door of the safe open.

Inside was a book bound in a faded leather cover. Gently, Jefferson lifted it from the safe, brushing off the cover and opening to the title page. *The Annotated History of Fort Blade Prison* by Gary Older.

Blade, again the name appeared. Why? Jefferson slipped the book into his pocket. It fit inside easily, feeling heavy in his jacket.

He took a last look around the room before moving back into the hall. As he shut the office door behind him, faint recognition suddenly seeped into his mind. He stood in the hallway, one hand still wrapped around the cool metal doorknob of Older's office.

The unknown voice on the phone.

With a strange clarity, he realized it had been Joseph Lyerman. Lyerman, whose son Kenneth had been found murdered on the roof of his own building. Why would Older, the murdered ex–Blade prison guard, have Joseph Lyerman's phone number with him?

Jefferson released the knob and walked slowly back down the hall and upstairs.

Lyerman tapped the phone icon on the control panel mounted just beneath his right hand. The phone clicked off, and Lyerman sat deep in thought for a moment, his cheek resting against the sip and blow movement straw extending from the rear of his chair. *Jefferson. Jefferson. Jefferson.* If Jefferson knew about Older, then he would know about Blade Prison. And if he started looking too hard at Blade, then . . . what? Not that it mattered; the wheels were all in motion. So to speak. Lyerman didn't like to use analogies that involved movement, made him think about the damn chair. *Still,* Lyerman thought, *it could be very inconvenient.*

His day had started off so promising, too.

"Cesar!" Lyerman called out. A moment later his thin nurse stepped into the room. It was amazing how quiet that man was. Lyerman had found him down in Panama, working in a butcher shop. He'd immediately recognized the man's talent. Well, if "talent" was the right word for what it was the man could do.

"I'm feeling a little down, bring me something nice to look at," Lyerman said.

The Panamanian nodded, slowly withdrawing from the room. He was gone for a few minutes, then he returned with a scared-looking boy of about eight. The boy was wearing a yellow T-shirt, the kind they gave kids in the Panamanian ghettos. But most interesting was what he was wearing below the T-shirt. Faded blue soccer shorts reaching just a foot below the waist, exposing so much of the boy's legs. Those beautiful little legs.

Cesar's talent was in finding the boys. All down in Panama somewhere. Street children. No homes. No parents. No one to worry about them, eager to do anything for a meal. A ticket to the United States. The social service was legitimate, placing impoverished Panamanian children with couples in the United States who wanted to adopt. But as he had told Detective Jefferson, nothing was really what it seemed. People didn't want to face reality.

Lyerman stared at the boy's legs for a moment more, before looking up into his face. Large brown eyes, dark skin, flat black hair. The boy was standing in the doorway, looking scared, his bony knees pressed together. Lyerman forced himself to smile. He'd worked on this, looking at himself in a mirror. When he'd first started, he'd found that his smile actually made the children more afraid. This had angered him, causing them to withdraw even farther. Finally, he had reached the point where most of them would approach him. But it took practice. Dealing with people could be so demanding sometimes.

Lyerman held the smile. "Come on, come on. Don't be afraid."

The boy stood silently, staring at the man in the electric chair. Lyerman's smile fell slightly.

"Cesar, please."

Cesar nudged the boy forward, farther into the room.

"Do you speak English?" Lyerman asked.

The little boy turned back to Cesar, who said, "*¿Habla inglés?*"

"No."

"No . . ." Lyerman repeated, then turned to Cesar. "Please get him to walk farther into the room."

Cesar spoke quickly to the boy, who nodded and slowly began walking. Lyerman stared at his legs. The movements of joint and bone. The way the knee slid back and forth, the flexing of the foot and the calf. They were slim, the musculature perfectly defined, the lines of the quadriceps meeting with the hamstrings. Even the tendons around the knee were perfect. Cesar had done his work well. He always had a good eye for that sort of thing.

"I want to see him do knee bends," Lyerman said. "Have him do knee bends for me."

Cesar nodded, speaking to the boy. The boy turned to look at Lyerman, and Lyerman tried a smile. The boy shrugged and dipped into a knee bend. Then back up. Then down again. Lyerman felt an ecstasy of energy flowing through him. Not sexual energy.

Those legs, though. The beauty of movement. That was what moved Lyerman. What had his juices flowing. A boy's legs, a girl's legs, they were all the same to him.

"Have him do jumping jacks."

Cesar spoke, and the boy listened, stopping the knee bends and moving into jumping jacks. Lyerman watched the flexing of the hip, in and out, the legs moving in perfect rhythm. The boy was beginning to sweat, a light sheen showing on the surface of his brown skin, highlighting the musculature even more. Lyerman licked his lips. This was becoming almost too much to bear. He had no outlet for these energies. Nothing to focus them on. Just a little more.

"Run in place. Quickly! Have him run in place. *¡Rapido!*"

Cesar spoke again, and the boy listened. Breathing heavily now. Legs pumping up and down. Naturally, like legs were supposed to work. Skin taut against the bone. Lyerman could feel the anger, the frustration building inside of him. The little boy was looking around the room, taking in the artwork. He looked bored. *Do I bore you?* Lyerman wondered. *Does this strange little man in his electric chair, bore you? Do you have any idea what power you have in those legs? And how undeserving of it you are.*

"Faster. Make him go faster! *¡Rapido!*"

The boy complied, legs moving quicker now. Ankles, knees, hips, all together in harmony. So perfect, until Lyerman couldn't stand it anymore.

164

"Enough!"

"¡Bastantes!"

"Get him out of here."

Cesar came forward, hustling the boy out of the office and back with the other children. *The day had been going so perfectly, Detective Jefferson.* Lyerman let his mind wander out to Blade Prison Island for a moment. Thinking about what was out there. What he had brought back. He licked his lips, watching it move again and again in his mind.

That's right, Detective Jefferson, I'm trapped in this chair. But things aren't always what they seem, are they?

Jefferson was slowly sifting through the black-and-white glossy photographs from the Lyerman crime scene. Bodies lying, necks flung back, blackball eyes bulging—it was all the same, nothing new to see. Sighing, he tossed the glossy prints onto his desk and leaned back in his chair, the springs creaking as he moved. He stretched his arms over his head, and groaned with the satisfaction of loosening tight joints. Most of the station was dark, the last remaining light from the day filtering in through the windows. He heard the *clip, clip, clip* of someone typing up a report somewhere in the files room next door.

The top of Jefferson's desk was almost bare. A small cactus plant stood on the corner, next to his childhood Felix the Cat clock, which read 6:30 P.M. The rest of the desk's space was taken up by the Lyerman photographs and a few file folders from other cases that were also "currently under investigation."

Brogan was a few feet away, eyebrows creased as he peered through his glasses at Reggie's photograph and parole report. Empty milk cartons were lined up on his desk, forming a small row across the front. A half-eaten Snickers bar, still partially wrapped, lay forgotten by an electric pencil sharpener.

Jefferson wondered how long the candy bar had been there.

Brogan's phone rang. Jefferson turned to glance out the window, listening absent-mindedly to his partner speaking softly. "Hello? Yeah, this is him . . ."

Outside, in the intense summer heat, a cry of voices sounded as a group of three kids rode by on bikes, pedaling hard, racing each other home.

Behind him, Brogan was silent; whoever was on the other end of the line seemed to be speaking.

Jefferson felt a vibration in his front pocket, his cell phone going off. Flipping it open, he saw McKenna's number flash on the display. Taking a look at Brogan, he stood, stepping out into the hall for a moment.

"Hello?"

"Hey, it's me," she said. "Got your message."

"Yeah? What do you think?"

"Don't know. I copied down the writing, I'll look into it. This guy obviously has some kind of obsession with demonology. That seems to be what's driving him. I don't know why he's choosing his victims yet though."

"I might have something on that."

"What?"

"Don't know exactly yet. Blade Prison keeps coming up. There's something there. I can feel it."

Silence for a moment.

"All right," McKenna said finally. "I'll look into the demonology aspect of it. But you be careful, OK?"

"Sure. I will."

Jefferson clicked shut the phone and walked back into the office. Brogan was in the process of hanging up the phone. As Jefferson entered, Brogan said a few words, then slammed the receiver back into its cradle.

"We got this fuck," Brogan said.

"Who?"

Outside, the laughter of the three kids on bikes faded into the distance.

"Our boy," Brogan said. "We got our killer."

Brogan explained as they walked down the long, dark corridors of the station.

"That was Vincent." Brogan was cinching up his pistol harness tight around his back. "He got a call from forensics. They pulled a few usable prints from the Sinatra house. Vincent talked to some people in the neighborhood, found out that the Sinatras had a few usual visitors. One, a Maria Alvarez, works for One Price Home Cleaners. She's their cleaning lady. Found her prints all over the house. Another was a Thomas Mancini, plumber, Vincent checked him and it turns out that Sinatra had some new fixtures put in his bathroom last week. Found his prints on the sink and the bathroom light switches. Three, Matthew Brian, eight-year-old kid that lives down the street, prints all over the kitchen. Apparently he liked Mrs. Sinatra's cooking."

"Those seem clean."

"Those are the ones we didn't have on record. Four, a Ron Saint. Three B & E priors, currently on parole after serving four years of a nine-year sentence at Blade Prison," Brogan continued. "Which of Mr. Sinatra's guests doesn't fit?"

"Mystery guest number four."

Brogan finished securing his gun as the two men pushed open the doors and stepped out into the rapidly cooling evening air.

"So how's this gonna work?" Jefferson asked.

"Vincent said they pulled the guy's file. He's been checking in monthly with his P.O. Officer, and his listed address is over in the Walnut Park Projects. I made some calls, got three black-and-whites and SWAT headed down there now, along with Vincent. He's going to meet us there. Once we get there, we go in and get him."

"Good," Jefferson replied.

Brogan jammed his silver .38 revolver back into the holster, the leather creaking against the metal. "Yeah, I've been wanting to meet this guy."

———

The Walnut Park Projects consisted of twenty redbrick low-income apartment buildings clustered around a small grassy park. Inside the park was a series of picnic benches and an old rusted-out seesaw. The grass was sparse, ground to patches of dirt and dried mud, flanked by white concrete sidewalks, with a chain-link fence running along the front.

As they pulled slowly up along the street, Jefferson saw three police cruisers, SWAT truck-sized tactical transport and command vehicle, and Vincent's black Ford Escort lined along the street. Vincent stepped off the sidewalk, waving their car to the side. He was wearing gray suit pants, with a black Kevlar-armored vest over his white shirt and tie.

Brogan pulled the car alongside the curb and shut off the engine.

"We think he's still inside," Vincent reported, as Brogan and Jefferson stepped out of their car. Vincent handed Brogan a stack of glossy black-and-white mug shots, which showed a muscular black man standing in front of a height-marked wall. Ron Saint's arrest photo from his previous B&E. Brogan distributed the photos to the SWAT team. Each man took a glance at the face before folding the photo inside the breast pocket of his Kevlar jacket.

An elderly Italian man in tan cotton pants and a pink button-down shirt was standing behind Vincent. He looked nervous, a thick ring of keys jingling from a loop around his belt.

Vincent jerked his thumb at the man. "The super here says each apartment's got three rooms, a living room–kitchen area, and two bedrooms. So when we go in, we've just got three rooms to clear."

Jefferson looked up at the four buildings rising in front of him, wondering which one their man's apartment was in.

Brogan gestured toward the building on the right. "He's number 301 C," he said to Jefferson. "We've got five men on the entry team, plus you and Vincent makes seven."

Standing behind Vincent, wearing upper body armor and black coveralls, was the small group of SWAT members. A couple of them looked young, their eyes wide and nervous. Jefferson felt queasy in his stomach.

"Jefferson and I will take the lead," Brogan continued. "We don't know what's going on in there. If this is our man, he's liable to be armed, and we're not just delivering him a pizza, so he probably won't take to kindly to us barging in."

Beyond Brogan's shoulder, a couple of teenagers were leaning up against the fence, watching the officers. One of them smiled when he saw Jefferson looking their way. "Hey, who you here to get?"

"It'll be you in a second if you don't get outta here." Jefferson waved them away. "Get home."

"I don't live here."

"Well, then, get where you live, all right?"

One of the teenagers nodded. He was about thirteen, his hair cut close to his head, a big gold chain dangling loosely around his neck.

"What kinda guns y'all got?"

"What?"

"You gonna shoot someone up? Raymond Robinson got shot up just last week. He and his ol' girl were just strolling through the park when—"

"Get home," Brogan interrupted.

"Damn, all right."

Neither of the boys moved. One of them unwrapped a lollipop, rolling it casually around in his mouth as he watched the cops.

Brogan turned back to Jefferson. "Anyway, you want to suit up?"

"Yeah."

Brogan nodded, stepped over to their car, and opened the trunk. A yellow lamp flicked on, lighting up the compartment's interior. Jefferson saw a row of three Bennelli shotguns, several SIG SAUER .40 cal pistols, MP5 machines guns, and boxes of ammo. "I've got an extra vest in here," Vincent said, pulling out the bulky armor. He shut the trunk and the light went out. "Here, so take it if you want. Just like being back in fucking Bosnia, eh partner?"

Jefferson nodded.

Jefferson fastened the Velcro straps of the vest, feeling its heaviness surround his body. As the night continued to grow cooler, the officers moved forward, toward the Walnut Park Project buildings.

As they passed along the fence, Jefferson took a last look at the two kids. "Go on, get outta here."

He gestured at them sternly.

They remained, watching in bug-eyed silence as the train of armored police officers passed by.

The men moved quietly along the sidewalk, skirting along the boundary of the complex as they jogged toward Saint's building. As they approached the doorway, Jefferson heard the faint canned laughter of a television sitcom coming from one of the open ground-floor windows.

A woman out by the front stoop, sitting in a lawn chair and sipping a Cherry Coke, murmured, "Gah damn," as the armed officers passed by, moving into the interior of the apartment building.

Inside the building, they moved quickly up the stairs, Brogan leading. The passageway was dimly lit and made of wet-looking concrete, which smelled faintly of dirt and DeCon rat poison. The sound of their feet echoed off the walls as they jogged upward in a single file. Someone had spray painted in silver graffiti the phrase, "Pale and KRZ 99" across the wall of the second-floor landing. Two rows of empty beer bottles, still sitting in a neat row in their cardboard six-pack container, sat on the floor in the corner, near a cluster of dead cockroaches, their hard-shelled bodies turned upside down, their little legs sticking into the air.

"One more up," Brogan said as they moved to the second floor.

Jefferson took out his Beretta, holding it with his finger across the metal trigger guard. They reached the third floor. The hallway beyond the stairwell door was quiet. The sound of a radio filtered through one of the doors.

The officers moved quietly down the hallway and stopped before 301 C, Saint's place. The numbers were made of a dirty, silver-colored metal; the C had fallen and hung upside down, dangling from the door by a single screw. Brogan pressed his ear to the door and shook his head once. Gently reaching into his pocket, he eased out the set of keys the super had given him. Finding the one labeled 301 C, he quietly slipped the key into the lock. Jefferson felt his lungs burn suddenly. He realized he'd been holding his breath. Slowly he released the air, feeling the pain die away. He swallowed hard and clutched the butt of his Beretta. Behind him he could hear the other officers' labored breathing.

When Brogan turned the key, nothing happened. The outer rim of the lock was shiny, much newer-looking than the rest of the door. Saint had probably had the locks changed. Brogan tried the key again, then shook his head twice, cutting his hand across his throat. He reached across his face, making a pulling motion over his head. The officers nodded, pulling gas masks around their mouths. Looking around, Jefferson fumbled with his, sliding the hard-plastic-and-glass unit over his head, instantly feeling an intense claustrophobia.

Moving away from the door, Brogan pointed two fingers toward an officer in back of him, then, with a swift jerk of his hand, gestured toward the door's hinges. The officer nodded and moved to the front, carrying a large, black Bennelli tactical shotgun. He pointed the weapon toward the top hinge. Turning his head away, he pulled the trigger.

The hallway exploded with noise as the hinge blew away in a cloud of dust and wood splinters, leaving a gaping hole where the metal had been. The officer quickly pumped the shotgun, chambering the next shell and, with another explosion, blew out the bottom hinge.

Brogan kicked sharply against the wood, and, without hinges, the door crashed open.

"Go, go!" someone was shouting.

Brogan tossed a gas grenade into the room. It exploded upon impact, releasing a thick cloud of tear gas into the apartment. Jefferson felt a surge of excitement from behind him, as he was half-pushed through the doorway.

Brogan moved in ahead of him, staying low to the ground. Someone else was yelling, "Boston Police! Boston Police!"

Through the gas, Jefferson caught glimpses of a sofa pushed against the wall, a bookshelf filled with a few framed photographs and some old books, an upright halogen lamp. The officers were filling up the room, moving quickly forward. Around them, the white gas was cut by red laser lines from the SWAT weaponry, the red dots and streaks sweeping around the room.

A door at the end of the room banged open, and a gigantically muscular man flew out toward them. The man was bare-chested, wearing only a pair of sweatpants. His upper body was covered in tattoos and his head was shaved bald. His features were twisted with rage, but in that instant Jefferson recognized the face of Ron Saint.

Behind him, Jefferson saw a bathroom, filled with the steam from a shower that had just been turned off. He had a moment to take this all in, before the large man crashed into the row of officers. Saint struck against Jefferson first, the blow coming unexpectedly, burying deep into his gut and knocking the air from his lungs. Jefferson gasped and slowly began sinking to the floor. The other officers were trying to subdue Saint, grabbing out for his arms and legs. "Get him, get him!" He was twisting around; lashing out, he struck Vincent across the face, knocking him to the carpeted floor.

One of the officers was choking Saint from behind, Saint's fingers clawing at the officer's arm. Saint reared up and, running backward, smashed into the bookshelf pressed against one wall of the room. The officer grunted with pain, "Ahh, fuck!" and released his grip, falling to his knees as a clatter of broken glass from the bookshelf fell around him.

Jefferson pulled himself to his feet and tackled Saint, bringing him to the ground. Saint was strong, and Jefferson felt the man's fingers close around his throat. Gasping, Jefferson tried to pry them off. They twisted over, until Jefferson lay pinned on his back, Saint's knees pressing his arms painfully against the ground. He could see Saint's chest twitching as he strained, the two large pectoral muscles bulging. There was a burn mark on his left shoulder, a stylized B with a knife running through the center of it—the symbol for Blade Prison.

Through blurry, dancing vision, Jefferson glimpsed Brogan moving quickly toward him, holding on to one of the shotguns. Calmly, Brogan lifted the heavy weapon and brought its solid metal butt down on the back of Saint's head. The weapon hit Saint's skull with a crack. The man sighed once, then his eyes rolled back, and he collapsed in a heap on top of Jefferson.

Jefferson grunted, pushing the heavy weight off him.

"Thanks." He nodded toward Brogan, gingerly rubbing his tender windpipe. "I needed that."

Brogan shrugged. "No problem."

Vincent stood up, feeling his jaw, lightly shifting it back and forth. He ran a finger through his mouth, checking for broken teeth. His finger came out bloody.

"All right, let's cuff this fucking gorilla before he wakes up," Brogan said, gesturing to two officers standing by the door.

They moved forward, bending the unconscious man's arms backward, clipping them together with a pair of handcuffs. Reaching under each arm, the two officers lifted the large man, his head swaying back and forth, his feet dragging on the ground. A third officer grabbed Saint's feet, and all three men carried him out of the apartment and down to the waiting car.

Jefferson took a glance around.

The apartment looked like a hurricane had just blown through. The bookshelf was overturned, with loose books scattered across the carpet. Bits of broken glass littered the floor, shaken loose from the several broken picture frames. The kitchen adjoined the living room. Jefferson opened up the refrigerator and saw a carton of skim milk and several packages of chicken breasts. A few loose cans of baked beans lined the kitchen counter, next to a blender and a large plastic jug labeled OPTIMAL PROTEIN POWDER. He opened the window and turned on the vent over the stove, trying to get rid of the tear gas smoke.

Brogan was over by the bookcase, sifting through the loose material on the ground.

"What you got over there?" Jefferson asked, indicating the mess.

Brogan shrugged, prodding the books with his foot. "Mostly Louis L'Amour books, looks like." He moved over to the television.

Stacked underneath was a series of unmarked videotape boxes.

"Porn?" Jefferson asked, nodding toward the videos.

Brogan peaked inside one, pulling out the black tape. He held it up. "*The Good, the Bad and the Ugly*, these are all Clint Eastwood movies . . . this guy must love Westerns."

"Got something here." From out of the bedroom stepped Vincent. With a gloved hand, he held up a .22 revolver. "Found it in the bedroom. Sitting in plain view right on the nightstand."

Jefferson glanced at Brogan. "Yeah, except none of our victims were killed with a .22. None of them were even shot."

Brogan spoke to one of the officers still standing by the door. "Notify someone in the DA's Office that we need a search warrant for this place in connection with the Sinatra murders. Then get on the radio to CSU and have them prepared to come down here, all right? Tell them I want a full check of this place, top to bottom, anything unusual, hairs, carpet fibers, blood. Anything."

The officer nodded. "Yes, sir," he said, and turned to leave.

"Wait. Hold up, one more thing." Vincent took an evidence bag from his pocket and delicately slipped the gun inside, sealing up the bag and handing it to the officer. "Here take this to evidence."

He held out the sealed weapon. The officer took it and disappeared out the doorway.

Vincent turned toward Jefferson. "But I bet we can trace that piece to something though."

Jefferson moved into the bathroom. He opened a small window over the tub to let the steam from Saint's shower filter out. Two toothbrushes were sitting on the windowsill, next to a small, pink plastic container. He picked up the container and opened it. Inside was a circular ring of birth control pills.

"Hey, look at this." Jefferson held them up. "Either our man is really a woman, or he's got a girlfriend coming over. Two toothbrushes here, too."

Vincent nodded, walking out of the bedroom holding a red lace bra. "And I found this on the bed in there. All right, let's see if we can find this girlfriend, pick her up, too."

Jefferson stepped into the kitchen. An open window looked out over the back of the housing project. Below, Jefferson saw a narrow alley slicked with oil stains and ending in a pair of open Dumpsters.

In the bedroom, Brogan was bending to look underneath the bed. "There's nothing really in here that I can see." He stood up, stretching out his back. "We did find this, though." He held out a small plastic identification card for Wakefield Elementary.

"Holy shit," someone shouted from the next room. "Jesus, look at this."

One of the patrol officers was standing, openmouthed, staring through the open doorway and into a second back bedroom of Saint's apartment. Brogan joined the man quickly, brushing him aside and looking into the room. He turned immediately to Jefferson.

"What?" Jefferson said, still standing in the kitchen, inspecting the bottom of the silverware drawer.

"You better check this out," Brogan said quietly.

Something in the room was flickering, throwing wild shadows across the faces of the two officers standing in the doorway. Jefferson closed the kitchen drawer, moving quickly across the floor, toward the open bedroom. He peered inside. The room was small, darkened by a shade pulled over the single window in the back. Across the front wall, opposite the window, were three long shelves. Each of the shelves was lined with lit candles, filling the white-walled room with orange light. The candles were assorted colors and sizes, their flames flickering in the breeze coming from the open doorway. Even standing outside the room, Jefferson smelled the strong scent of burning incense and melting wax.

"Looks like some kind of shrine," Brogan murmured. "Christ, there must be fifty candles in there."

Jefferson moved past him, slowly stepping into the room. On the floor was a large wooden bowl, lying on a tan-colored reed mat. The bowl was filled with a thick, dark liquid. Jefferson bent, smelling the contents.

"It's blood," he said slowly, standing back up.

A few drops from the bowl had spilled onto the floor and created circular crimson stains on the white carpet. Lying beyond the bowl was a long machete, the shiny blade colored red and orange from blood and the reflected candle flames. The long knife lay on a folded newspaper to prevent the bloodied blade from staining the carpet. Lying next to the newspaper was a wreath made from thorn branches, leaves, straw, and red berries. The three articles were arranged as an altar, placed in front of the rows of candles.

One side of the bowl was stained with an arc of blood, reaching up to the lip of the bowl, as if someone had been using it to pour, or to drink from. Curious, Jefferson looked around the room. On the nearest wall, cut by the doorway, an image was painted across the white walls. It looked like a series of wide streaks of dark paint slashed across the white. Jefferson cocked his head, trying to piece together the lines.

"Hey," Jefferson said to Brogan. "Look at this."

Brogan stepped into the room, turning toward the wall. "What the hell is it?"

"Don't know."

The door stood open, breaking the picture, the lights from the outside hallway flooding into the room.

"Shut the door for a second, will you, Billy?" Jefferson said to the uniformed officer.

"Sure thing," the officer replied, reaching into the room and pulling on the door.

As the door shut, the plane of the wall became solid, the lines of the image coming together on the back of the door, completing the picture.

"It's a monkey." Brogan's voice reflected his amazement.

It was just that. A monkey.

The body extended from the door, while the head and face were centered above the frame. It was hissing, its arms outstretched in front, tail erect, claws showing as it swiped at something invisible in the air. Jagged lines had even been drawn to indicate its hairs standing upright, making it look even more vicious.

The position of the drawing relative to the door gave the impression that the monkey was waiting to attack anything coming through the door, as if it were protecting the room.

Brogan had the same impression. "Looks like Saint was afraid of something."

Jefferson nodded.

He wondered what it was.

Jefferson felt a tap on his shoulder as he stepped out of Saint's bedroom, still thinking of the strange image of the monkey painted across the walls. Detective Vincent was looking at him, a concerned expression on his face.

"Can I talk to you for a moment?"

Jefferson nodded. "Yeah, sure, what's up?"

"Brogan, too."

Brogan was in the living room talking to a uniformed cop. Jefferson called him over and Vincent led the two men into the first bedroom, the one actually having the bed in it. Vincent closed the door as they entered, standing awkwardly next to the bed.

"What's up?" Brogan asked.

"I heard it again," Vincent said.

"What?"

"You know what," Vincent answered. "The voices. Same as we heard in Zvornik."

"I didn't hear nothing in Zvornik," Brogan answered. "Nothing."

"But you did," Vincent said, pointing to Jefferson. "You heard something. You know what I mean."

Jefferson shrugged. "Well . . . I did hear . . . something. I don't know what it was though."

"And that hanged man. You saw that, too, right?"

Jefferson nodded. "Yeah."

"Something happened that night. We all felt something . . . wrong . . . that night. I think whatever that was, it followed us here, somehow found us back in Boston."

Brogan shook his head. "Aww, c'mon, don't start in with that Zvornik crap again.

We left all that behind. What happened out there is between us three and JC, it doesn't go any further. I thought we agreed to that."

"We did," Vincent answered. "But whatever, *it* is, *it* didn't agree to that. Something is here, I can feel it. Last night I woke up having this horrible dream, and I could feel that something was in the room with me. There were these shadows racing across the ceiling, and I heard the voice again."

"You heard the voice?" Jefferson asked.

Vincent nodded.

Brogan shook his head. "You were dreaming. I had nightmares for months about that night."

"No, not this time. I was awake, and I heard it."

There was a knock on the bedroom door. A uniformed police officer stuck his head in, and announced, "Detective Vincent, you're wanted on the radio."

Vincent nodded, then, waiting until the door was shut again, said, "I tell you, I've got a feeling that what we did in Zvornik has come back for us. I feel it in my heart."

And without saying anything else, he left them standing in the bedroom.

Two of the officers were standing out in the hallway, arms outstretched, holding back a small crowd of curious people as Jefferson and Brogan slowly began pushing their way through the group. Jefferson felt a sudden tug on his arm. "It's about time you people showed up," said a female voice in a thick Polish accent.

An elderly lady, her hair in curlers, with pink slippers on her feet, was holding on to his arm. "I call you people yesterday, but nobody show. I tell you something was going on. You get rid o' that smell?"

"What?"

"That smell. You get rid of it?"

"What smell?"

The woman let go of Jefferson's arm, holding her forehead in amazement. "You mean you didn't do nuthin' 'bout it?"

Jefferson glanced over at Brogan. Brogan shrugged, raising his hands.

"Down in Apartment 14 B," the lady said. "It's that god-awful stink. I been saying for days. I work in County Hospital morgue for ten years. I recognize that smell."

"What is it?" Jefferson asked.

The woman looked at him for a moment, studying his face, in confusion. Finally, she said, slowly, in the way you talk to a third-grader, "It is the smell a body makes. A dead body."

It took almost ten minutes for Jefferson and Brogan to track down the super. He was in the basement arranging piles of old newspapers, pushing them neatly against the wall. "Who lives in Apartment 14 B?" Brogan was shining his flashlight around the corners of the basement, the beam sliding across the walls.

The super stopped, straightening up his back and scratching his neck. "Well, let me see. From what I remember, 14 B is unoccupied right now. We had a fire in there a few months ago, never got a chance to renovate the place."

"You got the keys to get in there?" Brogan shined the light at the super's brown loafers.

"Yeah, I got the keys," the super replied. Continuing to scratch his neck with one hand, he unclipped a key ring hanging from his belt and handed it to Brogan. "All the keys there are labeled," he indicated. "Should be anyway, unless it peeled off."

Brogan took the keys and flipped them to Jefferson.

"You boys want me to join you up there?" the super asked nervously, obviously hoping they would decline. "It's starting to rain, gets to my knees a little bit."

The super rubbed his knees as he spoke. "You know how it is."

Brogan shook his head. "No, that's all right. 14 B, where's that? Building on the left?"

"No, building in the middle, ground floor." The super looked at the keys. "That's my only set for that building, so . . ." His voice trailed off.

"We'll take good care, don't worry."

It had already begun to rain when Jefferson and Brogan stepped out of the Walnut Park Projects C Building. A skinny black kid in a long Fubu T-shirt came running toward them, covering his head with a folded newspaper. He squeezed past the two officers, moving into the stairwell and disappearing upstairs. The rain had begun to turn parts of the path to mud, mixed with the occasional thick strand of crabgrass. "You know, I was born a block away from here?" Brogan said suddenly, as they carefully made their way over the wet gravel.

Jefferson shook his head.

"Yeah, course that was when this wasn't such a bad place. People were working then, always at their jobs, no time to be dealing dope, shooting each other, and shit."

Brogan carefully stepped over a puddle. "Ah, well, times change I guess. No use being sentimental."

Building C of the Walnut Park Projects stood in front of them, rising out of the concrete glazed with wetness. Windows in the building were sporadically lit, and all were shut against the falling rain. The apartments on the ground floor started with 3 B. Jefferson noticed that the last door on the front was labeled 9 B. "Fourteen B must be around back," Jefferson said, shielding his eyes from the rain.

They walked quickly, shielding their eyes against the cold drizzle. The windows of Apartment 14 B were boarded-up, the door shut tightly. Even from outside, the smell was overwhelming, and Jefferson knew that this time it wasn't just from body odor and rotting food.

The old lady was right—Apartment 14 B had a dead body inside.

"We got something in here all right." Brogan was delicately holding a finger under his nose.

"I'd say the cleaning lady hasn't passed through here in a few weeks." Jefferson paused for a moment in front of the door. The only indication of the apartment's number was the 14 B written in black pen on the silver doorframe. Jefferson hesitated for a moment, fighting down an instinct to knock on the door.

"You waiting for him to let us in?" Brogan smiled. "I don't think anyone's home."

"Yeah," Jefferson answered. "Just give me a second."

Jefferson inhaled deeply through his nose, taking in a last breath of fresh air, like a diver about to jump into the black unknown waters.

He turned the handle and pushed open the door.

The smell of decay and fetid air rushed to meet him. He turned his head involuntarily, trying to shut off his nose.

Still in the doorway, holding open the door, Jefferson gestured to a trash can lid lying against the wall. "Yo, hand that to me?"

Brogan nodded, bent, and handed him the lid.

Jefferson propped the door open with the circular metal, trying to ventilate the place a little before he actually had to go in. Turning on his flashlight, he shined the beam of light into the room, letting it move slowly over everything.

The first room was empty. A black arc of soot and melted plasterboard stretched along one of the walls, over a thin, chewed-up carpet. Jefferson remembered that the super had said the place had been partially destroyed in a fire. It looked like it. The burn mark continued across the ceiling, where several tiles had fallen, smashing against the floor. All the walls were stained slightly brown. Jefferson figured it was both from the smoke of the fire and the water damage of the hoses.

Without the complete white of the walls to reflect the light of the flashlight, the apartment seemed even darker than the last one. Jefferson ducked his head into the bathroom. The room was also empty, the toilet dried out, a few dead insects lying in the sink. The shower curtain had long ago been removed, but a single bottle of Sesame Street Shampoo stood forgotten on the tub's basin. The bottle had an illustration of Bert covered in suds, taking a bath. Jefferson experienced a fleeting moment of sadness.

He felt a tap on his shoulder. Brogan was standing behind him, pointing into the last room of the apartment. Jefferson shined his light inside the dark room.

The body was there, dull in the flashlight beam. It was in bad shape.

Jefferson could see it was a man, probably early twenties, but it was tough to tell—the eyes had already disappeared into blackballs, his body puffing out slightly from gas. He was lying in the middle of the carpet, the main attraction in an otherwise featureless room. He'd been left on his back, one arm up, almost languidly cupping his chest, the other thrown out wide of his body with one leg hooked up underneath the other. A Red Sox hat lay a few feet away from him, its top crushed into the crust of dried blood that permeated the carpet.

One of the legs of his jeans had been rolled up almost to the knee, his sock underneath hanging limply. His bare legs were skinny, the skin dull and gray. He was wearing a white tank top, with a gold herringbone chain hanging loosely around his neck.

The front of his shirt had a quarter-sized hole of dark blood in it; Jefferson recognized the familiar entry wound of a smaller-caliber handgun. "Looks like a .22," Jefferson said. "This doesn't fit with our man."

"Yeah, well, maybe he likes a little variety. A shooting here, stabbing there . . ." Brogan's voice trailed off.

"No." Jefferson shook his head. "This doesn't make sense. I think this is something else."

"Just regular Joes popping each other off?"

"Yeah, something like that."

Brogan bent over the body, gently patting the man's pockets. He pointed to a beeper still clipped to the man's waist. "Drugs?"

"Everyone and their pets have beepers now."

"His wallet's gone, too—looks like he got robbed—but they left the herringbone."

"Probably just moving fast. Didn't see it."

"Something that big? This guy looks like Mr. T. No way you'd miss that."

Brogan stood up, stepping carefully away from the body.

"Well, what'd you wanna do?"

"Let's call this in and get back and see what our new friend Saint has to say for himself. Maybe he can explain why there's a body in the building next to his and why his prints are all over that lawyer's place."

Jefferson and Brogan, with Bruce Harding, one of the ADAs, stood behind the small one-way glass window looking into the station's interrogation room. Saint was sitting in the small room by himself. Nobody had remembered to get him clothes from his apartment, so after they brought him to the station, he sat in the car while two officers went inside to find him something.

Now he was seated, feet crossed, elbows raised on the room's long plastic-covered table wearing a T-shirt that had "DARE to Keep Kids off Drugs," across the front in red lettering, and "Boston's 4th Annual Bicycle Race, May 2" along the back. The station always had extras from when the department sponsored a charity race a few years back. Saint also had on plain light blue shorts someone had found on the floor of the locker room. They were too small, and his massive quads split out the sides in large block sections of muscle.

He sat behind the table looking uncomfortable, biting his fingernails, and occasionally looking up at the room. "We got Judge Goldstein out of bed and had him sign the search warrant, we got guys over at Saint's apartment now looking at the place," Harding, the assistant district attorney said. "Hopefully we'll find something we can use."

Harding had graduated from Princeton, then NYU Law School. It was going on 9 P.M., but he still looked freshly pressed. His hair was slightly wet, and pushed straight back from his forehead, and he was wearing a dark blue suit that hung comfortably around his body.

"Don't push him too hard," Harding continued, unconsciously smoothing out his tie in front of him. "We haven't decided to arrest him yet."

Jefferson nodded, then looked at Brogan. "You want to go in together?"

"Yeah sure. You talk."

Jefferson opened the door from the observation room into the interrogation room. Saint jumped at the sound of the handle, turning quickly toward Jefferson. He momentarily stopped biting his fingernails, placing his hands nervously on the table in front of him.

Brogan took a place by the door as Jefferson entered the room.

"How you doing?" Jefferson smiled, pulling out one of chairs and sitting.

Saint nodded, straightening his back against the chair.

"I'm Detective Jefferson." Jefferson indicated Brogan, standing in the corner of the windowless interrogation room. "My associate over there is Lieutenant Brogan."

Saint nodded, barely looking at the two detectives. Neither man moved to shake hands. He was staring off into space, his mind somewhere else. Jefferson snapped his finger as he sat. "Hey, you with me?"

Saint's head snapped toward him, his eyes glazed and unfocused.

Jefferson turned around, making eye contact with Brogan. Brogan shrugged.

"All right, uh." Jefferson cleared his throat. "So you are Ronald Saint, that right?"

There was no response.

A bead of sweat hung on Saint's forehead, dangling for a moment before sliding down his face. Saint let it run, his hands immobile.

"Hey, Saint," Brogan said forcefully. "You with us?"

Saint's eyes snapped into focus, he glanced at Jefferson. "Yeah," he murmured, shaking his head.

Jefferson nodded. "You working now?"

"Yeah, uh-huh." Saint ran a hand over his head. "Maintenance, over at Wakefield Elementary."

"Wakefield, huh? Where is that, downtown?"

"Naw, it's North of the city."

"Pretty long drive for you?"

"Yeah, well, my P.O. Officer fixed me up with this job." Saint smirked for a moment. "He got some kinda special deal or something with the principal."

Jefferson nodded. "What kinda deal is that?"

"It's a deal that makes me drive over an hour just to get to work every day."

Jefferson figured Saint was talking about kickbacks. The parole officer fixes him up with a job and keeps writing him good recommendations, but in return, part of Saint's salary gets kicked back to the officer.

Jefferson let it drop.

"So where are you living now?"

Saint looked at him for a moment, one hand against the back of his head, leaning back in his chair. He looked at the table, a sarcastic smirk creeping across his face. "Shit, y'all know where I live. You just busted into my place like Clint Eastwood or some shit. What, you saying you forgot my address already?"

Jefferson paused a moment. "For the record."

"I'm up at Walnut Park Projects, 301 C."

"You like living there?" Jefferson wanted to keep him talking on easy subjects, keep him relaxed.

"Like it?" Saint looked confused for a moment. "It's the projects, man, what do you think?" Jefferson stared at him. Saint shrugged. "Yeah, it's all right. It ain't no Ritz Hotel or nothing, but it's all right."

"You got a girlfriend?"

"Naw," Saint said shyly. "Well, you know."

"C'mon, you got a girl?"

Saint was playing with his hands, looking at his fingernails, the skin still puckered from getting out of the shower.

"Naw, I ain't got time to have a girl. Just girls from around the way. Nothing serious though. I'm always working."

"What about the birth control pills you had in your medicine cabinet?"

"The what?" Saint looked genuinely confused.

"The birth control pills. They were sitting in your medicine cabinet."

Saint banged the table, suddenly looking annoyed. "Gah dammit, Sharin," he hissed to himself.

"Who's Sharin?"

"Sharin? She's my sister. She staying up at my place from time to time."

Brogan laughed. "So, what are you guys sleeping together?"

"What?" Saint looked disgusted. "With Sharin? Who do I look like, one a those inbred white motherfuckers they got down in Arkansas?"

"So what's the problem?"

Saint looked at the table. "Nothing, forget it." He waved his hand.

"Well, she's sleeping with somebody, is that the problem?"

"Naw, look"—Saint glanced uncomfortably around the room—"she makes her money in a certain way. She ain't really got no other choice, after she got fired from her last job, she just needed some money."

"So she's a prostitute," Jefferson said.

"C'mon, man, don't call her that, she's my sister." Saint shrugged. "She makes her money from time to time with other men. I told her them pills don't do shit. They don't protect her from everything. They only make it so you can't get pregnant, other than that though. She says condoms cost too much money and sometimes her customer don't wanna wear 'em. Pay her extra to go without, you know? I tell her that's crazy, but sometimes she don't listen to me I guess."

Jefferson nodded. It sounded like Saint was telling the truth. He almost felt sorry for him. "All right, so she lives with you sometimes."

"Yeah."

"How long you been outta jail for?"

"I been outta Blade for about a year."

"You looking to go back?"

Saint glanced up at Jefferson. "You crazy?"

"We found a .22 on your nightstand," Jefferson said. "And a man with a .22 hole punched in him behind your apartment. You know anything about that?"

"Man was bad news," Saint said slowly. "Sold drugs to kids. He got what was coming. But no, I don't know nothing about that."

"That's not why we're here though," Jefferson replied. "You know why you're here?"

Saint looked away, staring off at the walls. He murmured something.

"What?" Jefferson asked, leaning forward.

Saint turned toward him. "Yeah, maybe. I think so."

"We found your fingerprints on a doorknob in the home of Thomas Sinatra. The lawyer in Beacon Hill."

"Un-huh."

"We found Thomas Sinatra in the bedroom . . . and parts of him in the living room, and some more in the kitchen. It looked like someone was trying a little interior decorating with the inside of his body."

"Yeah?"

"Yeah?" Jefferson said. "That's all you can say is 'yeah'?"

"Well, damn, I didn't do that shit. I don't even know the dude." Saint was bouncing around in his seat playing the "damn, I dunno" game.

"There was no forced entry, how'd you get into his house?"

Saint shrugged. "Five knew a guy. He said he was his man."

"Who was he?"

"I think he was an ex-guard. Out at Blade Prison, where we all served together. That's where I met Five and Q and those guys, out on Blade. Shit out there makes Concord Correctional look like Disneyland. I think this dude was a guard out there, used to be anyway."

"Used to be?"

"I heard he got fired, something 'bout sneaking around Blade at night, keeping track a things and shit. Like he'd found something out there and was trying to sell it or something."

"Found what?"

"I dunno, pirate treasure, shit. Who knows?"

"You served time at Blade?"

"That's right."

"How long?"

" 'Bout four years."

Brogan leaned back in his chair, regarding Saint.

"All right," Brogan said. "Tell me something more."

"Nothing more to tell."

"C'mon, Saint, we got your prints at the house. Which puts you at the scene. We got five dead bodies, and they're tied to murders all over the city. You want all this shit coming down on you?"

Saint opened his mouth to speak, but Jefferson interrupted. "Those words coming out of your mouth better be about how your fingerprints got on that door. And how you're sitting here in one piece, but everyone else looks like they went through a meat grinder. Then we show up at your place, you bust one of my men's jaws and we find a bowl full of blood and a machete in your bedroom." Jefferson paused, catching his breath. "So right now, I don't think it's looking too promising for you."

"All right, look." Saint leaned forward on the table. "How do I know that if I tell you something, you won't just go bust my ass back to Blade?"

"You don't know; I can't promise anything."

"Man, then forget it." Saint banged his hand on the table. "My shit's on parole, I'm not going back."

Jefferson turned to Brogan. "All right, let's lock him up for the night."

Brogan smiled, moving forward. "With pleasure."

Saint held up one hand. "Yo, wait a minute."

"You want to do this the hard way, not me."

"You can't lock me up tonight." Saint's eyes were wide. Jefferson was surprised, the big man looked frightened. "I can't be locked up."

Saint was getting worked up. He pushed his chair away from the table and was holding both hands up, preparing to ward off the two officers.

Jefferson stood up, holding one hand toward Saint, trying to calm him down. "Whoa, hey, wait . . . hang on a minute."

"You can't lock me up!" Saint was almost shouting, backing away toward the back wall of the interrogation room, his veins pulsing. It didn't make sense. Saint was a rough rider, he'd been locked up before. Shouldn't be anything that could frighten him like this on the inside. Brogan was moving forward, rubbing the knuckles of his right hand with his left palm. Jefferson held him back for a moment, almost imperceptibly shaking his head.

He looked at Saint, the bigger man cowering in the corner.

Saint was staring at him, but his eyes were round and glazed. His mind was some-place else again. Slowly, the ex-convict lowered himself to the floor, where he sat, back pressed against the corner, knees tucked under his chin.

"What the hell is this about?" Brogan whispered.

"Not sure."

"You wanna leave him alone for a while?"

Jefferson nodded. "Yeah, I think we better. I don't know what's going on with him. I never seen a man so scared before."

The two officers slowly backed out of the room. As they moved through the door-way, back into the station, Jefferson turned to look at Saint. He was still pressed against the corner of the wall, his giant arms wrapped delicately around his knees, the "DARE to Keep Kids off Drugs" lettering just visible across his shirt.

"How is he?"

"He's all right. He's calmed down again."

Jefferson was talking to the police psychiatrist, Rudy Phillips. Rudy had already been in the building talking with investigators on another case. After Saint's outburst, then shutdown, Jefferson had called Rudy in to have a look. They were standing in the observation room, looking in through the one-way glass into the interrogation area. Saint was sitting back at the table. He had returned to nervously biting his fingernails and staring blankly in front of him.

"He faking this?" Brogan asked.

Rudy shook his head. "I don't think so. He looks like he's experiencing some kind of severe traumatic distress."

"Can we talk to him?"

"Yeah . . ." Rudy's voice was hesitant. "Carefully. Take it easy on him. I don't know what he saw, but it messed him up." Rudy paused for a moment. "He says he wants to talk."

"He wants to talk?"

"He says he can tell you about what happened."

Jefferson glanced at Brogan. "Well, I guess we better go talk to him then."

The door made a soft *click*ing sound as Jefferson turned the knob and stepped into the interrogation room. Saint looked up from the table as they entered. He made an attempt to smile, but his words came out half-serious. "Sorry about that before. A man shouldn't act like that."

Jefferson took a seat at the interrogation table. "I've seen men do worse."

"Yeah, well"—Saint rubbed the back of his head with his palm—"I don't know 'bout that, this shit got me scared. Scared to death."

"What?"

Saint unconsciously glanced around the room for a moment, his eyes lingering an instant on Brogan, who was still leaning loosely against the door.

Saint sighed. "All right, look, me and these guys heard that this boy Sinatra had some cash up in his place. Like twenty grand."

"Who guys?" Jefferson interrupted.

"You know who," Saint said. "They all dead now. All those bodies you got."

Jefferson nodded. "All right."

"Yeah," Saint began again. "So anyway, we were planning on robbing this lawyer, Sinatra. Anyway, so we get in the back, and Five and Q go up the stairs. I'm watching the front."

"Wait a minute." Jefferson held his hand out. He flipped through a small notebook he pulled from his front pocket. "All right, uhh . . . Five is Harry Connor, right? And let me see, Q, who's that? Raymond Earl?"

Saint nodded. "Yeah, Five's real name is Harry. I dunno about Q though . . . I never heard him called anything else 'cept Q."

Jefferson put the notebook on the table. "OK, keep going."

"Where was I?"

"You were watching the front."

"Oh yeah, right. So I'm watching the front, and I hear this commotion upstairs. So as I'm looking up, something catches my eye."

"What?"

"It's like this lady, she's sitting in the dining room, just kinda watching me."

"Yeah."

"So, I go over to her." Saint breathed in. "This bitch is already dead."

"You killed her?"

Saint shook his head. "Naw, man, I didn't touch her. Someone else cut her throat. Her damn head almost fell off, like one of those bobbing head dolls, almost gave me a heart attack."

"Who did it?"

Saint shrugged. "I dunno."

"Five or Q?"

"Naw." Saint shook his head. "They were both already upstairs."

"So then you went upstairs?"

"What?"

"You went upstairs then; we found your prints on the third floor."

"Yeah, that's right, I went upstairs. Nothing but dead bodies upstairs." Saint lowered his voice, leaning in toward Jefferson. "Listen, I'm telling you, there was something in that house with us."

"What do you mean? Something?"

Saint paused for a second, drumming his fingers against the table.

Finally, he said, "You seen that shit in my apartment?"

"What?" Jefferson asked. "Those candles and all that?"

"Yeah."

"What about it?" Brogan said. "That bowl was filled with blood, wasn't it? You get that from the people you killed?"

Saint shook his head, disgusted. "No. It's chicken blood."

"Chicken blood?" Brogan repeated, almost laughing. "That's a first."

"This morning, my mom come over to my apartment carrying three chickens. Live chickens she keeps herself," Saint said slowly. "I know what's going to happen, I seen it once before, so I lay this plastic on the floor and my mom takes out this machete that she brought with her, she slaughters the chickens, catching their blood in the bowl."

Saint looked at the table for a moment more, his eyebrows knitted together. Then he turned away quickly, running his large hand over his eyes. The room was quiet for a moment. Jefferson didn't know what to say. Finally, Brogan whispered, "Why did she do that?"

"I was born here, in Boston," Saint said. "But my mom, she's from Haiti. She believes in the Voodoo. My mother is a Mambo, a voodoo priestess."

"She's a voodoo priestess," Brogan repeated dumbly.

"She knows Les Invisibles."

"What's that?"

"The spirits of the dead. She can call to them." Saint's eyes grew wider as he spoke, until Jefferson could see the meshwork of blood vessels networking the white outside rim of the eye. The veins in his arms and neck were bulging out like cords. "For protection against the evil spirits and the demons, she can call on the Loa, the immortal spirits of the dead. They come to eat the chicken meat and drink the blood, to gain strength."

"Protection from what? You're a big guy, you can take care of yourself," Jefferson said.

"I can fight a man, but . . ."

"But?"

"But . . ." Saint lowered his voice almost to a whisper. The two officers had to move closer to hear. ". . . I swear, what we saw in that apartment, that was no human."

Brogan groaned, his chair squeaking as he leaned backward. "C'mon, Saint, you bullshit us it just hurts you."

Saint leaned back and, sounding offended, said, "I'm not bullshitting, man. That's the truth."

"So, what?" Brogan said, shaking his head. "E.T. did this?"

Saint raised his hands. "Hey, you wanted to know what happened. There was something bad in that place before we got there. It killed all those people."

"Un-huh," Brogan said. "So how'd it happen that all these people get killed, but you manage to get away?"

Saint stood up suddenly, surprising Jefferson.

Expecting another outburst, Brogan crouched slightly, like a linebacker before the hit.

Instead, Saint turned around, his back to the two cops, pulling up the bottom of his sweatpants. "Look at that! Where the fuck you think I got that?"

He was pointing to the back of his left leg. Jefferson looked down to where he pointed. Running from the middle of the hamstrings, all the way to the calf, were three straight gashes. They looked recent, a still-wet sheen of blood glistening over them. They had been bandaged, but the bandages looked as though they must have pulled loose during the struggle. Bloody patches of gauze hung loosely from surgical tape clinging to the skin on his leg.

"This here," Saint said, still pointing to the cuts, "is a little souvenir left by that thing."

The marks looked familiar. They reminded Jefferson immediately of the cut wounds on Lyerman and on the bodies in the lawyer's place. They looked almost exactly the same.

Jefferson said nothing, leaning back in his chair.

Saint sat back down. "All right, look, I know someone who can help you out."

"Who?"

"My man," Saint said, as if that explained everything.

"Oh shit, I think I've heard this one before, huh Brogan?" Jefferson said. "Everyone that we bust comes in here saying they can give us everything we need to know, only it's their cousin, or a man, who knows it, and they happen to be out in L.A., but till he gets back, can't we give him a break?"

"I'm serious."

"Then give me a name."

"Ramsey. Robert Ramsey. He's killing time out at Blade."

Brogan had unwrapped a stick of gum. Placing it in his mouth, he chewed thoughtfully. "So how you know this Ramsey? You two pen pals?"

Saint turned toward him. "Yeah, something like that. I shared a cell with him for two of my four at Blade. Get to know a man pretty well."

"So what's he gonna have to say?"

"He'll have to tell you that. All I know is that some serious shit has been going down at Blade the past few months. Some *serious* shit," Saint repeated, staring solemnly at the two officers. "Something that makes what happened in that house look like a fairy tale."

The station was almost deserted. Across from him, Brogan's desk was empty, the bigger man downstairs getting coffee from the machine. His desk light was on, casting a pale arc across the floor. Somewhere below he heard the faint sound of a radio playing, the noise filtering up through the heavy granite walls and hallways of the station.

Jefferson was reading Older's book, *The History of Fort Blade Prison*, the pages open on his desk in front of him. According to the book, the prison was originally constructed as a fort; but not a Revolutionary War fort as was usually thought. In fact, the structure was built eighty years prior to the Revolutionary War, sometime during the 1690s. According to Older, the colonists in Massachusetts had been under attack by something "Which issued from the woods." Older had compiled accounts taken from diaries and reports of colonists living in the area at the time, and they all referred to some sort of unknown enemy which came from the forests at night and killed indiscriminately.

In 1689, there were thirty-five unexplained deaths, and most of these victims had been found beheaded, or otherwise mutilated. The same pattern held constant through the winter of 1690, until many colonists refused to even leave their homes, calling on the governor of the colony for military protection. Many thought the attacks were the retaliation of dislocated Indian tribes still living in the area, while others blamed European settlers such as the French and Spanish, reputed to be trying to gain footholds in New England. While those were the opinions held by many, there was a large following who believed that the attacks were the doing of witches or evil spirits inhabiting the wilds of Massachusetts.

The result was the construction of Fort Blade, a defense not against the British, but against some mysterious force that was slowly killing off the colony. Older's report stated that all who were able, moved out to the island fortress, living within its walls at night, venturing forth only during the day. The colonists lived that way for the next eight months, until one night, the attacks finally ceased. Older believed that the colonists, who had been sending small war parties into the woods each day to track the killer, had finally succeeded in defeating their enemy.

Somewhere on Blade Island, the colonists had buried their dead in mass graves, and it was in those graves they laid to rest the bones of their unknown enemy. While a guard on the island, Older had spent his time searching for this reputed burial site.

Jefferson shook his head, looking up from the book and across the empty floor of the station. He felt sure that Older had found something on Blade, but what was it? And what did that have to do with Lyerman and the murders?

The phone rang shrilly, startling him from his thoughts. It was McKenna.

"Hey, how are you?" her voice asked softly.

"I'm all right," Jefferson answered, holding the phone against his ear and leaning back in the chair, its springs creaking. "Just doing some reading."

"You want some company?"

Jefferson thought for a moment. "Depends who's offering. You?"

"Maybe. I'm just doing some reading here myself, something you might find interesting."

"What's that?"

"Sociology reading, you might say."

"Where are you?"

"I'm home," McKenna paused, then added. "Do you want to stop by?"

Jefferson closed his eyes, picturing her for a moment. *You kidding, do I want to stop by?*

"Sure," he answered. "Brogan can take care of things here for a while I'm sure."

"He's a big boy."

"Yeah. He is."

"I'll be here."

"All right, I'll be right over."

McKenna's house was on the ocean; she had given him the directions over the phone, saying she loved open spaces and the ocean was as open as you could get. Jefferson pulled into the driveway, the beams of his headlights washing across the smooth gray surface of her house, sparkling off the black glass of the windows, casting shadows over the bushes flanking her front steps. He opened the door, the warm night air flooding into the air-conditioned interior of his car, carrying with it the ocean's salted smell.

McKenna met him at the door, opening up the screen and stepping aside so he could pass through. She was wearing a cream-colored tank top, which spread smoothly over her breasts, forming a perfect arc just under the hollow of her neck. As he passed her, she smiled, smoothing the front of her jeans with both hands, running her palms down the front of her thighs, her fingers pressed tightly together.

"Hi," she said softly. "How are you?"

"Hello," Jefferson replied, looking at her for a moment, then turning back to the interior of her house. "Nice place."

"Thank you," she said. "I don't stay here too much, so it's a little empty. I just like having a place right on the water."

She was right, the house was a little empty. The front entry room was bare carpet, with a single halogen lamp standing in the corner. There were no dividing walls, and the room stretched back toward the rear of the house, where the carpet ended in a straight line against the shining tile surface of the kitchen floor, the only indication that one had moved into a separate room. Beyond the kitchen was a solid wall of glass, sets of sliding doors through which Jefferson could see the black night ocean.

"I just come here for the view," McKenna said. "I couldn't live here. I'd feel like I'd wear it out."

"I can understand that," Jefferson said, and moved toward the kitchen. A separate room opened up to his right and Jefferson glimpsed a freshly made bed, the large white comforter spread over the top of the bed's rounded surface. The doors and windows of the house were thrown open and Jefferson could hear the tropical *chik-chik-chik* of nocturnal insects, the sound filtering in through the screens like the patter of rain on leaves.

McKenna stepped past him, her open-toed black shoes tapping lightly on the kitchen's tile floor.

"You want a drink?" she said over her shoulder.

"Sure," Jefferson replied.

He followed her into the open kitchen, placing his gun and badge on the marble-topped kitchen counter, the two metal objects clinking like wineglasses on the shining surface.

"Raspberry iced tea or a beer?" she said, then smiled. "I'm kind of low on options."

"Iced tea," Jefferson replied.

A warm breeze strained through the screen, blowing back the two long curtains hung from either side of the sliding glass door. The curtains wrapped around themselves in rolling waves, lightly rattling the metal rods from which they hung. In the center of the room was a single director's style chair, made of pine green fabric and sandalwood, facing out toward the ocean. A single empty wineglass sat on the floor near the chair's legs.

"I'm having a Popsicle, too, do you want one?"

"Sure."

"Grape or cherry?"

"Grape."

She pulled out two Popsicles from the freezer, handing one to Jefferson.

"Do you live by yourself?" Jefferson asked.

"For the most part," McKenna answered. "Except for the random men I bring home and have sex with."

He looked at her for a second before she smiled. "Kidding."

He smiled back. "You mind living alone?"

She paused for a moment, seeming to consider the question, the refrigerator door half-open, the muted light inside shining out across her. She shrugged. "No. Not really. I've always done it, so I'm used to it by now."

She shut the refrigerator door with a nudge of her hips. Placing the two glasses on the counter, she filled them both with iced tea, the raspberry-flavored liquid glinting ruby-colored in the light.

"It's nice outside. You want to go out to the deck?" she asked.

"Sure," Jefferson replied, taking one of the glasses from the counter.

"We can look at the water," she said, taking up the other glass and walking around the counter. Sitting in the director's chair was a single book, which she picked up and dropped on the counter before they passed through the open doorway and onto the deck. She kicked off her shoes, slipping her bare feet into light blue flip-flops, then holding her drink in one hand and the book in the other, walked toward the railing at the end of the deck.

They ate their Popsicles for a moment, talking about various things. Life before the police force, their family, things they wanted to do.

She paused, then spun around. "Do you like Sade?"

"Who?"

"The singer."

"Oh," Jefferson said. "Sure."

"Hang on a sec," McKenna said, excited. "I'll be right back."

She put the glass of iced tea on the railing and skipped back into the house. She reappeared in a moment carrying a radio that she placed on the kitchen counter, pointing out toward the deck. There was a pause, then Sade began playing softly from the speakers. Sade. More babies had been conceived to this music than any other.

She smiled and stepped back through the doorway, moving toward Jefferson across the deck. The music filtered around her, reaching the deck before slowly dissipating into the warm night air. She joined him on the deck. Leaning both elbows on the deck's railing, she stretched her body forward, arching up onto the tips of her toes.

"I love it out here," she said breathlessly, pressing her stomach against the hard railing.

Jefferson turned reluctantly away from her for the first time, looking out from the porch. The view was spectacular, the kind of panoramic sight that made you suck in your breath and blink. McKenna's house was directly on the beach, the porch extending out over the sand until nothing was between them and the ocean. The cool pitted sand stretched out from underneath the porch, before washing underneath the black tides of the Atlantic. Small waves rolled up the sand in thin white curls, reaching toward the porch before stalling for a moment, then retreating backward. The tides seeped into the sand, leaving the beach moist and dark, the bubbles of hidden clams and mussels breaking to the surface in tiny bursts of foam.

Stretching beyond the beach, the cold Atlantic waters shimmered with gelatinous moonlight, the surface wavering in streams of silver ripples. The edge of the horizon was lined with lights, the blinking beacons of Logan Airport breaking across the waters, and, farther out, Jefferson could see the dark shape of Blade Prison Island. A single red light flashed on the tip of Blade, and from inside the prison walls, Jefferson saw the arcing spotlights cutting across the night sky, gilding the nocturnal clouds in pale luminescence.

"Nice, huh?" McKenna smiled, picking up her iced tea.

"Beautiful," Jefferson agreed, then asked her about the book he had seen her pick up and put on the kitchen counter.

"Let's go inside, and I'll show you."

She padded back across the deck in her bare feet. Jefferson followed her into the kitchen, where she flipped on a small light above the kitchen counter. She put her iced tea down next to the book and opened it, smoothing out the pages. "About that writing you mentioned from Sinatra's house. I looked into the demonology aspect of it, as I said I would, and I think I found something interesting."

"You did?" Jefferson said. "How about that? Where?"

"I found something interesting in this book."

The book's pages were yellowed in age, covered in dark, typed lettering.

"Where'd you get it on such short notice?" Jefferson asked.

"Believe it or not, I found it at a university library," McKenna said. "It's a book on demonology by Claus Von Murrow, written back in 1927."

"Oh yeah?" Jefferson leaned forward, curious. "I think that's when Brogan was in high school."

McKenna laughed, then, nudging Jefferson with her elbow, she said, "This is serious."

"I know. I'm listening."

"All right," she began, opening the book. "The lines that were written at the scene of the murder are actually from an ancient Sumerian poem, a poem about seven demons that rise from the underworld to terrorize men and haul them down into hell."

"So, you think maybe our guy is into this kinda stuff? This demonology?"

"It's possible," McKenna said, running her finger over a line of text. "Listen to this, the rest of the poem reads, 'The seven demons grip his thighs, They bite and tear his face, They slash at his body with an axe, They turn his face into the face of agony.'"

"Makes me glad I'm not a Sumerian," Jefferson said.

"No kidding," McKenna replied. "There's more though. And this is where it gets really weird."

She scanned the words for a moment. "OK, the writing on the wall . . . the first line said . . ." McKenna paused, flipping forward several pages in the book. She found the section she was looking for and highlighted it with her finger. Next to that she placed a small piece of paper, on which she had copied down what Jefferson had told her had been written on the wall.

"Four came from the Galla,
No bribe mollified them,
Nor did they satisfy a woman's body,
But hated children
And tore them from their parents' laps."

"That's right," Jefferson said, remembering the jagged, bloody words.

"It's this first line that's interesting," McKenna said. "Four came from the *Galla*."

"What about it?"

"Well, that line isn't in the original poem."

"Are you sure?"

"Positive," McKenna answered, pointing to the poem in the book. "That line is not there."

"So you think our guy got it wrong?"

"Maybe . . . but I checked on *Galla*. Turns out the *Galla* were seven demons in Sumerian legend."

"That makes sense," Jefferson answered. "If our guy is familiar with demonology, he would know about something like that."

"That's possible." McKenna's voice was hesitant. "But he said, 'came from the *Galla*,' so what if the *Galla* was a place?"

"No, no." Jefferson shook his head. "We already looked into that. There isn't a place named *Galla* anywhere. We even checked to see if it'd be short for something, an abbreviation or a symbol. It's not, I thought—"

"The *Galla* isn't a place," McKenna interrupted. "It's a ship."

Jefferson paused for a moment, startled. "What do you mean?"

"It's a ship. A World War II Merchant Marine ship," McKenna said. "It left New York harbor in 1943 and entered the Pacific theater one month later."

Jefferson was silent for a moment. *A Merchant Marine ship?*

"What happened to it?" Jefferson asked.

"It was sunk by a Japanese air attack while returning from the Solomon Islands in November of the same year."

"But there must be hundreds of ships sitting on the bottom of the Pacific. Why is this one so special?"

"That's it though. It's not on the bottom of the Pacific. It's right here. In Boston."

"*What?*" Jefferson said, startled. "What do you mean?"

"A diving crew found the USS *Galla* and raised a part of it from the bottom. They brought it into Boston Harbor six months ago for a new museum exhibit. The *Galla* is here . . . in Boston."

Still processing this new information, Jefferson was quiet for a moment, listening to the sound of the waves through the door to the deck. "Couldn't that just be a coincidence?"

"Maybe, but I think it's worth checking out."

"Yeah." Jefferson sighed, rubbing his forehead. "This is getting too much for me to figure. Where'd you say the ship was?"

"Right now it's in the Boston Naval Museum; they're still getting the exhibits ready. The place doesn't open till autumn, but I've already talked to the guard at the desk, and he said to come down anytime tomorrow. He'll be there in the morning, tomorrow, covering for somebody else."

Jefferson smiled. "I'm impressed. Brogan and I need to watch ourselves. You're gonna start taking our jobs."

McKenna gave a half smile, then looked down at her hands for a moment. "There's something else you should know."

"What?"

"The underwater expeditions of the kind used to raise the *Galla* require serious funding. Institutional sponsorship, financial backing."

"Makes sense. So who was the sponsor?"

"Well . . . the raising of the *Galla* was paid for by the Joseph Lyerman Institute. By Joseph Lyerman himself."

Jefferson could say nothing. The world can be a small place at times, filled with coincidental connections among people and places. Some form and are broken again with no underlying meaning, but others seem to hint at a deeper interconnectedness of events. A dragonfly landing on a branch in Africa causes a ripple of wind that turns into rain over the Atlantic, that becomes a hurricane in Florida, that travels up the East Coast and sinks a fishing boat from Gloucester. Four fisherman who wake up in the morning, have cereal, kiss their wives, live their lives, are dead that afternoon all because two weeks earlier a dragonfly landed on a branch somewhere on the other side of the ocean. Connections driven by the chaos of life.

Joseph Lyerman founds an institution that backs an expedition that recovers a WWII Merchant Marine ship and tows that ship to Boston, where Lyerman's own son is found murdered by someone who claims to be from that same ship. That, Jefferson thought, wasn't coincidental, wasn't random. Something deeper was there—Jefferson could feel it.

"Guess that caught you by surprise?" McKenna said.

"What? Oh, yeah . . . it did. Doesn't make any sense though."

"That's because you don't know the reasons yet. Everything makes sense when you know why."

McKenna took a sip of iced tea, then lowered the glass, looking out through the open screen door, her lips glistening with the cool liquid. She turned to him for a moment, before turning back toward the ocean. Far out to sea, heat lightning flashed silently for an instant, illuminating the clouds in bursts of pale light. Without a word, she flicked off the counter light, then walked back onto the deck, heading for the railing, staring intently out at the distant rain clouds. Jefferson followed her silently, joining her against the railing.

"Looks like rain," McKenna said quietly, then she turned to him.

"It does."

"When I was a little girl, I was always fascinated with rain. The process of it. There seemed something so dramatic in its evolution. Hydrogen and oxygen atoms falling together out of the sky, then breaking apart, separating and returning to the sky again to fall someplace else in the world. But it's always been those same number of atoms. They keep falling again and again from the beginning of time, finding each other for that one drop of rain, then losing each other again. And when I was little, I used to wonder what that must be like. Always falling and splitting apart again and if those three particular atoms would ever find each other in the exact same way. In the whole expanse of the world, would those three atoms that split ever be rejoined and fall again in the same drop of rain? Maybe there's this whole drama being played out around us in every thunderstorm that we're never even aware of. Loves lost and found again, but for only that one moment, for that one single drop. They never get more time together than that." McKenna smiled a slightly embarrassed smile. "Just the thoughts of a lonely little girl, I guess."

They were both quiet for a moment, staring out across the ocean, watching the sporadic flashes of heat lightning in the distance. It had begun to rain lightly, tiny beads of cool water which clung to McKenna's eyelashes, rinsing through her hair. McKenna arched her head back, squinting her eyes and looking up toward the sky.

"Life goes on though," she said softly.

Behind them, in the kitchen, a new Sade song had begun playing, the low jazz rhythms drifting out across the porch. The heat lightning flashed again in the distance, this time a low rumbling noise spreading across the water, mixing with the music drifting through the open doorway.

"Oh, I love this song," McKenna said, smiling as the tempo began to grow faster. She stretched herself backward on the railing. "It's a beautiful night out, tonight. Dance with me."

Jefferson laughed, shaking his head. "No, no. You don't want to see me dance."

He leaned with his back against the railing, drinking the raspberry tea, the ice clinking against the glass. McKenna was moving slowly across the deck, the rain streaking the front of her tank top, her smooth stomach beginning to show through the cream-colored top in wet, glossy patches.

She approached him slowly, pressing herself against him until Jefferson could feel her skin's warmth, radiating through her moist clothes. She smiled, pulling him away from the railing. "C'mon, dance with me."

She took his iced tea, placing it on the rail for him, then pressed the flats of her palms against his. They danced, only their palms touching, moving together. The rain was cool against their skin, pattering silently around them. Jefferson closed his eyes for a moment, listening to the music, the sound of the ocean's buoys, and the *ssh, ssh* of the water sliding over the sand.

There was a moment of quiet before a new song began. They both listened to the sounds rolling out from the kitchen.

"Uh-oh," McKenna said. "Slow song."

192

Jefferson nodded. "You're right."

McKenna cocked her hip out for a moment, looking up at Jefferson. "You know what happens during a slow song, right?"

"I get slapped for groping my date?"

McKenna laughed, then leaned in toward him, throwing her arms around his shoulders. He could feel her body against his, the smooth arch of her back, the pressure of her arms around his neck, her breasts against his chest. Through the open doorway, Sade was singing,

> If I tell you, if I tell you now
> Will you keep on, will you keep on lovin' me

"I don't think I've slow danced with anyone since junior high," McKenna said.

"All the girls on one side of the gym, all the boys on the other?"

"That's how it was." McKenna smiled, she looked up at him for a moment. "Everyone is always so nervous."

"I remember that all right."

"I miss those times," McKenna replied slowly. "Sometimes I feel like I grew up too fast."

She shifted her arms tighter around his neck, her fingernails tickling his sensitive skin, then she sighed and rested her head on his shoulder. She sniffled once, the tiny scar on her nose wrinkling. Over her shoulder, Jefferson could see the ocean's rim, the dark expansive line of the horizon freckled with stars. Out on the rough waters, the rock of Blade Prison was silhouetted against the night sky, its searchlights meandering lazily overhead.

Jefferson closed his eyes, smelling the ocean's salt and the peach fragrance of McKenna's wet hair which was pressed coolly against cheek. Out to sea, rain was falling. Drops of rain together for an instant. In the background, the music continued to play.

Jefferson left McKenna's just after eleven, getting back to his desk fifteen minutes later. Brogan was asleep, his head slumped forward, soft sleeping breaths coming from his mouth. He half opened an eye as Jefferson came in, nodding, then closing the single eye again. Jefferson sank down in his leather chair, leaning backwards, relaxing after being with McKenna. He was beginning to fall asleep when a jarring ring caused him to snap his neck back in surprise.

Wincing in pain, he reached for the telephone.

"I'm just finishing up down here with the Lyerman autopsy. I'd have gone home two hours ago if one or two problems hadn't arisen."

"Like what?"

"Well . . . I don't know. I can't really figure some of these things out."

Whenever Jefferson spoke with Wu, he always felt he had jumped into the middle of a conversation.

"Did Lyerman have any pets?"

"Not that I know of, why?"

"Had he been overseas at all recently? Third World countries, tropical areas, that sort of thing?"

"Don't know."

"What about any health problems? Had he been complaining of thirsts or sweats? Had he had diarrhea at all?"

"What'd you find?"

"Well . . ." Wu said slowly, "his heart. There were worms."

"Worms?"

"He had some kind of large-scale heartworm infestation."

"Heartworms? I thought that was just with dogs?"

"Well, to be honest, I've never seen anything like this in humans before. There are instances of limited parasitic infections of the heart, but those are generally very low-level, such as with some forms of trichinosis and toxocariasis. In trichinosis, though, most any larvae that reach the heart are killed by the inflammatory reaction that results. Toxocariasis infection caused by roundworm larvae can spread to the heart, but the symptoms are generally mild and patients usually recover within a month's time. But this, whatever was inside Lyerman, was much, much worse than anything I've ever seen, or really, anything I've even read about before. Heartworm is almost never seen in people, especially in the U.S. and not at the level he had. These things had almost eaten away the entire heart."

"Jesus . . ."

"My thoughts exactly. I've taken a few samples and should have some more results for you tomorrow, along with that DNA match. But I thought you'd want to know about it now."

"Definitely," Jefferson said. "Thanks. How's the arm?"

"I'll live. I'm on Zidovudine and Lamivudine for the next four weeks. Now I remember why I gave up working with the living."

Zidovudine and Lamivudine were both antiretroviral drugs designed to reduce the risk of HIV infection following exposure to blood or bodily fluids of an unknown subject.

"All right, Doc, hang in there. I'll talk to you."

Jefferson hung up the phone, reclining in his chair to think.

"What's up?" Brogan asked, now awake.

"That was Wu, I would have given you the call, but I didn't want to wake you up."

Brogan waved a hand, dismissively. "What'd he say?"

Jefferson filled Brogan in on the conversation he'd had with Wu, telling him about the worms that were eating through Lyerman's heart.

"Jesus, that's just what that old guy over at Richard Lee's place told us," Brogan said after a moment. "Did you tell Wu that?"

"No. That's too fucking weird. I didn't want Wu to think I was ready for the funny farm. Wu's sending over some of the worms or whatever to the lab, should get some results back tomorrow afternoon on that. We can see where these things came from."

"Fuck . . ." Brogan exhaled, looking down at the photographs on his desk. "What is going on?"

"That's not all."

"What?"

"I went over to McKenna's—"

"Oh yeah," Brogan interrupted, with a stupid grin.

"Because she had some information for us," Jefferson said.

"Yeah, what kind of information?" Brogan asked, still grinning.

"About Lyerman."

The grin fell, Brogan serious now. "What she say?"

"She told me there's a ship that came into Boston that she thinks might be connected with what went down last night."

"Connected how?"

"Some names in common, the name of the ship and a name that was at Sinatra's place. I'm going to check it out tomorrow."

"What'd she say about Lyerman?"

"She said that it was Lyerman's funding that brought the ship back to Boston. It's been sitting on the bottom of the Pacific for the past sixty-five years. He paid for it to be raised and towed all the way back here."

Brogan shook his head, turning and staring at a point across the floor. "Jesus . . ."

Brogan's phone rang with the two short bells of an internal call. Brogan's eyes refocused for a moment, long enough to put the phone on speaker.

"Brogan?" The desk sergeant's voice came on the line.

"Yeah."

"Jefferson there?"

"Right here."

"You two have a package, just got dropped off. It's at the desk."

"All right, I'll be down in a moment."

Brogan flipped off the speakerphone, then slowly stood up from his chair, cracking his neck. "I'll get it. My legs are all cramped up, need the walk."

Brogan lumbered off across the floor and down the stone stairs to the lobby.

Outside, the rain had begun again. Worms. Just like the old man had said at Richard Lee's place, that the mark of the demon's victim was a heart eaten by worms. Jefferson glanced through the window, watching the beads of water glide down the glass. A few feet from Jefferson's seat was a large plastic cup with a colored drawing of a baseball player across the front. Underneath in red letters it said, BOSTON RED SOX AND YOU, then underneath that, A WINNING TEAM.

Drips from the ceiling fell into the cup, landing with a soft splash.

"Hey, look what we got," Brogan called out a minute later, his voice loud as he finished climbing up the stairs and stepped toward the detectives' desks. He was holding a small brown pastry box, on top of which he balanced two steaming cups of coffee.

"Still leaking, huh?" Brogan said, as he carefully walked around one of the buckets on the floor.

"Yeah. What'd we get?"

Brogan stopped in front of his desk, carefully placing the brown box on a notepad near where the framed photograph of his wife used to sit, and took the two coffees off the top. He handed one to Jefferson. "Careful, it's hot." Then he placed the other next to the box.

Brogan opened up the box. Inside were four éclairs, wrapped carefully in white paper. "The sarge said Richard Lee was just in and dropped them off for us. Pretty fucking great, huh? Talk about bribing a public official."

Carefully, Brogan eased his hand into the box, lifting out one of the éclairs. "You want one?" He handed the éclair to Jefferson and lifted out another for himself.

Sitting down in his chair, he looked at the pastry for a moment. "You don't suppose these are poison or anything, do you?"

"Hope not," Jefferson said, taking a bite.

Brogan chewed slowly for a moment, "Dead from a poison éclair . . . never thought I'd go out like that."

Jefferson turned to look out the window, watching the rain continue to fall.

"Oh, while you were out, got a call on that bum you and McKenna found out by the cemetery where Reggie did a brain blowout," Brogan said.

"Yeah?"

"Just some nutball. Crazy bum. In and out of the county loony bin for the last ten years. Nutty but harmless anyway, looks like he died from a heart attack. Massive coronary. Nothing special there."

"Who did the work?"

"Don't know, someone in the ME's office. Not Wu; one of his guys, I think. Oh, almost forgot, we got those audiotapes from the roof of the Lyerman Building."

"When'd we get those?"

"An hour ago. Seems like Mr. Lyerman had a change of heart, had them delivered to the station. I was waiting for you to get back to listen to them."

Brogan reached into his desk drawer and pulled out a small tape player. "They record in a different format at the Lyerman Building, so they transferred them to regular cassette tapes for us. Check it out, some pretty weird shit."

Brogan inserted the tape and pushed PLAY.

Jefferson pulled his chair up to Brogan's desk, and the two men began to listen. The first portion of the tape was nothing but the light grating noise of the wind passing over the microphone and a tinkling noise that sounded like a wind chime. A plane passed overhead, the sound of the engines being captured clearly by the recorder. In the distance, they began to hear voices, two people talking.

"Can you make those out?" Jefferson asked, holding his ear closer to the speaker.

Brogan shook his head. "Sounds like a man and woman though."

The voices began to grow louder as the pair evidently moved across the roof, closer to the microphone. Brogan was right—one voice belonged to a man, the other to a the emergency room. Most of the time, the ER reminded Jefferson of an eighteenth-century insane asylum. People lying about on gurneys, sometimes covered in blood, doctors rushing around in blue scrubs, orderlies restraining patients, usually someone crying or screaming somewhere. McKenna seemed strangely out of place in the confusion. Sitting between a giant Hispanic man in construction gear, a long jagged gash down the side of his face, and an elderly woman who was bobbing back and forth in her chair like a pendulum, covering her ears, and shouting, "No! No! No!" to a nurse holding a clipboard.

McKenna looked relieved to see him.

"What are you doing here?" Jefferson asked.

"I talked to Brogan. He said you were coming to the ME's office to see Dr. Wu, thought I'd meet you here. Certainly didn't come for the atmosphere."

"No, I guess not," Jefferson said. "Well, c'mon then. Wu said he was all finished with the Lyerman prep. Had the pathology reports all ready to go."

They walked down the central corridor of the ER, passing a team of doctors working to remove a foot-long butcher knife from the back of a screaming man, through a set of double doors toward the medical examiner's office. A security guard, wearing sunglasses indoors, was shouting at a thin black man in a blue hospital gown with IV tubes dangling out of his arms like tree tinsel. The guard barely noticed them as they passed through a second set of doors, before stepping into the ME's office.

Beyond the doors, it was quiet. There they might get some answers.

"I should say from the start, that I don't know what to tell you, Will. I mean it, I've literally never seen anything like this before in my experience."

Dr. Michael Wu was seated behind the big metal desk in the back corner of the ME's office. He shared the room with four other desks, all empty now, his side decorated with framed diplomas from Yale University, Johns Hopkins Medical School, and a few black-and-white photographs of China. A family portrait sat on the man's desk, next to the manila folder marked "Kenneth Lyerman." Wu had the Lyerman folder open and was sifting through the mark-ups inside. A small bandage was visible on his arm where the guy in the alley had grabbed him.

"I'm sending some samples to Harvard, maybe they can figure something else out, but believe me, I'm baffled," Wu said.

"Did you find anything at all?" Jefferson asked.

"Sure, lots of *things*. But nothing that makes any sense. Is this some kind of joke?"

"No, believe me. This isn't a joke."

Wu sighed. "All right. But if I find out that this is somehow a hotshot detective pulling our chain, they'll be a lot of bodies piling up around here, and I'll be back at Harvard doing research work."

"What'd you find out?"

"Where should I start? With the possible or the impossible to explain?"

"Why don't we start with the possible."

Dr. Wu usually looked like he'd just come from the pages of *GQ*. Handsome, hair

"Nine, ten months ago."

"And before that? This thing was buried at the bottom of the ocean."

"That's right. Since World War II. Almost sixty-five years."

Jefferson compared the photograph with the writing in front of him one more time. There was no question that it was the same.

"Did anyone have access to this while it was on display? Could anyone have broken in and vandalized this room?" Jefferson asked.

"Well"—the guard rubbed his head, thinking—"sure, I guess. If they really wanted to. I mean, it'd be tough, but they could do it."

Jefferson nodded. *So someone could have crept in here sometime and written this on the wall. But why?*

"But if you're wondering about that writing you were just looking at, that was already there when they salvaged the piece," the guard continued.

"How do you know?"

"Oh, they documented everything when they broke the seal on the door. Got photographs of the whole place. Everything you're looking at in here is exactly the way it was when they opened it up."

Something else was bothering Jefferson, something about the dates.

"You said that the submersible crew died on September 20 or so?" Jefferson asked.

"Around then, yeah."

"And that's when they actually made the discovery?"

"That's right."

"But the *Galla* didn't make it into Boston until, what? January you said."

"Right."

"So where was it from end of September until January?"

The guard frowned, thinking. "Well, of course they found it in the South Pacific. That's a good month or so of sea travel from there to here."

"So it should have gotten into Boston in early, mid November."

"Well, it might have had to go through customs, or quarantine or something, I don't know about that."

Jefferson did know about that, and at most it would have been two days. Which would mean that the *Galla* should have been in Boston by December at the latest. But it never made it until January; over a month unaccounted for.

Where had it been?

Something had been on Bougainville Island. This ship had found it and was bringing it back when it sank, carrying whatever it was inside to the bottom of the Pacific for the past sixty-five years. And for the past sixty-five years, this thing had been waiting to be found.

The medical examiner's office was deep in the back of the old City Hospital, now a part of the Boston Medical Center, and the last place Jefferson expected to see McKenna. But there she was. Waiting for him on one of the blue padded chairs inside them. The gigantic segment of metal, still encrusted with rust, was placed in a supporting framework of steel disguised as coral, giving the impression the fragment was still on the seafloor.

On the walls around the display, photographs documented the salvage operation, men in hard hats lifting the wreckage, diving submersibles, a few underwater shots. There were also images of the crew, scanning charts, laughing, eating. One of the frames was set apart from the others, showing three men in orange underwater suits, standing on the deck of a ship, their arms around each other.

The guard pointed to the photograph. "Those are the three that died. Nat Rink, Randy Rutherford, and a French cameraman, Jean-Leon François. Last September, the twentieth or so."

Jefferson nodded, turning away from the photograph and moving toward the fragment. He shook his head. "What did you say before? They found this part sealed off?"

"That's right, completely dry inside. You can actually go in it."

Set in the side of the metal fragment was a solid naval-style door, with a small portal window in the front. The door was open, and beyond, Jefferson could see a room that looked like some kind of infirmary.

The guard waved his hand encouragingly. "Go on. Go ahead, it's all right."

Jefferson stepped forward, moving across the exhibit area and through the doorway. Inside, the air still seemed stale, unused, like stepping into a giant coffin. There were cots lined up against the far walls, with a bulletin board tacked up nearby, calendars and notices still hanging from the cork.

"When this is open to the public, they're gonna put up glass barriers around most of this, so visitors won't be able to damage anything," the guard said, joining Jefferson inside the room.

There was writing on the wall by the door, scrawled across the metal, carved into the sides by something sharp.

"What's that?" Jefferson pointed to the writing.

The guard shrugged. "They don't know."

The lettering was jagged and long, each word stretched out. Jefferson stepped forward, looking more closely. As he read, he felt something chill the inside of his stomach, like a cold fluid moving slowly through his guts. The sensation was physical—he could feel his heart beating faster, something in his throat constricting.

The evil command which issues from the midst of heaven;
The evil fate which springs from the depth of the abyss

He pulled out a photograph of the writing at the Sinatra lawyer crime scene. He held the black-and-white photograph up to the wall, comparing.

The writing was the same.

"Jesus . . ." he hissed, stepping backward. He turned toward the guard. "When did you say they found this ship?"

could feel his chest constrict with thoughts of her, gasping to breathe her into his lungs again.

Brogan's service revolver lay on the seat next to him. He picked it up, resting the bulk of metal on his lap, feeling the weapon tingle into his legs. He looked up toward the house, his house, with its silent black windows and two sleeping children. His baby daughters, who slept soundly, never knowing their mother the way he had known her, for whom her face had already begun to fade into time, becoming like the faint recollection of dreams come morning. He wished for this power, this childhood ability to forget the past, to push away the thought of her brown eyes, her long straight hair, the feel of her against him, her weight seeming so tangible.

Brogan raised his hand against his eyes, pressing his fingers against the bridge of his nose. Without thinking, he took the revolver and placed it inside his pocket, then opened the car door. The inside light came on, returning him to unfeeling reality. His wife had been taken from him. His wife, his love, his companion, ripped so hard from him until it hurts every morning just to breathe, but despite the pain of his loss, the hands of clocks still continue their orbital motion, elevators still *ping* on their vertical tracks, and interior lights still continue to illuminate with indifferent regularity.

You think the world should stop because someone you love has died, but it never will. Instead, everything continues as it always has. As it will when your own time comes. Brogan stepped out of the car, feeling the weight of the revolver pressing against his leg. His hurt arm burned slightly as he shut the car door, soft enough so as not to wake his two sleeping daughters, then he walked up the narrow brick pathway to his house. The rest of the neighborhood was quiet, no glimmers of motion showing in any of the dark windows along his crowded street.

His own house, the two-story wood shingle structure, was equally quiet, the front porch light snapping to attention as he approached, triggered by the motion sensors mounted on its front. He passed the long rocking bench, unused since her death but still sitting by the railing.

Objects that seemed trivial, unimportant while she had been alive, suddenly took on new significance, becoming saturated with memories of her. That was what he remembered now. All the details that make up a person. The bench. Warm summer nights, pressed against each other. Rocking to the sound of crickets and humming insects in the yard.

Collecting himself, Brogan unlocked the front door. No use thinking of empty benches. Inside was dark, but, moving with quick familiarity, he crossed the living room and made his way quietly up the long wooden staircase to the second floor. At the top of the stairs, he eased his shoes off, advancing down the hallway in his socks.

His older daughter's door was shut, only the glowing orange sliver from her nightlight visible along the floor. Quietly, he turned the knob, easing into her room. Sarah, his four-year-old was fast asleep in her bed. She lay flat on her back, her arms stretched out on either side of her, as though she were in the midst of a giant hug. Her head was tilted slightly to the side, hair pulled loosely back with a pink elastic tie, her small mouth hanging open as she took little snoring breaths. Brogan leaned over, kissing her

Jefferson stood, wiping off his front. "No, nothing."

"Then come up and take a look at this."

Jumping to pull it back down, Jefferson climbed the metal fire escape rather than walk around to the front of the station. From higher, he could see the uniformed officers covering the rest of the parking lot, checking outside the fence, their flashlights bobbing up and down in the darkness. From somewhere above came the sound of a helicopter approaching. When he reached the top, Brogan was off in the middle of the roof, standing by where Jefferson had found him. He was lucky he was still breathing.

"You all right?" Jefferson asked.

"I won't be playing tennis for a while, but yeah, I'm all right. Look at this." Brogan pointed at something.

Scratched into the metal of the air-conditioning unit were words,

They, the four, proceeding from the Western Mountains,
They, the four, increasing the Eastern Mountain.
Taking Sidina and his men to their final place of rest

Brogan grunted in surprise, reaching for something in his pants pocket. With his hand still fishing in his pocket, Brogan became still, his eyes beginning to glaze over from shock.

"Hey, you better lie down until the med team gets here," Jefferson said, placing his hand on Brogan's back, gently trying to lead him away from the body.

Brogan pulled out a slip of paper from his pocket, holding it up in front of the scratched writing on the air-conditioning duct, ignoring the beating rain that immediately began soaking it. As Brogan kept his arm outstretched, Jefferson looked at what he was holding. It was the small note that had been attached to the pastry box they'd gotten in the station. It read, "To Jefferson and Brogan, Enjoy." Brogan slowly indicated the air-conditioning unit. Jefferson glanced from the note to the air conditioner.

The writing on the two was the same.

Detective Brogan sat in the dark interior of his car, staring blindly at the pale elm trees in his backyard moving in the night breeze. Two hours in Mass General to get his arm stitched up, then twenty minutes on the phone with Amelia, the Mexican lady who watched his two kids when he wasn't around. She'd come out to the car to see him when he pulled into his driveway, telling him there were two sandwiches waiting on the counter. Turkey and tuna. Then he'd watched her leave, the taillights of her car growing smaller and smaller before finally disappearing in a flash as she turned the corner at the end of the street; and then he had continued to sit. That was almost twenty minutes ago and still the seconds ticked away, cutting unceasing slivers off time as they had from the beginning.

Time. It had been six months since his wife had been taken from him. Six months divided into thousands of these incremental moments, each digging at him more painfully than the last. Like drips of water, with every second drowning him until he

The radio squealed again, but Jefferson was already putting it away, moving quickly along the length of the roof toward the fire escape at the corner. The fire escape was slippery with rain, and Jefferson slid down the ladder leading to the first platform. From the platform stairs crisscrossed below him, running down from the top of the building until ending ten feet above the alley. The last stairway dropped to the alley below. One end of the alley was a brick wall, the other extended toward a parking lot, eventually intersecting St. Mark's Street.

Jefferson drew his gun, slowly moving up the alley until he was standing at the edge of the lot. Silent police cruisers were parked along the side of the station, while traffic was quiet on St. Mark's. Jefferson knelt, lowering his head below the frames of the parked cars, looking beneath them. Nothing. He moved quickly across the lot, toward the chain-link fence that surrounded it. Still nothing. Looking through the fence he saw more alleys and empty streets. Behind him came a wail, a police cruiser screeching into the lot, sirens throwing red-and-blue light over everything. Two uniformed officers got out of the car.

"What do we have?" Jefferson asked. "You see anything?"

The two officers shook their heads. "Nothing."

"All right, check up along the street."

A second cruiser was pulling in behind them, then a third, braking hard on St. Mark's Street. Jefferson pointed the men in both directions up and down St. Mark's, then ran back down the alley, to the Dumpsters that lined the brick wall of the station. Jefferson started flipping back their plastic lids. Inside the second one was a body. Richard Lee was curled into a fetal position, lying on top of a heap of trash bags, the black plastic glistening with rain. Richard was staring blankly up at the sky.

"What is it?"

The voice came from above. Brogan was standing at the edge of the roof and looking down, seeing something in the Dumpster.

"It's Richard Lee," Jefferson called up. "He's dead."

Brogan shook his head, pulling away from the edge and disappearing. Jefferson could hear him calling in the location of Lee's body.

Jefferson turned, still moving down the line of Dumpsters, flipping the lids on the last few, seeing nothing but garbage. Beyond the Dumpsters, just before the end of the alley, was a single manhole cover. The edge of the cover was raised slightly, just over the lip of the pavement. Jefferson pulled back on the top, lifting the thirty-pound metal lid and sliding it to the side. Beneath was an open hole, dropping into darkness.

Jefferson's flashlight came on, the beam pushing into the darkness and revealing bundles of wiring and long plastic tubing fixed to the side of the wall below the ground. Empty. He lowered himself to the ground, stomach against the wet pavement, leaning down to look farther up the underground channel. Beneath the manhole, the air smelled like mildew, but a breeze blew from somewhere in the darkness ahead of him. Jefferson shined the light forward, the beam following the line of tubing before the light melted into darkness farther on.

"Yo, Jefferson." Brogan's voice came from above again. "You see anything?"

A short deep groan escaped from the other side of the large air-conditioning unit. Someone lay sprawled out on the gravel of the roof, someone who moved slightly as Jefferson approached.

It was Brogan.

"Oh no." Jefferson jammed the Beretta back into his holster, rushed over, and squatted in front of his partner. There was a large gash across Brogan's chest, running from his right shoulder, to the bottom left side of his rib cage. Another gash ran the length of his biceps, ending just below the elbow. His clothes had been cut open, and the flesh underneath was pale, the blood from the open wound mixing freely with the rain, forming a watery red fluid that oozed down Brogan's stomach, puddling in his navel.

Brogan groaned again. "Fuckin-A." His face looked angry rather than in pain. That was good, that meant he was too pissed off to die. "I got that motherfucker, I swear . . ." Brogan was gritting his teeth hard, his words coming as short hisses of pain.

Jefferson fished out his radio, juggling it a moment in his hand, the wet plastic body slippery from the rain. "NH 12 to base, we got an officer down. An officer is down. I'm on the roof of the station, now; Jesus, I'm with Lieutenant Brogan. Over." Jefferson's voice sounded weak and panicked.

"Base to NH 12, please repeat your location. Over." The radio crackled, the dispatcher's voice sounding flat and tinny from the small radio speaker.

"I'm on the station roof. I'm right upstairs. Lieutenant Brogan is down, it looks like some kind of laceration. Over." He had to speak loudly to be heard over the rain.

There was a pause.

Jefferson held the radio to his ear listening.

"OK, affirmative, NH 12, a medical team is en route to your location. Over and out."

Putting the radio back in his pocket, Jefferson bent over his partner, looking at his wounds.

Brogan groaned again and rolled over on his side, still grimacing.

"You shouldn't be moving like that."

Brogan weakly waved him off. "Just got the wind knocked outta me, I'll be all right."

Brogan slowly pulled himself to his feet, the front of his shirt soaked a pinkish red. It reminded Jefferson of the corpses from old horror movies coming back to life.

Jefferson slowly began to slide toward the edge of the roof. Brogan saw the movement and nodded, waving his hand. "I'm fine, go! Find out what that was!"

Jefferson turned and started to run across the gravel. Reaching the back of the building, he looked down. Behind the station was an alley. Jefferson looking down at the tops of Dumpsters four stories below. The alley was empty. Four stories down and someone just jumped off the roof and what, ran off?

"NH 12, NH 12. Over."

"Go ahead. Over."

"Pursuing suspect on foot. Suspect possibly injured. Let's get units out behind the station. Last seen in alley leading to St. Mark's Street. Over."

down, his finger resting gently against the trigger. The walls of the stairwell were dark and moist with perspiration. Jefferson's bare arm briefly brushed against the cold surface, causing a momentary shudder. He glimpsed a few discarded cigarette ends, their butts crushed against the stone stairs, left by officers coming up to violate the station's no smoking policy.

They reached the top and stood in front of a black door, the paint chipping off in places revealing silver metal underneath. Two slide-bolt locks, at the top and bottom of the frame, secured the door. With his gun in his left hand, Jefferson used his right to pull back on the bolt. To his surprise, the bolt slid back easily, as if someone had recently oiled it.

The second bolt stuck slightly and Jefferson used his foot to ease it back gently. He pulled the door open, the metal hinges groaning weakly in protest, the rain breaking in through the opening crack.

Squinting against the pressing water, Jefferson stepped through the doorway, feeling the wind pick at his clothes. Brogan followed, and together they stood peering out into the murky darkness. The roof was covered in thin gravel, with ventilation shafts spaced intermittently, their silver domes stretching upward, glowing pale in the streetlights. Jefferson's clothes began to weigh him down, the cool rain soaking into the fabric.

He felt something press against his chest. Brogan pointed off around one of the central air-conditioning units, a large metallic block structure with three slowly turning fans. Jefferson nodded, moving slowly forward, his shoes crunching slightly on the gravel. Brogan separated from him, gliding around the other side of the air-conditioning unit, his steps tentative and wary. All around, the lights of the city rose, like iridescent algae floating lightly in dark waters. Below, he glimpsed a car passing along St. Mark's Street, pausing at the blinking yellow before turning into a parking lot, the headlights blinking off a moment later.

He turned back to the roof. Brogan had disappeared around the other side of the air-conditioning unit. Ahead of him stretched more ventilation ducts and a large electrical box that hummed softly. Beyond that he saw the edge of the roof, a dark outline pressed against slightly paler sky. Three gunshots cracked loudly in quick succession.

He moved forward quickly. As the rain pelted his face, he wiped the lids of his eyes with one hand. Ahead of him, something was moving across the roof, actually bounding across the roof. The figure's body was nothing more than a shadowy outline, appearing low and twisted, almost crouched over, as if it were using all four limbs to propel itself, reminding Jefferson of an enraged baboon.

The figure stopped just short of the roof, turning back for an instant. There was another crack of a gunshot, the flare from the muzzle flash glowing red for an instant. Jefferson paused, staring, watching things rapidly unfold before him like a movie. The shadowy figure screamed for an instant, the sound piercing, almost a wail, before it turned away, moving toward the edge of the roof. Then, in a single leap, it jumped, holding for an instant in the air before disappearing out of sight, falling with the rain. From four stories up.

perfectly combed, clean-shaven. This afternoon though, Wu looked tired. Puffy bags of flesh under both eyes, the top buttons of his lab coat undone, exposing a wrinkled white dress shirt underneath. There was a spot on the shirt that looked like baby food.

"First let me ask you something," Wu said.

"Shoot."

"What is so important about this case that, not only am I on-site, where I get attacked," Wu said, referring to the homeless guy who had grabbed him, "but I'm also called out of bed the night before to do the prep work. Called out of bed, Will. I have a wife, a new baby. It's tough enough to get a full night of sleep without 3 A.M. phone calls. So what's up with this?"

"Did you look at the name on the folder?"

"Kenneth Lyerman."

"That's what's up with it. You know who he is?"

"Who?"

"Son of Joseph Lyerman. Head of the biggest conglomerate in the country, probably the world. Enough money to make sure the wheels of justice are very nicely greased and moving swiftly."

"Well, I guess that explains the early-morning wake-up call."

"So what do you have for me?" Jefferson asked.

"First off, what I told you about last night," Wu said. "The heartworm infestation in the deceased. We've got samples at the lab, but so far they haven't been able to identify the exact species. Whatever it is, I'm guessing it's something very rare. Very unusual."

"OK. What else?"

Wu reached for a small cylindrical plastic container sitting at the edge of his desk and filled with a brown, gritty substance.

"This is the soil sample found on the roof of the Lyerman Building," Wu said, shaking the clear plastic container, watching the soil bounce off the sides.

"What is it?" Jefferson asked.

"It might be easier," Wu began, "to start with what it isn't."

"OK, what isn't it?"

"Well, it's not from anywhere around here."

"How do you know that?"

"About five different tests. This stuff is off the charts. Electrical conductivity for soluble salts, hydrometer particle-size analysis, element testing. Definitely not native. It's got over 70 percent silica content," Wu said. "It's rhyolite."

"What does that mean?"

"It means it's volcanic," Wu replied. "Not only that, but the clay content in the soil suggests a certain region of the world, somewhere near New Zealand or the South Pacific. And because it's rich in alkaloids, it makes me believe that this sample probably originated in a rain forest somewhere. So my best guess is that this soil came from a rain forest–dominated volcanic island somewhere in the South Pacific region near New Zealand."

"All that from this little bit of dirt?" McKenna asked.

"That's easy," Wu said. "What wasn't so easy was what you pulled out of our deceased friend's chest."

"You mean that black shard of whatever it was."

"Exactly," Wu said, crossing his fingers and leaning back in his chair. "Now these shards. They were pulled from Lyerman. You're sure?"

"Hundred percent."

"Embedded in his bone?"

"Like a knife in butter."

Dr. Wu nodded, leaning forward, opening up the file in front of him. He flipped through the pages for a moment, Jefferson catching glimpses of DNA gel sample images and paragraphs of writing.

"OK. Well, I'll be honest with you, Detective Jefferson. I don't know exactly what this is that you found. All I can really tell you is that it was something living. Not a resin or metal, but actual living cells. Otherwise, I can't offer too much except speculation."

"Speculate then. I'm listening."

"All right," Wu said slowly. "Let's start with cells. Cells, you know, make up almost all living things. You, me, ring-tailed lemurs, whatever is out there, it is composed of cells. Now within these cells, well, let's take humans for instance. Except for certain exceptions, such as red blood cells, every cell within us is nucleated."

"It has a nucleus."

"Exactly. A nucleus. And in this nucleus are chromosomes, strands of DNA to which certain genetic characteristics are attached. You follow?"

"Sure, I had my senior year biology class."

"So the nucleus contains our DNA. And every strand of DNA has pieces that contain genetic information that guides an organism's development. So DNA tells us whether a person will have blue eyes or brown eyes, be tall or short, etc."

"Sure."

"OK. What's interesting for our discussion is that every strand of DNA also contains pieces that supply no relevant genetic information at all. These segments are called introns."

"If they serve no purpose," McKenna asked, "why are they there?"

Wu shrugged. "Nobody really knows. They appear to be blank-slate pieces of DNA. These segments are called VNTRs, variable number tandem repeats."

"So every cell has DNA. Certain portions of the DNA are coded to produce things like our hair and skin color, while other sections don't really do anything. And those sections that don't do anything are called VNTRs, right?"

"Correct," Wu replied. "Now remember I said that every cell has some VNTRs, some sections which supply no genetic information. But most of the DNA strand has important genetic codes; otherwise, we couldn't exist. If all our DNA were useless, we'd have nothing."

Wu reached out and carefully took a plastic bag from inside the manila folder, staring through the plastic at the small shards inside. "But this. Whatever it is. This is all

VNTRs. The organism that this came from is composed entirely of what should be useless information," he said. "This thing has DNA, but no useful DNA. It's a blank slate."

"So what does that mean?"

"I couldn't say. It's literally like nothing I've ever seen before in my life. I said that I sent a sample out to Harvard. Dr. Charles Weinstein, he's a great molecular biologist, but my gut instinct is that he's going to come up with the same conclusion I have."

"Which is what?"

"I have no idea where this could possibly come from. It's like this thing was genetically engineered, but we've got nothing now, no technology that exists, that could engineer something this complex. The DNA is all there, but its presence is a genetic impossibility. Human DNA consists of the standard double helix. The DNA in this organism is also in a double helix, exactly like that of a human, but there's no way this organism could ever be born. Its DNA doesn't code any information, there's no rational way this organism should exist."

Jefferson leaned back in his chair. Behind Wu's desk were windows looking out over the Charles River. Jefferson's eyes wandered to the water, its surface glazed over by the afternoon sunlight. Sailboats rippled through waves, white sails billowing outward in the wind. A sidewalk meandered along the edge of the river. Jefferson watched couples walking together, seemingly far away from VNTRs and genetic impossibilities.

"It gets worse," Wu said suddenly.

"Yeah? I thought we were doing pretty well so far on its getting worse. How much worse?"

"Seriously worse."

"All right, tell me about it."

"Well," Wu began slowly, "there appeared to be an intermingling of genetic information."

"How do you mean?"

"You recovered these black fragments from the body of the victim?"

"That's what I said."

"They were actually *inside* the body itself. In contact with it?"

"Had to jimmy it out of the guy's sternum. I'd say that's pretty close."

"Well, that is really where our current scientific understanding of genetics fails us," Wu said. "Where the cellular fragments of bone come into contact with the uncoded DNA of this mysterious shard, there appears to be a genetic transference."

"What do you mean?"

"I mean that the uncoded DNA, the supposedly useless VNTRs of the organism, actually shift themselves to form an exact match with the DNA of the victim. In humans, once the body begins to mature, the role of each cell is fixed by the DNA. A nerve cell can't spontaneously become a liver cell, or vice versa. But in this organism, its apparently blank DNA fragments appear to have the ability spontaneously to express themselves in the same way as the host DNA."

"So this thing can clone itself into any shape it wants?"

"Not exactly. Cloning is done on the single cell level. But this organism appears to be capable of spontaneous generation of entirely new chains of DNA. Somehow, it can replicate the DNA matter of a host cell, changing its own blank-slate DNA to form the exact same gene pattern of its host."

"So this thing had the same genetic codes as Kenneth Lyerman?"

"Exactly the same. The DNA fingerprint of Kenneth Lyerman and this organism were indistinguishable from one another, but only in the cellular portions of the organism that had come into contact with Lyerman's bone fragments. It appears this organism needs direct contact with whatever it chooses to replicate itself as."

"What does that mean? Can this organism shape itself to look like Lyerman?"

Wu shrugged. "I'm not sure. I don't know if it can physically express the DNA of its host cell, if it can analyze the DNA from Lyerman and generate itself to appear as Lyerman or not."

So this thing may or may not look exactly like Kenneth Lyerman, or any of its other victims, Jefferson thought. *That's great.*

Wu reached into his desk, pulling out a small business card and handing it to Jefferson. The card had Wu's home address and telephone number printed on it.

"Here's my card. The powers that be think it's important that you and Lieutenant Brogan be able to contact me at home."

Jefferson thanked him, putting the card in his pocket. Then he exhaled, "Whatever this is, it's not human, right?"

Wu shrugged. "Not in the strictest sense. But listen. Every type of species on this planet has a certain, specific number of chromosomes. Dogs have seventy-two for instance. This creature has forty-six chromosomes. Exactly like humans. So this thing isn't human exactly, but whatever it is, it was created to be able to replicate us exactly. It was created in our own image."

"Or maybe . . ." McKenna began slowly, "humans were created in its image."

Jefferson and McKenna left the City Hospital through the main entrance, walking out into the warm afternoon sun. The hospital was located a few blocks from the South End neighborhood of Boston, with its narrow streets, faded brick apartment buildings, and flowering trees. The flowers were beginning to wilt in the late season, large white petals falling drowsily to the sidewalk around them as they walked.

"I went to the naval museum this morning," Jefferson said.

"What'd you find?"

"Our guy was there. Somehow he was there. The writing was the same. I think we should have left the *Galla* where it was, on the bottom of the Pacific. Now it's become some kind of Pandora's box that we can't get shut again."

"What are you going to do now?"

"Brogan and I are going out to Blade Prison late this afternoon. Prisoner there by the name of Ramsey is supposed to have some information. Could be nothing."

"Could be everything."

"Won't know until we go."

"And Saint, is he still a suspect?"

"The guy's fingerprints were all over Sinatra's place, and we know he wasn't just delivering a pizza. So no, we can't rule him out entirely. But something more than just him is going on here. There's a connection between Lyerman and whatever was on the *Galla*. Something that he found on that ship and brought back into Boston."

McKenna bent and picked up one of the flower petals, playing it back and forth between her fingers as they walked. The air was fragrant, slightly cooler beneath the mottled shade of the trees. It was nice.

"I got the message from Brogan this morning and listened to the voice on the audio recording taken on the roof of the Lyerman Building," McKenna said. "You remember what it said?"

Jefferson's mind faded back from the flowering shade to the two bodies slick with rain and left dead on the roof of the Lyerman Building. The voice Brogan and he had heard on that tape. The screaming, the sound of tearing flesh. And then that voice. *Ultio ultionis possidere.* Jefferson wouldn't forget that.

"Yes, I remember."

"*Ultio ultionis possidere,*" McKenna said.

"What does it mean?"

"It's Latin. It means, 'Revenge shall be mine.' "

She stopped abruptly, the white petal falling from her fingers to the street below. She turned to him. "I want you to be careful, Will. Whatever happens with this, I want you to be careful. I want you to be sure of yourself."

"I will," Jefferson said. "I promise."

Ultio ultionis possidere. Revenge shall be mine.

Jefferson gripped the damp railing as the Boston Harbor Cruiser rolled through another wave. The small cruiser's bow slapped up a salted mist spray from the ocean, which blew across Jefferson's face, leaving his skin wet and ruddy. He inhaled deeply, closing his eyes for a moment and listening to the churning of the engines.

"God I love this." Jefferson smiled. "I forgot what it's like to be out on the ocean."

Brogan was standing next to him, his gashed arm hanging stiffly at his side, his gray trench coat draped over his shoulders. He grimaced, squinting as the ship rolled again. "I'm actually feeling sick."

"Really?"

"Yeah, little bit."

"What they give you for that arm?"

Brogan shrugged. "Don't remember. Probably something that doesn't mix well with this Pirates of the Caribbean ride here."

Jefferson laughed. "It's the open air, the horizons. Get out of the city."

Given what Ron Saint had told them, they were taking one of the Police Harbor Patrol boats out to Blade Prison Island to talk with Robert Ramsey. Jefferson had picked Brogan up at his house, and they'd driven to the Harbor. On the drive over, he'd filled him in on the information from his trip to the naval museum and his meeting with Dr. Wu. Brogan had listened attentively, not commenting, only nodding quietly and staring out the window of the moving car.

Now Brogan was leaning unsteadily against the ship's railing. With the hand of his one good arm he held a steaming cup of Dunkin' Donuts coffee, the orange bubble lettering written around the Styrofoam. Behind them, the city of Boston was slowly fading away, its buildings standing stark against the sky. Brogan took a sip of his coffee. "You think this is a waste o' time?"

Jefferson shrugged. "Yeah, maybe."

"If it is," Brogan responded thoughtfully, taking another slow sip from his coffee, "I'm gonna tear Saint a new one."

They were quickly approaching the prison island. Blade stood silently, a giant rocky outcropping jutting out from the turning ocean. Waves rolled up against the large breaker rocks, slapping against them and turning upward into mist and white-flecked foam. Ahead was a long concrete pier, flashing red lights mounted on the end.

A guard stationed in one of the towers high on the prison wall was watching them approach with casual interest. He pulled a moment on his cigarette before turning away and looking out across the ocean. The engines of the cruiser were in idle, the small craft rolling sickeningly in the waves. Through the glass windows, Jefferson saw the driver talking on the radio to the prison control room. He nodded, placing the set back by the ship's wheel.

The light on the pier changed from red to green, and slowly the cruiser's engines turned over, moving the craft toward the docks. A man in a dark blue suit was approaching them, walking slowly toward the end of the dock, where three guards were already waiting. Quite a reception.

Jefferson's hand shot out to the railing as the cruiser bumped slightly against the dock. Some of Brogan's coffee rolled over the side of his cup, to a soft, "Aww, shit," as Brogan jumped back to get out of the way. The guards on the dock were wearing light blue uniforms and moored the cruiser with thick braids of rope. One of them dropped a metal gangway, which landed sharply on the cruiser's deck. Brogan flipped the rest of his coffee overboard, crushing the Styrofoam cup in his hand and looking around a moment for a garbage can before finally depositing it carefully in his coat pocket.

"Here we go," Brogan was saying as they stepped across the gangway to the dock, Jefferson automatically walking toward the man in the suit who was smiling and holding his hand out.

"Hello, welcome to Blade Prison." Jefferson took the limp hand, the handshake lasting for only a moment. "I'm Thomas Cappello, the warden of the island."

The warden shook hands with Brogan, pausing curiously at the stiffness of Brogan's arm. The guards made no move forward, remaining clustered together, staring blandly out to sea. In front of them, a grassy lawn stretched up toward the rocky walls of the prison. To the side of a brick administration building just beyond the docks, the Massachusetts state flag fluttered, its white flagpole rising out of a neatly groomed circle of wood chips and gently waving red pansies. Prison gardening always looked good—prisoners didn't have much else to do.

"So, I've been told you're here to see one of our guests," the warden said brightly. Brogan nodded. "That's right."

They were walking along the docks, the three prison guards trailing behind, talking almost inaudibly amongst themselves.

"Good." The warden smiled, as if Brogan had just told him he'd won the lottery. "We don't get many visitors out here. I'm sure he'll be happy to see you."

Twenty minutes later Brogan and Jefferson were seated in the prison guards' lounge area, waiting for Ramsey to be brought out of his cell. The lounge was comfortable, with three faded orange sofas surrounding a central metal table. Snack and soda machines were pressed up against one of the walls, next to a bulletin board, the rectangular cork filled with notices about worker safety and union announcements. Brogan was reclining on one of the sofas, his feet stretched in front of him, his rumpled tie off to the side. He was tapping the side of the sofa with the palm of his hand, keeping time to some unknown music playing silently in his head.

Jefferson checked his watch. "Wanna get back before five."

"Yeah, hopefully this won't be some wild-ass goose chase," Brogan replied. Leaning backward slightly, he pushed his hand into his pants pocket, pulling out a few pieces of loose change.

He stared at his open palm for a moment, counting the money. "Hey, you got twenty cents I can borrow?"

"Quarter, here." Jefferson flipped it to Brogan, who caught the silver piece just as the door to the lounge opened. One of the guards poked his head in for a moment. "Ramsey's all set."

"Great, thanks," Jefferson replied, pushing himself from off his seat on the table.

"Go ahead, I'll catch up," Brogan said, jingling the loose change in his palm as he moved toward the machine.

Jefferson followed the guard down the windowless hallway just outside the lounge. The warden had reserved one of the private visiting rooms for Jefferson and Brogan, not that the public visiting area was ever that crowded. Most people never made the trip out to the island. They stopped before a metal door, with a six-inch window set in the middle. Another guard was standing out front, leaning casually against the wall, one hand lightly scratching his chest. He nodded slightly to Jefferson. The guard pulled out a set of keys and unlocked the door, stepping back and holding the door open slightly for Jefferson to pass through.

"He's been restrained," the guard announced, then added, "we'll be right outside the door."

Jefferson nodded. "My partner should be coming up soon."

"Sure, we'll let him in."

The guard's head disappeared, and the door closed. Jefferson heard the key turning in the lock and the sound of the bolt pushed back into place. Jefferson turned away from the door. Ramsey was strapped to a chair placed at the far end of a long table. He had a thick goatee with long brown hair that hung around his shoulders. A tattoo of a vine wound its way up the side of his neck, turning into a strip of barbed wire as it reached toward his ear. He was staring at Jefferson.

Jefferson broke the stare, looking around. The room they were in was a converted workshop. Over Ramsey's head, pressed against the wall, was a large Peg-Board, the outlines of tools still visible, drawn in black magic marker. On the side wall was a large black cabinet, the door welded shut, NASCAR racing stickers affixed to the side. There was a metallic smell in the air. Overhead, an industrial fluorescent lamp hanging from the ceiling made the room uncomfortably bright, forcing Jefferson to squint slightly.

Ramsey was watching him carefully with sharp blue eyes, his lips pressed into a tight smirk underneath his thick brown facial hair. He shook his head once, his long hair sliding over his shoulders. "I heard you wanted to speak to me."

Jefferson moved slowly down the table. "I'm Detective Jefferson, with the Boston Police Department."

"Good for you," Ramsey said, staring straight ahead.

Ignoring the comment, Jefferson pulled a notebook from his jacket pocket, reading it slowly out loud. "Now, it says here that you're doing eight to ten for assault and battery on your wife, your neighbor, and three arresting officers. Almost beat a man to death with a seven iron. Like golf?"

"Don't much care for it," Ramsey answered.

The door to the interrogation room opened suddenly, Brogan stepping inside, still clutching a half portion of a Twix bar.

"This is a little party in here," Ramsey said. "I wish I'd known, I could have worn my best party dress."

Brogan pushed the rest of the Twix bar into his mouth, before pulling up a chair and seating himself across from Ramsey.

"We got a real chatterbox here, huh?" Brogan said, chewing the candy bar and staring mildly at Ramsey.

"Yeah." Jefferson raised his eyebrows. "Looks that way. I was just informing our new friend here that he's still got six years left on his sentence." Jefferson let the words hang for a moment. "And given his female assault problems, he's not gonna be favored real highly with the mostly female parole board."

"My female assault problem?" Ramsey shook his head, his beard wagging back and forth across his chest. "That what it say on that notebook o' yours?"

"That's what it says, female assault problem," Jefferson replied.

"Brother, I barely hit that woman. That ain't a problem; the only problem I got is that I keep getting married to these fucking whores. That's my problem."

"Yeah," Brogan said, raising his eyebrows.

"When all that shit happened back in '91, I was wound up tighter than a spring on a shithouse door. I didn't know what the hell I'd been doing, you could have told me

I was the damn pope, or, the goddamn queen of England. I would have believed you. I was higher'n a kite. But now, I don't got those problems. I'm clean. I ain't marrying no more fucking whores either, you can believe that."

"You beat a cop almost to death with a golf club," Jefferson said.

Ramsey paused for a moment, sucked in his breath. "I couldn't even see straight when he came on me. You get a Doberman and don't feed it for a week, then hang a steak in front of its mouth, you damn straight that sum o' bitch is gonna attack."

Jefferson coughed and tossed the notebook on the table in front of him. Brogan crumpled up the candy bar wrapper and placed it in his pocket.

"But what the hell's that got to do with anything?" Ramsey said. "You came all the way out here for that?"

"No, you're right, we didn't come out here for that," Jefferson started, sitting in one of the chairs. "We've got a proposition for you."

"Oh Lord." Ramsey rolled his eyes, leaning back slightly. "Listen, before you get into that, I'm gonna need something to smoke."

Brogan pushed himself away from the table, moving toward the door. He knocked once, and the door opened, a guard sticking his head inside the room. Brogan whispered something to the guard.

"Get me a pack o' Kools," Ramsey shouted to Brogan, then, turning toward Jefferson, said, "Got a fire in the chest, got to Kool it down sometimes."

Brogan came back with a few cigarettes, their white sticks dangling out from between his closed fingers. "Got these from the guards. They're Marlboros though."

"Aww, well, shit," Ramsey said, looking at the loose cigarettes on the table. "That's all right. This is Marlboro country anyway. I need a little help though."

"What?"

Ramsey glanced at his Velcroed hands, raising his eyebrows. "I ain't a magician."

"Huh?" Jefferson said, before looking down. He saw that Ramsey's arms had been fastened to the chair. "Oh sorry." Jefferson moved forward and undid the super-strength Velcro restraints.

Ramsey raised his arms, gently rubbing his wrists. He pushed back the sleeves of his shirt, showing off a faded tattoo of a naked woman on one forearm and a Rebel flag on the other. The tattoos were old, the ink smudging together. Ramsey caught Jefferson's glance. "Them two things never go outta style. Naked ladies and Rebel flags. Yessir. Not like a damn titty ring. Rebel flags, man, been around for 150 years."

Ramsey took one of the cigarettes, placing it unlit in his mouth.

"Light?" he asked, his lips pursed around the white stick. Brogan slid a lighter across the table toward Ramsey.

"People think cause I got this flag tattooed on my arm that I hate black people or Jews or some such thing." The cigarette flared up in a red ember as Ramsey lit it. "I've known some real nice black folk and some real nice Jews. Real nice."

Ramsey tossed the lighter back on the table. "But that's beside the point."

He leaned back in his chair, stretching his arms behind his head, pulling on the cigarette. "Real good smoke. Not like a Kool, but it ain't bad."

"So, how'd you like to get some of that sentence knocked off a little bit?" Jefferson asked.

"What the hell you talking bout?"

"If you help us out"—Jefferson nodded toward Brogan—"we can get you out of here."

Ramsey was suddenly listening closely, leaning forward and placing his palms on the table in front of him, the fingers splayed out. "Help you, how?"

"Tell us about the pit."

Ramsey sucked in his cigarette for a moment, regarding them, thinking. Then finally, he pulled the cigarette out of his mouth, and said, "Don't know nothing about that."

"You know someone named Ron Saint?"

"Yeah, sure I know Ron, I shared a cell with that brother for two years. He's a good man."

"Well, he's in some trouble now."

"Yeah?" Ramsey smiled. "What'd he do this time, get some old lady pregnant?"

"Nope. He's looking at going down with at least five homicides, and maybe another triple if we can connect him."

Ramsey sucked in his breath. "Jesus, Ronnie."

He looked up at the corner of the wall for a moment, the cigarette smoke wafting around his head. He inhaled, then shook his head. "Naw, that ain't Saint. He never killed nobody in his life. Just stupid shit. Y'all must have the wrong man."

"Maybe he's making up for it now," Brogan said. "Got all his killing in quickly."

"Hey, fuck you," Ramsey said, his blue eyes making hard contact with Brogan's. "Ron didn't do that shit. I know him, man. A lot of bad men passed through here, Ron wasn't one of 'em."

Brogan kept the stare for a moment, the tension in the room increasing.

"Well, that's why we're here, Mr. Ramsey." Jefferson's voice eased between the two men. "Ron said that you might be able to help us out in our investigation."

Ramsey's head swiveled to Jefferson. "How?"

"He told us to ask you about something called the pit? He said you'd know what he meant."

Ramsey just stared at Jefferson, the smoldering cigarette slowly burning toward his lips.

"Mr. Ramsey?"

Ramsey turned away. "Yeah, I heard what you said." He took the cigarette nub from between his lips and crushed it out on the table, flicking the ashes off onto the floor. "Jesus, Saint."

He turned back toward Jefferson. "You think this could help him out?"

Jefferson shrugged. "Maybe, no way to know until you tell us."

Ramsey rubbed the back of his head for a moment, the tattoo of the naked lady on his forearm moving up and down. "The pit, huh?"

"That's right."

"Goddamn," Ramsey smiled nervously, looking away. "And if I help you out?"

"If you help us out, we might be able to find the real killer," Brogan said. "So your boy Saint doesn't go in for five to eight life sentences."

"What about me?"

"You? If what you tell is true, we could see about knocking some time off your sentence. Maybe a year."

"Maybe two?"

Brogan shrugged. "You rehabilitated now? Gonna go beating on any more cops if you get out early?"

"No, sir, I'm changed. The crazy is all out of me now."

"Maybe two then," Brogan said. "You help us, we'll see what we can do."

"And Saint is up against the wall now, huh?"

"Yes he is," Jefferson replied. "Only thing that can help him now is if we find the one who really did it. You see, just like you, I don't think Saint really did this."

Ramsey paused for a moment, taking another drag. "Help you catch the real killer, huh?"

"Do everyone, including yourself, a whole lotta good."

"I ain't ever told nobody about that. Ain't none of us have. Might as well be now, huh?" His eyes were watering slightly.

"The pit . . ." Ramsey said slowly, letting the word seep out from between his lips. "That's another word for Blade's solitary confinement, out in the yard there. Nothing special about it really, just a damn hole in the ground. Or, least it was."

"What happened?"

"Well," Ramsey took another cigarette and placed it in his mouth, not bothering to light it, "originally, it was just a solitary. You get put there, you just live in the dirt and the dark for a few days, then they bring you back up. No big deal. Every prison's got something like that.

"Then, about six months ago, they put this brother down there name o' Cecil Edwards. He comes up the next day, dead and cut up to hell." Ramsey ran his fingers over his face. "His head had these damn claw marks across it, like some kind of animal or something had got him. One eyeball all popped out, chest ripped open. He was a fucking mess.

"So everyone panics, right? What the hell happened to this poor son of a bitch. Warden writes it off as some kind of self-inflicted accident, but that's bullshit, you can't self-inflict ripping your own chest open, know what I'm saying?"

"Yeah." Jefferson nodded. "But what about an autopsy, investigation. Any of that?"

"Naw. Warden took care of that. You see, the prison has its own medical staff on pay. Coroner and everything. And these are all good old boys, been working with the warden for almost twenty years now. You better believe that if the warden says some-one died from a prison fight, that's what gets wrote down in a medical report."

"OK," Jefferson replied, making a note to have Wu look at the autopsy report for a Cecil Edwards sometime. "Go on."

"After that, anytime someone gets put in that pit, they come up in pieces. And sometimes, whole parts of them are missing. A leg, an arm, just a hand, all gone. So the warden sends a few guards down during the day to check it out. The rooms down there are empty, right, no way anything is getting in there, and nothing getting out. So warden keeps putting prisoners there, and they keep coming back up like confetti."

"How did nobody ever find out about this?" Brogan asked. "Don't these cons have lawyers. Family visitation? Someone they can tell?"

"The warden owns this island, nothing that goes on that he don't know about it. Calls to the outside are monitored, lawyer visits are monitored. Everything. This room we're in now is clean because they only just started using it. Word is among the cons in here that if you let out the secret on the pit, you'll be the next one down there."

"What about guys they let out of here? Like Saint? How come he never told anyone?"

"Most of those brothers are on parole still. All it takes is one call from the warden to the right PO, and you get a violation written up on you that'll get you sent back. Someone on the outside starts talking too much to the wrong people, they get violated back here. They'll be in the pit before the story even hits the press. Don't take too much to keep a secret here if everyone's involved."

"What did you say the marks looked like?" Jefferson asked.

"They got like scratch marks across everything, like from a claw or something," Ramsey responded.

Brogan glanced over at Jefferson—same as on the bodies they'd gotten back in the city.

"So now, everyone here is scared to fart. Nobody wants to get put in the pit. We got organization here, like a Martha Stewart dinner party, everyone looks real nice, real polite, five hundred convict Ms. Mannerses in here. Everyone is afraid to piss anyone off. Safest prison in the country."

Ramsey pulled the cigarette out of his mouth, looking at its glowing ember for a moment. "Man, I done some bad shit in my life and most of it, I ain't even got caught for. So, yeah, I probably deserve to be here. But shit, no man deserves that pit. Everyone's always living in fear. Takes away your self-respect after a while. That ain't right, to treat a man like that." Ramsey took another pensive drag on his cigarette, then, staring off through the smoke, he murmured, "It ain't right."

"What do you think?" Jefferson asked softly, looking back at the prisoner.

Ramsey was still seated behind the long table. He pulled thoughtfully on his cigarette, staring blankly through the smoke. Brogan made a motion toward his belt, hitching up his pants. "Ask me three weeks ago, and I'd have said he's crazy. But with all the shit that's been going on recently." Brogan raised his eyebrows, then sighed. "I don't know. There's a part of me that believes him . . . you know?"

"I know what you mean." Jefferson checked his watch. "Listen, it's still early. Why don't we go and check out the pit. See if anything's down there."

Brogan nodded, rapping his knuckles lightly on the table and turning to leave.

Behind them, Ramsey suddenly said something inaudible.

"What's that?" Jefferson asked, walking back toward the man.

"I said," Ramsey began slowly, "you two ain't the only ones who's been asking me these same kinds o' questions."

Curious, Jefferson approached the prisoner. "What do you mean?"

"About two months ago, I had a guy come in here asking the same questions as y'all asked me. What about the pit and all, what kind o' things going on in there."

"Who was that?"

Ramsey shook his head. "Don't know, never gave his name. Didn't say shit to him."

"What did he look like?"

"He was elderly, looks like he was real wealthy from the clothes he was wearing . . ."

"Yeah . . ."

"He was in a wheelchair, an electric kind."

Lyerman. Lyerman had come out there and asked questions about the pit. How was he involved? Jefferson stood for a moment thinking about all the connections that seemed to be coming together. Lyerman, Older, the *Galla*; they all seemed to be pointing to something, something that was buried inside the pit.

Jefferson and Brogan pushed open a set of double doors, stood blinking in the late-afternoon sun of the prison yard. The heavy granite walls of the prison were outlined strongly against the turning clouds of the darkening sky. Along the third floor, Jefferson saw black outlines of windows cut into the stone, the occasional arm hanging limply out. Bored prisoners looking out their cell windows into the yard. As they walked across the grass, Jefferson could feel eyes on him from above.

The pit wasn't difficult to find, the round circle of dead grass made the area stand out starkly in the yard. The rusting trapdoor lay quietly, the centerpiece of the dead grass. Jefferson banged the metal with his foot, listening to the hollow sound it made. There was a large metal ring set in the door, lying flat on its side.

Jefferson was leaning over to pull the door up by the ring, when Brogan grabbed his shoulder. He looked up and saw the warden walking with quick, long strides across the grass toward him.

"Can I help you gentlemen?" he shouted from across the yard, his tie blowing back over his shoulder, flapping in a sudden gust of wind.

Jefferson let the ring drop, standing up. "We wanted to look in the pit."

"I'm afraid that's impossible." The warden was smiling, but his voice was tight, constricted.

"Why's that?" Brogan asked, turning to face the man.

"Well, we've got . . ." the warden began, then paused, smiling again. Jefferson watched him struggle, trying to think of something to say. "It just is."

Brogan looked at him closely for a moment. "We're here on a police investigation. A homicide investigation," he said, stressing the word "homicide." "I think you can appreciate that."

"Of course, it's just that, we don't let visitors down there. It's policy."

Brogan shook his head. "What the hell do we look like? A couple lollipop reporters from *Dateline* here for kicks?"

"No, no." The warden shook his head again. "Of course not. I'm sorry."

"So what's it gonna be?" Brogan asked.

The warden looked at the two officers for a moment, his loose tie and a few strands of hair blowing wildly in the wind. He pulled his lips back in something resembling a smile. "Well, I guess I don't really have a choice."

"I guess you could put it that way," Brogan answered.

The warden shrugged. Then, taking a step back, he raised his hands in a gesture of surrender. "OK."

Jefferson leaned down toward the ring again.

"Just a piece of advice though," the warden said softly.

"What's that?" Jefferson asked.

The warden looked up at the sky. He turned back toward Jefferson. "Just don't be down there too late."

Without a word, Jefferson nodded, then pulled back on the ring.

Slowly, the trapdoor opened.

While the warden and Brogan looked on, Jefferson pulled the door until it flopped back and landed on the dead grass behind with a heavy thudding noise. The black, square hole gaped up at him, cut almost perfectly into the ground. Brogan joined him on the edge, peering into the impenetrable darkness. He pulled his flashlight out, shining it into the hole. The light cut feebly into the darkness, glinting off the stone floor sixteen feet beyond. The stone below was glimmering with a damp wetness, the flashlight beam shimmering silver as it glided across the floor. Brogan circled the beam around, but they saw nothing, only the empty floor and the damp mildewed walls.

Part of the pit extended out of view, a black cavern stretching back out of sight.

Jefferson turned to the warden. "How do you get down there?"

"There's a ladder, right underneath the ledge. Just pull the lever. It drops."

Jefferson bent, running his fingers along the underside of the pit's hole. His hand brushed against something long and cold. He pulled it.

There was a clanging sound, and beneath them, a metal fire escape–type elevator swung into the darkness below. Without the aid of the flashlight, the rungs disappeared into the gloom.

Jefferson stared at the ladder, its black metal traveling into the void. He looked at Brogan and raised his eyebrows. "You first?"

Brogan smiled. "Yeah, right, man. I think I'll let you have the honors on this."

Jefferson nodded once, running his dry tongue over his lower teeth and tightening the belt around his waist. "All right, but you keep shining that light, OK? I need both my hands to climb, so you keep shining that thing."

"Yeah sure." Brogan took a step forward, turning the flashlight back on and pointing it into the hole.

Clearing his throat with a faint cough, Jefferson stepped to the hole and began lowering himself into the pit. His right foot braced against a rung of the ladder, holding his weight in place as he grasped the sides with his hands. Then, slowly, he began to descend.

The air below was immediately colder, like the inside of a cave. The smell was earthy, almost pleasant. If he hadn't known he was inside a prison, the whole place would have reminded Jefferson of a wine cellar. Halfway down, he paused for a moment to wipe the moisture that had collected above his eyes.

Above him, he saw Brogan, bent over, peering down, the light in his hand shining dully. "You all right?"

"I'm all right," Jefferson assured him. "Just clearing this shit out my eyes."

"You want a little hankie?" Brogan kidded.

"Yeah." Jefferson grinned. "Why don't you come here and give it to me, asshole?"

His forehead dry, he continued down. Eight rungs later, his shoes tapped against the hard stone floor. Stepping back from the light, he reached to his belt, pulling out his own flashlight and turning it on. The pit was a lot bigger than he had imagined.

The beam from his flashlight glazed over the wet stone walls, revealing chinks of individual blocks of granite. The room stretched back, then turned abruptly to the right, another section disappearing from view. Against one of the walls were what used to be wooden kegs, rotted almost completely out, nothing left except for their metal bands and soft wood. Powder kegs maybe? From back when Blade was still a fort.

Next to the kegs were gun racks, one tipped over onto its back, all of them empty. A section of stones protruded from the wall, forming a makeshift bench, which ran about five feet long. The rest of the room appeared empty.

A long hallway stretched in the opposite direction, breaking off into separate rooms. Light collapsed through the open trapdoor above him, catching on the motes of dust that circled around the ladder. From above, he heard Brogan shout something.

"Huh?" Jefferson shouted back, tilting his head and cupping his hand behind his ear.

"What's down there?"

"Oh." Jefferson looked back into the room for a moment, before looking up at Brogan. "Not much. Mold."

"All right, I'll be down."

Jefferson stepped away from the ladder, his foot clanging against something metal lying on the floor. Bending, he picked it up. It was some kind of food tray, bits of dried meat still clinging in clumps to the side. As he held it, a large cockroach ran out from the underside, scurrying quickly across the tray and, before Jefferson could react, running across his gloved hand.

Jefferson hissed involuntarily, flicking the roach off his arm, where it landed on its hard shelled back in the corner of the room, its little legs clambering in a futile effort to right itself. "Jesus," he whispered, rubbing his gloved hand.

The ladder creaked and moaned as Brogan carefully made his way down.

"Hey, boy, you gotta lose some weight," Jefferson shouted up. "You about to bring this thing down."

Brogan didn't answer, saving himself for the descent. Jefferson could hear his breath coming in quick rasps against the walls of the pit. With a final heave, the large cop reached the bottom, dropping with a sigh onto the floor. "Man, I wish I'd brought something to drink."

Pausing for a moment to catch his breath, Brogan straightened himself up and switched on his own flashlight, the beam of light joining Jefferson's.

"Careful, there are cockroaches around here," Jefferson warned, as they stepped into the pit.

"Hate those fucking things," Brogan whispered.

Jefferson looked down both halls, one longer, leading away with empty rooms cutting into it, the other stretching back twenty feet before turning sharply to the right.

"Which way?"

Brogan indicated the shorter path, and, together, the two began moving to the back of the pit. The floor was slightly uneven, stones underneath occasionally rising, creating small ridges and creases for them to step over. The walls were so slick with water that droplets formed in irregular spaces.

"Hell of a place to be in solitary," Jefferson said.

"No Ritz-Carlton."

A doorway was on their left, a thick oak door partway open in the frame. The surface of the door was gouged heavily, the whiter, pulpier inner wood erupting up from the marks in jagged shards of wood. Jefferson pushed the door open, shining his light into the room. The door yielded slowly, and he found himself pushing harder. There was a snapping sound, and the door jerked forward. From overhead a sudden blurred motion, something swinging from the roof, straight at Jefferson's head.

Jefferson twisted his body out of the way, the dark object sweeping by his face with a *whoosh*, before continuing out the open door in a wide arc and slamming into the far wall. Still twisting, Jefferson's foot caught against the uneven floor and he stumbled forward, bumping his forehead against a stone bench carved into the wall.

"Hey, you all right?" Brogan said, running toward him.

Jefferson sat up on the floor, probing his head gingerly.

"Yeah," he grunted. "I think so."

Brogan nodded, then turned toward the opposite walls, inspecting the black object that had swung from the ceiling.

"What is it?" Jefferson asked, slowly rising to his feet.

"I'm not sure. Come here, check it out."

The dark object was a long plank of wood. One end was affixed to an old door hinge that had been secured to the stone ceiling near the doorway. At the other end was a heavy barrel, four long nails protruding from the front. The plank had been suspended above the doorway by a stick propped against the door. When the door swung open, the stick dropped out of place, releasing the plank. The plank, weight down at its free end, swung through the doorway on the hinge, sweeping at anything coming through the door.

"Why the hell would anyone put this thing up?" Jefferson said, staring at the sharp nails protruding from the end of the barrel, now embedded into the mortar of the opposite wall.

"Wouldn't you?" Brogan said slowly. "If you thought something was here killing prisoners."

Jefferson nodded. True that.

Moving forward, they passed to the end of the pit, where the hallway turned to the right. Jefferson stopped, shining the light in front of him, into the smaller connecting room. Toward the rear, the roof of the connecting room narrowed, forming a small crawl space extending back into darkness. The walls were covered in a green, black slime that shimmered like wet algae in the light. Just over the opening of the crawl space, someone had carved a vacant-looking skull into the rock, with the inscription, MAY 2, 1692.

A large rock, the size of the opening, was pushed to the right, leaning up against the wall. There were tracks in the dirt from where someone had recently pushed it aside. The dead prison guard Older, perhaps?

Jefferson crouched in front of the opening, shining the beam down the narrow tunnel. He could see where the space opened up into a larger room, about twenty yards back.

"You want to check it out?" Brogan asked.

Jefferson nodded and, keeping his head low, slowly advanced into the tunnel. The space was just tall enough that keeping in a low crouch, he could duckwalk slowly on his feet. Brogan followed behind and the two men soon found themselves in the large room at the end of the crawl space. He stood, shining the beam of light around him. The room was a perfect square, each side roughly twenty feet in length, the walls constructed of massive solid stone blocks.

Dark objects about two feet high protruded from the dirt floor. Some were standing upright, some were bent at various angles, but each was rectangular in shape with a rounded, semicircular top. Jefferson shined his flashlight on one of the objects.

Gravestones.

The room was filled with them, forgotten markers of death, buried in this underground chamber. A graveyard beneath the prison. Jefferson moved around the room, lights on the stones, checking the dates. The dead were all buried between 1691 and 1692. Who were they? The original inhabitants of the fort? What killed them off? The room smelled of earth, like the inside of a cave. Jefferson felt his feet sinking slightly into the soft dirt covering the floor. The air was as still and sluggish as pond water, unmoved for the past three hundred years, it tasted sour and stale. Brogan paused in front of one of the grave markers, shining his light over the stone's surface. "Some of these dead aren't much older than kids."

Brogan was working his way carefully around the room, shining his light from side to side. He paused near the back of the room, staring down at something.

"Look at this."

Brogan gestured toward a large mound of dirt piled carefully to the side of one of the grave markers. Dug into the dirt floor was a gaping rectangular hole extending six feet into the ground. Jefferson joined him at the edge of the hole, looking at the cleanly dug sides, the flat bottom, reminding Jefferson of an open grave.

"Someone took something out of here," Jefferson replied.

In front of them, the walls were similar stone to the rest of the pit, and as Jefferson shined the light over them, he read the words written in thick black scrawls across the rock,

> *From the four corners the thrust of their advance burns like fire,*
> *They violently invade the dwellings of man,*
> *They lay bare the town as well as the country,*
> *They stomp the free man and the prisoner.*

Brogan stepped forward, inspecting the lettering closely. He pulled back, shining his light toward Jefferson. "You want to tell me what the hell is going on?"

Jefferson shook his head. "I wish I knew."

"You think it could be someone that works here?" Brogan asked. "Works at the prison?"

"We'll find out tonight," Jefferson replied.

"How's that?"

"Because tonight," he said, "we're going hunting."

Three hours later, Jefferson and Brogan were seated behind a large circular table inside one of the prison's administration rooms. The decor was early 1970s. Orange cushions on the sofa, wood paneling, green filing cabinets, photographs of birds. Like being in the back room of some disco lounge. Next to the photographs was a window looking out over the ocean. Pretty view. If it wasn't from inside a prison. A faint, dying light sifted in through the glass, reaching partway into the room before being overrun by the powerful overhead fluorescent lamps.

They'd brought in the big dogs for this one. Lt. Josh Commoss, team leader of Boston Special Weapons and Tactics. He was the biggest of the dogs. BD from CID. And he was now standing in front of the desk, peering at a blueprint of Blade Prison spread across the wide table. Big Dog was wearing full-length black coveralls, with black military-style boots and a bulky gray bulletproof vest. He had a black baseball cap pulled over his forehead, while an HK MP5 was slung loosely around his shoulder, hanging from a thin strap. He used his elbow to keep the small-sized machine gun on his back, its barrel pointing down.

The SWAT team had come in on two separate Police Marine Cruisers, riding out across the bucking harbor to the prison island. Just like bringing in a posse. The warden had shown them to the prison's filing and processing room, the only space with a table long enough for the blueprint map of the prison. Jefferson could hear occasional laughter and spurts of conversation as the rest of the SWAT team waited outside in the hallway, getting their equipment ready for the main event.

BD smoothed the creases of the blueprint with his hands. The print had been dug up from an archive room in the basement and had to be cleaned off before they could look at it, the layers of dust wiped away with paper towels. Since the warden found out that SWAT was being called in, he'd been going out of his way to be helpful. He'd even volunteered to clean the blueprint map himself, scrubbing at it with some paper towels and Windex. A regular Mr. Clean.

Jefferson might have even called him obsequious at times, if he thought anyone else would know what the word meant. Now he was hovering around the room like an airline stewardess making sure everyone was happy. BD ignored him.

BD was a certifiable sociopath. Just your average kind, one who should be in maybe the seventh year of a twenty-five-to-life for manslaughter. Funny thing was, though, he was a cop. Ironic. Take away the badge, he's in prison. Give him a badge, he's not only a cop, but a lieutenant. With everyone around him praying he doesn't decide to act out his sociopathic tendencies on someone who can sue the city.

He lived alone in a tiny one-bedroom apartment that looked a little like a South American prison cell with shag carpeting. He ate macaroni and tuna fish three meals a day, slept on a futon, and basically avoided contact with anyone the city wouldn't let him beat the shit out of. And someone decided to drag him out of that hole he lived in and bring him to Blade. Lucky day.

"All right, the decoy is here, center of the yard." BD was pointing to the small rectangular outline of the pit drawn on the blueprint.

"That's right," Brogan answered.

"Any idea where our guy is gonna try and gain access?"

"Probably over the walls. Pit seemed sealed from underneath. No way inside," Jefferson said. "Listen, BD, this guy is . . . well . . ."

"Well?"

"I've never seen anything like it," Jefferson said. "He's almost not . . . I just . . . I don't think these walls would hold him back at all."

"So you're saying we could expect Spider-Man to come over any of the five barrier walls protecting the yard."

"We think so." Brogan pushed a cough drop into his mouth, chewing on it thoughtfully.

"How high are these walls?" BD asked.

"About thirty, thirty-five feet," Jefferson answered.

"Can I put men up there?"

"Probably not; they've got a high-voltage fence running along parts of that. You don't want to risk getting one of the men fried." Jefferson pointed to the square blocks set along the wall. "These guard towers should give you a good view of the entire wall and yard, plus anything coming up on the outside of the island."

BD nodded, his eyes panning across the blueprint of Blade prison. "We'll keep our guys hidden. We don't want to frighten our man away."

Jefferson looked cautiously at BD. "Be careful. This guy is crazy."

BD smiled. "He's just one man, Detective. I think we can handle it."

Jefferson turned to look at him. "I never said it was just a man."

BD deployed four snipers along the perimeter of Blade's walls. Looking out through the office windows, Jefferson could see their shadows in each of the guard towers. Night had fallen fast over the prison, and a crescent moon was sitting high overhead. The searchlights wandered automatically from each of the guard towers, scanning over the prison yard, then back again out across the ocean, roving like wild lighthouse beacons. A German shepherd tracking dog lay on the floor near Jefferson, its muzzle stretched out, its eyes blinking occasionally, moving the tufts of hair underneath its forehead. BD was standing on one leg, his foot cocked up against one of the windowsills, his hands on his waist doing his best George Washington crossing the Delaware.

"Vegas One, to Vegas Two, do you copy, over?" BD was looking up toward one of the guard towers.

There was a pause, then a voice sounded clearly. "Vegas Two, copy. Clear here. Over."

"Copy that."

Listening to the deep voice of Vegas Two, Jefferson tried to picture what he looked like. Shade under six feet, stocky. Probably an asshole.

"You feel kind of out of place here? Bunch of these fucking cowboys and us," Brogan whispered, leaning in toward him.

They were both seated on two office chairs in the back. The rest of the SWAT team packed the room. Most were lying on the floor, backs against filing cabinets and the white plasterboard wall. Heavy equipment lay in accessible piles by their feet, helmets piled against automatic machine guns and flash/bang grenade launchers. Two of the team, the lures, were sitting in the dark of the pit playing prisoners. In the front BD was contacting everyone, getting the same negative action reply back.

"Yeah," Jefferson agreed. "I'm almost gonna be embarrassed if our guy doesn't show. It's like we're having this big party for him, and he didn't come up to dance."

Brogan smiled, leaning back in his chair. "I've got a feeling he'll show."

Jefferson nodded. He had the same feeling.

Down in the pit, SWAT Officer Chris Ross also had a feeling. He was cold as hell. He sat on the stone bench, bouncing his legs up and down, trying to get some warmth circulating underneath his black coveralls. At his feet, his MP5 was propped up against the stone, while his helmet was placed firmly on his head, more for warmth than for protection. Of all the shit-ass assignments, this was the most shit-ass. The cold from the stone was gradually seeping in through the Kevlar vest, slowly filtering into his back muscles, tightening them up.

His partner, Marlin Perez, was seated on the floor across from him, left leg sprawled out straight, right leg bent slightly at the knee. His eyes were closed slightly, until only the whites were visible in thin half-moon-shaped discs under the lids.

"Vegas One to Vegas Five and Six, over," Ross's helmet suddenly chirped, the voice of BD sounding loudly, surprising him slightly.

Perez's eyes jerked open. "This is Vegas Five and Six. Nothing doing here, over."

"Copy that, over," BD responded. "Keep awake down there."

Perez nodded, closing his eyes to their half-shut position again.

"This place gives me the creeps," Ross said. "Don't need to tell me to stay awake. You couldn't pay me to fall asleep."

"No shit. This is some medieval shit down here. All this stone, it's like a dungeon," Perez answered, his lids maintaining their position.

Ross eased the weight of his body to the left, leaning to the side, trying to loosen up the pressure on his numb right leg. He felt a wave of self-pity for a moment. "Don't cry for me. Don't cry for me, Argentina. *Don't cry for me, Argentina.*"

He jerked his head up and noticed that Perez was staring at him. He suddenly realized he'd been singing the line from the song softly out loud.

"What'd you say?" Perez asked, his voice polite.

"Nothing." Ross waved his hand. "Just singing to myself."

Perez nodded and returned to his crescent-mooned silence.

He'd been singing the line from that play. Without even thinking of it. Heather had been bugging him for a month to take her to a play. Something classy. Like *Cats*, or *Rent*. They'd seen *Evita*. Ross remembered waiting in line on the sidewalk for the door to open, standing among the other couples, the pleasant smell of colognes and perfumes rising from the bodies, their friendly chatter all mixing together into a discordant hum.

Then they'd gone inside. And he'd sat through *Evita*. Heather had loved it. They'd emerged from the playhouse onto the lit sidewalk outside, Heather almost skipping, her feet light on the pavement. She was smiling. Radiant.

He looked back up at the crescent moons of Perez's eyes.

"Hey," he whispered.

The eyes opened. "Yeah?"

"Saw *Evita* last night."

"Congratulations." Perez was smiling, his teeth gleaming in the darkness. Then the eyes half closed again, returning to their half crescents. "How was it?"

"Good."

Ross smiled to himself, leaning back against the wall again, tapping one of his boots softly against the stone. They'd set a marriage date, next June. He opened his mouth again, looking down at Perez to tell him. He glimpsed his partner's face, and immediately shut his mouth, staring at him curiously. The dreamy, calm appearance was gone, replaced instead by a look of hard concentration. Perez's eyes were open, creased around the edges, as he cocked his head forward and slightly to the side. Ross didn't realize what he was doing. Then it hit him.

He was listening.

"What is it?" he whispered to his partner.

Perez shook his head in reply, holding one finger up.

Ross stopped talking, listening himself. There was nothing, only a faint dripping sound of water, and a slight whistling of the outside air traveling down the stone shaft and into the pit. This place really did give him the creeps. It was a dungeon. He couldn't believe they actually locked men down here. He listened for the patter of rats, but caught only that incessant dripping.

Then, suddenly, he did hear something. It was a slight grating noise, of metal passing slowly across stone. Then silence again. For a moment, Ross thought he'd imagined it. Metal and stone. Sounded heavy. Definitely not a rat. Then he heard it again. The grating, lasting only for an instant, just like someone moving something carefully over the stone.

He suddenly wondered how long it'd been going on. If Perez hadn't noticed it, Ross would never have picked it up.

There it was again! Soft, but distinct in the tomb of the pit. Perez was slowly easing himself to his feet, his body creeping upward like a snake. Ross reached down and pulled his machine gun to his lap, carefully slipping his finger around the trigger and moving the safety with a soft *click* of metal. The noise was coming from the end of the pit in the adjoining room. One of the searchlights outside, perched on the prison wall, was shining down on them, sifting in through the cracks of the trapdoor and giving a faint, pale light to the chamber below. In that light, Ross could just manage to see Perez and his own weapon, but darkness quickly took over farther into the underground chamber.

Squinting, he could see nothing except for murky blackness. Perez was fully standing now, holding his weapon forward, while, with his free hand, he moved toward his belt and the suspended flashlight. He heard the noise again, faint and persistent, a soft screeching sound, reminding Ross of coming to bed after Heather was already asleep. Trying to slowly close their bedroom window in its creaky frame without her waking up. He'd slide the giant window down, bit by bit, listening to that soft creak.

Then abruptly the noise stopped. Ross froze. He didn't like the sudden silence. The same silence he heard in the bedroom, after the window was closed, when he crept slowly back into bed. Creeping in the darkness. Perez had reached his flashlight and was cautiously unhitching it from his belt. Silence, then ahead of them, Ross heard a new sound. A rasping passage of air. Like someone breathing in the darkness ahead of them.

Perez almost had the flashlight up in place. The rasping was continuing and getting closer. Ross faced forward, his finger pressing against the smooth curve of his machine gun's trigger. Someone was down there with them, and someone was coming. Now Ross's breath was coming in short spurts. He inhaled deeply, trying to calm himself, and moved his free hand up to wipe the gathering sweat from his forehead. Then there was silence. No grating of metal against stone. No breathing. And for a moment, Ross thought they were alone again.

Then it happened.

Something seemed to snap out of the darkness in front of him, a gray rushing mass. He felt a sharp pain in his arm, his weapon clattered to the stone floor. There was a strange sensation of a heavy coldness surrounding him, before he was suddenly jerked forward. Pulled into the darkness ahead of him, toward the rasping breath and a low throaty growl.

Perez's flashlight flipped on, filling the cavern with light. With sudden clarity, Ross saw what had his arm. He looked in its face, and screamed.

Back in the prison office overlooking the yard, Jefferson was fighting off the urge to sleep. He found the rhythmic passes of the searchlights over the grass strangely hypnotic and felt himself slipping farther and farther down into his seat. He even caught his mouth sagging open, his lower lip dangling loosely. He clamped his teeth together quickly, looking around to see if anyone else had noticed. Then a moment later, his eyelids were flickering again, slowly lowering. They were half-shut, when the radio on the windowsill by BD suddenly erupted into static.

"Vegas Five! . . . Veg . . . it's . . ." the words were broken up, and in the background Jefferson heard a pounding noise.

Awake.

BD grabbed the set off the windowsill, bringing it to his mouth, "Vegas One to Vegas Five, over!"

He held the radio to his ear, the volume turned up. The room lost its casual sleepiness. The SWAT team was pulling themselves up from the floor, grabbing their weapons. Time to ride.

"Vegas One to Vegas Five over!" BD was shouting into the radio, looking through the office window toward the pit.

The radio burst again with static, and, through its tiny speakers, Jefferson heard something else. A man screaming. Then a burst of gunfire. And more screams. Just like that. And all at once, Jefferson felt strangely detached. Like listening to a program on the radio. Or a book on tape. This wasn't real life. Whatever was happening was far away from them. Signals carried through the air from somewhere distant. Just actors in a studio somewhere.

It wasn't.

Jefferson looked out through the office window, and across the yard heard three quick volleys from inside the pit, the heavy boom of the machine gun fire. BD looked down at the silent radio in his palm, then gradually his gaze shifted to his men.

"Christ," he whispered to himself. "It's on."

"Sir?"

BD nodded, pulling the radio back up to his mouth, speaking to the four sniper positions. "Be advised, first team is moving toward the pit, all Vegas positions hold fire."

BD spoke quickly before dropping the radio back on the windowsill and shouldering his machine gun.

"OK, let's go, let's go," he was shouting to the men. And all around was a rush of movement. Men jumping up, helmets going on, weapons snapping into place. Brogan's mouth was open, sucking air in and out like a track star before the meet. Doing his psych-up routine. Then it was starting. BD pushing open the office door, stepping into the warm outside air of the yard. The rest of the men following him, eyes white underneath their black Kevlar helmets. One by one, moving quickly through the doorway and into the yard, machine guns held at shoulder level.

Jefferson and Brogan stepped after them, moving through the darkness, feeling the warm night air swallow them up. They were running across the yard, first in darkness, then moving suddenly in a brilliance of light as the guard towers focused the searchlight beams on them.

Then came a flash of red. Emergency flares standing on the surface of the pit shooting up into the air. Someone down there had triggered them. Someone in the pit was still alive. The red flares were arching above the prison, trails of sparks following them as they rose above the walls like meteors.

The entire yard was a confusion of lights and running feet and screaming from everyone's radio. Like going to war, and somehow this was all familiar. Mad rushing toward an unknown destination. Explosions of light breaking the darkness. Even the screaming. They reached the closed trapdoor of the pit, everyone fanning out around it, weapons aimed down.

"Hernandez, open it!" BD shouted, pointing down to the door.

Keeping low to the ground, Hernandez glided forward, reaching toward the door. The rest of the team moved behind to cover him. In the background, Jefferson could hear cheering. He looked back and saw the cellblock windows overlooking the yard. Arms of prisoners thrust through the bars of each window, fists clenched, pumping into the air. The flares hung in the air overhead. Hernandez pulled back the heavy metal door, dropping it back onto the ground behind the hole with a bang of metal. They all surged forward, flashing their lights into the dark hole.

"Ross? Perez?" BD called down into the pit.

No response. Below them was nothing, only the wetness of stone glistening in the light.

"Let's get down that ladder," Big Dog said into the radio. "All Vegas positions, we are moving down into the pit. Possible two men down, repeat, two men down. Call shore and have a medivac helicopter sent over."

"Mr. Ramunto"—BD pointed to one of the men—"down the hole."

Shouldering his weapon, Ramunto leaned down, catching the rung of the ladder with his foot. Slowly he began to climb, his figure, silhouetted by the nine flashlights of the rest of the SWAT team overhead, cast a sharp shadow on the stone floor sixteen feet below. In a moment he was down, squatting in a firing position, holding his machine gun forward.

Jefferson could see the man leaning forward, seeming to look at something farther down in the pit. Then he turned around, facing the other way, scanning his surroundings. He slowly moved backward on his heels, the barrel of his MP5 making slow circles around the pit.

"Mr. Ramunto," BD said softly into his radio, "what do you see?"

Ramunto was almost out of Jefferson's line of sight, when he looked up, raising his right hand to make the clear sign. As Ramunto's hand came toward his face, palm down, his entire body jerked suddenly. His face went confused—the kind of look guys have the instant they've been shot. Before the pain sets in. Before they realize they're done. His head was beginning to swivel to look behind him. Everything happening slowly. Then his body was twitching again, like he'd been caught on a hook and something was jerking him. He paused for an instant, nine flashlight beams trained on him. Then his legs and arms snapped one last time, something jerking his body away from the ladder. And he was gone.

"Jesus," Jefferson whispered, his eyes frozen open as he stared below.

Beneath them, the stone floor was empty. Ramunto had vanished.

Then they heard the scream.

After the scream, they all stared at each other. Even the cons in the cells around them seemed to hear it, everything going quiet for a moment except for the sizzling of the flares and the barking of the German shepherd. Then Big Dog took the lead, reaching his foot out for the first rung of the ladder. Everyone else snapped to attention, more guys following after him, moving toward the ladder. Everyone into the pit.

Jefferson followed, feet and hands on the cold metal rungs of the ladder. Reaching bottom, he turned to men with their backs toward him. Everyone stared down each of the tunnels of the pit. No screaming anymore, just silence. Someone was firing smoke grenades, chunking sounds as the grenades hit the floor, then hissing, as thick clouds of smoke poured out.

"Masks!" BD shouted as the thick smoke billowed toward them.

Jefferson had a moment to fumble for his mask, strapping it to his face and breathing the filtered air, before the white cloud of smoke overwhelmed him, swirling around his body and oozing across the glass faceplate of his mask. Voices now coming from inside the mask, from the radio receiver by his ear. Voices sounding tinny through the small headphones.

"First team, move north, up through the forward hallway," BD was saying.

Smoke was everywhere, and through it, he could see the black shapes of the team, one shape indistinguishable from the next. They were splitting up, one team moving north, toward the graveyard. The second team moved south, back down the passageway. He felt a touch on his arm, Brogan's hand coming through the white smoke, knocking twice toward the south. And they began to move through the white fog that streamed by Jefferson's faceplate.

Jefferson had one of the HKs, on loan from the SWAT cowboys. Nice weapon, the HK, short barrel. Plenty of rounds. They were moving. Flashlights suspended from the barrels of the HKs casting crazy beams of light that zigzagged through the oily white, highlighting it in smoky swirls. Four glowing orbs of light on either side of Jefferson, Brogan and the rest of the crew all trying to stick together.

They stayed in the corridor, open doorways on either side of them. Doorways that led to what? More rooms? More passages? One of them holding three dead SWAT guys? And whatever whacked them out. The place was a maze. Made the palace at

Versailles look like a one-room schoolhouse. Through the radio in his ear came the sound of breathing and grunting, men running, footsteps. Moving to the left, Jefferson poked his head around the corner of one of the rooms, shining his light around the smoke-filled area.

Something hung from the ceiling.

Something in black coveralls and Kevlar. Something with the name PEREZ written on the front of its jacket. Something that might have been human ten minutes ago, before half its insides had been opened up.

Brogan was behind him, radio crackling. "What do you see?"

Jefferson pointed through the fog. "Something bad."

Two of the cowboys joined them, everyone looking up at Perez, then scanning the rest of the room, flashlight beams going everywhere. Nothing to see. More glazed wet stone, broken timbers, somebody's old shirt. The masks had no peripheral vision, so it was like looking through a camera lens, requiring you to keep looking to the left and the right to take in a room. Nobody seemed too broken up about the hanged body. Everyone's adrenaline was pumping too hard. Time to feel bad about things later, when the medics came to cut Perez down from the ceiling, just like that Tate kid in the mausoleum. When your own life was safe, then there'd be time to think.

Then the radio went nuts. Everyone's earpiece crackling at the same time. Heads cocking around the room as they stopped to listen. Something was happening out there. Jefferson paused, holding his breath. The air in his mouth was warm and tasted plastic and he could feel the sweat building on his face, the humidity sealed in by the mask. The radio was chattering loudly now, five or six guys all talking at once. "What the fuck is that?" "What the fuck?" "Where is it?" "I can see it, it's here?" "Get it, get it, get it!" "There, the ceiling!" Shouts. Then gunfire. More gunfire. Confusion. Then, finally, the screaming.

The first team was getting hit. Even without the radio, Jefferson could hear the gunshots down the long tunnel. Perez continued to swing from the ceiling, neck cocked back. Whatever had done that had circled back on them, was behind them now. And it was coming through the tunnels toward them. Somewhere in this damn fog of white smoke. Brogan had the HK up, doing the lock and load.

More shouting on the radio. "Man down! Man down!" Another burst of gunfire. Then a screeching sound, like the roar of an approaching cyclone, followed by more shooting. The screeching sounded again. What the hell was that? Jefferson felt a second tap on his arm. Brogan was there, motioning back down the corridor toward the screeching noise. Brogan, always ready to roll on something. Never holding back. The other two SWAT cowboys were standing ready, their flashlights the only thing Jefferson could see in the mess of white.

Then they were moving again, back down the stone corridor. Lights were ahead, illuminations in the smoky swirls. Five separate bulbs, hovering back and forth in the smoke. There used to be seven. Two were missing somewhere. Maybe joining Perez wherever he was. The lights were forty yards ahead, bobbing and weaving. Occasionally flashing with muzzle fire and Jefferson worrying about getting hit by some SWAT cowboy getting too tight with the trigger and drawing down on him.

One of the lights flared up for an instant, the bulb bursting in a shattering of glass and the crunch of metal. Then the light winked out. One more guy down. This one not even screaming. Something was hitting them hard. There were more dark shapes moving in the fog ahead. Long shadows that bobbed and spun up and down. A body appeared from the smog, one of the SWAT guys from the first team, his eyes wide and scared. No weapon, just running. The guy ran past them, moving back down the tunnel, toward what? The ladder out? Jefferson wasn't even sure where that was anymore.

Then a second dark shape, this one coming quickly. This one on the ceiling. A large dark shape the size of an automobile moving toward them, pulling itself along the ceiling, scurrying like a giant spider. Brogan saw it, too, his head going up, HK following. The thing was roaring now, the cyclone approaching.

"There!" Brogan's voice coming in his earpiece. "What the hell is that?"

The shape kept clinging to the stone above them and as it came closer, arms and legs appeared, reaching out and pulling itself along through the smoke, moving swiftly toward them. Brogan fired his weapon, the noise in the narrow space almost bursting Jefferson's eardrum. Point-sized sparks of light flared up on the stone like struck matches as metal knocked against the ceiling. The thing kept coming, the shape moving directly overhead clinging to the ceiling sixteen feet above. Jefferson pulled the trigger. The HK bucked violently in his hand, and he almost lost control, rhythmically launching bullets toward the ceiling.

There was another roar, a horrible sound. Almost enough to make Jefferson want to drop his HK and bolt. Almost enough. Even Brogan looked startled for a second. It might have even gotten to BD, if he was still alive somewhere. The sound carried up and down the hallways of stone. It penetrated the smoke. The shape roared again, angry now, passing over their heads on the ceiling. Chasing something. The lone SWAT guy who had run past? Hunting each of them down individually. One by one.

Jefferson heard running footfalls and saw two orbs of light heading toward him. The lights bounced up and down, more flashlight beams that hit him full in the face, blinding for an instant.

"Turn your fucking lights off." Brogan waved his hands, knocking at one of them.

"Where'd it go? Where'd it go?" BD was staring at them both, wide-eyed.

BD looked bad. The lens of his faceplate cracked in spiderwebs, trickles of blood running down the sides of his cheeks in thin streams, jagged tears in his Kevlar vest. But worse than that, BD looked scared. Scared enough that he'd rather be back in his tiny apartment, eating tuna and macaroni. Another SWAT cowboy was with him, with the name GORFINKLE stitched on the front of his vest. He looked all right, though, breathing heavily, lens of his mask smeared with condensation, but no blood on him anywhere.

Five guys go down the hall, two of them come back out. Jesus, this was a fucking massacre. What the hell was down here with them? BD had been wrong—they couldn't handle this. But that was back when they thought it was just a man. Brogan was pointing down the hall, and the two SWAT guys rushed past, disappearing again into the thick smoke filling the passage. Brogan was pulling out the empty HK clip and dropping it to the floor, fishing for a new one in the pocket of his vest.

"New rules of engagement," he said. "Shoot anything that's not human."

The two bobbing flashlights of BD and Gorfinkle were moving quickly away and they chased after them. Back deeper into the pit. Running hard, weapons banging up and down at their sides. Following the two lights, which drew them deeper and deeper in. There was a snapping noise ahead of them, like heavy timbers breaking, and one of the bobbing flashlights suddenly lifted off the ground.

Jerked straight up into the air.

The light dangling sixteen feet off the ground for a moment, no longer bobbing. Then the timber-breaking sound came again and the light dropped. A sickening drop. Down to the tunnel floor, where it bounced on the stone before lying half-pointed upward. More gunfire, HK rounds chiseling out the stone ceiling. A red light came from nowhere. The smoke turning red, the walls turning red until the tunnel was engulfed in the color. Brogan was firing, too, firing from his hip on the run until the tunnel was a confusion of smoke and red light and gunfire.

Then Brogan held up, coming to a quick stop. An HK lay on the ground, the flashlight still on its barrel casting a crazy beam of light straight across the rocky floor. Beyond the discarded weapon was a human body, lying facedown. Reaching the body, Jefferson grabbed a shoulder, and twisted the man over onto his back. Gorfinkle. Blood and dirt smeared across his front, mixing with sweat and forming an oily sheen on his skin. His head flopping loosely around on his neck, like the Chinese doll they'd found on the roof of the Lyerman Building.

The red light was everywhere, all around them.

The HK was covered in someone's blood. Blood over the lens of the fallen flashlight. Blood that streamed over the light, glowing red on the glass, and the smoke highlighted in tones of blood that swirled and moved around them in the gusts of air.

More lights were visible at the end of the tunnel. Five of them. More SWAT guys coming down into the pit from above. They stopped, standing around in a group, pointing downward. Leaving Gorfinkle and the broken neck behind, Jefferson and Brogan jogged down the corridor toward the lights.

SWAT guys were circling around something on the floor, guns pointed down. BD was there, still alive. The other four guys looked new. The snipers from above. This was turning into Normandy Beach. Guys go down, bring in some more. Only they were running out of replacements. Pretty soon they'd have to be sending the cons down into the pit with them. Every man for himself if that ever happened.

BD didn't look scared anymore. Just pissed, but Jefferson couldn't tell if he was angry because so many SWAT guys had gone down, or because he'd been scared two minutes before and was making up for it now. Either way, he was doing a quick pace back and forth in front of whatever was on the floor.

"It's down here," BD's voice came through the earpiece. "Went down through that hole."

He stepped aside, pointing toward a gaping hole cut into the rock. A large drainage gate had been removed, exposing the rectangular opening. Blood pooled on the floor was slowly running down the depressed floor, dripping into the hole. The covering grate lay to the side, pushed back from the opening like a manhole cover. It was thick, the bars heavy. The thing must have weighed half a ton. What could move something like that?

The four new guys looked scared now. Five minutes ago they were up on top, smoking cigarettes and staring out at the ocean. Now they were thirty feet underground, in tunnels that were quickly filling up with dead guys. A few of them were even shaking their heads. No fucking way are we going down there. Down into some hole in the ground.

Then they all heard it. A single scream, long and painful. And the sound was coming from down in the hole, from somewhere beneath them. Wherever the blood was running. More headshakes from the new guys, one of them even looking like he was going to break into tears. Not BD though. He was moving toward the hole, gripping the sides and lowering himself into the blackness, the whole time the screaming continuing.

And Jefferson's mind flashing one thing. *Trap. Trap. Trap.*

BD dropped into the hole, his flashlight curving over the walls. More wet rock. This time with blood. At least no smoke. The hole was five feet down, then leveled out into a crawl space-sized tunnel. The four other SWAT guys dropped into the hole next, then Brogan was crouching, down and in, then Jefferson. Seven Santa Clauses come calling.

Jefferson was squirming his way down, the HK scraping rock on either side. Then he hit bottom, Brogan already crawling forward on hands and knees ahead of him. The passageway was barely a tunnel, more like a rathole. Jefferson was moving again, hands and knees, crawling along in the dark. Everything was wet, grime underneath soaking through his pants, sticking against his knees. His palms were wet, sharp stones digging into them as he put his hands down. Wet, plantlike growth dangled from the ceiling, dragging along his back as he moved forward.

Brogan was ahead, still moving, and Jefferson had a thought of dying like this, the last thing he sees on this Earth being Brogan's ass. What a shameful way to go. They were seven deep in the tunnel, moving forward as fast as possible on hands and knees. They had to be passing out from underneath the prison, maybe out beyond the walls, under the harbor somewhere. Their route must be how that thing got out to the prison, crawling foot after foot. And they were in its home.

"You see anything ahead?" someone's voice sounded in his ear.

"No," BD came back on. "Radio silence."

His hands and knees were burning, his HK swinging back and forth underneath him like a baby in a front pack, when he heard a chirping noise ahead. Brogan held up suddenly, then lurched upward quickly, moving to his toes, while pressing the flat of his back against the ceiling of the passageway, lifting his knees off the ground.

Something round and black was ambling toward Jefferson, walking under Brogan's body. Jefferson had an instant to reach for his HK before he saw what it was. A rat. A giant rat. The size of a raccoon. Someone in front hissed, "Oh, shit." And another rat was coming behind the first. Both possum-sized, rolling along the base of the passage. Only a moment to react, before the impossibly large rat was on top of him. He dropped the HK, heaving himself up like Brogan, getting his knees off the ground.

The rat passed under him, its fat body rolling beneath greasy fur, its cord tail trailing over Jefferson's hand. They both moved on, nonstop, between his legs, and kept going. Jefferson lowered himself, turning his head to look back down the passage, watching them disappear into the blackness. Going where? Up into the pit. And for a moment, Jefferson was sure that when they cleared out the dead SWAT team guys, the coroner's people might be confused by the little bite marks on the flesh. The little nibbles on the dead. The jagged tears of rat teeth.

Jefferson moved faster, keeping pace in case the rats decided to pull an about-face and head back in the direction they'd come. Then, suddenly, the small passage opened up into a larger tunnel. Everyone was ahead of him, already standing, flashlights passing over the walls around them, not stone this time but mortared brick rising into arches fourteen feet overhead.

BD was in front, holding a small heartbeat monitor. A neat gadget actually, about the size of a portable television with a bright green LCD display screen. The thing detected the ultralow-frequency electrical waves produced by the human heart, working up to fifty yards, even through heavy brick and concrete. And it was working, the LCD screen fixing on something alive in the tunnels with them. The screaming was going on still, ahead somewhere in the darkness. Everyone was doing a pretty good job of ignoring it, as much anyone could ignore the sound of a man being tortured to death. One of the SWAT guys was showing panic, breathing in and out so fast that he could have just finished a marathon. This guy looked about on pace to hyperventilation within five minutes.

At the front, BD waved his hand once, leading everyone forward. He kept his eyes on the box, following the directions of the LCD screen. Jefferson didn't like using the flashlights in there. Gave them up as a pretty clear target for anything waiting farther down the tunnel. Still, better that than having to go completely blind.

They were moving again, BD bent over the screen like he was playing a video game. They came to a branch and turned right, then left. Jefferson hoped that the high-tech gadget could find their way out again. Underneath, the floor was strewn with bits of broken brick, ground down until it formed a fine layer of pebbles and dust. There was a constant, quiet crunching noise as they walked, the sound of heavy boots sifting through crushed brick.

The heart sensor kept emitting its small rapid beeps as they moved, the sound constant, never fading or getting stronger. And they all followed BD, deeper into the tunnels, shadows flickering across the ceiling, elongated as they were cast across the convex walls. BD stopped short, holding up his hands, ten fingers extended twice. Twenty yards.

The HKs came down off shoulder straps, moving into hands, getting ready. Then they moved again, the sensor beeping and beeping. Gradually their target emerged from the darkness, caught in the seven flickering flashlight beams.

It was a man. Lying on his back, head propped at a sharp angle against one wall of the tunnel, still wearing the black SWAT coveralls, arms folded across his midsection. His face was a mix of blood and dirt. Flashlights were moving, scanning behind them, ahead of them, along the floor. The voice in Jefferson's brain still whispered, *Trap. Trap. Trap.*

The SWAT guy was turning to look at them now, eyes half-closed. The name on his tag read ROSS. The decoy. The first one in the pits. BD was bending down over him, fingers checking his pulse, looking at his watch. Two snipers were on the radio, calling up nothing but static, the walls too thick to transmit, and all at the same time Jefferson was realizing that nobody was coming to help them if something happened. BD was reaching into his pack for his medic's kit—there were deep gashes of black across Ross's gut. The man was bad, getting worse. He was doing the blood in the lungs gasp, every breath gurgling with fluid, choking on it.

The two snipers were still on the radio, the loud static crackle getting distracting. Ross was moving his hand now, reaching past BD, reaching for something above him. Jefferson was fixated on him, watching that moving hand. The hand was curling now, curling into a fist, then a single finger was extending. The finger was pointing up.

Up.

Then heads were turning to look, seven sets of eyes all looking up. Following the direction of the finger. Above them the ceiling arched and in the dark recess of the peak was something even darker. Something that was moving. The object was turning, a face appearing. Something hissing, sharp teeth shining in the flashlight beams, eyes. Someone inhaled sharply, surprised. Trap. Then came the shriek of the cyclone and the thing was dropping on them from the ceiling.

Things started happening quickly. Machine gun fire went off, someone shouted, muzzle flashes lit up the tunnel, highlighting Big Dog's face. The thing was right on them, swinging and cutting, flashlight beams dancing crazily over the walls. One of the SWAT team backed up hard against Jefferson, the man's helmet catching him underneath the chin and knocking him back. The guy was out of it, his eyes wide, mouth reciting over and over again, "Oh shit, oh shit, oh shit."

Brogan dropped the HK, swinging with his fists, throwing overhand bombs left and right, knocking hard against something. Then Brogan's head snapped back, and he went down for the count, hitting the ground hard. The next instant the shape turned on Jefferson and something smashed across his jaw, spinning his head to the left so hard he heard vertebrae crack. He felt a pressure around his windpipe, something at his throat. Then the pressure was gone, clean air flowing into his lungs.

The side of his head knocked against the tunnel, and he went down, falling, hitting the floor of the tunnel, rolling onto his back until he was staring at the ceiling. His head was sailing somewhere else, spinning from the blows. He turned his eyes, looking farther down the tunnel. The dark shape was there, bounding away from them, striding on two legs in a jerky motion.

The thing blended away into darkness farther down the tunnel, Jefferson listening to the crunch of gravel as it receded into nothing. And then blackness overwhelmed him, his brain shutting down. Passing out.

Awake. How long had it been? The stone felt cold against his skin, against the side of his face. Jefferson had been horizontal for maybe a minute, maybe an hour. Time stopped in the darkness. He lay for a moment more in the dark, listening, hearing nothing. Still alive anyway. All the flashlights had gone out, everything the pitch-black of an underground tomb. Then, somewhere in the darkness, he heard a low chuckle. Farther down the tunnel. Something watching him, laughing. He lay for a moment more, his hand sliding down the right side of his leg, searching for his lighter. Fingers wrapping around it, he held the metal in his hand, waiting.

Still hearing nothing, which meant, what? Everyone around him was dead? Or maybe they were just lying quiet, like him, all waiting for something to happen. The chuckle started again, this time fading slightly, moving off in the distance. Jefferson counted to thirty, still waiting. Then he heard a voice, three feet to his right. Someone whispering his name.

It was Brogan, the sound coming from floor level. Must be horizontal like him.

Jefferson whispered back, "You all right?"

"Yeah, feel like I took a bat to the head. I'll live. You?"

"Same. What about the SWAT crew?"

"Don't know, got guys all around me. I can feel them. Can't see anything, though, can't tell if they're still alive."

"I've got my lighter."

Brogan paused, then, "Use it."

"OK." Jefferson flipped back the top of the lighter, thumb moving to ignite it. "Here goes."

Scratch, scratch, then the tiny orange flame flickered up from the top of the lighter. It was enough light for him to see Brogan, lying on his stomach, head gashed open. It was enough light for him to see all around them, to each of the side walls. It was enough light to make him wish he could turn it out and go back into the darkness. Forget what he'd seen.

Everyone around them was dead.

Blood everywhere. More blood than he had ever seen. On the walls, on the floor, spilled all over the five dead men. BD, propped up against the wall, no eyelids, the whites of his eyes the size of plums. Jefferson wondered about that for a moment, caught in the trivialities. Someone had taken his eyelids. Each little piece of skin, carefully cut each flap off, leaving just the eyes. Why?

And then he turned to look at Brogan. The stone killer. Who'd once beaten a man to death with a bat. Who'd killed men in Bosnia. Who'd seen the worst of everything man had to offer. Even Brogan could say nothing except, "Lord have mercy."

What's there to do after something horrible happens? Some occurrence that you know changes things for you. Something that you can look back on years later and think, *and after that, things were never the same again.* Death happens every day. People die in auto accidents, plane crashes. Burn to death in apartment fires. And afterward, there's nothing. Nothing except to go home and try and fit yourself back into the thread of regular life.

And that is what Jefferson would have to do sometime. Find a place for himself. It was what he'd had to do after Bosnia. And you do it enough times, witness enough horrible things, and you either get better at fitting back in, or you forget how altogether.

Jefferson sat onshore, watching the water roll up onto the beach, staring back across at Blade Island. And somewhere underground, in tunnels under the water, lay the dead. By the time Jefferson and Brogan had found their way out, the helicopters had already arrived. Big ones, landing in the yard, spinning up grass and dirt as their blades whirled. They'd taken them back over the harbor, gray streaks of dawn already beginning to break on the horizon. Brogan had gone back to Mass General, the gash on his arm bleeding and open again. Jefferson sat on the shore, watching the waves roll and roll.

Something was wrong. Something missing. Whatever had been down in those tunnels, whatever it was that had killed ten men, had spared Jefferson and Brogan. It had them if it wanted, but it let them live. Why?

Dr. Wu might know. Jefferson reached into his pocket for the doctor's card. The card with the doctor's home address on it. The card that he knew should be in his pocket, but wasn't.

It was gone.

The bands of panic tightened around his chest. That thing in the tunnel, it must have taken it. Taken the card. And now Jefferson felt sure where it was going. It was going after Wu. The only man who had any idea what it might be. Jefferson could find his way back into normal society sometime, but not now. Now he needed to be able to fight like an animal.

Jefferson got Wu's number from directory assistance and called him with his cell phone, then, holding the phone to his ear, reached into his shoulder holster for his Beretta. He listened to the repeated rings. Wu lived close by. The thing had tracked down Sinatra and that Blade guard. Murdered them all in Sinatra's house. What would it do to Wu and his family?

The ringing stopped, silence, then, "Hello."

A woman's voice.

"Is Dr. Wu there?"

The female voice grunted, "Just a minute."

Jefferson heard the woman in the background speaking quickly to someone, then the phone was picked up again and Dr. Wu's familiar voice came on the line. "Yes, hello?"

"Dr. Wu?"

"Yes?"

"This is Detective Jefferson."

There was a pause, then, "Ahh, Detective Jefferson, very early riser."

"I'm sorry about that, listen, Dr. Wu, is everything all right?"

"All right? What do you mean?"

"Your family, is everyone all right?"

"Of course," Wu replied, an edge on his voice. "What's going on?"

"Nothing, stay where you are, I'm coming to you. Stay inside, lock your doors," Jefferson said. "Don't answer them for anyone, you understand? I want you to pack your things, you and your family. Some things have come up and you might need to leave town for a little while."

Sounding nervous, Wu asked, "What is going on?"

"Do you have a gun?"

"No, no, I'm not a cop."

"OK, well sit tight, I'll be there in ten, OK?"

There was a baby crying in the background. Then a tearing noise, like the sound of a bag being ripped open, and the cry stopped abruptly.

"I'm sorry, Detective Jefferson." Wu's voice again. Calm. The man not understanding the situation.

"Sorry, for what?"

"For tonight." The voice had turned cold. "All that blood. Blood everywhere. It must have been distasteful for you."

Jefferson grunted, holding the phone to his ear. What? More noise in the background, faint, a soft bubbling. Like a drain emptying of water, or someone crying lightly.

"I still have them, you know," Wu said.

"Have what?" Jefferson asked.

"BD's eyelids. I have them here, with me. I keep everything I cut off and take," Wu said.

The voice was mocking, deeper, with a slight rasp. It wasn't Dr. Wu anymore, the voice was different, something else. *Jesus Christ, who the hell is on the phone?*

"Who is this?" Jefferson demanded, keeping his voice strong.

There was another chuckle. Then the line went dead.

According to the directory, Dr. Wu lived on Dean Road in Weston, a small suburb just outside Boston. Jefferson kept the Beretta on the seat next to him as he drove. The streets were almost empty, vacant and gray in the early-morning dawn, the traffic lights still blinking yellow. Driving hard, Jefferson thought of the line going dead, then the photograph of Dr. Wu's family in his office. Everyone smiling.

Anger can cloud judgment sometimes. Cause you to make mistakes, miss things.

But sometimes, when you didn't need to choose, just needed to act, anger could be the best thing going for you. Made you stronger, made you forget pain, guilt, remorse, anything that would slow you down, and just let you act. And it was anger that drove Jefferson.

Wu lived in a Colonial at the end of a quiet street. The house extended out to a two-car garage that framed a short driveway. A black Mercedes sat in the driveway, just in front of the garage doors. Jefferson pulled in behind the Mercedes, turning off the ignition and stepping out of his car. Everything was quiet and still in the early morning. Painfully normal. The houses across the streets were dark and silent, a thin film of dew clinging to fresh-cut grass on front lawns. A golden retriever stepped out from the swinging dog door on the house across the street, sniffed delicately at the air, and carefully made its way into the front yard.

With the Beretta back in his shoulder holster, Jefferson moved quickly up the brick path to Wu's front door. Everything still quiet inside, no lights, no movement. Nothing was visible in any of the windows. Jefferson stepped along the brick pathway leading from the driveway to the front stoop. The front door was big and maple, with brass fittings that turned easily in Jefferson's hand, the door sliding quietly inward. It was unlocked. Jefferson paused in the small foyer, eyes adjusting to the dim gray light. The house was beautiful. Hardwood floors that shone like parquet, big palm plants, Renoir prints on the walls. Ahead of him, the floor stretched back into a narrow hallway, then there were marble countertops in the kitchen and a large bay window overlooking the backyard.

Everything was quiet inside. All the rooms were empty. *Start with the upstairs, then move down through the rest of the house.* Jefferson began moving up the narrow wooden stairway to the second floor. The stairs creaked slightly, but there was no response from inside the house. And Jefferson thought, *Maybe that's because they're all dead.*

On the second floor were more hardwood floors and cherry furnishings. To the right was an open doorway leading into a dark bedroom. *Start with this.* Jefferson stepped inside, felt his shoes press down into the soft cushioning of a thick carpet. The rectangular shapes of two windows on the far wall were dimly outlined by creases of light shining in around the edges of drawn blinds. At the end of the room, a second door opened into a small bathroom. A night-light in the shape of a clamshell glowed dimly from one of the floor sockets inside the bathroom, softly illuminating carefully folded towels and a checker-patterned tile floor.

The rest of the room was vague outlines of furniture, blending into the dark smudges of shadows. Jefferson stood quietly in the darkness, stepping farther into the room so as not to be outlined in the doorway. As his eyes adjusted, a bed materialized from the darkness of the far wall. A bed with something in it.

Jefferson moved cautiously forward, pulling his Beretta out from its holster. He stared at the something on the bed, a long shape covered over by a blanket, something that looked human. The sheets around the object were dry and clean, free of the dark stain of blood.

Jefferson glanced quickly around the rest of the room—empty except for the bed and the lumps under the sheets. As he moved, the covered shape on the bed twitched slightly, the blanket rising, something moving underneath, then going still again. Breathing heavily, Jefferson reached out, his fingers closing around the thin covering of the blanket. His gun was ready, aimed down, slide pulled back. *Here we go.*

He pulled back, whisking the blanket away from the bed, where it billowed to the floor. A man lay there. The man was turning his head, looking at Jefferson. Jefferson pointed the gun right at him and said, "Stay down, stay down!" The man didn't respond, but tried to sit up, causing Jefferson to place the barrel of his gun on the man's forehead, forcing him back into the sheets. The man lay there, hands spread out, looking scared. And time slowed enough for Jefferson to register the face.

It was Dr. Michael Wu.

Wu, wide-eyed, shook his head in little twitches of no, no. He was wearing a plain white T-shirt and blue boxer shorts, his rounded belly visible through the cotton shirt. And a voice inside Jefferson kept saying, *Shoot him now, don't trust him, shoot him now.*

Jefferson silenced the voice enough to ask, "Who are you?"

Wu looked confused, not getting it.

"Who the fuck are you? Answer me," Jefferson ground out, the barrel coming down on Wu's forehead again.

Finally, Wu said, "It's me, Michael. You know me. I work down at the . . . oh please, don't shoot me. Don't shoot me."

Wu was in a panic, breathing hard and fast.

Jefferson held a finger to his lips, silencing the blubbering, thinking maybe this really was Wu. *But how to know, how to know? Scars. Even if this demon can mimic human DNA and appear as anyone, it won't be able to reproduce scars. The body's response to injuries. Wu had been burned on his hand once; the mark should be there still.*

Still holding the gun on him, Jefferson grabbed for Wu's hand, turning it over. Nothing. No scar. The voice inside him screamed, *Shoot him now, shoot him before it's too late.* But then Jefferson was reaching for the other hand, Wu not resisting at all, still looking scared and confused. Jefferson bringing the other hand up, checking the skin over the knuckles. And there it was. A blotchy mark on the back of the hand. A mark burned into the skin by a Bunsen flame.

This really was Wu.

Which meant that whatever had been in the tunnels could be in the house some-where. Wu was shaking all over, looking about ready to scream. Jefferson placed the hand not holding the Beretta over his mouth. The man's eyes went wide, thinking he was about to be killed.

"Keep quiet, you understand," Jefferson said. "Shake your head."

Wu nodded.

"Are you alone?"

Wu paused, thinking, then nodded again.

"You sure?"

Yes again.

"I'm not going to hurt you, do you understand? Shake your head."

Yes.

"I think there's someone else in the house. Do you understand?"

Wu thought again, pausing for what seemed an eternity, then nodded.

"The phone rang here, twenty minutes ago. Did you hear it?"

Yes.

"Do you know who answered it?"

Wu shook his head no, and Jefferson slowly removed his hand.

"Your wife?" Jefferson asked.

Wu shook his head again. "No. Left for Providence yesterday afternoon. Family."

Jefferson thought back to the call, remembering the baby crying in the background. "And the baby?"

"With my wife."

"Then who answered the phone, a woman?"

"Maybe my housekeeper answered. She comes early, then leaves."

"Does she have a baby, an infant?"

Wu nodded. "Yes. Sometimes she brings him to the house."

"Is she here now?"

Wu shrugged. "I don't know."

"What kind of car does she drive?"

"I don't know. A white one."

No white cars were parked in the driveway. Wu's hand moved to his heart, and Jefferson thought that the guy might be having a heart attack, right there on the bed. *Better go easy on him.* Jefferson reached for his cell phone.

Jefferson punched REDIAL on the cell phone, holding a finger against Wu's lips to keep him quiet. Wu's eyes stayed fixed on the gun. The phone began to ring. Jefferson could hear the electronic chime in the cell, then the ringing of phones in Wu's house. One was right next to them on the bedside table. Whatever had been in the house before had answered the phone. Let's see if it was still in the mood. Still in the house.

The phone rang again, the cell chiming an instant before the rest of the phones in the house.

Jefferson could hear them ringing in unison. Shrill, urgent. *C'mon, someone answer me.*

Nobody seemed to be home. There was another ring, and Jefferson's finger moved to hang up the cell.

Then the phones cut off and a clicking noise sounded on Jefferson's phone.

Someone in the house had picked up the phone.

Jesus. Something else is in the house with us.

Jefferson pressed the cell to his ear, listened carefully, but heard only a faint breathing noise, the sound of air traveling through heavy tubing.

"Hello?" Jefferson asked.

There was a pause, then, "Yes . . ."

"Who is this?"

"My name is not important," said the voice on the line, the coldest sound Jefferson had ever heard.

There was a pause. Jefferson kept the phone to his ear, moving across the bedroom. *Where are the phones in the house?*

"Do you wish to speak to Michael Wu?" the voice said again, as Jefferson reached the doorway.

"I'm speaking with you now."

There was a pause, something tapping on the floor downstairs.

"Dr. Wu is in bed," said the voice. "I'll go up to get him."

Then the phone went dead.

Jefferson tore the cell away from his ear, looking down at the mute plastic, a slight hiss escaping from the speaker. Something was coming up. Something serious. Whatever had wiped out the entire SWAT team. *What the hell have I done?*

He could hear something. Noises from downstairs. Footsteps on the hardwood floors. Something coming. Jefferson backed away from the bedroom's open door, moving back to the bed, where Wu still lay, half-covered in bedding. Not much time.

"Get up," Jefferson said. "Go in the bathroom, lock the door."

Wu was up and off the bed in a moment, moving quickly to the bathroom, the door shutting behind him. Jefferson pushed the bed away from the wall, crouching behind it, putting something between himself and the open bedroom door. Footsteps still sounded downstairs, changing tone as they reached the stairwell and moved up. The thing was coming up the stairs. Jefferson waited for it behind the bed, Beretta raised and resting on the mattress, two full clips lying on the sheet next to him.

Then there was silence, broken only by the ticking of the clock, a car passing by on the street outside, and a dog barking. But no footsteps. A few seconds passed, then the first stair of the stairway snapped sharply. Then the second step. And the third. *Here it comes.*

Jefferson pointed the Beretta at the doorway. The creak of the stairs continued, growing higher in pitch as it neared the top-floor landing. Then it was in the hall, approaching the bedroom. Just outside the bedroom, it stopped. It stood in the hallway beyond the open doorway. As he readied himself to attack it as it came through the doorway, Jefferson heard a scratching noise, like the tip of a pencil moving across a chalkboard. Still nothing showed itself.

Finally, the stairs creaked again. Whatever had come up the stairs was going back down, leaving. Jefferson listened to the footsteps going down the stairs, then through the house. A door slammed. Then silence. *Alone.*

The bathroom door was still shut, Wu hiding behind it. Jefferson slid from behind the bed, moving toward the doorway. Reaching the doorframe, he paused, breathed, and poked his head around the corner.

The stairs were empty. From downstairs came only silence.

Remembering the scratching noise, he turned his head. There was lettering on the wall, just next to the doorway. Cut into the rose-colored wallpaper was writing, jagged white lines from the exposed plasterboard underneath. Jefferson stared.

I have come

An hour later, Jefferson and Dr. Wu were seated at the Wu family's dining table. Dr. Wu was holding one of the maroon cloth napkins in his hand, scrunching it up and releasing it repeatedly, staring blankly down at the mirrored surface of the polished wood table. Cops in blue uniforms circled throughout the house, their radios squealing softly as they passed through the rooms. Jefferson could hear them upstairs, staring at the printing on the wall.

"What was that thing in my house this morning?" Wu asked, working the napkin over and over in his hand.

Jefferson shook his head. "I'm not sure yet. We're working on that."

"You better work harder, Detective Jefferson. This thing came into my house. My house, where my wife lives. My baby. Your case brought this into my family's house. I'm a scientist. Not an officer."

"I know, and I'm sorry," Jefferson said.

"Does this have something to do with the Lyerman case?"

Jefferson nodded. "I think so. You remember you told me that the DNA of the fragment you found had the ability to mimic the DNA of hosts that it came in contact with?"

"Yes."

"On the phone, this thing sounded exactly like you. And your housekeeper, this morning, saw a man in the kitchen that she said looked exactly like you. Could it take your DNA and mimic you exactly? Right down to your voice?"

Wu spread the napkin across the table, thinking for a moment. "Possibly. But DNA can only take you so far. Theoretically it could make someone look like me, but things like my accent and mannerisms are all acquired after birth. Those things are created by the environment around us, we don't inherit them genetically."

Jefferson nodded. "So the burn scar on your hand?"

"Exactly. Very smart, Detective, it wouldn't be able to reproduce such marks."

"But it could make a rough guess of what you would look like, based upon how your DNA is composed?"

"Again, theoretically. But what you're talking about, as we've discussed before, is not believed to exist today by mainstream science." Wu paused, his eyes looking vague for a moment. "But . . ."

"But what?"

"Well, after we spoke yesterday, I remembered something from my early research work. Something that seemed familiar. So I looked into the subject and found some things of interest. Again, not accepted by the mainstream, yet perhaps we've extended beyond the realm of the known world of science."

"Way beyond I think. What'd you find out?"

"What I remembered was doing a case study with a colleague of mine concerning a skeleton found near in the mountains of southern China during the 1930s."

"Human skeleton?"

"Possibly. Possibly not. No one knew. The bone structure was unlike anything ever unearthed. It had a humanlike shape, but the skull was larger, with a heavy jaw and large canine teeth. The arms were also much longer than what had been typically found up to that time period. And most strange, it had retractable claws. Like a giant cat. Completely unheard of in any human-related skeletons."

"What was it?"

"Big mystery. Academics love to debate, and this find caused an enormous stir in the academic community at the time. It was agreed that this humanlike skeleton had been a natural predator. A killer. An aggressor rather than just a thinker. And this went against the notions of the time that the success of man's ancestors was based on their mental, rather than physical, capacities.

"Now this was before Johanson discovered Lucy in Africa. But even so, they had a fairly good picture of what primitive man looked like; and this was vastly different than anything found in the past, or that would be found in the future, for that matter. Here was what appeared to be an ultra-adapted predator, a predator that appeared out of nowhere in the fossil record."

"So they discounted the find?" Jefferson asked.

"Well, as technology progressed, they began testing the skeleton, checking its validity. First, they found that it had been in the cave for a long while. Since the early thirteenth century. But the most remarkable find was inside the fragmentary DNA structure.

"The DNA was nonexistent, a blank slate. Like this creature had never been born. Which then started speculation that, in fact, the entire incident was just a hoax. That perhaps the skeleton was man-made."

"Was it?"

"Don't know. But if it was, nobody could figure what material had been used. Like nothing anyone had seen before. And strong. You could batter the femur, for instance, with a baseball bat for an hour and not put a crack into it.

"So when it became obvious that the skeleton was not, well, scientifically possible, people looked for someone to blame. A lot of fingers were pointed at anyone who might want to embarrass the world of science. But nobody ever came forward to admit to doing it.

"Now a lot of scientists had supported the skeleton as being authentic. Many reputations were at stake. Very well respected scientists. So the community just quietly let the story die."

"What happened to the skeleton?"

Wu shrugged. "Oh, it ended up in a museum somewhere in St. Petersburg. More as a curiosity than anything else."

"And that's it? Could this help us?"

"Well, that was it," Wu began. "Until you brought me those fragments from these recent crimes. They have the same patterns of VNTRs as the skeleton. It's the same material. So, either the forger is back again, which is unlikely because the original skeleton was discovered seventy years ago . . . or . . ."

"Or what?"

Wu sighed, turning his head slightly. "Or this is some kind of new creature that has existed for thousands of years, but nobody knows anything about."

His cell phone out of power, Jefferson used the phone in Wu's kitchen to call Brogan again at Mass General.

This time he got through. "Guess where I am?"

"Where?"

"Dr. Wu's house. Our man paid a visit here this morning."

"Jesus," Brogan said. "You all right?"

"Everything is good."

Jefferson could hear a television playing in the hospital room. Looking out the kitchen window, Jefferson saw two police officers searching behind a yellow pool house, poking into the bushes with the long plastic end of the pool net.

"I'm thinking about taking a trip," Jefferson said, turning away from the window.

"Yeah, where to?"

"St. Petersburg."

"St. Petersburg? Florida?"

"No," Jefferson said. "St. Petersburg, Russia."

"Russia?" Brogan sounded surprised. "What the hell's out there?"

"Wu says they have another one of those things in a museum there. A skeleton of something that matches the DNA of what we have over here."

"Huh," Brogan grunted. "You going alone?"

"Why, you want to come?"

"I can't. I gotta stay with the baby, not to mention trying to find Richard Lee's killer and do something about that warden at Blade Prison. Why don't you ask McKenna?"

Jefferson laughed. "Yeah, right."

"I'm serious, man. She's the best tech we've got. She's a smart girl, knows what's going on. Besides, I think you two would look good out in Russia. Snuggling all warm and shit in the Russian winter."

"Why, you think she'd say yes?"

"Maybe," Brogan answered. "Hey, listen, better you than some candy-ass actor or some shit like she always seems to attract. Oh, hang on a sec."

Over the phone, Jefferson heard the sound of a door open and a female voice speaking quickly to Brogan.

"Listen, that's my nurse, I have to go," Brogan said when he came back on the line. "But you stay safe out in Russia, all right? And keep me updated. When you gonna be back?"

"Two-three days, tops."

"All right, good luck. And Jefferson?"

"Yeah."

"Ask her to go."

Thirty hours later, Jefferson's elbows were pressed in on both sides by the sharp plastic armrests of the British Airways 747. Flight attendants in light brown dresses moved up and down the aisles, passing out drinks in small plastic cups and peanuts in smaller plastic bags. Jefferson's tray was down, suspended from the seat in front of him, a St. Petersburg guidebook open to black-and-white photos of the Mariinsky Ballet.

He sighed, closing the book and stretching his arms forward, turning his head to the left, trying to see out the small oval window just past the large chest and stomach of the man crammed into the seat next to him. Outside was nothing but a crystalline blue monotony, layered underneath by the flat, unmoving clouds.

He felt someone squeeze his arm and turned away from the window to the seat on the other side of him. McKenna was looking at him, her hair pulled back in a loose ponytail that curved down the nape of her neck. He loved those eyes.

She smiled. "How you doing?"

"I'm all right," Jefferson answered. "Reading up on all this ballet they've been talking about in the guidebook."

"Stop right there," McKenna held her finger over Jefferson's mouth. "My male cousin did ballet. So don't make fun."

She looked at him for a moment, her eyes gazing into his before going back to her magazine and turning the pages with her long fingers. *How did I get here, sitting next to her?* It hadn't really sunk in yet. After his conversation with Brogan, Jefferson had called McKenna, asking her if she wanted to go with him to St. Petersburg. For some reason she'd said yes. Now here she was, sitting next to him.

And here they both were, on a plane, traveling to Russia. Life was strange sometimes. How the world spins.

McKenna was wearing jeans, sneakers, and a T-shirt, yet still managing to look better than half the women in the *Cosmopolitan* magazine she was reading. She made Jefferson feel like a ten-year-old kid sometimes, and he wished there was an adult equivalent of balancing on the top of the jungle gym just to impress her.

Instead, he looked again at the cover of her magazine, and said, "*Cosmo* doesn't seem like your style."

McKenna folded the magazine in her lap, looking at the picture of the woman on the cover who looked like a team of painters had worked for a week to create her.

"Believe me, it's not," she said. "My eyes are starting to fade from reading the small print. I need to look at some pictures. *Cosmo*'s got plenty of them."

"I'll take a good *Hustler* any day," Jefferson kidded. "Or the Russian equivalent."

"I'd hate to see what that looked like," McKenna said, scrunching up her face. "Ms. November, the wife of a Russian onion farmer, enjoys digging in the dirt and having children."

McKenna frowned for a moment, staring at the cover of the magazine.

A speaker overhead began to hiss, and the pilot said, his voice coated with a heavy English accent, "At this time, we have now begun our descent Pulkova Airport, St. Petersburg, so we should be landing in about thirty minutes. Local time now is 10:07 P.M., temperature about two degrees Celsius, with clear skies. Once again, on behalf of myself and the entire crew, we hope you've had an enjoyable trip with us on British Airways. Have a pleasant stay in St. Petersburg."

There was a pause, then another voice came over the speakers, repeating the message in Russian. Jefferson listened carefully, trying to pick out any familiar phrases or words. He caught nothing.

Underneath him, Jefferson could feel the plane rumbling slightly as it descended. They'd reached the cloud cover, and white wisps of clouds were whipping past the window outside, trailing along over the wing. Jefferson hated watching the wing of a plane. The thing was always wavering up and down slightly, buffeted by the winds. It was disconcerting, seeing that giant piece of metal that was supposed to be holding you up in the air, bouncing up and down like a trampoline. He turned away from the window, concentrating on the travel guide instead. "There are a rich variety of crafts in St. Petersburg, lacquered boxes, wooden dishes . . ."

The plane bumped roughly, and the cabin filled with the whine of the engines. Jefferson looked quickly back to the window.

They were already on the ground.

Pulkovo Airport was just outside St. Petersburg, with a bus running once every hour to and from the city. After collecting their bags from the slowly turning baggage wheel and going through immigration, they pushed their way out of the airport claims area, following the orange signs depicting the silhouette of a double-decker bus.

They boarded and began the slow rumbling ride into the city.

She turned to him. "What hotel are we looking for?"

"The Hotel Moskva. It was the most pronounceable name on the list."

McKenna nodded, looking back toward the window. Outside was St. Petersburg. They were driving along the wide Obvodnovo Canal, which shimmered like the silver undersides of fish in the white night. A gilded suspension bridge passed across the waters, two large bronze griffins mounted on either end, their wings curving upward away from their coiled, catlike bodies.

Along the canal were residential blocks, filled with Art Noveau buildings constructed of dull reddish brick and shining windows. Curled mosaics of the city framed the top portions of the building, running alongside the windows, flush with the roof. A few people wandered the streets, carrying bags or wrapped brown paper parcels, as they walked along the crooked stone sidewalks.

In the distance, across the canal and rising from the functional housing of the old Eastern Bloc, Jefferson saw the blue, white, and gold exterior of Saint Nicholas Cathedral. The four gilded onion domes topped the sea blue upper level, spanning the greenish roof.

Turning, they passed along the wide, calm Neva River for a block, before moving onto Nevsky Prospekt, the main thoroughfare of St. Petersburg. The plain brick five-story buildings on either side of them seemed to blend into a uniform solid construction, varying neither in height, color, nor texture. The fronts of small shops moved past the bus window, their awnings decorated with the Cyrillic lettering of the Russian alphabet, their glass walls showing into bakeries and knickknack stores.

Every few blocks, the bus would pull to a halting stop, and passengers would half push, half pull themselves out of the crowded aisles and onto the street, quickly filtering away like failing shadows into the grayish gloom of the streets.

The bus braked suddenly, and the lights came on again.

Jefferson asked the driver where their hotel was, and he pointed to a ferry moored along the canal. "Take ferry across, other side of canal."

Jefferson nodded, and they left the crowded bus, feeling relief at the open space of the street outside. He stood waiting for McKenna, then the two of them walked across the square, crossing the empty street and moving toward their hotel.

Paying the boat driver, they stepped aboard, feeling the craft moving under their feet. It was a large pontoon, with rows of benches evenly spaced. Aboard was a scattering of people mostly Russians, and Jefferson recognized a few from the bus. They took seats near the water, and Jefferson felt the vibrations of the engine through the plastic of the bench.

"I always loved boats," McKenna said. "Something about moving away from land, I think there's a great sense of freedom in that."

"Yeah, I think so, too," Jefferson said. "I hope Brogan is OK back in Boston. He's really taken a beating from that thing."

"You two are pretty tight?"

"Real tight."

"How long have you known him?"

"Oh, man, some years now. We served over in Bosnia together, just outside Zvornik."

"Zvornik?"

"Yeah, it's a small town in Bosnia, could have been real pretty at some other time."

"But it wasn't?"

"There was a war going on. Tends to detract from the appeal of a place."

"I guess so."

"You met Brogan there?" McKenna said.

"He was there. So was Detective Vincent, also with homicide. He was the first detective at the Sinatra scene. After getting out of the Army, we all came back here and started on the force. Then Brogan got married, Vincent got married."

"But never you?"

Jefferson shook his head. "Naw, never me . . . some things happened over in Zvornik that I needed to straighten out in my own mind. I couldn't see getting married when there was a whole part of my life I wasn't willing to share with anyone."

Jefferson looked away from her for a moment, thinking back to Bosnia. He stared out across the water, watching the ripples in the canal, the soothing ripples of water. When he looked back, he realized she was staring at him.

"What's wrong?"

He looked at her for a moment. He could see tiny reflections of light in her eyes, as if they were filled with the waters of the canal and he was floating in them.

"Nothing's wrong," he said, still floating in her eyes. "Everything's right."

"Were you ever scared over there?"

"Yeah, some."

McKenna nodded. "I'd be scared."

"What would you think about?"

"Oh I'd think about home, being back home. How the sun used to set across our back fields, lighting them up in a thousand different shades of gold. How you could walk through the long grass, insects jumping up all around you, not bothering you, just kind of leaping out of the grass. I'd think about people, too—family."

"You miss being home?"

"Some things, I guess; gets kind of lonely in Boston sometimes. No family and all. But I'm happy."

"Sometimes I'd lie awake at night in Bosnia, listening to the sound of rifle fire in the distance, and I'd feel that same way. That feeling of loneliness way down in your heart."

Jefferson remembered the harsh feel of the cot against his skin. Lying with his arms under his head, looking up at the high roof of the warehouse they all slept in, listening to the rattle of gunfire traveling through the warm night air.

Their boat was beginning to pull into the canal, men throwing towlines onto the shore, the bow turning into the water. The canal was smooth, and their boat threw off ripples, which traveled through the water around them like waves of sound. All along the canal shone the lights from buildings of St. Petersburg, their water reflections rocking back and forth as the ripples traveled across them. Gas lamps lined the sides of the canal, people occasionally passing beneath, lit for a moment before fading back into darkness. Jefferson could feel McKenna's warmth against his body as she sat next to him. Suddenly she leaned toward him, bringing her mouth close to his ear.

"I'm happy to be here with you," she whispered, her mouth so close that he could feel the tremble of her lips on his skin.

She leaned back, slipped her hand loosely along Jefferson's arm until she found his hand, then wrapped her fingers around his as their boat began gliding slowly across the waters of the canal.

Their boat passed to the other side of the canal, and they disembarked, walking across the cobblestone street to their hotel. A red carpet on the sidewalk led up to the central pair of glass front doors. Pushing the doors apart, they stepped into the warm foyer of the hotel. A desk clerk behind a high walnut counter waved to them, motioning them over to him, then speaking quickly in Russian.

"I don't speak Russian. English? Do you speak English?"

"English? Sure," the clerk said.

The hotel employee looked down, pulling out a thick black guest book from underneath the counter. Laying it in front of them, he handed Jefferson a pen. "Just sign in please. And I'll take your passports until you check out."

Jefferson signed his name, then, leaning back, the desk clerk pulled a metal key hung on a thick black tag from a row of hooks on the wall behind him. Handing Jefferson the key, he nodded toward the wide stone staircase at the end of the lobby. "Third floor up, number 302."

"Up the stairs?" Jefferson asked, looking down at their bags.

"Yes . . ." the concierge replied, then added, "the elevator is broken, so . . ." His voice trailed off with a slight shrug, not bothering to add that they'd have to walk up to the room.

The stairwell was clean, with a wrought-iron balustrade running alongside. Curved into the iron were images of horses pulling carriages, their heads thrown back, the fluidity of their wild manes caught in the heavy iron. By the time they reached the third floor, Jefferson's fingers were beginning to burn from carrying the suitcases.

They turned off the steps, walking down the narrow hallway lined with closed doors before stopping in front of 302.

"You think this place will have cable?" McKenna kidded, as Jefferson fitted the key into the lock.

"Right. I think we'd get lucky if there was a TV. And then, it'd be the all-Potato channel."

McKenna opened the door, and they stepped into a decent-sized room with a large bay window facing out toward the street. Smooth cream-colored wallpaper stretched from the floor to ceiling, before running into the bathroom. Jefferson stepped into the bathroom, turning on the light. Outside, McKenna lay down onto the bed.

"I'm glad you asked me to come," she said.

"What?" Jefferson asked, stepping out of the bathroom, brushing his teeth.

"I said that I'm glad you asked me to come," McKenna repeated.

"Good." Jefferson stepped back into the bathroom and washed his mouth out. "I'm glad you wanted to come. I could use your advice on this skeleton or whatever it is tomorrow."

"No, I mean . . ."

Jefferson heard the springs of the bed creak slightly as McKenna stood up. He reached for a white towel hanging from one of the gilded racks, drying his hands and face, before folding it back onto the sink.

"Jefferson," McKenna called him from the other room, "come here, you have to see this."

Jefferson pushed back from the sink, stepping into the bedroom. McKenna had opened the two large glass windows and was leaning against the frame, looking out through the open window.

Jefferson stepped beside her, looking out across St. Petersburg.

"The view is beautiful," McKenna whispered, her voice dreamy, sleepy.

The pale gray light had faded, allowing the city to sink down into a fold of darkness. Across from their room stretched a multitude of buildings, with their windows lit warmly from within. In the distance, a wavering sidewalk along the tremulous course of the Neva's waters was illuminated by glass-encased orbs of soft light hung from streetlamps. The walkway curved across the river, following a bridge that stretched across the water, its bricked supports arching gently down into the cool-flowing silver of the Neva. Above everything, the moon hung in the black curtain, like the soft orbs of light on the streets below, an eternity of stars spread around it.

McKenna leaned in toward Jefferson, resting her head gently against his chest, running her hand across his back. He closed his eyes for a moment, feeling her hair as it brushed the sensitive skin of his neck, and just for a moment he could almost forget why they were there, her presence enclosing him like a mist.

"What's this?" she asked, running her hand along the front of Jefferson's neck, pulling out a long gold chain. The chain ended in a Celtic cross, inscribed with interwoven lacing.

"It's from my family," Jefferson said slowly, looking down at the cross. "My father gave it to me."

"Where's he live now?"

Jefferson shook his head. "I don't know. He left when I was eight. I never saw him after that. Just kind of disappeared."

"Oh," McKenna said quietly, "I'm sorry. I shouldn't have brought it up."

"Don't worry about it," Jefferson replied. "That was a long time ago."

"You miss him?"

"No," Jefferson said, "I don't miss him."

He could feel McKenna pressing against him, her weight leaning against him. He brought his arm up, wrapping it around her, bringing her closer.

"There's so much sadness in the world," she said quietly. "Why does God let it all happen?"

Across the wide river, more streetlights were popping on in staccato bursts of color. Jefferson turned away from the window, reaching his hand out to her, running his fingers through her hair. She lowered her cheek against his palm, closing her eyes once and sighing slightly. Her lashes opened slowly, and she bit her bottom lip once, wetting the skin. Her head lowered almost imperceptibly, and Jefferson leaned forward. He kissed her, lightly at first, then slowly leaning into her, reaching inside the cool wetness of her mouth. He could feel her body against his, her hands wrapping around his back, her breasts pressing against him, the heat radiating off her body like hot desert sands.

Warm air blew in through the open window, cooling their upturned faces, winding through their open mouths. She was pulling on his shirt as she kissed him, pulling them both toward the bed. The bedside lamp was turned on, the only light in the room, its bulb filtering through a wax cloth paper shade, dispersing across the bed in faded peach-colored light. McKenna pulled him down on top of her, leaning back against the soft bedcovering, her hair fanning over the pillows. She reached up, then moved her hand down her front.

She was kissing him along his neck, her tongue darting against the sensitive skin, her teeth biting gently down on his earlobes. He could hear the rush of her breath as she moved over his ears, like the hollow sound of seashells, and feel the heat of her tongue.

She paused, looking at him for a moment.

"Where did you get these?" she asked, her fingers pressing against two circular scars on Jefferson's chest and abdomen.

"I'm not sure," Jefferson said. "I've always had them. Ever since I can remember."

"They look like bullet wounds," she said, her fingers running over them. She raised her head, kissing them. "Jefferson, the desperado."

She ran her fingers through his hair, smoothing it back, then with a fingertip, traced the line of his eyes. She leaned down again, kissing him once more on the lips. He swung her body to the side, rolling onto her again, feeling her nails run the length of his back.

They lay in bed, lights off, looking at the patterns of moonlight on the ceiling. McKenna lay against him, her head on his chest, running her fingers along the length of his stomach.

"With your head on my chest, I can feel your breath," Jefferson said. "The air you breathe . . . the same air that passes through you, I can feel it enter me."

She sighed, pulling her head closer to him.

"When I was over there, in Bosnia . . . I read a lot, brought books with me," Jefferson said slowly. "Do you know about Taoism?"

"No."

"In Taoist belief, one is always changing. Each person is different than they were a moment before. You can never get back the previous moment of your life, so you look back on that moment and think, 'Did I spend it wisely?'

"In the time it took for you to cook a piece of toast in the morning, or walk out to your car, you change very subtly, you are a slightly different person than you were before."

McKenna nodded. "I understand that."

"Every instant of my life, I'm different than the last. In Zvornik, every moment I could feel myself changing for the worse, moving to become someone I didn't want to become. With you, every moment I spend with you I feel better, stronger. Taoism believes there is a force of opposites. There is no light without dark, no man without woman, and no love without hate. I've felt the hate, strong, through my entire body. So I guess that means I can feel love, just as strong. All that in Zvornik, I'm on my way to being free of it. Because of you. You free me."

McKenna said nothing, listening to him, still running her fingers across her body.

"You know what I always thought was beautiful?" Jefferson said. "Tracer machine gun fire. Tracer fire at night. All those colors, streaking through the black sky, it's like watching fireworks."

Jefferson felt something loosen in his chest. "Do you want to know what happened out there?"

McKenna said, "I want to feel what you feel. Know what you know. I want to have lived your life with you before we even met."

"Once you know, you can't go back. You can't forget things."

"I don't want to forget," McKenna said. "I don't want to ever forget."

———————

Brogan and I were both with the Seventh Armored Cavalry Regiment, in Camp Washington, four miles south of the town of Zvornik. We had been in Bosnia for a month, time spent mainly in camp, watching movies and working out. Vincent was over there with us; that's where we met him. He was young and stupid at the time; before the wild had all got out of him, he used to be crazy. The military had brought over enough equipment to set up a pretty good-sized gym, and Brogan, myself, Vincent, and a man named JC from Spring Hill, Texas, were all working out together when someone, I forget who now, had the idea to go into the city of Zvornik that night.

For the most part, all U.S. military personnel had been confined to the camps during our time in Bosnia, allowed only to travel along our patrol routes, which took us just to the edge of the city. At night, we could hear music wafting up from the city, and sometimes the arcing white of spotlights cutting through the night air. JC, a young kid just out of basic, had been dying for some kind of action, and none of us had seen a woman in the weeks since we'd left our station in Germany. What kept us in the camp, more so than our CO's orders, was that it was thought that the road leading into the city was heavily mined by Serbian troops. That was true, there were mines, but they weren't the biggest threat.

Two weeks before, an American, Michael Wise from Ohio, had stepped on a land mine, having both his legs blown off. Or that's what was said officially. Unofficially, most of us knew what had really happened. He had been in Zvornik with two other guys from our unit and wandered off. A few hours later they found him dead in an alley, shot three times through the chest. Before he had died, someone had taken the time to strip off the skin of his legs, and cut off a few of his fingers.

That had kept us out of Zvornik for the past week, even with JC's constant talk, but the thought of a woman can be a powerful drug, and we were all feeling its effects. Weeks before, our third night in Bosnia, Brogan and I had been leaning against the sandbag wall of our camp, smoking cigarettes and drinking smuggled Jelen Pivo, a Bosnian beer. It was a warm night, the evergreen-colored tents of camp flapping quietly in the summer breeze. In the distance, we saw the colored lights of Zvornik. There was still fighting going on in the city at that time, flashes of white mortar fire silhouetting the city's squat concrete buildings, rumbling across the valley like thunder. We sipped our beers, watching the green flares cut across the night sky.

Since that time, no action had been seen in the city, so we all figured that the Serbs had moved on somewhere else. Or at least that was what JC was saying between sets of the bench press.

"Oh yeah," he said. "They all moved on. I heard it from a guy up by Tuzla."

JC was speaking of the city where the main bulk of the U.S. forces was stationed.

"It has been pretty quiet," Brogan confirmed.

"Except for that music," JC answered. "Where there's music, there's dancing. And where there's dancing, there's girls. Pretty girls."

We were all sex-starved, so we decided to leave camp that night, around ten, when we had time off anyway. Most nights we spent playing Nintendo and listening to the staticky American radio station being broadcast from Tuzla, some distance away. I was ready for a change myself.

That night we met thirty yards behind the long warehouse that housed about 150 men and women on rickety green cotton cots. JC had managed to procure one of the armored Humvees, and he leaned against one side, listening to the engine rumbling underneath the hood. Vincent was smoking a cigarette, his face long and thin as he sucked in his cheeks with each pull. Both men were in full battle dress, flak vests, Kevlar helmets, each carrying an M-16 and the standard 210 rounds of ammunition.

They smiled as Brogan and I approached, Vincent flicking away the cigarette with a careless motion.

"I've been dreaming about those Bosnian girls, man," JC said grinning. "All soft and warm, smelling like a woman."

Brogan was looking around him, his eyes darting nervously in all directions.

"Keep the voices down," he said. "We're fucked if the CO finds out."

JC nodded, swallowing hard and climbing up behind the wheel of the Humvee. Vincent jumped into the passenger side, while Brogan and I climbed into the back. The Humvee was roofless, and the air felt good as we began to move, the armored vehicle rolling over the rutted dirt of the camp. We hit the main road into the city, and JC accelerated, the night wind rushing past my face in long gusts. I closed my eyes, feeling some relief from the stagnant air of the camp. JC leaned forward, turning on the radio, an American hip-hop song blaring from the speakers.

"Hell yeah," JC said, bobbing his head. "This works!"

He gunned the engines and the Humvee sped along, the sound of the music in my ears, the wind against my face. I felt good, looking up at the stars, watching the lines of trees whisk by in a blur, like dust swept along by the ends of giant brooms.

"Hey you figure we're gonna get the pussy free tonight? Or you think we're gonna have to pay?" JC turned his head back, shouting against the wind.

"Your ugly ass is gonna have to pay," Vincent said, and we all laughed at the joke.

Along the sides of the road were forest and fields, an occasional skeleton house passing by in the night, the roof missing, the walls crumbing and fallen in on each other, mortar-exploded holes dug into the dirt. There were chickens outside some, still roosting in destroyed coops, while cows moaned quietly in discomfort, their udders full. I was still nervous about land mines, but the road ahead, lit by the twin headlights beams of the Humvee, was covered in tire tracks. Other vehicles had passed down the same road, which meant the dirt was probably free of mines.

Vincent was standing up in his seat, his back resting against the rollbars of the Humvee. He was taking target shots at the farms as we passed by, trying to knock out the remaining glass in the mostly vacant windows of the abandoned buildings. His M-16 bucked with each shot, and he cheered when there was an answering tinkle of smashed glass.

"Damn, man," Vincent said, lowering his rifle after a moment. "I was hoping to get a CIB outta this."

Vincent was referring to the Combat Infantry Badge.

"Hell yeah," JC said. "Me too."

"What the hell am I supposed to tell everyone back home?"

Vincent raised his rifle in frustration and fired off a few more rounds.

"Hey, hey," Brogan said. "Cool it for a moment."

Brogan gestured forward, and, turning, Vincent saw a pair of headlights bearing down on them from farther up the road. He slid back down into his seat, still clutching the M-16, reaching beneath his seat and pulling up his Kevlar helmet.

"Who do you think that is?" JC asked quietly, as we approached the oncoming vehicle.

"Don't know," Brogan replied. "Could be Serbs, could be Muslims."

"What's the difference again?" Vincent asked. "I forget."

"Don't worry about it right now."

The unknown vehicle was close enough that we could hear its engine. The Humvee slowed, pulling slightly to the side.

"Careful," Brogan warned. "Stick to the middle. Stay away from the mines."

JC nodded, and the Humvee swerved back toward the center.

I could see that it was a truck. The back was open, wooden slats rising along the sides. Two rows of men were seated in the truck, their bodies jostling back and forth as it bounced over the uneven dirt surface. Even in the darkness, I could see they were all carrying rifles.

"Shit," JC hissed. "Soldiers."

He leaned back, taking his eyes off the road and reaching behind him. "Get my rifle. It's in the back somewhere."

Brogan passed the weapon forward, laying it between the seats, next to JC. "Take it easy, brother," he said calmly. "Everyone around here knows who the Americans are. Nobody'd be stupid enough to fuck with us."

"Tell that to Wise," I said, referring to the slain American GI.

The truck was still approaching, and I began to feel a nervous discomfort in my stomach. My palms were sweating lightly, and I rubbed them against my pants, then moved upward to cinch the flak vest more tightly around my chest.

The truck was on top of us, and we all turned to stare as it passed. The men were wearing fatigues, with thick black-soled boots and crimson berets on their heads. They turned to meet our stares as we passed by, keeping their rifles resting against their knees. I scanned the men's faces and had the impression they were gaunt, with thin traces of stubble lining their cheeks.

I felt my chest jump suddenly as I made hard eye contact with one of the soldiers. The man was staring at me, and, as I watched, he sneered suddenly, his lip curling up in a mean-looking smile. The guy was laughing at me. The truck passed by us and continued down the road, but still this man stared into my eyes. When the soldiers were some yards behind us, the strange man reached for something around his neck and lifted it up for me to see, flicking on a flashlight to illuminate it.

It was a pair of American dog tags.

Just like that I knew that the men in the truck were the same ones that had murdered Wise. Vincent knew it, too, because he stood up, staring back at the truck as it continued away from us. I saw his fingers tightening around his rifle. Brogan saw the motion, too, and quickly shook his head.

"You don't want to die tonight. Don't do what you're thinking about doing."

The man in the truck was grinning now, slapping one of his comrades on the shoulder. He turned back toward us, then shrugged, dangling the metal tags between his two fingers. Then the flashlight went out, pitching everything back into darkness. The Humvee and the truck pulled away from each other, until the receding truck was nothing more than a pair of red taillights.

Vincent slid back down into his seat, angrily slapping the outside side of the Humvee door with his hand. We were approaching the edge of the city, but our mood had changed. We were no longer excited about the women, or the dancing, or the drinking. I felt like we had just stepped out of a funeral. JC had turned down the music as we passed the truck, and he hadn't turned the radio back on again, so we drove in silence.

Zvornik was a collection of low-income-looking blocky apartment buildings constructed of drab concrete cinder blocks. The road was littered with burned-out cars, the sides scorched black in jagged arcs, the windows missing, the seats stolen away. One of the buildings had been hit by a mortar shell and concrete rubble lay across the road, a broken hole cut into the side of the building. Looking through, I could see the remains of a living room, a shattered television lying upside down on the floor, a framed family portrait, the glass a meshwork of cracks, a pair of shoes. The streets were quiet, desolate, and in the distance were the staccato cracks of rifle fire. Garbage blew around us, empty plastic bags filled with air lofted through the air like small white balloons.

Vincent had raised his rifle and was firing at the bags as they blew past, throwing the plastic into spasms as the bullets ripped through.

"Jesus, Coop," Brogan said. "We're in the middle of a city; you're gonna kill someone like that."

The Humvee swerved to avoid the top half of a shattered porcelain toilet lying incongruously on its side in the middle of the road.

"There's nobody around, this whole part got hit heavy, everyone got the hell outta here."

"Does look pretty dead," I confirmed, my helmet beginning to feel heavy and hot against my skull.

"Looks like we missed the party," JC replied.

I was beginning to just want to call it a night, head back to camp and the safety of the bunks. Something about the ghost city made me nervous. The vacant empty windows, the loose piles of rubble, the empty city common, all entirely devoid of life.

Something flashed white across one of the dark side streets, presumably another of the plastic bags blowing aimlessly. Vincent raised his rifle quickly and fired a round, striking the white object dead center.

A sudden noise chilled all of us. It was a short scream of pain, a small voice, the sound of a little girl.

"Jesus Christ, man," Brogan said. "I think you shot someone."

Vincent was pale, shaking his head. "No way. That was just a piece of trash. No way was that someone."

"Then what the hell was that noise?"

"I don't know, I don't know." Vincent was shaking his head vigorously, chewing on his lip.

JC had heard the noise, too, and had stopped the Humvee. We sat in the vehicle, looking back at the side street where we had heard the noise.

"Do we go back and look?" JC asked.

"We have to," Brogan said.

"Let's keep going," Vincent said shakily. "Let's just get back to camp. I don't want to be out anymore."

Brogan stared at him for a moment. "We have to go back and look. We can't just drive on."

JC apparently agreed with him, because he was turning the Humvee around. The front wheels lurched up onto the curb, the crunch of glass sounding underneath us.

I looked back toward the side street, but we too far away. I couldn't see any farther up. JC had the Humvee turned completely around, and we were slowly driving back. In the front, Vincent was silent, staring down at his feet. He looked up expectantly as we turned off the main road and into the narrow alleyway. The Humvee advanced at a crawl, its headlight beams sliding across the cracked pavement.

"Oh my God," JC whispered almost inaudibly.

A tiny figure lay in the alleyway. She was young, about eight years old, wearing a faded cream-colored dress and shiny black leather shoes. Brogan was already up and out of the back of the Humvee, running forward, dropping his rifle by her side as he knelt beside her. I followed, my helmet falling down over my eyes as I struggled to get out of the back.

The girl was still alive, her eyes wide and staring, her small mouth puckered as she sucked in tiny breaths. The M-16 round had struck her in the stomach, leaving a jagged, bloody hole in the front of her dress. Her hair was pulled back with a yellow ribbon, stained with the dirt of the alley, bits of broken glass caught in her hair.

"Oh no," Brogan said softly. "On no . . . I'm so sorry."

He was kneeling in front of her, reaching down and smoothing back her hair, picking out the shards of glass.

"What is it?" Vincent's voice came from the Humvee.

"It's a girl," JC replied, his voice coming from right behind me. He was standing, bareheaded, looking down at her.

"She dead?" Vincent asked, still sitting in the Humvee.

JC shook his head. "She's alive."

I knelt in front of her, my two fingers reaching for the pulse in her throat. Her heart beat weakly, unevenly.

"Ah Jesus," JC said. "What the fuck do we do now?"

"Let's get her into the Humvee," Brogan said.

"Whoa . . . wait a minute," Vincent replied. "You sure on that?"

"What?"

"I just mean think it through. We're off base, in direct violation of orders, they're gonna have our ass. And we shot a girl?"

"That's right," Brogan said. "We shot a girl, now it's our responsibility to make sure she's all right."

"I know that, shit, I wasn't saying we just leave her here, but let's take her to a hospital or something. I mean, you want to have to go back to camp with her? That's prison time right there."

Brogan had opened his mouth, when there came a sudden scream from above us. We turned our gaze up, and saw a single head poking out of one of the glassless windows above us. A woman was screaming, her hand covering her mouth, as she stared down in grief at the wounded girl in the alleyway. A stream of Bosnian words came from her mouth as she appeared to recognize the girl.

"What's she saying?" JC said, his eyes darting from Brogan to me. "What's she saying?"

"Can't you figure it out?" I replied.

Over the woman's voice, I could hear the sudden sound of an engine approaching in the distance. Brogan had heard the noise, too, and he said, "Something's coming. Check it out."

Slowly I backed out of the alley, walking around the Humvee toward the main road from which we had turned off. The street was still dark, the glow from the Humvee fading quickly as I walked out onto the main street. In the distance, back down the road, were two headlights, approaching from the outskirts of the city. I could hear a distant clanging, as of a truck shifting gears.

"Vehicle approaching, from the north, just outside the city," I said.

Brogan was still bent over the girl, applying pressure to the bullet wound in her abdomen. I could see the girl's blood seeping around Brogan's fingers in an endless stream. Vincent was standing up, staring at the girl with wide eyes, while JC had his helmet off and was walking in small circles, staring at nothing. I turned my attention back toward the approaching set of headlights. As the vehicle passed over a bridge, the moon broke from the clouds overhead.

For the first time I could see that it was a truck. I felt the angel of fear sitting in the bottom of my stomach. I was scared.

"Shit, we got trouble," I said, running back toward the other guys.

"What's up?" JC asked, stopping in the middle of his circles.

"That truck with the soldiers in it?" I said. "The one we passed getting in here?"

"Yeah?"

"It's coming back."

Brogan looked up from the girl. "You serious?"

He nodded toward JC. "Check it out."

JC ran down the alley toward the main street. Above us, the old woman had stopped crying and was shouting something in Bosnian that I took to mean, "Help." I looked around the deserted alley, no movement except for something scuffling in a heap of garbage piled against the wall. The girl was moaning now, a thin film of blood glistening on her lips. Brogan was pressing down on her stomach, saying something softly into her ear and holding his hand against her forehead. Vincent was facing the wall of the alley, his hands pressed against his ears, his head dropping back and forth.

JC was staring up the street, and he turned and came jogging back toward us.

"Jefferson's right, it's that same truck. They're coming back here."

More screaming from above.

"Shut the fuck up, bitch!" Vincent shouted back at the woman in the window, his voice startling me.

She turned toward him and pointed her finger, more Bosnian words coming from her mouth.

Vincent pulled up his M-16, aiming it toward the window.

"Vincent, no!" JC shouted, reaching out toward him.

And then it happened.

The M-16 kicked four quick times and I saw the old woman jerk and pop as the bullets struck her. Her head seemed to shatter, and she collapsed against the windowsill, her body sagging halfway out.

"Jesus Christ, man," JC said. "What the fuck is wrong with you?"

More heads had appeared in the windows above us, a squat apartment building made of cinder blocks and concrete. Many of them took us in with a quick glance, before pulling their heads back. Vincent was covering his ears again, the rifle back down on the ground. He was shaking his head from side to side, his shoulders hunched. His lips were moving, "No, no . . . please God no, just be quiet. Please."

I thought he was talking about the girl at first. She was still moaning in a delirium of pain, but Vincent didn't seem to be noticing her at all. Instead he was turned away from her, his hands still covering his ears, his body leaning against the rough wall of the apartment building. The wall was covered in graffiti, long white streaks of painted Bosnian words that ran across its length.

In the far distance I could hear the truck continuing to approach. JC was licking his lips nervously, looking down at his rifle, checking the ammunition clip.

"Hey, look, we need to get out of here," he said to Brogan.

"The girl is dying."

"I know, I'm sorry, but those soldiers, they're out for American blood. They're gonna be coming after us." JC turned and pointed. "They want our blood, man. That's why they turned around."

I caught a sudden motion from overhead as something was thrown from one of the windows above us. I watched the object fall from two stories high, and had a moment to notice that it was a glass bottle—a champagne bottle—with some kind of rag jammed in the top. A warning sounded in my head an instant before the bottle smashed against the pavement just feet from JC. There was the sound of breaking glass, and the noise of rushing air as the gasoline-filled bottled exploded into flames that spread across the street.

JC jumped back, and Brogan leaned over the girl, covering her. I turned toward Vincent, but he was oblivious to the confusion, still leaning against the building. A breeze was blowing against him—I could see it lightly rustling his fatigues—and Vincent seemed to shudder, turning his shoulders against it, as if the air was cold and dank. The night was warm and calm, and I could feel no movement of air.

As I approached Vincent, however, something did seem to blow lightly past my ear, a cold, uncomfortable wind that tugged at my clothing. I moved to turn my collar up against the chill, but as I did, I heard a soft sound, a whispering noise traveling to my ears from the cold wind.

I cocked my head to listen, feeling the cold air against the side of my face. There was a noise, a long, drawn-out whisper.

"Kill . . . kill . . . kill . . ."

I turned back to Brogan, still bent over the little girl, but he seemed not to notice anything. JC was moving quickly away from the fire spreading along the alley, while he patted himself down to check for stray flames. Only Vincent and I appeared to hear the voice.

"C'mon, we gotta go." JC was pulling on Brogan's arm, trying to get him to move back toward the Humvee. I could see that our vehicle was lit in the approaching headlights of the oncoming truck. I could hear shouting in Bosnian, the sounds of men's voices, and I watched as the truck pulled up at the end of the alley, blocking our way out in the Humvee.

Brogan stood up from the girl, his hands literally dripping blood, with spots across the cuffs of his shirt. The truck's headlights swung over us, and the vehicle turned down the alley. We stood staring back at the truck, shielding our eyes from the high beams. In the brightness of the headlights, I could see very little, only the dim outline of the truck and flickering movements, as if the soldiers were jumping out the back. I heard a voice call to us in Bosnian and the clanking as someone opened one of the truck's doors.

Brogan was stepping back slowly, moving to where his rifle lay on the ground. JC was breathing heavily, the sweat on his forehead shining in the headlights. There was the crack of a rifle, and JC jerked backward suddenly as a bullet caught him in the chest, sounding like a bamboo cane against a pillow as the bullet smacked his flak jacket. He collapsed to the ground, gasping for air, and rolled onto his side. I raised my M-16 and fired blindly at the lights and the shadowy figures. There was an explosion of sparks as one of my shots found the right headlight, then, a moment later, the left one shattered and we were pitched back into relative darkness, left with only the half-light of the partially obscured Humvee.

Brogan was pulling JC along the ground by the edge of his flak jacket, as JC wheezed, "Can't breathe . . ."

"What do we do?" I shouted.

"Leave the girl," Brogan snapped. "Fall back into the city. We'll lose them in there."

Vincent had snapped out of his standing coma and joined us, firing rounds back toward the Humvee and the dark, shadowy figures. One of the figures spun and collapsed to the ground. JC pulled himself back to his feet, thick, corded veins running the length of his neck as he continued to struggle to breathe. Together the four of us moved down the length of the alley. A rifle shot came close to my head, and we ducked in front of a closed doorway. Taking the butt end of his rifle, Brogan broke out the panes of glass near the door and, reaching through the opening, unlocked the door itself. We each entered the building, moving up the thick concrete stairwell in front of us.

We ran down the hallway, past the stains, past the front reception desk and a windowed case filled with what looked like athletic trophies, toward the rear of the building. I heard nothing from the stairwell below us and felt a surge of relief—no banging of doors, no sounds of booted feet against the stairs or angry male voices.

As we approached the end of the hallway, I heard a sudden rattle of gunfire, followed by rapid bursts from separate guns, all coming from the alley. The soldiers outside must have found the fallen girl and were firing off rounds in the air, a warning to us that they were coming.

I could feel a gust of wind against my face, not the cold wind of the alley below, but a warm breeze. I crinkled my noise as the smell hit me. The air was dripping with the odor of death, of decomposing bodies.

"What's that smell?" JC asked, pressing the crook of his arm against his nose.

We turned the corner of the hallway and faced out suddenly into open space. The side of the building had been hit by mortar fire, opening up the entire wall in a jagged line of rubble. I could see desks overturned, chairs lying smashed, and in the corner of the room, I saw a hamster cage, the forgotten hamster lying mummified and dead in its shreds of newspaper.

"Ho, shit," JC said suddenly, pulling back from the room.

Brogan had a look of disgust on his face and he said softly, "My God."

The wall was open, allowing us to see out over the town square below. Three human-sized shapes dangled from the ceiling, just in front of the opening and partially obscuring the view into the square. Moving closer I could see that they were three men, each shot in the temples, and left to hang. It was what we had smelled in the hallway outside. There were signs around their necks, written in Bosnian so that I couldn't read them.

The breeze continued to blow in through the opening, and the three men swung in their nooses, the rope making scraping noises as it passed back and forth across the beam. Directly across from us was an apartment building, balconies filled with cheap-looking furniture and clay-potted plants lining the wall, each backed with a sliding glass door. From one of the balconies I saw a sudden burst of light. Something slapped the wall behind me, and I felt sharp bits of concrete hit the back of my neck.

"Sniper!" Brogan shouted. "Down, down."

There was a table in the back of the room, and, moving to it, I knocked it over onto its side and ducked behind it. Brogan and JC were pressing themselves against the far wall, just beneath the dead hamster in its cage, while Vincent was on the opposite side, behind a sink and something that looked like a chemistry set. We held our respective positions, motionless and silent. I was breathing heavily, resting my head against the back of the table.

In the hallway outside, I heard the booted tread of someone approaching. Looking toward Brogan, I waved my hand, then pointed two fingers out into the hallway. Brogan nodded and looked back out toward where the gunman was positioned on the balcony. I raised my head over the level of the table, but through the opening ripped in the wall, I could see nothing but shadows.

I didn't figure him to be a sniper—real snipers didn't miss at fifty yards. I thought most likely that it was a single soldier, or maybe even a civilian, carrying an automatic weapon, probably an AK-47.

I was beginning to wonder why he hadn't unloaded the clip on us yet, when the room began to be torn apart by bullets. I ducked back under the table and listened to the noise of chaos sound around us. The table was an inch thick, like Kleenex to an AK, but at least I couldn't be seen. If I was hit, it'd be by random chance. I always felt I had pretty good luck with those things.

A moment later, something broke through the table on the opposite end to me, three high-caliber slugs that slammed through the wood and embedded themselves in the concrete floor. I pulled my knees up to my chest, shielding my face with my arms. Around me I could hear the shattering of glass, probably the hamster cage, the tearing apart of wood, and the chipping of concrete, so loud that it sounded as if someone were throwing baseballs into a room filled with glassware.

I could hear JC shout, "Jesus Christ . . ." and, glancing over, I saw his face scrunched up, as he covered his head from the fragments of glass raining down on him. Then, as suddenly as it had started, the barrage ended, leaving the room strangely quiet. In the hall, I heard the squeak of boots against concrete again, as the soldiers advanced toward our position. Vincent had raised himself back off the floor, so I knew he was unhurt, and neither Brogan nor JC were crying out in pain.

Vincent fired a burst of rounds through the open wall, out toward the dark balcony. I could see the balcony railing shatter in quick bursts, broken ceramic pots and bits of dirt from the wall of plants exploding to the ground. A cold breeze had filled the room again, and I began to hear the same whispering noise I had heard on the street below.

"Kill . . ."

I shook my head and raised my eyes above the level of the table. The classroom was destroyed, quarter-sized bullet marks pocked the walls and showed along the sides of the splintered desks and tables. My own table had been hit three times, the round holes forming a small diagonal from edge to top, wood dust curling in motes around the openings.

One of the three men who had hung from ropes from the ceiling lay on the floor, apparently knocked to the ground by the gunfire. He lay sprawled out, face buried unnaturally into the concrete, his bound arms and legs tight against his body. Another of the men was swinging back and forth, and I could alternately see his face, then the back of his head as he twisted to and fro.

As I watched in horrid fascination, the man's eyes suddenly opened. I pulled back in surprise. The man was somehow still alive. Left living to hang outside the square. He stared at me for a moment, before raising a limp arm, the fingers curling to point toward me. His face was swollen, the lips cracked and bloody, the hair dirty, and I could see the rope cutting deep into the skin of the neck, folds of pale, greasy skin overlapping the cord.

The man's lips were moving now, and he seemed to be trying to speak. He continued to point at me, and I could hear him whispering, except the sound seemed not to come from his lips, but instead was all around me.

"I am watching you . . ."

Then his arm fell back to his side, and his eyes closed. I heard a squeak in the hallway, and turned to see three soldiers moving quickly into the room. I raised my rifle and fired, knocking the soldiers back. One of them was turning toward me, but a bullet caught him at the base of his throat, and that section of his neck seemed to vaporize in an instant.

In the hallway, I could hear the quick chatter of language and the sounds of retreating feet.

With a flick of my wrist, I motioned to Brogan that they were leaving.

He nodded and, pulling JC up, moved toward the doorway. Vincent was also up, sliding back along the wall. One of the soldiers was on the ground, his arms and legs twitching spasmodically. I turned back toward the man hung from the ceiling, the one who had appeared to look at me. His eyes were closed again, his arms again resting limply by his sides.

We slowly moved to the doorway, and, poking my head around the side, I saw a surprisingly large basketball court. From the walls hung purple banners, with dates on them, and a picture of an eagle, talons extended, clutching a torn-apart basketball. The scene was very familiar, like any high-school gym in the U.S.

"OK, let's set something up here," Brogan said, looking around the room. "Yeah, this is perfect."

He turned toward two swinging doors at the far end of the gym, then pointed at me.

"See about securing those doors, nobody in or out through them."

I nodded, and he turned to the other men.

"JC, you've got explosives on you, right?"

JC nodded. "Some."

"All right, let's rig up charges along the wall there, by the first door. I want a kill zone about fourteen, fifteen yards wide. You and Vincent set it up."

The two men nodded and moved toward the wall nearest the doorway we had come through. I moved to the far doors, to secure them as Brogan had instructed. The set of doors had a bolt lock. I turned the lock and watched the heavy slug of metal slide between the doors. Pushing my body against the wood, I felt a solid resistance—the doors refused to budge. With the butt end of my rifle, I knocked on the lock hard, until the metal used to turn the bolt was twisted and warped. Trying to twist the bolt, I found it impossible to move, the door remaining permanently locked. Proud of myself for the quick work, I turned back toward the gym.

Brogan was standing high in the bleachers, holding up his M-16 and sighting down onto the basketball court. There was a five-foot-high wall of concrete along the top, behind which was a walkway where spectators could stride along the length of the bleachers before stepping down the rows to their seats. Brogan stood behind this, his rifle resting on the concrete edge, looking down onto the court. He was measuring steps, then after ten paces or so, he took a single bullet from his pocket and placed it on the five-foot-high wall.

JC and Vincent were lining explosive charges along the wall nearest the entrance doors. They placed the charges about waist high, hiding them beneath the purple basketball banners. I turned back to check the doors again and Brogan put down a microphone, and, finishing setting up marks along the concrete wall, jogged quickly down the stairway of the bleachers and out onto the court.

He called the three of us over. "This is the Rope-A-Dope. We'll get them in here, next to the kill zone, make them think we're weak, then blow the shit of them. JC, how many you figure we can take out with what you rigged?"

JC shrugged, turning back to his work. "Didn't have too much to work with. I figure we could get about eight with the blast. That wall is weak concrete, should turn to shrapnel pretty easy, we'll get a few more with that, or at least cut 'em up bad enough that they won't be able to shoot back."

"Ten to twelve?"

"At least. Whoever walks through that door, it's gonna be like walking into a blender. My nipples get hard just thinking about it."

Brogan nodded. "I presighted the gym floor from up in the bleachers there. We've got a good wall for protective fire, anyone that doesn't get knocked down with the blast, we can finish off from up there."

We all nodded nervously.

"We need a runner," Brogan said. "Someone to get them to come in here. A rabbit. Who wants it?"

We all looked at each other.

"C'mon now, who wants it? You fast, JC?"

JC shrugged, then nodded proudly. "Yeah."

"How fast?"

"Ran a 4.43 forty-yarder back in high school, all-state tailback my senior year. Faster than anything they got in Bosnia, that's damn straight." JC smiled, looking around. "Ain't got nothing here that can run with Texas football. Hoowah!"

Brogan nodded and smiled. "All right, job is yours. Jefferson, go with him, cover his ass. Vincent and I will set up shop up top there." He gestured to the bleachers. "You two lead them back here, see if you can get them to follow. Vincent and I will be up there with places marked out for you." He turned toward JC. "You want a CIB, right?"

"Yeah, fuck yeah, I want it."

"All right then, let's go."

JC and I stood in the darkened hall, just outside the doorway leading into the basketball arena. I was walking forward, when JC stopped suddenly, bending down to unlace his boots.

"What are you doing?"

"Taking these off, I can run faster in bare feet."

He unlaced his boots fully and removed his socks, then placed them inside the doorway of the gym. He leaned forward, stretching his legs for a moment and rolling up the bottoms of his pants. Then he bounced up and down on the balls of his feet, shaking his legs back and forth.

"You ready, Carl Lewis?" I smiled.

"Yeah, I'm straight."

We walked down the long corridor together, passing a series of intersecting hallways.

"You think this'll work," I asked.

"Hope so."

"You figure to get caught?"

"Hell no, you ever run track down South? The shit is fast. They don't even have any black people over here; you think they can catch a nigga running full speed?"

I smiled. "Right."

I paused at the corridor. "I'll wait by the gym doors, make sure nobody gets in front of you."

JC nodded, rolling his head back and forth to loosen his neck. He exhaled sharply.

"Nervous?"

"Just like running the two-hundred-meter, no sweat."

He held out his right hand in a fist, and I knocked it with mine, before he grabbed my hand in his.

"Don't go nowhere."

I nodded, and watched him jog down the long corridor. The school's main hallway was about a hundred yards long. When he reached the end, he turned to the right and jogged out of sight. I stood alone in the quiet hallway, listening to my breathing and studying a map of the world pinned to the wall in front of me. I ran my eyes to the

United States, thinking about home, in my mind tracking the events that had led me to this place.

From somewhere farther down the hall, I heard a whisper of voices. The sound was so indistinct that I could recognize no words. A door slammed suddenly. The whispering ceased. Nervous, I moved slightly down the hallway. On my right was the open doorway of a classroom. The sound of the whispering seemed to have come from within, so, gripping my M-16 tightly, I moved silently into the room. It was lined with small desks, each heavily marked with pen and pencil, reminding me of my own high school back home. A wooden cabinet with a sink was along the far wall, but aside from a wilted plant lying forgotten in the windowsill, the room was mostly empty. I lowered my rifle. There were rust-colored stains on one of the walls, as if someone had thrown paint-filled balloons against the concrete, and they had splattered sharply. I knew those were more bloodstains—more executions had taken place there. A chalkboard was at one end, with a line of writing across the middle. My eyes scanned the words; I was surprised for a moment to see that the words were in English.

Curious, I drew closer, reading the board.

"You are chosen."

I raised my rifle, quickly scanning the room again, suddenly nervous. I peeked my head under desks and looked inside cupboards. I was alone; I was convinced of that. There was a sharp clatter behind me, and I whirled around, my taut finger almost pulling the trigger on my weapon. Behind me was nothing, only a blank concrete wall.

Something lay on the floor, and I moved across the room toward it. I bent and looked, surprised when I saw that it was a cheap gold-plated crucifix cross. The cross had apparently fallen from a nail driven into the concrete wall and was lying facedown. I picked it up, carefully putting it back on the nail. I turned toward the chalkboard. While my back was turned, the lettering had changed. Now it read simply:

"Kill."

I looked around me once more, but the room was still empty. Gripping the rifle tightly, I slowly turned and made my way out of the room. As I reached the doorway, I heard a second clatter behind me. I knew this to be the sound of the cross falling from the wall again and hitting the concrete floor, but I willed myself to stare forward, not wanting to turn back to see something standing behind me, something that wrote strange things on chalkboards and knocked over crosses.

Back outside in the hallway, I reached behind me, again without looking, and grasped the classroom door handle. I felt a cold rush of air around my hands, and, with a shudder, I quickly shut the door, feeling wind gust around me as I did so.

Out in the hallway, I stood staring again at the map of the world, focusing on Massachusetts and trying to calm myself. I rested my head against the back wall, swallowing hard. I shut my eyes. Inside the classroom I heard a noise, like fingernails scraping against the inside wood of the closed door. I ignored it, staring again at the world map. The fingernails scraped once more, and I found myself turning around to look back at the door. There was a small window in the door, a slit about eight inches wide. Through it, a pair of eyes regarded me.

A face was pressed against the window, and as I watched, it smiled slowly, its breath steaming up the glass slit. I raised my weapon, but suddenly, from somewhere in the school, I heard the rapid explosions of machine gun fire. I turned my head for a moment to look down the hallway and when I glanced back at the window, the figure had vanished.

The sound of shooting rang out again, echoing down the long, empty hallway. The soldiers must have found JC, and, hoping he was running, I mentally willed him to move as fast as he could. Raising my rifle, I forgot about the face in the window and backed up against the door leading into the gym. I pressed my rifle against my right shoulder, sighting down the powerful scope. At the end of the hallway, 130 yards away, I could see a small red metal box, which I took to have once held a fire extinguisher. I made this my mark and rested the perpendicular crosshairs in the middle. I waited in the dark hallway, slowing my breath as much as I could.

C'mon. JC . . . C'mon, I kept saying to myself.

I heard another shot, then suddenly, from around the corner, JC came running. He was at a full sprint, and lowering one hand to keep his balance as he moved through the sharp turn, almost running into the far wall. He ducked his head at another shot, and from behind him I heard the shouting of Bosnian voices. He turned up the straight portion and his stride leveled out as he flew up the 130-yard hallway. His body was straight up and down, his stride running almost parallel to the ground, long and graceful, and I could see why he'd been all-state. He had almost Olympic-caliber speed. I had a fleeting sense of wasted opportunity, of regret that he wasn't running track somewhere rather than being stuck in Bosnia.

Behind him, I saw a soldier appear around the corner of the hallway, raising his rifle and training the weapon on JC's back. I moved the crosshairs of the scope from their spot on the red metal box just a few feet to the right, to where they rested just above the level of the man's belt. Even at 130 yards, I could see the wrinkles of fabric where he had tucked his shirt in. I pulled the trigger twice, and watched through the scope as the man was blown back. JC kept running, as a second soldier appeared around the corner. I spotted a gold chain around his neck, and a short tuft of chest hair, before I knocked him back with a pair of shots. I opened up the magazine on the far wall to discourage anyone else from appearing.

JC was upon me, and he slowed, his breaths coming thick and gasping. He bent over, his chest heaving, sweat running down the length of his neck.

"C'mon," I said, grabbing him under his arm and pulling him through the double doors of the gymnasium. "Let's go."

I waved up to the top of the bleachers as we entered the basketball court. Brogan stood and waved back, signaling us with a sweeping motion of his hand to come up. I picked up JC's footwear and rifle from inside the doorway, and we bounded across the gym floor, moving quickly up the stairs of the bleachers. Brogan was crouching behind the low cement wall at the top, and he pointed us down the aisle toward the opposite end of the gym.

JC and I found our places about ten yards apart, directly past half-court, high in the bleachers. I raised my head above the wall and looked down, a perfect view over the entire court. Brogan scooted along the floor toward me, keeping his head below the level of the wall.

"Did they go for it?"

"Not sure," JC said between winded breaths. "Ran into a whole shitload of them out there. Must be about twenty-four or twenty-five men. They gave chase, shooting and everything, but I showed them how we do it back home. I think Jefferson here capped a couple of them."

I nodded.

"Good," Brogan said. "They should be coming through those doors soon. Get ready and keep your head down until I say. I got Vincent up in the announcer's booth. After we start shooting, he's gonna start talking, trying to get them to surrender. If they do surrender, then cease fire immediately."

"He speaks Bosnian?"

"He's got comcards with him."

Comcards, or communication cards, were two-sided laminated cards filled with the pronunciations of useful phrases in the native language. There was everything from "Show me your hands!" and "Please drop your weapons and lie facedown!" to "Where is the nearest restaurant?" and "Is this water safe to drink?"

Brogan held out his hand, and I took it, feeling him firmly press against mine, then handing me the wireless remote for the demolition charge.

"Take care, brother," he said.

He scuttled along beneath the wall to his position, twenty yards down from me. JC was still breathing heavy and lacing up his boots.

"Tired?"

"Winded."

"You're outta shape," I kidded him.

"I could do ten of those in high school, no problem. I *was* Carl Lewis back then."

JC finished lacing his boots and, taking his rifle, poked his head over the top, looking out over the basketball court below us.

"I'll show you some damn running," he said. "Newspapers used to call me the Thrill. Ran for over two thousand yards senior year, that's almost two hundred per game. Nothing could catch me, my shit was like Michael Johnson."

JC rested his rifle on the top of the concrete wall, then took the wireless remote for the demolition charges from me and placed it against the wall by the door, resting the small unit on the floor next to him. I had taken my spare magazines out, resting them in a line along the wall in front of me. JC did the same, then, taking a stick of gum from his pocket, put it into his mouth and began to chew rapidly.

The basketball court was silent, the rows of bleachers empty and quiet. While I waited, I made a game of counting them, counting the rows down, then back up, and down again. When I had counted that, I imagined taking shots from different parts of the floor, watching the ball arc into the net from the foul line, the three-point line, from midcourt. Minutes passed, and I had to use the bathroom. I was bobbing my legs back and forth.

Next to me, JC had thrown away his gum and was now eating a Snickers bar. He saw me staring at the bar and, nodding to me, silently broke off a piece and handed it to me. I nodded thanks and ate the piece, chewing slowly.

Below us, the doors suddenly moved. I almost choked in surprise, and had to close my eyes and concentrate on not coughing. Swallowing carefully, I clutched my rifle and stared down onto the court. The doors were being slowly eased open, bit by bit as I watched. JC was next to me, also staring down over the low wall, his hand gripping the detonator.

The door continued to open, and I saw a booted foot appear, then the end of a rifle, then finally a face. A Serbian soldier stepped carefully into the room, scanning the gym floor, his eyes moving over the bleachers. He said something barely audible to someone behind him, and a moment later a second man appeared, then a third. We watched as soldiers began to file in through the door, moving quietly along the wall. I counted them and saw that there were twenty-four, must have been almost every man from the truck. The first man had passed the kill zone, and I glanced over at Brogan. Brogan shook his head no, holding up five fingers.

The soldiers were still moving slowly forward, weapons raised, and I could hear them talking to one another. They were beginning to move past the kill zone, the line of explosive hidden beneath the banners, but still Brogan shook his head no. Then, as I watched, his fingers began counting down from five, then four, three, two, one . . . and he nodded.

JC triggered the detonator in his hand. There was an enormous explosion as the entire section of wall seemed to tear apart in a burst of red flames. A few of the soldiers tried to jump back, but were too late, shrapnel cutting them into fleshy pieces. I saw perhaps eleven men fall dead in the initial blast, while a few more lay in agonizing pain, screaming and looking down at destroyed limbs. Brogan raised his head and began firing rounds down onto the court. I heard the basketball buzzer sound loudly over the loudspeakers, an earsplitting single tone, as I raised my own rifle, then Vincent's voice bellowed over the intercom in broken German, the universal language of the region.

"*Kapitulation! Kapitulation!*" Surrender, Surrender.

The voice was still sounding from the loudspeakers as I raised my rifle and fired a short burst onto the floor. Some of the men had slowly begun to recognize their situation, and they raised their own weapons and began to open fire. We held the advantage, and were quickly knocking down their men as they stood on the court. Blood was beginning to seep across the court's shined-wood paneling, and the sight seemed only to heighten our anger, intensify our desire to kill these men who had hunted us.

I could feel my vision clouding. Dimly, I saw soldiers throwing down their weapons, raising their arms over their heads. But still the slaughter continued. Brogan stood up and began walking down the long row of bleachers toward the floor. I caught the movement from the corner of my eye, and ran to join him, JC right behind me. Running past Brogan, I moved quickly toward the first surrendering soldier. He was standing, arms raised above his head, a wide-eyed, scared expression on his face. He had a thin, pale face, with a faint wisp of a beard, the light growth of a sixteen- or seventeen-year-old boy.

I raised my rifle and struck him as hard as I could under the jaw with the butt of my weapon. I could feel his teeth smash together, hear the sound of bone cracking. He stood for a moment, dumbfounded, and I swung the entire rifle like a baseball bat, catching the side of his head with the heavy, blunt end of the weapon. There was a noise like a watermelon as it bursts on the street after being dropped from a very great height, and the soldier swiveled almost completely around before he collapsed, his ruined head striking the wood floor.

Another soldier was advancing toward me in confusion, and, taking my knife from its boot sheath, I used the blunt back end and smashed it against his throat, watching him sag back onto the floor. Brogan moved forward and kicked the man in the head as he hit the floor. JC and Vincent had also joined in, kicking and beating the soldiers senseless. Brogan had taken out his sidearm, and was moving down the line, pressing the handgun to the heads of soldiers and pulling the trigger. His eyes were alive, excited. We were all caught in a frenzy of violence. I felt a red hatred flowing through me like a drug, and with each swing of the rifle, I seemed to get higher and higher, the drug increasing in my veins.

Brogan seemed to be caught up the worst. He was beating on a fallen soldier until blood was flowing down the length of his rifle, and still he continued to beat. Then when there were no more dead, he swung up with his rifle, catching JC just under the rib cage. JC sighed loudly, the color going out of his face, and he collapsed to the floor. I thought Brogan would have stopped, realizing his mistake, but he advanced, pulling out his knife.

Shaking my head, I grabbed Brogan's arm, and he swung the blade at me, catching me across the right biceps and drawing blood. The motion turned him on me, and he sprang forward, still holding the knife. I backed away, tripping over the sprawled body of one of the soldiers and falling to the floor. Brogan sprang for me, before his body seemed to stop and jerk backward in midair.

I saw Vincent grabbing him by the throat, choking him.

"Brogan, cool it," Vincent said, his forearm tight around Brogan's neck. "You hear me? It's over."

Brogan was gasping for breath, and I saw the anger slowly leave his eyes. He began to go limp in Vincent's arms, and, slowly, Vincent lowered him to the floor. I was pressing my hand against my biceps, slowing the flow of blood. The cut wasn't deep, but it burned and made me light-headed.

The gym was a mess. Bodies lined the ground, I counted twenty-four dead, the same number that had entered the gym, in various positions all across the floor. I began to feel sick at the sight, the smell of blood and loosed bowels reaching my nose. I shook my head, backing away from the sight and looking for a place to vomit.

There were loose chips of concrete on the floor from the detonated explosives, and I kicked them out of the way as I ran to the bleachers. Gripping them, I leaned over and vomited once, then again, and a third time. Finally, after a moment, the feeling began to pass, and I stood up, wiping my lips.

I felt as if I had been injected with poison, and my body was fighting back, trying to rid itself of the toxic substance. Brogan was sitting on the floor, both arms propping up his body, his face blanched and white.

"All right, c'mon," I said weakly. "Let's get moving."

We all left the basketball court, locking the gym behind us and disabling the door mechanism. Feeling exhausted, we walked in silence down the long corridor, through the school, and back to our Humvee.

McKenna lay silent for a long moment, stroking the top of Jefferson's head with her hand. Finally she said, "I almost don't know what to say. It's so horrible the things men do to each other. I can't understand it sometimes."

"Do you wish I hadn't told you?"

She shook her head, sighing. "No. I'm glad you could finally share that with someone. That's too big a burden to carry alone."

"I try not to think about that," Jefferson said, feeling something like tears in his eyes. "I want to be so far away from that. Away from all that death."

McKenna cradled him, pulling his head toward her until he could feel her warm breath, comforting against the back of his neck.

"I know," she said. "I know."

She held him like that until they both slept.

The next afternoon, after a lunch of blinis, Jefferson and McKenna caught a taxi out to the Kryokov Museum. St. Petersburg was a city constructed around water, stretching over forty-two separate islands. Rivers and canals stretched throughout the city, like veins across the back of a hand, spreading between the buildings and the gardens. The museum was no exception. Overlooking the Karpovky Canal, the massive stone structure dominated the street.

Standing six stories high, the building was higher than the level roofs around it, with a giant stone stairway that swept down to the street. Thick columns spanned either side of the stairs, towering up toward the central colonnade. Jefferson paid the driver and stepped out of the taxi, followed by McKenna, who shaded her eyes against the sun, looking up at the museum.

"So now what happens?" she asked. "Do we just go in and ask to see their skeleton collection?"

"Yeah, right." Jefferson smiled. "That'd go over well. Hi, we're in from Boston, we'd like to see something in skeletons if you have any."

"It's a big place. Where do you want to start?"

"Dr. Wu told me he went to school with the curator of the museum," Jefferson said. "He was going to call ahead and explain the situation. We'll see."

Together they climbed the giant stairway. Two cloth banners hung down from the columns, announcing the arrival of a new exhibit. Jefferson couldn't read the Russian writing, but he could pick out the date. The banners fluttered in the wind, making cracking noises as the fabric snapped back and forth. Inside, they were immediately ensconced in the quiet of the museum. A long hallway stretched in front of them, next to a circular staircase that rose to the second floor. The walls were made of a white stone and gave the museum a light, elegant feeling. A guard in a brown uniform sat behind a semicircular desk in the main lobby.

"*Zdrastvuity*," the guard said as they approached.

"*Zdrastvuity*," Jefferson replied. "*Pamaguity pazhalusta?*"

"*Shto?*"

"I'm looking for Nikolai Ugriumov," Jefferson said slowly, pronouncing each syllable of the name. "Ugriumov, he's the curator here."

The guard nodded, reaching for the phone in front of him.

McKenna raised her eyebrows, looking up at Jefferson. "When did you learn to speak Russian?"

"It's in the guidebook," Jefferson answered. "Check it out sometime."

"Maybe I will," McKenna answered. "I had no idea. I'm impressed."

"Don't be. The only other phrase I know is, 'Where's the bathroom?'" Jefferson tapped on the counter, looking around the museum lobby. "Looks like he's coming."

Jefferson's eyes were turned toward a small, thin man in a brown suit walking purposefully toward them from down the long corridor. The man's face was narrow, a sparse goatee covering his upper lip and chin, his hair neatly trimmed close to his scalp. Wire-rim glasses were sitting on the bridge of his nose, making him look a little like Lenin. He pushed them gently upward as he walked.

"Ah, hello." His English was thick with a Russian accent. "Dr. Wu informed me of your visit. You must be the detectives from the United States."

"That's right." Jefferson shook the man's hand, introducing himself and McKenna.

The Russian shook Jefferson's hand firmly, before carefully taking McKenna's palm and lightly pressing his lips against the back of her hand.

"I had no idea that police in your country could be so . . . beautiful," he said, looking up at McKenna.

McKenna smiled, turning her head slightly away. *Take it easy, big guy.*

"I am Nikolai Ugriumov." The Russian shrugged. "But you can call me Nick. That's what they called me back in the U.S."

Nick smiled, raised his hands, and gestured Jefferson and McKenna down the museum corridor. "Come, let me show you my office, and we can discuss what brings you to St. Petersburg."

They began walking down the corridor, their shoes tapping lightly on the tile floor.

"I think he likes you," Jefferson whispered, as they walked.

"He seems the type that likes all women."

A group of German tourists passed them, cameras slung around their necks, following a tour guide who was pointing to a series of Degas pastels and speaking loudly in German.

"I understand you're here as part of a murder investigation."

"That's right," Jefferson said.

"Ahh, America, still such a violent place. That's what makes it so interesting."

"Thank you for your time, we appreciate that," Jefferson answered, his gaze drifting back over the Germans.

"Well," Nick replied, "that's one thing we Russians seem to have more of these days. Time."

He paused for a moment, opening the door to his office and waving them inside.

Nick's office was small, dominated by an overwhelming sense of holding too many things inside. A stuffed hawk, beak open, wings spread, rose from its wooden base, standing precariously on the top of a tall bookshelf filled with frail-looking volumes. A desk, crammed high with papers and loose manila folders, stood against the corner wall, leaving barely enough space to squeeze by. An old Macintosh computer sat humming on a table in the corner, the screen saver dancing crazily across the black screen.

The one window in the room was partially blocked by thick industrial-looking drapes, the sunlight streaming in through the glass serving only to illuminate dust particles swirling in the air, stirred up by their entrance. Nick took a seat in the leather chair behind his desk and motioned to two padded leather chairs. Jefferson and McKenna sat down, sinking deeply into the thick leather.

"Nice museum," Jefferson said.

"Thank you," Nick replied. "I am very protective of it; I feel as though everything in here is my own. Coffee?"

"I thought you just drank tea over here," Jefferson said.

"Times change. Now we mostly drink Coca-Cola." Nick shrugged. "Maybe just as well. Tea is becoming rare these days. But at any rate . . ."

Nick looked at them for a moment, twining his fingers across his chest. "You do not come all the way from America for this. I am sorry, I waste your time. How can I help you?"

"Not at all." Jefferson leaned forward in the chair. "Are you aware of the Skeleton of Qinghai?"

Nick smiled, saying nothing, tapping his fingers on his chest.

He looked at Jefferson for a moment, before answering, "Found in 1932 by a small group of Chinese miners and Sherpas who were working in southern China. While taking cover in a cave during a snowstorm, they discovered a fully complete, human-like skeleton. The Skeleton of Qinghai."

"So that's it? That's all it is?" Jefferson asked.

"Now that is the question," Nick replied, swiveling his seat back and forth. "That is the question . . . do you still have the game show, *The $64,000 Question*?"

"No . . ."

"That's a shame," Nick said. "At any rate. Nobody knew what the skeleton was. To this day, still nobody knows what it is. It was so strange in appearance, almost to the point of gross disfiguration, that it led many people to think it might even be a hoax."

"Why would people think it was a hoax?" McKenna asked.

Nick paused, looking out the window toward the crowded square outside. "Well, superficially, the skeleton was hominid in appearance. But even a cursory examination revealed several inconsistencies. Like it was human, but not human."

"Hey, I think half of Boston fits into that category," Jefferson said. "We got a whole wing of those types at Concord Correctional."

"I don't think you'd have any of these particular types," Nick said.

"What was wrong with it?" McKenna asked.

"Well, its canine teeth for instance. They were sharp. Fangs. Almost like they'd been taken from a tiger or other large cat. And its arms were strangely proportioned, unusually long, with what appeared to be the remains of vestigial claws. And the skeletal morphology of its legs indicated several unusual qualities."

"Like what?" McKenna leaned forward, looking interested.

"This creature had a skeletal structure similar to that of modern species, animals such as horses and ostriches, which are excellent runners. Long legs, digitigrade stance, walking on its toes, and from the muscle scars, scientists were able to reconstruct its musculature and hypothesize about its abilities."

As Nick talked, he stood up from his desk, putting a small pot of water onto a metal burner sitting near his computer.

"And they found it was fast?"

"That's not the word for it," Nick said as he took out a tea bag from a cardboard box. "The thing was like lightning. It was strong and fast, but the bones had no wear on them at all. It's like the thing hadn't aged at all. And that wasn't the strangest part," Nick said evenly, pausing for a moment, a cup and saucer suspended from his fingers in midair. "What made it an even more unlikely hominid ancestor were the reduced fourth and fifth digits on the foot."

"I'm sorry, that means, what exactly?" Jefferson asked.

"It means," Nick said, looking up at them from the cup and saucer, "that there were only three main toes on each foot. It had claws."

"Jesus," Jefferson whispered to himself, thinking back to the imprint of the claw in the mud in the cemetery. The same cemetery where they had found a man eviscerated and hanged inside a mausoleum. McKenna leaned forward in her seat, her attention focused on the Russian.

Nick noticed their movements, saying, "Looks like that caught your attention. Let me guess, you found a footprint near the scene of a murder. A footprint with three toes?"

There was a long pause. *If you only knew. Murder was an understatement. They don't have a word for what happened in that mausoleum. "Butchery" comes closest to it. A butcher that left three toe prints pressed into the mud.*

"How did you know that?" McKenna asked finally.

Nick smiled, sitting back down in the leather chair, folding his hands over his chest. "Lucky guess?"

"You should pick MassMillions numbers for me," Jefferson said. "Nobody's that lucky."

"Well, let's say it was an educated guess then."

"If you've had similar crimes here in St. Petersburg," Jefferson began, "we should coordinate a search effort. It's obviously some kind of internation—"

Nick interrupted him by holding up his hand. "No, Detective Jefferson. I'm afraid there hasn't been a murder of this type in almost two thousand years."

The Kryokov Museum reminded Jefferson a little of his grandparents' house, jammed with hundreds upon hundreds of little knickknacks and antiques that looked as though they hadn't been moved or touched in thirty years. Jefferson couldn't imagine how anyone even made sense of the museum anymore. Display cases were filled with various items, some marked with small slips of paper, others showing no markings at all, display cases lined up one after another, filling room after room, until the whole museum seemed to blur together into a collection of glass cases, random bits of art, and dust.

Nick was leading them slowly through the museum. The German tourists had disappeared farther down the hallway, replaced by a small flock of Russian schoolchildren tightly bundled up in brown coats and pants. The only spots of color were the glossy plastic backpacks, decorated with American writing and cartoon characters.

"Ahh, your capitalism." Nick smiled, looking down at the familiar Batman symbol colored onto one of the packs. "It is everywhere now. The frills of the new era. Box lunches, plastic kiddie pools, barbecue equipment. Twenty years ago, none of this. Now, it's everywhere."

"The business of America is business I guess."

"You know, years ago I saw your movie *Gladiator* on video here before it even came out in your country? Russian black market." Nick was walking slowly down the museum corridor, one hand held behind his back. "You know what true Russian entertainment is?"

"What?" Jefferson asked politely

"Construction sites. Things getting built. People come out to watch bridges and buildings, thinking, 'Maybe this means we are finally getting somewhere.'" Nick waved his hand. "It doesn't really. Our true poverty is gone, but the country is still a wounded bear. Our ninety nuclear subs in the Russian Fleet are all slow-motion Chernobyls. Our naval inspector tells us this, so we lock him up. But still it is always with the blue jeans and the kiddie pools." Nick shrugged, then softly said, "*Pir vo vremya chumi.*"

"What's that mean?" McKenna asked.

"It means, 'A feast in the time of a plague.'"

They had turned away from the main corridor, passing through a room dedicated to the work of Carl Fabergé. A glass case filled with multicolored eggs jutted out from the wall. A second case stood up from the floor, the velvet inside lined with enameled platters and snuffboxes, the outsides decorated with jasper and pale green nephrite.

They passed out of the Fabergé corridor, moving into a room of porcelain. Brightly colored figures and wildly decorated plates filled the displays, ranging in styles from the eighteenth to the twentieth century, then forward through the open doorway and into a third section. The room was filled with religious imagery. The Italian images of Christ bearing the crown of thorns, his arms pinioned behind his back, Flemish paintings of the Virgin Mary, Dutch masterworks of angels and disciples, all crowded together into the room.

Nick stepped briskly into the center of the room before turning around, his hands indicating the walls around them. "Are you a religious man, Detective Jefferson?"

"Irish Catholic, you kidding me? Yeah, I'm a religious man a little bit." Jefferson shrugged. "Less so these days. I go to church every once in a while. Try to anyway."

In honesty, Jefferson couldn't remember having been to church once in the past ten years.

"And you, Ms. McKenna?" Nick asked.

McKenna smiled. "When I get the time."

Nick nodded, stepping closer to her. "Do you know what an icon is? Have you heard the word before?"

"I think so," McKenna answered. "An image or article that shows divine revelation?"

"Very good," Nick praised. "The icon bears witness to this divine revelation . . . and a relic? Do you know what that is?"

"A piece of a saint, right? Like a portion of his bone, or a lock of his hair?" McKenna asked.

Nick nodded again, smiling this time. "Excellent. That's right."

Jefferson elbowed, whispering, "Smart-ass."

"Hey, maybe if you went to church a little more, you'd know these things," McKenna whispered back.

Nick walked to one of the walls, pausing in front of an image painted from the Last Supper. Jesus sat in the middle of the long table, his eyes looking unusually sad. *What an unwelcome gift it would be,* Jefferson thought, *to know the time of your own death. Had Reggie Tate known his time was coming, had any of the victims known of theirs? Would they have acted differently, enjoyed their last day more, or would they have been so overwhelmed by the knowledge of their impending mortality that they could do little but sit and wait, unable to savor their own last supper?*

Nick looked up at the image for a moment. "A holy man was not supposed to putrefy when he deceased. If a corpse of a holy man began to decay, then people think to themselves, 'Well, maybe he wasn't a saint after all.'

"This was the mark of a saint. And their parts were taken as trinkets, locked away at churches to attract pilgrims. The femur of St. John. The molar of St. Thomas. Their body parts divided up like pieces of a candy bar for everyone to snack on. Really very barbarous. Not much of an incentive to be a saint, eh?"

"Not really." Jefferson swallowed in agreement. "So what's that have to do with the skeleton?"

"Ahh, the skeleton," Nick began. "Well, that's what some came to believe the skeleton was. A relic."

"A relic?" McKenna asked, her voice confused. "Of who?"

Nick turned toward her. "Not who? But, what."

Jefferson shook his head. "I'm not following . . ."

"Well, if you believe strictly in the Bible, then you must also believe that there is more than just God, and Jesus, and the Prophets out there. You must believe that there is also evil. Demons. Fallen Angels. Things that bring pain and suffering with them.

"And you don't even have to go to the Bible to find that. Every religion has its evil spirits. Sumeria had the Maskim, seven demons that lived in the bowels of the Earth, rising to attack men and children. In Arabic, there are the Jinn. Known as the dark ones, or the concealed ones. With fire that circulates in their veins instead of blood. The evil ones who led the angels' revolt against Allah and were cast down to Earth.

"Christianity has its own demons. Beelzebub. Satan. Those figures that have turned away from God, instead seeking to bring pain to man. While the details are different, the essential character of the demons remains the same throughout the centuries. And many of these creatures were not considered to be true spirits."

"What does that mean?" McKenna asked.

"Well, that would mean that when a demon is killed, it leaves behind a solid body."

"And this body?" Jefferson inquired. "What would it look like?"

"A human body," Nick began. "Yet one distorted by evil."

A human body that left behind claw marks instead of footprints. Nick stepped to the far wall of the room, running his eyes over a gilded cross, the tortured body of Jesus crucified on it.

"It came to be believed that the skeleton was a relic. A most unholy relic. A relic of evil. Whereas the fragment of a saint was thought to posses the powers of good, the bones of a dark one would have the same powers for evil."

Jefferson raised his eyebrows. "So you're saying that the skeleton you have here is from some kind of demon?"

"Yes, I believe it is," Nick said slowly.

Jefferson stared at Nick, uncertain for a moment how to respond. He studied the man's face, looking for a faint trace of a smile, some indication that the man was kidding around with him, that the entire story was some practical joke, the Russian version of April Fool's. Nick stared back at him with his cool eyes, his thin frame as still as a lizard in the sun.

"Come on," Jefferson said, breaking the silence. "Are you serious? I mean, a demon? You actually believe that?"

"I am not so presumptuous as to believe only what I can verify with my own eyes," Nick said. "But being a police detective, your mind must be analytical, moved by reason, by evidence."

"For the most part," Jefferson responded. "Evidence is good."

"I shall provide you with evidence then," Nick replied. "The evidence that you seek."

Nick turned away from them, straightening the cuffs of his suit coat and walking out of the room, through a small doorway in the rear. Jefferson watched him as he left. The man's frame was small, almost effeminate, with its narrow waist and slender shoulders. He looked like the type of man who had failed in every physical endeavor he had ever attempted, so he had instead turned inward, strengthening his mind as others strengthened their bodies. While kids his own age played kickball and wrestled, Jefferson could imagine Nick sitting inside, reading, learning to play the piano, thinking of ways to fool American police detectives when he became an adult.

Jefferson and McKenna followed dutifully behind him as he guided them down a long hallway, walled on either side by high, open windows. The windows looked out to gardens on either side, stretching away to Jefferson's right before meeting a thick forest.

"Why don't we step outside for a moment," Nick said, turning back to face them. "The museum can have ears, and some of what I am going to tell you is not very popularly accepted."

Nick leaned against a glass door set in the middle of the windows, pushing it open for them. Warm air smelling of jasmine swept in to meet them.

"In this time of cutbacks," Nick said, holding the door as Jefferson and McKenna passed by, "one can never be too careful."

They preceded the Russian, stepping onto a cobblestone pathway that stretched out through the garden. The path and the garden reminded Jefferson vaguely of the Lyerman murders, the rooftop garden, the whirlpool, the two mutilated bodies. Rain had been falling that night, cool and empty, washing the blood into small rivers down the sagging white flesh of Kenneth Lyerman. On this morning, however, the sky was clear, small puffy clouds floated above them, innocent in their airy ignorance of death and cleansing rains.

They walked slowly along the path; fragrant herbs reaching out on long vines brushed against their legs, wind rustled the leaves of the tree overhead. They seemed far from the blandness of St. Petersburg and even farther from the violence of Boston. Nick joined them on the path, his pale skin almost shining in the sunlight, as if it were the first time it had ever known the sun.

"As I was saying," Nick began again, "near to this skeleton, inside this same cave, were a number of wide jars. Jars unique to the region of Jericho, around the Dead Sea, yet buried in a cave thousands of miles away in China. When the lids were opened inside were found three ancient scrolls rolled up in leather and cloth. The scrolls contained fragments of the Old Testament and other books, penned by the hands of several different scribes. The writings varied in their skill and description, seeming to evolve over a long period of time.

"What was most interesting, however, was a brief narration toward the end of the last scroll. This passage described a great battle against an invading force from the north, which lay siege to the city of Qumran, just near the Dead Sea."

Jefferson stretched apart the fingers of both hands as he walked, feeling the air circulate between them as he swung his hands back and forth. It felt good, clean. The air in gardens always seemed the cleanest. He remembered the public gardens near his home, back in the old neighborhood. He used to cut through the garden paths on his way back from baseball practice, taking his time, breathing in the smells, the air seeming to scrub his lungs free of all the crap that city kids breathe in during a single day.

Nick was continuing to talk, telling them of the city of Qumran. Of four creatures that came into the walled city at night, killing any who ventured out alone. The period of terror went on for two years, before the people in the city banded together, chasing out the evil and tracking their prints in the sandy flatlands surrounding the city.

"You see," Nick said, as they passed beneath the wispy fronds of a weeping willow, "despite the evil powers, they were very easy to track. They left behind prints. Deep prints, of their three-clawed digits."

Jefferson swept his head toward Nick, suddenly focusing on everything the man was saying.

"Ahh, I see I now have the attention of the class," Nick said.

"Go on," McKenna replied, shielding her eyes from the setting sun.

"Many recent scholars interpreted this passage in the scrolls to be a metaphorical description of the Roman invasion of Qumran, during their sweep through northern and eastern Judea."

"But you don't think it was the Romans?"

Nick shrugged, a short movement, his small shoulders rising and falling like tiny pistons beneath the fabric of his suit coat. "The dates were wrong. The Roman invasion of Judea occurred in the year 67, when Qumran was actually destroyed by the Romans, but the scrolls were carbon-dated fifty years earlier, in the year 17. I think that the Romans were second invaders into Qumran, the first being the evil presence described in the scrolls."

"So the story as described in the scroll," McKenna said, "wasn't metaphorical?"

Nick looked at them for a moment, a breeze ruffling his hair slightly, blowing a strand for a moment down across his face, before the stray hair ducked back up onto his head. "No . . ."

Nick said after a moment, "I don't think the story was metaphorical at all, I think the scrolls describe an actual, historical occurrence. I believe, and many like me also believe, that these scrolls describe the return of four fallen angels. The return to Earth of four demons."

They kept walking through the museum's garden, the setting sun gilding the tops of the herbs and flowers in a golden haze. The view seemed somehow different, less appealing than before. The lines of the garden seemed harsher, the flowers and herbs less inviting, the air cooler. Gone were Jefferson's thoughts of his childhood garden, replaced instead by visions of demons and three-toed claws and disemboweled bodies.

"Do you know what the Shroud of Turin is?" Nick asked as they walked.

"Sure," Jefferson replied. "Sort of."

"Isn't it supposed to be the fabric shroud that was placed over Jesus' body after his crucifixion?" McKenna asked.

Nick nodded, one hand pushed deep into his pants pocket, the other roaming about in front of him as he said, "The Shroud of Turin is believed by some to be one of the rolls of cloth purchased by Joseph and used to wrap the deceased body of Christ."

"You said, 'one of the rolls,'" McKenna turned toward him. "That would imply that there was more than one cloth."

"Was there?" Jefferson asked.

"The questioning voice of the nonbeliever." Nick smiled vaguely. "Yes, there was more than one cloth. There were two, in fact, two separate sheets of similar size and length."

"How do you know?" Jefferson asked.

"You want proof?"

"Or evidence."

"Something other than just the word of a faded old museum curator. I can understand your reasoning."

"Now I didn't say that," Jefferson said. "You're a very intelligent man, I'd just like some—"

"Corroboration?" Nick interrupted.

"I was going to say verification. You say tomato. Same difference."

Nick stopped in the middle of the path, so quickly that Jefferson almost bumped into him. Nick pivoted on his heels and turned back toward the museum.

"Why don't I show you?"

"Show me?"

"Come with me," Nick said, walking past Jefferson and McKenna, down the cobbled path and back toward the museum.

They walked closely behind Nick, who was moving quickly despite his short steps. Nick was speaking back over his shoulder again, reminding Jefferson of his eighth grade math teacher, who lectured with his back to the class, writing equations on the blackboard while he talked.

"Originally, it was thought Jesus' body had only one burial shroud," Nick said. "That Joseph purchased only one sheet of cloth. But historically, crucifixions of the time were very bloody affairs. Realistically, there had to be more than one shroud. Joseph and Nicodemus would have needed to wrap the body to carry it to the cave. Then more fresh wraps once they arrived.

"Burials of the time probably involved four to five separate cloths. Why would Jesus be buried in just one? The Shroud of Turin is the only one we know about, but there must have been others."

They had gone past the weeping willow tree once more, heading for the long hallway of windows connecting the two wings of the museum. Nick pushed open the door, and, together they stepped back into the hallway, Nick's shoes tapping on the wood floor as he turned and headed farther into the museum's other wing. Jefferson and McKenna followed, sometimes having to jump-step in order to keep up.

Nick turned to them. "Don't touch anything."

Then, moving quickly, he stepped behind the massive ape, quickly disappearing from view. Jefferson and McKenna followed, finding a narrow maintenance hall, the opening concealed behind the animal. Nick was already several steps ahead, striding down the hall, the walls so close that even his slim shoulders almost brushed against them. The floor was littered with folded drop cloths and buckets of plaster. Two paint-splattered wooden ladders stretched behind the drop cloths, while a can of paint-brushes stood on its side, the paint dried and crusted into a solid mass. Nick stopped again in front of a metal-encased door.

"This leads down into the basement," Nick said. "Please keep your hands to your-selves, there are many dangerous items down here. Oh, and there are bats."

"Bats?" Jefferson asked.

"They've somehow found an opening to the outside, so they seem to roost down here. We're looking into it."

McKenna squeezed Jefferson's arm. "You sound nervous."

"Batman I'm not."

Nick pushed open the door, and a set of stairs leading down into blackness gaped in front of them. Jefferson peered down, but it was like looking deep into the water, the stairs fading into darkness as they descended. Feeling along the wall, Nick flipped a plastic switch, and a series of bare bulbs overhanging the stairway suddenly sparked to life.

"We don't come down here too much," Nick said, his feet moving smoothly down the stairs. "I guess just about once every two months or so. Or when we decide to move an exhibit, like if we get a collection on loan from another museum and need to make space for it."

The stairway smelled of damp rags and wet concrete. There were cracks along the walls, and the stairs creaked. Cobwebs, sparkling in the light, swung back and forth like tiny banners over their heads, waving in the stirring of air caused by their move-ments. After they'd descended into the darkness for a moment, the stairway ended in a narrow concrete-floor hallway.

"There actually used to be a church where the museum now stands," Nick said. "Like most European churches, there was a series of burial catacombs underneath. The original structure burned down just before the end of the nineteenth century, but we decided to keep the catacombs themselves."

"What do you do with them?" McKenna asked, keeping one hand over her eyes to ward off any low-flying cobwebs.

"Well, the plan is to eventually open them up as an exhibit in themselves. As just another portion of the museum. But for right now, we mainly use them for storage."

The narrow concrete hallway opened up suddenly into the system of catacombs he had been describing. High brick walls ran alongside them, each with rows of burial ledges. There were hundreds of them, stretching far ahead, the individual spaces break-ing the walls into a honeycomb-like design, giving Jefferson the impression they were walking into a giant beehive. The air felt dry, dusty, and Jefferson could feel the particles tickling the inside of his nose as he fought down a sneeze.

Stacked neatly in each of the alcoves were the overflow pieces from the museum above. Paintings wrapped tightly in brown paper. Ancient collections of coins. Small chalices and decorative boxes. Life-size sculptures extended erratically from the floor, their forms obscured by bubble wrap and cardboard. One alcove was filled entirely with the stuffed heads of African game animals. Another was crammed with flowery material that looked like it came from old evening gowns. They walked along rows of catacombs, Nick's head remaining motionless, not turning to take in the museum pieces.

Nick did his quick stop once more, pivoting on his heels with the efficiency of a Nazi goose-stepper and finally turned his eyes toward the overflowing walls of the catacombs.

"A shame really," Nick said. "All this is slowly disintegrating. We had to install a new air system. Get some of this moisture out of the air so the paintings wouldn't mold."

"How do you ever find anything?" McKenna asked, her gaze fixing on a set of armor hanging from a stand.

"Theoretically, most of this is listed in a giant card catalog system, like a library. So if you know that an eighteenth-century French tea set is down here, it should be listed upstairs. It's a rough system. A lot of things get lost."

"You should rent some of this stuff for Halloween costume parties," Jefferson said, laughing to himself.

Nick smiled. "We have one of the dresses from the collection of Queen Elizabeth I down here. The fabric was laced with poisons by assassins wishing to depose her. I think that would be a nasty surprise to a costume ball."

Jefferson nodded in agreement. "That would put a real downer on the party."

The hallway of catacombs ended abruptly, and Nick turned down another passageway, leading deeper underground. Small rooms opened on either side of them, and Jefferson caught glimpses of metal shelves piled high with more museum articles. They seemed to walk past a series of these rooms, each blending into the other. One could hide for a month in there. Something small and black flitted over their heads, causing bursts of stirred air that rustled the tops of their head. The creature continued down the hall before vanishing behind a set of shelves. There was a series of small chirps, and Jefferson pulled his coat tighter around him, remembering Nick's mention of bats.

"You know where you're going, right?" Jefferson asked.

"Of course."

Jefferson began to think they were lost, when suddenly Nick clicked his heels against the stone floor. "Ah, here we are."

They were standing in front of a larger-sized room, that, like all the others, was lined with a series of open-faced metal cabinets. They followed Nick inside, walking down the aisle of shelves. The room reminded Jefferson slightly of the evidence lockup back in Boston. He looked around, expecting to see murder weapons wrapped in plastic bags, dope needles, and an odd collection of confiscated firearms. Instead there were only a series of plaster heads, staring blankly out at Jefferson as he walked past.

"What you have come for is in the back," Nick said, nodding toward the end of the room.

Jefferson's foot brushed against something on the floor, causing it to skid across the stone and bounce against one of the metal cabinets. A dead mouse. Surprised, he looked down at the creature as they passed by, almost stepping on a second dead mouse in the process. He scanned quickly across the floor, counting four or five more carcasses, their bodies turned over onto their backs, their legs sticking stiffly into the air. McKenna noticed them, too, touching Jefferson's arm, then nodding toward one of the small, mummified corpses.

"Maybe the bats killed them," Jefferson suggested in a whisper to her.

"Bats eat insects. Don't you ever watch Animal Planet?"

Set on the floor toward the end of the room was a wooden crate, almost eight feet long, resting directly on the concrete. The crate was made of several six-inch-wide slats, with Russian lettering stamped across the front. Someone had piled newspapers across the top, forming a yellowing tower that threatened to topple over onto the floor.

"This it?" Jefferson asked.

"Yes," Nick replied. "It's been down here, I don't know, must be twenty years now."

The crate appeared to be nailed shut, the corners pressed firmly against each other.

"One of these things . . . that attacked Qumran . . . is inside?" McKenna asked.

"Yes, the skeleton is inside."

"Can we see it?"

Nick thought for a moment, then shrugged. "I don't see why not. We'll just close it up again later."

Nick spun around, his eyes glazing over the room. "There should be a pry bar down here. Ah, there it is."

He pointed to a thin metal bar leaning against the concrete wall. "At least someone did something right. These are supposed to be left in every storage area to allow inspection of the boxes. Half the time they disappear though."

Nick took the bar, sliding its metal pry between the wooden slats of the crate. As he leaned down on the end, the bar slowly began to press upward, causing a shrieking noise to erupt from the wood. Jagged edges of splinters shot up from the wood, as the piercing noise of the metal nails pulling out from the soft wood filled the small room. Nick muttered something to himself in Russian, leaning more heavily on the pry bar, the wood screaming like a cat in a fight.

"Want some help?" Jefferson offered.

Nick grunted, shaking his head no. Gradually the top of the crate yielded, pulling up enough to be grabbed by hand. Nick dropped the metal bar to the ground, where it clanged loudly against the concrete. Careful to keep his suit clean, he pushed off the lid with the flats of his palms, leaving a thin trail of dust across the whites of his hands.

Inside, the long wooden box was filled with crushed newspapers, wadded together to form a makeshift padding. Jefferson reached down, pulling the yellowing papers out and letting them float to the floor. Despite his doubts, he found himself moving quickly, urged on by some kind of nameless excitement. Like opening a Christmas present, Jefferson tore away at the wrappings, leaving them in a cluttered heap.

The papers were cleared in a few moments, and Jefferson stood back, joining McKenna and Nick as the three looked down into the crate.

The bones appeared to be connected still, stretching seven feet in height. It lay on its side, and the legs were bent up at the knee, arranging the creature in a slight fetal position, while its arms formed two Vs across its chest. The overall impression was that the thing was asleep. Jefferson's eyes lingered over the obvious three-clawed foot, before they moved slowly up, scanning thick rib bones, the claws of the fingers, and the slightly inverted spine. The neck was craned backward, broken, and on top rested the skull.

Something moved inside Jefferson as he stared at the figure of bones. A cold finger seemed to push into him, stirring his insides, moving slowly through him, causing ripples of what? Panic? Anger? Fear? The finger turned again, making Jefferson feel nauseous, a churning sensation stirring at the base of his throat, the sickly sweet taste of vomit rising from the pit of his stomach. The thing was real, was alive, Jefferson could feel it. What lay in that crate was evil. A rushing taste of rotting vegetation suddenly overwhelmed him, as if he were gagging on dead leaves, someone forcing moss and fresh dirt down his throat until he choked.

"Are you all right?" McKenna asked, her voice sounding distant.

Jefferson turned toward her, and he felt drunk with anger. His hands clenched into fists. He wanted to strike her, to feel the brunt of his knuckles flush against her face. Then turn on Nick, to swing at him, break his nose, his jaw, beat him until his blood ran across the concrete floor.

Something touched his arm, something warm, and he looked down to see McKenna's hand, her finger running the length of his forearm until they found his fingers. Her skin was cool, soothing. Jefferson felt her slowly stopping the stirring inside him. The taste in his mouth condensed to one droplet of saliva, and, turning his head, he spit once onto the concrete floor, the feel of vomit and of rot leaving his body as he did.

"What's wrong?" McKenna asked again.

Jefferson shook his head, not wanting to tell her exactly how he had just felt. "Don't know. Felt . . . strange . . . there for a moment."

"Are you all right now?"

Jefferson nodded. He was all right, although there was still a slight pounding just behind his temples. A slow throb beat along with his pulse, as if a poison had been injected into him, and with each beat, passed through his body. Nick watched him with careful eyes, gripping the pry bar tightly as he did, whether for defense or attack, Jefferson wasn't sure.

"Look at me," Nick commanded, his voice quite.

"What?"

"I said, look at me."

Jefferson turned and looked at Nick, directly into his eyes. Nick seemed to search his face for a moment, and then, looking relieved, released his grip on the pry bar.

"You look ready to knock someone out with that," Jefferson said.

Nick shrugged. "You never know; sometimes people don't feel like themselves."

That's the truth. Jefferson wasn't sure what he had just experienced. But already, the feelings were beginning to fade, like the last remnants of a dream you seem to remember upon awakening. Jefferson turned to look back at the skeleton, and, together, all three again stared into the crate.

"So this is it?" McKenna asked.

"Yes, it is."

She walked to the end of the crate, squatting, looking at the thing's bleached white feet. "The toes look about the same size as the imprints we saw back at the cemetery. Definitely the same shape."

"Can't be too many three-toed freaks like this running around," Jefferson said.

"The people of Qumran were never able to slay these demons, only driving the four from their city. After their attack on Qumran, the four demons are mentioned in frequent texts as appearing in this area over the next six hundred years, from what is now Israel, into Egypt and Jordan and north into Syria and Lebanon. Always the four, traveling as part spirit, part living creature."

"What do you mean part spirit?" McKenna asked.

"Well, these demons were limited in their power, in their ability to take physical form. Only when they found four willing vessels, four humans whom they could possess, were they able freely to walk the Earth."

"Did they ever find these vessels?" McKenna asked.

"Some believe that they did. In 632 the great Islamic schism occurred. From this break sprang four human warriors, perfect warriors. These four were believed to have become the physical bearers of the fallen angels—the four demons. These demons were given new power in the body of a great warrior named Sidina and his three closest companions.

"Sidina ruled for six hundred years, before the writings end with the description of the final defeat of him and his dark ones in A.D. 1232 by a legion of men. Then they tell of non-Hebrews, knights of the Crusade, who took the body away from the city, carrying it northward, across the desert and into the mountains of an unknown region. Their travels lasted for 440 days, carrying the body with them, until they finally believed they were far enough away from known civilization that this evil one could never find its way back to the city."

Jefferson looked at whatever lay bleached and dusty in the crate, imagining how horrible it would have been in life. Then imagined Crusaders carrying this creature's remains for over a year, for thousands of miles, until they came to the cave in China. What could be so powerful, so evil, that carried its remains into unknown lands. Lands so far from known civilization that there was little assurance of the warriors even returning.

"A cave was found in the mountains, and the knights took the body of this dark one deep inside it," Nick was saying, walking a slow circle around the crate, still looking at it. "They brought with them a cloth of the body and blood of Jesus. A shroud from the crucifixion, and they wrapped the dark one inside that cloth."

"So there were other shrouds?" McKenna asked, still crouched at the end of the crate.

Nick nodded. "Oh yes. There were. And one was used for each of the demons."

"Why would they do that?" Jefferson asked.

"Remember, the men were devout Christian warriors who were carrying the bodies of demons, demons that had plagued generations, and had only by luck been slain. These creatures came to Earth following the path of Jesus, and could, like Jesus, be resurrected from the dead. The demons had taken bodily possession of men, then distorted their images to suit their own purposes, to become the form of evil that lies before you."

"But they had already killed this creature, right?" McKenna asked.

"Yes and no. They had killed the demons in the bodies of Sidina and his companions, but they believed that they could return. Could be resurrected. The Resurrection of Jesus brought his body in ascension to Heaven. But the resurrection of the demons would return an unstoppable evil to the Earth. To protect against this, the shrouds were used as a final seal around the demons' bodies, chains around them so that they could never be resurrected." Nick stopped, clicking his heels again in characteristic fashion, then smiled, showing unusually white teeth. "Or so the manuscript says."

Nick looked at them both for a moment, the smile stretching across his face. A second something flitted across the ceiling again, another bat bound into the night to search for insects amongst the hundreds of thousands of decaying bits of relics in the catacombs. Nick turned away from them, still tapping the crowbar and looked back down at the crate.

"From a collector's standpoint," Nick said, staring down at the jumble of bones, "this is a very interesting piece."

"Why would anyone want this?" McKenna asked.

"That's what the rich do, Ms. McKenna," Nick said. "They collect interesting pieces."

"Has anyone ever offered anything for this?"

Nick nodded. "We actually had a very recent attempt to acquire, but we do not believe in selling away our collection piece by piece. Even in Russia's troubles, we won't prostitute ourselves."

"Do you know who it was?" McKenna asked.

"One of your wealthy American businessmen," Nick said. "A Joseph Lyerman."

If Lyerman had made a bid on this piece, he must have known that whatever lay in the crate in front of them had some kind of importance. He was sure now that the creature was of the same type that had hunted in the cemetery, that had killed in Sinatra's house. He was also sure that Lyerman knew this and that whatever had been on Blade Island was from wherever this thing that now lay in front of him had come.

Jefferson looked down at the bones, running his eyes over the crushing wound to the back of the head, a gaping hole in the skull just above the spinal cord. The crushed fragments of bone weren't in the case, only the six-inch hole remained. The arched-back neck and the jagged hole made the skull look even more vicious. Jefferson could imagine the anger this thing must have felt when someone finally bashed its brains in. The jaw was open, the sharp teeth that Nick had mentioned were clearly visible, protruding downward. The skeleton could almost be human, except for these teeth.

"Looks like a mean bastard," Jefferson said slowly. "Whatever the hell it was."

"Reminds me of a couple ex-boyfriends of mine," McKenna said.

She bent over, looking down at the skull, one hand outstretched tentatively. "Can I touch it?"

Nick nodded. "If you would like."

McKenna reached into the crate, running her hand over the smooth surface of skull. "It's warm," she marveled, her fingers skirting over the vertebra of the neck. "Like it's alive."

Nick laughed. "Bones take on the ambient room temperature fairly easily."

"But it's not warm in here," McKenna said. "I'm serious, feel these."

Jefferson bent over, lightly touching the sides of the ribs with his finger. She was right, they did feel slightly warm, like touching the pavement on a hot day.

"Ouch!" McKenna cried, jerking her hand away, a drop of blood on the tip of her index finger.

"What happened?" Jefferson asked, looking at her.

She was waving her hand up and down, rubbing the tips of her fingers. "I cut my finger."

Jefferson looked back into the crate. A smear of blood stained one of the canine teeth of the skull. She'd cut her finger on the damn thing's canines. Jefferson gently touched the edge of the tooth, feeling its razor sharpness.

Jefferson pointed at the red stain on the white bone. "I can't believe these things are that sharp after all this time."

"I can't either," Nick whispered, bending to inspect the tooth more closely. He was still holding the crowbar, and Jefferson could see the white of the man's knuckles as he gripped the metal tightly. The smile had faded from Nick's face as he leaned in toward the gaping skull.

"How's the finger?" Jefferson asked, taking McKenna's hand.

"I'll live." She smiled, keeping her hand in his.

Nick was still peering at the skull when his head suddenly shot up.

"Look at this," he hissed suddenly, reaching around and motioning to them.

The stains of blood on the tooth appeared to have gradually spread out, running along the vertical section of the bone. Then, as they watched, the stains disappeared entirely, soaking into the bone as if it were a sponge, filtering in through the white enamel as a napkin might soak up liquid.

"Whoa . . ." Jefferson said, pulling back slightly. "What the hell was that?"

"I'm not sure." Nick looked closely at the tooth, pushing his wire rim glasses up to his eyes. Gently prodding at the tooth, he rocked it free of its dental cavity, holding it up to the light from the small dangling bulb hanging from the ceiling.

"Amazing . . ." he uttered softly.

"What?" McKenna asked, forgetting her finger for a moment, letting her hand drop to her side.

"This tooth still has blood vessels in it," Nick declared, showing them the tooth. There appeared to be small flecks of red running just underneath the white enamel. "It's like there are living cells inside."

"You mean this thing is alive?"

"No." Nick shook his head. "It just appears to have blood vessels inside that would be able to feed living cells. It's like the skeleton is coming alive."

"What could you cause that?"

Nick shrugged, thinking for a moment. "I'm not sure. It's almost as if someone injected the tooth with blood."

"What?" Jefferson replied. "Wait a minute, I thought this thing has been locked up for the past twenty years? How did someone get in here and inject the tooth with blood. I mean, we saw the crate—the thing was almost sealed."

"I know, I know." Nick shook his head. "Unless maybe that is from Ms. McKenna. Somehow pulled into the tooth."

McKenna look back down at her finger, replying nervously, "You mean, some of my blood is in that thing now?"

Jefferson didn't like the idea either, it was, somehow, creepy.

"Well, I don't know." Nick shrugged. "I've never seen anything like this before. Bones become less porous with age, the chance that they could somehow soak up blood is very remote. I guess it's possible, though. Strange."

He slipped the tooth back into the dental cavity. "I hope nobody has been tampering with this. I'll have to check with the staff."

Jefferson darted a quick look at McKenna. Her eyebrows were pulled together, a single line forming between them. She caught his glance and raised her hands slightly, shaking her head in confusion. Jefferson didn't like the idea of that thing in the crate having anything alive in it. The skeleton was frightening, unnatural, the bones themselves seeming to exude a foul presence.

Jefferson had encountered many evil things in his life. Sick, depraved people who had raped and murdered children. Men who tortured others, growing stronger off pain, suffering. He had interrogated serial killers, sadists, rapists. Every type of evil that human society could produce Jefferson had run into at some point in his years on the force. And what lay in that crate scared him more than anything he had seen on the streets or in the interrogation room; it scared him more than anything mankind had ever done to itself.

"What about the other things they found in the cave?" McKenna asked. "The scrolls and the shroud?"

Nick turned around, looking up at the metal shelves near the crate. "They should be around here somewhere."

Nick rummaged around for a moment, before pulling up a roll of fabric. He flipped open the shroud, rolling it slowly down the table and exposing the image outlined on the fabric. The fabric was a faded yellow color, as if stained with coffee, stretching out before them like a giant piece of dried animal skin. The edges curled upward like the toes of Persian slippers, the tips bending down to touch the fabric of the shroud. The figure of a man was pressed into the fabric, shaded lightly into the coffee texture of the shroud. Jefferson sucked in his breath, looking down at the shroud, his eyes lingering over the pale fabric, the dried splotches of blood, the outline of the figure.

"Did they ever test these stains?" Jefferson asked. "See if they're really blood?"

Nick shook his head. "I'm afraid not. This shroud was forgotten. No one was willing to risk their reputations to support its legitimacy. That's why it ended up down here for all these years."

Jefferson nodded, looking back at the stains. They seemed to glimmer in the light, as if they'd been glazed over with sugar. The effect was strange. Hypnotizing, like staring at the surface of water as the setting sun reflects across the still waves.

He reached out and touched one of the splotches.

His finger came away coated in a red wetness.

He jerked his hand back in surprise. "What the . . . ?"

Jefferson looked down again. The shroud was bleeding. The fabric was wet with the blood shed two thousand years ago. Startled, Jefferson looked up, confusion written across his face. McKenna was still turned away from the table, her eyes sweeping over the shelves in the rest of the room. Nick was staring at a scrap of paper he'd pulled from his pocket, his attention diverted for the moment.

Neither of them had seen Jefferson touch the fabric. He looked down again. The glassy wetness of the splotches was gone. The stains appeared dry again, mixed indelibly into the fabric of the shroud, looking like little more than marks of dirt or mildew.

He touched the fabric again. It was dry.

"Oh, please don't touch that, Detective Jefferson," Nick chided gently. "The oils in your fingers can break down the fabric."

Jefferson murmured an apology, looking down at his finger. His skin was still red with blood. It could only have come from one place. From the fabric of the shroud. He wiped his hands on the side of the crate, the blood oozing down the wooden slats.

"What's wrong?" McKenna asked.

"What?"

"Your hand, you get something on it?"

"Oh yeah, just a cobweb or something," Jefferson replied. "No big deal."

McKenna shook her head, looking uncomfortably around her. "This place looks like it'd be filled with them."

"Yeah," Jefferson answered awkwardly, the conversation quickly dying out.

McKenna turned back to Nick. "What about the rest of the scrolls inside? Can we see them?"

"Might as well." Nick sighed. "We've already pawed apart a thousand years of history."

Laying the scrolls across the top of the metal crate, Nick slowly unrolled them. The writing was beautiful, yet strange, the lettering carefully drawn in unwaveringly smooth lines of calligraphy. The scrolls were a faded yellow, dry to the touch, almost like the skin of a lizard.

"What does it say?" McKenna marveled, running her eyes over the print.

"These are all portions of Old Testament text, fragments from the book of Ezekiel," Nick scanned the writing quickly. "This isn't what we want."

He rerolled the ancient text, placing it back in the jar. Taking the second scroll, he undid the leather ties and spread it flat across the metal top.

"Hmm," he hummed as he looked down.

"What's this one?"

"This contains descriptions of the settlements, the agricultural estates, and the riverbeds in the areas between Jerusalem and the Dead Sea."

"Help us?" Jefferson asked.

"Not really," Nick replied, rerolling the scroll. "Unless you're looking for treasure."

"Treasure?"

"Well . . ." Nick smiled, shrugging. "Well, this set of scrolls, and another set known as the Copper Scrolls discovered near the city of Qumran, allude to the possibility of a cache of treasure somewhere in the wilderness near Jericho."

Nick looked at Jefferson for a moment, then winked. "Pure fantasy I'm sure." Pulling the third scroll out from the jar, he carefully spread it out. "Ah! Here we go . . ."

"This one it?"

"Yes, the scroll describes the battle between the warriors of Qumran and the evil force from the north, which may or may not be our friend in the crate there."

"Did the battle actually take place?"

"Oh yes!" Nick answered quickly. "It's almost an historical fact."

"How so?"

"They found graves, mass graves, outside the city of Qumran. These graves had been dug quickly, forced by the necessity of burying the postbattle dead before they began to rot in the Middle Eastern heat. So tunnels had been dug into the mountainside, and the openings marked with a skull."

"A skull?"

"Gravesites were considered unclean, bad luck, so to speak, so the mark of a skull was placed over them to warn people away."

"So what were inside the graves?"

"They found skeletons, hundreds of them crowded together still in full battle dress. What was strange was that many of the bones had been burned, a ritual associated with purification. But all of the skeletons they recovered seemed to have similar injuries."

Nick held up his hand, curling the front three fingers to mimic the shape of a claw. "They all had parallel gouges in them. The marks were repeated on the armor of the men as well, deep grooves cut into the leather, like something had simply cut them open."

Jefferson nodded, his mind spinning back to the same parallel marks they had found on all the bodies back in Boston. The deep gashes. The fragment left in the sternum of Kenneth Lyerman, which Dr. Wu had analyzed and said connected back to the skeleton in the crate sitting behind him. It was almost like there was something out there, following in the footsteps of this creature that had died almost a thousand years ago. And a battle that had been fought on the deserts outside Jerusalem seemed to be forming again, the forces of evil descending once more, and for some reason they had picked Boston.

Without a word, Nick rolled up the scroll. His movements suddenly seemed nervous, almost as if he knew what Jefferson was thinking. He ran a hand over the back of his head, then up where his fingers lingered on the bridge of his nose for a moment.

"Well, I think we've done enough digging for today, haven't we?" he said curtly, resealing the scroll and placing it back in the jar.

"Whoa, wait a minute," McKenna said. "What's going on here?"

"I'm not sure," Nick answered. "But it's none of my concern."

"What do you mean it's none of your concern?" Jefferson said, grabbing Nick's arm.

Nick shook his arm free, pulling it quickly across his chest, his face pinching in anger. He stepped quickly across the room, turning his back to Jefferson and McKenna.

"I can't help you," the Russian whispered.

"Why?" Jefferson asked.

Nick turned to him. "Those jars were sealed. They've been sealed for twenty years. Nobody except us has looked at those scrolls for all that time, yet the ink is still wet? Doesn't that seem strange?"

"Well, sure." Jefferson shrugged. "There's an explanation, I'm not sure—"

"Of course you're not sure," Nick interrupted. "Because there isn't a logical explanation. Logic doesn't exist here anymore. This is something I can no longer understand, and it scares me."

"It scares me, too, but you're the only one that seems to have any idea what these things are," Jefferson said. "I will not let you just walk away from this; too many people have died already."

Jefferson banged the table with the flat of his hand, turning away and pacing back toward the row of shelves. Overhead, a black object flitted across the ceiling, swooping down toward the white moth banging unceasingly against the lightbulb. There was a rushing sound and the moth disappeared, the bat shooting back down the corridors of the catacombs. Nick stared at Jefferson for a moment, running his dry tongue over even drier lips.

"I never told you what happened to the men, the knights of the Crusade, who carried this skeleton into China," Nick said finally.

Jefferson turned slowly back to face him, saying nothing.

"The men, it seems, set out to return to their homeland, but something happened to them on the trip back."

"What happened?"

"They went insane, hacking each other to death with their broadswords. Feasting on the flesh of the dead. Only one man survived to later recount the tale as he wandered, half-mad from the wilderness."

"Jesus," McKenna whispered. "Why?"

Nick shrugged. "No one knows for certain. But it is believed that, during their journey to the cave, they had been exposed for too long to the relic of the demon. They were no longer the same men who had left the city of Qumran. They had become assassins themselves, driven by the lust to kill, until so caught up in this frenzy, they turned on each other, until each man murdered the other."

Nick looked at Jefferson for a moment. "This is what has happened to those have who have sought this power of evil. Are you certain you wish to continue on your quest?"

"I don't have a choice."

Nick stared at him for a long moment, the little man suddenly seeming the biggest thing in the room. Overhead, the lightbulbs crackled and popped with electricity. Somewhere above them, a door closed.

"Well then, my knight-errant"—Nick gave a half smile—"it's time for you to see the manuscript I mentioned earlier, as well as something else I have for you."

They followed Nick deeper into the basement, past more dark hallways and the even darker gaping mouths of the catacombs. The walls turned from crumbling brick to a damp stone that glistened in the dim overhead lamps. Gone were the random stacks of forgotten museum pieces, the honeycomb openings of the catacombs remaining empty except for the occasional sight of bone or bit of decaying fabric Jefferson caught glimpses of in the darkness. They turned away from the central hallway, walking deeper into the maze of underground burial chambers. Jefferson imagined that they must have passed out from underneath the museum, walking perhaps fifty yards directly below the streets of St. Petersburg.

"These are the oldest parts of the catacombs, constructed sometime in the twelfth century," Nick said. "Time here is measured in centuries, not years."

Nick led them farther onward. In front of them stretched a dark corridor, reminding Jefferson of the massacre on Blade Island.

They walked farther, their flashlights casting small spheres of wavering light around them. The path was smooth stone, the walls growing more narrow and rough, the builders apparently finding it more difficult to carve the solid stone. The dull beating in Jefferson's head had slowed, so that something pulsed every minute or so, like a lingering heartbeat slowly dying. He was trying to forget what he'd felt at his first sight of the skeleton when Nick stopped with no heel click, holding his torch down toward his waist.

Nick was standing in front of a large sarcophagus set in the middle of the floor.

"What is this?" Jefferson asked.

"The coffin of Sir Gerard de Ridefort. A knight of the Crusades."

The lid was pushed slightly to the side, decorated with a cross carved directly into the stone. The stone was covered in a film of ash-colored dust and sticky cobwebs. Jefferson held his breath, waiting for a reaction similar to the one he had gotten from the skeleton, but his mind remained clear. He felt nothing from this half-open coffin, none of the rushing taste of decomposition that had filled his mouth before. Even the dull pounding in his head seemed to have died out entirely.

" 'Lord God, our war is over. We are nothing but dead men—and the Kingdom has come to an end,' " Nick quoted softly, looking down at the coffin. "Said by the Count of Tripoli following the Battle of Hattin."

"Who was he?" McKenna asked, nodding at the coffin.

"He was a Knight Templar, a Warrior Monk, the only survivor of the Battle of the Horns of Hattin in the twelfth century."

The casket lay silent, the stone top pushed slightly off to the side, a small crack between the top and the side. McKenna squatted, her jeans pulling tight across the tops of her legs. She surveyed the top of the lid, lowering her head so that the dust refracted in the light from the torches.

"Someone has been here recently," she said. "Within the last few days. The dust layers are different around the edges of the stone."

Jefferson glanced over at Nick, who paused for a moment before nodding. "As soon as Dr. Wu called me and reported a few of the details on your investigation, I came down to assure myself that it was still here."

"That *what* was still here? Who was he?"

Nick looked at Jefferson for a moment. The flashlights created pools of shadows on his face; deep black shimmering ones beneath his eyes, below his hairline and along the base of his neck. The shadows moved in perfect unison with Nick, like dark leeches hanging from his body.

"Sir Gerard and his fellow knights were crossing the desert near the Sea of Galilee in 1187. They carried with them a relic of the True Cross, the Cross on which Jesus was crucified. During their travels, the knights were attacked and defeated by the Moslem army led by Salah ad-Din Yussuf ibn Ayub, commander of the Syrian army," Nick said, pausing for a moment, the shadowy leeches pausing with him. "The battle was waged in the desert for three days, and each night something came up from the sand, stealing away the dead of the day's battle."

"What was it?" McKenna asked.

"The bodies were mutilated by the claws of the beast—three parallel cuts. That story was written down by Sir Gerard and kept with him. He was twenty years old at the time. It was Sir Gerard who realized that the true evil was not the army of the Syrians, but whatever dark force had come during the night and stolen away their dead. Sir Gerard saw the face of that evil and came to believe it was the warrior Sidina, the man whose reputation had spread throughout those lands of trouble.

"Sidina was part of the assassins, a secret society of Muslims that had been founded in Persia and headed by Shaykh-al-Jabal. By the close of the eleventh century, these assassins had established a series of footholds in northwestern Syria, where they terrorized the knights of the Crusades over a period of many years. It was Shaykh-al-Jabal whom the Crusaders knew as 'old man of the mountain,' but it was Sidina Ali who was known as the 'perfect warrior.' Even as a young knight, Sir Gerard would have been familiar with the legend of Sidina, of the great many knights who had fallen to him and his three companions. And after the desert and the Battle of Hattin, he dedicated his life to finding and slaying Sidina and his three followers.

"Forty-five years later, Sir Gerard returned to the lands of the Crusades, tracking down Sidina across the deserts of Syria and into Persia. By that time, the rulers of Persia had become wary of Sidina's ferocity and ruthlessness, and, fearing that Sidina might seek to overthrow them, they betrayed their most powerful warrior to Sir Gerard and his Knights Templar.

"Sir Gerard attacked Sidina's palace and gardens in 1232, where, at the age of sixty-five, he succeeded in defeating Sidina, slaying him and his three closest followers. As I mentioned before, Gerard believed that Sidina was truly evil. A demon on Earth. So he selected his bravest warriors to carry the remains of Sidina and the three fallen assassins to the separate corners of the world. Sir Gerard bore the remains of one of these assassins himself, traveling with five other knights, but returning alone almost eight years later at the age of seventy-three, the only one to have survived the trip."

Bending down, Nick pushed aside the heavy stone table covering the sarcophagus, the two stones scraping loudly against each other. Underneath was a man's skeleton, dried and dusty, but still wearing a sheet-metal breastplate adorned with the Red Cross of the Crusades. Over the breastplate was a helmet with a thick nosepiece and rounded arches, loosely framing a vacant-eyed skull.

"What you saw in the crate," Nick began again, "is the one skeleton that is known to have been recovered. If the story is true, there are three others, each located in some far corner of the Earth. When this particular find was unearthed in China back in the thirties, there was a resurgence of interest in demonology. One particular line of study evolved to try to track down, according to the legend, where the other three skeletons would have been taken.

"The site of the successful attack on Sidina and his companions was believed to have been just west of the present-day city of Esfahan, the ancient capital of Persia. With that as a starting point, scholars tracked the movements of the knights of the Crusades, following one group east all the way to southern Asia. A second group traveled west and north, ending somewhere near the Adriatic, in Eastern Europe, while the third moved due west by ship, some say reaching as far as the American coast."

"The American coast? Wouldn't that be too far for the time period?" Jefferson asked. "They could never have crossed the Atlantic."

"Maybe. But, when Sir Gerard returned alone from his voyage, half-insane from thirst and hunger, among the objects he carried with him was a single traveling basket. It was ornamented with red-and-green-painted decorations representing hearts, vines, and faces. The same style of ornamentation was later found by European explorers as belonging to the Mohegan-Pequot peoples of eastern New England. Sir Gerard never spoke of his voyage, although there are vague references in his manuscripts, but perhaps the basket indicates he was successful in his journey, reaching the New World hundreds of years before any other Europeans," Nick said, then looking down into the sarcophagus. "And this is where he lies now."

Jefferson looked again at the knight's remains. Resting to the side of Sir Gerard's breastplate was a large leather-bound book. Nick reached down, pulling the book out of the sarcophagus and gently dusting off its surface with the flat of his hand.

"This is a collection of his manuscripts, what I indicated before I wanted to show you," Nick said. "They record his encounters with the demons. They were translated in 1910 by a professor of history at Oxford, then returned to Sir Gerard. If you are truly dealing with a demon, then you will need the instructions written in this book.

"And, in case it is of any interest to you, there are hints in some of the later manuscripts that he may have buried a copy of the manuscript wherever he buried the body he had taken, in the hope that if the demon ever managed to come back, people would know what they were up against."

Nick held the book out to Jefferson. The shadowy leeches came to rest on the Russian's face, hanging in dark sacks from every crevice of his face. Jefferson reached for the book, but Nick pulled it back and instead grabbed Jefferson's hand in his own. The man had moved quickly, his hand flashing out so that Jefferson hadn't had time to respond. Nick gripped Jefferson for a moment, his fingers pressing with a strength that Jefferson wouldn't have thought possible.

"Do you remember when I asked you before if you were religious?" Nick asked.

"Yes . . ." Jefferson replied slowly, his hand still held tightly in the Russian's.

"Do you have faith, Detective Jefferson?"

Jefferson blinked, surprised at the question. "Faith? Well, now I don't know. I never solved a case on faith."

"Without faith, you will fail."

Nick dropped Jefferson's hand and held out the book. Jefferson looked at the manuscripts, yellow light wavering over the leather-bound cover, before slowly, Jefferson reached out his hand and took it from him.

Jefferson and McKenna left the museum, passing a group of women filing in through the wide doors of the onion-domed church on the corner of the street. He remem-

bered church, the sermons, the old women, smelling of heavy perfume and baby powder, fanning themselves endlessly during the hot summer afternoons, but he didn't
remember his faith. His job left no room for faith. He couldn't trust people on the
street. Being a policeman had made him cynical; and this cynicism had burned out
whatever faith he might have had left from childhood.

Jefferson didn't know if he had it in him any longer to believe.

McKenna was walking quietly beside him, her hair catching in the slight breeze
coming in from across the square, rippling the waters of the canal. They turned off the
main road, stepping onto a wide cobblestone sidewalk that ran parallel to the canal.
The streetlights overhead had already begun to turn on as evening advanced in slow
degrees. A row of trees ran along the sidewalk on their right side, separating them from
the lazy street that seemed to serve more bicycles than automobiles.

Couples strolled along the canal with them, most locking arms, or resting heads on
each other's shoulders, talking and laughing quietly, caught up in each other's worlds.
And they were worlds very different from disemboweled victims and mythical
demons. Jefferson and McKenna walked slowly, feeling the uneven cobblestones
beneath their feet, glancing occasionally out across the water.

They stopped and bought raspberry ice cream from a street vendor, then walked
on, the cold of the ice cream permeating Jefferson's fingers through the thin cardboard
of the bowl.

"So how do you like Russia?" Jefferson asked as they walked, both spooning the
ice cream with the little paddles.

"I think it's beautiful," McKenna answered.

Jefferson nodded, turning his head to catch a brief gust of wind as it filtered
through the wide green leaves of the tree along the walkway. In St. Petersburg, the
wind carried with it a scent of the earth, the smell of the lazy water in the canals. In
Boston, it carried the exhaust of buses and cars, the sounds of subways, the air laden
heavily with the waste of the city. St. Petersburg breezes evoked leaves, fresh and
green, which rustled in the wind, but Boston's winds lifted only the city's refuse, plastic shopping bags and paper cups whirling about in circles overhead. St. Petersburg
seemed fresher, more innocent; but maybe Jefferson was just being cynical. Homicides
had a way of corrupting the scenery.

They turned from the old walkway, moving across a bridge that seemed to arc just
above the surface of the water of the canal. The bridge was made of solid stone, with
cast-iron railings that curled up to form the decorative shapes of leaves at either end.
Waves underneath made light splashing noise as they struck against the stone supports.
Couples were standing on the bridge, elbows against the railings as they looked out
toward the vanishing sun.

"This is wonderful here," McKenna whispered, running her hand over the green
railing.

"Makes you forget Boston. A little."

"A little. Some things you can't forget though."

"I know. It's usually the bad stuff, too. The things you wish you could."

Jefferson placed his hand on his chest, the quarter-shaped scars that marked the smooth flesh.

"Not always," McKenna said. "But yeah, sometimes it is. You take the good with the bad."

"Demons and angels."

"Yes, I guess," McKenna said slowly, then paused, thinking for a moment. "I do believe there are demons, just as I believe there are angels. There are too many stories, too many similarities, throughout the world for them not to be true."

"Every culture has its demons."

"They do, and while the stories are all slightly different, the essential character remains the same. They can't simply be random, there must be something to them."

"I don't have much faith left," Jefferson said. "So if it is true, then it's more than I can handle."

McKenna took his hand and squeezed. They stopped just before one of the green lampposts that stood up from the bridge. Standing side by side, their shoulders touching, they leaned out across the water, eating the last of their ice cream. Her skin felt warm, even through the layers of clothing. Or maybe Jefferson was just imagining it. Sometimes the mind makes you feel something you don't really feel.

They looked across the canal, at the row of houses, dark in the thickening dusk, and at one distant window, its glass blazing with light as the sun's last reddish gleam struck it for a moment. Her shoulder was pressed against his and she laughed at something he said. He turned toward her, his eyes soaking up her face, and she returned his gaze calmly, brushing a loose piece of hair away from her face.

They arrived home the next day, following two six-hour flights, one to London and the next to Boston. Jefferson spent the afternoon catching Brogan up on what they'd learned in Russia, then crashed early, trying to get his body back to Boston time. The next morning, he and Brogan took a ride over to McKenna's. While Brogan tried to find a parking space on the Boston streets, something that hasn't been readily available since 1986, Jefferson took the stairs up to McKenna's apartment.

"Hi," McKenna said, opening the door to her apartment. "Long time, stranger."

"Did you miss me?"

"I was having withdrawal symptoms already."

"It's been a day since you saw me last, it's understandable."

"Don't let it go to your head." McKenna smiled. "Do you want to come in?" she asked, opening the door slightly.

Jefferson nodded, smelling her perfume as he stepped past her. It was nice, familiar. Her apartment was warm and smelled pleasantly of spice. The lights had been turned down, with only the soft yellow glow of a lamp sitting on a small table across the room. Three candles had been lit in a curving black metal frame that stood on a sandalwood coffee table. A sofa sat against the wall, underneath two large windows.

Art hung from the walls. There was a painting of the park at dusk, and a deep blue impression of the ocean. A large white dog slept on the floor. Its body was strung out lengthwise on the red Oriental carpet. The dog looked up at him through the tufts of hair covering its eyes, but did not move.

From behind him he heard the door close and McKenna move toward him.

"You want something to drink? Tea?" she asked.

"Sure . . . thanks."

"Why don't you sit down on the sofa and I'll bring it out." McKenna pointed into the room. "Don't mind him," she said, indicating the dog. "He's friendly. He's too old to be mean anyway."

Jefferson sat heavily on the sofa, stretching his legs out in front of him. McKenna disappeared into another room. He saw a light go on, reflected against the ceiling, and heard the sound of dishes being moved and a cabinet door opening and closing.

"How's Brogan?" McKenna called out from the kitchen.

"He's fine. You don't want to try and kill that guy. Now he's annoyed. I feel sorry for this demon, whatever it is. He's on his way up; he was just parking the car."

There was a knock on the door, and Brogan stepped quietly into the apartment, his big frame pulled tightly together as he tiptoed.

"Hey, Brogan," McKenna called from the kitchen. "Come on in. Don't worry, this isn't the Boston Public."

Brogan smiled, relaxing a little, but taking his shoes off at the door, walking across the Oriental hallway carpet in his socks.

"Parking's a bitch," he said to Jefferson.

"As always."

Brogan was always surprised when it was difficult to find a parking space. It was like time had stopped for him in 1986, which might also be the reason he refused to accept that Springsteen wasn't still topping the charts. Jefferson looked at him, waiting patiently for Brogan's next bit of wisdom, which was always related after finding parking.

"The Chinese have it right, better to ride a bicycle."

Yes indeed. Jefferson turned, reached down and scratched the dog on the side of his body. The dog turned slightly and rolled closer to Jefferson, his tail beginning to move almost imperceptibly. Jefferson leaned over and spoke softly into the old dog's ear. First rule of winning over a woman, make friends with her pets. Feed the fish, scratch the cat under the chin, and pet the dog.

"I'm making some cups of tea," McKenna said from the kitchen. "Do you want one?"

"Do you have hot chocolate?"

"I think so."

"I'll take that."

Brogan was the only man Jefferson knew that could make the words *hot chocolate* sound like he was saying, "double shot of whiskey." Brogan looked around the living room, the small leather sofa, the two wicker chairs. "S'pose you'd want to sit next to McKenna."

"Would be nice."

Brogan sighed, squeezing himself into one of the wicker chairs. The chair creaked under his weight, the wicker frame probably wishing it had been used to make a basket instead of a chair.

"Never get mixed up with a partner and his girlfriend," Brogan said.

There was a noise, and they both looked up. McKenna stood in the doorway holding three mugs on a platter. She passed out the mugs, then sat on the sofa next to Jefferson. The liquid was steaming, Jefferson could feel its warmth through the cup. In the dim light the tea was dark. He took a sip and rolled the spicy flavor in his mouth. He looked up at one of the paintings on the wall. Staring at it, examining it closely. It was a park in the winter. A woman and a small girl were tossing out seeds to a small cluster of birds. Looked like the Boston Common, circa 1910. Brogan was staring at the painting, too, probably trying to figure out a time before automatic handguns and the Boss.

"I've looked over Sir Gerard's manuscripts," McKenna said, pulling their attention away from the picture.

Jefferson nodded, remembering the book that Nick had given them in the catacomb. McKenna placed her cup of tea on the windowsill, where the steaming vapors were highlighted against the outside lights. With her legs crossed, the slit of her dress rose to just above her knee, showing the smooth skin of her leg.

"You're staring," McKenna said.

"Sorry."

"Don't stare," McKenna said. "All my life, people have stared at me. Don't be typical like that."

Jefferson shook his head. "I'm sorry."

"Apology accepted."

Brogan stared down into his mug of hot chocolate, a half smile on his face like a little boy.

"And no smirking either from the peanut gallery," McKenna joked.

"Sorry."

"How you feeling? Jefferson told me what happened to you up on the roof."

Brogan shrugged. "Hey, shit happens." In the normal world, "shit happens" usually referred to losing a few bucks on the blackjack table. In Brogan's world, "shit happens" referred to anything from stab wounds to drive-by shootings.

McKenna nodded, then took the ancient book from the coffee table and placed the bound manuscripts on her lap, slowly turning the pages. The book was beautifully illustrated, with long looping handwriting, each line decorated with layers of gilded drawings. In the margin were sheets of paper, the translations inscribed in English.

"I've been looking at this since we got back," she said.

"What'd you find out?" Brogan asked.

"Enough to scare me," McKenna replied, looking down at the manuscripts.

Jefferson focused on the colorful pages of the manuscript, keeping his eyes away from the edge of her bare knee. The book was five or six inches thick, each page waxen-looking, shining in the overhead lights of the room.

"As Nick mentioned, Sir Gerard was one of the Knights Templar, a monastic military order formed at the end of the First Crusade. Having all taken monastic vows, the Knights Templar were true Warrior Monks, dedicated to spreading the Word of God throughout the known world. This dedication took them to the lands of Persia and Syria during the Crusades, where they fought alongside Richard the Lionhearted.

"In 1187, while crossing the desert near Tiberius, along the Sea of Galilee, the Knights Templar were besieged by the army of Salah ad-Din Yussuf ibn Ayub. Trapped and forced to fight in the desert, Sir Gerard writes of how the Knights Templar quickly began to weaken from lack of water. On the second night of the battle, four concealed ones, or four dark ones, named Sidina and his followers, arrived under cover of night and attacked them. The only warning they had was the whinnying of the horses, before these four warriors were in their camp.

"That first night, they killed many knights before disappearing into the darkness. Then, on the third night, they attacked again. Already weakened from combat during the day with Salah ad-Din's men, the knights could barely muster the strength to defend themselves against the four, and only by daybreak did they realize the extent of the massacre. Come the dawn, Sir Gerard describes finding men dead and murdered in such a way as no man could have done."

She ran her finger over one of the lines, reading aloud from Sir Gerard's manuscript,

" 'And come break of dawn, we came across thirty dead knights from Briar's Notch. Their bodies were flayed of skin in such a manner as made our sturdiest man feel faint of heart. Their backs had the mark of the demon, the three gouges struck by this devil of the ancient land.' "

"So he thought it was a demon?" Jefferson asked.

"He believed it was this warrior, Sidina, and it was him that was possessed by a demon and he'd given the demon a name."

"What name?"

"Jinn. He'd called the demon a Jinn."

"Why did he think that?"

"Well, Sir Gerard was familiar with Sidina and the legend of the demon from stories passed down among the Templars. Sidina had attacked the Templars for years, in each of their Crusades into the Holy Land, making his name infamous among the Warrior Monks. These attacks had begun during the First Crusade in 1096, yet Sir Gerard swore that it was Sidina who again appeared in the desert at the Battle of Hattin in 1187, more than ninety years later. Either Sir Gerard was mistaken in his belief, which is unlikely given that Sidina would have been so well known to him and his men, or Sidina has some miraculous power that could account for his longevity.

"Now the name Sidina goes back even farther, first appearing during the time of the great Islamic schism in 632, almost five hundred years prior to the First Crusade. This schism arose following the unexpected passing of the prophet Muhammad and centered around the violent dispute over leadership after his death. Two opposing groups, the Shi'ites and the Sunnis, emerged to contest the future of Islam. At the time, Sidina was a general in the army of the *khalifatu r-rasûl*, or caliph in English.

"During the violence that erupted in the years following the schism, Sidina switched sides many times between the Sunnis and the Shi'ites, apparently taking advantage of this time of confusion to kill without penalty under the cover of war. So violent was Sidina during this time that he became known as the perfect warrior, often turning on the forces of his own army, slaughtering his own men blindly before his rage could be cooled."

"Until years later Gerard defeated him?"

"That's right. After Sidina and his companions were slain, Sir Gerard writes that their corpses were not those of men, but of men deformed by evil. The skin melted away, revealing an inside so grossly deformed as almost not to be human, of a length taller than their tallest warrior, with talons for feet and teeth like a lion. It was these deformed creatures that Sir Gerard and his men carried with them to the corners of the Earth."

"Why was the body deformed?" Jefferson asked, remembering the appearance of the skeleton in Russia.

"Sir Gerard believed it was showing the true form of the Jinn that had inhabited Sidina and his closest warriors for so many years. Just beneath their human exterior were these terrible creatures that had produced so much pain and suffering. These demon could assume human form in three ways. One was through permanent possession, as they did with Sidina and his companions. They could also possess someone of a weak mind or spirit, but this possession was only temporary."

"What do you mean someone of a weak mind?"

"Someone who was mentally unbalanced, who didn't have a strong grasp on reality."

"OK, and the third?"

"Well, it was thought that after any of them had physical contact with a human, any other Jinn could, for a short time, take the form of the human with whom the contact had been initiated."

Jefferson looked down for a moment, thinking, then snapped his finger, "Oh man . . ."

"What?" Brogan asked.

"The homeless guy that was found by the cemetery, where we found Reggie's body. Brogan, you remember what you told me, that the guy had been in and out of mental institutions?"

"Yeah? He was nuts, so?"

"Well that sounds like exactly the kind of person the demon would be able to possess. Someone weak of mind. The guy was crazy; therefore, he was an easy mark."

"So you think the Jinn possessed him temporarily and had him hunt Reggie?"

"Makes sense. I don't believe in coincidence. What was he doing dead just around the block from the mortuary in which Reggie killed himself to escape something?"

310

"I don't know what the hell makes sense anymore. Ask me a month ago if temporary possession made sense, and I'd have said you were ready for the loony bin yourself."

"And Dr. Wu, when Dr. Wu went to check on this guy who we thought was dead, the guy grabs Wu, cuts him."

"That's right," McKenna said.

"So that would explain how the Jinn could make itself appear as Wu. Wu's housekeeper swears she saw someone looking exactly like Wu at the house, and when I called, the voice was the same as well, same tone, everything. It must have been from that physical contact. If the Jinn had possessed that dead homeless man, then it would have had physical contact with Dr. Wu when it grabbed his wrist. Just like Wu said with the Lyerman case—the mixing of genetic information with that shard I pulled from Lyerman's sternum," Jefferson said.

"If that's true, then we have to figure who else the demon made contact with. Because it could appear as anyone, right?"

"And not just the one Jinn, any of the other three," McKenna reminded him. "This is told in the ancient parable of the merchant Heiblus, whose wife was murdered by a madman possessed by the spirit of a Jinn. The merchant is heartbroken and buries her, but one night his wife appears to him, walking in the desert. Thinking she has come back to life, Heiblus follows his wife for days, deeper and deeper into the desert, until finally overcome by heat and thirst, he is unable to continue. As he reaches for her, her appearance changes to reveal herself to be a second Jinn, even more horrible in appearance than the first. This second Jinn then torments the dying merchant for his blind foolishness."

"I haven't heard that parable before," Jefferson said.

"Well, the Jinn are more known for their role in the *Arabian Nights* and the story of Aladdin."

"Oh yeah," Brogan piped up suddenly. "Sure I heard this one. That kid that finds the lamp in the cave and rubs it and the genie comes out. Robin Williams, right? I saw the Disney cartoon."

"Right. But the original tale is based on ancient Arab oral traditions and on the belief that Jinn, or genies, actually existed. In the story, the genie freed from his lamp by Aladdin grants Aladdin a series of wishes, which leads to Aladdin's fame and fortune and final marriage to the beautiful princess. In the more traditional Arab version of the story, however, while these demons have the ability to grant wishes, these wishes always carry with them a very high price.

"These Jinn have tempted men for thousands of years, appearing in various guises throughout history and existing in all religions. In India, they are mentioned in the text known as the *Dhammapada*: Just as milk does not curdle in an instant, the consequences of the Jinns' temptations are not immediate. They will linger in the minds of the evildoers, and follow them from this life to the next, slowly burning them—like the fire burning under the ashes."

"So it's like the old saying of selling your soul to the devil?" Jefferson asked. "The

Jinn tempt you by promising to fulfill your wishes, but you end up beholden to them. You get the worst end of the deal."

"Exactly," McKenna said. "Now Sir Gerard believed that Sidina and his three companions had been possessed by Jinn. When Sidina and the three assassins were killed, the Jinn were returned to their original spirit forms. The bond of possession works both ways, however, so even in spirit form, the Jinn were forced to stay close by the remains of Sidina and his followers, even at the far corners of the Earth, only able to wander farther afield when one of them had obtained permission to occupy its reincarnate's body."

"So no matter where Sir Gerard and his men carried Sidina's body," Jefferson said, "that Jinn would have to follow?"

"That's right."

"And what happened in Qumran," Jefferson said, snapping his fingers. "That must have been what happened out on Fort Blade in the early 1690s!"

"What do you mean?"

"Well, according to Older, the first colonists in the area were plagued by attacks that came at night. Older described the colonists finding many who had been murdered during the night. They must have inadvertently settled an area where Sir Gerard and his knights had left the remains of one of Sidina's assassins. If what you said is true, about the spirit of the Jinn being forced to follow the remains of the deceased warrior, then the colonists would have also settled in an area where the spirit of a Jinn was present. If these spirits were strong enough to attack the city of Qumran in A.D. 17, then one of them, presumably, would have been strong enough to attack the small settlement of the first colonies. Older wrote that eventually the attacks stopped. Maybe that was because the colonists found the remains of Sidina's companion and buried it deep enough on Blade Island that this demon spirit was trapped below the island somewhere."

"That makes sense," McKenna agreed. "And in that spirit form, a Jinn is in a much weakened state. But, Sir Gerard believed that the souls of Sidina and his three warriors were destined to be reincarnated, again and again. Should the spirit of the Jinn encounter the appropriate reincarnate, it would attempt to regain possession of that body. If this occurs, then the four Jinn could return to Earth, wreaking devastation and bringing the beginning of an Armageddon.

"The Jinn know this, so they wait for chance or fate to bring one of the reincarnates to the appropriate Jinn, and when that occurs, the Jinn will try to take possession and return to Earth."

"How can they take possession?"

"Only with the agreement of the reincarnate. An agreement to forsake the world of the living in pursuit of death. A Jinn will offer anything the person desires, in return for allowing that Jinn to possess the body. One Jinn cannot return alone, however. The Jinn must find and possess not only Sidina's reincarnate, but all three of Sidina's followers as well. Sir Gerard writes that in each successive generation, Sidina and his three followers will reappear. They will have no memory of who they were in previous lives, only remembering the events of their current lives. Should a Jinn possess one of these former warriors, the other Jinn must find the other reincarnates and gain permission to be possessed. Apparently there are some rather complicated permutations on how this occurs, but Sir Gerard was not very specific. I suppose he proably didn't know all the 'rules.' "

"And these things were spread to the four corners of the globe by Sir Gerard," Jefferson said.

"That's a lot of trouble," Brogan, who had been listening thoughtfully to Jefferson and McKenna's discussion of the Jinn, said. "Round here they just take them up to New Hampshire some place. Drop 'em in a quarry."

"These knights believed that the remains of Sidina and his followers were so adulterated by evil that they had to be buried as far from civilization as possible. We saw one of these skeletons," McKenna added. "Pretty scary stuff."

"Really? Like Mick Jagger scary?"

Jefferson nodded. "Steven Tyler scary."

Brogan concurred. "That's pretty bad."

"Even in death, the knights so feared Sidina," McKenna said, "that they dispatched one hundred men to guard Sidina's tomb."

"So, let me get this," Jefferson said. "We had one of these skeletons, the deformed remains of Sidina's man that we saw in Russia."

"That's right."

"Another one of the skeletons we're pretty sure was buried out on Blade Island."

Brogan shifted in his chair, the reeds screaming in protest. "I'd like to see that fucking thing again."

"Another one was on Blade, yes," McKenna said.

"Then we have a third one, supposedly Sidina himself, buried on Bougainville Island?"

McKenna nodded. "I've read that particular passage in the manuscript several times over. If you estimate their final location based upon how far they traveled, then that would put them roughly in the area of Bougainville."

"And a fourth in Zvornik," McKenna said flatly.

The room went quiet for a moment, the word "Zvornik" hanging over them.

"But if Sidina and whoever else are all dead," Brogan said finally, "then what the hell is doing the killing, the dispossessed spirit of one of the demons?"

"Possibly, yes," McKenna replied.

The world that Jefferson had known seemed to be going crazy. Demons wandering the Earth, Brogan using long words like "dispossessed"—a week ago Jefferson wouldn't have thought it possible.

"So this spirit, or whatever it is," Jefferson said, "was trapped on Bougainville Island?"

"That would make sense," McKenna replied. "So until someone brings it off the island, it wouldn't be able to leave. These demons are bound by the same physical limitations as humans."

"Meaning what?" Brogan asked.

"Meaning that they can't enter a room without opening the door. These things can't pass through walls or keyholes. They're not like ghosts. And they generally have to stay near the remains of whoever they had possessed in life. That's their prison. Like being inside the lamp in the *Arabian Nights*. Only when one of them possesses one of the reincarnates are the others free to wander in search of their own reincarnates."

"Shit, this is deep," Brogan said. "You got a beer?"

"In the fridge, bottom shelf," McKenna said.

Brogan lifted himself from the chair, stretched for a moment, his neck cracking audibly in the quiet apartment. He twisted his body slowly, the gouges in his chest stiffening him up.

"You two?" Brogan said, pointing his thick finger at McKenna and Jefferson. "Couple brews?"

"Not me," McKenna said. "It's like eleven in the morning."

"It's like mother's milk to me," Brogan said. "Nothing starts a morning better."

Brogan lumbered into the kitchen, where Jefferson heard him opening the refrigerator. McKenna leaned in toward Jefferson, brushing her hair back from her face.

"I think the manuscripts are incomplete," McKenna said.

"What do you mean?"

"I think there should be more pages. More details."

"Like what?"

"Earlier portions of the manuscript allude to a means of killing the demons, but then the section just ends. Too abruptly," McKenna said.

"Too abruptly, as in the translation was never finished, or too abruptly as in someone stole the rest of it."

"I'm not sure, but there's more to think about. Why do you think the demon from the *Galla* is going around killing people in Boston? I think the answer is that it's looking for the reincarnation of Sidina so it can permanently possess a human body."

"The reincarnated soul of Sidina?"

McKenna shrugged. "I think so. The last section is missing, so I can't say for sure. But from the tone of it, I'd say that this demon is looking for a very specific person. This thing isn't just killing."

"What do you think it's doing then?"

"I think it's hunting."

And using Boston as its hunting ground. If that was true, then there was someone in the Boston area the demon was seeking. Someone it hadn't found yet. If they found whoever it was first, then they could wait for the demon to come to them. Jefferson's grandfather used to tell him, you never chase a bear into the woods. You sit and wait for it to come to you.

"What'd I miss?" Brogan said, standing in the doorway, a green Rolling Rock in his hand.

"Let's take a ride," Jefferson said.

Brogan's face fell slightly. "But I just found this killer parking spot. On the same block and everything."

"Crime fighting awaits."

Brogan sighed the sigh of the unjustly persecuted. "All right partner, I'll get the car, meet you out front. I'm beginning to feel like I'm *Driving Miss Daisy*."

"Bring the car around, Jeeves."

Brogan shook his head, then, still holding the beer, turned, and Jefferson heard the apartment door open then shut, the big man's footsteps quickly fading off down the hall.

"Be careful, Jefferson."

"As always, milady."

"No, I'm serious. Be careful. Without the last chapters of the manuscript, we don't know how to kill the demon. And we don't even know what it's looking for. All we know is what it can do, and that is some evil shit, Jefferson."

"I know, I've seen it."

"It scares me."

It scares me, too, Jefferson thought, but he said nothing.

"If you see this thing, I want you to run. Until we know how it can be stopped. Don't do the male ego thing. This isn't a bar fight."

"I was never much for bar fighting anyway."

McKenna reached for Jefferson, stroking the back of his neck for a moment. "I just started to kinda like you. I don't want to see you hurt or—"

The sentence hung in the air, neither of them needing to complete it with "or killed."

McKenna took her cup of tea from the windowsill. Raising the cup to her lips, she took a sip, paused, and looked at him for a moment.

"Promise me you'll be careful."

"I promise," Jefferson said. "I'll be careful."

Jefferson looked down at the carpet for a moment before slowly turning his head toward her. The dog on the carpet stretched his legs and yawned, before settling back to sleep. In the distance, out the open window, Jefferson could hear a siren, softly fading away. McKenna's hair had fallen around her shoulders as she leaned forward. He put his tea on the window ledge, leaned toward her, and touched her lips with his. Her mouth was warm, and he tasted the orange spice of the tea.

There was the sound of a horn honking on the street below, long and insistent. Brogan, always the romantic.

"I have to go," Jefferson said.

"I know you do," McKenna replied.

She waited for him to turn and leave, then called out, "Run, Jefferson. If you see it. Don't think, just run."

Run. *If this thing can take anyone's appearance,* Jefferson thought, *the problem isn't whether or not to run, but knowing who to run from.*

Brogan sat in the large brown Crown Vic, idling on the street corner and listening to Steve Miller on the radio. The Crown Vic was the tank of the automobile world, and Brogan kept his spotless. The floor and backseat were perfectly vacuumed, the lines of the steam cleaner visible on the upholstery, like plow marks on the soil. Brogan was unwrapping a piece of gum, slowly putting it into his mouth and placing the wrapper inside a plastic bag he kept under the front seat to hold trash.

"Knock your shoes," Brogan said, as Jefferson opened the door.

"What?"

"You know the rules."

Brogan's car had more rules than most Gentlemen's Clubs. No smoking, no eating, no coats, shirts, or pants with exposed sharp buckles or edges that could tear the fabric, and always knock your shoes to remove any loose dirt before entering. He made exceptions to the rules for himself, but only for chewing gum and drinking out of a resealable glass container, both of which he was doing now. His car was known around the neighborhood, every night sitting under its gray cover. Nobody so much as kicked the tires, forget about stealing it. Kids wouldn't even play stickball on the street nearby, lest the rubber tennis ball bounce off the car's hood.

"Where to, Pilgrim?" Brogan asked, putting part of the gum in his mouth, leaving the rest dangling above his chin.

"John Wayne?"

"Well, I reckon so."

Brogan was in one of his John Wayne moods, trying to squeeze as many John Wayne movie lines into his sentences as possible. Except he didn't remember any of the lines perfectly, so each one came out slightly modified, and Jefferson didn't remember any old John Wayne movies where the Duke had a Boston accent.

"Let's take it back to Sinatra's place."

"The lawyer's . . ." Brogan struggled for a moment to add a John Waynism, then added. "Pilgrim?"

"Yeah. What did Vincent learn about how Sinatra spent his spare time?"

"Besides getting off psychos and rapists."

"Besides that."

"He said that he collected old art or something. Maybe coins, I don't remember, why?"

"Let's say McKenna is right, that this demon kills for a reason."

"Yeah?"

"So what reason did it have for killing Sinatra?"

"Because Saint's crew, breaking into the place, was outta Blade. That was the connection. Same as that guy in the graveyard that bought it."

"The guy in the graveyard, he was from Blade. He'd been down in the pit. But nobody from Saint's crew had actually been down there, except for Saint."

"So?" Brogan asked, the stick of gum still hanging limply from his mouth. Brogan chewed gum like a boa constrictor eating a rat, swallowing it bit by bit. He pulled the gum another centimeter into his mouth. The ritual was odd, making everyone who saw it for the first time stare with open amazement, sometimes even asking about it. Sometimes. Mainly little kids who hadn't learned all the tricks of self-preservation.

"So . . ." Jefferson answered. "There was no reason to kill all of Saint's crew and all of Sinatra's family. Besides, according to Saint, that thing was already in the apartment when they got there. If Saint was its target, how would the demon know ahead of time that they were planning on breaking into Sinatra's place, so that it would be there before they even arrived?"

Brogan thought for a moment. "That's true. If it wanted to whack Saint and his whole fucking crew, why would it wait to do it at Sinatra's place. It could do it anytime it wanted. McKenna didn't mention nothing about this thing being a fucking psychic, knowing ahead of time where Saint and his crew were gonna be."

They were driving down Newbury Street, away from the Common and toward Massachusetts Avenue. Expensive shops glittered marble and glass under the rising sun. Women in furs leading small dogs on thin leashes walked up and down the sidewalk. Brogan's Crown Vic stuck out on a street lined with BMWs, Mercedes, and the occasional Lexus.

"We never considered that the demon might have been at Sinatra's place, just to kill Sinatra," Jefferson said.

"It never seemed like a possibility. Sinatra was a lawyer; sure, that's reason enough for most people to want to kill him, but he didn't seem like he had anything to do with the rest of the murders."

In another moment of creative epiphany, Brogan had developed what he called the "beating the scratch ticket" theory to homicide investigation. Ninety percent of homicides happen for a reason or have some explanation for them. Money, women, drugs, there were a handful of elemental pursuits that drove most homicide investigations. But there was a small percentage of homicides that appeared to occur randomly. With these killings, time and location aligned at just the right moment. An hour before or an hour after, the victim would have made it. A half city block away, he or she would have made it. They had just been in the wrong place at the wrong time and been struck down by the random scythe of life. Of all case investigations, only a few fell into this category, with about the frequency of a winning lottery ticket.

"What if it wasn't random," Jefferson said. "What if the demon was at Sinatra's place because it was looking for something."

"Like what?"

"It would have to be something that interested it. That it wanted or needed."

"Something old, from before it was trapped on the island?"

"And Sinatra collected ancient things."

Brogan snapped his finger. "That's right. The demon must have wanted something that Sinatra had collected. Like an ancient coin, or book—"

"Or an ancient manuscript."

Brogan nodded. "Just like the one McKenna was reading."

"Except this one might be complete."

Jefferson sat in the Crown Vic finishing the last of a corn muffin while leaning out the window to avoid dropping crumbs inside and watching the sailboats cut paths through the sluggishly moving water of the Charles. The water sparkled, the sailboats gleamed white, and everything *seemed* right with the world. The afternoon had shaped into a beautiful one, and Brogan had parked the car along the walkways running beside the Charles. Both their windows were rolled down, and a cool breeze flowed through the car, smelling of grass and the muddy scent of the river.

"That all you got?" Brogan was speaking into his cell phone. "You sure on that?"

Brogan nodded, listening to the speaker telling him something, while Jefferson followed the quickly receding form of a rollerblader making her way down the walkway. The corn muffin was sitting in a thick lump in his stomach.

"All right, buddy, I'll see ya."

Brogan snapped shut the phone and leaned back into his chair, sighing. "God bless Boston on a day like this."

"Let's see it in the middle of January."

Brogan glanced over at the corn muffin bag. "You still eating those?"

"Yeah, the first bites are good."

"It's like muffin-flavored concrete."

"It's not that bad. What'd you find out?"

"Well, called Vincent."

"Yeah?"

"Asked him if he knew whether they had inventoried any kind of old manuscript among Sinatra's possessions or in the house itself."

"And?"

"And he said that there was no such thing."

"Well . . ." Jefferson said. "Would have been a lucky guess. Scratch ticket odds."

Brogan smiled, or his face shaped itself into something like a smile, usually seen most often right before the detective brains someone with a wrench or stumbles across a popcorn kernel of evidence.

"What?" Jefferson said.

"What?" Brogan replied back innocently.

"You've got that look."

"And what look would that be, my good man?" Brogan did his best English butler impersonation. Sounded like a bad Monty Python skit done by local Boston players.

"That look you get just before I start wishing I'd retired early."

"Leave Boston's finest in blue on a day like today?" Brogan asked. "C'mon. Don't pout."

"So what else did Vincent tell you?"

"The aforementioned Vincent made mention to me, the aforementioned Brogan, that there did appear to be a manuscript in Sinatra's collection at some point. Specifically, a document from the thirteenth century that is listed in one of Sinatra's personal collection inventories but was not present in the actual house."

"So he did have it."

"Sounds like. But it was only recently purchased according to the inventory. See, I'm thinking that Older, the ex–Blade prison guard, he makes it his hobby to do research on the prison. He comes across the cemetery we found underneath the prison and, somewhere along the line, also comes across the manuscript. He goes to work for Sinatra, who is a collector of antiques, and sells Sinatra the manuscript from Blade. Then they both get whacked for it. Question is," Brogan said, "where is it now? You think the Jinn got it?"

It was possible that the Jinn had found the manuscript while it was in Sinatra's house. That manuscript must have been what brought it to the house in the first place, and there was a good chance that it had found the document somewhere in Sinatra's collection. But something still nagged at Jefferson, a tiny barb at the back of his mind.

"If the Jinn had gotten it," Jefferson mused, "why would it still be looking for Saint?"

"What do you mean?"

"You remember when we talked to him? He said that all the crap with the monkey and the blood was for protection. Like maybe he thought this thing might come after him again. Track him down."

"Yeah?"

"Well, that must have been the Jinn."

"Think so?"

"It's the only thing that makes sense," Jefferson said. "If you believe the Jinn was only at Sinatra's for the manuscript, it wouldn't keep following after Saint unless it wanted something from him."

"Or Saint had seen its face," Brogan said. "That's the only reason it hunted down the guys from Blade."

Jefferson thought for a moment. "That could be, too," he finally admitted.

"Don't get down on yourself, Columbo. We'll check Saint out. If he's clean, we'll send him on his way. If he's not, then . . ."

Brogan's voice trailed off again, and his facial muscles shaped themselves into another smile.

After his detention and questioning, Saint had been released, and had presumably returned home. That had been less than a week ago. Jefferson hoped the man had stayed home. They had contacted Saint's parole officer, a woman named Maria Ortiz, who told them that Saint was still residing at the Walnut Park Projects.

"Look for the gym," she said.

"The gym?" Jefferson asked.

"You'll know what I mean. Saint. Big guy, right? The guy's got a whole fitness center right outside his place."

Jefferson remembered the project housing from the raid last weekend, but he didn't remember seeing any type of fitness center outside. Then again, it was almost dark and he wasn't exactly in the mood for a good set of bench. Ortiz told him that except for his sister, she thought Saint lived alone and she had always found him to be one of the nicest parolees she had ever dealt with.

"Of course," she said, "with a lot of them, it's just an act. But Saint was a real gentleman. The kind they haven't made in a hundred or so years. He was just trying to do right. If he's mixed up in something again now, do what you have to do, but go easy on him. He's a good kid."

As Brogan drove, the houses came closer and closer together, until yards gave way to tiny alleyways between triple-decker housing and fenced-in sections of lawn the size of miniature golf putting greens. Old men and women sat on front porches in white tank tops and sundresses, smoking cigarettes and reading newspapers, sometimes shuffling back into their house to cool down in front of a fan and watch *The Price Is Right*. Nobody seemed concerned with going anywhere. Jefferson had a feeling that days passed with numbing regularity, broken only by the weather and the thickness of the Sunday paper.

Although almost as drab and hopeless, the Walnut Park Projects at least broke the monotony of the triple-deckers. The complex was divided into twenty separate buildings, each with three floors, in the shape of a horseshoe. In the center of the horseshoe was a small section of dirty grass, cut in diagonals by the concrete sidewalks leading into each of the buildings.

They parked the Crown Vic in a small parking lot bordering the complex. Across the street was an elementary school. Kids ran back and forth on the concrete playground, falling down and bouncing up like pinballs. Suburban kids fell down on grass. City kids fell on pavement and broken glass. Jefferson caught Brogan's face as they stepped out of the car. He was staring across the street a slight smile, a real smile this time, expanding on his face just below his softening eyes. Jefferson followed his gaze and saw that he was watching the playground, watching the kids playing and laughing together.

Faith. I don't know how anyone can have that anymore, Jefferson thought. *Faith in what? That we're all left on this world at the mercy of the predators, the sadists, the murderers, or even just the fuck-up who drives the wrong way onto an exit ramp. If that was what faith was about, then I'm was better off on my own.*

Jefferson and Brogan stepped onto the slowly dying grass of the complex, walking toward the first of the U-shaped brick buildings, then stepped over trash and old needles lying in the dirt.

The night of the raid had passed by so quickly, blending into a series of adrenaline-filled memory snapshots, that Jefferson remembered very little of the details of the complex. In the middle of the afternoon, without the bulky feel of the Kevlar vest and the overwhelming anticipation of violence, Jefferson could observe more of the surrounding buildings and grounds.

The buildings were constructed of the same faded red brick that all looked as if they had been cooked for too long. Everything was colored in faded reds and browns, like the last dying leaves of fall before turning to winter. Occasionally a child's plastic play set, lying abandoned in the dirt outside one of the units, would add a mix of bright blue or yellow into the complex's palette, but the effect was like placing a point or two of color on a canvas filled with mud.

The windows on the buildings were small, mostly open in the hot afternoon, the occasional fan turning lazily into the rooms inside. People gathering outside the brick buildings, like lizards coming into the sun for heat, turned their heads to watch Jefferson and Brogan. Some sat on curbs drinking lemonade from tall plastic glasses, while others listened to the radio, wearing white tank tops and leaning back on their elbows.

Two kids in their late teens stood in the parking lot bent over a mocha brown mid-1980s Buick with its hood up. A third kid sat in the driver's seat, revving the big engine, while the other two watched the play of pistons and belts inside the block. They looked up at Jefferson and Brogan for a moment with dull eyes, before turning back toward the engine, the pounding bass of rap music filtering up from the giant car's stereos.

Saint's building was toward the rear. They could hear the clank of metal against metal as they approached and the high voice of Aaron Neville.

The parole officer had been right; Saint had a hell of a fitness center.

The horseshoe-shaped grassy area in front of his unit was filled with weights and bars and equipment all gleaming in the afternoon sun. There was a central large Nautilus machine, made of thick white metal and black bars of weights held in by pins. A stereo sat on the seat mat of the leg press, the cord running into the open door of Saint's apartment, the speakers crooning Aaron Neville and Linda Ronstadt's, "I Don't Know Much."

A bench press stood in the center, not like the old rickety one that had been moldering in Jefferson's basement for ten years, but new and stable, the professional kind Jefferson only saw down at gyms. And on this, Saint was lying on his back, grunting and pushing the thick bench bar up from his chest, three metal plates clipped to each side. Saint's arms extended fully, then glided the weights back down toward his chest, then up again, and down, like a pendulum swinging back and forth over his body. Another man stood at the end of the bench, spotting for him as he lifted. The second man was massive, built like a gorilla, with long thick arms and a neck the size of watermelon. His face was vaguely familiar.

Saint finished his set, the weights booming as he dropped the bar onto the rack. The second man nodded to him, raising his eyes to Jefferson and Brogan. Saint sat up on the bench, resting his elbows and his knees and regarding the two detectives.

"How much was that?" Brogan asked.

"Three-fifteen, ten times, easy," Saint said.

"Not bad."

"Courtesy of Blade Prison. Not much for a brother to do, except get big. You go down for a two-to-five and come out benching less than three hundred, you wasted your time."

"How much you max?"

"Four-twenty." Saint jerked his thumb back at the man standing behind him. "Venice here can do 455. Haven't beat him yet."

The man named Venice stood still behind the bench, wrists crossed in front of each other, hands clasped so that the front of his biceps showed to the two detectives.

"Venice . . ." Brogan said. "Troy Venice?"

"That's right." The man nodded once.

"*The* Troy Venice."

Venice nodded again.

"Holy shit," Brogan said to Jefferson. "You know who this is?"

The name was familiar, but Jefferson couldn't place it.

"Defensive tackle for the Patriots. All-Pro last year, right?"

"And the year before."

"And the year before that," Saint added.

Jefferson remembered him finally, realizing why the man's face looked familiar. Defensive tackle from Florida State, drafted sixteenth overall by the Patriots about four years earlier.

"What the hell you work out here for? Don't the Pats have a facility around here?" Brogan asked.

"Don't need all that fancy shit they got over there. Saint's my boy; I grew up down the street. This is my neighborhood, man. I just leave for practice and the games."

Brogan nodded, looking around at the equipment. "You leave all this shit out here at night?"

Saint laughed. "You think anyone stupid enough to steal it? They all know whose it is."

Jefferson didn't doubt that. Saint seemed completely different from when he had seen him last. He tried to reconcile the confident man sitting before him with the one crying and shaking on the interrogation room floor. Something must have happened since then. Saint knew what was in that house, knew that it was some kind of evil. A demon. But here he was, out in the open, seeming not to care anymore. He was confident. Too confident.

A pretty young woman appeared in the open doorway of Saint's apartment. She was wearing cutoff shorts, a size too big for her body, and a New England Patriots jersey, number 61, Troy Venice's number, printed on the front and back. Saint caught Jefferson's eye and nodded toward the woman.

"That's my sister," Saint said. "C'mon out here, girl, don't be shy."

The girl stepped out into the sun of the front stoop, one hand up shading her eyes.

"Sharin, I want you to meet Detectives Brogan and Jefferson."

The two detectives waved, and the girl smiled. "Hi."

Jefferson remembered the birth control pills in Saint's apartment. The ones for Sharin.

"You still working?" Jefferson asked.

"Hell no." Saint shook his head. "She's out of that. Right after I got through talking to you, I helped her get out."

"That's a tough business to just walk away from sometimes," Jefferson said. He'd seen a lot of hookers after they'd tried to leave the streets, thought they'd be better off working a nine-to-five job somewhere. He'd seen a lot of them, broken noses, dislocated jaws, cracked ribs, thanks to some pimp who thought differently.

"Yeah, well, not as tough as you'd think. Depends who you got doing the negotiating." Saint rubbed the top of his hand as he spoke. Jefferson eyes glanced down at the man's fingers. His knuckles were swollen and thick, small scabs forming on two of them, as if he'd hit something hard enough to almost break his hand. Something like his sister's pimp. Jefferson glanced at Venice's hand, seeing the same marks along a line on the man's knuckles, and felt sorry for the pimp or any man, for that matter, who ever tried to touch Sharin again.

Jefferson's eyes remained a moment longer at Saint's knuckles. When he looked back up, he saw Saint regarding him with dead eyes.

"I heard what went down at Blade. All over the news, a lot of SWAT guys ran up against that thing down there."

"It killed a lot of our guys," Brogan said. "That's right."

"Maybe some good came out of it though."

"How's that?"

"Day of reckoning is coming. The warden exposed for the shit he was doing every day in there. That place will get cleaned up a little bit now. So yeah, maybe there is some good."

"Maybe."

"So what can I help you two with today?" Saint asked.

"Doing some more good. Can we talk alone?" Brogan asked.

"Nothing that you could say to me that can't get said in front of these two."

Brogan shrugged. "Fine with me."

Saint was still seated on the end of the bench press. Brogan leaned against one of the weight racks, jamming his hands into his pockets while Jefferson sat on the top of the leg press machine. The radio changed to Lionel Richie's "Hello." Venice watched both detectives.

"Wanted to talk to you again about what you saw that night," Jefferson said.

Saint's eyes flickered for a moment, and even Venice seemed to shift uncomfortably on his feet as if he'd heard what had happened. Then he nodded to the radio.

"Easy listening. That's the shit. Not like that gangsta rap shit the media pushes on Black men," Saint said, before turning back to them. "You think I look like the type o' man that scares easy?"

"No I don't," Jefferson answered honestly.

"Yeah. Well, I didn't think so either."

"We need to ask you some questions about what you saw in that house."

"Saw a lot of things."

"What about a manuscript?"

"A what?"

"A manuscript, a book of old papers, about two feet tall."

Saint paused for a moment, and Jefferson thought he saw him shiver. He looked as if the small of his back had been hit with a cold chill, yet the day was warm and sunny.

"Why don't you two go on home. Believe me, you don't want to be messing with this investigation."

"We don't have a choice. Now, the manuscript, did you see anything like that in Sinatra's place?"

"No, no, I didn't see nothing like that," Saint replied.

Brogan shifted forward on the rack of weights. Venice's eyes turned slowly toward him, and he rested his hands on the bench bar in front of him, arms tensed as if ready to push off quickly.

"Hey, Jefferson," Brogan said, staring at Saint.

"Yeah?"

"What'd forensics find on that drug dealer's body we found right out in back of Saint's apartment."

Jefferson nodded, taking the bait. "They found he was killed with a bullet shot from a .22."

"And what did CSI find in Saint's apartment?"

"A handgun, violation of his parole."

"Yeah and what caliber was that again?"

"Also a .22."

Brogan kept his eyes on Saint. "What do you think we'll find when we match the bullet pulled out of that dead guy's chest with one fired from the gun we found up in your apartment?"

Jefferson knew Brogan was bluffing. They had both already looked at the forensic report. The bullet had hit against that junkie's spine, the small .22 round crushing against the bone, making a match impossible. Still, no way for Saint to know that. Otherwise, there was nothing connecting Saint to the drug dealer's killing, even though the man was guilty. But maybe Saint had it right, maybe the man did have it coming. Even if they didn't have him on the .22 rap, they could always violate him back to Blade for breaking his parole by going over to Sinatra's. The board didn't look kindly on ex-cons getting themselves mixed up in robberies.

Saint said nothing for a moment, then smiled, looked up at Brogan then back to Jefferson. "Hey, OK, you want to take this investigation, you want to chase evil into its own den, I'm not gonna to stop you."

"The manuscript?" Brogan asked. "Where is it?"

Saint sighed. "After we entered the house, Five and Q went upstairs, I stayed down by the door, watching the windows, you know. Like I said before."

"Yeah. Go on."

"And I see it lying there. Nobody around, so I just grab it. After all that happened, I got out of the house, got home, and realized I still had it."

"Why didn't you tell us this back at the station?" Brogan asked.

"I was scared, man. I didn't want you to know any more than I absolutely had to tell you."

"So what happened to the manuscript?" Brogan asked.

"I gave it to my mom at first, and she had it when you came to my door. Later I got it from her again, but then I almost threw it out. What the hell I gonna do with some old papers? Five was supposed to unload the shit, and with him getting killed, nobody I knew would buy it."

Jefferson felt his heart drop in his chest as if it were weighted with mercury. If Saint had thrown the manuscript out, it would be impossible to find, buried under tons of trash in a landfill somewhere.

"Did you throw it out?"

"No, I didn't," Saint replied.

"So where is it?"

"I don't have it anymore."

"Bullshit," Brogan said, shifting again against the weight set. Venice shifted with him. He seemed to be unarmed, but his body was weapon enough. Jefferson remembered watching a film clip of the man tackling Roger Eastman, quarterback for the Rams. Venice had hit him so hard that he'd shattered the man's collarbone and knocked him unconscious for three minutes. And that was with a helmet and shoulder pads on.

"No bullshit, man," Saint said. "I'm not fucking with you. Shit, you think I want to go back to Blade for some junkie killing?"

"So where is it then?" Brogan asked.

"I told you, I don't have it."

Brogan shook his head. "This is going nowhere."

"I sold it."

"You what?" Jefferson asked, disbelieving. Who would want to buy that old manuscript.

"Something was wrong with it. Even though they was just a bunch of a papers, I could feel it wasn't right. Like, you know how you get a feeling about a dog sometimes. It looks all right, but you know that inside it's just bad. That's how I felt about those papers. Like they were possessed with Les Invisibles. The dead spirits."

Jefferson remembered Saint mentioning Les Invisibles in the interrogation room. At the time, he remembered not believing him. But times change, and the conversation in the interrogation room seemed like it was in another lifetime. Sitting on the leg press, in the small horseshoe-shaped yard of the housing complex, Jefferson found himself ready to believe everything Saint was telling him.

"These spirits," Brogan said. "You felt like they'd followed you here?"

Saint stared at Brogan for a moment, trying to detect the hint of sarcasm in the man's voice, the indication that Brogan was just setting him up. Brogan appeared ready to believe Saint's words as well; Jefferson could see that in his face. Saint apparently saw it as well, because he continued, saying, "They found me here. They came to my door, but I didn't let them inside."

"Did you see what the spirit looked like?"

"It was in the shape of a man."

"What man?"

"I never saw his face clearly, but his eyes, they swirled with yellow. Like a crazy dog."

"And you think this man was coming for those papers you had taken from Sinatra's house?"

"Something like that. This wasn't no ordinary man, you can't just trust to give him something and he go away. You can't play with the spirits like that, you need an intermediary. Someone who can communicate with both the real world and the spirit world. My mother is one of them."

"So you don't have the manuscript anymore?" Jefferson asked.

Saint shook his head.

Fuck. We're back where we started then. Jefferson thought, *with no way to fight this thing.*

"But if you just wanted to read it," Saint said slowly, "I copied everything it said for myself."

Jefferson and Brogan stared at Saint for a moment. Saint and Venice stared back. Lionel Richie was finishing up "Hello" and immediately starting into "Dancing on the Ceiling." The teenagers in the parking lot were gunning the engine of their massive Buick again.

"I'm sorry, what'd you just say?"

"I have a notebook, inside, that I wrote everything down in."

Jefferson felt his heart skip with excitement. If that was true, then Saint would know everything that was in the manuscript. He would know everything about the Jinn.

"You did what? Why?" Brogan asked, open disbelief on his face.

"I know what was in that lawyer's place was a demon. When I get it back from my mother, I read this manuscript I got, and I see that it's all about what this demon is. How to kill this motherfucker. I figure anyone going up against this thing would need to know what it was about, you know?"

Jefferson felt an urge to hug the man. Even Brogan was smiling, shaking his head in surprise. Saint caught their faces and looked amused. Maybe at the irony of his helping out two cops.

"So you want to know what it said? Because I tell you, man, that if half this shit is true, you could be in for some serious trouble."

They sat on plastic lawn chairs Saint brought out from inside his apartment. The chairs were white with green stripes, the kind Jefferson's mother used to take out every summer for beach parties and barbecues. Brogan and Jefferson sat opposite Saint, who remained at the end of the bench, leaning forward, feet flat on the ground in front of him.

Venice went to go stand at the front of the horseshoe yard, hands crossed in front of him, leaning against the brick siding of the apartments watching the crisscrossing sidewalks. Jefferson had seen how big the man really was when he stepped out from behind the bench press. He was wearing athletic shorts and a Florida State basketball tank top that bulged in the back, just over the bottom of his spine, from the handgun Jefferson was sure must be there.

Sharin was in the apartment somewhere. Jefferson caught glimpses of her shadow moving back and forth across the open doorway, the white numbers of her football jersey catching the sun.

"If I tell you what you need to know," Saint said, "I need to know that the little issue you were mentioning earlier."

"The drug dealer you shot?" Brogan asked.

Saint looked pained. "Well, yeah. Something like that. That little issue won't ever come up again. You know what I'm saying? I won't be going back to Blade, not ever."

Jefferson nodded. "Fair enough," he said, not bothering to mention that it wouldn't matter anyway.

Saint eyed them for a moment, then said, "Cool."

Leaning farther forward onto his knees, Saint turned his head both ways, looking up toward the parking lot at one end of the complex, then back down toward the school. Venice had turned the radio down before he went to stand at the top of the horseshoe, but Jefferson could still hear it faintly playing from the top of the leg press.

"Now most of what I read," Saint said slowly, "was about this dude named Sidina."

Jefferson felt another jolt of excitement. Saint really had read the manuscript, and it was the one they had been looking for.

"That's right. What about him?"

"Well it was calling him the Perfect Warrior. The most brutal killer that the world had known. He was so brutal that people at the time thought he'd been filled with some kind of demon."

Saint reached down and pulled a water bottle from underneath the bench, slowly unscrewing the cap and holding the bottle halfway to his lips.

"They finally kill this man, Sidina, and his warriors, but it takes all the best soldiers of the time. But even when they're dead and buried, everyone still believes that the demons are alive. That's when their bodies were buried, these demons are forced to stay close to the bodies they had possessed, but they were still looking for their reincarnations."

"Searching for what?"

"For the reincarnated souls of Sidina and his three companions."

"That's what it said?" Brogan asked, knitting his brows in confusion.

Saint shrugged, taking a sip of water. "That's what it said. Reincarnated. So in other words, when Sidina dies, his soul is born again into someone new. And the same for the others. And when that person dies, that same soul is born once more, and so on."

Jefferson nodded, remembering McKenna having said something similar.

Saint pointed to Venice with the end of his water bottle. "My boy there, he thinks he's been reincarnated from Blackbeard."

"Who?"

"The pirate. That's why he thinks he's so crazy. Because in a previous life he thinks of himself as a pirate."

"What about you? You have any previous lives?"

Saint grinned, showing his sharp white teeth. "Leader of the slave revolt in Haiti. Killed a whole bunch of white landholders."

Saint took another sip of water, regarding Jefferson and Brogan with a bemused smile.

"So like Venice believes that in a previous life he was Blackbeard," Saint said, "there is someone living today who was Sidina in a previous life. Maybe that person doesn't even know he or she is either. Most people don't know about reincarnation. Never get in touch with their previous lives, so whoever Sidina is today, they might not even know it."

"You said 'he or she,' so Sidina might be a woman today?" Brogan asked.

"That's right. Sidina's soul would have been passed down from generation to generation and finally could have ended up inside a woman. So whoever this woman is, that would mean that she's Sidina."

He looked at the two of them for a moment. "Fucked up, ain't it?"

Jefferson felt strangely lifted from his body. The feeling he always had just after waking from a dream. Lying in the dark, uncertain of what the line was between the dream world and the real world, and feeling for a moment as if he hadn't crossed over. That he lay in some strange space between the two, like a water bug skimming the surface of the water, gliding just between the reflection of reality on the smooth liquid surface below and the unreflected reality above.

As the water bug glides, is it in the dream world of reflected images, or is it in the real world of actual space? Or can it occupy time in both places, where the wavering experiences of dreams are actually the recollections of past realities? Jefferson felt like what a water bug must feel; never sure of what in life is real and what is just a watery image, dissolving to ripples upon a single touch.

"So Sidina is alive today, possibly in someone that doesn't know it themselves," Brogan said. "And the spirit of the demon is searching for that person?"

"Sidina is somewhere here today," Saint agreed. "His spirit lives inside someone. And it's for this person the demon's been searching. For hundreds of years, generations, the evil spirits of the demons have sought out Sidina and his warriors. And maybe it has finally found Sidinia, and maybe his companions, here in Boston."

Saint's words made Jefferson shudder. The idea that this demon really was in the city, that it was somewhere out there, hidden in the shadows, watching, waiting for someone as it had watched and waited for centuries.

"Now, the demon and Sidina are linked in a chain that cannot be broken. The first step for the demon to return to the physical world, our world, full-time, is to take possession of the body of whoever Sidina is today. The whole manuscript was written as a warning, saying that this demon would always be searching for its reincarnated vessel. However long it took, the demon would always be looking to come out of retirement. But like the Three Musketeers, you know, 'All for one and one for all,' and that kind o' shit, it's an all-or-nothing deal. So not only must the Jinn who possessed Sidina find the reincarnation of Sidina, but the others have to find their reincarnations."

In the school playground, four kids had begun playing two-on-two basketball, the sounds of the rubber ball striking hollow against concrete. Venice had turned his head to watch, his arms still crossed in front of him.

"Did the manuscript say anything about how we can kill this demon?" Brogan asked.

"Yeah, you can kill it," Saint drawled, shielding his eyes against the setting sun. "But according to what I read, there's only one way to do it."

"What's that?"

"When Sidina was finally killed, his body was laid on a giant metal door. His blood had been so tainted with evil that it smoked and burned the metal where it fell. This metal, now contaminated by evil, was melted down and used to fashion six arrowheads and a dagger. Only these weapons, made with the blood of Sidina himself, can be used to kill these demons, these Jinn, should they return. And if you kill any one of them, you kill them all."

At the end of the horseshoe, Venice was bobbing his head up and down, lips moving as if he were singing something to himself. Jefferson wondered if he knew all about what Saint was saying. It was hard to imagine an all-pro defensive tackle getting mixed up with demons.

The air smelled of barbecued chicken, a sweet, tangy smell that seeped around them, carried from someone's grill fire. It was going to be a warm night, perfect for outdoor barbecues.

"Where are these weapons, you know?" Brogan asked.

Saint shook his head. "Naw. It didn't get into that. It only said that's what you need to kill these demons. And kill them quick, before they start their resurrection."

Jefferson wondered if the resurrection has already begun. St. Petersburg, the bleeding shroud, the wet ink on the parchment. They were beginning to show changes. For centuries, nothing, and now? Jefferson felt cold when he remembered McKenna's finger, cutting herself on the sharp tooth of the creature. Her blood, inside that thing, running through the thing's veins.

Saint was speaking again, but Jefferson wasn't listening, thinking back to the museum basement, to McKenna cutting her finger. Then, from the drone of Saint's voice, a single word cut through the fog of Jefferson's mind.

"Lyerman."

"What?"

"I said, that was the dude that I gave the manuscript, to," Saint answered. "Joseph Lyerman."

"*The* Joseph Lyerman?"

"The rich dude from TV, yeah, that's him."

"He came here?" Jefferson asked, trying to imagine Lyerman's electric chair driving up the long path of the complex. Vacant stares at the strange little man in his strange cart.

"Naw, he called me, told me to come down to his building."

"And you went?"

"Yeah. He said he knew I had the manuscript. That I'd taken it out of Sinatra's place and that it was dangerous for me to have. Powerful forces or something were after it," Saint said. "And he mentioned money."

"Money?"

"Yeah."

"How much?"

"He said it was enough to make it worth my while."

"So you gave it to him?"

"I knew Les Invisibles had been to my apartment. I could tell they were looking for something, and I knew it must be that book. I just wanted to get rid of the damn thing. Lyerman can take it if he wants. He seemed to know what he was getting into."

"The man is one of the richest businessmen in the country. You mean to tell me that you think Lyerman knew what was going on?" Brogan asked.

"Hell, yeah, he did. Older found the book on the island and something else, a box of something."

"What was in it?"

"Don't know. Sinatra never had that. Older told Q that he sold the box right off the bat to Lyerman. He was gonna sell the book to Lyerman, too, but he decided to make a killing, first sell it to Sinatra, his employer, then contract with Five and me and Q to steal it from Sinatra. We was supposed to sell it back to Older for fifteen grand, and Older would resell it to Lyerman, so everyone makes out except Sinatra. But then the shit hit the fan.

"Lyerman must've known all about the deal, because he came and contacted me. He knew all about that demon, about what happened out at that lawyer's place. If anything, it seemed like he was the one pulling the strings. The one making it all happen. Shit, that boy had you fooled from the beginning."

"Just checked up on our friend Mr. Lyerman," Brogan said, clicking shut his cell phone. They were driving down Massachusetts Avenue, away from the Walnut Park Projects and back toward Jefferson's house. After leaving Saint, Brogan had called a contact by the name of Albert Manuel at the *Boston Globe* to do some research on Mr. Joseph Lyerman.

"Yeah? What'd you find?" Jefferson asked.

"Manuel's looking now, calling me back in five minutes."

Lyerman had not only known about the presence of the manuscript, but he'd also known who might have it. He'd contacted Saint only days after the incident at Sinatra's house. Had Lyerman known all along about the demon, or had he only recently been brought into the loop?

"If Lyerman has anything to do with this," Jefferson said, "I swear to God, I'll fucking push that little cart of his off a cliff. With him in it."

"We don't even know Saint was telling us the truth."

"How do you mean?"

"How do we know that Saint isn't the guy, isn't this Sidina person? He could have been in on this from the beginning."

Jefferson thought for a moment. "No. That doesn't make any sense. If Saint was Sidina, and the demon had already gotten to him, then what would it still be looking for?"

Brogan shook his head. "You said there were four skeletons in total, right?"

"Yes. From Sidina and his three warriors."

"So if Sidina has been reincarnated, then it'd stand to reason that his three warriors would have been as well."

"Yes . . ."

"So the demon wouldn't just be looking for Sidina, for one person, it'd be looking for its three warriors as well. It'd be searching for four. Four people here in Boston."

Jefferson paused, running his hand over the top of his head. Jesus, that was probably true, and it hadn't even occurred to him. Since they'd left Saint's, he'd been thinking that the demon was only looking for Sidina, but Brogan was right. It was possible that it had already found what it was looking for. If Saint had been leading them down the wrong track, the man could act better than Robert DeNiro and Brando put together.

Jefferson had known a lot of ex-cons who could live out entirely made-up stories, who made a habit of it, lying to the parole board, lying to parole officers, anyone they needed to. There was an ex-con out of Plymouth Correctional who had his parole officer convinced for eight months that he had become an ordained minister at a local parish. He showed up at his appointments with his parole officer in holy robes, and even agreed to baptize the officer's newborn baby. The whole time, the parolee was running drugs weekly from Boston to Nashua and hadn't seen the inside of a church in eleven years.

Cons could lie. Even so, Saint's would be a big one.

"Didn't you ever think of that?" Brogan asked.

"No, I guess I didn't."

"That would explain how Saint got out of Sinatra's in the first place. Think about that. He claims he was the only one who made it out. What if he's lying. What if Saint is Sidina and that night, the demon tracked him down at Sinatra's? What if Saint never made it out at all?"

"Jesus, if that was true," Jefferson said, "we weren't just talking to Saint. We were talking to the demon."

Brogan nodded. The thought sat heavily on both of them. Jefferson felt a shiver, the kind that hits the moment after a major car accident, in the quiet when you realize you're still alive. The phone rang. It was Manuel at the *Globe* calling them back. Brogan put him on the car's speakerphone.

Manuel had moved to Boston with his family from Panama when he was eight years old. His English was almost perfect, with only a slight hint of a native Spanish speaker's accent.

"*Hola, amigo,*" Brogan said. "What's up?"

"You tell me, my friend," Manuel said, his voice sounding distant from inside the car's small speaker. "I come to this place, this Boston, sit through godforsaken winters, when in Panama City it's seventy-eight degrees. You tell me why I come here? Make it worth my while."

"How about exclusive coverage on what we've got going on now, Manuel," Brogan answered. "And this isn't a page-nine investigation. This is front page, coast to coast, CNN work. You always wanted a Pulitzer, right?"

Manuel was silent for a moment. "All right, my friend. I will help you, but you promise to keep me in the loop, yes?"

"*Sí, sí.* Of course, now what'd you dig up on Lyerman?"

"OK . . ." Manuel said, and Jefferson could hear pages turning. "Joseph Lyerman. Born in Charlestown, 1923. His parents were both Irish immigrants. His father was a dockworker and was killed during a labor strike in 1927, his mother was a seamstress.

"After his father's death, the mother supported Lyerman and five other children, moving them out of Charlestown and down into South Boston. His oldest brother, Henry, traveled to Montana during the midthirties as part of Roosevelt's New Deal program. A part of Henry's wages helped support the family for two years, until the wage payments stopped coming in 1935. Henry was never heard from again.

"At thirteen, Lyerman took a job as a newspaper delivery boy, working for the *Globe.* I guess we liked them young back then," Manuel observed dryly. "He worked for three years, until his sixteenth birthday, when he began work as a general laborer for FreshCan Tuna, the fish cannery that burned down in the fifties. Three years later again, he joined the Merchant Marine at nineteen, then served in the South Pacific on the USS *Galla.*"

Manuel was continuing to speak, but Jefferson was no longer listening. The USS *Galla.* Lyerman had served on the ship a part of which had been brought to Boston in January. Something had been aboard that ship, Jefferson was sure of it. Something that had gotten free. And if Lyerman had been on board sixty-five years earlier, he must have known what was on the ship with him. Lyerman had funded the expedition to raise the wreck of the *Galla* from the bottom of the seafloor because he knew what was locked inside one of the cabins.

He knew, because he had seen it himself.

"Hang on a sec," Brogan said. "All right, Manuel?"

"Sure."

Brogan pushed mute on the speakerphone, then turned to Jefferson. "You catch that about the *Galla*?"

"Yeah, but I can hardly believe it. Lyerman served on that ship. He must have known what was going on."

Brogan nodded, his eyes looking distant, out toward the horizon. "I'm going to kill that fucker, I swear to God."

He turned to Jefferson, and his eyes looked glazed, like he was half-drunk. Even knowing the man as well as he did, Jefferson still felt a nervous fear in the pit of his stomach every time he saw Brogan like that. That the man's blind fury could turn any-where on anyone.

Brogan pressed the mute button again on the phone.

"Manuel?"

"Yes."

"What else you got on him?"

"Well, his military service ended when the *Galla* was sunk by a Japanese air attack. Lyerman was only one of a handful of survivors, but that is where he lost his legs. After that, he came back to the States and entered the business world. The man's got a rep-utation as an animal. Ruthless. He started out in petroleum, but now he has his hands in everything. In my country, he owns thousands of acres of land to grow tobacco plants. Even with no jobs in the country, many Panamanians will not work for him. They call him Tiburón, the Shark."

"Why?"

"Because he eats people alive. Like a shark would. With no feeling.

"There was a man in my country who was attempting to organize the workers at two of Lyerman's tobacco plantations to strike. This man, he had a family, three little girls and a wife. He comes home from working in the fields and finds that his family is missing.

"The man is in a panic, and villagers search the mountains for miles around. Three days go by, and on the evening of the fourth day, the man finds a note pinned to his front door. The note lists an address in a neighboring village, and attached is a Polaroid photograph of the man's wife and his three little girls, sitting around a small table, plates of food in front of them.

"The man and eight of his fellow villagers go to this address. It is a small hut, on the edge of the tobacco fields, constructed of sandalwood and banana leaves. The door is rickety, no lock. In a panic at the silence of the hut, the man kicks open the door. Inside, under a small electric light, are his wife and children, still seated around the table, and plates of food as they were in the picture."

"Were they dead?"

"No, they were very much alive, each of them appeared to be unharmed, and fol-lowed the man with their eyes, keeping their heads very still. They were not shackled, and the man could not understand why they had not gotten up from the table and left, or cried out for help.

"'Maria, what is wrong?' he said to his wife. 'I have found you. Why do you not speak?'

"His wife only stared at him with her large brown eyes, and as the man watched, a tear slipped down her cheek, landing just above her left breast. He was most confused.

"'What is it?' he asked. 'Why do you cry? You are safe.'

"Then he saw a small fruit fly buzzing around the mouth and nose of his littlest girl, yet she did nothing to brush away the annoyance." Manuel paused in his story for a moment. "Each member of his family had been drugged, and small incisions had been made in their spines by experienced doctors. With these incisions, nerves were cut. Vital nerves, responsible for movement.

"Each of them, his wife, his three little girls, had been systematically paralyzed, then propped up like dolls around the table."

"Jesus . . ." Brogan whispered, his knuckles going white around the wheel.

"There was no note, but tobacco leaves had been wadded up and placed in each of their laps. Tobacco leaves. Who else could it be but Lyerman. A warning to his workers not to strike."

Jefferson felt cold, colder than he had ever felt before. It was as if he had been covered in ice, his hands, his arms, icicles dangling from his nose, his eyelids, his entire body encased in glistening frozen water, cutting off all feeling of the world around him. From somewhere distant, Brogan was thanking Manuel, hanging up the phone and keeping his head forward. Jefferson thought of the man and his family, down in Panama, his wife and his children. Then he thought of Lyerman, and the ice began to melt, burned away by a rage deep within him. A rage at a man who could carry out such crimes, could order such things be done. Only a man like that would welcome a demon.

Outside, the sky was beginning to darken. The dying sun was passing into night with its last breaths of orange and red, fading before the glowing city of concrete and metal. And running along it all were the waters of the Charles, sluggish and murky below them, dark as the deepest jungles, lit only by a single electric bulb.

Brogan pulled up to the curb in front of Jefferson's car. Jefferson stepped out, slammed the door, then leaned back in through the window.

"I'm gonna go down to Lyerman's building, see about setting up a meet," Brogan said, staring straight ahead.

"Don't do anything stupid. Lyerman's a fucking psycho; he brought this demon. But he's also just a rich asshole. You don't want to go to prison for that prick, and knocking off Lyerman won't help us get the demon."

"Don't worry, I'll make sure he tells us everything we need to know about how to deal with the Jinn."

"Brogan, don't do this. I'm serious, man; Lyerman isn't some two-bit junkie that nobody'll miss. If he just turns up dead, people are going to want to know why."

Brogan turned to Jefferson. "Promise me something."

"What?"

"If something happens to me tonight—"

"C'mon, man." Jefferson tried to smile. "Don't—"

"Shut up, Jefferson, listen to me," Brogan interrupted. "If something happens to me tonight, I want you to take care of my daughters, OK?"

"Yeah, yeah, sure. Of course."

"And after you make sure they're safe, I want you to make sure that Lyerman is dead, too. I want that fuck dead. You kill him for me, you kill him slow, too."

Jefferson shook his head. "Brogan, I . . . You know I can't do that."

Brogan looked at him for a moment, then turned his head back to the road. The big Crown Vic's engine roared, and the automobile skidded away from the curb, Jefferson jumping back from the spinning wheels. Brogan careened the car wildly out into traffic. Jefferson stepped back onto the curb, watching his partner drive off, the horns of angry motorists dying out one by one.

Jefferson picked up McKenna, then the two drove back downtown, toward the Lyerman Building. While Jefferson drove, McKenna called ahead to the number given to them by Lyerman. She had spoken with his secretary, who wasn't sure where Lyerman was exactly, but was probably involved somewhere down at the party.

"Party?" McKenna asked.

"Sure, there's a big one going on," the secretary said. "A fund-raiser. Must be two hundred people here."

McKenna asked a few more questions, thanked her, then hung up the phone.

"Lot of people there tonight," McKenna said, as they drove up Dartmouth Street, massive brownstones flashing by on either side. "Not good."

"What's the fund-raiser for?" Jefferson asked.

"Help impoverished families in Panama," McKenna said flatly, not understanding the irony.

Jefferson felt sick, remembering the family that Lyerman had ordered surgically paralyzed. Part of him wanted to reach Lyerman first, to arrest the sick motherfucker, tighten the metal handcuffs around his spindly wrists, weak from a lifetime bound to a wheelchair. That was what part of Jefferson wanted. He knew what the other part wanted, hoped for. That Brogan reached Lyerman first. Then there would be nothing left to arrest.

The entrance to the Lyerman Building was crowded with a line of expensive automobiles, about to be whisked away to a lot for the evening. From the car across the street, Jefferson and McKenna watched a series of beautifully-dressed beautiful people surrender their keys to the uniformed valets and glide into the building for the fund-raiser. Brogan's Crown Vic was parked; the wheels half on the curb, a ticket already fastened under the windshield wiper, the orange paper fluttering in the wind.

"What do you want to do?" McKenna asked.

"Let's check out that party."

"We don't have a warrant. They won't let us within fifty yards of it."

"So we won't let them know we're police."

McKenna allowed her eyes to travel down Jefferson's outfit, and smoothed her own with her hands. "In that case," she said hesitantly, "we're going to need a change of clothes. This isn't exactly an Oscar dress here." She glanced at her watch. "I know this is crazy," she signed, "but it wouldn't take us more than 20 minutes to buy something at The Prudential Center and get back here."

Although the saleslady raised an eyebrow at their insistence that they were going to wear their newly-purchased evening clothes out of the store, the plan went off without a hitch, and half an hour later, it was McKenna and Jefferson who were walking the red carpet into the Lyerman building. Two men sat up quickly from chaise lounge chairs as they approached. The men each had bulky black bags slung over their shoulders and both raised cameras to their eyes.

"Photographers," McKenna murmured to Jefferson. "This fund-raiser must be a big deal." The two photographers looked at McKenna and Jefferson for a moment before lowering their cameras with looks of disappointment and resuming their vigil beside the glass front doors.

"Guess we're not famous enough to make the cut," Jefferson smirked.

The lobby was paneled with peach-colored marble, veins of black running through the stone in long streaks. Through the tall back glass windows, Jefferson could see across the street to the Common. The porters and valets stood around the doorway, talking and reading newspapers. Palm plants in the corner were waving slightly, buffeted by the unseen air currents of the ventilation system.

They walked up to a long marble front desk staffed by a man in his sixties wearing a tuxedo not unlike the one Jefferson had just hurriedly purchased. The concierge nodded to them at their approach, lifting his head from a piece of paper he had been writing on.

"May I help you?"

"Mr. Lyerman's fund-raiser, that's in the thirtieth floor, right?" Jefferson asked.

"The thirtieth."

"Oh, right, right. We're running a little late, we just came from the Wang Theater, we were just running up to say hello to some people."

"Of course," the gentleman acknowledged, and nodded them toward the elevators.

Jefferson thought to himself that security probably should be much tighter for such an event; they didn't even bother to check a list of names. He extended his arm for McKenna, and heard the swish of fabric and the light tapping of high heels on stone. She was wearing a long, low-cut evening gown that ran down the length of her body before spreading out slightly over her ankles. Jefferson stared for a moment, noticing that the porters and valets outside had stopped their chatting and turned to look at his "date." They were young kids, still in the phase of their lives where the presence of a beautiful woman is an occasion to stop and stare. He thought for a moment that if she weren't on his arm, he'd be right there with those boys, just transfixed by a gorgeous woman on her way to a party.

She took his arm, turned toward him and said, "You look simply dashing," in a fairly good British accent.

"Thank you. So do you," Jefferson replied, not trusting himself to say anymore. "You've got an audience, I think."

He nodded toward the windows, where the porters stood on the sidewalk, gawking and smiling. McKenna turned toward the window and curtsied, to the excitement of everyone outside.

Together, they turned back around and walked to the nearest elevator. Jefferson pushed the call button, while McKenna moved her lips closer to Jefferson's ear, and whispered jokingly, "I've never bought formal wear that quickly before. It makes me feel like I'm seventeen and someone's just told me if I get to the prom in ten minutes or under, I'll get laid." She flashed him a devilish smile.

"Play your cards right, sweetheart, and you never know . . ." Jefferson grinned back. The giant elevator doors pulled apart with an electronic *ping*, and the couple stepped in. The walls were glass, overlooking the street. "What floor, please?" an automated voice asked.

Jefferson looked around him, checking for the familiar panel of floor numbers. There were no buttons to push.

"What floor please?" the voice repeated.

The elevator seemed to be voice-operated.

"Thirtieth floor."

"One moment please."

There was a jerking motion, and the elevator began to glide upward. Behind them, the ground quickly receded, until they could see the tops of cars and buildings through the glass walls of the rising elevator. Far below, the porters stood on the street, occasionally glancing up at the rising elevator.

"So what's the plan when we get up there?" McKenna asked.

Jefferson shrugged. "Make it up as we go along. We'll see if we can find Lyerman. Maybe they'll have good appetizers. I really like those little baked crab cakes."

The numbers counted off quickly, moving up toward thirty. As the car began to slow, Jefferson could hear the sound of music and voices even before the doors opened.

The secretary had been right—it was a hell of a party.

The elevator doors opened, and Jefferson found himself staring at the wide, muscular back of an enormous man. The man turned toward the sound of the elevator, holding his hand out as Jefferson and McKenna tried to step free of the car. Behind the man, across the room, Jefferson saw a swing band just finishing up, their instruments going to their laps as they rested between songs. They were wearing gray, shimmering suits, like something a 1920s gangster might wear, and sat behind large wooden music stands on a constructed stage. The large crowd was composed of men in tuxedos and women in evening gowns, all filtering round elegant tables. Each table had a white tablecloth, and a bowl filled with water, in which floated a candle and white water lilies. The tables surrounded an open dance floor. People were grouped in clusters of twos and three, holding cocktails and talking animatedly.

"Just a moment, sir," the large man said, his body preventing Jefferson from exiting the elevator.

The guard looked Samoan. He had short-clipped hair and a wide neck that squeezed down into a carefully tailored tuxedo. Even with the man's bulk, the fabric of the coat fit perfectly. The guard quickly glanced up and down Jefferson's clothes, making him feel like a woman at a bar.

"May I see your invitation?"

Jefferson made a motion as if he were patting down his own pockets. "I don't have it with me."

The guard shook his head. "I'm sorry then. This is a private function for invited guests only.

"They let us in downstairs."

"Are you on the list?" the Samoan asked, his eyes moving down toward a clipboard in his hands.

The elevator doors had begun to close. Jefferson stuck his hand out between them, and immediately they retracted again with a jerk.

"No. I don't think so."

"Then I can't let you in. You'll have to go back downstairs."

"We just need to see Mr. Lyerman."

"I'm sorry, I cannot let you inside. Perhaps if you waited down in the lobby, I could contact Mr. Lyerman. But other than that, no invite, no entrance."

"I need to see him tonight," Jefferson said, feeling stupid for only repeating himself.

"I understand you feel that way," the big Samoan said, his voice showing a trace of annoyance. "But perhaps Mr. Lyerman doesn't need to see *you* tonight."

The elevator doors began to close automatically again. Jefferson had to stick his hand between them. He was getting tired of standing there, and he felt awkward, the elevator continuing to close in his face.

"Is that all?" the guard was saying, oblivious of the conversation happening behind him, snapping Jefferson's attention back. "Because I need to ask you to leave. Now."

Jefferson only nodded.

He took a last glance out into the party. Everyone's attention was elsewhere, caught up in their own conversations. No one had noticed him arrive. The timer in the elevator had begun to close the doors for a third time anyway. Jefferson let them shut in front of him.

"Nice going, slick," McKenna said, a half smile on her face. "Good plan."

"What floor please?" the elevator asked immediately.

Jefferson shook his head in frustration. "Thanks for the help back there."

"What could I do?"

"I don't know, bat your eyelashes at him or something. Ask him how much he benches," Jefferson kidded back, before turning to the elevator. "Twenty-nine."

"Thank you."

There was a momentary falling sensation, as the elevator moved down one floor, before the doors swung open again. Twenty-ninth floor.

"What now?" McKenna asked.

"Change of plans."

Jefferson stepped out of the car cautiously, expecting another security guard to meet him. There was nobody. The twenty-ninth floor was empty.

The floor appeared to house some kind of corporate offices. A compact reception desk stood vacant in the front lobby of the firm. A cube-shaped fish tank rose from the thick carpet, three angelfish gliding silently in the water. The floor was dark, except for the fish tank's greenish glow and the outside lights that filtered in through the main windows looking out on the city.

Jefferson and McKenna stepped out of the elevator and onto the darkened floor.

Past the receptionist's desk was a large room divided into a series of gray foam-padded cubicles. The cubicles were low-walled, each having a computer terminal, turned off for the night, and a padded chair. There must have been a hundred of them. The cleaning crew had already passed through the room, leaving empty trash cans in their wake. Most of the desks themselves were clean, except for an occasional *Wall Street Journal* or a family photograph.

They moved quietly in the darkness, heading toward the rear and a glowing red EXIT sign. Above him, resonating through the ceiling, Jefferson could hear the party. The band had started playing again, and Jefferson could faintly pick out the tune of the old song, "Minnie the Moocher."

Jefferson hummed quietly along to the song as he walked.

"Haven't heard that one in a while," McKenna whispered.

Jefferson planned on cutting across the floor, then taking the back stairway up to the thirtieth floor. It was unlikely they had posted someone at the stairway entrance, and they might be able to slip into the party unnoticed. Lyerman might not be on the thirtieth, but there would probably be someone up there who would know where he was.

They began walking past the rows of cubicles when something flashed across the dark room.

In the far corner of the room, one of the computers had turned on.

Slowly, McKenna reached down and pulled her .22 out from the holster strapped inside her right thigh, holding the weapon down at her waist. Jefferson did the same with his Beretta, quietly pulling back the slide and chambering the first round. Jefferson pointed to the computer, then at McKenna, before making a circling motion toward the far wall. McKenna signaled her understanding.

Jefferson gave her a thumbs-up, then ducked low, his head beneath the foam-padded walls of the cubicles. The cubicles were box-shaped, like rows of honeycomb; something could be hiding in any number of them and he wouldn't know until he was right on top of it. He turned to warn McKenna, but she had already vanished, lost somewhere in the maze of gray walls.

Jefferson began moving forward slowly, foot by foot, in a low crouch. With his head below the level of each cubicle, he found it difficult to orient himself without being able to see the surrounding walls and windows that would give him a sense of direction. When he was a kid, he had gone with his mother to see the Breaker's Mansion Hedge Maze down in Newport, Rhode Island. Wandering around the narrow paths, constricted on all sides by the encroaching green foliage had felt similar to this wandering between the padded walls.

When Jefferson had passed what he felt were enough desks, he took a turn to his right, slowly advancing down the long aisle. In the silence of the room, he could hear the sounds of the single computer. The whir of the hard drive, the staticky sound of the monitor. White and blue light flashed on the ceiling over him from the electric glow and he slowly raised his head above the walls.

Nothing moved.

On a single desk, four spaces away from him, the computer continued to boot automatically, unguided by human hand. *Remember, the demon can take human form. It could appear as anyone.*

Jefferson listened for a moment more, hearing nothing. He called out to McKenna in a single low whisper. He heard a scuffling sound, and her head popped up from behind the gray walls several cubicles away. He pointed to the computer, then back out across the rest of the floor, then at his watch, and shrugged. Maybe the computer was set on a timer to turn on by itself? McKenna stood up to her full height, still holding her weapon pointed at the ground. She walked toward Jefferson, finding her way down the aisles.

"Nothing?" she asked.

"Nope."

The computer had finished booting, leaving a single cursor blinking on the screen. Above him, "Minnie the Moocher" had ended, the band quickly moving into the Kurt Weill song, "Mack the Knife."

Jefferson could imagine the couples gliding across the floor, the women seeming to twirl sparklers as their dresses glittered in the chandelier light. One floor below, they were standing in the eerie darkness of the empty room. McKenna and Jefferson stared at the computer monitor, the screen still blank except for the slowly blinking cursor.

"Well . . ." McKenna exhaled, sliding her .22 back into the concealed holster. "Looks like I crawled around in an evening gown for nothing."

"No, wait," Jefferson said, grasping her arm just above the elbow.

On the screen, the cursor was slowly beginning to move. A trail of letters formed behind it, forming as if someone were typing on the empty keyboard.

"My God," McKenna whispered, her hand unconsciously moving back toward the base of her spine as she watched the cursor's slow crawl across the screen. Jefferson turned away from the monitor, his eyes scanning carefully across the rest of the room. They were alone. Unless something was ducking below the level of the cubicles. Something that was waiting for them.

Still holding his weapon, Jefferson slowly turned his eyes back to the monitor. The cursor had completed its trip across the black screen and stood their, blinking, a line of writing spaced evenly behind it.

You should not be here

Jefferson felt cold at the base of his spine. The feeling he was encased in ice again crept over him, the intense chill spreading out from his spine, across his skin, and all the way out to the tips of his fingers, the ends of his toes. McKenna whispered something unintelligible under her breath. She also felt the cold.

The single sentence was gone, replaced by a series of images that flashed by on the screen. The images all lasted for a only a moment, blending together, like the million snapshots of a blinking eye. In the flashes, Jefferson saw glimpses of religious imagery. Buddha, Christ, and Muhammad. Images of the Wailing Wall, Chinese temples, Russian onion-domed churches, French cathedrals. Paintings of the Madonna, Christ hanging from the Cross, lines of text from in Arabic and Hebrew. Men on their knees, heads to the ground, praying; women holding their arms to the heavens and sobbing. On and on, the onslaught was overwhelming.

McKenna stared at the screen, transfixed as well, the images forming a mosaic of colors that reflected off the glassy wetness of her eyes. Then as suddenly as it had started, the screen went black once more. Jefferson exhaled; he felt exhausted.

"What is this . . . ? McKenna asked.

Above them, the swing band music continued to play.

Then the images began to flash again. These were different from the first. Jefferson saw men running through trenches, a starving infant covered in flies, soldiers shooting from behind a stone wall, the bloated corpse of a dead horse, a wooden cottage in flames, an emaciated woman dying in a hospital bed, a man with a gun to his head. Hundreds more followed, all of war and death. Then a single one illuminated the screen, holding long enough for Jefferson to study it. A woman, sitting in a chair, her legs and arms pressed against the chair, her skin puffy and swollen from where the cords pressed into it. Above the woman's shoulders was the head of an animal. It was the body of Sinatra's wife, the body they had found mutilated in the lawyer's home.

The screen went black and a simple line of text appeared.

It is too late. It has arrived.

They stood together in the darkness of the office. Jefferson could feel himself gripping his weapon, feeling reassurance in the metal against his skin, the raised ridges of the butt pressing into his palm, leaving a grid of marks on his fingers. His mind was already past the images, working at the actual production of what he had just seen. Someone in the building had the ability to turn on that computer. And at the right time as well. Which meant that someone knew exactly where they were. His eyes scanned the floor around him, desks, chairs, blotters. Then, there it was. A pinpoint of red light high on the wall. A single security camera, pointed out toward them.

Jefferson took her by the arm, her skin feeling cool and dry against his hand, and led her toward the stairwell door, marked under the red EXIT sign. In the emergency stairwell, the light was brighter, shining from fluorescent bulbs placed high on each landing. The walls were concrete block, painted a sky blue in color, while metal grips were layered into each stair. They paused for a moment, alone in the stairwell, and Jefferson took McKenna's face between his two hands, looking at her.

"Are you all right?"

She nodded once, her hand coming up to brush a piece of hair away from her face. People respond to being scared in a variety of ways. McKenna's response was anger. Quiet anger. A lot of people Jefferson knew were the same. You can't let fear inside—once it's in you, it begins to eat away at you like acid. Burning your insides.

"I'm all right," she answered. "Yeah, I'm OK. Thanks."

"You sure? You don't have to be here."

"No. I'm fine. I didn't come all this way with you to leave you alone now."

Jefferson smiled and kissed her quickly, then looked up the stairwell, toward the party on the thirtieth.

"Let's see about crashing that party, OK?" McKenna said, forcing a small half smile.

They took the back stairwell, moving up the stairs toward the thirtieth. They could hear the sound of the music, echoing in long warbles down the stairwell. A single trumpet note sounded far off, as if they were deep underwater listening to the note being played on a ship above them.

They paused on the thirtieth-floor landing, the music much louder, traveling easily through the thin metal door. He could hear the band playing, a trumpet blowing out a high riff from a Louis Armstrong song.

Jefferson gently eased the door open a crack, pressing his eye to the opening. They were to the left of the stage; Jefferson could see the backs of the musicians' legs as they stood on the raised platform in front of him. Beyond that, couples were moving together, turning across the polished dance floor.

"Ready?" Jefferson asked, and felt an affirmative squeeze of his arm from McKenna. Slowly, he eased the door open, and they slipped through, behind the stage, walking quickly toward the dance floor, holding hands. Jefferson adjusted his cuff links. They were just a couple who had stepped away for some privacy.

Around them, the party was still in full swing, no one seeming to notice them. The large Samoan still stood at the far side of the floor, clipboard in hand, his back turned to the elevators. They would have to watch him.

McKenna leaned in close to Jefferson, her lips approaching his left ear. "Quite a party."

They were standing in the midst of a large crowd. Overhead, delicate sheets of lace were suspended from the chandeliers and illuminated from within, forming webs of white gossamer across the ceiling. Somewhere a bubble machine was working, and Jefferson saw an occasional shimmering bubble hover across the dance floor, tentative for a moment in its movements before finally bursting and vanishing in an instant.

A long table at the far end of the room was covered with catered food set carefully on napkins. Three men in white tuxedos stood serving the food, little chocolate-covered strawberries and other snacks, from behind the table. The trumpet player finished his solo with a flourish, collapsed into his seat, and massaged his lips.

Jefferson and McKenna moved across the dance floor, still holding hands.

"See anyone we know?" McKenna asked.

Jefferson had his eyes open for Brogan or Lyerman, but saw neither. Lyerman, he figured, should be easy to spot, the bulk of his chair making him noticeable even in a crowd.

"No."

Long white columns stood up periodically from the floor, bracing themselves against the ceiling. They made their way to one of them, leaning back against it and surveying the room.

The music slowed suddenly, moving into a jazz rhythm. A billboard hanging over their heads announced the band as the Baker Sax-o-Tet.

"Not a bad spread here," McKenna said.

"I should talk to the decorators next time I have people over for the Patriots game."

The room was elegant. The walls were covered in purple velvet, crystal chandeliers hung with silk dangled from the ceiling, and large green ferns in mud-colored bowls rose toward the ceiling. Women in close-fitting cloche hats and pleated silk skirts were standing around the dance floor, one hand resting on a thrust-forward hip, while with the other they casually smoked long-tipped cigarettes.

The men were all dressed nattily in tuxedos, hair slicked back and shining in the overhead lights. A pretty young woman was filtering through the crowd, selling Lucky Strikes from a cigarette box slung about her waist and helping to complete the Jazz Age atmosphere. She moved past Jefferson, smiling at him for a moment before turning her eyes to look for other potential customers.

"I'm going to get a drink," McKenna said. "You want something?"

Jefferson nodded, and McKenna slipped away to the bar. He watched her move through the crowd. It was rare when you could really watch someone, keep your eyes on them without their knowing, without their acting anything but normal. And Jefferson watched McKenna now, the roll of her hips beneath the black fabric of her dress, her slender waist, her hair shining in the light.

Onstage there was a sudden commotion. An attractive woman with long red hair and a shimmering blue dress was making her way up the steps toward the band. She was drunk, staggering slightly, one hand holding a martini glass, the liquid spilling out over the side as she wobbled forward. She waved her hand, motioning the band to stop playing. Moving to the center of the stage, she grabbed the microphone. Smiling drunkenly at the crowd of expectant faces, she raised her martini glass.

"This is the way the world ends," she began, holding on to the microphone for support. "Not with a bang but a whimper."

Her head slumped down toward her chest for a moment, and Jefferson thought she might pass out up there. Then she abruptly looked back up, gazing unsteadily into the crowd. She stared sullenly down from the stage for a moment, before she smiled again, holding up her glass once more, ignoring the liquor spilling out over her hands.

"Gif me a vhiskey . . . and dawn't be stingy, baby," she intoned, keeping her glass raised. She moved off across the stage, as behind her the band started playing again.

People turned away, resuming their conversations as the general hum of voices returned. Jefferson continued to watch her take short stuttering steps, one hand pressed against the side of her head, as if she were trying to keep her hat from slipping. Something about her was familiar.

He looked closely at her face. She was almost to the edge of the stage when Jefferson recognized her. Veronica. The hostess at Richard Lee's tearoom. The one that had led Jefferson and Brogan to Richard. *What is she doing here?*

Jefferson pushed his way toward the front of the room.

"Veronica," he called out to her.

At the sound of her name, she turned her head, staring vacantly at Jefferson for a moment. Gradually her eyes focused, and she smiled a long, drunken smile, holding a hand up as she descended from the stage.

"Detective Jefferson," she cried. As he approached, she leaned forward, pressing her hand firmly against his chest and looking up at him. She was close enough that he could smell her perfume and the liquor on her breath.

"Call me Veronica," she said. "We're old friends."

She remained standing close to him, her body leaning in toward his. She moved her hand slowly up from his chest, running the tips of her fingers across the side of his cheek. She smiled again, eyes waxen, as she looked at him. She had the exaggerated motions of a drunk, and as she pushed away from him, her body weight shifted onto one hip, which she thrust forward, continuing to stare up at him with her green eyes.

"So," she said, pressing her fingers against his chest and slowly trailing down toward his stomach, "what are you doing here?"

"I could ask the same about you."

She shrugged. "I go to all these events. Don't you know? I'm one of the in crowd. A real go-go girl."

"Are you here with one of the guests?"

"Well"—she smiled—"technically, no. He's off somewhere. Some businessman. I haven't seen him all night." She shrugged. "Oh well."

"Oh," Jefferson said after a moment, slowly beginning to tune her out.

"It's too bad," Veronica was saying, "since he owns the whole place."

Jefferson felt his heart jump in his chest.

"What?"

"I said he owns the whole place," Veronica said. "He's the one throwing the party. Ain't I important, to be going with him."

"What's his name?"

"I don't know. I forget. I'm just supposed to walk up the carpet with him. Or actually, since he can't walk, I'm just supposed to walk alongside him. He's got one of those motorized chairs, you know, the kind you can control with just one finger?"

Jefferson was no longer listening. Veronica was with Lyerman. Someone had hired her to be his date for the evening, which meant that, for some reason, Lyerman wanted her at the party. But why? Unless there was some connection with Richard. Even that didn't make sense though. Jefferson was sure that Richard's death had been a straight snuff. Just to send a message to Brogan and Jefferson, not because the Jinn needed anything from Richard.

Thinking of the young gangster, Jefferson managed to say, "I was sorry to hear about Richard."

Veronica nodded, looking serious for a moment. "Yeah. Me too. He was an all right kid, you know? Better than most. A real stand-up guy, just right for a real go-go girl like me, right?"

"Yeah."

"It's nice to have the steady ones every once in a while. Ones that actually remember your name. Don't just call you, 'hon.'"

Jefferson nodded; he wanted to get away from her. She depressed him. The stink of booze, her life a blur of paying male faces. Veronica was staring at him. Her lips parted and for a moment Jefferson thought she might lean in and try to kiss him. Abruptly, though, she pulled back, taking another sip of her drink.

"I have to go to the ladies' room," she said suddenly. "Freshen up."

Jefferson nodded quickly. "Sure."

She turned, her hips swinging back and forth as she walked away. As she stepped across the dance floor, she looked back once over her shoulder, smiled for a moment, then continued walking.

Jefferson stood for a moment on the edge of the dance floor before he felt someone tap him on the shoulder.

"May I have this dance?" McKenna said, looking at him with one hand on her hip.

"Of course."

Jefferson took her out onto the dance floor, where she took his hand, sliding her other arm up onto his shoulder. The music was a slow waltz, and they moved out among the other dancers, lost in the swirls of fabric and patterns of circulating feet. McKenna's head rested on Jefferson's shoulder, her lips close to his ear.

"Detective Vincent is here," she whispered.

"What? How do you know?"

"I saw him at the bar."

"Talk to him?"

"Uh-huh. He said he's here as part of the extra detail of security Lyerman has for the party."

Jefferson nodded, but something was bothering him. Veronica was there. So was Vincent. Both of them working for Lyerman.

"Did Lyerman request that Vincent be here personally?" Jefferson asked.

"I'm not sure. Why, you think that's important?"

"I don't know. Maybe."

Jefferson scanned the crowd over McKenna's shoulder. He saw Vincent himself, talking to a white-haired man who stood unsteadily at his table, one hand gripping the tablecloth tightly. Vincent was bending over, saying something directly into the man's ear. Whatever was said didn't seem to make the man happy, as he pulled away from the detective, swaying unsteadily on his feet.

"I see Vincent," Jefferson whispered.

"What's he doing?"

"Rousting a drunk," Jefferson said. "One of Richard Lee's girls is here. This girl named Veronica."

"What's she doing?"

"I asked her, she said that she's the date of the gentleman who's throwing the party. A gentleman in an electric wheelchair."

Jefferson felt McKenna's body stiffen in his arms. "Jesus. She's here with Lyerman."

"Sounds like it."

"How?"

"Don't know. Sounds like she does this a lot. Lyerman must have requested her, like at a service. Unless it's just chance. In which my faith decreases sharply as the night goes on."

"So you think that Lyerman wanted her here? But why?"

"I'm not sure. Maybe she's . . ."

"What?"

"We never considered the possibility that Sidina might be a woman. Maybe Lyerman thinks that it's her. But she doesn't seem the type."

McKenna was silent for a moment more. "I don't know. You'd think he'd went to come back a little classier."

Jefferson nodded. "I agree."

They continued to dance in slow circles around the dance floor. McKenna tightened her grip on Jefferson's shoulder. "Did you ever stop to think that we're here, too?"

"What do you mean?"

"We're also here at Lyerman's. You and I. Just like Veronica."

"That's because we chose to come. Lyerman didn't have anything to do with that."

"Are you sure? Maybe he didn't hire us, like Vincent or Veronica, but what if he led us here. Made sure that we'd show up?"

Someone on the dance floor blew into a party favor, the noise sounding raucously. A giant wooden grandfather clock standing on the far wall began chiming slowly, each chime sounding as the deep ringing of a bell.

McKenna leaned in toward Jefferson. "Vincent, Veronica, and Brogan. We're all here, Jefferson. What if it's not just them that Lyerman is interested in. What if it's one of us?"

"One of us?"

"You or me. If you're the one, the reincarnation of Sidina, you might not even know it. You could go through your entire life without ever knowing what you once were. If it's possible for Veronica or Vincent, why isn't it possible for us?"

"No, there's no way. I would know it if I was. I would feel it. But I don't feel anything."

346

"Haven't you ever? Haven't you ever felt off, Jefferson, just a little? As if something were familiar to you, but you didn't know why?" McKenna asked. "That perhaps you were living a life that had already been lived sometime before you. I have. I think we all have to some extent or another.

"You walk into a room and meet someone for the first time. Yet they seem oddly familiar to you. As if you'd known them for years. I've felt that way before. As if I had known those close to me sometime in the past, before I'd ever met them in this life."

More party favors sounded like trumpets, and a general cheer erupted from the crowd. The bells struck midnight. A ribbon holding a net was cut, and from overhead hundreds of white balloons began drifting onto the dance floor, falling from the ceiling. Everyone in the hall looked up, smiling and raising their hands over their heads, reaching for the balloons like small children.

"There's something I have to tell you, Jefferson," McKenna said, leaning in close to his ear.

"What?"

McKenna stared at Jefferson as the white balloons fell around them, bouncing lightly off their bodies like tufts of dandelion seed. He wanted to lie in bed with her again. Far away from there, from the Jinn, from all the deaths. He wanted to feel her body against his again as he had in St. Petersburg. With the moonlight coming in through the window. There was red around him now, red-colored balloons that rolled along the floor like waves. Spreading out like waves of fire.

The fire that seemed to move like a fluid, across the floor, climbing the walls. Fire around them. Sounds in the distance. Gunfire. Screams. And more fire. An intense heat that seemed to envelop him. Heat burning up a small underground room. A body on the wall, hung like the one in the mausoleum, but this one different. Wearing ragged clothes. Bare feet. More gunfire. Someone hit. Blood spraying everywhere.

Jefferson began to feel dizzy, confused. The room spun around him, a blur of laughing, drunken heads and the trumpeting of plastic horns. On the stage the band had begun to play again, a quick melody, note piling upon note. He could hear McKenna calling him distantly. The red balloons of fire were moving across the floor, the crowd oblivious of them. He fell away from her, stepping back against the bar. People fell away from him, scattering before him with nervous, sidelong glances. He held on to the polished wood tightly, closing his eyes, the sounds of the band awash in the roar of the blood in his ears.

"He's OK, don't worry, he was just feeling a little sick earlier," McKenna was saying to the crowd. "He just needs to sit down."

He felt himself guided to something solid, and he sat down. The red balloons had dispersed to separate corners of the room. McKenna was looking at him, her cool hand on his forehead. Jefferson closed his eyes, concentrating on the feel of her skin against his, the texture of her palm. He opened his eyes.

"Jesus . . . what happened?" Jefferson said.

He was sitting on a chair near one of the round white tables.

"You looked like you were passing out. One minute you were fine, then the next I almost had to carry you. You all right?"

"Yeah. Yeah. I feel like I'm sleeping off a twenty-drink hangover, but I'll be OK. I think I just got dehydrated or something."

"Here, I'll get you some water."

McKenna stepped up to the bar for a moment and came back with a glass of ice water. Jefferson took the water and drank it, the cool liquid flowing down his throat. He could feel it all the way into his stomach, where it seemed to sit for a moment, his body soaking it up.

He began to feel better.

Floors above, Brogan crouched in the darkness, waiting. Down the black hall, he could hear the whine of an electric motor. The battery-powered turning of Lyerman's wheels sounded faintly, like the small engine of a child's remote-controlled toy. Brogan took a step forward, his feet sinking soundlessly into the hall carpet. The whining was growing louder as he moved, coming from a single room at the end of the hall. A lamp was on in that room, the light spilling out into the hall, forming a single square painted on the opposite wall.

Brogan wasn't sure yet what he'd do when he found Lyerman. The man would be helpless, trapped in his chair, unable to move except at the slow, awkward crawl of his cart. Brogan began turning ideas over in his mind. If he pulled out the battery case, he would leave the man completely stranded. Able to swivel only his neck, watching Brogan move around the room. The thought gave the detective a thrill, the old feelings coming back. The same feelings that made you go after the guy who had looked at your girlfriend wrong, the revenge and uncontrolled anger that made you hold him down and pound him again and again until the bones in your hand hurt and your skin grew slick with blood and snot.

His wife had helped him to suppress those feelings. A grown man shouldn't get that way. A mature, educated man shouldn't act like a street animal. But that's what Brogan always knew he was—a street animal. Now that his wife was gone, the old feelings were coming back. The dulling of the emotions. An animal didn't feel guilt or pity, wasn't weak when it came time to attack, and neither was Brogan going to be. At heart, you never change.

Brogan fingered his thick leather belt, wondering if he should wrap the leather around his fist so he wouldn't break a knuckle. He thought not, his hand pulling away from the loop. *Jesus, the guy's a crip, I shouldn't break anything on the old bag, no matter how hard I hit.* He smiled at this, picturing the old man's head, about the same size and shape as the speed bag he worked out on at the gym. Just like hitting a speed bag, except one that screamed and cried out. Not that it bothered Brogan. The man had it coming.

The electric whining had ceased. Maybe the old guy was asleep. That'd be perfect. Creep up on him while he slept, get the chance to shake him awake. Let him think he might still be dreaming until the first punch came, maybe breaking the guy's nose right off, watering his eyes. Almost smiling to himself, Brogan crept forward on the rug, moving toward the square of light. He reached the open doorway and slowly eased his head across the sill. He found himself looking into a bedroom, clay lamps, chests of drawers, and an open closet exposing racks of clothing. In the center was a massive motorized bed, the kind the handicapped used to move up and down while they slept.

He glanced around the rest of the room. In the far corner, near the big glass windows, was Lyerman. The man's chair was turned toward the window, his back facing Brogan. He could see the man's head rising above the line of the chair, silhouetted against the lights of Boston outside. The chair was pulled up beneath a table, and Lyerman appeared to be looking at something. Brogan inched forward, feeling safe because the man's back was turned.

Lyerman's head was pointed down, the muscles of the neck rigid, staring at something placed on the table. Brogan caught a glimpse of red fabric, and he moved a step closer. Stretched out on the table was a small pair of red cotton pants. A school uniform that a boy of about eight might wear. Lyerman had the pants facedown, the legs stretched apart. The fabric was clean, except for small streaks of grass stains soiling the seat.

Lyerman was excited, Brogan could hear him breathing heavily. His head began to sway back and forth rhythmically. *What the fuck is he doing?* Something about watching him made Brogan feel sick and angry inside. A nauseous feeling of rage was slowly building in the pit of his stomach. Whatever Lyerman was doing felt wrong, twisted, so that Brogan felt disgusted.

Maybe he could use the belt after all. He was going to be hitting hard.

Behind him, Brogan heard the sudden patter of steps approaching quickly down the hallway toward him. He was beginning to turn when something sharp jabbed him in the side of the neck. The point of a needle broke the skin, sliding deep into him, tearing as his body twisted. In a rage, Brogan swung his arm backward, his fist sweeping over nothing but empty space behind him. The movement felt strange, heavy, throwing his body wildly off-balance. He sagged against the doorframe and felt another sharp needle jab in his arm, like a hornet caught beneath his shirt and stinging him again and again.

He tried to stand, but already his body felt heavy, like there were a thousand rubber bands wrapped around him, pulling him to the ground. He could hear the electric whine of the chair again, Lyerman turning away from the table, turning his chair toward him. The chair moved, almost floating along the bedroom carpet, as Brogan fell forward, rolling over onto his side.

Lyerman looked down at him, his face flushed. "Detective, you're interrupting."

Brogan tried to lift his arm, but instead felt a crushing pain on his wrist as Lyerman drove over the small bones. There was an audible crunch, and Brogan's bones were crushed under the massive weight of the chair. The pain was strangely distant. Stepping out of the dark hallway was Lyerman's Panamanian nurse, still holding the hypodermic needle, a small bead of clear liquid dangling bulblike from the sharp point.

The Panamanian was saying something to Lyerman, nodding at Brogan as he spoke, but his voice was small and so quiet that Brogan could barely hear him. The rubber bands wrapped around his body were stretching tighter, pulling him into the thick carpet. Lyerman was speaking to the nurse. Brogan knew he should listen, it was something about him, something very important. But he felt so tired—all he wanted to do was sleep.

Jefferson sat still, drinking the water and watching the dancers move slowly across the floor. The spinning in his head was gradually coming to a rest, like the final few turns of a carousel. The red balloons were gone from the floor, pushed off to the side by the dancers until they lay in forgotten clumps against the wall. Gone, too, was whatever dim recollection they had brought to Jefferson, whatever long-forgotten memory they had called up with their appearance. Whatever portion of his mind that they had excited. McKenna's hand was stroking the top of his leg up and down.

She smiled at him. "How you feeling?"

"Been better, but I'm all right," Jefferson replied.

He was feeling better, but it was beginning to bother him that they hadn't seen Brogan since they'd arrived at the party. He reached for his cell phone, pulling it out and dialing Brogan's number. Holding the receiver to his ear, he listened, the phone ringing four times before switching to voice mail. He snapped the phone shut, placing it back on the table. Wherever he was, he wasn't planning on answering now.

McKenna's hand had come to rest on Jefferson's knee, and she sat with her head turned toward the dance floor as well, a faint smile on her lips as she watched. The candles floating like tiny lit boats in their bowls of water on the table made light flicker across her face, shadows moving on her skin. She looked beautiful.

"Look at us," he said to McKenna. "Look just like a couple of regular people right now."

"Uh-huh."

"We could just be two people sitting here. Just a normal couple enjoying themselves."

"Regular, huh? And what's that?"

"Pool parties, taking the kids to soccer practice, minivans."

"Yeah? Is that what you want?"

Jefferson shrugged. "Don't know. I've never had it. You? That the life you want?"

"I'm here with you now," McKenna said, taking his hand. "That's where I want to be. That's all I'm sure about."

Jefferson looked at her for a moment, watching the shadows moving on her skin. He leaned in and kissed her on the forehead, holding her to his lips, smelling her lightly scented hair. Then, pulling back, he reached for his phone to call Brogan again, feeling himself pulled deeper into that other life.

Slowly Brogan began to retreat from the blackness, rising back into consciousness like a diver to the ocean's surface. Something cold and slick was touching his face, annoying him, keeping him out of the peaceful blackness of sleep. He shook his head, but the slickness was still against his skin. Slowly, he opened his eyes, small droplets of water forming in beads on his eyelashes. He went to move his hand to wipe the water away, but found his arm was not responding, a dull pressure tightening against his wrist.

He was sitting in a chair, his jacket gone, his arms and legs bound to the wooden frame. Heaving himself back into consciousness, he opened his eyes fully, this time turning his head slightly. He was on the roof of the Lyerman Building, at the edge of the path, ten yards from where they had discovered the bodies of Jill Euan and Kenneth Lyerman. Cool drizzle was raining slick against the skin of his face and hands, and he could feel that his hair was damp, clumped coldly against his skull. Once again he tried to move, to stand up, but the restraints held him fast to the chair.

There was a noise behind him, the familiar whirring of an electric motor, and he heard the crunch of rubber wheels on the wood chips of the path. He turned his head toward the noise, his movement limited so that he could just see past the line of his shoulder. Lyerman was coming toward him, sitting in his motorized cart, driving up the roof's narrow path. The small Panamanian was with him, walking next to the cart.

"Good evening, Detective Brogan," Lyerman said, as the cart wheeled into Brogan's line of vision and came to a stop. "Or should I say, good morning, since it's after midnight. Either way, I think."

"I know about you," Brogan said, his lips and tongue moving sluggishly, as if he'd been injected with Novocain. "I know what you've done."

"Yes, well, you've certainly earned your retirement pension. Let me ask you, was it my son. The death of my own son that distracted you for so long?"

"He was your own kid, your own flesh and blood that was murdered up here by that creature. How could you let that happen?"

Lyerman sighed. "He was my own son. But let's be honest, he wasn't a very good boy at all. Have you ever heard of the biblical story of Abraham, asked by God to sacrifice his own son as a proof of faith?"

Brogan nodded, more droplets of rain falling into his eyes. He began rocking his hands slowly back and forth, testing the restraints on his wrist The little Panamanian nurse was staring at him, not giving any indication that he saw the movements.

"This demon asks for a similar proof of devotion," Lyerman said. "Except that, unlike God, the Jinn expects payment in full."

"Why would you help it?"

"If you've tracked me here, you must know already that I served on board the USS *Galla* during the Second World War. On that night in November, we were attacked by Japanese planes. That's an awful thing, to be inside the belly of a metal ship when it explodes. The force of that . . . is intense, the sound waves alone enough to knock a man senseless. I was in the mess hall, with twelve other men, when the explosion came. It ripped the ship open like a tin can, flooded us with water. We were drowning, couldn't breathe, locked in the blackness of the sinking galley. I remember swimming up through the galley, fighting against the wave of water.

"That was the last time I remember ever being able to move without this chair.

"A second explosion, from deep in the engine room, ripped through the ship. I was thrown out onto the deck, my spine snapping cleanly, like a dry twig. Someone pulled me into a rescue ship, and I awoke two weeks later." Lyerman stared off across the roof for a moment, rain collecting on his doll-like body, falling across his face, as he sat, like Brogan, unable to move. "I prayed to God for the first year. Prayed that I might walk again, hold something up to my nose to smell, climb a flight of stairs, wiggle my toes. And in all that time, in that year lying in a hospital bed, I heard nothing back.

"I knew what was on that ship. I knew what we carried, that it was a demon. A demon that had taken the shape of a man to get off the island. And it was to this being that I next began to pray. I promised that I would do everything in my power to help it, if it would only give me back my legs."

"But you're still in the chair," Brogan said.

"For now." Lyerman shrugged. "Do you know the legend of Sidina?"

Brogan nodded. "I've heard it."

"Sidina is here, he's close. The demon will come for him, whoever he is. And when the Jinn is resurrected back to glorious life, then I shall be given the power to rise from this chair."

"You would sell your soul for that?"

"Your God has already forsaken me. If a soul is God's creation, then I have little that I can sell for it. Your God has offered me nothing, so it is He that I have turned against."

Lyerman turned his head upward, looking into the rain, closing his eyes for a moment and letting the cool water wash over him. Then he lowered his head to stare at Brogan. His nostrils flared, scenting the air around him, his eyes shifting left then right in their sockets. "The Jinn is here tonight. I can feel it."

Lyerman looked back at Brogan. "You know, I've been following you for a while now. Following your career. Your picture, I saw it once in the *Globe*. You were the lead investigator on a case some years back. They published your picture, a little thing really. I almost didn't notice it myself, except the article mentioned that the victim's legs were broken. And then I saw your face. And I recognized it. Knew who you were. So it's an irony to me that we've come to this point. I want to thank you for helping me on this investigation."

"I thought you were a grieving father, you fuck. I thought you just wanted to be kept up on the investigation, to know what had happened to your son. I never knew who you really were. What you were capable of. If I'd known, I never would have passed along anything to you, kept you in the loop."

"Oh, we're all capable of horrible things, Brogan. Horrific acts. Don't just single me out for what any one of us is capable of doing."

The little Panamanian leaned in toward Lyerman, whispering something into the man's ear. Lyerman nodded once, then looked back at Brogan. Still shifting his wrists back and forth, Brogan could tell he wouldn't be able to break the restraints holdings them in place. Instead, he concentrated his attention on the chair itself. It was made of solid wood, very simple in construction. If Brogan leaned forward slightly, he might be able to sit back sharply enough that he could crack the wooden legs and free his ankles.

The Panamanian shrugged as he finished speaking to Lyerman, then stood up, looking back toward Brogan. He walked on his toes past the bound detective, and Brogan could hear the crackle of wood chips as the man walked onto the path directly behind him.

"You have friends here, Jefferson and McKenna," Lyerman said slowly. "Did they come with you, or are they acting separately?"

Brogan shook his head. "I don't know. I came by myself."

"Mm-hm, and your friends. How much do they know about me?"

Brogan said nothing, staring straight ahead into the rain. Behind him, he could hear the Panamanian moving around. There was a rattle of metal on metal, reminding Brogan of the noise the cutting tools made in the metal pan just before an autopsy.

Lyerman stared at him for a moment. "I understand you want to help your friends. But you can help them best, by helping me find them."

Brogan still said nothing, half-closing his eyes, his mind wandering back to the darkness of his own house, the feel of his wife's warm skin against his, her body against him in the moonlight.

"You cannot see it, but behind you, Cesar is standing in front of a cart. On the cart is an assortment of cutting instruments, sharp and jagged blades that can rip a man open."

Dimly, Brogan heard a high-pitched electric whining behind him, like the sound of a dentist's drill. Or maybe a small saw. Brogan closed his eyes again, searching once more in the recesses of his memory for his wife. He found her, waiting for him, sitting on the swing on their back porch, the colors of autumn glowing behind her. She was beckoning to him, indicating with her finger that he should join her on the bench.

"I have no wish to torture you," Lyerman said. "But have no illusions. I will do what is necessary."

Deep in his memory, Brogan was walking to his wife, sitting beside her on the bench. Reaching out for her hand, readying himself. Distantly, as if far across the field outside his house, he hear the whir of the bone saw, the sound muted as his wife leaned in to kiss him. Then there was a different noise. A ringing sound again. The whir of the bone saw died away. The ringing continued.

Lyerman was speaking now, saying something sharply to the Panamanian. Brogan left his wife sitting on the bench for a moment and returned to the rooftop in the rain. The ringing noise continued, the sound seeming to come from beside him. Twisting his neck and leaning over so that he could see over his right shoulder, he saw his cell phone sitting on his jacket. Someone was calling him.

Lyerman smiled, staring at the phone the Panamanian had taken from Brogan's pocket and turned on. Then he said something in Spanish to the Panamanian, who reached down for the small phone and brought it over to Lyerman, clicking it open and holding it against his ear. Lyerman listened for a moment, then a broad smile broke across his face.

"Detective Jefferson, is it?" Lyerman said. "How nice to hear your voice. I knew it was a good idea to turn on Lieutenant Brogan's cell phone."

"Who is this?" Jefferson said into the cell phone, still seated at the table near the dance floor. McKenna looked over at him sharply, turning her attention from the band as she picked up on the sound of his voice.

"You know who this is . . ." came the voice again on the end of the line. The tone was playful, almost bantering.

"Lyerman?"

"Well, I'm certainly not your friend Detective Brogan," said the voice. "Who is here, I might add, but rather indisposed at the moment."

Jesus, it's Lyerman on the phone. The man somehow got to Brogan. Brogan was trying to get to Lyerman, and he must have done so, but it sounds like he's in trouble. He must be somewhere in the building. But where? The building is huge, they could be anywhere. McKenna was staring at him, leaning forward to hear the voice on the line.

"Brogan is there with you?" Jefferson asked.

"That's right; he's a bit strapped right now though."

"I think we've got some leads in the death of your son. Why don't I come up and talk to the both of you?"

Lyerman chuckled again, and in the background, Jefferson heard a faint droning noise. "While I'm sure you would be very eager to meet, I'm afraid I'd like to hold off on seeing you in person for a little while longer."

Jefferson heard the droning in the background slowly fade away.

"We'll meet soon," Lyerman said. "Believe me. Much sooner than you'd like."

Back on the rooftop, Brogan watched Lyerman smile again, even wider as he listened to whomever was speaking on the cell phone. The Panamanian continued to hold the phone up to his boss's ear, while keeping his head turned, his eyes focused on the lights of Boston around them.

"I don't think there's any use for that type of language," Lyerman was saying in an almost fatherly tone.

Pause.

"I understand your situation."

Pause.

"OK."

Pause. Lyerman sighed again, as if the person on the line was being difficult. Then, speaking into the phone again, he said, "All right, let me talk to him for a moment and see if he's available."

The Panamanian pulled the phone away from Lyerman's ear, and Lyerman looked directly at Brogan. "It's your partner on the phone, do you want to speak with him?"

"Leave them out of this," Brogan said sharply.

"No? OK, fine," Lyerman returned, his voice exasperated as if he were late for an appointment. "Bring it back." He motioned with his head to the Panamanian, and the phone was quickly returned to his ear.

"He doesn't want to talk to you," Lyerman said into the phone, speaking to Jefferson. "And I'm sorry, as much as I'd like to catch up, I'm going to have to cut this conversation short. I'm really very busy tonight, but maybe you'd like to arrange a meeting later in the evening? No? Well, OK. Ta-ta for now. Oh, and Jefferson, tell McKenna that I love her dress."

Lyerman nodded, and the Panamanian took the phone away from his boss's ear, clicking the unit shut. The Panamanian slipped the phone into his own pocket, then walked behind Brogan once more. Lyerman looked at Brogan for a moment, then past him, to the Panamanian.

"Now . . ." Lyerman said. "Where were we?"

Lyerman nodded once. Brogan heard the electric whine of the bone saw starting up.

Jefferson clicked the phone shut, clenching his jaw. Lyerman was somewhere in the building, and so was Brogan. The sound he had heard in the background while he was talking to Lyerman, the far-off droning, was, he realized, the noise of an airplane passing overhead. Which meant they must have be on the roof.

"What's up?" McKenna asked, as Jefferson looked up from the phone.

"The roof. Let's go."

They crossed the floor to the glass elevators. The large Samoan guard looked them up and down as they passed, but said nothing, his attention focused on people coming into the party rather than leaving. They stepped into the elevator, Jefferson looking through the glass walls and out across the city as they rose.

"You think someone's up there?"

Jefferson nodded. "Lyerman."

The elevator continued to climb smoothly upward, the floors passing quickly.

"Is Brogan with him?"

"I think so."

The roof of the elevator was also glass, and through it, Jefferson caught a sudden movement above them. A large object was falling toward them; as if something had been thrown off the roof. Unaware, McKenna opened her mouth to say something, but a moment later the object smashed into the top of the elevator, shattering the glass and raining the broken bits onto them. The force of the blow was tremendous, swinging the elevator wildly and throwing Jefferson and McKenna both against the glass wall. The lights of the street far below moved sickeningly back and forth as the elevator swayed in its tracks.

McKenna was swearing to herself, holding on to the railing and pulling herself back up.

"Christ, what the fuck was that?" Jefferson said, holding the side of his head. Pain flared, and his fingers came away covered with blood.

A strong wind was blowing in through the smashed-open window, filling the inside of the elevator and making the car sway unsteadily. Through the broken top, Jefferson saw something large and black sitting on the twisted metal frame of the elevator roof.

"Are you all right?" Jefferson asked McKenna.

She nodded, bits of broken glass sparkling in her hair.

"Close your eyes," Jefferson said, then, using a sleeve of his tuxedo, gently brushed the glass out of her hair and away from her face.

"What hit us?"

Jefferson looked up again. "Don't know, I can't tell. But whatever it is, it fell from the roof."

"Or was thrown."

The elevator continued rising, then there was a small electronic *ping* as the car reached the top floor. The roof. There was another *ping*, and the doors began to slide open.

"We'll know in a minute, I guess," Jefferson said, then stepped out onto the roof.

The air was even cooler than it had been a week earlier, the roof's night garden quiet save for the sounds of insects. A wind blew through the flowers, turning their pale faces toward the night sky, their stalks waving back and forth in wide motions. The path led away from the elevator, a pale strip of ground lit by dim lamps rising just a foot off the ground. Farther ahead, the solarium building seemed quiet, a single light on inside. Next to it was the hot tub and several of the rosewood benches, all empty and quiet. The roof appeared to be uninhabited.

Jefferson turned back to look at the roof of the elevator. The large black object was jammed down into the supports of the elevator's roof, twisting the metal into sharp angles. Jefferson dragged one of the benches over, stood on it, reached for the heavy object, and pulled it off the roof of the elevator. As it came clear of the roof he could see that it was the large electric-powered chair. It smashed into the ground in front of him, just missing the bench, before rolling over once.

"Jesus . . ." Jefferson whispered, moving quickly toward the broken wheelchair, "it's Lyerman's."

The chair was turned upside down, someone still strapped to it, head pressed into the dirt of the garden. One wheel was spinning slowly, while the other was bent inward, the spokes splayed into ruptured points.

"Who is that?" McKenna said stepping in front of him and pointing to the figure, whose face was obscured.

The man was strapped tightly to the chair's frame, his arms pinioned to the arms with thick cord, and as Jefferson lifted the chair upright, the man's head flopped backward, revealing his face. The eyes bulged and ran with blood, the tongue hung limply from the mouth. Even so, Jefferson recognized him.

Lyerman. *Jesus, what does this mean about Brogan?* Jefferson thought to himself.

Jefferson moved his fingers to the man's neck, but even before he did so, he knew Lyerman was dead. Jefferson's hand dropped to his side and he reached for his gun, pulling it out from the holster in the small of his back, then repositioning the holster so that it was at his right side.

"I just talked to him on the phone," Jefferson said as he ran up the darkened path, covering the top of the roof. "Four minutes ago. Whoever tossed Lyerman still has to be up here."

"I'll check along the edges," McKenna said, cutting off the path and through the line of trees that ran alongside the edge of the roof.

Jefferson moved quietly toward the hot tub. The tub had been emptied and sat quiet and dark. The fountain was off, the gaping holes for the water jets in the horses' mouths sitting quiet and empty in the moonlight. Jefferson moved toward the solarium, looking through the window at the desk and chair inside, lit by a single yellow lamp hung from the ceiling. A rectangular spill of light illuminated the grass, and white moths fluttered and banged against the glass of the solarium.

Four minutes earlier, Lyerman had been alive. And in that time, someone had murdered him and thrown him, bound to his chair, from the roof. Whoever had done all that had vanished.

Jefferson scanned the roof and fixed his eyes on the stairwell at the back. The door was ajar, a single seam of fluorescent light showing in the crack. Jefferson moved quickly, across the line of benches and through the darkened grass. He banged open the stairwell door and looked down through the open corridor of space between the stairs and the walls. Nothing.

From behind him he heard the sound of glass breaking, somewhere over the side of the building.

"Jefferson," McKenna called from behind him. "Over here."

Jefferson turned from the empty stairwell and looked back across the lawn. McKenna stood at the edge of the roof, bending over the guardrail and looking at something below. Jefferson jogged across and joined her.

"What?"

"Look," McKenna said, pointing down along the sheer edge of the building.

Under them, the black glass side of the Lyerman Building slid in a smooth face toward the street. Far below them, the smoothness was broken abruptly by a shattered window on the side of the building. It looked as if curtains were blowing in the wind; at least Jefferson could see something billowing out through a window far below them.

"What do you bet that's Lyerman's personal floor, where his apartment is," Jefferson said.

McKenna pulled back from the edge and looked at him. Her dark hair blew wildly around her face and neck as if the rooftop were the deck of a ship cutting through the black sky and lights of the city. Jefferson stared out for a moment, seeing Fenway Park, silent and dark. "Something happened down there," she said. "Something bad."

"We'll go down and take a look."

"Won't there be an alarm?" she said.

"Yeah . . ." Jefferson said thoughtfully, then he walked quickly back across the roof to the bent wheelchair. He scanned the frame for a moment. Lyerman must have some kind of electronic key on the chair, to allow himself access in and out of his own apartment. After a moment, Jefferson found it, a small battery-powered laser-emitting electronic key the size of a credit card labeled BUILDING MASTER and affixed to the plastic panel on the side of the chair. Carefully detaching it from the panel, he slid it into his pocket. Now they'd have access to anyplace in the building they needed to go.

They took the broken elevator, the wind whistling through the opening, down to the forty-second floor and Lyerman's apartment. When the elevator came to a stop, a red warning light began to blink. Jefferson aimed the key and pressed the little button he found in the center. The flashing red light turned to a steady green glow and the doors to the floor opened with the familiar electronic *ping*, allowing Jefferson and McKenna to exit the elevator.

Lyerman's apartment was beautiful. Jefferson saw twelve-foot-high ceilings, a wide expansive hall floored with flecked marble that seemed to stretch back forever. They stood quietly in the entrance hall. To their side a birch console was pressed against the wall, a foot-long bronze sculpted pear sitting on top. The walls of the wide entrance hall were painted a faded yellow, and above the sculpture of the pear was a painting of a nude woman, fig leaves covering her in the usual places.

The lights on the floor were turned off, reducing the furniture to jagged black silhouettes. A faded blue filtered in through the far walls of giant glass windows. Outside, the lights of Boston gleamed like pieces of Formica set in black sand. One of the windows was broken, bits of glass spread across the carpeted floor. The curtains flapped and rolled in the wind like sheets hung on a clothesline. McKenna went quietly to the window, bending over the glass.

"Strange. The glass is on the inside. Like something broke the window from outside."

"How could that happen? We're forty-two stories up."

"Don't know," McKenna said. "But it looks to me like something came in through here."

She stood up from the broken glass and looked farther down the hallway. A room opened away from the entrance hall, spreading out to the right. They made their way down and carefully stepped inside. On the far wall were two chandeliers, each holding two candles. The flames burned smoothly, not flickering in the still air of the room. The walls were a golden-flecked Indian sandstone, decorated with works from an assortment of civilizations. Standing next to the candles, as tall as a full-grown man, was a sculpted-stone pre-Columbian grave marker. The marker was a stylized man, his hands linked across his chest, eyes and mouth closed.

The rest of the space in the room was taken up by a jade table, a bowl piled with glass fruit, and an expensive leather sofa. Jefferson listened closely, but the apartment was quiet. The light from the candles exposed the black outline of another doorway at the far corner of the room. Jefferson, followed by McKenna moved across the floor, his feet sinking deeply into the Persian carpet underneath him.

The room on the other side of the doorway was dark, and Jefferson stood still, trying to look into it. More windows with a view of the city, but the bluish nighttime glaze couldn't penetrate deeply into the area.

"Nice spread," McKenna said.

"Yeah . . ."

McKenna wrinkled her nose. "Smells in here. Bad."

Jefferson nodded. "Yeah."

The air inside was stifling, the smell nauseating. Even without the lights, Jefferson knew that it was the scent of death. He hesitated in the doorway, not sure what he was going to encounter in the room. Running his hand along the wall, he found a light switch and turned the lights on.

Two large clay lamps flicked to life, radiating light from underneath their white shades. They were in a bedroom, the two lamps on either side of a large bed. Across the covers was a spray of blood, small red droplets forming an arc from the crumpled pillow down to the base of the spread. The walls were painted a deep blue, and spatters of blood stretched across the coloring just above the bed.

"Looks like we're missing something," McKenna said.

"Like a body."

Near the bed, the doors of a large armoire had been thrown open, revealing a full-size mirror on the inside. The mirror was cracked in several places, jaggedly reflecting the scene in the bedroom in a spiderweb of images.

Jefferson scanned the room. To the right of the bed was a painting of a man wearing a mask and riding a horse. Underneath the painting was a table, on top of which was a small cigar box. Jefferson moved to the box, opening it. Inside was a stack of photographs. Jefferson lifted out the stack, sifting through the photographs. They were black-and-white images of men in military uniform and a photograph of an island. The island looked to be somewhere in the South Pacific, long tracks of jungle stretching across the white sand. He turned the photograph over: *Bougainville, Northern Solomon Island, 11 November 1943.*

He paused for a moment at a shot taken from the back of a landing craft. In the front, Jefferson could see that the flaps were falling to the ground at the instant the picture had been taken. The chains were a blur of movement, and he could see the men beginning to move onto the beach.

The next was a flaming bunker, two Marines standing out front, looking down at the hole in the earth. He flipped to the next image, a group of soldiers standing in front of a downed Japanese fighter plane somewhere in the jungle. There was a small group of men, each bearing a rifle and most wearing helmets. Most of the men had their shirts off, their bones prominent after time on the island. Jefferson scanned each of their faces, moving down the line.

One of the men was leaning back against the metal skin of the plane, a cigarette dangling from his mouth. Huh.

"Look at this guy." He pointed the man out to McKenna. "Looks like Brogan, doesn't he?"

McKenna nodded, but said nothing, staring at the photograph. Jefferson continued to scan down the line, flipping the photograph over, reading the names printed in black ink on the back. The one she pointed to was named Keaveney. And then Davis. Mulry. Walker. Seals. All names now forgotten.

McKenna had joined him, was staring over his shoulder. He could feel her close to him, her body tightening at something she saw in the photograph. What was it she saw?

Jefferson looked more closely at the faces again. Pausing at each for a moment. And then, caught in the sixty-five-year-old photograph, he saw it, too.

He looked down again at the image of Davis. Then, slowly, he looked up at the broken mirror in Lyerman's bedroom, staring at his own face, broken up slightly by the jagged cracks in the glass. He touched his cheeks, his finger running down toward his mouth.

The face in the mirror was the same in the photograph. Jefferson could have been an exact twin of Eric Davis.

"Your faces," McKenna said. "Yours and the man's in the photograph. They're the same."

"Jesus, we do look alike."

"Not alike, Jefferson. Yours and his. They're the same face."

"No, that can't be right. I didn't have any relatives who fought in World War II. I don't even know who this guy is."

"And that man you say looks like Brogan. They have the same face. You and Brogan have twins in this picture. And this one? It's Vincent." McKenna was pointing to a third man in the photograph. Jefferson stared hard at the face. The skin was tighter against the bone and the body was thinner, but even so, the man looked much like Steven Vincent.

"Don't you see what's happening?" McKenna asked.

"I don't know."

"The fulfillment of the manuscript. Everything that the demonology text writes has happened so far. The manuscript spoke of the reincarnation, and this is it. Right here. You don't just look like the faces in this photograph, you are the faces in this photograph. You lived the lives of these men before. In a previous lifetime."

"Are you saying that the guy in the photograph is me?"

"Yes, Jefferson, that's exactly what I'm saying. And Brogan and Vincent. All three of you were on that island. You may not remember it, but it's true. The photograph is proof," McKenna said. "The Jinn was on that island before, and now it's here in Boston. The demon has come looking for one of you."

"That means that you think that one of us is . . ."

"Sidina," McKenna said. "That's right."

"Sidina," he repeated.

"The demon isn't here in Boston looking for just anyone. It's looking for one of you three."

"But which one of us is Sidina?"

McKenna looked at him and shrugged. "I think you're all in danger."

Jefferson flipped the photograph over. On the back were names, written in thick strokes with a black pen. "J. J. Mulry, Alabama" written where Vincent was standing. Two names over was written "Eric Davis," the man who looked like Jefferson. And where Keaveney stood was Brogan's face.

Jefferson, Brogan, and Vincent, they were all in the picture. They were Davis, Keaveney, and Alabama. They had all been on that island, had been tent mates. Had fought together out there, and something had happened to all of them. Something terrible had happened on that island, and each of them knew what it was.

Something was beginning to grow in Jefferson's memory. A distant recollection that became steadily more familiar as his mind worked to dredge it up. He stared at the box on the table.

Reaching down to Lyerman's bedside table, he opened the black bag that also lay in the box. Inside were two pieces of metal, connected by a long chain. He pulled them out, the metal cool against his skin, and turning them over he read the inscription.

ERIC DAVIS

USMC

They were U.S. military dog tags. Suddenly, the smell of jungle struck him forcefully, the stink of rotting vegetation and mud, leaving him choking. He bent over the table, gagging, feeling sharp pains where the bullet-sized wounds marked his chest. He squinted in pain as a flash of memory hit him, a quick remembrance of running across a beach, the snap of rifle fire all around him, the smell of blood and the ocean in his nose.

"Hey, are you all right?" McKenna's voice sounded from somewhere far away.

He held his hand up, holding her away.

"Yeah," Jefferson answered. "I'm all right."

McKenna was looking around the rest of the room. In the far corner, beyond the painting of the masked man on horseback, sitting on top of a table, was a long box covered by a scarlet sheet. Grabbing the end of the sheet, McKenna pulled it back, the fabric sliding easily over the glass surface of the box.

"Look at this," McKenna said.

Jefferson stepped close to her, looking down at the table. Underneath the glass was a body. The skin had long since mummified and dried, but Jefferson recognized the mummified remains of the soldier. "Eric Davis," Jefferson said, feeling the tags in his hand.

McKenna pushed a button on a console on the side of the wooden table. There was a hissing noise, and the glass paneling opened, a musty smell escaping from inside. The leathered body was still clothed in military green, an ancient helmet placed near his head. His skin was withered to a leathery cracked surface, withered hands like monkey paws extending out from the sleeves of the jacket.

"Where did he come from?" McKenna asked.

Jefferson was staring at the body before him, the recollections of former events continuing to wash over him until he was drowning in forgotten smells and sights.

"The *Galla*," Jefferson replied. "Lyerman found him on the *Galla*. They found something on board that ship, there was something inside. The *Galla* had just come from Bougainville Island, had just picked up wounded soldiers. Davis must have been one of them."

"What else was on that ship?"

"The demon."

Jefferson continued to look at the body of the soldier. The one with his face. It was like looking at a version of himself, a forgotten twin from sixty years ago. The leathery hand was resting on the table, fingers curled in toward the palms. He could see dried bloodstains on the jacket, flecks of rust, and Jefferson felt his own chest, remembering the phantom pains that woke him in the night. He reached for the dried hand.

"What are you doing?" he heard McKenna say.

Jefferson only shook his head, then, with his outstretched hand, he took the hand of the dead soldier, feeling the dried skin like bark against his own. He shuddered as a current passed through his body, a wave of energy striking him. His breath was coming in gasps, a constricting band seeming to travel up from the hand into his own body.

He closed his eyes, pressing his fingers against the bridge of his nose as the memories flooded over him, as if he had opened a spigot somewhere in his mind. He remembered walking in a jagged line through a field of grass, the crack of rifle fire, and the explosion of mortars in the dirt. He had fought on a grassy plain. Then they passed back down into the jungle. There was a plane. A Japanese plane, stretching down from the trees, forgotten, like a child's toy. The pilot hung down from the branches, suspended in midair by his parachute, caught in the thick foliage above him.

"I can see things . . ." Jefferson whispered.

"What kinds of things?"

"Amazing things. I'm in a jungle."

"It's the past. From when you were on the island. You're beginning to remember."

"I remember a name. The name of a man," Jefferson said.

"Who?"

"Seals."

Seals telling them to stand in front of the plane. They are going to take a picture. He remembered now. He remembered everything.

The dead pilot was swaying back and forth like a giant pendulum hung from the tree, and I had to put my hand against the man's leg to steady him. Vincent was there and Brogan. They were watching as another man, Jersey I think, and I began sticking our hands into the pilot's pockets, fishing out his wallet, loose bits of paper, and three empty rounds of ammunition. I could feel the cold flesh through the thin fabric of the pockets; soft and yielding, like cold meat. The pilot had nothing of interest on him.

"Who are you?" came McKenna's voice.

"I'm . . . Davis," Jefferson said. "Eric Davis."

"Everybody up," Seals said, suddenly. "Get over by the downed plane. We've got to take some pictures for *Life* magazine."

I remember staring at him for a moment. He'd been acting strangely before, but I can't remember what it was he'd been doing. But now he was behaving normally. I think he might have murdered someone. A soldier named Reder, but I remember not being sure. I tried not to think about it.

"You serious?" I asked. "Hell, we're gonna be in *Life*?"

"General says we need to promote the war back home, so . . ." Seals had a large camera he was positioning on the top of a root, the lens turned toward the downed plane. "We're taking pictures for *Life* magazine."

Interested, we all gathered in front of the downed plane. Jersey and I had left the pilot hanging, moving over to join the rest of the group. The tail of the Jap plane was suspended in the air, while the nose and wings were impacted deep into the earth. Three parrots were sitting on the glass canopy, using their large orange beaks to groom each other's wings.

We crowded together beneath the plane, jostling each other for a better position. Most everyone had his shirt off, wrapped around his head to form a military green turban. I stood on the end, between Vincent and Jersey, my rifle propped against my shoulder. I remember Brogan being there, too, smiling at something. Seals was bent over the camera, fixing the auto-set mechanism. He sighted through the lens once, adjusting the shot of the men, then quickly ran over to stand at the end of the group nearest the crushed nose of the plane.

There was a whirring noise, then the shutter clicked once, capturing the moment.

We relaxed as Seals went to retrieve the camera. Vincent sighed once, then turned toward me, and said something strange.

"Something's wrong about this island," he said. "I can feel it."

Then he slung his rifle over his shoulder and turned back toward the line of trees. "Something's wrong."

After the picture, Seals wrapped the camera carefully in a piece of cloth and gave it to me to carry. Everyone else hoisted packs back onto sore shoulders, lifting rifles carefully, fingers tired from being wrapped around the weapons. Vincent had moved ahead first, stepping underneath the upraised tail of the plane, pushing aside the vines that dangled from the metal skin. He took a few steps, then stopped abruptly, his rifle dropping to the ground from loose hands.

"Holy Christ," he said slowly.

"What?" Brogan said, walking up next to him. Brogan froze, eyes turned up. "Oh man, you guys gotta see this."

We all jogged forward, moving underneath the tail of the downed Japanese fighter.

I was tired, not really in the mood for jogging, and thinking about *Life* magazine had made me depressed, my mind wandering back home. What was this place we were all in? Some hell, disguised in a thousand shades of green. We joined Vincent and Brogan, following their eyes forward.

In front of us were two massive stone columns, both thick with vines that ran over the stone in meshworks of veins. The columns stood on either side of a crumbling wall almost twenty feet in height, which stretched through the jungle, sometimes hidden by encroaching vegetation. More vines spread across the rocky face, burrowing into the stone and arcing up over the top. The entrance to the gate, where wooden doors had once stood, was open. But the doors, except for a few long timbers that lay almost obscured by greenery on the jungle floor, had rotted into the ground.

We all stood staring at what we had found. It was the first man-made structure we had found on the island except for Jap bunkers.

"What the hell is this about?" Vincent asked.

"Don't know," Seals replied.

"You think it's Japs?"

"Too old for that."

"Maybe they just put vines over it to make it look old. You know, like a disguise. Fool us."

"You're telling me they built a wall twenty feet high and God knows how long, then just left the door open for us to walk in?"

"I don't know. Yeah, maybe. They're sneaky little bastards."

"Vincent," Seals said, "don't talk anymore. Just keep quiet."

The rest of us stood staring at the thing. Tiny gnats were buzzing about my ears, and I was ready either to move forward or fall back. Anything but just standing there in that hot, dense heat. *Make up your mind.*

"So, what the hell you think it is?" Brogan asked.

"Don't know," Seals said. "Looks old. Been here a while, that's obvious. Maybe people used to live on the island."

"Why the hell would anyone want to live on this shithole?" Vincent asked.

"What'd I say, Vincent. Shut your piehole."

"I'm sorry, sir, but Jesus H, I'm serious. And if people used to live out here, where the hell they all go? What, they swim off the island? We're like a thousand miles from anything."

Seals gave Vincent the CO stare for a moment, then let it slide. He shrugged, then gripped his rifle. "Don't know. Why don't we go see. Vincent, thank you for volunteering for point."

"I didn't volunteer . . ." Vincent began, than, catching that same look from Seals, nodded. "Oh . . . right. Sure, I'll take it."

We spread out, Vincent taking point. Seals inspected the ground for a moment. There were no human footprints, but he found a number of impressions in the soft mud. They were claw marks, three-toed prints from some kind of jungle animal most probably. The marks were everywhere, in and out through the open gates. Each of the prints was the same size and shape, making me think it was one animal tracking through here hundreds of time rather than a whole group of them. Whatever "them" were.

As a unit, we passed between the columns, stepping beyond the wall. As we did, a cold wind came from nowhere, making the sweat chill against our bare skin. Vincent and a few others took their shirt turbans off their heads and buttoned them back on.

"Got cold all of a sudden," he said, hunching his shoulders.

Inside the wall were more structures, old buildings made of crumbling sandstone. Sandstone, definitely, which was strange, because that didn't seem like it should be a native rock of the island. Then again, I was no geologist. Each of the buildings was unique in size and shape, and there were hundreds of them. At some point, this must have been quite a town, but now it lay abandoned.

Each of the structures had broken stairs of stone leading up to a black rectangular doorway. On either side of the doorway were carvings, sometimes of men or of bulls, or sometimes with giant reliefs depicting groups of soldiers armed with long, curving swords. There were more of the three-toed tracks inside the walls. They were every-where. Whatever was making the prints probably lived inside one of the buildings.

Between the stone structures, where roads and pathways must have once run, the vegetation had grown up again, spreading across everything. Giant leafy plants arched over the tops of stairways, while green lichen stained the tan carvings and reliefs. Everything was quiet. The jungle was sometimes as loud as a bus terminal. Parrots squawking, monkeys hooting. But inside the gates was nothing. No noise. It was the first time things had been quiet since we'd arrived on the island. It was uncomfortable.

That cold wind had passed, and the intense, thick heat of the jungle was back. I wiped at my face with my shirt, lifting my helmet off my head for a second, letting my scalp air out. I could hear a buzzing, like the sound of live electricity. The buzzing got louder the farther we walked, and I tracked the sound as coming from inside a rectan-gular stone building on our right. The building had a triangle-shaped roof, looking like it might have been a temple at one time. Like the Parthenon. Curious, I broke from the group, walking toward the building and up the wide stone stairway.

Something inside was dead.

I could tell that from the smell. You don't have to see anything to know when something dead is nearby. You can smell it. And dead men have their own particular smell. Strongest thing I've ever encountered in my life. It's nauseating, the smell of a rotting body. The stench stays with you for hours afterward. When I was a kid, I found a man down by the old Route 53. He'd been hit by something, a truck most likely, and knocked into a ditch, which must have been why nobody had found him. And this guy must have been lying there dead almost a week before I came across him. I don't much remember what he looked like, but I can sure as hell remember that smell. And I was getting it full force again.

The buzzing was growing louder, too, as I approached the open doorway of the stone building. There were about five or six steps leading up to the door, and with each one, the buzzing got louder and the smell got stronger. I reached the top and stepped forward. Inside was hot and rancid. My eyes took a moment to adjust to the darkness, and when they'd adjusted and I'd looked around the room, I gave them a moment more just to make sure I was really seeing what I was seeing.

I was standing in a room of dead. They were everywhere. Dead bodies literally stacked in heaps on the floor, piled in the corners, hung from the ceiling by thick ugly ropes that wrapped around their necks and stretched them out. They were twisting back and forth in a slight breeze, the ropes creaking under the motion, glazed eyes staring openly at me.

Flies buzzed around throughout the room, filling the air with a quivering black cloud.

I turned away quickly, covering my mouth and nose with one hand. With the other, I waved the men up the stairs. Seals joined me first, looking in through the opening. He whistled softly, low and quiet.

"Lord have mercy."

Seals, the hard-ass, the cold killer. Shocked with surprise.

Vincent was up next. Then a moment later, he was back out in the open, throwing up in the long grass.

"My God," Seals said. "What the hell happened in here?"

I shook my head, kept my mouth covered, and took another glance at the bodies. They all looked Japanese. My stomach was dancing beneath my chest, and I had to close my eyes to concentrate on not throwing up. I was aware of everyone else around me, staring into the room. There was silence. Except for the noise of the flies.

"Would you look at that," a voice I recognized as Brogan's finally said. "Those flies, none of them are touching the bodies. They won't even land on them."

I opened my eyes and looked again. Brogan was right. The air was filled with buzzing, but none of the flies were landing on the bodies.

"Who you think did all this, sir?" Brogan turned to Seals.

"I don't know."

"Our guys? That missing unit?"

"No . . . this was something else. No man could do all this," Seals said, then turned to the rest of us. "All right, I want each one of those dead men checked out. Make sure none of them is our crew. Drag them outside quick. Lord knows we don't want to be in here any longer than we have to."

We went to work carrying the bodies out of the temple and onto the grass outside. We chewed peppermint gum and put rags over our mouths and noses while we worked. Brogan had some Aqua Velva, and we all soaked our upper lips in the stuff. It was almost enough to keep out the smell.

I carried body after body, the smells of decaying skin and aftershave strong in my nose. Eventually we had them all outside, a whole line of them, melting into the grass.

"I hate to say it," Vincent whispered to me as we worked, "but I hope that missing unit is mixed in here somewhere. Anything to get us the hell out of here."

When we were outside, Seals walked up and down the line, looking at all the dead faces. None of them was American. None of them was from the unit we were looking for. Seals didn't ask us to check them for intelligence, and nobody volunteered. We counted them all. There were forty-seven.

I turned away, walking slowly into the open space between the buildings, breathing the cleaner air. The air was filled with a grayish light; looked like a storm was coming.

We left the lines of dead behind in the grass. Seals was up front, Brogan walking beside me, everyone's head moving from left to right, then back again, scanning everything around us. There was a hum of crickets in the tall grass, and I could see small black bugs jumping from blade to blade ahead of me. At least that was something living inside the walls. Vincent was on my right, an unlit cigarette hanging lightly from his lips, the straps of his helmet falling into loose ends by his chin. He looked pale, probably from the vomit job he'd done.

We were passing underneath a low, overhanging tree, with large pieces of fruit that looked vaguely like oranges hanging from the branches. I reached up, picked one off, and shined it against my shirt. I moved to peel the orange whatever-it-was, pressing my thumb into the skin. A stream of blood flowed out of the fruit from where I'd broken the skin. I dropped the fruit in surprise, and it rolled along the grass, the blood dripping into the ground. What the hell was this place?

I shifted the grip on my weapon, rubbing sweat from my eyes with one hand. I kicked aside the fruit with my boot. As I kicked, there was the sudden crack of a rifle shot. I heard a grunt and turned to see Jersey sinking to his knees, blood flowing from his gut.

"Down, down!" Seals yelled, dropping to his knees and raising his rifle.

Jersey was ten yards to my right. He was rolling back and forth on the grass, groaning, his eyes ground shut. Seals was firing at something in the distance. Brogan joined him, their rifles aimed toward a building with two stone bulls out front. I kept my head down in the grass, the blades tickling me along the neck and cheek. These kinds of firefights weren't so bad if you could keep your head down, keep out of sight. Only the ones who tried to return fire got it. Trouble was, you didn't want anyone to see you keeping it down. Get called a coward. Have to go home with that name.

Vincent was running in a crouch to Jersey, skidding beside him like a ballplayer. Brogan was firing again, moving through the tall grass and crouching behind a wide stone stairway. I kept my head down a moment more, following a single cricket climbing up the length of a stalk of grass. When I'd stayed down as long as I thought I could, I raised my head like a swimmer surfacing for air. Propping my rifle against my shoulder, I sighted down the barrel. I didn't see much of anything in the tangle of jungle and stone buildings ahead of us, but I squeezed off a few shots anyway. Just to make an impression with my own guys. I was a fighter. Then, lowering my head again, I scooted along through the grass on my stomach until I reached Vincent and Jersey.

Vincent had peeled back Jersey's shirt, looking down at the quarter-sized leaking hole just above his belly button. Jersey's stomach was rising and falling, the skin quivering as red liquid seeped out of the hole, pumping out in bursts, reminding me of spurts of seawater from clams under the sand. Something like a bullet cracked over my head, throwing me to the ground again. You can't really hear a bullet passing near you, there's no real sound. But you can sense it. The break of the air. The feel of the metal rifling going by for an instant. And all around me, the air was filled with these little sensations.

Someone was putting some heavy fire on us.

When I raised my head, across the field I could see three Japs with loose-fitting helmets. They were stripped to the waist and crouched behind a tumbled column that lay in broken chunks across the grass. They had a big gun, one of the heavy machine guns, and had the thing opened up. I fired my rifle twice. One of the men went down, making me a killer. Only, in times of war they don't call you a killer. They call you a hero. Whatever they were going to call me, all I know is that I could see a spurt of blood bursting from the man's punctured neck.

Together, Vincent and I grabbed on to Jersey's shirt, pulling the squirming man through the long grass toward where Brogan was crouched behind a stairwell. Something exploded in the grass, a round of mortar fire landing just in front of the building to which we were dragging Jersey. The Japs had mortars, big ones, that ripped up big chunks of earth and rained it down on top of us. Brogan left the cover behind the stairs, running out and helping us drag Jersey through the grass. Together, we pulled him out of the open and back behind the stairs again, leaving him writhing in the grass while we returned the Jap fire.

Another mortar shell struck the ground, followed by a burst of heavier machine-gun fire. The hammer strikes of bullets swept over the building, knocking us to the ground, where we lay in curled balls, trying to press our entire bodies against the rocky surface of the building's side.

"Jesus Christ," Brogan spit out, his face cringing as bits of shattered rock fell down on us.

A large chunk struck me in the face, splitting open my skin in a jagged mark down the side of my cheek. Raising my head over the level of the side stairs, I saw two more Japs bending over a tube-shaped mortar set into the earth about fifty yards away. They launched a round, and I watched it rise into the air like a rocket, hanging above the grass as it completed the apex of the arc, before it slowly began to fall down toward us.

"Incoming!" I shouted.

"We gotta go!" Brogan shouted.

"What about Jersey?" Vincent shouted.

And in the midst of the shouting and the gunfire, we knew the answer to Vincent's question.

"No time, leave him," Brogan said, starting to pull back. "He's gone."

Vincent nodded, reaching down and grabbing Jersey's hand. "Sorry, brother."

Jersey squeezed back for a moment, watching us run in low crouches away from the building. A moment later, the mortar shell struck the stairway, the explosion slamming through the thick stone and bursting rocks and flames across Jersey, scorching him alive.

Vincent looked back once at Jersey, then turned his head quickly away. "God help us."

Seals was running parallel to us, waving his hand toward the opening in the gate.

"Let's go," he was shouting, moving through the grass.

We followed him toward the opening in the wall, heads down, running over the uneven ground. We reached the gates and passed through, the heat of the jungle flooding over us as we turned the corner of the wall and stopped, breathing heavily. Never thought I'd be happy to smell the jungle again. Truth was, though, for all its rot, it's better than the smell of the dead.

"Too heavy back there." Seals was panting, holding his side.

He brought his hand away, and his fingers were shiny with red.

Vincent, Brogan, and I all noticed.

"You all right, sir?" Vincent asked.

Seals nodded. "Yeah. I'm all right. Jersey?"

Vincent shook his head.

Seals shook his head, then sighed. "All right."

We moved away from the wall, following its line through the jungle, stepping deeper into the darkness.

We moved along the line of the wall, walking in a ragged line over the hills and descending back into the jungle below. We were passing through a grove of bamboo plants when it happened.

We found the missing Marines.

There were seven men, sitting on tree stumps in a small open area between the trunks of giant rubber trees. They were smoking cigarettes and talking to each other over metal bowls of brownish food. As we broke into the clearing, the seven men looked up, their conversation dying out. We all stared at each other for a moment. There was a sudden rustling noise behind, and I turned quickly to see three Japanese coming out of the jungle behind them.

The men had been carefully concealed—green leafy branches hung from their helmets and their faces were painted black with mud. A fourth Japanese man, bald, walked toward us crying, "Ahee, ahee, ahee, ahee," while grinning and extending a clear glass bottle of sugarwater soy milk.

"Jesus, a fucking ambush," Vincent said, knocking away the bottle and raising his weapon.

Things were happening fast. Seals was bringing up his M1, turning quickly toward the four Japs behind us. They were reacting, too, reaching for their own weapons, which they hadn't bothered to come out with. I was also reaching for my rifle, my helmet falling over my eyes, half-blocking my vision. That's just the way of it. One moment everything is fine, the next moment someone is stepping on a land mine, or getting shot, or four Japs are stepping out of nowhere to ambush you. Things had gotten fucked up quick.

Then in the midst of the storm came a clear voice, "No! No shooting!"

And for some reason, we all listened. Even Seals, who lowered his rifle and turned back to look at the person who had spoken. The Jap soldiers stood staring at us for a moment, then lowered their weapons and stepped past us into the clearing with the Americans. Sitting cross-legged on the ground, the Japanese took bowls of food from the missing unit, began eating, and otherwise ignored us. We watched this whole thing take place, but still couldn't believe it.

"What is going on?" I whispered to Vincent.

"Don't know."

We all stood there, frozen, nobody sure what the hell was going on.

Seals stepped forward. "You the Fifty-third?"

One of the men nodded. "That's right."

"Lotta folks looking for you," Seals observed, then nodded toward the Japanese. "These POWs?"

The man must have thought that funny, because he smiled. "Naw. They're not our prisoners. They're fighting with us now."

Vincent laughed aloud. "Man, what the hell you talking about? We had these same fucks shooting at us an hour ago."

"Was it inside the gate?" the American sitting near the fire asked.

"What?"

"The gate, was it inside the walls of the gate."

"Yeah, why?"

"Inside the gate, the war is still going on, but out here, we're fighting something much worse."

There was a quick conversation in Japanese among the Americans and the Japanese soldiers. Vincent turned toward me, whispering, "They've lost it. Either that, or they're with the other side now."

The American turned toward Vincent. "There's something out in the jungle. It's been hunting us."

"What the hell you talking about?" Brogan said. "Nothing out here except for the Japs. You can walk all night and not bump into anything else except them."

"You try and leave here at night," the American soldier said slowly. "You won't live until morning."

For the first time, I noticed an odd-looking structure, made of logs, standing in the small clearing behind the men. It looked like a bunker, except it was hexagonal, with window slits facing out in all directions. It was the unusual shape that caught my attention. Most bunkers were constructed with a front and a back, designed to defend against an attack from one direction. This structure had openings on all sides, as if the men who built it were expecting an attack from all around.

Vincent stepped back slightly, leaning in toward Seals and lowering his voice. "These boys are gone."

Seals nodded slightly, then stepped forward.

"We were sent out to find you," Seals said. "Out in the jungle. I'm not sure exactly what's going on here. I thought you'd be lost, or wounded, but none of that seems like it's true. Am I right, Private?"

The man sitting on the log smiled slowly, placed the metal bowl down at his feet, then reached back and pulled a helmet out from behind him. Bringing the helmet up, he dusted off the front. Two shining captain's bars were affixed to the metal.

He rested the helmet in his lap. "I said, if you leave now, you won't live six hours. You understand me now, Sergeant?"

Military rank is a powerful thing, and Seals nodded, stepping back. "I'm sorry, sir."

The captain waved us over to the log benches, and, shouldering our rifles, we all sat down. It felt good to sit—my feet were aching from all the walking.

"You want something to eat?" the captain asked. "Drink?"

We shook our heads no, but I wouldn't have minded having something to eat and drink about then. I wasn't going to be the one to give in though. Not until I found out what the hell was going on.

"I'm Captain Mark Chambers," he said, then began pointing to the other men, introducing each of them. He nodded toward the four Japanese sitting cross-legged on the ground and eating from the metal bowls. "These are our Japanese friends, Mr. Moto, Mr. Matsumuru, Kenjii, and Mr. Taki."

The Japanese looked up as they heard their names, nodding in turn to us.

"Well, that's the goddamnedest thing I've ever seen," Vincent said.

"I know what you're thinking," the captain said. "I'd have thought the same thing two weeks ago. Now it's different. We're not fighting the Japanese anymore, we're fighting something out there."

"Where?" I asked.

"It's out there." The captain gestured toward the thick trees. "In the jungle."

"What is . . ." I paused for a moment. "It?"

"We're not sure yet," another one of the men said. He was tall and slim, his skin stretched tight across his face. "They come out of the jungle at night."

The captain nodded. "A little more than two weeks ago, we were sent inland for recon and then to link up with the airborne. The Japanese had hit us hard on the north beachhead, so we patched together a mixed unit of who was left, some Rangers, Marines, whatever we had, and moved down through the island. That first night, something came into our camp, killing our two on-duty guards, slitting their throats. We thought it was the Japanese at first, but the next night something killed four more of our guys. It crept into their tent. We woke up the next morning, there was blood all over the tent fabric, but the bodies were missing. After that, we made time during the day, but something would come into our camp at night. First we tried climbing into the trees, but it hunted us down. Then we stopped sleeping, staying awake by the fire. Moving during the day and circling up at night."

The captain paused for a moment, taking a thoughtful look down into his bowl of food.

"On the fifth day, we reached the gates." The captain nodded toward the stone wall in the distance. "We spent the night inside the walls. We were hit again by a unit of Japanese. We fought during the night and knocked the Japanese back out of the gates.

Even after we had won the battle, our own men turned on each other. They started killing each other. They couldn't get enough blood. They were drunk on it.

"More Japanese came the next day and the next. Inside those gates, the Americans fight the Japanese every day, both sides fighting for the enjoyment of killing. They destroy each other every day, not because of any war. But because they like doing so.

"I left with the seven men you see here, the rest of our unit pushed farther into the gate. Then we bumped into these guys." He nodded toward the Japanese soldiers. "They told us that their unit had done the same. The men turning on each other, killing each other."

"A revolt within the units?" Seals asked.

"No." The captain shook his head. "There's something evil inside those gates, something that turns men crazy with violence. Fills them with evil. Inside those gates a war is going on, more violent than the war outside. I've seen it, the men literally ripping each other apart. Biting, tearing, like wild animals."

"What about outside the gates?"

"Outside, there's something in the jungle," the captain said. "Assassins. A combination of man and beast. And every night they attack us. So we built this camp outside the gates, to defend ourselves. We joined together, us and the Japanese, to fight against these things."

"Against what?"

"There is a man, I've seen him. A man with the head of a bull. He leads them."

I looked over the captain's shoulder, staring at the large octagon-shaped bunker. For the first time I noticed there were gouge marks in the wood. They were in sets of three, shredding the coconut logs in deep lines.

"Christ . . ." Seals said. "Captain, sir, you're a United States military officer. You're telling me you believe this?"

"This story isn't familiar to you?" the captain responded. "You've come from somewhere, you've been in the jungle. You know what I'm talking about."

Vincent nodded in agreement. One of the Japanese soldiers looked to be following the conversation. He scooped the last of his food from the bowl, then shouldered his rifle. Brushing himself off, he slowly stood up, saying something in Japanese.

"What'd he say? What'd he say?" Vincent asked.

"The Kuro is an evil wind," the captain began. "From Japanese legend. He says these things are demons, carried to this island by the Kuro. They are the spirits of the dead warriors, brought here for evil, attracted by the smell of war."

The captain looked up toward the canopy of leaves above them, at the sky. He took the rest of his coffee, swirled it for a moment in his metal cup, then threw the remains onto the fire. The flames flared up for a moment as he rose.

"Getting dark," he said. "They'll be coming soon. It's time to get ready."

We were carrying helmetfuls of dirty water from the wide Kai River, which cut through the heart of the island, running near the bunker, dousing the coconut wood with the water. Seals joined us, dipping his helmet into the stream alongside Brogan, Vincent, and me.

"What do you think, sir?" Vincent asked in a low voice, keeping his eyes across the clearing and on the Japanese and the missing unit.

"I don't know, Vincent," Seals replied. "What do you think?"

"Sir?"

"That's right, Vincent, for the only time in your life, I'm asking you your opinion. Better take advantage of it while the question stands."

"Thank you, sir," Vincent said "Well . . . part of me thinks that everyone here is crazy. That we walked right into an insane asylum. Maybe they just cracked under the stress of fighting. Just like a dam, you can only take so much before you starting springing leaks. Who knows?"

"That's true."

"But part of me," Vincent said, "part of me thinks that these guys are telling the truth. I mean, shit, we seen some strange things this tour."

"Amen," Brogan said.

"Some real strange things," Vincent continued. "And part of me thinks that these fucking nutcases are the only ones that know what the hell is going on around here. That's what the other part of me thinks."

"You?" Seals said, turning toward me.

"My vote's with what Vincent says," I replied. "Whether we want to admit it or not, something is going on that's beyond this war. And frankly, I think we'd be safer taking their advice than trying to dog it back through the jungle."

"Damn, right," Brogan said.

Seals ran his fingers through the water for a moment.

"All right," he said finally. "We stay here the night. See if things change in the morning."

We filled our helmets in the river, then walked the short distance through the jungle before throwing the water against the logs of the fort. Just like the captain had told us to do.

"They started using fire," the captain began, carrying three full canteens. He gestured toward black scorch marks on the roof of the bunker. "Trying to burn us out. Lucky it was raining last night, the roof would have gone up. Tonight I don't think we'll get the rain."

After we had wetted the place down, Vincent, Brogan, and I used our bayonets to sharpen sticks of bamboo almost six feet long. Two of the Japanese soldiers took the sharpened sticks, burying them pointing outward into the dirt, forming a ring around the bunker. Vincent was staring at the Japanese soldiers as he worked, his eyebrows knitted together. I could tell what he was thinking. That one minute you're trying your best to kill off every member of a race of people. Then the next minute you're buddied up with them. It was a little hard to shift gears so fast.

Seals had Martinez's flamethrower strapped to his back. He was shooting jets of fire into the surrounding jungle, burning the thick growth back, opening up the clearing. Whoever approached the bunker would have to move over thirty yards of open ground.

"Never thought I'd see the day when I'd be working next to a Jap," Brogan said.

"Yeah. I know what you mean," I said. "So . . . you really believe all this shit?"

"Hell, I don't know," Brogan said slowly. "Something strange has been going on, I know that much. You see how them flies wouldn't touch those bodies inside the stone building there? And how there were no animals in there, and that real cold feeling when we walked through the gates. It's like we walked into an evil place."

"But our own guys attacking each other? And evil winds and dead warriors?"

"I know what you mean."

"Just seems crazy is all. I never heard of anything like that before in my life."

"My father fought in World War I. He said that he used to see a shadow creeping over the battlefield, the shadow of death, coming to collect his due. I think evil things are attracted to evil deeds, are attracted to war, feed upon the hatred and the dead."

I picked up one of the bamboo poles and began sharpening it absentmindedly.

"I don't know which is worse," I said. "Fighting the Japanese, or whatever this is . . ."

My voice trailed off, and I cocked my head to the side.

"What?" Vincent said.

"You hear that?"

Vincent sucked in his breath, listening carefully. Above us, the sky was quickly growing dark, the clouds lit with a reddish hue from the setting sun. Fruit bats were beginning to flit in and out among the treetops. Somewhere in the distance, from the base of the mountain range, was a long, low, booming sound.

"What is that?" Vincent asked.

The noise continued for a moment, before the tone rose fluidly, as if someone were blowing into a conch shell. Listening to the sound echo off the mountains, I felt something rise on the back of my neck. A gargoyle of fear perched on my shoulder. The captain was running up from the stream, three of his men following close behind. At the clearing he stopped, looking out through the trees and across the valley.

"They'll be coming," the captain said, staring off into the distance. "Everyone into the bunker!"

"The Kuro," one of the Japanese soldiers said. "The Kuro is blowing in."

I jumped up from the log, taking the sharpened bamboo stick with me and burying it deep into the soil outside the bunker. Vincent was behind me, staring nervously backward toward the oncoming sound, which seemed to roll up the hilltop in a wave. The trumpeting sounded again, first low, then high. In the distance, a flock of birds took to flight from the treetops, their bodies silhouetted against the darkening sky. I felt a fearful rush to get into the bunker. Nearby, Seals was walking slowly around the perimeter of the clearing. He was carrying a flaming torch, a long heavy branch wrapped in fabric. More torches had been erected along the perimeter, about ten yards apart, forming a circle of light around the bunker. He walked from torch to torch, lighting each of them in turn.

I turned and moved toward the entrance. There was a heavy door of coconut logs and sharpened bamboo lashed over supporting logs on one side. Inside, the bunker was large, almost twenty yards across, with high-vaulted ceilings. More torches were wedged into the logs, and men were moving in circles quickly lighting each of them, sparks from the flames falling in cascades onto the dirt floor.

Through the slits in the walls, I could see Seals light the last torch, then move slowly back toward the bunker. The four Japs (or Japanese, I guess I should say now that we were friends and all) were kneeling on the ground just outside the entrance, lowering their heads to the ground in prayer. One of them straightened up, still on his knees, and tied a white scarf filled with Japanese characters around his forehead.

The door creaked, and Seals stepped inside, followed by the four Japanese. Turning back to the door, the captain slid a heavy log bar across the frame, sealing the entrance shut. The torches on the walls were burning, their smoke trickling up through a hole in the roof.

"Everyone take a window," the captain said. "Load up and keep your eyes peeled!"

I moved quickly to one of the slits. Vincent was next to me, Brogan on the other side, both leaning against the wall, peering out through the narrow opening. I loaded my carbine, resting it on the floor next to me, and looked out across the clearing. The vegetation had been burned and cut away, leaving a series of black stumps and loose branches. The clearing extended in a thirty-yard radius around the bunker, ending in the dense growth of the jungle. At the edge of the burned area were the torches, flickering occasional showers of sparks onto the ground, hundreds of insects flying in circles around their light.

Seals was standing guard at the window nearest Vincent. I was near them, pressing my cheeks against the open slits of the bunker, when I felt a cold wind against my face. The coldness was blowing in from the jungle, stinking of decay and death.

"The Kuro," one of the Japanese said in English. "It is blowing in tonight."

The horn sounded again, filling up the bunker with its noise. Vincent swallowed once, his Adam's apple bobbing up and down along his neck. In the jungle, I saw a light appear, a single flame. I shrugged my shoulder up to my cheek, wiping the sweat away. The air was hot and humid; after the cold breeze, I could feel more sweat running down my back.

A second light appeared, moving in a circle through the jungle around the bunker. Then another light flashed up suddenly, then a fourth.

"What's happening?" Vincent turned toward Seals.

"Not sure." Seals raised his rifle, sliding it through the slot in the wall. "Looks like there's someone out there."

More lights were appearing, flashing all through the jungle, until there was a series of small fires burning and moving. Something was approaching, a shadow emerging from the line of the trees, stepping out into the clearing, and walking slowly toward the bunker. The figure was still in silhouette, but as it came closer to one of the torches, it was lit with a reddish glow.

The figure was a man, bent over, bearing the weight of a large wooden cross on his back. The cross was tall, so the man had to bend forward to prevent the base from hitting the ground behind him. His arms were stretched to the side, and, even from across the clearing, I could see the spikes driven into both of his hands, pinning them to the wooden cross section.

"Holy God," someone whispered. "What the hell is that?"

Brogan sucked in his breath and crossed himself, reaching for the rifle at his feet.

The figure continued to step forward, staggering from foot to foot under the heavy weight of the cross. He was wearing pants, but no shirt, streaks of blood and dirt caked against his skin. His head hung limply, but as he moved closer he suddenly looked up.

We all recognized the face.

It was Hartmere. The man missing from the first night.

The one who had gone out for watch then just vanished by morning.

"Oh man," Vincent said. "That's Hartmere."

"But he's dead," I said. "We buried him already."

The Marine was half the distance across the open area, when he collapsed to his knees, the cross striking the ground behind him. We all watched in some kind of fascinated trance.

"I'm going to get him," Vincent said, backing away from the window.

"You stay here," the captain said. "Nobody leaves the bunker."

"No, sir," Vincent replied, moving toward the door. "I'm gonna bring him back."

"They won't let you bring him back."

The captain moved to restrain him, but Vincent shrugged him off, lifting the bar from the door. He pulled the door open slightly and stepped outside. The captain didn't follow. Vincent stood for a moment in the doorway, looking around the clearing. The open area was colored reddish with the flickering light from the torches along the perimeter. If others were out in the jungle, they hadn't shown themselves yet.

Hartmere was still on his knees, his head sagging toward his chest. Vincent moved toward him slowly, his rifle raised.

Stepping around one of the sharpened bamboo sticks, he reached the fallen Marine, bending down in front of him. "Hey, buddy,"—Vincent shouldered his rifle, reaching out for the Marine's shoulder—"you all right?"

Hartmere's shoulders were moving, shaking. A soft sound was escaping from his lips, the rapid sucking of air. I thought he had begun to cry. Vincent must have thought the same, because next thing, he was placing a reassuring hand on the man's head, looking up to keep an eye on the jungle. The lights were still in the trees; they seemed to be suspended in the air.

Hartmere's body started moving, his entire torso shaking rapidly. Vincent looked down at him, seeing the man's eyes wrinkling at the corners. The quick gasping sobs slowly changed, growing louder and longer, until suddenly we all realized that Hartmere wasn't crying. He was laughing.

Startled, Vincent jerked his hand away, stepping back from the fallen Marine. Hartmere slowly began to raise his head, until he was looking directly up at Vincent. The man's face had changed, his lips were tighter, drawn back from teeth that now appeared to be sharper. His eyes had changed from their light brown color to a swirling yellow. And leaning on his knees, his arms nailed to the cross, he was laughing.

"Hartmere?" Vincent said softly, leaning forward.

Hartmere stood up quickly, ripping one hand free of the cross. Something sharp was in his hand, and he jabbed upward, stabbing toward Vincent's gut. Vincent grunted and moved to the side, dodging the blow. Hartmere came at him again, laughing. Vincent slowly backed away, confused. The fire lights in the jungle were increasing. Vincent turned and ran back toward the bunker.

Hartmere stood up, one hand still pinioned to the cross. He pulled his other hand free, then began bounding quickly across the clearing, heading for the open bunker door.

"The door!" I shouted. "Somebody close the door!"

"Hurry up, hurry!" Seals shouted to the approaching Vincent, Hartmere directly behind him.

Vincent burst through the open doorway and one of the Japanese soldiers moved quickly to the door, pushing it to and shoving the bar into place. Hartmere slammed into the door with a cracking sound, knocking the Japanese soldier backward. Seals and the captain threw their weight against the door, trying to hold back Hartmere. Or whatever it was he'd become.

"Jesus Christ," Vincent was almost crying. "That ain't no man. What the hell was that?"

From outside came the long trumpeting noise again.

"They'll be coming!" the captain shouted. "Back to the windows."

The cold wind, the Kuro, was blowing strongly now, filling the inside of the bunker with chilled air, threatening to douse the burning torches. Breathless, I ran back toward my slit, sliding my carbine through the opening. The flames outside were moving, coming toward the bunker. From the jungle, there was a long scream, followed by another, and another, the sound of a hundred men screaming. The trumpeting continued, rallying them forward. I heard a pounding noise, and from the darkness of the jungle, figures began bursting into the clearing. They stood at the edge of the clearing, shouting and jeering.

They were wearing armor, knight's armor, like pictures I'd seen from the Crusades. There were flags of different colors blowing in the stiff wind, some showing golden lions or eagles, all standing above the men. The visors of the soldiers were down, preventing me from seeing their faces, but through the slits something was glowing red and yellow. As if their eyes were on fire.

They continued to stand in a line, pumping their swords in the air and cheering. I looked around the clearing. There were hundreds of them surrounding the small bunker. Horns were blowing, and a figure on horseback broke through their ranks. The horse was massive and black, smoke coming from its nostrils as it rose on its two back legs. A plate of armor lined its breast, a second plate covered the front of its long face.

The horse was riding along the front of the ranks of knights. A man was seated atop, swinging a giant mace. He was wearing armor plates on his shins and arms and a metal breastplate with a Red Lion on the front.

And he had the head of a bull, with fire-colored eyes and flaring nostrils. The bull's head bellowed once, and he pointed toward the bunker.

"Here they come!" I heard someone in the bunker shout, followed by a burst of gunfire.

The men in armor were charging toward us, their feet pounding the open ground to the bunker. One of them had reached the first of the sharpened bamboo and was tearing it from the ground. He was holding a lit torch in one hand, the flames sparking to the ground. I sighted down my rifle at the figure and pulled the trigger of my carbine, watching as he spun to the ground.

He lay there for a moment, before rising again.

Running forward, the knight flung the lit torch onto the roof of the bunker, where the heavy log thudded loudly. There were more thuds on the roof as other torches landed heavily, sizzling against the wet wood.

"Water! Water!"

One of the Japanese was flailing his hands in the center of the bunker, his left arm engulfed in flames. Vincent took off his shirt, wrapped the man inside, and rolled him on the dirt floor until the flames died out. I was turned away from the opening, watching Vincent, when I felt a sharp pain across my face. Turning around, I saw something reaching through the narrow slit. A long arm swinging a dagger wildly. When I touched my face, my fingers came away with blood.

I fired a round at the arm, which snapped back away from the window, disappearing from view. The inside of the bunker was beginning to grow hot. Scorching. Looking up toward the roof, I saw a line of flames running along one of the logs as the bunker began to catch fire. Smoke was filling the small space, and men were tearing off strips of fabric, covering their mouths and noses.

Through the slit, I could see more figures running across the clearing. Seals hoisted the two metal fuel canisters for the flamethrower onto his back. Stepping to the window, he thrust the end of the weapon out the slit. Three armored figures were moving toward the bunker. As they approached, Seals pulled the trigger.

A solid jet of flames shot out, striking the figures directly. They burst into flame, but continued to move forward, their bodies a burning mass. The trumpet called again, with its low, booming noise, and the creatures began retreating toward the jungle.

I was bleeding heavily from the cut across my cheek and pressed a dirty rag against my face, trying to stop the flow.

"Is that it?" Seals panted. He had a cut across his chest, the shirt fabric torn in parallel grooves.

"No." The captain shook his head. "They'll be back."

"What are they?" Vincent screamed. "I got three of them. Shot them down so they couldn't live, but they kept on coming."

"I shot two myself," another voice cried. "They're not men. They're something else."

"We all shot some of them," Seals said. "These things, these creatures can't be killed."

The horn in the jungle was sounding again, and we could hear the cries rallying together outside the perimeter of the clearing.

"They're coming again," I said.

Above us was a loud cracking noise, one of the flaming timbers breaking down into the center of the room. Men dived out of the way as the fire-drenched wood struck the dirt floor. The heat was incredible, scorching the faces of the men. The bunker was turning into an oven, its inside filled with red light.

"We can't stay here," the captain said. "It's burning down."

Seals moved to the door, lifted the bar, and pulled the door open so the men could leave the burning structure.

I moved through the doorway, choking and gagging on the thick smoke as I lurched into the clearing. I hung my head and leaned forward, sucking in the clean night air. The horn was blowing again in the jungle, and I could hear a pounding noise, the sound of feet. Another attack was coming.

"Fix bayonets!" the captain shouted.

I reached up toward the end of my rifle, sliding my bayonet onto the end of the barrel and screwing the long knife tightly into place. I was nervous, my fingers slipping twice over the bolt before I secured the lock.

Dark shadows were running through the jungle toward us, the pounding noise growing louder, sounding like a thousand galloping horses. We formed a ragged line across the front of the bunker. Next to me, Brogan was breathing heavily, gripping his rifle, the end affixed with the sharp bayonet.

"Here they come!" a voice shouted, just as the shadows broke into the clearing. Near us, one of the Japanese soldiers let loose with an attack cry and began running forward, holding his bayonet in front. The rest of the soldiers followed, racing across the wide, burned expanse of the clearing, running to meet the shadowy figures head-on.

The distance between them and us closed rapidly as we ran to meet the creatures from the jungle, running across the clearing of burned vegetation. We met halfway, and immediately men fell to the ground, screaming in pain. Brogan rolled over onto his back, a broken spearpoint protruding from his side, while I felt a sharp pain in my leg as something stuck me.

Holding out the bayonet, I jabbed the knife into the charging figure's gut, twisting the rifle around as the bayonet pierced the metal. The figure cried, falling backward and landing on the ground. I saw Seals jabbing a knife into a throat, then push the body away from him. Seals stood up, then turned slowly and faced me, and I saw a jagged line cut across the center of his stomach.

The bunker collapsed in a roar of flames, shooting sparks into the air. The red embers descended on us, covering our clothes and bouncing across the clearing on gusts of wind. One of the cloaked figures had been struck by a falling log. It was knocked forward, plunging into the fire. A moment later it reeled back, its body ablaze. It ran toward the Japanese, impaling itself on one of their bayonets. Still burning, the figure swung wildly, struck the soldier across the face, and knocked him to the ground.

I felt someone grab my shoulder and turned to look.

Seals was staring at me, his face black with ash, the whites of his eyes showing through the blackness. "Let's go. We're leaving."

I nodded, and Vincent, Brogan, Seals, and I turned and ran, moving quickly along the line of the wall, leaving the burning bunker behind us. We reached the entrance of the gates and turned inside the walls, immediately feeling the rush of cold air as we passed through. Just over the wall, we could see the sky glowing an angry red, lit by the raging fire in the bunker. We moved deeper into the area beyond the gate, carefully scanning ahead for a Japanese troop emplacement. The Japs outside the gates had been friendly, but not the ones inside.

There was nothing, only the quiet rush of the wind through the thick grass. Palms, silhouetted against the night sky, rose above the line of the wall, waving back and forth in the breeze. Ahead of us was a rectangular stone building with a curving roof of wooden timbers. A large eye was painted just over the doorway, and two carved lions flanked either side, standing at the top of the wide staircase.

"We'll see if we make a stand in there," Seals said, nodding toward the building.

The building's front was long pillars, through which we could see the thick over-growth of what must have one time been a beautiful garden. Now vines and palm plants strangled out everything, including a fountain in the center that had long since dried out.

We moved up the stairwell, stepping into the dark interior. The inside was inky black, like the very bottom of the ocean. Faintly, I could make out a thick rope hanging from the ceiling, just to the right of the doorway. Grasping the rope, I tugged hard. Above me, from somewhere in the ceiling, was the noise of grating stone. A section of the roof opened up over us, and the interior room was suddenly filled with a pale light.

A set of large mirrors was suspended at the height of the wall, angled slightly downward. The glass reflected the moon's light into the room below, giving us enough to see by. We were standing at the beginning of a single long narrow room. Along the sidewalls were carved stone statues of men about eight feet in height, each with the head of a different animal, standing rigid, eyes pointed straight forward. At the end of the room, I saw a much larger statue, a man again standing upright, this time with the head of a bull.

In front of the statue was an altar, rising from the floor. The top of the altar was bare except for a single wooden box. I moved to the box, flipping the lid open and looking down. Inside the box were six metal arrowheads, each with four jagged edges, divided into two straight lines. The arrowheads were made of a heavy dark metal, with openings at the back end for the shaft of an arrow.

"What's that about?" Vincent asked, looking into the box.

"Don't know."

I took the box, closed it, and carefully placed it inside my pants pocket. As I lifted the box from the altar, there was a rumbling noise, a thick scraping of stone, and slowly the altar slid backward, revealing a gaping rectangular hole underneath. A stairwell ran down the hole, and, as we stood looking down, a cold wind blew up from the opening. A set of torches along the stairwell suddenly illuminated, flames flickering up and casting shadows along the sandstone walls.

And that's when we heard it. The strangest thing.

From below us, we heard music. And voices and laughter. The light speech of women. We stared at one another.

"Sounds like a party going on down there," Vincent said.

"Who the hell would be down there?" I said.

"Well, sounds like it's better than what's going on up here," Brogan said. "That's for damn sure."

From out in the courtyard beyond the opening of the shrine we were in, we heard the quick rattle of gunfire and a muffled explosion. We ran back to the entrance of the shrine and stared out through the abandoned garden and into the fields beyond. A group of Japanese were making their way through the grass. They were carrying a long pole, on which a man hung, his arms and legs tethered to the wood.

One of the Japanese saw us and pointed excitedly, raised his rifle, and fired twice, the bullets smacking the stone column just beyond our heads. Vincent began firing back in quick succession, dropping two of the soldiers. There was more firing back and forth between our groups, bullets cutting over the abandoned garden and between the long columns of stone.

I saw the Japs spreading out, running low to the ground, quickly moving toward our position. They were flanking us, coming up on either side. I turned to tell Seals, but saw that he wasn't behind me anymore.

"Where's Seals?" I shouted above the loud popping of Vincent's carbine. The carbine ejected the spent clip onto the stone floor. Vincent turned around, looking back into the shrine behind them.

"Don't know; he must have gone down them stairs," he said.

Outside, the Japanese were moving closer, heads down, bodies low to the ground as they approached, sliding from stone column to stone column. It had begun to rain again, and I had to wipe my eyes clear to look out across the clearing. I counted at least eight men moving through the clearing toward us. Eight against three.

"I say we go down the hole," I said. "Take our chances below. We stay here, that's it."

Vincent and Brogan nodded, pulling back. There was a sudden thud, and Brogan collapsed to the ground, his right pant leg instantly bloodied. He'd been struck just above the knee, the bullet tearing a hole in his thigh. He rolled on his side, his right leg up, his palm pressed against the wound as he cried in pain.

Vincent grabbed him under the armpits, dragging him along the stone floor. Through the opening, I could see the Japanese moving faster, aware we were retreating. I turned and fired a few rounds through the open doorway, knocking one of the Japs backward, his body spinning as it quickly vanished into the grass.

Vincent had pulled the screaming Brogan to the top of the stairway. I joined him, picking up Brogan's feet, and together we carried the wounded man down the stairs. The stairway was made of blocks of sandy-colored stone, torches illuminating the bare walls. I could hear again the sound of women laughing, the noise drawing us farther underground.

At the bottom, the floor leveled out into smooth stone, covered with a layer of dirt and dust. We laid Brogan on the floor, tightly binding his wound with a strip of cloth ripped from my shirt. He was swearing through clenched teeth, his fingers balled into tight fists. Above us, we heard the sound of boots against the hard stone as the Japanese soldiers entered the shrine. Wouldn't be long before they came calling down the stairs.

As Vincent cinched the strip of cloth tight around Brogan's leg, Brogan cried out, and I had to clamp my hand tightly around his mouth. He nodded after a moment, and I slowly removed my hand.

"Can you walk?" I hissed.

"I think so."

We lifted him to his feet, and Brogan limped a few steps forward, using the butt end of his rifle as a cane. We were standing at the edge of a long, dark, open area. The area was divided by columns that stretched from the ceiling to the floor, spaced equidistant around the perimeter.

Through the columns, the view was breathtaking. Jewels were pressed into the ceiling, glittering in an exact replica of the constellations in the night sky. In the center of the room was the island, carved in replica from stone and surrounded by mirror glass, which reflected the stars above like an ocean. Exactly like we were looking down on the island at night.

Along the sidewalls and by each of the columns were life-size soldiers, sculpted entirely from stone. They were armed with shields and long, curving swords, their bodies adorned with chain-mail armor. We moved into the room, silent and dark except for the glittering jewels above. From the corner of my eye, I caught a sudden flash of movement as something ran from column to column. I turned my head quickly, but saw nothing, only the mute forms of the statues.

"Seals?" I whispered into the darkness.

No reply. Only a cold wind, which seemed to blow from nowhere, striking against our skin and making me shiver slightly. At the end of the room was a long hallway, lit by more torches. The floor was laid with smooth marble, shined until the surface reflected the wavering torchlight. At the end of the hallway was a giant statue, standing almost twenty feet high, of a man with the head of a bull. The bull's horns were curving and sharp, the eyes narrow, angry, while the body of the man was muscular, arms resting at his sides.

There was a scuffing noise on the stairway behind us. The Japs were coming down the stairs, following us underground.

"Let's keep moving," Vincent said softly.

I listened for a moment. More shuffling of booted feet against stone. Then a slight rushing of air; the noise of something breathing. Something else was in the room with us.

We moved quickly toward the rear of the room, Brogan limping heavily, his pant leg caked with blood. I heard a voice, someone shouting in Japanese. There was a loud report of a rifle, and something chinked against the stone. They were firing at us again. We ducked behind columns as more rifle fire cracked near us.

"We're in a tight spot," Vincent whispered. "Got Japs crawling all over."

I nodded, peeking my head around the side of the column. I saw two Jap soldiers moving quickly along the other side of the room, ducking from column to column. I raised my rifle and fired off two quick shots, missing with both. There was a quick response from somewhere else in the room, four muzzle flashes snapping in the darkness, followed by the accompanying whine of bullets.

I ducked behind the pillar again. Twenty yards ahead of us, I could faintly make out the rectangular outline of a third doorway, a separate set of stairs leading downward. I gestured toward the area. We had to keep moving.

"Let's see if we can get out down there."

We ducked our heads, moving to the next column; no answering fire came toward us. After pausing for a moment, we moved again. Shoot and scoot. There was something lying on the floor in front of us. A Japanese soldier.

He was down in a pooling circle of blood, a deep gash running across the front of his chest. Directly over him was one of the statue soldiers. The stone gaze was fixed and the sculpted sword was raised. Streaks of blood covered the blade.

We kept moving, past the dead Jap and toward the back doorway.

From behind us came a sharp scream—a Jap crying. I heard a whistling noise, like a blade cutting through grass, then the scream again.

Something was shaking me.

"Jefferson," a voice said. "Wake up."

The shaking began again, from somewhere in the darkness around me. The temple was gone, and I was left in blackness, with the shaking, and again a female voice saying, "Wake up!"

Something was lifted over my head, the cool feel of a metal chain being pulled upward.

Jefferson felt a rushing of wind around him as he jerked back into consciousness. The smell of the jungle escaped from his nose, like air escaping from a balloon. He jerked open his eyes, his mouth popping open as he sucked in air with a "Haahh."

McKenna was shaking him, holding firmly on to his shoulder.

He shook his head, trying to clear his mind. "What is it?"

She looked down at him, holding her hand over his mouth, her eyes wide.

"Something's coming."

Jefferson shook his head, trying to clear it. His ears were popping and ringing, as if he were a diver surfacing from deep underwater. McKenna was holding the dog tags in her hand, the chain dangling beneath her fingers. Jefferson was sitting upright on the floor, underneath the table with the dried body of Eric Davis above him. McKenna was looking past him, over his shoulder to the two closed doors of the bedroom.

"Footsteps in the hall," she said.

Jefferson cocked his head, trying to concentrate through the ringing in his ears. He heard the jerking sound of footsteps outside the door. They paused, then jerked again, like someone creeping down the carpeted pathway toward the bedroom. Whatever was out there was trying to be quiet, sneaking forward in quick, halting steps, moving rapidly toward the door.

Jefferson pulled himself to his feet, but had to brace his body against the table as he stood unsteadily upright, waving back and forth. He grabbed the bundle of photographs from the table, took the dog tags from McKenna, and jammed them both into his pants pocket. McKenna started moving toward the door. She stepped behind a large walnut bureau just beside the doorway. Putting her weight behind it, she slid the heavy piece of furniture across the two doors, blocking them from the inside.

Jefferson took a step forward, but felt his front leg buckling underneath him, unable to support the weight of his own body.

McKenna was back by his side, one arm around his waist holding him up.

"Do you think you can walk?"

Jefferson nodded. "Yes. Slowly."

There was a clicking sound outside the door, and they both turned to look. The handles of the doors were gold and curved into a soft S formation. One of them was slowly turning. He heard a voice outside, a low whispering sound, followed by a brief chuckle, then another whisper, and the handle turned again.

"Jesus," Jefferson whispered. "It's outside."

"Sit down," McKenna said. "Rest."

She propped Jefferson against the table, where he remained sitting, trying to get his bearings. McKenna was quickly moving around the room, searching for some kind of exit. At the far corner was a second doorway. She opened it and found a long hallway on the either side, leading toward a kitchen.

"Can you walk?"

There was a knocking on the outside door, then the handle turned again, this time with more force. Whatever was outside was beginning to grow more impatient. There was a pause, then a thud, a heavy weight being thrown against the wooden frame. Jefferson glanced toward the closed doors. "Yeah, I can try. Whatever's outside is being a pretty good motivator right now."

Jefferson stood slowly, hooking his arm over McKenna's head. He felt light-headed, drunk almost, his legs wobbling beneath him. By leaning heavily on McKenna's shoulders, he could lift and drag his feet along behind him, his body sagging under its own weight.

"Let's make it to the end of the hallway," McKenna said, as they moved forward.

Behind them, something smashed against the door again, the wooden frame vibrating violently, the heavy cabinet sliding back an inch.

"Hurry," she said. "It's coming."

They made their way down the hall. The kitchen was small, white tile floor, marble counters, a central island topped with a vase of flowers. Two large oak doors stood on heavy metal hinges in the frame. Behind them, the bedroom doors had broken down, and they could hear a patter of feet of something running down the hall toward them. McKenna dropped Jefferson into a kitchen chair and reached for the two oak doors. She slammed them together, pulling the bolt across both of them.

She took one end of the kitchen table, pulling the heavy weight across the floor and pressing it against the double doors. Something outside in the hallway was jiggling the door handle now. Jefferson watched the brass fixture turning slightly back and forth.

There was a booming noise as something crashed against the frame from outside. The door vibrated, and the table slid back an inch across the floor.

"Jesus . . ." McKenna murmured, her eyes fixing on the door.

Jefferson pushed himself up from the chair, testing his legs again, making short steps across the room. He held on to the refrigerator, steadying himself, and looked around. There were no more doors in the kitchen. No way out. Only the lines of windows over the sink.

The booming noise sounded again, the two large oak doors rattling in their frames. The slide bolt held fast, but Jefferson could see the metal beginning to bend. There was a cracking sound, and threads of wood erupted from the door's surface as the oak began to splinter. They were trapped. Outside there was a sudden screaming roar of frustration, followed by another door-rattling smash. Like sitting in a car during an auto accident.

"There's no way out," Jefferson said.

"Check the windows, see if we can open them."

"And do what, climb? We're forty-two stories in the air."

"I don't know. I'd maybe rather jump than wait around for whatever is out there to get inside."

One of the doors was slowly coming apart under the beating, a jagged crack forming in the wood, starting at the top of the door and reaching halfway down. McKenna was looking wildly around the room, tearing open cabinets, throwing out their contents. Pots and pans rattled against the white tile floor, spreading out in a mess of shining metal. Jefferson was feeling stronger, the lightness in his head passing away. Letting go of the refrigerator, he found he could walk across the floor. At least he'd be able to put up a halfway-decent fight when the Jinn broke down the doorway. All this time, and he still hadn't had a good look at it.

McKenna was working on the silverware drawers, throwing each one back and rummaging her hand through the knives and forks. Jefferson joined her, pulling out the drawers, looking for something useful. There was a small doorway the size of a square kitchen cabinet just to the left of the sink. Jefferson opened it and found himself staring at the inside of a little cupboard. No, not a cupboard. An elevator. A small service elevator.

"McKenna, look at this!"

"What is it?"

"The kitchen's service elevator, for raising and lowering supplies," Jefferson said. "We can get out through here."

McKenna nodded. "Got no argument from me."

She climbed up onto the counter, sliding her way into the small car and pulling her knees up toward her chin, the black evening gown riding up the length of her thigh. Jefferson climbed onto the counter next to her, pushing his way into the car beside her. They were pressed tightly together, but with both their knees tucked under their chins, they just fit. Outside the car, set on the side of the white cupboard, were two large buttons that controlled the elevator. Jefferson pressed himself into the car next to McKenna, then, reaching out, pushed the button labeled UP.

Immediately the car jerked to life, slowly beginning to ascend. Jefferson felt his body shaking from the rushes of adrenaline. He took a last look into the kitchen as they moved. The thick wooden boards of the door were quickly splintering apart, the pounding on the doors outside sounding like a fireman's ax striking the heavy oak.

Then the view was gone.

They were passing farther up into the elevator shaft, moving into complete darkness. Jefferson could hear the grind of the winch pulling their weight and he wondered how old the mechanism was, imagining the rope breaking and the forty-story fall down to the basement. Next to him, lost in the darkness, Jefferson could feel McKenna's body, curled up tightly and shivering in the darkness.

"Where do you think this goes?" Jefferson heard her ask.

"Don't know. Up. Away from the kitchen at least."

Jefferson reached into his pocket and pulled out a metal Zippo lighter. He flicked the top and a bright flame illuminated the box-shaped elevator. On the open end of the car, Jefferson could see the walls of the elevator shaft sliding by as they ascended. Every floor, an opening appeared in the wall, the three-foot-by-three-foot endings of the ventilation ducts that ran through the building.

The flame flickered in Jefferson's hands, casting shadows across the interior of the car. It was like being inside an oven. Below them was silence. He wasn't sure if the demon had broken its way into the kitchen or if it had given up entirely, moving back somewhere into the rest of the apartment. Wherever it was, they would have to get past it if they wanted to leave the building.

Brogan was on the roof; so was Lyerman, and if Lyerman was up there, probably his little Panamanian nurse was as well. Something killed Lyerman, throwing his body onto the elevator car. Then what? Climbed down the sheer side of the building and into Lyerman's apartment? What happened to Brogan? Jefferson flipped off the lighter to save the fluid. Back came the dark.

Jefferson leaned back against the wall, crouching in the darkness, hearing the sound of gears turning and McKenna breathing. A minute passed, then two. They kept moving up. Then McKenna's voice came out of the darkness.

"What happened when you touched, him, Davis . . . that soldier? Do you remember?" McKenna asked.

Jefferson said, "I remembered things that happened, in the past, back on that island."

"Sidina. Did you see who it was?"

"No, I didn't get time to figure it out. We were all there, Brogan, Vincent, and I. But I don't know who was who."

Jefferson felt McKenna's hand on his arm, "Don't worry . . ."

Her hand slid toward his, her skin cool.

Then they heard the gears above them begin to groan. The car came to a jerking halt. McKenna's hands moved to her sides, palms pressing against the metal walls to stabilize herself as they rocked back and forth for a moment, the tiny car swaying on its support lines.

"Jesus, what was that?" McKenna said.

"We stopped."

Jefferson had the Zippo out in front of him, pressing his head against the front wall, trying to look up toward the gear mechanism above them. Maybe the engine had shorted out after carrying the weight of two people. With his head pressed tightly against the wall, Jefferson could see a little way up into the shaft above them. The flame of his lighter faded out in only a few feet into the darkness, the support lines disappearing into blackness as they rose through the narrow shaft.

"Can you see anything?" McKenna asked.

"No, pretty dark up there. I can't see more than a few feet."

"You think the engine's broken?"

"Don't know—" Jefferson began to say when the car jolted to life again, the sound of the winch echoing back down the shaft. "Oops, no, there we go again. Must have just stalled."

Jefferson sat back into the car, watching the passage of the shaft move up past the open side of the car. Moving up. That meant they were moving down. Back toward the kitchen.

"Oh my God," McKenna said at the same moment. "We're going back down."

Jefferson could hear the difference in the pitch of the winch as it released more line instead of having to pull it up. They were falling down the shaft, faster than they had risen, the air grate openings passing by them in rapid succession.

"The controls in the kitchen. Did you leave them working?" McKenna asked.

Jefferson groaned. She was right. He had left the controls to the service elevator intact. He should have smashed them. Somehow the Jinn had figured out where they had gone and was calling the service elevator back to the kitchen.

From somewhere below them, they heard a roar, like the screech of an animal moving up through the elevator shaft. Jefferson felt McKenna tighten her body against him. Whatever was making that sound was waiting for them. *If we're still inside the elevator when it reaches the kitchen . . .* Jefferson let the thought die in his head. He forced himself to look around.

"What are we gonna do?" McKenna asked. "Can we cut a hole in the roof?"

"Don't know," Jefferson said. "Close your eyes, block your ears."

Jefferson took out his Beretta and, placing the barrel against the roof of the service car, pulled the trigger. The blast was incredibly loud in the tiny space, causing Jefferson's ears to ring painfully. He pulled the trigger again and again, until the small car was filled with acrid gunsmoke and several holes were punched in the ceiling. With his fist, he pounded against the weakened metal. It gave way slightly, bending backward, but not enough for them to squeeze through. They were trapped.

Jefferson turned his eyes from the ceiling and watched one of the open air-ventilation shafts sweep by.

"We could try getting out through there," he said, indicating the ventilation shaft as they passed another one. Each opening was narrow, the opening about as wide and tall as the face of a small television set.

"You crazy?" McKenna said. "We can't both fit through there in time."

"You want to wait and find out what's down in the kitchen? I'd rather take my chances with this. If we move fast enough, we can both make it. I know it."

McKenna turned her head, doubtfully watching the ventilation shafts sweep by the car.

"Either we try, or it's over the second we reach the kitchen. Your choice."

"Not much of a choice."

"No, it's not."

McKenna said, "Let's go."

Jefferson watched the ventilation openings slide by, trying to time how far apart they were. One passed and he began to count slowly in his head. He'd reached nine before another one passed. He figured that they had just over two seconds when the open wall of the elevator lined up with the opening of the shaft. They would have to be quick.

"OK, when we go, go hard. You first, I'll be right behind you. Push as far forward as you can into the duct and keep moving until I say I'm clear," Jefferson said. "If I'm not behind you, I'll try and get into the next shaft. Just keep going forward and we'll meet in the stairwell."

"OK," McKenna agreed.

"All set?"

"Yes."

"We're going to be fine."

"I know we are."

They passed a ventilation opening and Jefferson began to count. One, two . . .

"Get ready, you move first, go as soon as you can and push into the ventilation duct. I'll be right behind you."

Five, six . . .

They both had their feet pressed against the back wall of the small elevator, like sprinters waiting at the starting blocks. The car slid by the open ventilation shaft, and McKenna sprang forward, pushing off the back of the elevator wall and sliding into the shaft. Jefferson pushed off a moment later, exploding behind her, sliding forward on his stomach.

There was an instant of sharp pain as his shoulder banged hard against metal. He could feel the elevator car continuing to descend; soon it would crush his lower back, snapping his spine. With a final push, he forced himself into the ventilation shaft, like a cork shooting from a bottle.

He lay on the metal floor of the shaft, breathing heavily, the tops of his shoulders aching from where they'd been struck. He looked up and saw McKenna's backside.

"You all right?"

"Yeah. I'm good."

Jefferson looked around at the close metal walls. "Not so bad. I've rented studio apartments smaller than this."

The empty duct stretched ahead of them, an enclosed space of gleaming corrugated metal that narrowed away from the duct's openings. On his hands and knees, Jefferson's back pressed tightly against the metal ceiling. As the shaft narrowed, to move forward he had to lower himself to his stomach and slide along. The motion was awkward and made seeing behind him almost impossible. To do so he had to turn onto his side, a feat in itself. Memories of the island, inside the narrow dirt tunnels flushing out the Japanese, came flashing back.

Ahead of him, McKenna was also wriggling forward, the toes of her shoes making squeaking sounds against the metal as they were dragged along. She was still wearing high-heeled dress shoes from the party. In a quick movement, she kicked them off, leaving them behind her in the tunnel as she pressed forward in her stocking feet.

The shoes lay on the floor of the duct ahead of him, and Jefferson picked them up, carrying them with him as they moved to avoid leaving a trace. The last thing he wanted was for that thing to chase them into the enclosed ventilation system. He could barely even move his arms away from his sides, let alone defend himself if attacked from behind.

"This is like crawling through the inside of a trash can," McKenna said, still squirming forward.

The elevator car would be arriving back in the kitchen soon, and the Jinn would see that it was empty. They needed to get as far into the duct as they could before that happened. They jerked and wiggled forward, Jefferson holding the Zippo lighter ahead of him. The flame was flickering wildly from a steady gust of air that blew from farther down the duct ahead of them.

"I feel wind," Jefferson said. "Do you see anything in front of us?"

"I can't tell. Too dark. Looks like there might be something moving ahead of us. A fan maybe."

"Might be a ventilation fan. That'd lead down into the floor below us."

Behind them, the grinding of the elevator had stopped. There was a silent pause, and, a moment later, they heard a long shriek. An angry roar carried up through the duct. The demon had found the empty elevator car.

"You hear that?" McKenna asked.

"Just keep moving."

Jefferson placed his ear against the duct, listening. He could hear the roar again, vibrating through the thin metal. He pressed forward, trying to move faster.

"You see the fan still?"

"I can't tell."

From behind them, Jefferson heard the mechanical whirring of the elevator again, the high-pitched whine. The elevator was rising once more, only this time the noise of the winch was louder, the gears straining against a weight. As if the car were no longer empty. Jefferson knew what that sound meant. The demon was in the elevator. It was coming after them.

"We gotta move. Keep going," Jefferson said.

"It's coming, isn't it?"

"I think so."

They began sliding faster. The corridor was beginning to branch out, intersections in the duct system as the ventilation cut off to different areas of the building. It was a maze, each pathway looking exactly the same, a nightmare of shining metal gleaming at him from every direction. McKenna turned to the right, moving a few yards forward, then to the left, Jefferson following her.

Slithering forward, Jefferson heard something in the ducts with them. A scuffling sound, shoe rubber over metal. He reached up, grabbing McKenna's ankle to stop her. She turned and looked back, and he held one finger over his mouth. The scuffling was coming from ahead of them. Jefferson flipped the lid over his Zippo, extinguishing the flame and pitching them into darkness. Gray light filtered up from the offices below, allowing them to see the length of the duct.

"What is it?" McKenna whispered.

"A sound." Jefferson nodded forward. "Up ahead."

They stared down the long metal corridor, up to where it formed another intersection thirty yards ahead. Jefferson held his breath, placing his ear against the metal. He heard the sound again, something moving along with them. McKenna tensed, and Jefferson looked up to see the black shape of the demon ahead of them.

It was crawling perpendicular to them, moving along the connecting pathway and Jefferson could tell it hadn't noticed them yet.

The Jinn was stopped ahead of them in the duct, still unaware they were watching it, only a turn of the head away.

It was doing something with its hand, a back-and-forth motion over the top of its head. Jefferson watched with horrid fascination. It was cleaning itself, but not like a human would, but more like a rat would straighten or smooth its own fur. They watched it for a moment more, but still without turning its head, it began crawling forward again, moving out of the intersection and out of sight.

Jefferson exhaled and pointed McKenna down a corridor that stretched to their right, away from the demon. She nodded and began sliding forward, keeping as quiet as possible. Ahead of them, Jefferson could see a series of metal grates in the floor, light shining up from between the slats. They were small, too small for either of them to fit through, but as they passed over them, Jefferson could see the wooden top of a long conference table about eight feet below.

He paused for a moment, pressing his face against the metal slats, staring as best he could into the room. He could see everything from above, looking toward the far wall where paintings hung, back to the doorway. The room was empty.

"Nothing."

McKenna agreed and continued forward. Periodically, Jefferson stopped to press his ear against the metal, each time hearing nothing. The duct made a ninety-degree turn, forcing them to curl their bodies up tightly to cut the corner, then abruptly the duct split, one passageway heading right, the other, left. McKenna hesitated for a moment, then turned right. Jefferson began to think they were traveling in a circle.

Jefferson's neck began to cramp from holding his head back. He paused again to listen. When his ear touched the cool metal, he heard something. A single shriek, vibrating through the aluminum of the duct. Like someone dragging knives over metal.

McKenna was moving ahead, and he hissed at her to get her attention. She paused and looked back at him as he pressed his ear to the metal again, stifling his breath to listen more closely. He heard the noise again, a rapid clicking sound, followed by a screech of solid nails against the aluminum—the sound of the demon, clawing its way through the tight corridor. It wasn't giving up.

Jefferson turned his head, looking back, ready to open up with his service revolver. Behind them was nothing. Only a long, empty stretch of shining corrugated metal. But for how long?

"Keep going," Jefferson said. "There must be some kind of way out."

McKenna nodded, and they continued crawling forward. They passed along fifty yards of smooth metal before Jefferson felt an increase in the strength of the breeze that surrounded them. A cool draft of air was being pulled from behind him and flowing forward.

McKenna felt it, too, and her pace quickened, moving toward the flow of air, toward what must be an opening in the duct. As they pushed on, the flow kept increasing, until it became a constant stream through the metal tunnel. Jefferson had begun to notice something else as well, something he had been trying to ignore—the scratching noise in the metal was rapidly becoming louder.

Even without pressing his ear to the duct, he could hear it, the sharp screech of nails on metal.

He turned his head, trying to see behind them down the duct.

The Jinn was there.

It was covered in dry, gray skin. Its head was the shape of a bull, but strangely elongated in the back, with a mouth filled with jagged sharp teeth. Its eyes were red, and as Jefferson made eye contact, it hissed its tongue out like a giant snake. The thing was still about forty yards behind them, pulling itself through the narrow duct with its long arms, jerking forward on its belly like a rat.

"There's something ahead," McKenna said suddenly. "The tunnel. It ends."

Jefferson pulled his eyes away from the pursuing creature and looked forward. McKenna was right. Ahead of them was a flat, blank wall of metal. The draft of air must be coming from someplace though. He looked around again.

Just before the end of the tunnel was a ventilation fan set in the floor of the duct. An opening.

The fan's blades were turning lazily, pumping fresh air into the office space below them. Mounted on the back of the fan was a rounded metal box, and inside was small electric motor. A series of black wires ran along the base of the motor. The fan was set in a circular hole about two feet in diameter in the base of the duct. Beyond the spinning metal blades, Jefferson could see a bathroom beneath them. The blades were moving too fast for them to squeeze through the opening while it was running.

"We need to shut this off," Jefferson said, his eyes scanning the motor.

McKenna screamed suddenly, a loud, piercing noise that vibrated through the narrow, metal walls. She was looking back down the duct at the Jinn, seeing it for the first time. Jefferson followed her gaze. The thing was rapidly moving toward them, pulling itself forward with its claws in quick, almost robotic gestures. As it heard McKenna scream, it opened its mouth and bellowed.

"Oh Jesus," Jefferson said.

He looked down at the electric motor and began pulling out the series of black wires. The electric whine of the fan immediately died, but the blades themselves continued to spin, propelled along by momentum. If they tried to squeeze down through the opening now, they'd be cut apart by them. Jefferson pulled out his Beretta, jamming the base of the gun down into the path of the blades.

There was an immediate shower of sparks as the metal pieces grated against each other. Jefferson held his hand in place, the vibration running through the weapon making his arm shake.

Gradually, the blades slowed, finally coming to a stop.

"Quick," Jefferson said, "get down through the hole."

McKenna pulled her legs up, slipping her feet between the blades of the fan and lowering herself. She hung for a moment, a few feet above the tile floor of the bathroom, before letting go and landing safely.

She looked back up at him, raising her hands.

"C'mon," she said. "Hurry!"

Jefferson turned and looked backward. The creature was almost on him; he could feel the entire wall of the duct vibrating as it approached. Jefferson began lowering himself through the fan opening, and, as the creature lunged for him, he let go of the duct, falling into the bathroom below.

He landed painfully hard on the tile floor, sprawling forward, his shoulder crashing against the porcelain edge of a bathroom sink. Above them was a scream of frustration. The rectangular metal duct they had emerged from ran along the ceiling of the bathroom. Too large to squeeze between the fan blades, the demon bellowed. A claw suddenly appeared, tearing through the metal of the duct above them. The creature was ripping its way through the thin metal.

"Let's go."

McKenna nodded, and they ran out of the bathroom, pushing open the door and stepping into a dark, quiet hallway beyond. Behind them, they heard the high-pitched whine of metal as the demon continued to cut.

Jefferson was no longer sure which floor they were on, but moved toward the glowing EXIT sign at the end of the hall and into the main stairwell of the building.

"Which way?' McKenna asked.

"I don't know."

"Pick one."

In front of them, wide concrete stairs stretched both up and down

"Down," Jefferson said, quickly moving forward.

They moved down two floors, before stopping and ducking into the forty-ninth floor. They stood for a moment in the hallway beyond, trying to let their eyes adjust to the darkness. Throughout the building, the lights were off, turning the office spaces into areas of shadows and the dark outlines of computers and desks.

The hallway they were in opened up into a larger reception area. Plush, comfortable-looking chairs were lined in a semicircle around a small table strewn with copies of *Architectural Digest*, *The Economist*, and *The New Yorker*. On the far wall was an unused fireplace, just beneath a large mirror with an expansive gilded frame. A chandelier hung in the center of the room, low enough that Jefferson could have reached up and touched its base if he'd wanted.

Beyond the reception hallway was a series of closed doors, each leading to a separate office. They walked to the last door and pushed it open.

Inside was an enormous corner office. Large windows lined two of the walls, the light from the buildings outside filtering in. The walls were decorated by framed watercolor prints of sailboats, their pastel colors lightening the room. An expansive mahogany desk, topped by a computer and green writing pad, stood in the corner of the room.

"Let's rest here," Jefferson said. "Regroup."

Jefferson looked around the room again, seeing a sliding glass door toward the rear. There was a small porch outside, decorated with rows of planted flowers and two metal chairs pulled up the to a glass-topped table. Jefferson slid back the glass door and stepped out onto the landing, McKenna joining him. The outside air was cool, refreshing. He breathed it in deeply.

"It's still in the building somewhere," McKenna said, leaning against the railing and looking up at the rest of the Lyerman Building towering over them.

"I know."

"It's hunting us now. And we've got no way to fight it. Maybe it's time to call in reinforcements."

"I don't think so. I saw what it did to that SWAT team and don't see how reinforcements would fare any better. Anyway, we know how to kill the demon. Find the arrowheads mentioned in the manuscript Saint copied."

"Jefferson, that was centuries ago. There's no way to know where they are now, or if they even existed."

"I think I know where they are."

"Where?"

"Tonight, when I talked to the guy who used to be Kenneth Lyerman's bodyguard, Harold Thompson, he mentioned something about Lyerman keeping something of value up on the roof. Said that was where they had the toughest security."

McKenna thought for a moment. "Possibly. But even if they were up there, the whole thing is just a legend. Who's to say that they would kill the demon?" McKenna shrugged. "It's a big risk."

"Yeah," Jefferson said. "But we're running out of options."

He moved to the edge of the porch and looked down. Forty-nine stories below were an alley and a parking lot. He saw the tops of Dumpsters and slicks of oil shining purplish in the streetlights. Thin traces of steam filtered up from the sewer grates, and, at the far edge of the parking lot, a green neon sign in the shape of a dragon advertised a Chinese restaurant. The dragon's tongue flickered in and out, in changing strobes of orange neon that reflected off the thin pools of oil in the alley outside.

"Why are you still with me?" Jefferson said.

"What do you mean?"

"You know I was on that island. Both Brogan and Vincent were there, but so was I," Jefferson said. "One of us must be Sidina. What if I'm the one?"

"You're not."

"How do you know, McKenna? I could be it, the reincarnation of Sidina. You said I might not even know."

"Jefferson, it's not you. I would know it if it was. I don't feel that evil inside you."

McKenna stepped to him, putting her arms around his waist and hugging him. She pressed her head against his chest.

"I can hear your heart beating," she said. "And it's a sound so familiar to me."

She looked up at him. "I've always loved you, Jefferson. In this life, and before. I think as much as the demon searches for Sidina, I have searched for you. You can't be Sidina."

"Why not?"

"Because if you are, then everything I've known in my heart is wrong. The rain, Jefferson. The atoms that find each other in rain, the story I told myself when I was a little girl. We all fall alone but somehow we've found each other again. That night, when I was with you on my deck overlooking the ocean, I knew you were the one. So if you are Sidina, then everything I've ever known is wrong. And I can't believe that."

"I want to think the same," Jefferson said. "But I don't know what happened on that island. One of us out there was Sidina, and it might have been me."

"I'll never believe that."

Jefferson sighed, watching the dragon's tongue flicker in and out.

"I'm going up to the roof to look for the arrowheads," Jefferson said. "Hopefully Brogan will still be there."

"I'll go with you."

"No, you should stay here. If something happens to me, you're the only one that knows what's going on."

"Jefferson . . ."

"Stay here, just sit tight. I'll be back in ten minutes. OK?"

Reluctantly, McKenna agreed. "I'll be waiting for you."

They stepped back into the office, shutting the porch door. McKenna sat on the floor behind the large desk. She was well hidden by its front, invisible to anyone passing by in the hall outside.

She should be safe there. He hoped so anyway.

Not wanting to use the elevator again, Jefferson took the stairs up to the roof. He stopped for a moment just outside the stairwell, standing in the night air and listening to the *scree, scree, scree* sound of insects. Somehow they had managed to find their way up to the top of the building. The roof was still quiet, just as he and McKenna had left it minutes before. The trees rustled in the night breeze, a section of yellow police tape caught in one of the branches. The drizzle had stopped for the moment, but everything still shone with a slick wetness.

The solarium light was still on, and, as Jefferson watched, a single silhouette passed in front of the window. Slowly, Jefferson eased his Beretta out and approached the building over the grass. The silhouette moved past the window again. Whoever it was had a small frame, slightly bent over at the waist. It was definitely not Brogan or Vincent. Someone else was up there with him. The door was half-open, and Jefferson pushed at it lightly with his fingertips, then stepped inside the small room.

Standing in the entryway, he could see the edge of the great desk and several of the large potted palms. The solarium had the feel of a safari room. Black-and-white hunting photos hung from the wall, and there were rifles and Hemingway novels. Someone was moving quietly, off to his left, just obscured by the edge of the hallway. Jefferson moved forward a little more, then saw the figure. It was the Panamanian. The little man was bending over a square hole cut in the floor, a section of the wooden parquet placed on the scarlet carpet under his feet. The Panamanian lifted something out of the hole, something that looked like a cigar box, and laid it carefully on the side of the large desk.

Jefferson approached the man from behind, gun drawn, then, without a word, he coughed. The Panamanian whirled around wildly, dropping the lid of the box and turning to stare at Jefferson. His eyes met Jefferson's for a moment before flickering down to the weapon, then back up to meet the eyes.

"Hi," Jefferson said. "How you doing?"

The Panamanian nodded once, a slight movement of his head.

"Must be a tough night for you," Jefferson said. "With your recent unemployment and all. Sorry to hear about your boss."

"You put down your gun," the Panamanian said.

"I don't think so. But what I will do is ask you to step away from whatever it is you just put on that desk."

The Panamanian looked down at the box, then back up at Jefferson. He shook his head.

"Apparently you don't understand the significance of me holding a gun and you being unarmed, asshole. Let me explain it to you. That means that you have to do whatever the fuck I say. Now step away from the desk."

Keeping his eyes on Jefferson, the Panamanian slid sideways like a crab, until he stood five feet away from the edge of the desk. This guy had killer eyes; it was like looking into the blank lens of a camera. They made Jefferson nervous.

"Don't look at me," Jefferson said. "Pick a spot on the floor and stare at it."

The Panamanian slowly lowered his head, staring at a point just above the toes of his shoes.

Jefferson walked to the desk and flipped back the lid of the box. Inside were six arrowheads, carefully aligned along the bottom of the box. They were made of metal, two jagged points meeting to form a sharp point. The heads were slotted, shaped to fit easily into the notch of an arrow.

These were the weapons from the manuscript. Jefferson was sure of it.

From behind him, across the roof, came the electric chime of the elevator. Jefferson turned toward the sound, seeing light flood out from the elevator's interior and onto the darkened roof. Someone had come up. There was a rustling noise in the solarium with him, and he turned to see the back of the Panamanian as the man took advantage of the distraction and ran out the rear door.

"Shit," Jefferson hissed, watching him cut silently across the shadows of the roof. Jefferson let him go, turning his attention back to the elevator car. He reached out, quickly turning off the single desk lamp and plunging the solarium into darkness. Taking the box in his hands, he made his way below the line of the desk, where he could look out over the roof without being seen.

Two figures had stepped out of the elevator, highlighted for a moment by the interior light, before the doors slid closed. They were talking to each other, walking up the path as two dark shadows, their arms moving in conversation. As they passed out of the line of trees and into a section of moonlight, Jefferson saw both of their faces for the first time.

It was Brogan and Vincent.

What are they doing up here? Jefferson moved to stand up and call out to them, but then he froze, thinking. Both Vincent and Brogan had been on the island. One of them must be Sidina. There was no other possibility. Slowly, hoping he hadn't been seen, Jefferson lowered himself below the line of the desk to watch.

Vincent was wearing a black suit, while Brogan was wearing only khaki pants, white shirt, and tie. Vincent was sweating slightly, his hand moving back and forth in front of his face as he appeared to swat away an insect. Brogan was looking directly at Vincent, his hands in his pockets, the tie loosened around his comfortable-looking neck.

They were talking to each other, occasionally glancing at the lights of the city. Jefferson listened, but could only hear the low murmur of their conversation, the words too indistinct to be caught. Brogan was shaking his head as Vincent said something, poking his fingers at the other man's chest. They appeared to be arguing.

Jefferson scanned the rest of the roof, looking for the little Panamanian. The man had apparently disappeared, maybe going down the stairwell. Jefferson would let him; there wasn't much the man could do. He would have to remember that he was loose somewhere in the building. He turned his attention back to Brogan and Vincent, watching the argument continue.

They had both been on that island. What had happened out there? McKenna had pulled him back from his memories before he had a chance to see. The secret was out there somewhere, forgotten on that island for sixty-five years. Jefferson had to go back to find out what it was.

He reached into his pocket and felt the cool metal of the dog tags. They were his link to the past. The same tags worn by Eric Davis on the island. The tags he had worn in his previous life. He needed to go back again, back to the island to learn the end of the story. The secret, the key to everything, had died with the men on the island. To find the truth, he had to visit the island one last time.

Jefferson took a last look out the window and saw that Brogan and Vincent were still arguing. He held the tags for a moment before slipping them over his head.

Immediately the room around him began to spin, gradually growing darker and darker, then shrinking around him. There was a flash of light, and he heard noises, far-off voices of people he once knew but whose names he couldn't remember. There was a long sound, a rushing of air or water down a drain, and ahead of him he could see a floor of stone. The stone was getting closer and closer. He could hear gunfire, then someone screaming, and a flash of pain in his abdomen. He was there. Back in 1943 on the island. He was Eric Davis. Brogan was again Keaveney. And Vincent had become Alabama.

I'm walking along a corridor. What kind of corridor? A hallway? No, it's made of stone. Must be inside the temple still. But where? Brogan is beside me, his rifle slung over his shoulder. Vincent beside him. And I know one of us has to become evil. But who? Around us, the walls are painted with pictures. Ancient wars. Men in chariots riding across battlefields under thick clouds of falling arrows. Combat with swords and spears. Blood and pain. The images painted with gruesome detail. Over the entire field is drawn a giant eye, an eye that watches the death.

We were in some kind of tomb, underneath the stone columns. Like being inside the ancient pyramids, wandering through corridors of constant stone, their massive weight all around us. The floor was dusty, and we kicked up small clouds that rose in billows to our knees as we walked.

There were torches spaced evenly along the walls, their lights flickering against the sandy-colored stone. We all take one from their holders.

Brogan was leaving small trickles of blood behind him in the sand as he walked. His was red, even redder in the torchlight. His eyes were bulging and he looked feverish. I caught a look from Vincent, who shook his head once, looking at Brogan. He was sick. Bleeding to death.

We kept moving. None of us even looked back when another scream sounded somewhere behind us. Something was back there, something that lived in those corridors. In those tunnels. And it would be coming for us soon. The torch in Vincent's hand began to flicker wildly. The cold wind attacked us again. The air around us grew cold, the sweat on my body growing clammy and uncomfortable.

"The Kuro," I replied. "Just like that Japanese soldier said."

Vincent pulled up at that. "I don't think we should be going down there."

"No," Brogan said. "This is right. We should keep going."

Ahead of us, I saw a door cut into the stone sides of the corridor.

The door was made of lusterless black metal, a black handle set in the center. I reached for the handle, and it felt cold to the touch. I pulled my hand back, my skin crawling as if I'd just stuck my hand into a horde of maggots.

"What's wrong?" Vincent asked.

"Don't know, felt strange. Creepy. Like something was crawling on me."

Brogan reached for the door, his hand not flinching as he pulled it open. There was a rush of cold air from inside, striking me in the face. The air smelled sour, of rotting meat, and instinctively I turned my head. I could see Vincent doing the same, but Brogan was already stepping inside. Trying to hold my breath, I followed after him, Vincent coming in behind me.

We stood inside a chapel, rows of pews running ahead of us, fronted with an altar. The chapel was painted only in shades of black. The pews black, the walls black, the stone columns were all painted in black. There were stained-glass windows along the wall, but those, too, were painted in different shades of black, so that I could barely make out the scenes they depicted.

A man was sitting in one of the pews.

His back was to us, so that I couldn't see his face. He sat still, and I wasn't sure if he knew we were behind him. I stared at the back of his head for a moment, not sure I wanted to meet whatever kind of man would be down there. Down in that church of blackness.

Brogan was walking down the center aisleway between the pews, and I followed him, still looking around me. The glass windows depicted battles. Battles between demons and angels.

"What is this place?" Vincent whispered in my ear. "It feels evil. All around me. Like I can taste it even."

I nodded.

"You think that can happen, a place can be so strong with evil that you can taste it?"

I shook my head. "I don't know."

We were approaching the man sitting in the pew. Brogan walked right past him, his eyes fixed forward, toward the black altar. I was just behind the man sitting in the pew, staring at the back of his head, seeming to see everything in incredible detail—the hairs on the back of his head, the pores of his neck, even the texture of his skin itself. I found myself reaching for his shoulder.

"Careful now," I heard Vincent say.

But still I reached forward, grasping the man by his shoulder and turning him toward me. There was no reaction to my touch. Slowly I turned him around so I could look at him. His face was that of a pig, a beast, something unnatural. I drew back my hand in disgust, and saw that he was wearing a military jacket. The name stitched across the front read, "Seals."

"My God," Vincent said. "What happened to him?"

"I don't know," I replied.

"And when Jesus found a man possessed by demons," I heard Brogan cry out, "He drove those demons into a herd of swine. Thereby, the pigs became possessed by demons that had once held on to the soul of a man."

Brogan did not turn his head toward us, speaking to us while kneeling in front of the altar.

I ran toward him. "Let's go!"

I grabbed him by the shoulder, but he shook me off violently, and I fell backward, landing against Vincent. Brogan stood up, and, for the first time, I noticed the top of the altar wasn't bare. There was a small black communion cup and a metal tray of black wafers sitting in the middle.

Brogan took hold of the cup, put it to his lips, and began to drink. He drank fast, and a blackish liquid trickled down his cheeks in two thin streams, running down his neck and staining his shirt. When he had finished with the cup, he placed it back on the altar in front of him.

Brogan reached for the black wafers. Picking one up, he placed it in his mouth, chewing thoughtfully. While still chewing he turned toward us, his jaw working up and down. He stared at me for a moment, looking directly into my eyes, penetrating me.

"The dark waters are in front of me," Brogan said. "I can see them. Like I'm on a ship headed into the storm. Into the heart of the darkness."

I stood stupidly in front of him.

"Jesus, you all right, Brogan?" I heard Vincent say cautiously, holding out one of his hands.

"Am I all right?" Brogan asked, turning toward him.

"Yeah, you're just acting . . . a little strange."

"Strange? I feel good."

Around us, I noticed that the stained-glass windows had begun to change, the black glass swirling in slow turns. Torches placed along the aisles were flickering, a cold wind passing down the pews toward them. Brogan stood before the altar, head raised, looking around him, his eyes glistening.

Brogan turned toward us. "My head feels clear, I know now who I am. Who I've been."

"What are you talking about?"

"There was once a great warrior, the perfect warrior, who killed without remorse, without guilt. He was so fierce, so brutal, that those who saw him said that he was possessed by a demon."

"What the hell?" Vincent whispered.

"His name was Sidina." Brogan's voice lowered suddenly, and words came from his mouth without him seeming to speak. "My name is Sidina."

Vincent grabbed my arm. "Let's go, man. Something's wrong."

I nodded, slowly backing down the aisle.

"You should join me," Brogan said slowly. "You two have been chosen."

"Chosen?" I said, still standing, fascinated.

"Yes, chosen. Join me," Brogan said, staring at us, his face seeming to grow more sharp, more angled, "and you will also share in eternal life. Together again, as we were for six hundred years, if we can find the fourth of our group." Slowly, he began to jog toward us, gradually breaking into a run.

"Let's go," Vincent cried, pulling me back. "This ain't right."

I nodded, and we pulled open the metal door, running out into the stone corridor. The torches were still burning brightly, illuminating the depictions of battles along the wall. Behind them, we could hear Brogan roar.

"What's going on?" Vincent shouted, as we ran down the length of the corridor. "He's all messed up in the head. We have to get out of here, get away from him."

Ahead of us, I could see the circular winding stairway leading up into the temple.

We were almost upon it, when I heard the crack of a rifle. I instinctively cringed, but felt nothing. Turning, I saw Vincent falling to his knees, his body twisting around, his face showing confusion. He held in that position for a moment more, before there was another crack. The second bullet struck him in the chest, blowing him open. I looked down at him in shock. Vincent's mouth hung open in surprise, and he clutched his chest as air escaped from the hole through his ruptured lungs. There was a third crack, and this bullet struck his shoulder, spraying blood along the back wall.

I turned toward Brogan and saw that the rifle was trained on me. I twisted my body as I heard another crack, feeling something burn into my right arm, just above the elbow. I turned, taking the stairs upward and hearing nothing from behind me. The temple was empty. The bodies of the slain Japanese soldiers had been removed, leaving only blackish stains on the stone where their bodies had lain. My arm was burning with pain and hanging limply at my side. My rifle slipped off the weakened shoulder, clattering to the ground. I stared down at my arm for a moment before I heard a shuffling of feet below me. Brogan was coming up the stairwell.

I moved quickly along the line of stone columns, beneath the black ceiling pressed with the hundreds of glinting jewels. I was feeling light-headed, weak from the loss of blood, and I ducked behind one of the columns at the far end. I collapsed to the ground, pressing my back against the smooth stone, hiding for a moment while I caught my breath.

My arm was shattered below the elbow, the area beneath the bullet wound still obscured by the fabric of my shirt but appearing flimsy, like the joints of a marionette puppet. Using my teeth, I ripped a section of my undershirt, wrapping it tightly over the wound. I still had my hand weapon, tucked just beneath my belt, and I drew it out with my good hand. Waiting, I tried catching my breath, taking long, deep inhalations.

Something had happened to Brogan. Something had happened to everyone, and now I was alone.

I heard the scrape of boot against stone behind me, and I stiffened.

"Come out, come out, little piggy," Brogan said slowly, from somewhere behind me.

I checked my gun, making sure it was loaded.

"I don't want to hurt you," came the voice again. "Join me, and the two of us can find the third, and then we'll have two lifetimes to find the next reincarnation of Vincent." The shuffling of booted feet was moving off to my right. If Brogan made a full pass around the room, he'd come to where I was hiding. I needed to take him out first.

I kept my back pressed tightly against the wall, stifling my breathing. I couldn't hear Brogan, wasn't sure where he was anymore. Slowly I began to ease myself into a standing position, keeping my back tight against the column. I poked my head around the corner, looking quickly around the room. I saw the row of columns in front of the far wall, spaced evenly apart, circling the room. Brogan could be behind any one of them, and I wouldn't be able to see him until he moved.

I took a step forward.

"I can hear you," came Brogan's voice from somewhere in the room.

I couldn't place where the sound was coming from exactly, but it still seemed to be off to my right. But slightly higher than before. I scanned along the wall, seeing an odd black shape protruding from the wall between two columns. I stared at the shape for a moment more, trying to place it. It seemed to fasten to the side of the wall, and it took me a moment to realize that I was staring at Brogan.

He was clinging to the wall like a spider, his head turning from side to side. I watched him, fascinated, trying to understand what he was doing, then it hit me; he was listening.

He was listening for me.

I took a step forward. Then a second. And a third. The soles of my boot crunched loudly on gravel strewn across the floor. Brogan's head twisted around, until he was staring at me. He smiled. A moment later he began bouncing up and down on the wall, like an enraged gorilla. With amazing speed, he padded over the rocky surface, crawling with his hands and feet.

"I'm coming for you."

I raised the handgun and squeezed off two rounds, both striking him directly in the back. Unaffected by the shots, Brogan dropped off the wall to the ground. I turned and ran. There was another cracking sound, and a moment later I realized that I had been shot again.

I reached the foot of the stairs and forced myself upward. Above me, I could see a rectangle of light, the doorway out, but the rectangle was growing smaller and smaller. Something was closing over the opening, the giant altar moving slowly back into place, sealing me inside the underground tomb. I pushed harder against the stone stairway, the pain in my abdomen growing to be excruciating, mind numbing, almost causing me to pass out. The stone was still sliding in front of the opening, but pushing myself forward, I squeezed through the narrowing seam of light.

I collapsed. Something pressed against my leg. The wooden box with the arrowheads was still in my pants pocket. I lay for a moment before reaching down and pulling the box up.

Seeing that it was undamaged, I slipped it back into my pants pocket, then pushed myself off the ground. I stood up, beginning to walk unsteadily out of the temple and down the long steps. I stopped in the open doorway, stunned.

What had previously been an abandoned garden before, appeared to be in full bloom. Giant wildflowers the size of a man's fist hung heavy on long vines spreading up the column. Statues spit water into large pools, in which swam giant goldfish and quacking ducks. Three women were making their way along a path, and they giggled as they saw me cutting through the garden, blood dripping out of me until it stained my shirt. One of them waved to me, curling just her fingers toward her palm, smiling as she did so.

I felt weak, ready to lie down in the garden. To give in. Instead I staggered forward, through the gates and into the hot jungle, leaving Brogan and the garden behind. I took a few more steps, before tripping and sprawling headfirst in the mud. I lay for a moment on the edge of consciousness before a wave of nausea hit me. I vomited, then passed out.

Jefferson jerked his eyes open, gasping for breath and clutching at his throat. His chest was on fire, the pain real, as if he had just been shot. He was sprawled on the floor, the box open next to him. Blood was seeping through his thin cotton T-shirt—his old wounds had reopened. He was dizzy and sick from the memories; he could still smell the stink of the jungle, hear the crack of gunfire, and feel the patter of rain on his body.

It had been Brogan. Brogan had been the one on the island, the one who had been possessed by the demon. Brogan was the reincarnation of Sidina. Brogan, as Keaveney, had ended up on the same island as the Jinn seeking Sidina. Davis had eventually gotten off that island, but had died on the *Galla*. So had Brogan, and the demon that was inside him had become trapped at the bottom of the Pacific Ocean. It made sense—someone had been giving Lyerman information on the case, keeping Lyerman in touch with what was happening. Lyerman had specially requested Brogan. *Was it because he knew exactly who Brogan was? Did he know that Brogan was Sidina? Or just that Brogan was the reincarnate of the Marine whose body the Jinn used to get off the island?*

Jefferson was feeling nauseous and weak and rolled over onto his side. Then, pulling himself upright, he stared out the window. He was unsure of how much time had passed, but, checking his watch, he guessed it couldn't have been more than ten minutes. The bleeding in his chest had stopped, but had left his T-shirt wet and sticky against his skin.

Gradually he was able to pull himself up over the sill of the window and look out across the rooftop, expecting to see Brogan and Vincent still arguing. Instead he saw only Vincent, sprawled out across the grass, his throat slit.

Brogan was gone.

Shit, Jefferson thought, *while I was under, Brogan murdered Vincent and left. Where?*

Jefferson tried to stand, but fell back immediately to the floor. Outside, he heard the crunch of footsteps on the path. Someone was coming. Panicked, he tried to raise himself a second time, but failed again, collapsing to the floor and wincing at the loud thump his body made as it struck the floor. He was lying nearest the bay window looking out toward the whirlpool. The large oak desk was behind him, and pulling himself along the ground, he was able to reach its base. Looking up, he saw that the door to the solarium hung open from when he had crept inside after the Panamanian.

He heard the sudden *tap . . . tap . . . tap* of slow footsteps across the marble patio. Still lying flat on the ground, Jefferson painfully began to crawl across the floor, dragging himself over the crimson Oriental rug toward the open doorway. He could hear the footsteps pause outside the whirlpool. Brogan must be standing there, surveying the rest of the roof, looking toward the solarium. He wouldn't miss the open door.

Jefferson was halfway across the carpet, still in the middle of the room, when he heard Brogan's footsteps beginning again, this time walking more purposefully to the bottom of the stairs. As Jefferson moved, he could feel the blood flowing back into his legs, feeling them gradually growing stronger. He pulled again and again with his hands, pushing off the carpet with his feet, until he was close enough to the door that he could make out little details, the grains of the wood, the screws in the lock.

The pattern of Brogan's steps had changed, they no longer made the tap of shoe on stone. Instead, there was a soft, *swish, swish,* the sound of his shoes walking through the higher grass of the lawn. Jefferson was powerless, weak. If Brogan were to come upon him in his current condition, everything would be over as quickly as Brogan wanted it to be. There was nothing he could do.

Instead, Jefferson tried to concentrate on each pull of his arms, drawing him closer to the doorway. Finally, he was able to graze the door with his fingernails, and a moment later, he could grip the frame solidly with his hand. Slowly, he began to ease the door forward. Then he paused, not wanting to risk the sound of the *click* as the door swung completely shut. Instead he left a small space, hoping Brogan would pass by without noticing.

Jefferson began pulling himself back across the carpet, feeling himself growing stronger as he moved. Outside, he could hear Brogan reaching the path leading to the solarium. He would be curious about the darkened building, maybe wanting to approach and check inside. Jefferson began to crawl faster, pulling himself across the rug until he had reached the wooden box.

He jammed the box of arrowheads down into his pants pocket, as he heard Brogan's footsteps pass slowly by the door outside. Jefferson exhaled in relief as the footsteps passed by without pause. He leaned back against the desk, closing his eyes and focusing on regaining his strength. He listened as Brogan continued down the path, the rhythmic sound of his footsteps reassuring Jefferson.

Jefferson jerked his eyes open. Something was wrong.

Brogan's steps had stopped abruptly. Too abruptly. Jefferson's eyes fell on the partially opened door, seeing that it was swaying back and forth slightly on its hinges, caught in a breeze coming through the open window. There was no sound from outside, and Jefferson could imagine Brogan out there now, head cocked, listening carefully. Jefferson held his breath, and after a full minute, he heard Brogan walking away again.

Jefferson relaxed, and as he did so, his weakened arm slipped down, his watch striking the floor with a *click*. He froze. Outside, the footsteps stopped. He heard a scuffling sound, and suddenly Brogan was running down the path. Jefferson could hear the patter of his boots as he moved quickly toward the solarium.

Brogan was coming for him, and Jefferson could barely stand up. He looked around the room wildly, noticing for the first time a large ornately carved chest pressed against the wall just beside the window. He concentrated on this, pulling himself forward until he was able to open up the top slightly, praying there would be enough room for him inside. There was more than enough, the chest empty except for an animal skin lining the bottom.

Hauling his body up, he slipped inside the chest, pulling the lid on top of him as the door to the solarium crashed open. Inside the chest was cramped and hot, with a pungent odor of old wood. Jefferson's knees were pulled up toward his chin, his feet against the side wall, his arms in the fetal position, curled together in front of him. The top of the chest came down flush with the base, but left a small crack of light that ran around on three of the chest's sides. By pressing his eye against this, Jefferson could see a small sliver of the room.

Brogan had stepped through the outside door and was slowly moving into the room, his head shifting from side to side. He was holding a long, curving knife, stained red from Vincent's blood.

"Come out, come out, little piggy," Brogan said slowly to the room. "Come out wherever you are."

Jefferson remained quiet, not moving. He watched Brogan for a moment more, looking around at the pictures and framed wild game heads hung around the room, then abruptly, Brogan turned and walked back out into the hallway. He could hear the footsteps across the path, then to the elevator. Brogan was going back into the building.

Jefferson listened to the elevator doors slide shut before he slowly pushed open the lid of the chest. He pulled himself up, finding that he was able to stand upright. He took a few shaky steps to the door, then threw it open and looked out across the roof. He breathed in the outside air, then, leaning against the sill, looked back around the room. Directly in front of him, underneath two crossed spears, was a tall glass case, filled with a group of rifles. Slung from the wall next to the spears were a large compound bow and a quiver of arrows.

His strength returning, Jefferson crossed the room and opened the case. He took out the bow, pulling back on the line, testing its weight. The bow felt heavy and powerful in his hands, the line taut, difficult to pull back before the compound pulley was activated.

Taking out the quiver of arrows, he laid them on the table, pulling each arrow out. Opening the wooden box he had carried off the island, he began fitting the metal arrowheads taken from the door of Sidina's fortress onto each of the arrow shafts. After a few minutes' work, he had notched each of the arrowheads onto a shaft. Shouldering the quiver and holding the bow, he walked out into the hallway, his legs feeling strong beneath him.

Figuring that enough time had passed that Brogan was looking for him somewhere else, Jefferson called for the elevator. He was inside the elevator heading to the foyer when his cell phone vibrated in his pocket. Checking caller ID, he saw that it was Brogan.

"Jefferson, where are you, why won't you come out?"

It was Brogan's voice, only different. Higher-pitched somehow.

Jefferson replied, "I can't believe it was you."

"I'm sorry to disappoint you."

Again, the difference in pitch, like someone doing an imitation.

"You're not Brogan, are you?"

There was a chuckle on the line. "I am part of him now."

"Why?"

"He knew he was the one. You remember Bosnia, don't you? What he almost did to you back then."

"That was years ago."

"Nobody ever changes. Besides, the Jinn can give you wonderful things."

"What did you promise Brogan?"

"His wife. His dead wife. I told him I could bring her back, that he could see her in the garden if he would serve me. I think he knew in his heart though."

"Knew what?"

"I think he always knew who he was, about his past, that eventually I would come calling on him," said the voice on the phone. "You know, in almost eight hundred years, this is the first time any of us has managed to find all of you together."

The elevator was descending rapidly. Jefferson remembered the building's security system, cameras on every floor. If he could get down to the basement, he could use the cameras to discover where Brogan was.

"You still there?" Brogan asked.

"Yeah, I'm still here. Do you want to turn yourself in?"

"I'm afraid not." Brogan chuckled.

"Then I'm still here."

"Ahh . . . well, then," Brogan said, his voice calm, almost friendly. "Isn't this nice, just the two of us, like being back on the island. But, to be honest, you do seem a little disappointed. Maybe you were expecting something more than me?"

"Maybe."

"I know, I don't seem like much of a demon. I look like just a man. But when you get down to it, there's not too much that can be more evil than man. You're the ones that commit murder, kill each other, torture each other. That's been going on for thousands of years. Do you really think that's all me? Nothing else on this planet can be evil. Just you humans. Interesting, don't you think?"

Jefferson said nothing.

"That's the problem with being a demon. Everyone meets you for the first time and they're speechless. I tried to save you out on Blade Island. I was your partner."

"That was Brogan, not you. Brogan was my partner. You're nothing to me."

"You owe me, Jefferson."

"Owe you what?"

"Well, let's see. How about everything?" Brogan said. "Many years ago, when I was in Sidina, I was able to rule half the known world at that time. Then Sidina was killed and brought to the island by the knights of the Crusade, and I was left without a body. Do you know what that's like? It was a very New Age experience, very freeing."

The elevator opened on the lobby, and Jefferson moved quickly to the stairwell leading to the basement. He was jogging, trying to keep his breathing under control. For a demon, the guy could talk up a storm.

"So I spent my days on Bougainville Island, able to leave only occasionally, when one of my fellow Jinn found its reincarnate and got it to agree to be possessed. But we were never able to get more than the one to agree to bodily possession, so we had to go back into limbo and wait for another generation to be born. Then one day I see a man, a soldier. Sidina. This man, that you know now as Brogan, was the one I was looking for. He was who I had been searching for all those years."

"I know all about your finding the reincarnation of Sidina on Bougainville," Jefferson replied.

"Yes, well what you don't know, Jefferson," Brogan's voice suddenly snapped, "what you couldn't know, is what it's like to be so close, and then be trapped on that fucking ship, that fucking *Galla*, at the bottom of the ocean for sixty-five years. Trapped in a cage, for over a half century."

"Lyerman let you out?"

Brogan chuckled. "Before the *Galla* sank, Lyerman and I had made a little arrangement. He would help me in whatever way he could, and I would grant him anything he wanted. Which I can, by the way."

"But you killed him?"

"He was going to harm my prize. This wonderful body that I find myself in and require to avoid being cast back into limbo, only occasionally coming out to deal with those who might reveal our secrets or to try to convince the newest Sidina reincarnate to allow me the use of his body."

"And killing his son, that was just a test?"

"I had to know if he would be loyal. Through everything."

"Some test."

"What can I say? I'm making this up as I go along. Maybe next time it'll be multiple choice."

The Jinn seemed to be enjoying himself. Seemed to like talking to him. Jefferson heard a sliding sound, as of closet doors opening.

Brogan sighed. "Ahh, Lyerman has quite a collection of clothes for a cripple."

He must be back in Lyerman's bedroom, Jefferson thought.

"There are one or two things that humans do right," Brogan said. "And Armani suits are one of them."

Jefferson had reached the basement floor, stepping out into the cracked concrete hallway leading to the security room.

"Well, we don't want to waste all night," Brogan said. "I think you know why I'm here. There were three warriors with Sidina, three of the greatest fighters of the time. Together we ruled the world. You were one of them, and you continue to be one of them. It is time that you honor your birthright. Your right to greatness."

"You want me to join you? Forever?" Jefferson said.

"You make it sound so serious," Brogan replied. "It's just like joining a club. You were on one side, now you're on the other. My side. Believe me, it's a lot more fun."

"But I have to choose?"

"That's true. Make the correct choice. The wrong choice is always so . . . messy, for everyone involved. And I just had this new suit tailored. I'd hate to ruin it with your blood."

"And Vincent?"

"Vincent made the wrong choice," Brogan said. "There was always a question with him. But you, you have always been my star. If you and the fourth reincarnate make the correct choice, then we have two lifetimes to find the next Vincent reincarnate and convince him to make the correct choice, too."

"What do I have to do?"

"First, you have to give me the box that I know you must have by now."

"You want the box?"

"Please," Brogan replied.

"And if I say no?"

"Don't say no. Trust me on that one. No is a very bad choice."

"Can I have some time to think about it?"

"You don't get time. Make a choice. Yes or no."

Jefferson was moving down the hallway, pushing open the security room door. Empty, the guards must be somewhere else in the building. Inside, the room was dark, lit only by a wall of ten black-and-white television monitors. They all showed images from the building's security cameras. One of the cameras was placed in Lyerman's bedroom. He could see Brogan standing, cell phone to his ear, looking out the window.

Jefferson focused his attention back on his own cell phone. "I'm sorry. What was the question?"

"Yes or no."

"Oh, right," Jefferson said slowly, then smiled. "I'm gonna have to go with no."

Brogan began to speak, but Jefferson had already disconnected.

Jefferson closed the security room door, his eyes moving over the camera views. In the top left corner of the wall, he could see Brogan, standing in the bedroom, staring down at his silent phone. Jefferson felt a pang of something in his heart as he looked at the familiar form of his partner, his friend, now changed into something else. He shook his head, looking at the other screens.

They showed views throughout the building. Lyerman must have been a security freak to install so many cameras—they were practically everywhere. He wondered what life must have been like for the old guy, bound to his wheelchair like that. *So much wealth and power, and he couldn't even walk up a fucking flight of stairs.*

Jefferson glanced from screen to screen, seeing outside lawns, hallways, exotic rooms filled with paintings, then something caught his eye. In the top right corner screen were four men. They were standing in one of the Lyerman bedrooms, probably the kid's, two of them pulling out drawers while the third and fourth had taken knives to the furniture, opening it up and shoving their hands inside. Jefferson recognized one of them as the big Samoan guard.

Opportunists. Jefferson watched one of the men loading shoes from a closet into a large duffel bag he had slung over his shoulder. *They're fucking robbing the place. They must know Lyerman's dead, seen the body.*

If they were taking the time to stick around and loot for a few extra bucks, they must have felt comfortable. Which meant that nobody had called Boston PD, no alarms had been tripped, nothing that meant the blue cavalry would be showing up. That was fine with Jefferson—he didn't need thirty or forty street cops running through the building, getting in the way of finishing business.

And business was somewhere on the floors above him. If he had to put Brogan down, another cop, he didn't want anyone around to see it. No hesitation. Jefferson turned his attention away from the security guards doing an L.A. riot in Lyerman Jr's. bedroom and back to the row of security monitors, settling on one of the screens. The view showed a bathroom. It was filled with the massive porcelain fixtures rich people seemed to love. A three-ton toilet, a bathtub the size of a Volkswagen, and a row of sinks that looked like cattle feeding troughs. Jefferson's eyes fixed on the tub for a moment. It stood in the center of the room, the old-fashioned kind with gilded feet in the shape of talons. Something was moving inside the tub.

Something black and grainy on the screen. It twitched and rolled back and forth. Then the object turned toward him, exposing a white face, and Jefferson inhaled sharply.

It was McKenna.

She was bound, her legs and arms tied together, a strip of silver tape over her mouth. Brogan, the demon, had McKenna. It must have found her hiding behind the desk.

"Hang in there, baby," Jefferson whispered, pressing his fingertips to the screen. "I'm coming."

He was going to kill Brogan. There was no doubt about that. He trained his eyes a few screens over, back to the bedroom. The room in the tiny monitor was empty— Brogan had disappeared. But where?

He looked back to the bathroom, seeing McKenna continue to struggle to free herself. He scanned the details of the room, trying to figure its location in the building. Nothing was familiar to him. He was sure it was in some part of the building he hadn't visited. There were over seventy floors in the building, a thousand rooms, and that bathroom could be anywhere. It might take days before he found her.

He looked away from the screen, his eyes scanning the console, anything that might say where the camera was located. On the central computer monitor was a group of folder icons, each labeled differently. Jefferson scanned the labels, pausing before one called SECURITY VISION.

Inside was a replication of the rows of security screens. Beneath that, was a list of locations: GUEST BEDROOM EAST WING, FOYER, SOLARIUM, STUDY, CONFERENCE ROOM, BATHROOM WEST WING, BATHROOM EAST WING. The list continued on and on, with hundreds of names. Jefferson found that by dragging one of the names onto the replication of the security screen, he could get that particular screen to show the view of the camera. Curious, he tried it out, seeing if he could make it work.

Choosing the line labeled Lobby, he dragged it onto the security screen. Immediately, the corresponding screen above him flashed to an image of the upstairs lobby, empty and dark. Jefferson looked back up at the screens in front of him, eyeing each of them in an attempt to find Brogan. There was a glimpse of movement, and Jefferson saw Brogan, back turned to the camera, walking down a long hallway, somewhere in the building.

When Brogan reached the end, he turned the corner to his right and disappeared from view. Jefferson tried manipulating the cameras so that he could find Brogan again, but the man had disappeared. He checked each of the screens, but they were all empty.

Frustrated, he looked down at the computer monitor in front of him. On the desktop, there was a small icon of a looking glass. Jefferson clicked on this, and a new window opened in front of him. The window appeared to operate a search function. By typing in key words, he could search room by room, by type of room, or by room size.

At the bottom of the screen, he saw a line that read, LOCATE BY MOVEMENT?

Jefferson clicked on this, and a tiny spyglass appeared on-screen, flashing back and forth over the camera locations. The glass paused over something that read, SECOND FLOOR GRAND HALL. Then a screen appeared, the view from a camera.

Jefferson saw Brogan walking down a second hallway, this time the camera tracking his movement. Looking closely, Jefferson saw that the man's physical appearance hadn't changed. He still appeared as his partner, but there was something else in his manner that was different, something more hostile in the way that he was walking.

Jefferson thought back to the encounters that Brogan had with the demon. On the rooftop, the thing had nearly killed him after it had murdered Richard Lee. Or had it? Perhaps it had known who Brogan was then, and had spared him, knowing that Brogan was the one.

Brogan turned the corner of the hallway, and the camera automatically tracked him, cutting to another view of a second hall, this one lined with gilded mirrors. So this demon believed that Brogan was the reincarnated spirit of a warrior who had died almost eight hundred years ago. It had found him on the island, then when Brogan had died while trapped on that ship, the Jinn had found him again in Boston. But one of the demons had been with them in Bosnia, had been watching the night they murdered that little girl and killed all those men. That had been the presence they'd all felt.

He looked up at the screen. Brogan had stopped in front of a door. He reached for the knob, turned the handle, and pushed the door open.

"Oh no . . ." Jefferson whispered to himself.

In the next screen, he could see the bathroom with McKenna tied down inside the tub. Behind her, the door was slowly opening, Brogan appearing in the doorway. He was coming into the bathroom; he was coming in for her.

Jefferson's eyes were fixed on the black-and-white television monitor. McKenna lay in the bathtub looking at Brogan but not moving. Brogan had moved toward the tub and was standing at the edge, looking down at her. In his right hand, he held something long and sharp that looked like a kitchen knife.

Jefferson watched helplessly, the scene taking place somewhere in the building, knowing he would never be able to reach her in time. Brogan was staring at her, like a cruel boy stares at an injured bird, analytical about its suffering. Jefferson reached for his cell phone, hoping Brogan was taking calls.

"Come on, Brogan," Jefferson cried, as if that would get him to answer his phone. "Hey, asshole. I'm ready for you."

There was a long pause; Jefferson stared at the soundless television screen, watching Brogan's reaction, unsure if he knew he was being called. Jefferson prepared to close his eyes, not wanting to watch what would happen if Brogan didn't answer. After a long pause, Brogan slowly stepped away from the tub and reached into his jacket pocket.

"Jefferson, I assume that's you? I can't imagine who else would be calling me this late." Brogan said. "I was beginning to give up on you."

"Hey, man, I'm still here," Jefferson said. "I'm waiting for you."

"Where are you exactly?" Brogan replied.

"The roof," Jefferson said. "Come and get me."

Jefferson hung up again, leaving it set to vibrate so it wouldn't ring. He could watch Brogan on the screens. Brogan would be coming after him, going to the roof. Jefferson could watch him move, see what floor the sign by the elevator indicated.

Then, while Brogan was searching the floors above, Jefferson could take one of the interior elevators and get to McKenna.

On-screen, Brogan stood for a moment, staring at his phone, thinking, then turned toward McKenna. Jefferson could see that his mouth was moving; he was saying something to her. Brogan laughed, then turned and walked out of the bathroom.

He watched Brogan walk down the long hallway. While he followed the man on-screen, Jefferson picked up the compound bow he had taken from the roof, pulling out one of the arrows. He nocked the arrow, pulling back on the string and swinging the bow around the room, testing the aim.

On-screen, Brogan stood waiting in front of an elevator consul. The number 41 was visible in silver numbers just beside the door. The forty-first floor, one below Lyerman's residential floor. That's where McKenna was.

Jefferson slung the bow over his shoulder and stepped out of the security room, taking the stairs up to the lobby. He carried the arrows in the quiver slung around his back, and they rattled lightly as he walked. His Beretta still sat in its holster at his waist. He was sure the Panamanian was still somewhere in the building. If the little man showed himself, Jefferson would just as soon shoot him and not waste one of the arrows.

The stairs led to a door concealed by the base of a giant rubber tree at the far end of the lobby. The lobby lights were dimmed, low pools of yellow forming over the main security desk where Jefferson and McKenna had been given their party clothes. The desk appeared empty, but Jefferson remembered the guards he had seen patrolling the building before. The armed guards. He wondered where they all were. Jefferson waited behind the tree, pressing himself against the rough bark and watching the quiet lobby for a moment more before slowly stepping out onto the marble floor.

To his right, someone was pounding loudly against the outside glass door.

A man stood outside the door, near the valet stand, cupping his hands on the glass and peering inside for a moment before banging once more with the bottom of his hand to attract Jefferson's attention. It was Saint.

Jefferson moved quickly across the floor and unlocked the glass front door of the building.

"What the hell you doing here, man?"

"Thought you might want a little help," Saint said, stepping past Jefferson and into the lobby. "So I came and brought a bag of my friends."

Saint held up a black duffel bag for a moment before laying it down on the marble floor, the *clink* of metal sounding from inside the fabric. He was wearing black warm-up pants and black sweatshirt, the hood over his head.

Jefferson stared at him until Saint shrugged. "This thing, whatever the fuck it is, it killed two of my friends and cut me up bad. I'm here for the payback, for the brothers back at Blade."

"You sure you want to do this? You could get killed in here."

"Get killed just about anywhere these days. Might as well pick and choose when you want to face it. Live and die hard. Know what I'm saying?"

Saint bent down and unzipped the bag, opening it up. Inside it was filled with dull black gunmetal. Jefferson saw seven or eight handguns, two or three machete-sized knives, the long barrels of a Mossberg shotgun, and an AK-47. You don't show up an uninvited guest without bringing something for everyone, and Saint was bringing his own potluck to this party. Saint knew better than anyone what the demon was; if he wanted to fight it, Jefferson wasn't going to stop him.

"So you led a slave revolt in Haiti," Jefferson said. "Killed a lot of white people?"

Saint smiled. "A whole lot of y'all. Rich, pasty white devils. Just like you."

Jefferson reached down and looked into the bag, fingering the shotgun. "May I?"

"Just so long as you give it back when this is through. No extended warranty plan with these. You break it, you buy it."

Jefferson pulled out the weapon and pumped in a shell. Then he took two boxes of shells and put them in his pockets. He nodded at Saint. "You want this fight, you're in."

Saint held out his hand in a fist. "Tonight we kill the Diabb-la. The Serpent of Darkness."

"Helping out a white man to get a devil," Jefferson said, knocking Saint's knuckles with his own. "If your ancestors could see you now."

Jefferson and Saint took one of the undamaged elevators up toward the forty-first floor and McKenna. As the elevator whirred upward, Saint lowered the hood on his sweatshirt. His skull was shaved bald, shining in the light. He pulled the sweatshirt off, unzipped the duffel bag, and placed it inside. Underneath he was wearing a sleeveless black shirt, and an empty holster hung at each side of his chest. His arms were blocky with muscle. Reaching down into the bag again, he began pulling out guns and more guns, reminding Jefferson of some kind of psychotic magician pulling rabbits out of a hat.

Silver Glock 19s went into the two chest holsters, a .38 Special into one at the small of his back, a .22 at his ankle, and a big .44 Magnum at his hip. Forget walking through airport security at Logan for a while—the guy was carrying more guns than a 12–6 A.M. convenience store clerk would see in a year of being held up.

Then Saint pulled out the AK-47 from the bag, a long weapon with a longer range. Not typical gang banger equipment. That was more ex–Soviet military. Whoever Saint was running his guns with was someone into some hard-core shit.

"AK?" Jefferson asked. "Where'd you run across one of those?"

"JCPenny was having a sale."

"Don't ask, don't tell."

"Exactly, my white brother."

Jefferson held the Mossberg in one hand, the bow slung over his right shoulder. Mossberg 835 Ulti-Mag. All models include a Cablelock and a ten-year limited warranty, though Jefferson doubted that Saint's particular Mossberg came with either. But what the hell, if they ran into the demon, he figured a good blast from a double-aught would slow it down enough for him to bring the bow around, nock an arrow, and get off a shot. Besides, they might still run into the Panamanian and whatever security guards were left in the building. All and all, the party was going to be hot.

"Someone's coming," Saint said.

Jefferson followed the man's gaze out through the glass to the side of the building. Above them, one of the other elevators was on the move. The car was gliding downward toward them, no light coming from inside. Saint turned to face the elevator, shouldering the AK and tracking the car downward.

"Go easy till we know who it is," Jefferson said.

Saint nodded, the *click* of the safety mechanism sounding off sharply.

They passed within fifteen yards of the other car with a hushed, whirring noise, and Jefferson followed it with his eyes as it whooshed past them. A single figure stood inside the car, silhouetted against the lights of the city outside the elevator's glass. Whoever it was turned his head to look up at them. Saint kept the AK pointed down until the car and the single figure receded far below them. They watched as the second elevator stopped for a moment, and a thin sliver of light appeared as the doors opened. Someone was getting off on one of the floors below them, not intending to leave the building just yet.

Their own car bumped to a stop a moment later, and the doors opened onto the darkened floor. Jefferson saw a small waiting area, in back of which was an expanse of cubicles that expanded out onto the floor from the elevator. Saint stepped out first, the barrel of the AK sliding right, then left, covering the room. Jefferson followed with the shotgun raised. The weapon felt heavy in his hands, reassuringly heavy, like carrying a thick baseball bat into a fight. No matter who they ran into, they weren't going to be outgunned. Saint and his duffel bag had made sure of that.

When the waiting area, with its cream-colored couches and glass coffee tables, had been cleared, Jefferson gestured down the hallway to the right. If he had watched Brogan carefully enough, McKenna should be behind the fourth door on the left. He checked his watch. Ten minutes since he'd last seen Brogan heading toward the roof. That could put him anywhere in the building.

He hoped the guards upstairs were too busy doing the all-you-can-grab shopping spree of Lyerman's valuables to give them any trouble.

Jefferson pumped the Mossberg loaded, the sound an attention grabber on the silent floor. If anyone was hiding in one of the cubicles, Jefferson had just given them the heads-up to stay down and mind their business. Saint had the AK at waist level, his eyes fixed out across the floor. Jefferson caught his attention, then nodded again down the hallway toward where McKenna should be.

And then it happened.

A single door at the far end of the floor opened with a bang. Jefferson caught the motion, trying to duck out of view behind one of the cream-colored sofas. A man stepped out of the open doorway, one of the security guards. He saw Jefferson instantly, forty yards away. His eyes flicked from Jefferson to Saint, then down to the Mossberg and the AK. The guard's arms were at right angles, a stack of men's suits hanging from each of them. He looked down at the suits, then back at the Mossberg shotgun. Jefferson could see him thinking for a moment, brand names flashing through his head—Armani, Dolce, Mossberg.

In that moment of choice, Jefferson had time to shake his head no. *Don't be stupid. Don't be stupid.* Then the man moved. His arms dropped, the suits fell in a tangle of fabric and pinstripes as he reached for a weapon, something low-caliber, underneath his left armpit. Stupid. Saint raised the AK, shouldered it, and the weapon exploded in four bursts each as loud as a motorcycle backfire. Forty yards away, the guard went into a series of spasms, pummeled by some giant, invisible fist. Pieces of flesh jumped off his body in bloody eruptions, and he went down. For good.

The AK is a loud weapon, no way to hide the sound. You hear a four-shot burst and know something bad is going down somewhere. And there was still another crew of guards somewhere. It wouldn't take long for them to show.

Jefferson and Saint were standing just outside the elevators. Lines of cubicles stretched away from them, back toward the rear exit into the stairwell, where the first guard had appeared. Saint slid one of the cream couches over toward the elevator, wedging the end between the doors to keep the car in place and the doors open. Jefferson crouched behind the front reception desk, sweeping away some secretary's mess of pencils, family pictures, and bowls of candy. The desk was constructed of thick wood, sturdy enough to absorb a .22 round with no problem, maybe even a .38. Anything higher would be on the bullet express train, no stopping, straight through until it hit something solid. Like Jefferson's body.

He rested the barrel of the Mossberg on the desk, training it on the door. Ten yards away, Saint crouched inside the elevator, the AK sighted out between the semiclosed elevator doors. *Steel,* Jefferson noted. *Lucky fuck.*

They didn't have long to wait.

Across the room, Jefferson heard the sound of voices coming from inside the stairwell. Two or three voices, the guards arguing about something. Jefferson wondered if the big Samoan was back there. A moment later a hand stuck around the corner of the doorway. No body, just a hand, holding a TEC-9 assault pistol, the kind gangs had been running for years from Atlanta to New York. Jefferson dropped his head below the level of the desk as the TEC-9 began to go wild from the stairwell. Not a bad weapon actually, low-caliber bullet though, not enough to kick through the secretary's desk. Jefferson kept his head down, weathering out the storm and listening to the rounds chewing up the room, the decorative picture frames, the bowls of candy, and generally ruining some secretary's workday Monday.

The TEC-9 comes with a twenty-round clip. That can disappear in a few blazing moments of glory if someone takes the time to modify the pistol to full-auto, but whoever was firing at Jefferson was going on semiautomatic. Twenty pulls of the trigger for twenty rounds, and he was taking his time about it. Jefferson listened to each shot, one after another, firing blindly in their general direction. He glanced over at Saint and saw that he was actually studying his watch, looking bored, as if he were waiting for a subway train running a few minutes late.

At fourteen shots, Jefferson eased out his Beretta. A shooter's weapon, accurate at long ranges. When Jefferson finally counted out twenty rounds, he exhaled and rose above the level of the desk. The Beretta's barrel is smooth, sighted with white ticks at either end. The spots of white against the black metal make a nice contrast. Forty yards across the room, the hand was still extended beyond the doorframe, the finger clicking again and again on the TEC-9 empty chamber. Jefferson exhaled again, then, holding his breath, pressed the Beretta's trigger.

The hand and the TEC-9 disappeared a moment later, leaving bloody speckles on the doorframe. There was a muted scream, followed by more arguing. Jefferson thought of McKenna again, still tied up in the tub down the hall. The fourth door was twenty yards away from Jefferson, too far to run in the open with three or four guards still somewhere in the stairwell. Jefferson wondered if Brogan had heard the shots, too.

Another hand appeared in the doorway. *Here we go again,* Jefferson thought, as he crouched again behind the desk. A second TEC-9, which someone had taken the time to modify to full-auto, popped around the corner. There came the drumbeat tap of bullets from the weapon as the room began churning again into bits of broken glass and wood. Over that sound, Jefferson heard the duller thud of a .44 Magnum. The .44 is the mortar shell of handguns and sounds just as loud, like being inside a thunder-cloud during a full-scale hurricane. Things were beginning to get heavy, with the TEC-9 on full-auto and someone blasting away with the .44 like Dirty Harry. There was an explosion on the desk just above him, a computer monitor taking a bullet head-on, cascading broken shards of glass onto Jefferson.

He took one of the larger pieces, holding it above the level of the desk to catch the rest of the room in reflected in the glass. Two men were moving out of the stairway and into the maze of cubicles under the covering fire of the hands in the doorway. A moment later the TEC-9 clicked on empty, followed by the Magnum, and a third and fourth figure stepped out of the stairway and ducked under the cubicles. This was get-ting messy.

Jefferson looked over at Saint, holding up four fingers, then pointing back into the office room. Saint nodded, shouldering the AK and taking a quick peek around the corner of the elevator door. Jefferson lifted his head above the desk, looking out across the walls of cubicles. He watched for a moment, his finger resting on the Mossberg's trigger.

A moment later, out in the office, a single head popped above the level of the cubi-cles, took a quick look, then ducked back down. Then, ten yards from the first, a sec-ond head popped up, looked, then down. Jefferson thought of that Whack-A-Mole game, with the moles' heads that popped up for an instant and ducked back down before you could whack them with the padded hammer. When the third head popped up, Jefferson pulled the trigger on the Mossberg, the big shotgun kicking heavily into his shoulder. The top half of the cubicle disappeared into shredded bits of foam and twisted metal. There was a scream, and Jefferson knew that at least part of the shell had ripped open more than just the cubicle wall.

The scream continued for what seemed like a long time, then slowly died down to a low moan. A full-throated scream takes a lot of energy. Jefferson knew that someone who had been shot really badly could only manage one or two solid screams. After that, it was just a low, rolling moan of pain. You whack your thumb with a hammer, you've got plenty of energy to scream, tell someone how much it hurts, worry if you're going to lose the nail. You take a Mossberg shell to the body, you're not worried about much except trying to get to the next breath. And whoever he'd just hit didn't sound like he had too long to worry about that.

Jefferson pumped another shell, then ducked again under the desk. McKenna must be able to hear the gunfire. Maybe she would be able to work her way out of the tub and onto the bathroom floor. At least they wouldn't have to worry about Brogan for a little while. Except for the elevators, the only way up to the floor was through the stairwell, and the guards, with their suits and whatever else they were trying to jack, had that pretty well under control.

What the hell, they can have all that shit, Jefferson thought.

"Hey," Jefferson called out over the desk, "take what you want. I don't care. We're not here for that."

There was silence. Whoever Jefferson had hit was still doing the low moan somewhere out in the maze of cubicles. Saint shook his head no, they're not going for it. We're going to have to deal with these guys. Jefferson pointed to himself, then down the hall, then back to Saint's AK and out toward the floor. Cover me while I go for McKenna.

Saint seemed to understand the improv sign language. Or maybe he just wanted to shoot his AK some more. He raised the weapon. Jefferson heard the *click* as he switched it to full-auto, then a moment later the machine gun began to bark. It barked like a caged dog barks, not at anything in particular, but at everything, pulling chunks of foam out of the walls, tearing gaps in the ceiling plasterboard, ripping bits of cement and carpet from the floor, and generally encouraging the four guards to keep their heads down and out of sight. For a while anyway. Long enough for Jefferson to scoot down the hall to the fourth door.

He pushed it open in a single motion, sliding across the tiled floor and into the bathroom. The room was set up exactly as he remembered from the security monitor. The same massive porcelain fixtures, the wide glass mirror, and, in the middle of the room, the giant bathtub standing on its four clawed feet. *Must be some kind of executive bathroom.* Jefferson moved to the tub and looked down.

He breathed a sigh of relief.

McKenna lay in the bottom of the tub looking at him, her eyes wide and alert above the strip of duct tape. He laid the Mossberg on the floor and bent over her, carefully peeling the tape from her mouth, where it left a red mark over her lips and beneath her nose.

"Miss me?" Jefferson asked, going at the knots holding McKenna's arms and legs together with a knife he had pulled from Saint's duffel bag.

"Jesus. Oh my God, thank God," McKenna said. "It's Brogan. I saw him. He's the one."

Jefferson nodded. "I know. I just found out, too. He's still here somewhere."

In the hall outside, Jefferson could hear the AK still barking. McKenna heard it, too. "What's that?"

"Ran into some problems with some of Lyerman's guards. Saint's keeping it under control."

"Saint? He's here, too?"

"Just showed up, looking for work."

"Jesus, Jefferson," McKenna said. "It's Saint."

"What's Saint?"

"He's one of Sidina's warriors. It's Saint. He's the fourth."

Jefferson froze, halfway cutting through McKenna's ropes. *Jesus. Saint's the fourth. It makes perfect sense. Why else would he be here? How else could he have gotten out of Sinatra's house? Saint, the stone-cold ex-con. The fourth warrior. The fourth body the demons were trying to occupy.*

"Oh man," Jefferson said, reaching for the Mossberg and turning toward the open doorway behind him. Outside was quiet, the sound of the AK finally falling silent. *This is bad.* He heard a return shot from outside, one of the guards finally firing back. There was still no return fire from the AK. *This is very bad.*

"Give me the knife, Jefferson," McKenna said, looking at the knife Jefferson was still holding. "Let me cut myself free."

Jefferson handed her the knife, and she went to work cutting the rest of the knots around her ankles, freeing her feet. Mossberg in hand, Jefferson went back to the bathroom doorway, took in a breath, and poked his head around the corner. Outside, the hallway leading back toward the offices was empty. He scanned the floor to the right. The cream-colored sofa was still jammed between the doors of the elevator, but now the car was empty. Saint had disappeared.

The hallway was short, allowing him to look past the elevator and out onto most of the floor. He saw one of the guards standing beyond the row of cubicles. It was the guy whose hand Jefferson had almost knocked off with the Beretta. He held the bloody appendage tight against his waist, wrapped in something white that looked like a T-shirt. The guy looked pissed, still holding the TEC-9 with his undamaged left hand. *These fucking guys don't quit,* Jefferson thought *Just take the damn suits and get out of here.*

Jefferson shouldered the Mossberg and fired a shell at the guard. He was too far to hit, but the sound at least made him duck down into the cubicles again. Let them know someone was still alive and shooting. Jefferson didn't like his position. He was in a Butch Cassidy spot now, having to come out guns blazing just to get back to the elevator. And he had McKenna to worry about, not to mention he didn't know where Saint had run off to. He liked it better when he just had Brogan to think about.

He heard a noise behind him and turned to see McKenna climbing out of the tub, still holding the knife in her hand. She looked tired. Jefferson pulled out his Beretta and handed it to her.

"Loaded and ready to go."

She nodded, looking at the weapon for a moment before finally taking it from him.

Slowly, Jefferson eased out of the bathroom and back into the darkened hallway. He pumped another round into the Mossberg, making sure the noise was heard across the floor. McKenna was following him; Jefferson could hear the sound of her footsteps, her short breaths. They began moving down the hall, keeping close to the side of the wall near the three closed doors, which were evenly spaced along the wall. Out in the office, Jefferson saw one of the guards, crouching low, moving out from behind a desk. Jefferson raised the Mossberg, firing once, taking off a chunk of desk and spinning the man around.

Then it happened.

The last door in the hallway began to open. Saint was coming out of one of the offices, looking at Jefferson, then past him. Saint's expression changed, he took the eyes of the stone killer that Jefferson knew he was. The eyes of the perfect warrior. Saint was slowly raising the AK to shoulder level. Jefferson looked down at the Mossberg, no shell in the chamber, reaching for the pump. The bow was still slung over his shoulder, but Saint already had the drop on him. No time to reach for the bow. A Mossberg round might be enough to slow Saint down long enough for Jefferson to make another move.

The AK was coming up to shoulder level, the nickel-sized barrel looking black and empty. Saint was sighting down the weapon, his face scrunched strangely against the stock. Jefferson thought of the Daisy air rifle his mother had given him for Christmas. Shooting soda cans in the backyard with it, his face making that same scrunching impression as he pressed it against the stock. Jefferson felt disappointed. The moment of his death, and he was fixed on some inconsequential memory. He felt like there should be something more.

The AK was swinging toward him; it fired. Once, then again and again. He'd already died before. Davis, taking bullets to the chest. The feel of blood in the lungs, thick and soupy with every breath. It was all inevitable. Jefferson watched in fascination, the heavy gun bucking against Saint's shoulder, the brassy metal shells spinning out from the chamber, shining like new pennies. Smoke rising from the empty barrel. And the bullets passing by him, over his right shoulder. Striking something behind him. A short shriek of surprise. And the spell was broken. The spell of awaiting his own death snapped and Jefferson reached again for the Mossberg pump. Chambering a shell, he raised it and aimed the big shotgun at Saint.

"Wait." Saint held up his hand, dropping the AK in one motion.

And Jefferson waited.

"Look," Saint said, staring over Jefferson's right shoulder.

And Jefferson looked. *My God.* There it was. McKenna lay on the floor behind him. *Oh Jesus.* The front of her chest was gone. A ragged mess of black fabric, blood, and destroyed flesh. The AK rounds had ripped through her, to leave her lying on the floor—not McKenna anymore, just a torn-up discarded body of someone Jefferson had once known.

He stood at her feet, looking down, then up, his grip tightening on the Mossberg. One of the guards winged a shot at him from the office, but he ignored it. His heart was crushed by a fist of loss, but he ignored that, too. Instead, he turned toward Saint. Saint was already on him, reaching for the shotgun, grabbing the barrel and pulling it from Jefferson. Jefferson pushed up, trying to level the big shotgun at the man's chest. Saint was strong, with iron bars for arms, but Jefferson was angry. Furious. And that made him dangerous.

Saint looked past Jefferson, the same surprised expression spreading across his face, and Jefferson felt him weaken for a moment. He pushed the barrel of the Mossberg a quarter of an inch closer to Saint's chest. His finger was moving toward the trigger when Saint pulled Jefferson toward him, away from McKenna. Something sharp and metallic flashed by Jefferson's neck, and he felt a rush of air passing over his skin. Saint was pulling him farther forward, off-balance, and Jefferson almost fell to the ground before Saint jerked the Mossberg up with gorilla strength, pulling Jefferson back to his feet.

"It's her, man; Jesus, it's her," Saint said.

Dumbly, Jefferson turned back toward McKenna.

She was sitting upright. Three AK bullets, center of mass, and she was sitting upright. Jefferson moved toward her, but Saint's hand gripped him around the biceps, holding him fast. A mess of slippery blood shining in the overhead lights still stained the front of McKenna's dress, three half-dollar-sized pocks in her skin from the bullet entries. Her hair was matted and greasy around her face, falling in loose, gleaming strings. In her right hand, she still held the knife.

"My God. What is this?"

"That's not who you think it is. She is the spirit of the dead now."

McKenna's head jerked up, and she stared at Jefferson. She smiled, running her finger across the bloody mess below her neck. The tip came away red and shining.

"What did you do to me?" McKenna said. "I loved you, and you betrayed me."

She smiled again, sliding the knife behind her back while raising her other hand toward Jefferson. Still sitting on the ground, she waved her fingers at him. Come closer. And even seeing everything, even staring at this thing, this awful thing that lived and breathed but couldn't be human, Jefferson felt himself wanting to draw closer. McKenna's other hand was still behind her back, and, as he stepped forward, he saw the sinews in her arm flex. The arm was ready to strike with the knife, to slice through his neck. Jefferson paused, stepping back.

He shook his head. And then it happened.

McKenna's head twitched once, and Jefferson watched her face begin to change. The nose flattened out, the ears grew longer, thicker, the head elongated. Slowly, McKenna was disappearing, her feature melting away, another face taking its place. Brogan's face.

Jefferson reached for the bow, fumbling it off his shoulder in surprise. Brogan was already standing up from the floor, still dripping blood from the three massive chest wounds. Saint had raised the AK, pumping the remainder of the magazine into Brogan, whose body jerked and spun backward. But still he came on. Jefferson had the bow down at his waist and reached to pull an arrow from the quiver slung at his back.

Brogan had brought the knife up, edge out toward Jefferson, and was moving toward them as Saint's AK clicked empty. Jefferson nocked the arrow, raising the bow as he pulled back.

The shot was rushed, the arrow hitting against the side of the bow as it whooshed out from Jefferson's fingers. Still, the arrow caught Brogan in the right shoulder, embedding itself deeply into the flesh and causing him to drop the knife. Brogan screamed, took a step back, and looked down at the shaft protruding from just beside his collarbone.

"Hit it again," Saint said, and Jefferson reached for another arrow.

Brogan leapt at him, knocking hard into Jefferson and throwing him to the ground. In a blur of falling, Jefferson saw Saint swing up with the butt of the AK, but Brogan leveled his fist straight into Saint's rib cage, knocking the big man back against the wall. The arrow shaft vibrated violently again in Brogan's shoulder, and he turned from them, screaming once more. Rage, pain. Leaping again, he bounded down the hall and into the large open office beyond. He cleared the cream-colored sofas and headed toward the rear stairwell.

Saint was down on the ground, breathing heavily from the blow to the chest.

"You all right?" Jefferson asked, pulling himself along the carpeted floor. His shoulder felt dislocated, a bulge the size of a tennis ball protruding underneath his shirt.

"Yeah, I'll be straight in a minute," Saint said, pulling the AK toward him. "You?"

Jefferson nodded, standing up, his shoulder sagging. Down the hall came the sound of gunfire. The guards must be mixing it up with Brogan out in the office area. They should have all left when they had the chance. There was a long scream and the sound of something cracking. Jefferson looked out across the floor and saw red against the ceiling, like it had burst from a grape. Brogan was out there, occupied now, but for how long?

Jefferson turned back toward the bathroom. McKenna hadn't been the one in the bathtub. Brogan must have doubled back and concealed himself as her, waiting for Jefferson to show himself. Which meant that McKenna might still be alive somewhere. She would be somewhere close by. Brogan would have kept her hidden somewhere. Jefferson went past the bathroom, picked the knife up from the floor, and opened doors into offices and closets along the hallway.

And then he saw her.

She was bound at her hands and feet, lying in her underwear on the floor just inside the doorway. Her head was turned away, and Jefferson felt panic welling inside him. He reached down for her, touching her arm and turning her body toward him. There was tape over her mouth and her eyes were open. The pupils flicked toward him, recognition showing in her face. She was alive.

Jefferson felt the fear rush out of him so explosively that his legs went weak and he had to drop to one knee beside McKenna. He reached out and slowly pulled the tape from her mouth.

"Jefferson, oh thank God. Did you get it? It looked like me? It—"

"I know, I know," Jefferson said. "It's all right now."

"Jefferson, the tooth."

"What?"

"The tooth. When I cut my finger on the skeleton's tooth. In Russia. I should have figured that out. That's when it made contact with me. When it took my blood. If one Jinn makes contact, any of them can take that form temporarily."

He cut the cord from her wrists and a moment later her arms were up and around his neck, holding him. Her body pressed against his. Her head turned, and she looked at something over Jefferson's right shoulder. He felt her stiffen against him.

Jefferson whirled around, pointing his shotgun up toward the doorway. Saint stood there, looking down at the two of them.

Saint's hands came up. "Go easy, it's me."

Jefferson lowered the shotgun. "Jesus."

"We need to get moving. Cut her loose and let's roll. It's wounded somewhere, but not down. We got to finish this."

Jefferson went to work on the cords at McKenna's ankles. They were the same that had bound Brogan in the bathtub, thick black bungee material that Jefferson had to dig through with his knife.

"What's happening?" McKenna asked.

"We got it, once in the shoulder. It ran off somewhere into the building."

"It's Brogan, isn't it?"

Jefferson nodded. "He's the one."

"I saw him, upstairs. I knew the instant before he made his move. I could feel something was wrong with him." McKenna's hand touched Jefferson's shoulder. "I'm sorry it had to be your partner."

"At least we know now."

Jefferson's knife sliced its way through the last of the cords, and McKenna's ankles came free. Her feet were bare, and she stood.

"He took my clothes," she said.

Jefferson nodded. "Hang on a sec."

He stood and moved out the doorway again, back down the hall to the bathroom. Near the massive porcelain tub was a closet, towels and thick white bathrobes hung from racks inside. Jefferson took one of the robes, bringing it back down the hall to McKenna. Saint was standing guard outside the door, looking out across the office space. The sounds of gunfire had died down, but Jefferson could hear someone groaning in pain somewhere in the cubicles. Saint pointed to his watch as Jefferson passed by with the robe.

McKenna was standing, massaging her wrists alternately in a circular motion. Jefferson passed her the robe, and she put it on, cinching it tight around her waist. The terry cloth hung just above her bare feet.

"Give me the bag," Jefferson said.

Saint nodded, sliding the duffel bag over his head and throwing it to Jefferson. Jefferson dropped the bag to the floor, undid the zipper, and pulled out a Beretta, handing it to McKenna. She racked the slide, chambering the first round and clicking off the safety.

"Just so you know, bullets don't kill it," Jefferson said. "But they slow it down some."

She nodded, and Jefferson zipped the bag shut, throwing it back to Saint, who slid it over his shoulder again. Jefferson grabbed the Mossberg from the floor, taking shells out of his pocket and pumping them into the big shotgun. The end of the barrel was still warm from being fired so many times. If he could catch Brogan with a full blast, he could stun the demon long enough to get off another arrow shot. He hoped.

"Time to go hunting," Saint said from the doorway.

"You ready?" Jefferson asked.

McKenna nodded. "Bare feet and all."

Saint turned, and they followed him out into the hallway. The groaning became louder as they walked back into area with the cubicles. Someone was seriously injured. Saint had his AK up, shifting it slowly from right to left, Jefferson walking behind him with the Mossberg. The cubicles came to chest level, like the grasses on the island Jefferson dimly remembered. Brogan could be out there, crouching somewhere, waiting for them. They had better odds in the long hallway. At least there they could see Brogan coming. In the tight rows of cubicles, they might unknowingly pass right by him.

Ahead, Saint was crouched low, moving quickly, heading toward the groaning. Jefferson stayed behind him, taking turn after turn in the foam-padded aisles. Saint pulled up suddenly, looking at something lying on the ground to his right. Jefferson stopped beside him, following his gaze. Propped against one of the walls was the big Samoan Jefferson had met twice before. Something had torn him open; three gouges across his chest reached halfway into his abdomen. Blood covered the floor, soaking into the gray carpet in a congealed, shiny mess. The Samoan was still alive, though, his skin pale, his lips red and bloody, reminding Jefferson of a vampire.

His eyes were fixed on the carpet, oblivious in his pain to the three figures looking down at him. A TEC-9 pistol lay by his right hand, spent cartridges all around. He'd managed to unload a full clip before he was taken out. Bullets didn't slow it down that much.

Saint turned to leave, but the Samoan was calling him back, showing for the first time that he even knew anyone was standing there. The Samoan was talking to Saint, asking Saint not to leave him like that. Saint turned back to him, nodded once, then raised the AK. Jefferson looked away as two shots came in quick succession.

Saint stood. "It's not here. Big man here said it went out through the stairwell. He also said that they got three or four more guards in the building, he didn't know where."

"So what do you want to do?" Jefferson asked.

"I say we have some fun before we die."

Jefferson nodded, then turned to McKenna. "You all right?"

She nodded. "Yeah, sure. Let's do it."

Saint turned and moved quickly to the stairwell, the duffel bag rattling on his shoulder. The stairwell was empty, and yellow emergency lighting flickered on and off. They paused for a moment, checking stairwell both up and down; both were empty. Then came gunshots. Three quick bursts, large caliber. Something like a .45, the sound echoing up from one of the floors below them. Saint began moving down quickly, taking the stairs two at a time, jumping to the landings with a *clang* of metal. Jefferson and McKenna followed through the flashing alternates of yellow light and darkness. They went down four levels before Saint suddenly stopped.

The door to the thirty-seventh floor was open.

The thirty-seventh floor was a mess. Chairs overturned, pictures shattered in pieces and lying on the floor, bullet holes in the walls. It reminded Jefferson of Bosnia. There were two long tables set in the middle of the room, large-scale models of buildings on them. To their right was a square room with a shiny conference table and two rows of chairs lined up alongside it. Straight ahead was a wall of glass separating an individual office, in which Jefferson saw mounted photographs of the American Southwest on the walls. The floor seemed empty otherwise, except for the body.

The man lay on his back beneath a table holding a model, a squat building that looked like a cross between a shopping mall and a post office. Jefferson didn't bother to check on him. Instead he focused on the footprints leading away from the body, bloody prints that tracked across the floor, away from it for ten yards before fading away.

"Looks like we got company," Saint whispered.

From somewhere on the floor, they could hear the sound of arguing voices. Three men. Saint moved quickly toward the sound. As they slid past the models, Jefferson caught movement in the corner office. A fourth man, rising from where he'd been hiding behind the desk, shouldered a heavy machine gun. A trap.

"Down, down, down!" Jefferson said, ducking behind the wide legs of one of the tables.

The glass walls exploded in sheets of broken fragments as the fourth man open fired. Saint caught a round in the shoulder, something bursting from his arm and spinning him to the ground. Jefferson reached out, grabbed the strap of the duffel bag, and pulled him across the floor and under the table. McKenna ducked back into the stairwell, keeping her back pressed against the wall.

"Where the fuck did he come from?" Saint hissed.

"Don't know, must have been waiting for us."

More rounds were coming, knocking apart the fiberglass models above them and chipping holes in the far wall. Whoever was doing the shooting wasn't taking the time to aim, just opening the magazine and dumping as much lead into the room as he could.

"This shit is really starting to fuck with my yoga," Saint said.

He was on the ground, blood flowing freely from his left arm. He unhitched the strap of the duffel bag and tied it tight just above the wound. Jefferson wasn't sure what type of bullet Saint had taken, but whatever it was, it looked like it had done some bad work. McKenna was at the doorway, squeezing off a few rounds with her Beretta, the gun sounding like tap shoes compared to whatever cannon had them pinned down.

A second man appeared suddenly from the end of the hallway, turning the corner and holding two big revolvers, cowboy style, one in each hand. Jefferson remembered the voices, three of them. This must be one of them making a cameo. Jefferson could see the hammers of both guns being pulled back, the cylinders rotating into position. The guy had them dead, before Jefferson pulled up the Mossberg, pulling the trigger quickly. He hadn't had time to shoulder the weapon, and the butt end of the gun jammed painfully into Jefferson's gut as the shell exploded. Firing a single bullet, Jefferson would have missed right by a solid foot, but the Mossberg load spread out like a net and tagged the second man on the left shoulder, knocking him down like a paper target at the carnival.

A third man came right after the first, running out of the hallway Kamikaze style; this genius was not even holding a weapon. McKenna fired three quick shots from the doorway, each putting the guy down before Jefferson could even pump the next shell. The third man fell to the ground, rolling back and forth on his side, his feet pushing him a few inches at a time along the marble floor. Definitely not dead yet. Jefferson ignored him for the moment, focusing on the two who were left—whoever was doing Wyatt Earp in the back office and the last of the voices he had heard that hadn't shown himself yet.

Then, in an instant, the shooting was over. The one doing the Wyatt Earp was calling out to them, telling them he was coming out. Jefferson leaned slightly to his right, looking past the table leg and into the back office. He put a Mossberg round against the back wall, tearing out a two-foot circle in the plaster.

"Don't fuck with us," Jefferson called out. "Show me hands!"

A moment later two hands appeared above the level of the desk, followed slowly by a head and a body. The man looked scared, young kid, about twenty-five. His face was cut, probably from the plasterboard chips the Mossberg had just torn off the wall.

"McKenna," Jefferson called out. "Take him. There's one more to our left, down the hall."

The kid was coming out of the office, hands still raised, walking through what was formerly the glass wall, his feet grinding the broken bits into the floor. McKenna was yelling something to him, and the kid was responding, lowering himself facedown onto the stone floor. The kid wasn't the concern anymore; Jefferson focused his attention on the hallway. The single guard was still down there, and Brogan was still running around the building.

A second voice called out, this one from the hall. It was the last guard, shouting out that he was giving himself up. He was coming out, moving slowly out of the hallway and onto the main floor, hands above his head. Jefferson covered him with the Mossberg, the large double-aught barrel leveled at the man's chest.

McKenna was moving out of the stairwell, still in the robe, covering the kid with her Beretta. Jefferson stood from under the table, still holding the Mossberg, as he stepped over the two bodies lying on the floor. One of them was unarmed. Why? Was he trying to give himself up, too? Saint pulled himself up as well, the strap cinched tightly around his left arm. They were going to have to do something with these guys until they could track down Brogan. Maybe lock them in one of the offices for the time being.

The second guard was still standing, arms over his head. He was a thin man, thin face and nose, high cheeks, with two scratches on his face just below his eyes. He was wearing the black uniform of the Lyerman guards, and his rubber-soled shoes squeaked slightly on the floor. Saint was leaning against the table, bleeding all over the hardwood. He would need to rest somewhere, maybe even get to a hospital. Jefferson moved to stand over the security guard still lying facedown on the floor.

"Get up," Jefferson said, and the kid responded, pushing himself up to a kneeling position, his eyes still focused on the killing end of the Mossberg. "Why the fuck are you still here?"

The kid looked scared, saying nothing and only shaking his head.

"All right, we're gonna lock the two of you in one of the offices for now," Jefferson said.

"Two of us?" The kid looked confused for a moment, pulling his eyes away from the Mossberg and looking for the first time toward the other guard, the thin man. The kid tightened suddenly and jumped to his feet quickly.

"Stay the fuck down!" Jefferson shouted, moving to strike the kid with the stock of the Mossberg. The kid wasn't even looking at Jefferson, focusing instead on the thin man across the floor. Jefferson, too, turned slowly.

Something was wrong. The thin man's face was changing, thickening, elongating again, just like it had with McKenna. Trust no one. The kid was backing away, a soft wheezing noise coming from his mouth. Saint's back was to the thin man, and he was looking down at his bloodied arm, cinching the strap tighter. Jefferson saw a flash of yellow, the thin man's eyes going yellow for an instant. Turning to Brogan's eyes.

"Saint, behind you!" Jefferson called out, swinging up the Mossberg.

The thin man bounded forward as Jefferson fired, the buckshot going wide right and blowing apart one of the ceiling's columns. Jefferson pumped the Mossberg as Saint was turning, the thin man knocking into him. McKenna's Beretta fired two quick shots before clicking empty. The thin man was changing quickly now, back to Brogan. Back to the demon. The bow was still slung over Jefferson's shoulder, and he reached for it. Saint was on the floor, scrambling toward his AK.

Jefferson had the bow up and was pulling for an arrow. Brogan was focused on Saint, but he stopped when he heard the whisk of the arrow sliding from the quiver. Squatting, Brogan turned his head back to Jefferson, seeing the arrow coming up and into place. He hissed once—like a snake—startling Jefferson. Jefferson nocked the arrow and sighted down the shaft, the ancient metal tip lining up on Brogan's chest. He pulled back to his ear. His fingers released.

Something heavy hit Jefferson from behind, knocking his arm as he loosed the arrow. He watched it fly wide to the right, Brogan ducking and spinning out of the way as the wooden shaft cleaved by him, burying itself deeply in the opposite wall. Something was on Jefferson's back, fingers digging into his neck, teeth gouging his shoulder. Someone was biting him.

Standing upright, he pushed backward, slamming himself into the doorframe behind him. There was a grunt of pain and surprise, and the fingers loosened from around his neck. Jefferson's elbow shot backward, the point striking against flesh and bone, eliciting another grunt of pain. Jefferson turned, brought his fist around, and struck someone hard in the face.

The figure pulled back, hands over nose, blood streaming out between small fingers. It was the Panamanian. Lyerman's nurse. The man was whimpering, holding his shattered nose delicately with his hands, speaking quickly in broken English.

"The master, he promise me, if I help him—" The Panamanian collapsed to the floor.

Jefferson turned back to the master, back to Brogan. Brogan stared at them from twenty feet away. Jefferson knew that he wouldn't have enough time to nock and fire another arrow. Brogan was fast, he could cover the twenty feet before Jefferson could even pull an arrow out of the quiver. Instead, Jefferson's eyes focused on the Mossberg lying at his feet. Behind Brogan, Saint lay on the floor. He wasn't moving, his eyelids firmly shut. He might have been knocked unconscious when Brogan struck him.

Jefferson's eyes moved back to Brogan, who was standing completely still, his head turned slightly. Peripherally, he could see McKenna, also not moving, the empty Beretta at her side.

"McKenna," Jefferson said slowly.

"Yes."

"Slowly move behind me."

"You sure?"

Jefferson nodded, still keeping eye contact with Brogan. McKenna began moving across the floor, sliding sideways, keeping the front of her body facing Brogan. Gradually she passed behind Jefferson, until she was standing ten yards beyond his right shoulder. Saint still hadn't moved. By the stairwell, the Panamanian continued to whimper, his broken nose leaking blood down his chin and covering his shirt. The kid had moved out of sight into one of the back offices. Jefferson hoped he had the sense to stay away.

Brogan was making a growling noise in his throat, a low, ticking sound like the rattling of a drum. He looked ready to strike. Jefferson moved first. Dropping down to one knee, he reached for the shotgun, telling McKenna to get back. Brogan moved forward an instant later, bounding over the floor, the rattling become a full growl. He leapt as Jefferson brought the shotgun up and pulled the trigger.

The shell struck Brogan flat in the chest as he arced through his leap, pushing him backward and spinning him around. He landed facedown on the stone floor. Jefferson reached back for one of the arrows, but Brogan was already pushing himself up. Jefferson wouldn't have time to get off a good shot, and, if he missed, Brogan would be on him. A hand grabbed at Jefferson's shoulder, and he turned to see McKenna pulling him down the hall.

"Let's go, let's go. No time. We'll hide."

Jefferson took a last glance at Brogan, who was already on his knees, before he turned and followed McKenna at a run down the hall. They moved past the row of elevators toward a food court at the opposite end of the floor. There were two glass doors sectioning off the food court, doors Jefferson knew would be locked. He raised the Mossberg as they ran, pumping another round, then pointing the weapon at the doors. The doors exploded into thousands of shining fragments as he fired, and he and McKenna ran through the opening.

The food court was large. Tables to their left with some kind of themed French market area to their right. They moved into the market area, ducking behind cartons of plastic fruit and bins of fish lying in ice. The market was big enough to get lost in, with large booths selling meat and pasta and desserts and things in between, everything dark and quiet for the night. Ducking behind one of the counters, they had a view of the shattered doors and space behind them if they had to fall back. Otherwise known as run.

Jefferson passed the Mossberg to McKenna. "If I miss with the bow, you pump a round into it, all right?"

McKenna nodded, taking the big shotgun and resting it on top of a crate holding a pile of plastic bananas. Jefferson nocked an arrow, holding it in place with two fingers, and they waited. Waited listening to the quiet. Waited watching the lights outside the window, the flashing beacons out at Logan, the sporadic flow of traffic over the Longfellow Bridge, the blue of streetlamps. And, finally, when Jefferson didn't think he could wait anymore, he heard a sound. Footsteps on broken glass.

McKenna sat up slightly next to him, raising the Mossberg an inch. Across the stands of the market, Brogan stepped through the broken doorway. He paused for a moment, turning his head left and right, scanning the new environment.

"Remember, only if I miss," Jefferson said.

He raised the bow slightly, waiting for Brogan to step farther into the room. The shot wasn't hard with a pistol, but with a bow? Jefferson wasn't sure he could hit the side of a truck with it. Robin Hood he wasn't.

Brogan was moving cautiously, now that he had seen the arrowheads. Jefferson would wait until Brogan moved ten more feet, then he would have a straight shot directly across from him. A twenty-yard shot. He wished he'd taken more of those archery classes back at summer camp. Brogan was moving more aggressively, the steps counting down. Jefferson lifted the bow, pulled and waited. Three more steps. Now two. One. There. Release!

The arrow loosed with a soft click, Brogan turning his head toward the sound. Now Brogan's arm was coming up, defensive, the arrow flying straight for him. Brogan's hand was opening slightly, snatching something out of the air. Snatching the arrow out of the air. Holding the arrow in place, the shaft and point six inches from his chest.

Brogan had caught the arrow in midflight. *Jesus, the guy is fast.* The arrow snapped in Brogan's hand as the man turned toward where Jefferson and McKenna hid behind the crates of fake fruit. Brogan moved toward them more quickly as McKenna brought up the Mossberg. Brogan's face registered a faint surprise at the sight of the big weapon, and an instant later McKenna fired, pumped another round, and fired again. The shot hit Brogan squarely, knocking him back once again, then the second one tagged him on the shoulder, spinning him so that he crashed against dinner tables, shattering the costly-looking place settings.

Then they were running again, back out through the broken doorway, moving toward the rows of elevators. McKenna pushed the call button, while Jefferson did a slide next to Saint. The man was still alive, a nasty purple bruise rising on his forehead and spreading over to his temple. Time was ticking. Saint's eyes rolled toward Jefferson.

"Can you move?"

"Don't think so," Saint said. "My head feels like a damn truck hit it."

"You look like you got a map of Asia printed on your forehead, but your skull's not broken," Jefferson said. "Fuck. All right, listen, you sit here and play dead. It doesn't want you. It wants me. You pretend like you been whacked, it'll pass right by. Just don't move, OK? Got that?"

Saint nodded. "Yeah. You two go."

Saint reached up and pressed something into Jefferson's hand. A silver-colored Glock. Jefferson put the weapon into his belt and nodded. There was a *ping* noise from the wall of elevators, and Jefferson turned to see one pair of doors sliding open. McKenna was inside, waving to Jefferson to hurry.

"Stay down," Jefferson said a last time, then stood and ran toward the elevator. Beyond the lobby and into the darkened food court, he could see that Brogan had picked himself up and was moving quickly toward them. Jefferson reached the elevator and threw himself inside. McKenna could see Brogan coming toward them through the still-open doors of the elevator. She began pushing floor buttons frantically, then the CLOSE DOOR symbol.

Jefferson fired the Glock, emptying half the magazine into Brogan's body without even slowing him down. Brogan was running, streaking like a cheetah across the lobby toward them. Finally, the doors responded. Another electronic chime, and they began sliding shut. They clamped together just as Brogan reached them; his body slammed into the doors.

At the impact, the metal instantly warped inward; the car rocked wildly in its tracks and Jefferson was thrown hard against the back wall. The lights flickered on and off, and, for a sickening moment, Jefferson thought they might be stranded. Then there was silence and movement again as the elevator began gliding smoothly up and away from Brogan, the floors counting rapidly upward on the digital display.

"You all right," Jefferson asked.

"Yeah. You?"

"I feel like I just went over Niagara Falls in a barrel."

Jefferson stood, rubbing his left shoulder. The elevator car was small, no windows, a square television screen over the door flashing news and weather information. It was drizzling in Seattle. Trouble in the Middle East. A demon trapped three in a building. The usual bullshit. Turning his head back and forth, he tested his neck.

Then it hit them.

Something hard, from underneath, the car doing the roller-coaster sway back and forth again, knocking the insides of the shaft and throwing McKenna against the side wall. Her head snapped back, and a deep gash appeared on her forehead. The car had stopped moving; lights flickered on and off again. The digital floor display flashed back and forth between the fifty-eighth and fifty-ninth floors, the eight and the nine jumping up and down fast enough to cause a seizure in anyone staring at it. Jefferson helped McKenna up, and her fingers went to the edge of her scalp, coming away bloody. She had a fairly deep cut that Jefferson could only hope would stop bleeding on its own.

"Jesus, what was that?" McKenna asked, still fingering her wound.

"Guess?"

From underneath them came a low shriek of bending metal, followed by a scraping sound. Something was under the car, and Jefferson had a pretty good idea what it was. The grinding sounded again, the sound a car makes when it's being crushed, a shrill scream that rises and falls in pitch. Brogan must have climbed up the shaft after them. *What the hell is it trying to do? Stop the elevator? Come up through the floor?*

Jefferson pumped the Mossberg, keeping the barrel down toward the floor. Slowly, he backed to the edge of the elevator doors, pulling McKenna back with him.

"Cover your ears," he said.

"What?"

"Your ears. Cover them. It's loud."

Slowly, McKenna's hands went to her ears, cupping them. Then Jefferson pulled the trigger. In the small elevator car, the Mossberg sounded like a grenade going off. The shot ripped a hole the size of a basketball in the floor, exposing support beams and the darkness of the shaft underneath. Jefferson pumped again and fired, another basketball appearing a foot to the right. This one was followed by a scream of surprise from below. Jefferson moved the barrel down another six inches and fired again. Another scream. The floor was getting turned into a *This Old House* improvement project.

A hand appeared through one of the basketballs, and Jefferson fired a fourth time. The hand disappeared quickly. They needed to get out of the elevator. The air was filled with plaster dust from the blown-apart floor. The fine white powder floated all around them, dusting their clothes and eyelashes. They needed to get onto the floor.

"See if you can pry apart the doors," Jefferson said.

McKenna moved to them, pulling at the crack with the tips of her fingers. They moved apart an inch, enough for Jefferson to wedge the barrel of the shotgun between them. He hoped that Brogan wouldn't decide to make an appearance while the Mossberg was tied up as a crowbar. Jefferson pushed on the butt of the weapon, and slowly the doors began to slide open. He pushed them back with both hands, and they slid apart farther and stayed apart, enough for Jefferson and McKenna to slip out. They were halfway between floors, a narrow space below their knees that looked down into the fifty-eighth. And a wide gap from their waists to the top of the car that looked up at the fifty-ninth. The opening to the fifty-eighth was too small to fit through, so the fifty-ninth it would be.

Below them they heard the sound of twisting metal again. Brogan was still down there.

"Get up there," Jefferson said. "I'll be right behind."

"You better be."

McKenna stepped into Jefferson's fingers and he hoisted her to the fifty-ninth. She slid out on her stomach. Then turned around, extending her hand back down through the opening.

"Come on!"

Jefferson reached for her, and, as their fingers touched, the car lurched downward suddenly. Jefferson was thrown off-balance down to his knees and McKenna had to jerk her hand back through the narrowing crack between the ceiling of the elevator and the floor of the fifty-ninth. Brogan was below, tearing apart the elevator. He was trying to bring down the whole car. McKenna's hand came down again, but again the car lurched, this time a foot. The space had become too narrow.

"I can't fit," Jefferson said. "Go!"

"No! I won't leave you!"

"Go! I can get out on the fifty-eighth. I'll come for you," Jefferson said. "Meet on the roof."

The gap to the fifty-eighth floor had widened as the car slipped down, so that now Jefferson could fit through in a crouch. Bending, he pulled apart the outside elevator doors and saw a strip of tan carpeting below him. He took the shotgun, took a last look at McKenna, then stepped out of the opening and onto the fifty-eighth floor.

As his feet hit the ground, he turned to look back through the open elevator doors. The shaft was divided evenly in half. The upper portion was taken up by the bottom half of the elevator car, underneath that was the open shaft. And hanging, clinging from the bottom of the elevator car was Brogan. And he was staring at Jefferson. *Run,* Jefferson thought. *Run.*

Jefferson turned and ran. He headed toward a row of offices in front of him. From behind came the sound of two gunshots, and Jefferson felt something strike him in the left shoulder. He felt incredible pain in his arm as the bullet entered him, tore its way through the muscle, and punched through his skin, exiting his arm. Incredible shock accompanies being shot for the first time, largely getting the mind to accept the unreality of it all. With what had happened on the island, this was Jefferson's fourth or fifth time taking a bullet. He was beginning to get used to it. A couple more lives like these, and he would have a baker's dozen.

Jefferson pushed open a set of glass doors and headed down the row of offices. He heard Brogan coming after him, the panting of breath and pounding of feet. Jefferson was already bleeding hard. He needed some time to stop the bleeding. McKenna could help, but he didn't want to head up the stairs and bring Brogan to her. No, he had to hide somewhere. Ahead of him, he saw a bathroom.

Still running, he reached into Saint's bag and pulled out four flashbang grenades. *When these go off, they sound like elephant roars and light up like a slot machine after spinning three cherries. If Saint's right, they should each have thirty-second delays before they go Hiroshima. Won't do anything to knock Brogan out, but I have other plans for them.* Taking the first one, he lobbed it gently into one of the offices, counted off five seconds, then lobbed another, then the third, and headed for the bathroom.

He was still counting in his head when he pushed open the bathroom door, turned, and locked it. Jefferson moved to the corner of the room, to the right of the stalls, and took out the Mossberg. He could hear Brogan outside, banging on the locked bathroom door. Jefferson ignored him, concentrating on his counting. Five seconds. The bathroom was long and narrow, typical, row of urinals with that caked shit inside, row of stalls. Four seconds. The bathroom floor was covered in peach-colored linoleum. Cheap stuff, already peeling up slightly at the corners of the room. Three seconds. Brogan continued to bang, the sounds coming heavier, really getting his body into it.

Two seconds.

Jefferson steadied his feet, placing the muzzle of the Mossberg a foot above the bathroom tile. He hoped it was cheap enough. One second. And fire. Jefferson pulled the trigger of the Mossberg as outside, in the office, the flashbang grenade boomed. The tile exploded into fragments of peach plastic, spraying back into Jefferson's face. He ignored them, pumping the shotgun and counting again from five. When he reached "one," he fired again as the second flashbang boomed. The shot tore into the floor again, exposing electric wiring and whiteboard.

He hadn't gone completely through yet. The third round was coming as Jefferson pumped the shotgun a final time. As the flashbang went off outside, Jefferson pulled the trigger. Nothing happened. The shotgun clicked empty. A hole as round as a trash can was blown in the floor, but he hadn't completely punched his way through the ceiling of the floor below. Outside, Brogan slammed against the door again.

Jefferson dropped to his knees in front of the hole, taking the butt of the shotgun and bashing it down on the drywall of the ceiling below. He worked the shotgun like a sledgehammer, battering away until a hole began opening up. Jefferson could see down through the hole to the floor below. He was looking at the top of a desk. Plaster fell onto the keyboard and computer monitor. He kept widening the hole until he was sure he could fit through, then tossed the bag down. It hit the top of the desk and slid off to the floor.

Jefferson stood, moving quickly to the sink. There wasn't much time. Already the bathroom lock was rattling, weakening. Overhead was an air grate. Jefferson knocked at the grate with the butt of his shotgun, until knocked loose, it fell out and clattered against the sink below. With luck, Brogan would think that Jefferson had gone up rather than down—into the air ducts again rather than through the floor.

Jumping back off the sink, Jefferson took the round metal trash can and placed it beside the gaping hole in the floor. Then, laying the shotgun athwart the hole, he used it to lower himself slowly through the hole. When his lower half was hanging from the ceiling of the fifty-seventh floor, he used his hips to balance himself, pulled the shotgun through the hole, and reached back up, grabbing the trash can and sliding it over to conceal the hole. Then he let himself drop.

The fall to the desk was only a few feet, but he landed on something and jarred his ankle as he rolled onto the floor. He paused to examine the ankle, but luckily it was only twisted, not broken or sprained. Grabbing the bag, he hobbled across the floor toward the stairwell. Jefferson's arm was still bleeding hard, blood running out of him like juice from a squeezed orange. He took the stairs down another level, then across the floor and into a women's bathroom.

Above him, Brogan would have already broken down the door and, Jefferson hoped, taken the bait and gone into the air duct. If not, he'd be searching the bathroom, opening stall doors, maybe knocking over the trash can and discovering the hole. Jefferson had to get the bleeding stopped, then get to the roof and find McKenna.

On the wall near the door of the bathroom was a silver box, with feminine products for sale. Jefferson fished in his pocket for change and purchased three pads, then he slid onto a sink and sat down, his back against the wall near the mirror. Carefully he took his shirt off. The lower half of his arm was slick and red with blood, though new blood appeared only intermittently. Taking one of the pads, he ripped the wrapper off and placed the pad carefully across the wound. Then he did the same with the other two, placing each on top of the other. Over all of that, he ripped a section of his T-shirt, tying it tightly to keep the pads in place and put pressure on the wound.

He pulled some paper towels from the dispenser, wet them in the sink, and did a quick cleanup of his arm and hand, then dried himself. Most of the bleeding had stopped. He wouldn't be swinging any home run balls out of Fenway, but he'd be all right long enough to get to hospital. That is, if he ever got out of there.

Jefferson sat back against the wall. *Jesus, what a night.* Reaching into his pants pocket, he pulled out the stack of photographs, shuffling through them while giving himself a chance to rest for a moment. *Let those platelets do their work.* The past few minutes he had begun to feel like that Czar's hemophiliac kid.

The pictures were more of the same. Jungle scene after jungle scene. Bulldozers clearing out trees. Someone torching a Japanese bunker. Men wading in waist-deep water across a river. Someone playing cards. *Looks like a real hoot.* Then Jefferson paused. There were more pictures, but they looked like they'd been taken inside a ship. He recognized the inside of the USS *Galla*, the ship they'd brought up from the bottom of the Pacific and dragged all the way to Boston. Jefferson saw Lyerman, looking young and fit. Walking on two legs. Smiling, before everything else had happened. And for a moment, Jefferson felt sorry for the guy. For a moment.

He flipped again. More pictures of the ship. He paused for a moment, looking at a picture of himself wrapped in bandages, sitting up on a cot in the infirmary. Or Davis. Or whatever. He still hadn't gotten used to the idea of the past life experiences just yet. But the face was unmistakable. That was him sitting on that cot. Him shot out on the island. There was no doubt of that. He studied his own face for a moment, then his eyes moved around the rest of the picture.

A nurse in white is standing over me, reaching down for something on my chest. Pretty girl, probably why I look so happy in the picture. Attaboy. Always with the ladies. Even a past life can't hold me back.

Jefferson looked at the nurse's face for a moment more.

"Oh no . . ."

Something sank in his chest, the painful feeling you get when someone lets you in on a truth and you wish you could forget it a moment later. The kind of feeling Columbus might have had if you told him he hadn't really discovered India, but a couple million natives were going to die anyway.

Jefferson stared at the face of the nurse in the photograph.

The face that was exactly McKenna's.

He knew the truth. The nurse on the *Galla* who had attended to Davis had been McKenna. The souls of Sidina and his three warriors would stay together each succeeding lifetime. Brogan, Vincent, and Jefferson, all together on the island, and again all together on the Boston Police Force. The three of them were linked. And so was McKenna. Linked to all of them and to Sidina. Jefferson knew that she was one of them. She was the fourth warrior. The fourth to be called by the Jinn. The fourth and final one to be tempted to evil. Brogan had failed to resist the call.

Will McKenna? Will she relent and give Brogan's and her Jinn the opportunity to convince his and Vincent's reincarnates in the next lifetime to join the unholy union? Does she even know the rules? Has Brogan told her?

"Not you . . . McKenna," Jefferson whispered to the empty bathroom. "I won't believe it."

Jefferson's arm had stopped bleeding. He stood and jammed the rest of the photographs back into his pocket, then, taking the Mossberg from the sink, moved to the bathroom door. Pushing it open a crack, he peered out. Everything was quiet and dark. Brogan might still be upstairs somewhere, or he might have given up the search for Jefferson and left for some other part of the building entirely. If she had followed the plan, McKenna should be on the roof. That was where Jefferson headed.

Things were beginning to make sense. Jefferson understood why Brogan hadn't killed McKenna when he'd first found her. He knew she was one of the four. Knew what she could become if given enough time.

Jefferson took one of the working elevators to the roof. *McKenna can't be turned. Or can she?* Ask his ex-partner Brogan about that. Apparently the Jinn can be very persuasive. He hated to think what would happen if she were. And he hated even more to think what that would mean for him. What he might have to do.

The elevator ride was short. The doors *ping*ed and opened, and soon Jefferson was stepping onto the roof. The rain had started again, the same cold drizzle there had been the night of the murder. The first night Jefferson had ever stepped foot up there. At least he was sure of that. Things that had happened in his own life. People he had known. Places he had been. That was what really counted. What had happened in *this* life.

Eric Davis had drowned on that ship. What had happened to McKenna when the *Galla* went down? Had she drowned as well? Probably. But did that mean they were all destined to repeat the pattern of sixty-five years before? No, that couldn't be. That didn't feel right. Davis had been shot out on that island. Davis had drowned on that ship. Davis. Not Jefferson. Not him. The present was what counted not what happened in the past. Someone else's past. And whatever had happened to McKenna, that could change, too. Whatever had happened to that nurse on that *Galla*, that was somebody else, somebody different from McKenna.

That night was what mattered. Whatever happened on that roof, that would shape the rest of their lives. Not the actions of strangers over a sixty-five years earlier.

And so Jefferson stepped out into the rain. The roof was familiar by then. The same paths and gardens, the same high grass, the solarium at the far end by the fountain and patio. Everything seemed empty, but McKenna might still be there. Hiding somewhere in the trees. Jefferson walked carefully, keeping the Mossberg raised, the bow still slung over his shoulder. *Whatever happens, I'm through running. If Brogan shows up, I stay and fight. It ends here, on the roof.*

Jefferson walked the path of wood chips, along the edge of the roof, city lights shining around him like iridescent fish in black oceans. He approached the solarium, passing the bench where Kenneth Lyerman and his girlfriend had sat for the last time. The Jinn liked it up there. Maybe it was the open spaces. Maybe it was the gardens and trees that reminded it of being back on the island. He was twenty yards from the solarium, the glass-and-wood structure, when something moved beyond it.

Brogan stepped from behind the building. He was wet from the rain, his suit torn and ragged from where the shot had struck him, his hair matted. He stared at Jefferson for a moment, then smiled.

"Hello, Jefferson."

Jefferson said nothing, gripping the Mossberg and feeling the bow on his shoulder. *Stun him with the shotgun, then go for the bow. No more running. No place to go. You can't even escape if you die. These things will chase you into the next lifetime if they have to. At least now you remember what it is. You know who it is. And you've learned how it can be killed. Now the odds are even.*

"You've come up here to kill me, haven't you," Brogan said. "I know. Just as you wanted to sixty-five years ago. Your nature is as vicious as mine. Always has been."

"Tell that to Reggie Tate or Lyerman."

"Lyerman . . ." Brogan said. "He had that coming for betraying me."

"Betraying you? He brought you up from the Pacific. He found you."

"He didn't trust me. He betrayed me. He found the *Galla*, but then wouldn't free me. Instead he towed took the salvaged compartment, my prison, to Blade Island and left me there. Left me until he figured out what to do."

"But you escaped?"

"Because of a guard. Older. He found me on that island and freed me, but I still couldn't get off the island. So I was stuck on Blade, where I could do nothing but wander those tunnels, wander in and out of the pit."

The prisoners, Jefferson thought. *That was when they first became afraid of the pit, when Older freed the demon onto Blade. That was where the* Galla *was for the missing month, on Blade Island. Lyerman must have brought the infirmary compartment almost to Boston, then had second thoughts and hid it somewhere on Blade, keeping the demon trapped inside. Lyerman might have already known about the second demon, known that it had been buried somewhere on the island by the original knights of the Crusade. Maybe Lyerman figured that if Blade had held one of the demons for so long, it could hold another. But it hadn't.*

Older had found the compartment of the *Galla* during his wanderings around the island and released the demon, somehow managing to escape with the box that Davis carried with him, the box with the arrowheads. Then when Lyerman returned to the island later, he would have found the compartment empty except for Davis's body. Realizing what had happened, Lyerman arranged to bring Davis's body to his own residence before taking the compartment to the naval museum. Then Older contacted him and told him about the knight's manuscript that he had found on the island. He also told Lyerman that he had the box with the arrowheads. Although Lyerman did not know how important the arrowheads were, he figured that they might give him some leverage against the demon. Older, though, tried to make an even better deal for himself, by first selling the manuscript to his employer, Sinatra, then contracting Five and Saint and Q to rip off Sinatra, return the manuscript to Older, who would then resell it to Lyerman.

The plan would have worked out for Older, if the demon had remained trapped on that island.

"How did you get off Blade?" Jefferson asked.

"The island was always connected to the city through a tunnel. The tunnel you and your SWAT team found. For months the tunnel was blocked, trapping me on the island, with nothing but those prisoners to occupy my time," Brogan said. "But nothing lasts forever."

Jefferson remembered something now, avoiding traffic delays on the way to the Lyerman building the night of the murder. Traffic delays caused by construction. The construction must have opened up the old tunnel to Blade, allowing the demon to enter the city. And that night he tracked down Lyerman and murdered his son.

"The construction site, that's what opened up the tunnel," Jefferson said.

"That's what gave me my freedom. First I found Lyerman. And then I found Older."

"Why did you go after him?"

"Because he had the manuscript. The knowledge of my . . . weaknesses. I couldn't have that, now could I? If it weren't for your friend Saint, I could have ended things there. But I got it back from him. I arranged to meet Saint, arrived in the form of Lyerman using his backup wheelchair, and took back the manuscript."

So that's what happened. Saint, stealing away with the manuscript. Then thinking he gave it to Lyerman. But it was the Jinn, taking the form of Lyerman, who he really gave it to. Lyer-

man, the real Lyerman, never saw the manuscript. Never knew what was written in it. Never knew the significance of the arrowheads.

"And Reggie Tate? What did he do?"

"Reggie Tate . . . saw my face. Out at Blade. The first night I found the pit, Reggie had been down there. He saw my face, this face. Brogan's face. And I made the mistake of not killing him then. I was weak, just having left the *Galla's* infirmary compartment for the first time. And Reggie was released from prison before I could get to him again."

Brogan took a step forward, and Jefferson raised the Mossberg. Brogan stopped.

"You were wrong," Jefferson said. "I'm nothing like you."

"Oh, we're not so different. We've met before, you and I. So many times before, probably more times than you'll ever know. Ever remember. If you die here tonight, you'll forget me, who I am. You'll forget everything about your life now. You'll forget everyone you know. You'll forget everything that's important to you. You'll be reborn in someone else's life. You'll have to start over again. Is that what you want?"

"I want to be free of you. I want McKenna to be free of you."

"Ahh . . . to be free," Brogan said. "You'll never be free. The best you can do is to join me. Or die and forget me. Temporarily of course. Until I find you again in your next life. And I will find you again. You can't hide from me. And maybe when I do find you again, the next time, you'll be married. Have a wife. Children. A family." Brogan raised his eyebrows. "Someone you love?"

"You and I are through. Here. Tonight. I finish this tonight."

"You finish this tonight? This has been going on for almost eight hundred years. Do you have any idea how many lifetimes that has been? How many times you thought or the others thought you could finish it. And yet here I am. And the others. Still around. And there you are, still around. What do you think happened all those times?" Brogan asked, taking another step. "You or the others die, Jefferson. Every time, you die. You refuse to join, and you die. That's what happened on Bougainville. And that's what happened to Vincent tonight. And it's going to happen to you. And then it begins again. I kill you, and then, unless I can convince McKenna to allow herself to be possessed, she dies, and I am forced to separate from Brogan, but not before I kill him, and we wait for the next round. We finish nothing here. Since 1232 it has been this way. What makes tonight any different?"

"It will be different."

"You look so sincere, that I might actually believe you this time." Brogan stepped back, and reached for something behind the solarium.

"Don't fucking move!" Jefferson called out.

Brogan shrugged, then pulled McKenna out from behind the solarium. Her mouth was taped over, but she focused on Jefferson with her eyes. Jefferson felt his chest tighten. McKenna pulled away from Brogan, but he gripped her, forcing her back.

With McKenna in the way, I can't get a shot at Brogan.

"I can see by your face that this changes things," Brogan chortled.

"Don't you fucking touch her."

436

"Touch her? Why would I want to hurt her?" Brogan said. "We just finished getting reacquainted, she was just telling me about all the old times that we shared, back on the *Galla*."

Jefferson tried to keep his face straight, but he blinked once, his eyes focusing on McKenna.

"Oh," Brogan smiled. "Hmm . . . you didn't know? You mean, she never told you who she was? And who says that you can trust those you love."

"I knew; she told me about it," Jefferson bluffed.

Brogan looked at him for a moment, then shook his head. "I don't think so. I think maybe you found out, just recently. But she didn't tell you. The pictures in Lyerman's bedroom, right? You saw those?"

Jefferson said nothing. What could he say? Brogan knew.

Brogan smiled again. "Well, if you didn't remember on your own about McKenna being on the *Galla,* and she didn't tell you about it, then you don't remember how the story ends. You have no idea what happened out there, do you? You don't know whether McKenna turned to me. Whether she helped me, or kept loyal to you. You don't have a clue about that, do you? You can't remember."

"No, I know. She didn't join you."

"Really? What makes you so sure?" Brogan smiled, then, leaning down, kissed McKenna on the side of her cheek, his tongue running up toward her ear. "What makes you think she's still yours?"

"If you've turned her, then what's to stop me from killing you both, right now?"

Brogan looked at Jefferson for a moment, then shook his head. "Nooo . . . you wouldn't do that. You're in love with her. You've always been in love with her. For all this time. And in all this time, you've never hurt her. No matter how many times she betrays you, you never learn."

"She's never betrayed me."

"How can you be sure? Join me, and you can finally be with her. We would have two lifetimes to find and convince Vincent's reincarnation to join us. You could be with her not for the few fleeting moments we have in a human life. Beyond that. More than the brief time God sees fit to give us before we die. That's what I can give you."

"And what do I have to do in return?"

"All you have to do is take my hand."

"Take your hand?"

"That's right."

Brogan nodded and, removing his hand from McKenna's wrist, held it out to Jefferson. Jefferson took a step forward, lowering the shotgun slightly. Then McKenna moved. With her free hand, she tore away the tape covering her mouth, throwing it down to the ground.

"No! Shoot him through me," McKenna screamed. "I don't die here. I didn't die on the *Galla*. History repeats itself; I'm not supposed to die now!"

Brogan's face contorted furiously, and he jerked McKenna back to him, his extended hand clamping hard down over her mouth. Jefferson moved for his bow, dropping the Mossberg and pulling the bow off his shoulder. Brogan was looking down at McKenna, shaking her wildly. Slowly his eyes turned back toward Jefferson, as Jefferson nocked an arrow. He pulled back on the bow and held it for a moment.

"Jefferson," Brogan said, "think about what you're doing. I can give you at least two lifetimes, probably love eternal, with McKenna. Don't throw it away. That was what you wanted."

Jefferson faltered for a moment, then his eyes met McKenna's. Her beautiful eyes. And she was crying. She nodded once. And Jefferson loosed the arrow.

The shaft cut through the rain, striking McKenna dead center, just below her rib cage. Her eyes widened, then constricted, still locked on Jefferson's. Slowly, her body sagged, and she dropped to the muddy earth. *God, what have I done?* Brogan was letting her drop, staring in surprise, first at her, then down at himself, where blood was beginning to flower in the middle of his gut. He reached for the blood, touching it in shock, his fingers coming away red.

Jefferson pulled another arrow on the bow, holding it back by his ear. Ready.

Brogan was making a gasping sound. A horrible sound of fury and pain. His arms were moving away from his sides, lifting up and away from his body, palms facing outward. He looked at Jefferson for a moment. "This isn't how it ends."

"Yes it is. This time, it is."

Jefferson loosed his finger. The arrow struck deep in Brogan's chest, driving him backward. He was falling, back onto the mud and grass. He struck the ground flat on his back, his arms outstretched on either side, his feet together. The shaft of the arrow burrowed deep into him. Jefferson approached slowly, looking down at the face of his former partner. Rain collected in the hollows of his cheeks, wetting his hair, pooling in the hollow of his throat. Brogan's eyes were still open, and he turned his head, focusing on Jefferson.

Jefferson lifted out his final arrow, nocked it, and pulled back. He held the tip just above Brogan's heart. Or where the heart of a man would be.

"This time, this is how it ends."

The final arrow pierced Brogan, driving through him into the ground below. Brogan sucked air, above them lightning tore the sky like a curtain, and his eyes rolled back into his head. Dead. Finally dead.

From behind him, Jefferson heard a moan of pain. McKenna lay on her side, the arrow still protruding from her midsection. Jefferson ran to her, kneeling beside her and lifting her slightly into his arms. Her head turned toward him. There was blood on her lips. Blood in her lungs.

"Oh God, what have I done," Jefferson said. "You told me you're not supposed to die. I'm not supposed to kill you. That's not the way it happens."

McKenna's hand reached for Jefferson's face, brushing the hair from his forehead. How many times had she done that? How many times had she reached for him? How many times had she died before him?

"So handsome, always." She smiled. "No, you haven't killed me. This time it's you who have set me free."

The rain was collecting on her face as it had on Brogan's. Her hair was wet and shining. Familiar. Her clothes streaming with water. So familiar. The *Galla*. The ship was sinking. Attacked by Japanese Zeroes and sinking to the bottom of the Pacific. Davis had still been alive, trapped inside the infirmary room.

He had gone to the portal window in the door. Looked out, the hallways of the ship already flooded with water. Flooded with death. Someone was swimming toward him from out of the darkness. A woman. McKenna. Her white nurse's uniform floated around her in the water, swimming around her like a mist, her hair floating. She was dying in that water, but still she came to the portal window. Davis had watched her through the glass. She met his eyes, her fingers pressed against the glass, the tips dark. He remembered now. And he kissed them, through the cold glass, he kissed her fingers before she died. Before she drowned, just like everyone else.

McKenna lay in his arms and watched his face. She knew that he remembered. Saw in his face that he knew her fate. What was to happen.

"I lied to save you," she said. "I died on the *Galla*. And I'm dying now. It has to be like this. I love you too much for it to end any other way. My life for yours."

"No, no. No it doesn't. We won this time. The Jinn is gone. We don't have to repeat the past. You don't have to die now."

McKenna nodded. "I can feel it happening. This life slipping away from me."

"No, don't—"

"And I'm happy."

"Why?"

"Because, Jefferson, I will see you in the next life. And when I love you again, we'll both be free." McKenna smiled. "Because of you, we will both be free. And I'm not afraid of what will happen anymore."

McKenna's hand moved down Jefferson's face, to his arm, finding his hand. Her fingers wrapped around his, and she held him. Her eyes looked up into the rain for a moment, then back to his face. "I will wait for you to find me again someday in some other life, far from here," she said. "I will watch for you in every familiar face."

"You would wait?"

"Of course I would," McKenna said, her eyes slowly closing, sleeping. "I have always loved you. Throughout eternity."

Awake. Somewhere. Where? When? You ask me, do I remember what happened in my past. All the places I've been, the people I've known. Perhaps, yes. If I think hard enough. And now, where am I? I'm not sure now. I suppose I'll find that out. And will she be waiting for me somewhere in this life? I think so. I think they all will be waiting. Brogan. Vincent. McKenna. You ask me if that's comforting. Yes, I think it is. What am I going to do now? Wait. That's all I can do. I think we never really meet people in this life. We just find them again for the first time.

And so, I wait.

04

WITHDRAWAL

JAN 20 2004